Also by Craig Shaw Gardner

The Other Sinbad
A Bad Day for Ali Baba
Scheherazade's Night Out

A Malady of Magicks
A Multitude of Monsters
A Night in the Netherhells
A Difficulty with Dwarves
An Excess of Enchantments
A Disagreement with Death

Back to the Future Part II
Back to the Future Part III

The Cineverse Cycle Omnibus

Comprising
Slaves of the Volcano God
Bride of the Slime Monster
Revenge of the Fluffy Bunnies

Craig Shaw Gardner

First published in this omnibus edition in 1992
by HEADLINE BOOK PUBLISHING PLC

A HEADLINE FEATURE paperback

This omnibus edition was originally published in three volumes in
paperback: *Slaves of the Volcano God* in 1989 by HEADLINE
BOOK PUBLISHING PLC; *Bride of the Slime Monster* in 1990 by
HEADLINE BOOK PUBLISHING PLC; *Revenge of the Fluffy
Bunnies* in 1990 by HEADLINE BOOK PUBLISHING PLC

10 9 8 7 6 5 4 3 2

ISBN 0 7472 3889 8

Printed and bound in Great Britain by
HarperCollins Manufacturing, Glasgow

HEADLINE BOOK PUBLISHING PLC
Headline House
79 Great Titchfield Street
London W1P 7FN

CONTENTS

Slaves of the Volcano God   1

Bride of the Slime Monster   181

Revenge of the Fluffy Bunnies   353

Slaves of the
Volcano God

This book is for the two Toms;
Count von Eins bis Zwei
and
the *other* Bad Movie Commando.

CHAPTER ONE

Roger thought he should be able to deal with anything. He worked in public relations, after all. He prided himself on facing crises.

'I told you not to move,' the man in the trenchcoat reiterated. The man's voice was almost theatrically gruff. Roger might have found this whole thing funny if the man had not been waving such a large gun in Roger's direction. And he had been waving that gun for an awfully long time. Some crises, Roger reflected, were worse than others.

Perhaps if he worked in public relations out in the business world, rather than in a cloistered university setting, he might be better able to cope with a gun. Still, he didn't think guns showed up in the world of business public relations either. At least, not very often.

The whole thing had, of course, begun with Delores. Ah, Delores! Just thinking of her slim form and long, blond hair, her full lips, her eyes as blue as the Caribbean, Roger wanted to swoon.

He stopped himself immediately. Swooning, as far as Roger knew, was a form of moving. The man with the gun was not too keen on moving. He had mentioned this to Roger many times. Could something go on this long and still be considered a crisis?

'Oh, Roger,' Delores had said in her husky voice, as distinctive in its way as the voice of the man with the trenchcoat. Then Delores had kissed him – the kind of kiss that starts on the lips but somehow manages to work its way down to the toes. 'My Roger,' she had said as she tousled his sandy brown hair, and with those words, he had known his fate was sealed. He was 'her Roger', and he knew what happened when Delores really wanted something. After all, if she hadn't attacked that vending machine, he never would have met her in the first place.

What really surprised Roger, however, was the equal certainty that he considered this woman 'his Delores'. After what had happened to him with Susan, he had never thought he could feel this way about a woman again. Heaven knows, he never felt the same way when he walked into a supermarket. But somehow, supermarkets no longer seemed important. They were 'her Roger' and 'his Delores'; that was what was important. And that was it, no matter what.

'No moving,' the man in the trenchcoat said again. He paused. 'Well, I suppose you can smile. I mean, we all have to move some, don't we? You can't help but blink your eyes. That sort of thing. But no big movements. I think that's what the guys meant. I wonder what's taking them so long?'

'Guys?' Roger asked. Somehow, this was all beginning to seem like some particularly bad *film noir*.

'No talking now!' the man in the trenchcoat waved the gun even more in Roger's direction than he had before. 'Smiling's okay, but talking's definitely out. Talking is moving, and then some! I know my orders. You tell Big Louie to do something, he does it!'

Big Louie? The guy with the gun wasn't any more than five foot four, and one time when the floor-length trenchcoat swung open, Roger could have sworn he glimpsed elevator shoes. Just what was going on here?

'Just what's going on here?' the little man in the trenchcoat whined as if he had read Roger's mind. 'Those guys should be here by now. I mean, this is where Delores lives, isn't it?'

Roger cleared his throat. 'Well—' he began.

Roger found the gun pressed against his nose.

'What did I say about talking?' Big Louie hissed. He frowned and removed the gun from Roger's nostril. 'Well, I suppose you can talk if you're answering a question. That's only fair, isn't it?' The gunman shrugged. 'I'm a little new at this. I hope it isn't too obvious.'

The gunman lapsed into silence, and Roger once again thought about Delores. So beautiful, so witty, so full of life. There had to be a catch. That's one thing Roger had learned in his thirty-two years upon this Earth. There was always a catch.

'There's always a catch,' Big Louie mumbled, more to himself than to Roger. 'Hey, they say to me, you want a chance at the big time? Sure I says. Okay, they say, we got a job for you, a piece of cake. I'll do it, I says, but I have to have a gang type name. What's wrong with Seymore? they ask. Hey, I says, if I'm gonna do gang things, I gotta fit the part. What's wrong with Seymore? they ask.

Seymore, they continue, is a perfectly good name. You know the type. They never understand the important things!' Louie came out of his slouch to stand as tall as he was able. Yes, he was definitely wearing elevator shoes. 'I want to be called Big Something, I says. Like Big Seymore? they ask.' Big Louie sighed. 'You know the type. They never understand.' The gunman slouched again, lapsing into gloomy silence.

Roger wondered if he could risk saying something. He had given up trying to overcome the short gunman – heck, he had even given up thinking about it – approximately ten seconds after Big Louie had arrived. The short fellow was too quick, and, even worse, too nervous. Plus, this gangster had caught Roger in his jogging suit.

There was something about wearing a set of navy blue sweats, even the fancy kind with the white stripes down the pants. Whether it was that he was caught without a belt, or that – he had to admit it – his stomach wasn't quite as flat as it should be, being in a jogging suit made Roger feel somehow particularly – how should he put it? – vulnerable. Especially when he was looking into the barrel of a gun. Roger had to face it: he was a runner, not a fighter.

He paused for a long moment, waiting for the man in the trench-coat to make a move, but Big Louie did nothing but sigh and stare moodily at his gun.

'Did you want me to answer a question?' Roger asked at last.

'What?' Big Louie started, gun at the ready. 'What did I tell you – oh – that's right – I did. Yeah. I guess so. I mean, with the guys not showing up and all, I guess we have to change the rules a little.' He lowered his waving weapon. 'So, let me ask you. Just where is Delores?'

Roger told him she had left half an hour before.

'What?' The little guy shook his gun in disbelief. 'You mean she's already gone? That would be just like those guys. A piece of cake, they say.' The small man shook with fury. He pointed his revolver straight at Roger's stomach. His knuckles were white where he held his gun.

'There's only one thing I want to know,' Big Louie whispered between clenched teeth. 'What am I waiting around here for?'

The gunman vanished in a puff of blue smoke.

Roger blinked.

Did this mean the crisis was over?

The first thing Roger was aware of was lips. And what lips! Only one woman in the world kissed like that.

'Delores!' Roger gasped when she let him come up for air. At least she was safe! He had been so worried about her after the short gunman had shown up. It was only natural, after all, especially since that incident between Roger and Deirdre – although, in that case, it was a rifle, not a revolver. And there had been that overripe avocado, too. But he had promised himself he wasn't going to think about Deirdre anymore, or Susan, or Wanda, or – well, he especially wasn't going to think about Phyllis! All that sort of thing was over, now that he'd met Delores.

But Delores hadn't told him where she was going. She was like that. Roger really thought she enjoyed being mysterious. This time, though, her sense of mystery might have been fatal. Even if he had known whether or not he should warn her about Big Louie, there was no way he could have gotten in touch with her.

So eventually he had exchanged his jogging suit for a pair of striped pajama pants and crawled into bed. Even more eventually, he had fallen asleep. None of his real dreams had come close to Big Louie. That had worried him even more. Just what was Delores mixed up in?

She put a finger to her lips. His dreams had gone away, replaced by Delores' magnificent reality.

'Have they been here?' she whispered. Roger always had to be careful not to shiver when she whispered.

He nodded.

'I was afraid of that.' Delores frowned. 'I really didn't want to get you mixed up in this, Roger.' She sighed wistfully. Roger loved it when she sighed wistfully. 'It's a little late for that now, though.'

She stroked his bare shoulder tentatively. 'I think I should tell you everything. But I will have to hurry. I don't think we have much time.'

She looked around the room, as if she expected someone to pop out of nowhere at any second. Roger remembered Big Louie and the blue smoke. Satisfied that they were alone for the moment, Delores reached into the pocket of her black vinyl jumpsuit and took out a small, shiny object. She pressed the object into Roger's hand.

'This is what they were after,' she said.

Roger studied the strangely familiar object in the bedroom's dim light. He held a hollow silver oval, made of some lightweight plastic, with an insignia attached to one end. It looked like nothing so much as a Captain Crusader Decoder Ring.

Roger remembered Captain Crusader Decoder Rings from his childhood. You got one whenever you bought a box of Nut Crunchies. You needed them to understand the messages written in Captain Crusader's secret codes that always appeared on the back of the box.

He could still remember decoding those messages on his breakfast napkins: 'Civic Responsibility is everybody's business.' 'Every day starts better with a smile.' 'Always look both ways before you cross the street.' Roger had always wondered what was so special about those messages that they had to be written in code. Still, anything that came for free in a box of Nut Crunchies was always worth saving, and Roger would always keep the rings. At one time, Roger had had seven.

He looked back at the object in his hand. 'What is it?' he asked, afraid in his heart she would tell him it was a Captain Crusader Decoder Ring.

'This,' Delores intoned solemnly, 'is the key to the universe.'

'Oh,' Roger replied. Actually, he didn't like that answer much more than the one he had anticipated. This tiny, cheap, plastic thing was the key to the universe? He turned on his overhead reading light to better study the small, silver-coloured band. It still looked just like a Captain Crusader Decoder Ring.

'Actually,' Delores confessed, 'it's a Captain Crusader Decoder Ring.' She smiled one of her dazzling Delores smiles. 'But the people at Nut Crunchies never realised what they had wrought with the invention of this little marvel.' She winked at Roger. 'You see, you can use this little ring to go anywhere you want in the Cineverse, to any one of those uncounted million worlds—'

'Hold it!' Roger cried. This was all too complicated. After that mess he had gotten in with Vicki, Roger had sworn off complicated relationships once and for all. At least he thought he had.

'Whatever is going on here,' Roger continued, 'you have to start your explanation from the beginning.' He pointed at the piece of plastic in his other hand. 'I do not believe a Captain Crusader Decoder Ring qualifies as a beginning.'

Delores pouted. 'Well, it is.' Lord, Roger thought, Delores was beautiful when she pouted! 'At least,' she continued, 'it is in a way. Well, actually, it's a very complicated beginning. Maybe there's some other way I can explain.'

Her frown only lasted a few seconds. She snapped her fingers and smiled.

'Roger,' she said, 'you really like to go to the movies, don't you?'

Roger looked at her in astonishment. That was like asking him if he liked to breathe. Just the night before, he had taken Delores to see a triple feature of jungle action pictures at the local revival house: *Zabana, Prince of the Jungle*; *Zabana vs. the Nazi Death Ray*; and *Zabana Goes to Hollywood*. And she asked him if he liked movies!

'Well, yes,' he answered after a moment's pause.

With that, Delores once again showed her fabulous smile. 'I know you do, darling. Your love of movies is a big part of why we're involved. That surprises you. Doesn't it? I suppose I should have told you about all this sooner. Still, our romance was so perfect.' Her cool fingers ran across his knuckles. She chuckled ruefully. 'It was almost like a movie.'

Her touch sent waves of chill excitement down Roger's spine. Maybe he was being too hard on Delores. After all, complications had a way of sneaking up on you, especially in relationships. There was nothing Delores and he couldn't work out somehow. Especially when they were alone together. Somehow, as Delores spoke, she seemed closer and closer to him, and Big Louie and the blue smoke seemed farther and farther in the distance.

'Not now, Roger!' Delores gently pushed him away. 'Oh, I want to, too, but we don't have time when the fate of the universe is at stake!'

Her frown deepened as she continued to speak. 'You know quite a bit about movies, films made thirty, forty, even fifty years ago.' She paused again, and bit her lip. 'Well, what if I were to tell you that those movies were more than just movies?'

'What?' Roger asked. Somehow, the more Delores explained, the more confusing this became.

Delores took a deep breath. 'Let me tell you the whole thing. I think that would be best. Please don't interrupt. You can ask me questions when I'm done.'

She sat down next to him on the bed. 'There are many other worlds, Roger, worlds not so different from the one that contains this room, this bed, and the two of us. Actually, Roger, you would find these other worlds strangely familiar. For you have seen these worlds in the movies!'

'In the movies?' Roger whispered.

'Roger,' Delores reprimanded, 'your interjections are not helping. Just listen.' She nodded her head emphatically. 'That's right. For a time, Hollywood, USA had managed to tap into the universal subconscious, and was showing this world – your world, Roger, not mine – glimpses of the Cineverse.'

'The Cineverse?' Roger queried.

Delores' lovely frown deepened. 'Roger. Please. I am trying to use terms that you will comprehend. I'm talking about the almost infinite number of worlds that occupy this same space in all the many universes. That was what Hollywood had keyed into, at least until *the Change*!'

'*The Change*?' Roger enquired.

She nodded emphatically. 'Yes. The Change. It must have been obvious, especially to someone with a background like yours. I mean, you must have noticed that movies aren't as good as they used to be.'

Roger paused. She was right. Movies *weren't* as good as they used to be. He felt a chill in the pit of his stomach. Maybe there was really some truth to all this stuff she was spouting!

'Now, this is all serious enough, but I haven't told you about the real danger.' Her frown deepened. Three worry lines creased her lovely forehead. 'I know this must be confusing to you. Maybe it would be better to show you. Roger, could I please have the ring?'

Roger handed it over in silence.

'Here,' she said, squeezing Roger's hand as she took the ring away. 'Let me show you how to open a window to the beyond.' She held the ring under the light. 'First, you turn the Captain Crusader Decoder Dial—'

There was a puff of blue smoke, accompanied by the usual low-key explosion. Delores leapt to her feet and screamed.

'Heeheeheehahahaha!'

The room was filled with hideous laughter. A voice cried: 'We knew you'd have to activate that thing eventually!'

The smoke took some time to clear. When Roger stopped coughing, he saw they had been joined by four figures. One of them was Big Louie. He and two others were wearing double-breasted suits straight out of some bad prohibition film.

But the other man's costume was something else altogether. He was wearing long robes – and hat to match – of the deepest black, made more striking still by the bright red stitching upon the sleeves, stitching that formed shapes that almost – but not quite – looked like letters or words. For an instant, Roger wondered if these shapes might be ancient symbols of some long-dead language. Then again, perhaps they were only letters and words attempted by someone who wasn't very good at embroidery.

The red squiggles danced around the hat as well, a circular cap that came to a point at the top, except that the point was a bit askew, as if the hat might have been sat on once or twice. Roger stared at the hat, and discovered that, if he squinted, the symbols there looked even more like words. He frowned as he concentrated on the embroidered scrawl, forming the syllables silently with his lips as he read:

'DAD'S . . . THE . . . CHEF.'

'What do you mean, "Dad's the Chef"? ' the fellow in black demanded, his frown accentuated by a severely trimmed moustache. 'Unless . . .'

His frown deepened as he glanced down at his apparel.

And, what, Roger wondered, was the meaning of that apparel? The fellow's companions were all dressed as 1930s gangsters, but the man in black's costume came from another era entirely. Roger could swear he had seen that kind of conical cap before somewhere. Wasn't it the sort of thing schoolchildren were forced to wear when they sat in corners after they misbehaved? Yes, it did look rather like a dunce cap. Except the rest of the costume didn't look schoolboyish at all. The robes looked more like the fellow stepped out of a low-budget King Arthur movie. That was it! All he needed was a magic wand, and he'd look just like—

Roger shook his head. A wizard? Could it be possible? The fellow had thrown his hands over his chest, as if he might hide the robes behind them. From this guy's behaviour so far, Roger decided he would vote for the dunce theory over the wizard any day.

'Oops,' the man in the maybe-a-wizard's outfit apologized as he waved distractedly at his garb. 'What am I doing in this? It's totally inappropriate.' The fellow's smile was the slightest bit sheepish. 'They must have made some sort of mistake in central casting. Excuse me, won't you? I shan't be a minute!'

The blue smoke showed up again as the man-who-shouldn't-have-been-a-wizard disappeared. Unfortunately, Big Louie and the other two chose to stick around, menacing Delores and Roger with their snub-nosed .38s.

And then there was another of those all-too-frequent explosions. The voice began to speak even before the blue smoke cleared: 'Sorry for the delay. Now where were we? Oh, yes.'

The voice cleared its throat.

'Heeheeheehahahaha!'

The room was once again filled with hideous laughter as the smoke dissipated once more, and the formerly-dressed-in-black fellow stood before them again, in a costume Roger thought looked even stranger than the last one.

The laugher wore a loose green garment, sort of like an oversize smoking-jacket made of some shiny, almost metallic material, with pants to match. The jacket had a large, blood red 'D' embroidered on the lapel. And the laughter upon his lips was now replaced by a sardonic smile as he spoke again.

'And now,' he began slowly, 'we shall get down to what – ahem – really matters.'

The man in green removed something from his head that looked vaguely like a space helmet. Actually, Roger reflected, what it most looked like was a fish bowl with a television antenna stuck on top.

'De-lor-es,' the man in green hissed. 'You didn't really think fleeing to Earth would save you?' His smile broadened as he examined the woman's form, from blond hair to jumpsuit to black boots. His eyes seemed to glint evilly, but perhaps that was just the reflection of his metallic green suit. He threw his head back to laugh again.

Delores stared angrily at the man in green. 'I had no thought of being saved,' she whispered between clenched teeth. 'What is happening to our worlds is more important than either you or I!'

One of the green man's henchmen spoke up: 'What should we do with them, Doctor Dread?'

The man in green's smile grew even wider than before. 'We will – heh, heh, heh – deal with both of them, if you get my meaning.'

The henchman smiled. 'Yeah, Doctor Dread. I get your meaning.'

Roger was afraid that he got the man in green's meaning as well. Especially since two of the henchpeople were using this opportunity to brandish their large, nasty-looking guns in Delores' and his general direction.

A moment later, Big Louie glanced at these fellows and hastily began to wave his gun as well.

It was then that Roger remembered he was wearing only his pyjama pants. He felt even more vulnerable than he had in his jogging suit. He sucked his stomach in. How could he possibly save Delores if he wasn't dressed for it? He wondered if he should at least start by getting out of bed. He took another look at the revolvers. He thought better of it.

'Delores,' Doctor Dread murmured. Roger couldn't take his

eyes off the man's suit. When the light hit it just right, it looked like snakeskin. 'Pretty, pretty Delores,' Doctor Dread continued. 'You will of course be coming with us.' His smile broadened again. 'But then, I know how much you like to –' he paused meaningfully '– travel.'

'Yeah,' one of the henchpeople smiled. 'Travel!'

'You idiot!' Delores replied. 'How can you think of your own petty plans at a time like this!'

'Hehhehheh,' Dread laughed. 'My plans are anything but petty. Soon I shall *rule* – but – hehheh – perhaps I say too much. We will discuss this when we are in more private surroundings. Won't we, boys?'

The two henchpeople laughed. Big Louie laughed a second later. The others looked at him.

'Uh,' Big Louie said. 'Yeah, private surroundings. Yeah – uh – don't say too much. Uh—' Big Louie wiped his forehead. 'Uh—What do you want to do with the other guy?'

'I'm glad you brought that up,' Doctor Dread remarked. 'The other guy, as you so quaintly put it, will have to be – heeheehee – taken care of.'

The two other henchpeople laughed. Big Louie tried to join them, but the noise died in his throat.

'Taken care of?' Big Louie replied.

'Yes, taken care of,' Doctor Dread ran a perfectly manicured hand through his close-cropped hair. 'You know.' He frowned, and looked at Roger. 'What is your name?'

Roger told him.

'Very good.' The Doctor's smile returned. 'Roger, here, then, must be taken care of. Roger must be –' he paused to chortle, '– dealt with. Roger must be – hahahaha – removed from active consideration.' Doctor Dread sighed. 'I ask you: how can I be any plainer?'

Big Louie swallowed again. 'Removed from active consideration?'

Doctor Dread nodded. 'You want to be called Big Louie, you've got to act Big Louie. When you're finished, we'll meet you back –' Dread paused to look suspiciously about the room, '– at the usual place.

'Heh, heh, heh. Grab the girl!' Dread ordered a henchman. 'And get the ring. And may I say, Roger, that I enjoyed my– ' he paused again, his smile a mixture of supreme triumph and ultimate evil, '– final visit?'

Doctor Dread placed the antennaed goldfish bowl over his head as his henchmen dragged the struggling Delores to his side. His laughter echoed in the room until the blue smoke cleared.

Roger stared at Big Louie. More specifically, Roger stared at the gun shaking along with Louie's right hand. What was this guy going to do with him?

'What am I going to do with you?' Big Louie asked. He gripped the shaking gun with his left hand as well and pointed it straight at Roger's forehead.

'Sorry,' Louie said. 'You heard those guys. This is a part of my job.'

Roger yelled and tried to leap for the small man's gun. He might have made it, too, if he had not been so tangled up in his bedclothes. It was very difficult to be a hero when you had a blanket wrapped around your legs.

'You're not making this any easier are you?' Louie wailed. He pushed Roger back on the bed. 'A minute ago, I was looking for a way out of this. But I'm afraid you don't give me any choice!'

Roger felt the cold muzzle of the gun on his too-warm forehead.

'Buddy,' the other man whispered hoarsely, 'you just made Big Louie everything he knew he had to be.'

CHAPTER TWO

'Everything I knew I had to be,' Louie added. 'Like a complete failure.'

Roger felt the gun leave his forehead.

'I just can't do it.' Louie stuck the handgun back in his shoulder-holster. 'Heaven knows I tried. All these years, working in comedy relief. I wanted a break, you know? I thought I could be a henchman.' He laughed bitterly as he rebuttoned his coat. 'I guess I just wasn't meant to hench.'

'Does this mean,' Roger asked cautiously, 'that you're not going to kill me?'

'I'm afraid so,' Louie said glumly. 'Don't spread it around, okay?' The small man paused, a half-smile struggling to overcome his frown.

'Wait a second! While I'm bouncing around from world to world with my ring, you're stuck back here on Earth! There's no way anyone will know if I killed you or not!' He giggled. 'Fool around with Big Louie, will you?' He pointed a finger at Roger. 'Bang, bang, you're dead. Now, if you'll excuse me, I have a date with an evil genius.' Big Louie reached in his right pants pocket and frowned.

'Wait!' Roger cried. He couldn't let Big Louie go. Not yet! No matter what nonsense this fellow was spouting, Louie had a Captain Crusader Decoder Ring. Even though Roger still wasn't quite sure what those rings did, he did know one thing: he must get hold of one if he were to ever see Delores again!

'I'll make a deal with you,' Roger said hurriedly.

'A deal?' Big Louie pulled his hands from his jacket pockets. The frown was still there.

'Yeah, a deal!' Roger tried to think fast. He had to do it, for Delores! 'Let's see. What would someone like you want?' Roger glanced feverishly around his bedroom. There were his colour

TV, his stereo, his clock radio. Somehow none of this seemed appropriate. 'Give me a second! I'll come up with something!'

Louie sighed. 'This is what happens when you let somebody live. You want me to make a decision? Henchpeople aren't supposed to make decisions. They're just supposed to blindly enact the plans of the evil genius.' He pulled something from his breast pocket. Louie allowed himself a little smile. It was a Decoder Ring! 'It's my own fault, I suppose. If I had killed you, I wouldn't have to listen to any of this.'

'Wait a moment!' Roger blurted. 'You haven't heard my offer!' What would a five-foot-high man in double-breasted blue serge want? There certainly wasn't anything here. Roger thought about those golf clubs he had stored at his mother's, the ones Fiona had given him and he had never used. Then there was his old guitar. Sure, the neck was a little warped, but did Big Louie need to know?

'Sorry,' the henchman said. 'Deals are out. I couldn't do it, no matter how good it was. Let me explain.' He held the grey piece of plastic under Roger's nose. 'This ring belongs to Doctor Dread. If I should lose it—' Louie made an unpleasant noise deep in his throat as his little finger slashed the air in front of his Adam's apple. 'In other words,' he continued, a slight harshness in his voice, 'I would be taken care of.'

Roger thought of Doctor Dread. He swallowed hard. 'You mean you'd be dealt with?'

'Yeah.' Big Louie nodded. 'That's it. Dealt with.'

'So they're that valuable?' Roger asked, a hint of wonder in his voice.

Louie nodded. 'I only know of three of these things in working order. They break all the time. What do you expect? They're only made out of cheap plastic!'

Roger shook his head. 'And these *really* are the key to the universe?'

'Sure are.' Louie placed the ring on his finger. 'Really says something about the nature of our universe, doesn't it? Well, it's been a lot of fun shooting the breeze, but you'll have to excuse me. I'm expected at the hideout.'

Big Louie squinted at the ring, ready to make some fine adjustment with his free hand. The truth sunk into Roger's brain at last: this small henchman was going back to Delores, and leaving Roger behind!

'Um, uh—' Roger tried to think of something to say.

'Hemming and hawing won't do you any good,' Louie remarked. 'No, no. Clearing the throat and coughing isn't any better. I'm leaving, and you're staying here. The only reason you're not dead is that you don't have a ring. Without one of these Captain Crusader numbers, you're not going anyplace!'

Big Louie carefully twisted the dial half-way around. 'See you in the funny papers!' he cried. And with that he was gone.

By now, Roger had gotten quite tired of all this blue smoke. Still coughing, he opened a window to clear the room.

Roger sat back on the bed, atop the blankets that had almost been his undoing. He couldn't give up to despair. There had to be some way he could still reach his beloved.

According to Louie, without a ring, Roger was stuck on Earth forever, Delores eternally beyond his grasp. But, in a moment of panic, Roger had thought of his mother. More specifically, he had thought of his mother's basement.

If things were as he remembered them, Roger did have a ring. In fact, at one point, he had had seven.

Roger looked at the middle of the room, where he had seen Big Louie and Doctor Dread and Delores all disappear. He jumped out of bed, grabbing the jogging suit he had thrown over a chair the night before.

There was no time to lose!

'Why Roger, what a surprise!' His mother's smile vanished as he rushed past her and headed for the basement.

'Is my old stuff where I left it?' he called over his shoulder.

'Well,' his mother considered, 'I guess so. At least what's left of it.'

What's left of it? Roger didn't like the sound of that in the least.

'Aren't you even going to stop and say hello?' his mother called after him.

'Don't have time now, mom!' Roger shouted as he took the basement steps three at a time. 'This is something of an emergency!'

His mother followed him down the steps.

'Where is it?' Roger screamed. Nothing was where it should be! He opened the door on what should have been a fruit cellar and one hundred square feet of boxed storage. Instead, he saw a brightly lit recreation room.

'There's no need to shout, dear.' His mother smiled cordially. Roger noticed through his panic that her hair had changed to blond again. 'If you'd make yourself clearer, I might be able to answer you. Where is what?'

'All the storage space!' Roger shouted. No, he thought, it didn't do any good to raise your voice when you were around mother. In a more controlled voice, he added: 'All those boxes full of stuff from my childhood.'

'Oh,' his mother said brightly, 'those old things? We moved those things out months ago to make room for this new den here. Mr Mengeles, the nice man next door, has been helping me with home improvements.'

She giggled coquettishly. 'I hope Mr Mengeles will help me with everything, pretty soon. Still, dear, if you came over to the house more often, you'd probably notice when I made major changes.' She lightly touched Roger's elbow. 'Not that I'm criticising you, dear.'

'I don't care if you criticise me or not,' Roger replied, doing his best not to shout. 'What have you done with my things?'

'You didn't want those old things any more, did you dear? As I used to say to Vicki, if you let Roger have his way, he'll clutter the house up with all manner of junk!' She patted her son gently on the shoulder. 'Of course, dear, we let you do it because we love you, although heaven knows what value you place in a lot of those things you collect!'

'Mother!' Roger counted silently to ten before he continued. His mother waited patiently for him to finish. Not only had she redone her hair, Roger realised, but she was wearing very stylish clothes in the middle of the day. What was going on here?

'Is Mr Mengeles coming over?' Roger asked.

His mother blushed. 'How did you know?' She smoothed imaginary wrinkles out of her cotton print dress. 'You know, dear, I'm always glad to see you, although I wish sometimes that you'd call me before you came over here. That's of course assuming that you still know how to use the telephone. Not that I'm criticising you dear, but you used to be so much better about keeping in touch when you were married to Susan.'

'Mother,' Roger interrupted, trying to stop the inevitable. 'I do not wish to talk about Susan!'

'And why not?' she chided. 'She was always such a nice girl. I don't understand why you ever broke up with Susan anyway. She let you keep just about anything in that house of yours. Heaven knows it looked like it, with all the clutter everywhere—'

'Mother!' Roger had started to shout again. This was all too much. 'I didn't dump Susan, she dumped me! Remember? Susan ran away with the guy who ran the meat counter at the Superette.'

'Oh, that's right.' A little half-smile lit his mother's countenance. 'I remember that fellow.' She sighed. 'The way he used to say, in that great deep voice of his, "And would you like that wrapped, madam?"! Susan was such a romantic. You didn't deserve her, Roger.'

'No, mother, I didn't. Now what happened to all the boxes?'

'Oh, don't worry, dear, they're around here somewhere. I think Mr Mengeles put most of them back in this closet.' She fluttered across the room in her high heels. 'Mr Mengeles is so handy to have around, dear, and so considerate!'

She reached a door at the back of the room. 'I think you'll find almost everything in here,' she said as she opened the door. 'Oh, of course, I gave all your old comic books to Mr Mengeles. He has this grand-nephew, Ralph, who just loves comic books. And I must admit that I used most of the stamps from your collection to mail letters. And there's one or two things that I gave away to rummage sales. But, besides that, everything's just as you left it!'

Roger wanted to scream, but he didn't have time. His mother had given away half his childhood!

He looked inside the closet. There were only half a dozen boxes left, out of the thirty or forty he had put here for safe keeping. But so what if his Tom Corbett, Space Cadet books were gone forever. Roger had to remain calm. There could still be a Captain Crusader Decoder Ring in those boxes that remained!

'Is there a light in here?' he asked.

'There's a pull string overhead,' his mother replied. 'Mr Mengeles put that in too. He's so handy to have around.'

Roger pulled the string and got to work. The first box was filled with books, the second with old school papers and projects. He took a second to shuffle between his kindergarten drawings and his second grade science project: 'Colours in Nature'. He was eating Nut Crunchies in the second grade, wasn't he?

Somewhere, in the distance, a bell rang.

'Oh, dear,' his mother said. 'It's been awfully nice seeing you, dear, but I'm afraid you'll have to go. That would be Mr Mengeles. Not to criticise you, dear, but the two of us have plans, and you didn't call ahead, now, did you?'

'Just a minute, mother!' Roger cried, shrugging off her insistent hands on his shoulders. He dug his fingers into a box full of tissue paper, burrowing past baseball gloves and a pair of broken binoculars. There had to be a ring in here somewhere!

'Roger!' his mother cried in her most commanding voice. 'You have to leave right now!'

Roger knew what would happen next. He grabbed a nearby shoebox to fend off his mother's hands when they grabbed his hair to drag him away.

The bell rang again, stopping his mother in mid-grab. The shoebox fell to the floor with a thump, followed by an odd little ping.

'I have to go up there right now!' His mother gave him one of her sternest looks, reserved for those occasions when you had done something slightly worse than blowing up the high school.

'If you are not right behind me when I open the front door,' she yelled from halfway up the stairs, 'you will be in trouble!'

Roger nodded his head as his mother disappeared upstairs. Why had the shoebox gone 'ping'? He looked down at his feet. Actually, it hadn't been the shoebox, but a small wad of tissue paper that had fallen out and hit a pipe that led to the hot water heater. Heart in his throat, Roger tore the paper in two.

It was a Captain Crusader Decoder Ring.

Roger whispered a silent prayer to whatever god was in charge of putting free prizes in cereal boxes and ran up the stairs after his mother.

She opened the front door as he approached. 'Oh, Mr M!' she cried. 'What a surprise!'

A balding gentleman sporting a pencil-thin moustache stood on the front steps. When he smiled, Roger saw he had a gold tooth.

'It was such a nice day, Mrs G,' the newcomer bubbled, 'that I thought I might come for a visit.'

'Oh, Mr M!' Roger's mother gushed. 'You're always so thoughtful! I'd like you to meet my son, Roger. You were just leaving, weren't you, Roger?'

Roger quickly stuffed the decoder ring in his pocket and shook the balding gentleman's hand. He had the oddest feeling that he had met this fellow before. Perhaps it was something about that pencil-thin moustache.

'Any son of Mrs G,' Mengeles was saying, 'must be quite a son indeed!'

'Oh, yes,' his mother interjected. 'Roger is a sweet boy, if a trifle absent-minded. It really is a shame that he has to leave this house this very minute, isn't it, Roger?'

'Um,' Roger replied as he let the gentle but firm pressure of his mother's hands push him past the older man. 'Yes mother. Can't stay. Have to go. Awfully nice meeting you sir—'

'Won't you come in, Mr M?' His mother's voice cut through Roger's pleasantries as she ushered the older man through the door. 'It was awfully nice to see you, dear,' his mother called to Roger over Mr Mengeles' shoulder. 'Do plan to stay longer next time you're—'

His mother's voice was cut off by the slamming front door.

Roger shrugged. This had worked out to his advantage as well. He had been able to get in and out of his mother's house without having to provide a single explanation. Roger laughed out loud. He could almost kiss Mr Mengeles' balding pate. But there was no time for that now. He had a decoder ring to decipher. Somewhere out there, in something called the 'Cineverse', Delores was in danger.

Roger resisted an urge to throw the decoder ring across the room. Big Louie had said they were extremely breakable. Big Louie had also left without giving Roger the slightest clue as to how these rings worked.

Roger had returned to his apartment in good spirits, full of the best intentions. He had folded his bed back into a sofa, and drawn the blinds so he wouldn't be distracted. He sat back on the couch, determined to discover the ring's secret, and found himself becoming distracted anyway.

The problem wasn't that he didn't know how to work the Captain Crusader Decoder Ring. The problem was that he knew the decoder ring too well. The more he looked at the tiny grey dial, the more secret messages returned from his childhood: 'Always listen to what your teacher says.' 'Brush your teeth after every meal.' 'The policeman is your friend.' How many messages just like that had he decoded so many years ago, perhaps with this very ring? They filled his head, making it difficult to concentrate on anything else, as if his thoughts had been taken over by some deranged social studies teacher.

How could this be the key to the universe?

Roger swallowed hard. Whatever his personal feelings, if he were to believe Delores, indeed, if he were to save Delores from whatever horrible fate awaited her, this cheap, plastic ring was central to the problem.

If only he could get it to work!

He had to concentrate. Delores hadn't really even begun her demonstration when they were interrupted by Doctor Dread and his double-breasted minions. And he had been too upset to even watch Dread as the snakeskin-suited villain had spirited Delores away. The only time he had really seen the ring in use was in Big Louie's somewhat clumsy exit.

He had thought, initially, that he could simply reproduce the diminutive henchman's actions. First off, he was pretty sure Big Louie had turned the dial on his ring halfway around. He could only hope the ring had originally been set on 'zero'. If so, Roger could set his ring for the same destination.

But he had turned the ring every which way innumerable times. The only thing that happened were those civic messages constantly filling Roger's head. What had Big Louie done that Roger had forgotten?

Unless—

No, Roger thought, that was stupider than stupid. Then again, what did he have to lose? He was alone in his own home, the curtains drawn against the outside world. He could say and do whatever he wanted to.

Roger twisted the ring again.

'See you in the funny papers,' he whispered in a voice he hoped was as gruff as Big Louie's.

The room was filled with blue smoke.

Roger clasped the ring in his right hand. He was on his way.

CHAPTER THREE

Roger coughed. Somehow, the blue smoke had turned to brown.

'Who's that?' he heard a voice call.

'I say we kill 'im!' another voice replied.

The first voice laughed gruffly. 'Just hold your horses there, and wait for the dust to clear.'

So it wasn't smoke after all. At least, not any more. Now it was dust. Well, no matter what it was, it still made Roger cough. He could barely make out two figures through the brown haze.

Roger forgot all about his cough as the haze cleared.

'I say we kill 'im!' the second man repeated.

'Don't look familiar,' the first man observed. 'Think he's a Cavendish?'

Roger's throat felt much too dry. The two men staring at him looked disturbingly familiar. He recognised the boots, the spurs, the chaps and the ten-gallon hats from a thousand 'B' Westerns. He recognised the rocks, sagebrush, cactus and scraggly trees that now surrounded them from those same movies – the perfect place for an ambush or a chase on horseback. He wished he didn't recognise the shiny silver six-shooters each man had pointed at Roger's chest.

'Hey,' asked the first man, who wore a bright red bandana over his embroidered yellow shirt. 'You a Cavendish?'

'What?' Roger replied.

'Watch out!' warned the second man, who was dressed all in black except for an ornate silver belt buckle and a smaller, but no less ornate, band of silver around his hat. 'Those Cavendish vermin are tricky!'

'What's a Cavendish?' Roger asked.

'See, what'd I tell you?' Black and silver cried. 'I say we kill 'im!' He smiled as he cocked his gun.

'Wait a second, Bart,' Red and yellow drawled easily. 'You've gotta give him a chance to answer. That's one of the laws of the West.'

'You think the Cavendish pigs obey those laws?' Bart reluctantly eased the hammer down on his six-shooter. 'But you're right. Otherwise we're no better than those Cavendish curs.' He waved his gun in Roger's direction. 'Okay stranger. Thanks to Bret here, you got a minute to explain yourself before you start saying your prayers!'

Roger thought fast. What would you say to somebody in a Western who had a gun pointed at you?

'Uh—' he began. 'I come in peace.'

The two cowpokes frowned. Roger could see why – that didn't sound at all right. That was the sort of thing you said to Indians just before Geronimo or some two-faced white trader with a wagonload of guns and firewater showed up, and everybody ended up circling the wagons so they could be shot by the hero.

'Uh—' he tried again. 'The name's Roger. I'm just driftin'. No particular place to go.'

That went over a little better. The two cowboys looked a little more interested and a little less threatening. Roger hoped he was on the right track.

'No place to hang my hat that I'd call home,' he added.

The cowboys frowned at that all over again.

'Of course,' he added hurriedly, 'I lost my hat.'

Under the scrutiny of this pair from some all-too-distant cinematic past, Roger had become painfully aware of exactly what he was wearing. It was no wonder that these cowboys were suspicious. Before this, they'd probably never even seen a blue jogging outfit with white stripes down the side and matching running shoes. He wondered if there might be any way he could put their suspicions to rest. He hastily pulled the pockets out on his running pants.

'Look,' he added, 'I even lost my gun.'

Bart turned to Bret. 'Should we believe him?'

Bret squinted behind his revolver, as if he were taking better aim. This didn't seem to be working at all. Roger decided he'd better come up with another story, fast.

' 'Course,' he added, 'I never did tell you fellows about why I left home, and my dear little sweetheart, Emmy Lou—'

Bret shook his head. 'I don't know. Something's wrong with him. Maybe he's a little slow in the head.'

Both guns were now pointing straight for Roger's gut. There

had to be some way out of this! Roger cleared his throat. ' 'Course,' he added, 'that was before I got jumped by Apaches—'

Bart and Bret glanced at each other as they simultaneously pulled back the hammers on their six-shooters.

'Uh, er,' Roger added hurriedly. 'Then there was that lynch mob who mistook me—'

Bart gently released the gunhammer as he spat in the dust. 'He seems a little loony if you ask me.' The man in black strode up to Roger, his spurs a'jangling. He poked his six-shooter at Roger's chin. 'Mister, you came to the wrong town when you came to Sagebrush. We already got a town drunk.'

Bret strode to his fellow cowboy's side to wave his gun at Roger's nose. 'Yeah, and we're right proud of him, too. So don't get any ideas in that loony head of yours. We like Old Doc just the way he is.' A smile cracked across his weathered face. 'Why, I can't think of anybody I'd rather have fishing quarters out of a spittoon.'

'Yeah,' Bart agreed. 'Doc sure as heck does do a good grovel.' He chuckled. 'The way he crawls across the floor, lapping whiskey out of the sawdust—'

'And how about when he gets the shakes?' Bret twirled his six-gun merrily a few inches from Roger's forehead. 'I'll tell you, when Doc needs whiskey, he does a mean square dance.'

The two of them laughed together. 'And how about his visions?' Bart poked his gun cheerfully into Roger's ribs. 'Heck, he don't see no snakes or rats or spiders. Nobody sees visions as good as Doc. When he's comin' down off a drunk, he sees camels!'

'Yeah!' Bret chimed in. 'And dromedaries!'

Bart frowned. 'What's a dromedary?'

Bret frowned in turn. 'Well, I'm not too sure myself. Doc's the one who saw it. I think it's some kind of special camel with extra humps. Either that, or some kind of pitted date.' Bret shook his head in wonder. 'That's our Doc. Imagine, having drunken visions of dried fruit.'

'Whooie!' Bart whistled. 'All this talkin' about Doc has made me thirsty. I guess we're not going to kill you after all.' He thrust his six-gun back in its holster. 'You should be plum grateful, stranger. The least you could do for us is buy us a drink.'

He put a comradely hand around Roger's shoulder, gently but firmly turning Roger around, and began to guide him toward a distant group of buildings. As they approached what Roger realised must be the local town, he could hear the faint sounds of gunfire and the almost inaudible tinkling of a player piano.

'Yeah,' Bret said, pushing Roger along from the other side. 'You should buy us a couple at least. Out of sheer gratitude.'

Roger let himself be eased into town by the two cowboys. What else could he do? Roger listened to two sets of spurs a'jangle as their owners led him towards what passed for civilisation in this place. Their walk through the sagebrush gave him his first chance to think since he'd shown up here.

Why had the ring brought him to the Old West? Was this where he was supposed to end up? Somehow, this didn't seem to be the sort of place one would expect to find someone like Big Louie. Maybe he could pull out the Captain Crusader Decoder Ring and try it again. But try for where? It was only now, walking between two Tom Mix rejects towards a saloon where there was bound to be trouble (there was always trouble in B-Western saloons) – only now did Roger realise the true difficulty of his situation. It was one thing to be all noble and heroic when your beloved was in hideous danger. It was another thing to try and be all noble and heroic when the key to the universe looked suspiciously like a cheap and easily breakable plastic ring; a ring which, incidentally, he hadn't the slightest clue how to operate.

But he had more immediate problems than learning to use his decoder ring. His two trigger-happy companions expected Roger to buy them a drink. With what? Roger hadn't thought to stick his wallet in his jogging suit. Regular old Earth-type money wouldn't be any good here anyways, would it? He did feel a flat piece of plastic in his jacket pocket, but still – unless B-Western saloons took MasterCard, Roger was in a lot of trouble.

Maybe, he thought, he could use the ring to get out of here. Of course, the next place he ended up might be even worse than this. Roger suppressed thoughts of suddenly appearing in a pit full of lions in some Roman epic, or perhaps materialising in the cockpit of a World War II fighter bomber just before it is hit by the enemy and bursts into flames. He'd have to examine the ring more carefully before he used it again.

Roger felt some added pressure at his back.

'Can't you move a little faster?' Bart snickered. 'At the speed we're goin', we're all gonna die of thirst.'

'Yeah,' Bret added. 'What kind of a town drunk are you if you can't even make it to the saloon?'

The cowboys laughed as if that was the funniest thing they had ever heard.

Roger clenched the Captain Crusader Decoder Ring even more tightly in his hand. Whatever he did, he had to wait until he was alone. If somebody got curious about that little plastic ring, and broke it or took it away at gunpoint, he would be stuck in Sagebrush for the rest of his life.

The three of them passed the blacksmith's shop, the first of half a dozen weathered buildings huddled together at the desert's edge. A bullet whizzed past Roger's ear.

Now that Roger thought of it, the rest of his life might not be all that long.

Two men appeared on opposite sides of the dusty street, one from behind a barber pole, the other from behind a rain barrel. Roger noticed with some distress that their guns were drawn as well.

'Whoa!' Bart called to the newcomers. 'This fellow's with us.'

'So he's not one of those Cavendish scum?' one of the other men called. They were both dressed more or less alike, in faded browns and blues, as if they wanted their clothes to blend in with the windswept desert and town. The two slowly approached Roger and his companions. They made no move to holster their guns.

'If he's a Cavendish, they've really lowered the entrance requirements.' Bart pointed at Roger. 'I mean, take a look at him.'

Both of the newcomers paused to squint at Roger. They glanced at each other and holstered their weapons.

'That's more like it.' Bert drawled. 'Let me introduce you to the boys. I'd like you to meet Slim and Sam.' Both Slim and Sam nodded in turn. Roger wasn't quite sure which one was which. 'Slim, Sam – Roger here is gonna buy us all a drink.'

'Really?' Slim (or it might have been Sam) slapped Roger's left shoulder. 'Right neighbourly of you.'

'Yeah,' Sam (or possibly Slim) chimed in as he jostled Roger's right side. 'You should mention this sort of thing when you come into town. Saves a lot of shooting.'

Roger found himself propelled by four pairs of hands through the swinging doors of the saloon.

The most dishevelled man Roger had ever seen fell off a chair in front of him. He groaned, turning his bloodshot eyes to stare at the new arrivals. He uttered a tremendous belch, then began to drag himself across the sawdust-strewn floor, heading straight toward Roger.

'A shtranger!' the incredibly filthy fellow called as he

approached. 'Hey shtranger – how'sh about buying – a drink for a – guy who'sh down on hish—' The remainder of the man's sentence was lost in a coughing fit.

'This here is Doc,' Bart remarked, nudging the rag-clad man crawling by his feet.

'Yeah,' Bret chuckled. 'Now you see what we mean. Is Doc a town drunk or is he a town drunk? How could you even hope to compete?'

Doc's hand shook as he reached for Roger's foot.

Roger had to admit this crawling, belching fellow was really into his role.

'Yeah,' Bart mused. 'It's hard to look at this disgusting shell of a man and think that once, not so many years ago, he was a great doctor.'

'One of the best in the territory,' Slim added. Unless it was Sam. Roger wasn't too sure.

Doc clawed weakly at Roger's sneaker. He made a retching sound deep in his throat.

'And he was one of the fastest guns around here, too,' Bret added. 'He was the best there was, north-west of the Pecos.'

'Well, I don't know about that,' Sam (or conceivably Slim) argued. 'What about Dakota Jim Grady?'

Bret nodded solemnly. 'Forgot about Brady.' He paused to reconsider. 'Well, Doc was the fastest, west-north-west of the Pecos.'

This time, the others nodded in agreement. Doc moaned by Roger's feet. The retching sound was a lot louder this time, as if it was guiding something upwards from deep inside Doc's throat. Roger carefully pulled his sneaker out of the way.

''Course, you fellows forget,' Sam (then again, it could have been Slim) remarked, 'about what a mean violin player Doc was.'

'Jush – down on my – luck,' Doc pulled weakly at Roger's pantleg before he began to cough again.

'Yeah, and a crackerjack accountant, too,' Slim (still, it might be Sam) replied.

The four men again nodded solemnly. Doc seemed to have passed out on the floor.

Bart laughed whimsically. 'Yeah, and how about the way he could juggle flaming hoops while making assorted bird calls of the American West – but all this talking has made me thirsty.' He kicked Doc's prostrate form out of the way. 'Wasn't there somebody here that was going to buy us a drink?'

Roger found himself pushed to the bar. The old, grizzled barkeep looked up from behind the far end of the polished wooden plank, where he busied himself polishing shot glasses with his apron.

'Four whiskies,' Bart demanded. He looked at the others. 'Unless somebody besides me wants a drink, too?'

'Give us a bottle.' Bret smiled. 'And five glasses. We want Roger to join us, don't we, boys?'

'Wait a second.' The bartender hobbled towards his new customers, his one good eye darting back and forth between Roger and the others. Roger noticed he had placed one hand on a shotgun he kept at the back of the bar. 'Who's going to pay for these?'

Roger looked at his four drinking companions. They all smiled back at him, their respective hands resting lightly on their respective gun handles. Well, this was it, then. He silently said a last farewell to Delores.

Bart frowned. 'You do have money, don't you, Roger?'

'Hey,' Bret said. 'That's right. There wasn't nothing in his pockets!'

'You got something to pay for this, don't you?' Bart glanced meaningfully at the other cowboys. 'Maybe I should have killed 'im after all.' He grabbed Roger's wrist. 'What are you holding so tightly in your hand?'

They were after his ring! Roger pulled away, punching the cowboy in the belly.

His actions only startled Roger for a second. After all, death was one thing. His Captain Crusader Decoder Ring was something else again!

The four cowboys stared at Roger in disbelief.

'Wait a moment, fellows,' Roger began, hoping against hope he might be able to talk his way out of this thing after all. 'Even in lawless towns like this, you don't shoot unarmed men. That's one of the laws of the West.'

The four paused a long moment, considering, Roger was sure, just what laws they were ready to break.

There was a commotion on the street outside – gunshots, shouts, the sound of running feet.

'Mr Bret! Mr Bart!' A youngster came bursting through the swinging saloon doors. 'Mr Slim! Mr Sam!'

Bart turned to the out-of-breath youth. 'What is it, Jimmy?'

The boy could only manage one word:

'Cavendish!'

'So those maggots have finally come to town!' Bart smiled grimly. 'Somebody get this Roger fellow a gun. It looks like he might have some backbone after all. And he's gonna need it against the Cavendishes!'

Bart and Bret and Slim and Sam (or possibly Sam and Slim) ran out into the street. Roger stared out after them, temporarily overcome by this sudden turn of events. How terrible were these Cavendishes, anyway?

The enormity of the situation hit Roger with one thought: those fellows who were forcing him to buy them drinks were the good guys. According to Bart and the rest, the Cavendishes were much worse.

That's when the shooting began.

CHAPTER FOUR

Somebody handed Roger a six-shooter.

Startled, he looked up in the face of the old bartender.

'If you're gonna stand around here,' the barkeep said as he plugged shells into his shotgun, 'might as well help me defend the place. You get the front room. I'm going upstairs to see if I can get the drop on 'em.'

The old man turned and limped up the stairs with amazing speed.

The gunfire outside sounded like it was getting closer. Roger looked down at the gun in his hand, worn silver with a mother-of-pearl handle. He didn't have the faintest idea how to use it. He quickly stuffed the Captain Crusader Decoder Ring in his jacket pocket, behind the Mastercard. If he could help it, he didn't want anything happening to his key to the Cineverse.

The bundle of rags stirred at his feet.

'Excushe me, shtranger.' Doc rolled over and groaned.

A cowboy appeared at the door. It was either Sam or Slim. There were gunshots somewhere down the street. Either Sam or Slim turned and fired.

'You can appreciate –' Doc grunted, and somehow managed to get himself into a sitting position, '– when a fella needsh a drink?'

The answering gunshots were much closer than before. Either Slim or Sam cried out and clutched at his shoulder. He raised his own pistol and fired again.

Roger didn't want to take his eyes off the door. 'The bartender's gone,' he said to Doc. 'I imagine you can help yourself to all the whiskey you want.'

Doc twisted his head around to look at the bar. 'Land o'Goshen!' he exclaimed, timbre returning to his voice. 'I've made it to Heaven at lasht.' He began to crawl through the sawdust in the general direction of the bar. 'And all thish time I thought I wash shtuck in Shagebrush.'

Yet another gun answered Sam's. Unless it was Slim's. Whoever he was, he crumpled onto the weathered walkway by the door.

Roger retreated to Doc's side. It looked like the Cavendishes were killing the good guys. Roger stared down at his gun. How did cowboys shoot other cowboys in old B Westerns? You just pulled the trigger, didn't you?

A very large, mangy-looking fellow dressed all in black, without any of Bart's redeeming silver, filled the wide doorway to the saloon.

He smiled when he saw Roger. He had three teeth, maybe four if you counted a yellow stump. Roger fumbled with his pistol. Why were his hands sweating so much?

'Die, *hombre*!' the toothless fellow remarked.

Roger's heart was pounding in his ears. He pulled his gun up too fast. It flew out of his hand, skittering across the floor to land against Doc's posterior.

'Yeah.' The toothless one raised the largest six-shooter Roger had ever seen. 'I like to play with guns, too.'

Roger heard two shots. He opened his eyes to see the large man fall like a mighty timber. The floor shook when he landed.

Roger turned to Doc, who held a smoking gun in his trembling hand.

'You shot him!'

'Of courshe I shot him.' Doc waved the gun as if to shoo away any objections Roger might have. 'Thish ish sherioush bishinessh! I mean, ther'sh nobody behind the bar. Took two shots, though.' He resumed his crawl, aiming this time to get to the rear of the bar.

'I'll shoot better,' Doc wheezed, 'onshe I have a drink.'

Numbly, Roger followed Doc to the bar. The old fellow had managed to prop himself up against the mirror on the back wall. Somewhat unsteadily, he grabbed a bottle and a pair of shot glasses, and manoeuvred them very carefully until all three rested in front of Roger.

'Hate to drink alone,' Doc explained. 'Will you do the honorsh?'

Roger poured them each a shot. Doc drained his in a gulp and sighed in satisfaction.

'That'sh more like it,' he intoned, his voice stronger than

before. He studied the empty shot glass philosophically. 'It'sh not eashy being the town drunk, you know.'

Roger nodded and took a sip from his glass. He started to cough as soon as the whiskey hit the back of his throat. It felt like his tonsils were on fire!

'Yesh,' Doc agreed. 'Good shtuff, ishn't it? When you're the town drunk, you don't often get the good shtuff. It's a real reshponsibility, let me tell you. You have to be good at crawling acrossh the floor, for one thing. And vishions! They always expect you to have vishions!'

Doc pushed his shot glass toward the half-full bottle. Roger poured him another.

'I shee camelsh, you know,' Doc admitted.

Sam (or possibly Slim) coughed where he lay by the doorway to the saloon. So he was still alive! Maybe there was something Roger and Doc could do to help him.

But wait! Someone was coming! Roger could hear gruff voices, and a number of spurs a'jangling.

'I can't help it if I shee camelsh.' Doc drained his glass again. 'Or wash it dromedariesh?'

The gun! What had happened to the gun? Roger looked frantically around the sawdust-strewn floor, but he couldn't see it anywhere. Did Doc still have it?

'Humpsh! Thatsh – what it wash.' This time, Doc refilled the shot glass himself. 'Humpsh have always been – my undoing.' Doc paused to drain the glass again. 'Or maybe it wash mumpsh.'

Three men burst into the saloon. All were dressed in black. All smiled toothless smiles.

'Die, *hombres*!' they cried together.

Doc casually shot them.

'Now, where wash I?' Doc stared blearily at his shot glass. 'Oh yesh. Camelsh!'

'You shot all of them!' Roger exclaimed.

Doc nodded. 'Told you I'd be better onshe I had a drink. Shteady's the hand, you know. Great medicinal value.' Doc poured himself another.

They heard the sound of other running feet. Doc slowly swung his six-shooter back toward the door.

He let the gun fall when he saw it was Bart and Bret. The two cowboys stared at their prone friend.

'They shot Slim!' Bret exclaimed.

'Slim?' Bart remarked. 'I always thought this one was Sam!'

Whichever one it was groaned again.

'He's still alive!' Bart called.

'He need's doctorin',' Bret agreed. 'But who can—?' He left the rest of the question unasked.

Doc wearily pushed himself away from the back of the bar. 'I'll do it!' He walked steadily to the swinging doors. 'You boys get Sam or Slim here into the back room, I'll do the rest.' As an afterthought, he added, 'Anybody here got a pocket knife?'

Bart fished in his pocket and handed Doc his. The two cowboys picked up their wounded comrade and carried him past Roger, through a doorway to the left of the bar.

When Bart and Bret walked back into the saloon, they noticed the bodies.

Bart whistled. 'Roger doesn't just have a mean right hook. He can shoot, too.'

Roger started to object, but Bret had already picked up the bottle and was pouring the three of them a round.

'As long as the barkeep is upstairs,' Bret drawled, 'I think it's time for us to buy Roger a drink.'

Roger heard a rapid hobbling sound coming down the stairs. He turned to see a grim-faced bartender descending towards them.

'Just a darn tootin' minute!' the aged barkeep cried. 'Who's going to pay for all this?'

Bart smiled up at the old man. 'How about the Cavendishes?'

Instead of answering, the bartender glared back up the stairs. There, Roger saw, on the very top stair, were a pair of snow-white boots.

The owner of the boots slowly began to walk down, a step at a time. Roger saw that the man had pure white chaps, and pure white jeans, and a shining white, enamel, horse-head-shaped belt buckle for his white leather belt.

The bartender scurried down the stairs to get out of the new-comer's way.

The white-booted man took another step, then another. Roger saw that his shirt was covered with white fringe, and he wore a white bolo tie.

The stranger continued his descent. The straight line of his jaw looked oddly familiar, but Roger imagined he had seen the same noble jaw line on a hundred Western heroes. He was clean-shaven, with a firm mouth and a long, aquiline nose. But the top half of his face was covered by a white mask tied behind his head so that it covered most of his blond hair as well, with only two, small holes cut for the eyes.

The stranger placed two immaculately manicured fingers on his pure white stetson, and tipped it ever so slightly at the group standing before the bar.

'Heard there might be a little trouble,' the stranger's deep bass voice mentioned.

'Oh, no, Mr Marshal,' Bret hurriedly explained. 'No trouble here at all.'

'Shucks, Mr Marshal,' Bart chimed in. 'We were only having a little harmless fun.'

'Perhaps,' the Marshal mused thoughtfully. 'Why don't you fellows pay up for your drinks?'

Bart and Bret quickly dug into their pockets.

Casually, as if it might be an afterthought, the Marshal remarked: 'I hear there might be some Cavendishes in town.'

Bart nodded rapidly. 'Yep! The whole bunch!'

'Well, that bunch isn't as thick as it used to be.' He glanced at the bodies littered about the room. 'I see a few members spread out on the floor.' He patted his white-handled pistol in its pure white holster. A slight smile played across his lips. 'And Betsy here got one or two as well.'

He looked around the room. 'I think you fellows can clean up here. Now, if you'll excuse me, I've got some Cavendishes to collect.'

He turned back to them as he reached the swinging door. 'Be careful,' he said as he tipped his hat a final time. 'Remember: Civic responsibility is everybody's business!'

And with that, he was gone.

Roger felt a sudden chill run down his spine. There was something about that fellow – something oddly familiar.

'Who was that man?' he asked.

'Why, didn't you know?' the old barkeep wondered. 'That's the Masked Marshal!'

'Hey!' Bart called. 'Listen!'

'Yeah!' Bret agreed. 'Doc must have fixed Slim up.'

'Yeah!' Bart echoed. 'Or maybe it was Sam.'

From somewhere in the back of the building, Roger could hear the faint strains of a violin.

'Freeze, *hombres*!' came a deep voice from the door.

Roger spun to look. The doorway was full of Cavendishes!

Yet another large man in black – one of a number of them

crowding the door – grinned a toothless smile. 'It took forever for that Masked Marshal to leave. Now that he's gone, though, we can take over this place!'

Cavendishes started to file into the room. A lot of Cavendishes.

'I'd like to introduce you to a few of my boys.' The main Cavendish leered toothlessly. 'It's the least we can do for you *hombres*, before we plant you up on Boot Hill.'

He pointed to the men in black farthest from him. 'These here are Tex and Dakota. You boys check upstairs, then keep watch out some windows to make sure the Marshal doesn't come back.'

Tex and Dakota quickly climbed the stairs. The speaking Cavendish spat a wad of tobacco juice at the corner spittoon. Despite himself, Roger wondered how the fellow could chew anything with so few teeth.

'The next two are Arizona and Kansas,' the Cavendish further drawled. 'You fellas get in that back room, and see who's playing that violin!'

Arizona and Kansas did as they were ordered.

The lead Cavendish nodded toward another pair. 'California and Colorado here are going to keep an eye on a few of you until Boss Cavendish comes. What's this, though?' He pointed at Roger. 'I see a new face.'

He walked halfway across the saloon in three very long steps. A hand the size of most people's heads grabbed Roger's running jacket and pulled the smaller man toward him. 'You're dressed almost as strange as the Masked Marshal. You wouldn't happen to be his sidekick?'

Roger rapidly shook his head.

The big man laughed. 'You wouldn't tell me if you were. Sidekicks are that way, noble and self-sacrificing. It's one of the laws of the West.' He shook his head. 'I'm afraid, my sidekick friend, that you might be too much trouble for us. We might just have to put you out of the way before Boss Cavendish shows.' He turned and pointed at one of the black-garbed men hanging slightly behind all the rest.

'Idaho!'

A man much shorter than all those around him replied: 'Yeah, Boss?'

The big man pointed to Roger and smiled. 'Take this sidekick out and shoot him!'

The small man stepped forward. The gun quivered in his hand. Wait a moment! It took Roger a minute to recognise this fellow, now that he was wearing a black fringe shirt and ten-gallon hat. But he was sure of it – he'd recognise that trembling gun and wishy-washy manner anywhere.

'You better move, you two-bit – um, I mean – you big galoot!' the small man managed. His gun was really shaking now.

Roger couldn't believe his eyes! It was Big Louie!

'Out of my way, lackey!' a voice shouted outside.

'Uh-oh,' the leader said. 'That's the boss. Looks like you get to live for a few more minutes, sidekick. 'Course, Boss Cavendish knows a lot more interesting ways to die than a simple bullet through the heart.' The big man smiled so broadly this time that Roger could actually see a few rotting, discoloured molars set deep in the gums.

'Good, good,' Boss Cavendish's all-too-familiar voice chortled outside. 'You've done just what I asked.' The voice laughed. 'Now there are things to be – dealt with. 'Now there are things to be – taken care of.'

A tall thin man stood in the door, framed by late afternoon sunlight. The black snakeskin coat didn't fool Roger for one second. The man who stood in the doorway – the man they called Boss Cavendish – was really Doctor Dread!

CHAPTER FIVE

Doctor Dread frowned.

'What is this?'

'We think he's a sidekick, Boss,' one of the hulking fellows in black fawned. 'Maybe even the Masked Marshal's sidekick!'

Dread grunted, 'A sidekick? Well, he's certainly dressed – strangely enough.' His frown vanished as he talked, the evil-doer warming to his topic. 'However, I am privileged to have – other information. I know – heh – certain things about this – hehheh – stranger, things that should have been reported in the – hehhehheh – past tense, if you get my drift.'

'Oh, yeah, boss!' A half-dozen Cavendishes pointed their six-shooters at Roger's head. 'Past tense!'

Everybody in the gang except Big Louie laughed heartily. Big Louie tried to step back, but the Cavendishes were ranked too closely behind him. The small fellow stopped abruptly, almost tripping over his spurs.

Dread turned his slightly maniacal gaze at the diminutive gunfighter. The fringe on the Boss's black leather glove shook as he pointed at Louie.

'But you're – not laughing,' Dread purred.

'Pardon me, Doctor – I mean, Boss Cavendish,' Big Louie blurted. 'It was an oversight. I enjoy a joke as much as the next – uh – cowboy. Ha ha, sir.'

But Dread/Cavendish refused the apology with a curt shake of his head. 'No, it's – too late now.' He glanced back at Roger, the sardonic smile once again playing at his lips. 'In fact, it's – hehhehheh – too late for both of you!'

His black-gloved hand whipped around to grab Big Louie's bright red bandana. 'We have to have a – little talk, Big—' Dread coughed apologetically. 'I beg your pardon. What's your name – hehheh – around here?'

'I-Idaho,' Louie quivered.

'Figures,' Boss Cavendish/Doctor Dread replied dryly. He pointed at Roger with his free glove. 'Idaho – why hasn't this man been –' he paused meaningfully, '– removed?'

'Uh,' Big Louie/Idaho stalled. 'You mean – um – why hasn't he been – uh – dealt with?'

'No, I mean why hasn't he been –' he hesitated suggestively, '– sent away on a permanent vacation! What do you think I mean? Haven't I made myself clear, time after time? And yet – hehhehheh –' he tugged purposefully on Louie's bandana, '– you've – hehheh – let me down.'

'But, Boss—' Idaho pleaded, trying to think fast and failing utterly. 'He had a gun. Well, no, actually, he didn't have a gun, but he didn't have a ring. That is, I didn't think he had a ring, so I didn't want to waste my gun. I mean, my bullets.'

Idaho looked around to the other bad guys for some sort of help. Unfortunately for him, at that precise moment all the other bad guys seemed far too involved in studying the intricacies of their individual six-shooters, or the dust on their boots, or the tobacco in their mouths, or anything else besides Idaho.

'You know, bullets!' the short gunslinger went on anyway. 'Uh – Lefty only gave me five, and I had no idea when I could get any more, still being in my probationary period as a bad guy and all, so I thought, my boss will be proud of me if I *save* my bullets for something really worthwhile, say bank robbing or posse shooting—'

'Boys,' Dread said to the others as he completely ignored Louie's groveling. 'I have a – hehhehheh – job for you.'

All the other black-clad cowboys laughed even louder than before. Half a dozen thumbs clicked back the hammers of their six-shooters.

'Now, boys,' Dread chided. 'You misunderstand me. Let's not be overeager. I don't want – hehheh – anything done around here. I think it would be better if we took our friends here on a – teeheehee – little walk. Say behind the – snickersnicker – feed store?'

From the way the cowboys laughed, Roger could tell they all thought it was an excellent idea. Dread turned to glare at him, his smile even more demented than before.

'But why does our intruder look so glum? I assure you, stranger, what happens next will be very –' he hesitated compellingly, '– educational. You're going to have a chance to see a whole array of authentic western weapons – hehhehheh – real close!'

One of the largest of the Cavendishes waved his gun at Roger's nose. 'C'mon, *hombres*, it's time to get a'movin. You've got a – chuckle – appointment on Boot Hill.'

Roger sighed and let himself be led, side-by-side with Big Louie, out of the saloon and onto the dusty street. All six of the Cavendishes who had drawn their hardware came with them, forming a semi-circle around the luckless duo once all of them had gotten through the saloon's swinging doors and out onto the street.

Roger thought, for the merest instant, of making a run for it. After all, it was only fifty feet or so to the nearest cover, with six loaded guns aimed by six crack western marksmen, and all of them pointed at him. Why, they wouldn't have a chance to get off more than – say – twenty or thirty shots before he reached safety.

This was it, then. His search for Delores would end with him in an unmarked grave, his corpse weighted down with Cavendish bullets. And, with his failure, who knew what horrible fate awaited his beloved? Some kind of hero he was!

'Some kind of hero we both are!' Big Louie whispered. 'I did try to keep you out of this. If you would have just had the sense to stay back on Earth, tied up in your blanket—' The henchmen-turned-cowboy left the rest of the sentence unsaid as he scuffed his boots dejectedly in the dry Western soil.

'Yeah,' Roger replied, glancing at his hang-dog companion. He was surprised how sorry he could feel for someone who had previously threatened him with a loaded gun. But Big Louie was such a – Roger paused, trying to think of the right word – such a character! Yeah, that was it. That was it exactly.

Their black-clad companions continued to laugh among themselves. The largest of them, a full six foot six from his mud-caked boots to his ten-gallon hat, once again led the conversation.

'Well, boys, how are we going to do it?'

The other cowboys looked surprised.

'You mean – the job?' one asked hesitantly.

'That's right.' The tall cowboy smiled. 'And Boss Cavendish would expect us to do it with some style.'

'I guess I'm going to get both of us killed.' Roger admitted to Louie in a whisper. 'I never thought about that when I followed you here.'

Big Louie shrugged. 'That's all right. If it hadn't have been you, it would have been somebody else. I realize now that I'm not cut out for bad guying.' He sighed, playing absently with the mother-of-pearl buttons on his cowboy shirt. 'I should have stayed in comedy relief, where I belonged.'

Roger had never seen anyone look so defeated. Maybe there was some way he could cheer the fellow up in their last moments together.

'Style?' One of the cowboys asked the others. 'I thought we were going to shoot them, you know, behind the feed store.'

'Shooting?' the big gunfighter rumbled. 'Behind the feed store? Where's the drama there – those heart-tugging moments when we see these innocents unable to escape certain death? What kind of reputation are we Cavendishes going to get if we lower ourselves to shootings behind the feed store?'

The other cowboys grunted in agreement. One mumbled something about never thinking of it that way before.

Roger decided to ignore the discussion of their deaths for the time being. He nudged Big Louie.

'Actually, I didn't think you did so bad.'

'Really?' Big Louie replied half-heartedly.

'Yeah,' Roger agreed. 'Especially when you showed up in my apartment. I didn't doubt for a minute that you were a gangster.'

'You think so?' Louie looked up and squared his shoulders. 'I was that tough, huh?'

'Absolutely,' Roger replied, trying to be as truthful as possible. 'I had never seen anything quite like you before.'

'We could hang them!' one of the other cowboys suggested.

'Gee,' Big Louie considered. 'But I wasn't very good as a cowboy, was I?'

'Well—' Roger began, trying to think of something, anything, positive he might say.

'Now there's an idea!' the big fellow enthused. 'Two innocents dangling in mid-air, their lives slowly choked away by a hangman's noose. That's a Cavendish idea, that's for plum sure! Anybody know of any big trees around here?'

'It was that name, Idaho, wasn't it?' Big Louie continued before Roger could think of anything clever. 'Yeah, I know it's not as good a name as Big Louie, but it was the only name they had left.' He paused, glancing for an instant at his ornately tooled boots. 'Well, that's not completely true. I did have some choice – they really had two names left. It was either Idaho, or the District of Columbia.'

'Doesn't sound like much choice to me,' Roger agreed. 'I see what you mean.'

'Anybody know of any smaller trees?' the large cowpoke asked after no one answered his earlier question. 'Don't have to be much more than seven, eight feet.'

'Yeah,' Big Louie replied. 'No other names left. The Cavendishes are a *big* gang!'

'Anybody know of any large bushes?' the leader asked at last. 'Maybe we can think of some way to hang them sideways – or something.'

'Sorry, Dakota,' one of the other cowboys replied. 'It's a desert town. Not a tree for miles.'

'You're right, Kansas,' the big gunfighter, Dakota, replied reluctantly. 'But it was such a crackerjack idea!'

'There's always our guns,' another suggested, 'and the feed store.'

'Guns?' Dakota moaned. 'Feed store? So the Cavendishes have to sink that low!'

'Wait a second,' Kansas suggested. 'What about a – cattle stampede?'

Dakota slapped Kansas on the back. 'Now that's Cavendish thinking! The two of them with nowhere to run, confronted by a wall of marauding beasts whose only thought is fear! No matter where they go, no matter what they do, there is no escape! Then, in a moment of poignant terror, the mass of cattle overwhelm them, a thousand hooves pummelling their bodies beyond recognition!' The large cowboy sighed with satisfaction.

'It is really nasty, isn't it?' Kansas agreed.

'It's more than that!' Dakota chortled. 'It's Cavendish nasty!'

'Uh, fellas?' a third cowboy – the same one who had remarked that there weren't any trees – interjected. 'There is one small problem.'

'Not again!' Dakota groaned. 'What is it this time, Nevada?'

'Well, correct me if I'm wrong,' Nevada continued haltingly, 'but I don't think we have any cattle.'

'No cattle?' Kansas blurted incredulously.

'Are you sure?' Dakota demanded. 'None at all?'

'Well, you know,' Nevada continued apologetically, 'this being a desert town—'

'Wait a moment!' Kansas interjected. 'Don't the Widow Johnson—'

'Why, that's right!' Nevada replied, hitting his chaps with a resounding slap. 'The Widow Johnson's got cattle!'

'See?' Dakota chortled proudly. 'If you're a Cavendish, you just got to be resourceful. Now, all we have to do is go over to the Widow's—'

'Uh –' Nevada cowered a bit as he spoke again, '– there's still a slight problem.'

'Problem?' Dakota frowned. 'You mean the Widow Johnson doesn't have cattle after all?' He turned his gun ever-so-slightly, so that its muzzle was pointing a bit more toward Nevada than toward Roger and Louie. Roger thought again about making a break for it. With only five guns pointed at him, he'd probably only take fifteen to twenty rounds before he made it to safety.

'I would be very unhappy,' Dakota drawled, 'if, after all this time, the Widow Johnson didn't have cattle.'

'I didn't say that!' Nevada replied abruptly. 'She has cattle all right!'

'Well, why didn't you say so?' Dakota smiled easily as he once again aimed his gun at Roger's head. 'You got me worried there for a minute.'

'Uh – she just doesn't have very many cattle,' Nevada added softly.

'How many does she have?' Kansas asked before Dakota could get annoyed again.

'Uh – two,' Nevada answered.

'Two?' Dakota demanded.

'Well, yeah,' Nevada replied defensively. 'She's got to get her milk from somewhere.'

'Two cows?' Dakota despaired. 'How are we going to stampede somebody with two cows?'

'Well,' Kansas suggested, 'maybe we could have the two of them stampede over these fellows a number of times. You know, after ten or fifteen runs back and forth—'

'No,' Dakota said with finality. 'Too messy. That ain't a Cavendish death.' He waved at Nevada with his gun. 'You're sure there're only two?'

'Well, you know,' Nevada said as he took a step away, 'this is a desert town—'

'Well, I suppose I can't shoot you for that.' Dakota sighed. 'But how are we going to kill them?'

'There's always our guns,' someone piped up in the back. 'And the feed store.'

Dakota's six-shooter once again pointed at the speaker. 'I don't want to hear that suggestion made again. Understand, Arkansas?'

Arkansas nodded vehemently.

'Good.' Dakota's gun returned to guarding Roger. 'Now come up with a Cavendish way of dealing with these scum!'

'Uh, uh—' Arkansas began. 'Uh, we could – uh – throw them over a waterfall!'

'Throw them over a waterfall?' Dakota began derisively, but stopped himself. 'Wait a darn tootin' minute. That idea ain't half bad. I can see them struggling uselessly against the current, their muscles giving out as they are pulled ever closer to the edge, their screams lost in the thunderous sound of cascading water as they are tossed like rag dolls onto the rocks below, their broken, bloody bodies on those granite slabs mute testimony to what happens when you cross the Cavendishes!' He laughed heartily. 'Yeah, that ain't bad at all!'

'Uh,' Nevada interjected, even more hesitantly than before. 'Dakota—'

'What?' the big cowpoke snapped. 'The waterfall's a fine idea! What's your problem now?'

'Uh,' Nevada quavered. 'This is a desert town—'

'Oh,' Dakota remarked, stopping for a moment to stare at his gun. 'Yeah.' He glowered at the others. 'Well, what's everybody waiting for? Let's get to the feed store. You heard Boss Cavendish!'

Roger felt himself being pushed right, straight for an alleyway between another saloon (so far, Roger had counted six) and a two-storey building with a large, red and yellow sign that proclaimed 'Aldridge Feeds'.

'You, know, Dakota,' Kansas drawled as the gang pushed into the alleyway behind Roger and Louie. 'You can look on the bright side of all this. Sure, we have to shoot these guys, and behind the Feed Store, too. But that doesn't mean we have to bury them! Why not leave 'em lying there instead, two corpses exposed to the elements, so that the buzzards can pick their bones, and there'll be nothing left but a pair of broken skeletons, bled white by the desert sun?'

'Hey, Kansas!' Arkansas cheered. 'Now that sounds like a Cavendish job!'

'Oh, stop trying to cheer me up,' Dakota grumbled sourly. 'By now, I just want to get this over with. We'll stop them in back of the place, and then—'

A dark-garbed stranger stepped from behind the store to block their path. Roger and Louie stopped halfway down the alley, the six Cavendishes close behind them.

'I'd stop right there,' the stranger said, 'if I were you.'

CHAPTER SIX

The Cavendish gang stopped. So did Roger and Big Louie. The stranger smiled.

Roger thought there was something familiar about that smile. He'd seen it before somewhere. For an instant, he thought the stranger might be the Masked Marshal in disguise. But he wasn't tall enough, for one thing, and Roger doubted if, even in disguise, a pristine figure like the white-suited marshal would ever allow himself to look so dishevelled.

'Now you boys are going to have to let your two guests go,' the stranger drawled, 'or there's gonna be a little shootin'.'

'Oh, yeah?' Arkansas replied.

Before he could get his gun half drawn, the stranger had shot him.

Arkansas clutched at his stomach, staggering forward three paces, then back two. He stared at the stranger as he slipped to his knees, then collapsed, face first, in a cloud of dust.

'Not bad,' the stranger commented. 'At least you Cavendishes know how to die right proper. So who's next? Any of the rest of you lookin' for a little extra ventilation?'

None of the remaining Cavendishes moved.

'Good.' The stranger smiled, rubbing with his free hand at his unshaved chin. 'Excuse me for a second.' He reached in his pocket, fishing around for something. 'Don't try anything!' He pulled out a flask, and deftly unstoppered it with his thumb. 'I shoot faster than I drink!'

It was only when the stranger lifted the flask to his lips that Roger realised who it was.

'That'sh better,' Doc mumbled as he repocketed the flask. He hiccuped softly. 'Pardon.' He shook his head and blinked, as if trying to clear his head. 'Sorry it took me so long to get around to rescuin' you fellas, but I had to do a little doctorin' first. Slim was in a bad way. Unless that was Sam I tended to.'

'It's Doc!' Dakota exclaimed as he, too, recognised the dishevelled figure. 'I would have realised it sooner, but that is the first time I've ever seen him standing up. Wanna fish for pennies, Doc? There must be a spittoon around here somewhere.'

The Cavendishes all laughed.

'Hey,' Doc replied sourly as he once again retrieved his flask. 'I'll thank you to keep a civil tongue in your head. I'm the one who's got the gun.'

Dakota chortled. 'That's right, boys. See who's got the drop on us? Why, it's the town drunk!'

'But Dakota!' Kansas interjected. 'The town drunk already shot Arkansas!'

'A lucky shot!' Dakota sneered. 'Let's see how one gun stands up against five!'

'Duck!' Big Louie shouted. Roger followed the other man's lead as both of them dove into the dirt.

Doc shot the remaining Cavendishes before any of them had a chance to aim. All five staggered back and forth for a moment, clutching various parts of their anatomies, before they collapsed into a large Cavendish pile that filled the alleyway.

'Five more lucky shots,' Doc announced. 'I think that calls for a drink!'

He uncapped his flask and took four long swallows.

'Yeah!' Doc cheered when he finally took a breath. 'Thass more like it!' And he too fell, face first, into the dirt.

'Oh, dear,' Roger remarked as he regained his feet, rather surprised by this turn of events. He peered down the alley at the prostrate Doc as he brushed the dust from his jogging suit. 'Is he drunk again?'

Big Louie whistled as he stood beside him. 'Either that, or he really needed to take a nap.'

Roger shook his head. 'Well, at least he was nice enough to save us from certain death before he passed out.'

Louie scowled, looking back the way they had come. 'Well, at least he has for the moment. Doc may have gotten rid of our immediate problem, but the Cavendishes are a *big* gang!'

Before Roger could ask what Louie meant, he heard the commotion, a combination of angry shouts and running boots, complete with spurs a'jangling.

'Cavendishes!' Louie replied to Roger's horrified expression. 'At least a dozen of them!'

'What are we going to do?' Roger whispered.

'Well, we do have a couple guns here.' Louie knelt, picking up a pair of six-shooters dropped by recently-deceased Cavendishes. 'We could stand our ground in the alleyway, and face those dozen Cavendishes as they come around the corner. It would be the noble, dramatic thing to do.'

He frowned as he curled his index finger around the trigger of the revolver in his right hand. 'We can't pay much attention to the fact that I've never fired this type of gun before.' He handed Roger the other revolver. 'I would guess that you're not too experienced at this either. And, of course, we should pay no heed that there'll be a dozen to our two, and that all of them are seasoned gunfighters who know no mercy.'

The crowd noise was getting closer. Roger thought it sounded angrier as well.

Big Louie's frown turned from his gun to his new-found companion. 'On the other hand, we could hide.'

'I've always wanted to see the inside of a feed store,' Roger admitted. 'But what should we do with Doc?'

'Drag him inside. I guess.' Big Louie started toward their fallen saviour at the alley's end. 'Come on. That mob's going to be here in a second.'

Roger ran to join Big Louie. He saw a weathered door in the back corner of the equally weathered feed store building. Maybe, he thought, they could drag Doc in there. Doc's eyes opened as they approached.

'Wait a shecond!' Doc demanded. 'Keep your handsh off me!'

'But Doc!' Roger began.' The Cavendishes!'

'Sho that'sh what you are!' Doc's hand gripped his revolver. 'Well, I've shot a few Cavendishesh in my time!'

'But—' Roger began again. He stopped abruptly when a bullet whizzed past his ear.

'Time for the feed store!' Big Louie proclaimed, already sprinting away toward the back door.

'But—' Roger looked one final time at Doc. The fallen man's gun swung wildly back and forth as he attempted to aim. Roger quickly followed Louie. A pair of gunshots followed them.

Roger jumped inside the feed store, flattening himself against a rough-hewn wall. Louie slammed the door and bolted it shut. There was a faded poster tacked to the door's inside advertising hog chow.

'You all right?' the small fellow managed after he'd regained his breath.

Roger nodded, looking about the dimly-lit storeroom they now found themselves in as if the dusty shelves and hog and chicken chow posters might give him some kind of answer.

'But—' he said haltingly. 'I don't understand—'

'You mean Doc not recognising us?' Louie chuckled. 'Well, his memory's not so good. Comes from all that drinking.'

'No.' Roger frowned. 'No, that's not it.'

'His eyesight's not that hot either. Mistaking us for Cavendishes!' Louie whistled. 'And did you get a whiff of his breath?'

Mistaking them for Cavendishes? Roger decided not to remind Big Louie who else was dressed in official bad guy black around here. Instead, he doggedly pursued his original question.

'No. What I wanted to know is, didn't Doc already shoot six Cavendishes?'

'Yep.' From the way Louie laughed, Roger had uttered a real knee-slapper. 'You saw it too. What a shot!'

Roger realised he was going to have to be a little more obvious. 'And doesn't he have a *six*-shooter?'

'Yep. A Colt Peacemaker. Standard gun of the West.'

Roger sighed. Maybe he was missing something. He'd have to pursue these questions to the end. 'And wouldn't you agree with me that he was far too drunk to reload?'

'Doc was far too drunk to be conscious!' Louie chortled.

This was it, then. Roger asked the final, logical question: 'Well, then, how did he have any bullets left to shoot at us?'

Big Louie looked at him in surprise, then started laughing all over again. 'Oh, that's easy. Haven't you ever heard of Movie Magic?'

'Um—' Roger replied hesitantly. 'I guess so. Everybody's heard of Movie Magic.' It was the sort of phrase that always popped up in documentaries about the Golden Age of Hollywood. He didn't add that, until this moment, he hadn't thought it really meant anything in particular.

'Well, that's what we're talking about here. We're in the Cineverse, you know!'

'Oh,' Roger replied, still not really understanding at all. Delores had told him something of the Cineverse. But, as he recalled, they had been interrupted before her explanation had begun to make any real sense.

'You see,' Big Louie continued, 'you're trying to apply mathematical logic to this situation. That's the way things probably work back where you come from.'

Roger guessed so. At least, that's the way they were supposed to work. He nodded.

'Well, they sure don't work that way around here. Like I said – Movie Magic. Look – Doc's a hero. Well, at least in this case he was, and, in the Cineverse, mathematics and logic don't apply to heroes.'

'Don't apply?' Roger parroted. 'So he can get more than six shots from a six-shooter?'

'No problem at all,' Louie assured him. 'Heroes can get twelve, eighteen, twenty-two shots off without reloading, and nobody thinks twice. It's a part of that Movie Magic. Good guys shooting bullets move the story along, so the bullets are there.'

'So *that's* Movie Magic?' Roger mused, beginning to understand.

'What you can't begin to understand,' Louie continued, 'is that Movie Magic is different on every world in the Cineverse. In a place like this, it's pretty straightforward, rules like that gun thing, or the fact that, should you pull your wagons in a circle, all the Indians in the vicinity are required to ride their horses around said circle in a clockwise direction, until all said Indians are shot.'

'Really?' Roger replied, intrigued despite himself. 'I always wondered about that.'

'Oh, sure. You think any self-respecting Indian would do something as foolish as that otherwise? Of course, on a Western world like this, it's all pretty straightforward. Movie Magic gets a lot more complicated on other worlds. Witch-doctors, magicians, vampires, mystics, sea-serpents, all kinds of fantastic people and things, and all exercising their own brands of Movie Magic. If you ever land on one of their worlds, things can get sticky. But that's not the worst. If you ever get stuck on one of the musical worlds, forget it!'

Roger was about to ask exactly what it was he should forget when he heard the Cavendishes.

'Hey!' a gruff voice cried outside their hiding place. 'They got Dakota!'

'And Kansas!' another yelled.

'And Arkansas!' a third chimed in.

'They got all of them!' the first voice added. 'Maybe – Boss Cavendish – underestimated them?'

'Those guys?' another of the voices replied in disbelief. 'But they both looked like *sidekicks*. Everybody knows sidekicks can't shoot!'

'You're right,' the first voice replied. 'There has to be some other explanation.' He paused, then added in surprise: 'Hey! Who's this?'

'Wha – oh, that's just Doc, the town drunk.'

'They've found Doc!' Roger whispered. 'We've got to do something!'

'Just hold your horses, there!' Louie replied. 'You like that? It's one of the Western phrases I managed to pick up. And me here only a matter of hours—'

'But Doc saved our lives—' Roger interjected.

'And tried to take them again, shortly thereafter,' Louie reminded him. 'Besides, what could we do? If we go rushing out there, the Cavendishes are probably going to expect us to do something with our guns.'

'Something with our guns?' Roger replied, unable to keep the dread out of his voice. He had to admit that Big Louie could be persuasive when he wanted to be.

'Maybe, that's our answer!' one of the Cavendishes yelled outside. 'Maybe Doc helped them.'

'The town drunk? Let's stop clownin' around. No, my guess is that someone else did some fancy shootin', and my second guess is that they're still around here someplace. Texas, check over there. Oregon, look back out on the street.'

'They're going to find us!' Roger whispered, the panic rising in his voice.

'Not necessarily,' Louie replied. 'These are the bad guys. And bad guys, by the rules, can be pretty stupid.'

'Movie Magic again?'

'You're catching on.'

Roger was more than catching on. He had an idea. 'But maybe that's our salvation. By the laws of Movie Magic, if those are the bad guys, and they're looking to kill us, doesn't that make us the good guys?'

Big Louie frowned. 'Well, probably. By default, if nothing else.'

'Then maybe we can shoot it out. If we're the good guys, we just have to wait for them to run out of bullets.'

But Louie wasn't convinced. 'It's not that simple. We may be good guys, but we may still just be sidekicks, too. And sometimes sidekicks get killed.'

'Killed?' Roger replied with some disappointment.

'Yeah, it's called pathos. It helps move the plot along.'

Roger sighed. 'And anything that moves the plot along is Movie Magic?'

Louie nodded in approval. 'You're learning fast. Besides, you can never tell when the bad guys will run out of bullets. That is, until it happens.'

Roger shook his head. These rules seemed to get more complicated by the moment. 'You mean—'

'Yeah, sometimes bad guys get more than six, too. But they do always run out of bullets before the good guys. 'Course, that doesn't always happen when they're shooting at sidekicks.' Louie paused to look between the slats of the back door. 'And there *are* twelve of them out there. That'll give some of them a chance to reload.'

Sunlight streamed through a knothole a couple of feet above the corner where Roger crouched. Boots clumped heavily back and forth outside, a'jangling spurs muted in the dirt. Roger resisted the urge to follow Louie's lead and peek out at the gang. If they were any match for their voices, they were twice as big and twice as ugly as the last group of Cavendishes.

'So there's no way to get out of here?' Roger despaired instead.

'Didn't say that. This being the Cineverse, there's a certain order to everything. Maybe we *can* get them to use up all their bullets. Then, of course, they have to throw their guns.'

'They have to?'

Big Louie nodded solemnly. 'It's a compulsion. You get an empty gun, you have to throw it at the hero. You don't have to hit him, of course, just throw it in his general direction.'

'I always wondered about that,' Roger nodded, fascinated despite himself.

'Nobody up this way!' one of the Cavendishes called outside.

'Nobody up on the roofs!' another called from overhead.

'I still got the feelin' they're around here somewhere,' the first voice mused. 'Colorado?'

'Right here, California!'

'Why don't you take Ohio and New Mexico and check inside the buildings around here. Michigan, you and Vermont cover them! And why don't you check the feed store first?'

Big Louie brought his six-shooter up to eye level.

'Careful now,' he whispered to Roger. 'This is the big showdown.'

Roger swallowed hard. 'Okay. This is our moment to be heroes – the big chance for our thrilling victory, right?'

Big Louie grimaced. 'Either that – or a double dose of pathos.'

CHAPTER SEVEN

That's when the shooting started.

'Hey, California! Who's shoot— Ugh!'

'Colorado! Is that – ow!'

'Watch out, boys, we don't want to shoot each – Awwwk!'

'Wait a minute! Those bullets are coming from down belo— Aurrgghh!'

'But that would mean it would have to be the town – drooff!'

'Are you kidding? It couldn't possibly – bracckk!'

Half a dozen miscellaneous screams followed in close succession. Then there was silence.

Louie slid back the bolt on the door and opened it very cautiously.

Doc was sitting up, more or less in the centre of a dozen very still bodies. He waved his flask in Louie's general direction.

'I know how to shoot a few Cavendishesh!' he announced before he took another swig. He then promptly collapsed.

'Doc saved us again!' Roger wondered.

'Yeah,' Louie marvelled. 'He must have sobered up barely enough to use his gun. A true son of the west, that Doc.' He paused and grinned. 'You like that phrase? "Son of the West." Gee, it's getting so I can speak real cowboy!'

'So what do we do now?' Roger asked, trying to collect his thoughts.

'I suggest we get out of here, and fast!' Louie said as he waved at the bodies outside. 'Sure, we've managed to kill a few of them, but I told you before that the Cavendishes are a *big* gang!' He frowned seriously at Roger. 'I think it's time to use your ring.'

'My what?' Roger took a step away, tiny alarm bells going off in the back of his brain.

What was this man suggesting? And really, how well did Roger know this fellow anyway? The one thing Roger did know was that the ring was important – Delores had called it the key to the Cineverse – and if he lost it, he would never see Delores again. Besides that, he wasn't too sure how to use the stupid thing. Did he want to admit this to Big Louie, who, up until now, seemed to think Roger was in control of what he was doing? If he brought out the ring, he'd either have to get Big Louie to instruct him in its use, or – if that failed – simply hand the ring over to the sidekick. But could he trust Big Louie to use the ring to save them both? Or would this small fellow dressed in black use the ring for his own nefarious purposes?

There had to be some other way. Didn't there?

'You know,' Louie insisted, 'your Captain Crusader decoder ring. I had to give mine back to Doctor Dread after I got back from your apartment – like I told you, there's only three in working order that I know of. Only I guess now there's four – I mean, how else would you have gotten here?'

'Oh,' Roger replied, thinking fast. 'I see what you mean.' Every time he thought about the ring, it seemed more important than the time before. Especially where Delores was concerned. There had to be some way to keep it hidden. Didn't there?

Louie stared at him expectantly.

'Oh,' Roger said again. After a moment, he added: 'Well, I have my methods.' He hoped it sounded mysterious. To him, it just sounded lame.

'Methods?' Louie's eyes narrowed to calculating slits. 'You got here using *methods*? Say, you aren't working for Captain Crusader, are you?'

Amazingly, his ruse seemed to be working! Roger managed to keep a straight face as he replied: 'I am not at liberty to divulge that information.'

That was the sort of line you used in public relations when you wanted to confirm everybody's suspicions about something while still being able to claim you were denying them.

'Not at liberty?' Louie grinned. 'I should have known. You've got much too much dumb luck for it to be natural. Just about anybody else shows up in town, they'd get gunned down by one side or the other in a matter of seconds!'

Roger smiled to himself. His hastily assembled plan was working better than he could have hoped. Apparently, denizens of the Cineverse had had little exposure to public relations. For the first time since he had shown up in this dust-filled place, he felt he was gaining some control over the situation. But how could he turn all this to his advantage? Or, more to the point, how could he use Big Louie to find Delores?

'But we are wasting time,' Roger added decisively. 'I have to complete my mission.'

'And you said you're not working for Captain Crusader?' Louie laughed. 'What do you take me for, anyway?'

Roger decided not to answer that question. Instead, he replied: 'We have to rescue Delores.'

'Delores?' Louie frowned. 'Who's Delores?'

'What? You don't remember Delores?' Roger asked a bit too emotionally. How could this fellow forget the most beautiful woman in the – well, they weren't in the *world* any more, were they? Very well, then – the most beautiful woman in the Cineverse! Roger took a deep breath. He would have to be careful – he could already feel his control slipping away.

'Hey, I'm sorry.' Louie shrugged. 'There's an awful lot of women in jeopardy around here. This is the Cineverse, after all!'

'You remember,' Roger tried again, forcing patience to take the place of panic. 'You must remember. Delores was the woman you came after on my home world? The reason you were holding me at gunpoint?'

'Oh!' Louie brightened. '*That* Delores? Oh, you mean the woman Doctor Dread is planning to torture horribly until she reveals all her secrets? Oh, yeah, I remember her now.'

Delores? Tortured horribly? Roger found his voice getting more frantic with every word. 'Well, I want you to do more than remember her. I want you to help me find her!'

'Oh,' Big Louie replied softly, cowering ever-so-slightly. 'She'd be at the hideout – the Devil's Wishbone!'

'The Devil's *Wishbone*?' Roger asked in disbelief.

'Yeah.' Louie grinned again, 'Pretty neat, huh? Doctor Dread – I mean, Boss Cavendish – always did have a knack for naming hideouts.'

But Roger had no more time for neat names. There was an edge to his voice as he asked instead: 'Do you know where it is?'

Louie's voice was the slightest bit hurt as he replied. 'What do you mean, do I know where it is? Am I a Cavendish or what? Oh. Actually, I'm not a Cavendish any more, am I? Still, I don't think they would have moved the hideout on account of me. Especially since, as you recall, you and I are currently supposed to have been – uh – taken care of.'

'*CAN YOU*—' Roger interrupted rather loudly.

'I can find it in a pinch,' Big Louie hurriedly assured him.

'Well,' Roger remarked much more quietly, his breathing once again under control, 'the pinch has come.'

'What?' Louie exploded in disbelief. 'You want us – that is, you and me – you want us to raid the Devil's Wishbone – and rescue this Delores? You want us – two sidekicks if I've ever seen two sidekicks – to go up against the fortifications of Doctor Dread's secret hideaway on this world, fortifications that probably include the rest of the Cavendish gang, and the Cineverse knows what else? You want the two of us to waltz in there past all those guns, rescue this Delores, and then waltz out again? Is that the general idea?'

'Uh, yeah, that was the general idea,' Roger admitted.

'How crazy are you?' Big Louie demanded.

'I have my methods,' Roger said again. The phrase didn't even sound as good as the last time he had used it.

'Oh, yeah,' Louie mused. 'Your methods. I keep forgetting – you may be a sidekick, but you're probably Captain Crusader's sidekick! Well, hey, let's use your methods to get us out of here.'

Roger shook his head.

'Delores.'

Big Louie shook his head. 'You really want to go through with this? You are crazy.'

Roger decided Big Louie might be right. It probably was crazy to go around acting like a hero in a place like this. But it didn't matter. The only thing that did make any difference was Delores, whether he was back on earth or on this half-baked movie world. And he was going to get her back, no matter how crazy he had to be.

He stared at Big Louie with such intensity that the smaller man took another step back.

'Let's look at this way,' Roger began. 'You haven't had too much luck as a Cavendish. Do you want to stay in this place for the rest of your life?'

'You mean the Wild West here?' Louie shrugged nonchalantly. 'Well, I am learning to speak cowboy.' He paused and frowned. 'Of course, there's all those Cavendishes who'd like to shoot me.' He paused again, pushing at the brim of his ten-gallon hat with his index finger. 'Then again, there's all those townspeople, who still think I'm a Cavendish – and probably would like to shoot me even more.' He stopped to glance down at the unused gun in his

holster. 'Well, maybe I could learn to use a six-shooter after all –
uh – there must be some way out of here, isn't there?'

'I have my methods,' Roger said with what he hoped was a
mysterious smile.

Louie sighed. 'Well, my methods are your methods. I guess it's
time we raided a hideout, huh?'

Roger nodded, satisfied at a job well done. 'I'm glad you see
it my way. So is this – Devil's Wishbone – around here someplace?'

'Are you kidding?' Louie hooted in disbelief. 'Wouldn't be
much of a hideout if it was right next door.' He frowned, then
pointed. 'It's out in the desert – thataway.'

'Thataway?' Roger asked. 'Couldn't you be a little more
specific?'

Louie shook his head with finality. ' "Thataway" is the only
direction allowed out here. Don't you know anything about the
Wild West?'

Roger nodded. He kept forgetting he was someplace where only
Movie Magic prevailed.

'Well,' Louie remarked with a certain grim finality. 'If we're
going to get ourselves killed, we might as well get a move on.' He
stepped from their hiding place into the body-strewn alleyway.

'Okay,' Roger answered, trying to sound forceful. He was
beginning to wish that sometimes the smaller fellow might not be
quite so negative. He glanced at the one body still breathing – and
snoring – in the midst of all the other still forms.

'I think it would be a good idea if we took Doc along,' he
murmured.

'And save him from the outraged excesses of the Cavendishes,'
Louie replied, 'should they find him here and guess the true
culprit in the death of all their fellows? Hey – that sounded pretty
dramatic, didn't it? I'm getting better and better at this cowboy
stuff!' He chuckled appreciatively. 'Still, saving Doc, huh? That
shows you've got a good heart.'

'Yeah,' Roger replied. 'A heart that I would like to have continue beating. Hadn't we better get a couple horses?'

'Horses?' Louie mused, glancing at the bodies piled about
them. 'Shouldn't be any problem. Lot of folks around here won't
be needing theirs anymore. Give me a second.'

He whistled. Roger heard the sound of pounding hooves. Three
horses – complete with saddles, saddlebags, rifles, canteens, and a
few other necessities – galloped into the alleyway.

'Three horses?' Roger asked.

'That's what they are,' Louie agreed. 'I realise you may be a city boy, and not too familiar with different animals—'

Roger shook his head. 'That's not what I meant. Isn't it awfully convenient that, when you whistle, the exact number of horses arrive to suit our needs?'

'Hey,' Louie retorted. 'Anything that moves the plot.' He whistled again. 'Hey, Lightning!'

A jet-black stallion with a zig-zag of white between the eyes reared onto its back legs with a whinny of greeting.

'Now there's a fine horse,' Louie commented. 'Used to belong to Dakota, who's recently deceased.' He nodded to his left, then turned to Roger. 'You do much riding?'

Roger replied that he had been on a horse once or twice when he was fourteen.

'I see,' Louie replied doubtfully. 'Well, perhaps I should ride Lightning, just to be on the safe side. Now, this other horse here is Tornado.'

The second horse, a fiery speckled grey mare, snorted and pawed at the ground, as if it couldn't wait to be galloping somewhere.

'Well,' Louie murmured. 'Once or twice? Not since fourteen, huh? Hmmm—' He paused to scratch his head. 'Maybe we'd better strap Doc to Tornado.'

Roger frowned. 'Surely there must be some horse I can ride.'

'Well, I think you're going to have to work your way up to the likes of Tornado and Lightning,' Louie counselled. 'But you're in luck, for the third animal here is my old pony.'

A small, nervous white mare shifted from foot to foot. Big Louie stepped over to her, gently patting her flank.

'Roger, this is Moderate Summer Squall.'

'Moderate Summer Squall?' Roger exploded before he could help himself. 'What kind of name—'

'Well, the Cavendishes were running out of horse names too,' Louie replied defensively. 'The Cavendishes are a *big* gang. Anyway, I always called her Missy for short.'

Roger didn't object. Nervous as Missy seemed, she appeared far less dangerous than either of the larger horses. Maybe, if he projected a little confidence, he'd be able to ride her long enough to rescue Delores.

He quickly helped Louie lift Doc and tie him across Tornado's saddle, Doc's arms hanging from one side of the horse, his legs from the other. Doc didn't seem to mind. In fact, Doc didn't seem to wake up at all, except to mumble a slurred 'Let'sh shoot shome Cavendishes. Bang, bang,' as they tightened the rope that secured his waist to the saddle. Louie vaulted upon Lightning as Roger gingerly approached Missy. Despite a nervous sidelong glance, Missy allowed Roger to swing up into the saddle.

'Okay!' Louie shouted back to him. 'Let's ride!'

All three horses took off at a full gallop. Roger hung on for dear life. This hero business wasn't all it was cracked up to be. Maybe Big Louie was right, and they were destined never to be any more than sidekicks, no matter what they did.

They left the small desert town behind in a matter of moments. Louie slowed the horses' frantic pace down to a steady canter as he scanned the horizon for landmarks, looking, Roger was sure, for 'thataway'.

Now that he no longer had to hold on for dear life, Roger breathed more easily, allowing himself to rock back in the saddle. Actually, once they had slowed down to this gentler pace, riding a horse was almost pleasant. He had a chance to get a look at the wide-open vistas before him, full of picturesque sagebrush and cacti, a pair of dark brown mesas artfully rising in the distance. The sky above was blue and cloudless, the sun warm on his back, the only sound the horses' hooves against the packed earth. Roger almost smiled, revelling in the sudden peace. This was a movie world he could live with.

Thank goodness, Roger reflected, this wasn't one of those 'singing Westerns' where the hero or his sidekick used the slightest excuse to burst into the song about 'his Texas Rose', or 'these endless prairie skies' or some such. This respite – just the three of them riding through the endless prairie under a Western sky – would finally give Roger a chance to think. Maybe he'd even come out with a way to rescue Delores.

'It is sort of nice out here, isn't it?' Louie remarked, as if he could read Roger's mind.'Especially now that I've figured out which way it is to the Devil's Wishbone. There's only one thing missing.'

Louie pointed to Missy's saddlebags.

'Do me a favour – would you? – and hand me that guitar?'

CHAPTER EIGHT

'What's the matter?' Louie asked as he accepted the guitar from Roger's outstretched hand – a guitar that, for some strange reason, Roger hadn't even realised was there until Louie mentioned it. He frowned. How could you miss a guitar?

'You look like you just swallowed your gun,' Louie added. 'Need to make a rest stop?'

Roger shook his head no and asked about what was really bothering him, even though he knew he would hate the answer:

'This isn't one of those "singing Westerns", is it?'

Louie grinned as he took a tentative strum. 'Oh, you know about this place, do you? Well, my friend, you are in luck, for – in this part of the Cineverse, at least – the West would be nothing without a song.' He stretched the fingers of his left hand around the neck of the guitar, and strummed again, producing something slightly off-key. He frowned down at his instrument. 'That wasn't right, was it?'

Roger could feel the depression settling in already. Not only was he going to be subjected to songs about Texas roses and the open prairie, he was going to be forced to listen to badly played songs about Texas roses and the open prairie.

Unless he could do something about it. The whole reason the two of them were out on the open prairie about to listen to songs about the same was that Roger had finally taken control of the situation so that he might find Delores at last. Perhaps, if he tried exerting his will once again, he could escape this musical assault.

Big Louie mangled an entirely different chord.

'Must you?' Roger complained as forcefully as he could muster. 'I was enjoying the quiet.'

'Sorry, pardner, but I must.' Louie pushed back his ten-gallon hat to scratch at his thinning hair. 'If I didn't, we'd be stuck in this quiet, endless expanse of prairie forever.' He carefully repositioned his fingers on the frets. 'Let me explain something to you.'

Louie strummed a couple more times on the guitar, the chords sounding almost right. 'We were talking before about all the different worlds of the Cineverse having different – even unique – rules, and we've come up against one of those rules here. Under ordinary circumstances, it would take us days to ride to the Devil's Wishbone – but, when you add a little music, things change – and you find you've reached your goal in under three minutes flat.'

He nodded at the great expanses before them. 'That's right, it's one of the Laws of the West. All you have to do is sing a song, and, by the time you finish the final chorus, bingo! you've reached your destination. Otherwise it takes forever to get from place to place out here.'

'Really?' Roger replied. He supposed it made sense; heaven knows he had seen it happen in Western after Western. It was like all the other laws he had encountered so far in the Cineverse; obvious to a film junkie like himself – if he would have taken a minute to consider it. Apparently, Roger decided, if he was going to survive in this strange, new place, he was going to have to learn to think more like an old movie.

'Besides,' Louie shrugged, 'whatever moves the plot along . . .'

He began to strum the guitar with a steady rhythm.

'Now, all I have to remember is one good Western song,' Louie mused. 'How about this?'

He began to sing. His voice, thankfully, was only slightly flat.

> 'Texacali Rose,
> You're wondrin' I suppose,
> Which way the river flows
> And the way the sagebrush grows?
> Could I sniff you with my nose;
> My Texacali—'

Louie stopped himself with a frown.

'That doesn't sound right, does it? I must have gotten the words wrong. Just doesn't have the proper romance.' He paused, biting his lower lip for a minute. 'Guess I'll have to try another one.'

Roger gritted his teeth and decided he would have to suffer through it, for the sake of Delores.

Louie sang and strummed:

> 'Out here on the prairie plain,
> A cowboy can make his name;
> Where a man is a man
> and he does what he can;
> And a horse is a horse
> And he does what he's forced,
> But to me now it's all the same!'

'Um,' Big Louie paused. 'There's a chorus here somewhere. Maybe I'll remember it next time around.'

To Roger's regret, he continued his song:

> 'Out where the prairie is wide,
> With a six-gun by my side;
> Where a stream is a stream—
> It's a watery dream;
> And the dirt is the dirt,
> It'll get on your shirt,
> As you sit in your saddle and ride!'

The small fellow shook his head. 'Still can't remember the chorus. You see anything up ahead?'

Roger squinted across the great expanse before them, but besides an occasional cactus, all he could see were the distant mesas.

'No luck, huh?' Louie frowned. 'Nothing that looks at all like the Devil's Wishbone? And I've already made it through two verses of the song.' He sighed. 'We'd probably be there already if I could remember the chorus.' He shrugged, strumming aimless chords. 'Well, perhaps another verse or two.'

Louie continued his assault:

> 'I ride 'cross a prairie that's free,
> Wide open spaces for me:
> Where the sky is the sky
> And the desert is dry,
> And the stars are the stars—
> If you squint you'll see Mars,
> What a place for a cowboy to be!'

'Are you sure that's the way the song goes?' Roger asked incredulously. This didn't sound like any Singing Western song he'd ever heard.

'Shh!' Louie shushed him crossly. 'If you break my concentration, we'll never get to the Devil's Wishbone! Let's see now. Oh, yeah, I think I remember . . .

> 'You'll ride cross the prairie so vast,
> um – It's one place that was built to last,
> Where a cactus is a cactus
> And – er – that's a factus,
> And – um – a prairie dog is a prairie dog—'

'Wait a minute!' Roger shouted. 'You're making all this up, aren't you?'

'Well, yeah, I ran out of verses,' Big Louie admitted. 'Was I that obvious?'

'Probably only to a trained ear,' Roger replied, backing off slightly when he saw the worry on Louie's face. 'Still—'

'I was only trying to help!' Louie complained. 'I have to get you to the Devil's Wishbone, so you can get me out of this place before I'm shot by somebody. But it's hopeless! The only way we can get to the Devil's Wishbone is if somebody finishes a song!'

But Louie's griping gave Roger an idea. This small ex-Cavendish wasn't the only one around here who knew how to play the guitar. Roger had dabbled with the instrument for a couple of years in college. After all, sensitive numbers like 'Fire and Rain' – or anything by Joni Mitchell – had been sure-fire ways to get to meet girls. He still had his old acoustic in a closet somewhere.

'Give that to me!' Roger demanded, pulling the guitar from a surprised Louie's grasp. Of course, he hadn't played the guitar in a long time, but surely he'd remember something. He had known a lot of them in his college days. He strummed experimentally. Then again, he couldn't remember some of those chord changes. Or, for that matter, some of those chords. He frowned, trying to think of some song he could actually make it through.

Only one came to mind. Roger decided it would have to do.

'Shake it up, baby,' he began, 'twist and shout—'

'Look!' Louie shouted as Roger was singing his final 'Oh, yeah!'. Roger looked up from his guitar. Their surroundings had totally changed. The mesas, so distant before, towered over them to either side, like two great guardians announcing their entrance into another world. But Louie pointed beyond the mesas. There, in the distance, one corner of a ramshackle hut peeked out of a box canyon.

That, Roger decided, was a definite hideout.

Louie whistled in admiration. 'You're not bad at that music stuff, for a city slicker. Why, if you had managed to sneak in a couple references to the open prairie or flowers blooming in some Western state, we would have landed smack dab in the middle of them!'

'Well, I'll work on it,' Roger agreed, sticking the guitar back in the saddlebags. 'Now, however, we have to come up with a plan.'

Doc hiccuped loudly.

'A plan?' Louie asked defensively. 'Hey, don't look at me. I'm only a sidekick around here.'

'Don't worry,' Roger replied. 'I was only thinking aloud. I'll come up with a plan – somehow.' He squinted ahead as they rapidly approached the box canyon. 'Actually, it's probably to our advantage that we have a few more minutes of riding ahead of us. It'll give me a chance to think.' Like a movie, Roger added to himself, think like a movie. If only he could figure out how the Masked Marshal would handle something like this.

'Hey!' a muffled voice shouted behind him. 'What'sh goin' on here?'

Roger looked over his shoulder. From the tell-tale slur, he realised Doc had revived. From the way the town drunk was squirming about on the saddle, he seemed to have revived in a big way.

'Hey!' Doc exclaimed, fumbling behind his back with the rope that bound his waist to the saddle. 'I'm tied to a horshe!'

'Sorry,' Roger called. 'We didn't think you were sober enough to ride.'

'Nonshenshe!' Doc retorted. His hand worried the knots at his belt, his fingers deftly moving their way between the strands of rope until he had pulled every knot apart. As the rope pulled free, he raised himself from the saddle as he grasped the saddle horn, quickly swinging his right leg over the horse as he settled into a sitting position.

Doc grinned at Roger. 'Shober? Shee, I'm perfectly shober.'

'My apologies,' Roger murmured, quite taken by the performance.

'It'sh nothing,' Doc replied modestly. 'Jusht a little shomething I learned back when I wash a daredevil rider and eshcape artisht.' But his self-satisfied grin turned into a frown as he looked ahead. 'What'sh that?'

'Do you mean the hideout?' Roger offered.

'Chertainly not. I know a hideout when I shee one! What are all theshe dromedariesh doing out here?' Doc demanded. 'Or are they camelsh?'

'Oh, dear,' Louie remarked softly.

Roger knew just what Louie meant. Doc wasn't going to be much use to anyone if he spent all his time hallucinating. But maybe there was some way to get beyond all this.

'I have no idea what they're doing here,' Roger said gently. 'However, I think if you will ignore them, they'll ignore you.'

'Shage adviche,' Doc agreed. 'Excushe me.' He reached in his coat pocket and retrieved his silver flask. 'Jusht one little drink. Shettlesh my nervesh.'

Doc drank, three long swallows. He smacked his lips as he recapped the flask.

'That's more like it!' he announced, his voice noticeably stronger.

Something buzzed by Roger's ear – an insect, maybe – although it was travelling awfully fast. Another buzzed past his other ear. Roger wondered absently if they were riding into a swarm of something or other. And then there were those tiny dust clouds rising in front of his horse, as if someone was throwing tiny pebbles into the dirt. Both Tornado and Lightning reared up on their hind legs with whinnies of fear. Only Missy continued to plod placidly ahead.

Dust clouds? Travelling awfully fast? Whinnies of fear? Roger frowned. There might be something wrong here.

'Ambush!' Big Louie yelled as he urged his horse toward a nearby cluster of boulders.

Ambush? Roger's frown deepened. That meant these things flying around him weren't bugs, or even pebbles. They were bullets!

'Somebody's shooting at us?' he asked rather less calmly than he might have wished. Missy turned, sedately following Big Louie's lead behind the clump of rocks.

'Well,' Doc replied with a sardonic grin as he swung off his horse. 'We'll have to shoot back, now, won't we?'

CHAPTER NINE

The next few minutes were much too loud for Roger's liking.

There were bullets flying most everywhere, a number of them tearing chunks out of the large cactus immediately above his hiding place. The rock wasn't high enough here for Roger to do much more than kneel and cower. Missy had joined the other two horses behind the much more sensible gigantic boulder that Doc and Big Louie now stood behind. Perhaps, Roger considered, he shouldn't have dismounted quite so quickly. But then, he was new to being shot at.

Roger decided to follow the lead of Doc and Big Louie. He peeked above his hiding place, and lifted his six-shooter, taking the most careful aim that he could, while he was still busy cowering, at one of their dozen or so assailants, most of them hiding in the rocky outcroppings to either side of the box canyon ahead. After the first couple of tries, he managed to keep his gun from jerking wildly in the air as he fired. Once he had conquered that hurdle, he figured he could get aiming down in no time.

By the time he had really gotten the hang of it, however, no one was shooting anymore, and silence once again ruled the desert. In other words, Doc had killed all their opponents.

'Dead?' Louie cried in disbelief. 'We got all of them?'

'I think that calls for a drink!' Doc exclaimed.

'Wait a second!' Roger called as he leapt to his feet and ran with a speed that amazed even himself to tear the flask from Doc's hand. 'We've still got a woman to save. Any celebration now would be far too premature.'

'Wow!' Big Louie marvelled. 'You got a death wish or something? You dare to take a drink away from a gunfighter of Doc's calibre?'

Yes, Roger thought, that was exactly what he'd done. Although he hadn't thought much about the wrath of the gunfighter when he'd done it. He was much more concerned about the unspeakable things Delores might be suffering at this very minute at the hands of Doctor Dread – that, and the fact Doc seemed to be an excellent gunfighter when he was precisely drunk enough – no more, no less. With too little to drink, the gunfighter was incoherent, with too much, he was unconscious. Roger couldn't let either of those extremes occur – not with Delores' life – actually much more than her life, her *honour* – at stake. That was what he'd been thinking about, and not those other consequences Louie had so helpfully mentioned, when he deprived Doc of a drink. And it was the right decision, too!

Or at least it was as long as Doc didn't shoot him.

'No celebratin' til' the job is done?' Doc drawled as he holstered his pistol. 'Okay. Sounds like one of the laws of the West to me.'

Well, Roger was glad to get that out of the way. He wiped away the sweat that had suddenly drenched his forehead and considered their options. Now, as far as he figured it, all they had to do was walk into the box canyon before them after their presence had been so dramatically announced by their recent gun battle, the three of them marching single file down a narrow, well-lit path between two great walls of stone absolutely riddled with the sort of hiding places bad-guy-gunmen seemed to favour. It was not an experience Roger was looking forward to.

He looked over all the black-clad bodies littering the entrance-way to the canyon, and had a thought. They would be in trouble – unless, of course, they had managed to shoot all of the Cavendishes. Heaven knew they had managed to shoot a large number of them; even more than he had originally thought. Roger gave up counting when he reached two dozen. Perhaps the worst was over – perhaps there would be no one left inside save Delores and Doctor Dread.

'Louie?' he asked the fellow hopefully. 'You don't think, maybe, that we could have shot all of the—'

But Louie shook his head before Roger could finish.

'The Cavendishes are a *big* gang,' Louie insisted.

'Well, what are we waitin' for?' Doc chortled manfully. 'I hear we've got some rescuin' to do!'

'We're going in there like this?' Louie wailed. 'Two sidekicks and a town drunk?'

'No,' Roger cautioned. 'Wait a minute. I have a plan.' At last, he realised, he was beginning to think like an old movie. Louie was already dressed for the part. But both Doc and he needed a change of clothes. After a quick survey of the bodies, he picked the two recently deceased Cavendishes closest in size to Doc and himself, then asked his two companions to give him a hand in stripping the corpses.

'Stripping the corpses?' Louie protested. 'Haven't you ever heard of death with dignity?'

'I'd rather hear of the three of us surviving what happens next,' Roger answered dryly. 'We might not have much chance of that as two sidekicks and a town drunk. However, I think our chances improve greatly if we walk into that camp dressed as Cavendishes.'

Doc whistled in appreciation. 'I gotta hand it to you, stranger, that's a real Western plan.'

'But how can it possibly work?' Louie fretted. 'They don't know us at all. Won't we still look like strangers?'

Roger shook his head thoughtfully. 'There's a chance that won't matter. After all, you said so yourself: The Cavendishes are a *big* gang.'

Reluctantly, Louie helped Doc and Roger get the clothes off the corpses, then left to tie the horses out of sight. By the time he returned, all three of them were dressed in black.

Louie sighed, still not convinced. 'We may look like Cavendishes, but to me we still feel like two sidekicks and a town drunk.'

Doc chuckled in return. 'Come on now. Is that any way to look into the jaws of danger?'

'No,' Louie admitted. 'It's only my way. Actually, I would much prefer to look into the jaws of danger from a somewhat greater distance – say, back in town?' He smiled apologetically.

'Come on,' Roger said. 'Let's get this over with.' The two silver six-shooters he had strapped to his waist felt cold against his palms as he slowly made his way toward the entrance to the canyon. Deep in his heart, he felt almost as uneasy as Big Louie, for he realised he was probably leading all three of them into certain death. But if he didn't, then what would happen to Delores? Unless it was already too late. He pushed the thought from his mind, concentrating on the sounds of six spurs a'jangling as the three of them trudged down the incline to the canyon floor.

He had to face up to it. What happened next was going to be dangerous. It might be downright impossible.

It also didn't help that the boots he was now wearing were a little tight.

'Yo!' called a voice from the canyon wall. 'Who goes there?'

Roger stopped and swallowed, even though his mouth was desert dry. If they could fool the guard, they could get in to rescue Delores. If not—

Roger refused to think the rest of that thought. He saw Doc's hand edge over to brush against his pearl-handled revolver. Roger shook his head. It was time to use cunning, not force. He stared at the ground as he called up to the sentry, doing his best to keep his face hidden in the shadow of his hat.

'Cavendishes coming in!' he called. That was the sort of thing bad guys said when they walked into a secret hideout, wasn't it?

'Cavendishes?' the sentry began. 'What's the pa—'

'Don't worry,' a gruff, cowboy voice said from up ahead. 'I'll show 'em around.'

'Okay! You're the boss!' The sentry disappeared behind an outcropping of rock.

Roger turned to the other Cavendish, a dozen yards ahead. He was the biggest bad guy Roger had seen so far, a full three inches taller than the recently deceased California. He smiled at Roger and his companions, and Roger saw that three of his teeth were gold. When he smiled, he looked even meaner. Maybe, Roger considered, it was because of all those scars.

'Follow me, pardners,' the very large man remarked right after he spat. The spittle landed on the toe of Roger's borrowed boot, a distance, Roger estimated, of some twenty feet. Roger looked up at the large man, but he had already turned around and was walking away.

'Welcome to the Devil's Wishbone,' the immense fellow called over his shoulder. Roger could see the fellow's back muscles ripple as he moved, even under his black shirt. 'I'm the foreman around here.'

'Foreman?' Roger asked before he could stop himself. Did a hideout need a foreman?

'Every place in the Old West needs a foreman,' the foreman rumbled. 'It's one of the Laws of the West. There's certain laws even bad guys don't break.'

'Sure, we knew all about that,' Louie hastily added.

Doc's hand hung nervously over his gun. His free hand reached toward the pocket with the flask, but Roger again shook his head emphatically.

Roger couldn't blame his fellows. Even he had to admit that this newest Cavendish tended towards the sinister. Still, what else would you expect of a foreman of the bad guys? At least his plan was working, and they were getting inside the Devil's Wishbone. In fact, it had been far easier than he first imagined.

'I figured you boys, bein' new here and all, would like a look around,' the foreman drawled with a chuckle. 'This up ahead is the main house.'

'The main house?' Roger blurted before he could cover his mouth. The place up ahead looked like nothing more than a weathered, unpainted shack, the sort of place that, when you opened the door, you fully expected the roof to cave in.

'Sounds better than the main shack,' the foreman explained. 'This is a hideout, after all. In this business, you gotta make some compromises.'

A man in a black snakeskin hat appeared on the inside of a dust-smeared window for an instant. It had to be Doctor Dread! Roger's breath caught beneath his Adam's apple – that meant Delores was inside for sure! As if to confirm his suspicions while they approached the shack, Roger could hear voices arguing inside.

'So what do *you* want to do with her?' a woman's voice demanded.

'Oh,' Doctor Dread's slimy voice replied. 'I don't know. Something –' he paused significantly, '– appropriate.'

'But there are so many options!' the woman's voice insisted. 'I mean, there's tying her to the railroad tracks, or chaining her to a log that's about to go through the sawmill, or how about stranding her in a boat that's just about to go over the waterfall?'

'Aren't those a little –' Dread paused meaningfully, '– too common? We want her to –' he halted tellingly, '– talk, after all.'

'But I see. You want me to be a little more –' she hesitated knowingly, '– creative.'

'Yes, we need something to make her –' he stalled suggestively, '– especially cooperative.'

'Oh!' the woman responded brightly. 'Why didn't you say so? Why not strap her out in the desert sun, her hands and feet bound by strips of wet rawhide which will shrink painfully as they dry, her face smeared with honey and sure to attract those fire ants milling around that anthill close by her left ear, bits of a sacred totem broken and scattered about her helpless form, sure to infuriate that fierce band of renegade Indians that have just appeared on yonder hill—'

Roger couldn't stand this anymore! They were talking about torturing the woman he loved! He ran forward.

'Oh,' the foreman drawled without the least surprise. 'You want to look around inside, do you? Well, at least let me open the door.'

He did precisely that, and Roger rushed into the shack. Doctor Dread looked up as he entered the room. Standing nearby was a woman Roger had never seen before, an imposing-looking female of a height equal to or greater than that of the foreman who had led them here.

But all thoughts of the others fled as he saw who was bound and gagged in a chair between those two, her perfect face illuminated by a kerosene lamp beneath her feet upon the floor. Hope lit her eyes as she saw him enter the room. His plan had worked after all. They had found Delores!

'Who is it?' Doctor Dread's voice held the slightest note of annoyance. 'More members of our –' he paused significantly, '– little family?'

Their large guide grunted in reply. 'No, actually, it's two side-kicks and a town drunk. But they're dressed like Cavendishes. I thought I'd bring them around to you before we shot them.'

Shot them? Perhaps, Roger considered, his plan still had a few flaws. He glanced behind him, ready to bolt at the slightest opportunity. Doc and Big Louie were crowded close by his back. And in the doorway – their only possible means of escape – stood the foreman, the same foreman who had drawn both his revolvers and was covering all three of them.

'Shoot them?' Dread frowned disapprovingly. 'Oh, no, no, no.'

'What?' The foreman's gold-toothed grin faltered. 'We shouldn't shoot them?'

Dread wiggled a finger in the large cowboy's direction. 'No, no, you should never *talk* about shooting them. People like this should be –' he paused significantly, '– removed. They should be –' another pause, '– dispensed with. These matters have to be discussed with –' yet another pause, '– some delicacy.'

The big fellow shook his head slowly, struggling to comprehend.

'Then, of course, once you're done implying things, you can take them out and shoot them,' Dread added. 'It's as simple as that. You have a lot to learn, Ontario, about being a Cavendish.'

'Ontario?' Roger asked, unable to stop himself.

'He's from the northern branch of the gang,' explained Dread with an oily grin.

Roger did his best to manage his breathing. It would do him no good to panic now, and he didn't want to think what would happen to Delores if he lost control. So what if his first plan hadn't quite worked? All he had to do was think like a movie. What did he remember about the Wild West on film?

Yeah, Roger thought, the plots of a dozen 'B' Westerns flying through his mind. You could always talk or fight your way out of trouble with bad guys. Well, you could that is, if you were the hero. Roger wasn't sure if the rule held up for sidekicks. Still, it was worth a try.

'But wait a minute!' Roger insisted. 'What are you guys talking about? We're Cavendishes!'

'Sure,' Ontario the foreman chortled. 'And I'm the first robin of spring.'

Doctor Dread and the very imposing female shared in the laughter.

'Oh yeah? Well, um, er, oh yeah?' Roger countered none too steadily. Perhaps words weren't going to work after all. But that meant they were going to have to use their fists, didn't it? Roger wished some of the bad guys weren't quite so tall. Maybe he just hadn't talked enough. 'Don't we look like Cavendishes?'

All the bad guys roared at that one.

'Give it up,' Big Louie cautioned. 'They know who I am!'

'Oh,' Roger remarked. He should have thought of that, Big Louie having been in Dread's gang and all. 'You mean Doctor Dread remembers—'

'How could he forget?' Louie stared down at his tooled leather boots. 'You see that statuesque woman over there? She's my sister.'

The statuesque woman grinned and approached them. The floorboards shook beneath her feet as she walked. She stuck out her hand in Roger's direction.

'Put 'er there. You can call me Bertha. You know, for a sidekick, you're kind of cute.'

Hesitantly, Roger took her hand. Once she had let go, Roger shook his hand again in an attempt to restart the blood flow.

'Bertha,' she replied with a smile that implied all sorts of things Roger didn't want to think about. 'My friends call me – Big Bertha. Remember the name. I think I'm going to be seeing –' she paused in that way the bad guys had, '– a lot of you.'

Roger swallowed, his throat even dryer than it had been in the desert. What did she mean by that? And why did her tone give Roger a queasy feeling, deep down in his stomach?

'Alas, dear Bertha,' Dread interrupted unctuously, 'I fear we don't have time for that. These poor unfortunates must be – dealt with.'

'Oh, yeah?' Doc erupted, spinning abruptly and felling the large Cavendish behind him with one well-aimed blow of his fist. Ontario crashed to the parched earth outside the shack. Doc turned again and swaggered forward so that he stood at Roger's side. He grinned at the remaining Bad Guys.

'You want to bet on that?'

'Yeah,' Roger agreed as his fingers curled reassuringly around the cool handle of his revolver. 'I think we're going to leave here with what we came for.' He smiled reassuringly at the hog-tied love of his life.

'Delores!' Roger called.

'Mmmmppphhhffff!' Delores replied. Roger's smile broadened. It was wonderful to hear the sound of her voice again. Her fashionable silver bracelets clinked together as she tried to turn toward him, but she was so severely tied that she could do nothing save clink her silver bracelets. This was too much for him to take! He took a step forward.

'No.' Doc placed a deterring hand on Roger's shoulder. 'Let me do it. You never know what tricks these Cavendishes are up to.'

Roger nodded and stepped aside. He was happier with every passing moment that he had kept Doc from taking that extra drink. It was amazing how capable the fellow was when he wasn't falling-down inebriated. Now, Roger was sure, as long as they kept Doc on the wagon, they'd be able to free Delores and foil anything the Cavendishes could throw against them.

Doc sauntered forward, his spurs a'jangling over the rotting floorboards.

'We'll have you out of this in a minute, missy,' Doc murmured nobly as he approached. 'Excuse me while I move this lamp.' He squatted in front of Delores's chair and dragged the kerosene lantern toward him, making a face as the fumes hit his nose.

'Excuse me,' he muttered. 'I'll untie you just—' He blinked rapidly, his face taking on a vaguely unfocused look. 'Excushe—' he started again. 'I'll untie you – right –' his eyes seemed to cross of their own accord, '– after I jusht take a little nap!'

Doc was snoring before he hit the floor. Maybe, Roger reflected, it had been an alcohol lantern. Whatever – it took Roger but an instant to realise Doc's inhaling of the fumes had once again driven him over the edge. This was terrible! All was lost, unless he and Big Louie could act quickly.

'Stay where you are!' Roger barked as he quickly pulled his revolver from his holster to cover Dread and Bertha. He figured this was his last chance to get the drop on the bad guys, while they were still surprised by recent events. And even later he would still agree that his theory was near perfect movie-thinking. Still, he had to admit it probably would have been much more effective had the gun not flown out of his hand the minute he yanked it from its holster. He heard it clatter in the far corner of the room at the same instant he felt something hard pressing into the small of his back.

'You're pretty good at throwing away your gun,' Ontario drawled. 'Now let's see how good you are at throwing away your life.'

'What a great line!' Dread enthused. 'Do I know how to pick my foremen, or what?'

'Well, Boss?' Roger heard the twin clicks of two gunhammers being drawn back behind him. 'Is it time?'

'Soon, Ontario, very soon,' Dread assured his crony. He smirked at Roger. 'I could have him – deal with you right away. But no, I think that first I shall – spend a minute and gloat over my – master plan! That's right. I have only begun to tear down those fences and stampede my cattle over the properties of innocent homesteaders! And only today did we burn down the Assay Office so we could jump the claims of unsuspecting prospectors. Now, after we alter the river's course to control the water rights and make preparations for the railroad to come through—' He paused to laugh maniacally. 'And that's only on this world, a small part of my – master master plan!'

'Can I deal with them now, boss?' Ontario asked hopefully.

'Roger?' Big Louie's voice quavered at his side.

Roger turned to look at his companion. Could the small man know of some way out of this?

Louie's smile faltered as he added, 'It's been good knowing a sidekick as nice as you.'

Sidekick? Roger guessed that answered his question. He had come to this world trying to be a hero, but would end up as pathos. He guessed it was fate.

'Wait!' the tall woman commanded. 'There may be another way.'

A flicker of hope stirred deep within Roger. He had forgotten that this big woman was Big Louie's sister! Maybe family feelings could save them where all else failed!

'Now, now, Bertha,' Doctor Dread chided. 'I know one of these sidekicks is your brother—'

'That's not it at all!' Bertha interjected. 'I was foolish in talking you into giving Seymore – or whatever he calls himself now – a job. Let's face it – my brother should have been shot a long time ago. No, I want the other one.' She smiled thinly in Roger's direction. 'I thought he was cute before, but when he ineptly tried to take control a moment ago it sent shivers down my spine. That's when I knew he had to be mine.'

Bertha paused to make grasping motions with her very large hands. 'I haven't *used* anybody in ever so long!'

Roger would have taken a step away if he didn't have a gun stuck against his spine. The way this woman was looking at him through those half-closed eyelids started him thinking how simple and clean death could be.

'Now, now, Bertha—' Dread began.

'Oh, I know it means keeping him alive a little while longer,' Bertha pleaded. 'But think of it this way. When I'm done, there won't be much left of him, will there? I mean, by that point, his being alive will be more of a technicality.'

'No, Bertha,' Dread said with finality. 'As long as this interloper lives, there would be a small chance he might escape, and even though, being with you, it would probably take him months to recover, I still can't take that chance. They will have to be – dealt with now.'

Ontario chuckled behind Roger. 'Oh boy! Does that mean it's time?'

'Yes,' Dread agreed gleefully. 'You put it so well. It is – hehheh – time.'

This was it then. Roger's throat was so dry that he didn't even try to swallow. He looked a final time at Delores as she bravely tried to blink the tears from her eyes. At least he had seen her a final time before the end. There was no way to save them now.

That's when he heard the bugle.

CHAPTER TEN

A bugle? But it couldn't be!

'Drat!' Doctor Dread cursed. 'It's the cavalry!'

Then it was a bugle! Come to think of it, Roger reconsidered, in a place like this, not only could it be, but it was probably required.

'Thank goodness!' Louie whispered at his side. 'We're going to be rescued by one of the Laws of the West.'

'Movie Magic?' Roger whispered back.

Louie nodded. 'Hey!' he remarked a second later. 'Maybe this means we're not sidekicks after all. Or – maybe – *one* of us isn't a sidekick!'

Louie and Roger frowned at each other.

'Aw, come on, Boss,' Ontario pleaded. 'Can't I deal with these guys anyway?'

'Now, now,' Dread reprimanded, 'you've been on Western worlds long enough to know what would happen if we attempted that! Oh, sure, it would begin promisingly enough. You'd lead these two out into the sun outside the shack. Then, as an evil smile spread across your face while you simultaneously pulled back the triggers of your two six-shooters so you could plug both these sidekicks dramatically at the same time, the heroic leader of the cavalry would ride over a nearby hill, and, with a single shot, fire a bullet past your spine and straight into your heart, causing your two guns to fire harmlessly in the air as you fell, lifeless, into the desert sand.'

'Oh. Yeah,' Ontario pondered. 'I guess that would happen, wouldn't it?'

Dread nodded solemnly. 'It's one of the Laws of the West.'

'You mean,' Bertha blurted, 'that I won't have any time to *use* him?' From the way she smiled hungrily at Roger, there was no doubt whom she was referring to.

'Alas,' Dread replied sadly, 'I am afraid for now that all our desires must go –' he paused significantly, '– unfulfilled.'

'Maybe just a little?' Bertha winked in Roger's direction. 'With my techniques, I assure you it will take no time at all.'

'That, unfortunately, is exactly what we have,' Dread said with finality. 'No time at all.'

'But can't we do anything?' Ontario asked, hands still hopefully on his gun handles.

Dread nodded curtly. 'We can get out of here.' He waved to his fellows. 'Bertha, Ontario, I need each of you to hold onto a sleeve of my fringe jacket.'

Dread's cronies did as they were instructed, Bertha somehow managing it without looking away from Roger.

'Good,' Dread commented his fellows. 'Now I want each of you to place a hand on the shoulder of our captive.'

'Mmmmppphhh!' Delores protested.

'Delores!' Roger cried in despair, unable to cope with the thought of his one true love once again being snatched away to parts unknown.

'How magnificently pitiful!' Bertha said, her voice a low, throaty growl. 'Couldn't we find a way to take this one along?' Her tongue darted across her teeth in anticipation. 'I promise to use him very quietly! You'll hardly even hear his pleas for mercy – really!'

But Dread frowned at her suggestion. 'No. There is something about this newcomer that seems to upset any plan we may devise. If we cannot kill him – and I assure you, should one of us even attempt it at this moment, we would be destroyed where we stood – then we must disappear somewhere where he can never follow us, so that we might complete our plans and destroy his kind forever!'

'But can't he follow us,' Bertha insisted, 'if he has a ring?'

'An excellent point!' Dread mused. 'Then there is one final thing we must do before we – take our leave. Ontario, point your guns at Louie.'

Ontario grinned. 'That's more like it, Boss!'

Shots rang outside of the shack. Somebody screamed as they fell a considerable distance. The bugle blew again.

'They got the look-out!' Bertha exclaimed.

'Yes,' Dread replied. 'We have no time to lose. Ontario, unless Louie tells us where his friend is hiding the Captain Crusader Decoder Ring, shoot him.'

Ontario frowned. 'But I thought you said—'

'That only applies to heroes,' Dread interrupted. 'There's some possibility this Roger is one of those. That's why we're not pointing the gun at him. Louie, on the other hand, is lucky to be even considered a sidekick. I think we just have time to shoot him before we escape.'

'Oh, boy, a shooting!' Ontario enthused. 'Can I do it now?'

'In a second,' Dread cautioned. 'After all, we need to give him a little time to spill his guts. It's one of the Laws of the West.'

'Okay, small stuff.' Ontario cocked both his pistols. 'The ring or a bullet. Which is it going to be?'

'But – but—' Big Louie was sweating so profusely that his hat threatened to slide down to cover his eyes. 'Y-you can't shoot me!'

'Wanna bet?' Ontario's fingers curled around twin triggers.

The hat fell over the top of his nose as Louie vehemently shook his head. 'Y-you don't understand. R-r-roger doesn't have a r-ring—'

'Doesn't have a ring?' Dread demanded. 'Are you sure—'

'But that means—' Bertha announced, as respect mixed with lust in her gaze.

'It means we should kill him anyway!' Ontario turned his guns toward Roger.

Somebody pounded heavily on the door as the bugle blew on the other side of the window.

'Open up!' a gruff voice announced. 'It's the cavalry!'

'Too late!' Dread cried. 'To my side, Ontario. We leave this instant!'

Ontario and Bertha resumed their positions, forming a circle with Dread and Delores.

'Mmmmmppphhhh!' Delores protested a final time.

'Don't worry,' the doctor sneered in Roger's direction. 'We'll be back . . . once the laws have changed!'

He twisted the plastic ring on his finger.

'See you in the funny papers!'

The four of them were surrounded by blue smoke, and then they were gone.

Only one word escaped from Roger's lips:

'Delores!'

There had to have been some way he could have saved her. Dread had told his henchperson not to kill him, after all, although Ontario had seemed ready to shoot him at the slightest provocation right until the very end. But would they have dared to do anything? The cavalry had shown up, and Louie swore they only came around when there was a hero to rescue, and Dread had assured Louie that he could never ever be a hero, which, by the process of elimination, meant that the hero had to be Roger. Didn't it? But, if he was the hero, he should have been able to rescue Delores. Shouldn't he? Then, to confound things, she had disappeared in a puff of smoke, and he was still standing here, doing nothing in particular, while the cavalry made a lot of noise with their bugles outside. Is that the sort of thing a hero would do?

Roger had to admit it. He knew he was confused.

And then the cavalry broke down the door.

A burly man dressed in cavalry blue, his dusty uniform sporting sergeant's stripes upon the sleeve, was the first into the shack.

'Where is he?' the newcomer demanded.

'Where's who?' Louie asked. 'Didn't you come to save us?'

Slim, or possibly Sam, strode through the door next. Whichever one he wasn't followed at the first one's heels.

'There he is!' One of the two pointed at the still snoring form of Doc, curled up at the centre of the uneven floor.

A number of other cavalry members, along with some miscellaneous townspeople, piled into the shack as well. Somebody blew a bugle in Doc's ear.

'What? Huh?' Doc yawned and stretched, squinting up at the room full of people. 'Can't a fellow get a deshent afternoon'sh shleep around here?'

The townspeople cheered.

'That's our Doc!' Bart said cheerfully.

'Yeah,' Bret joined in. 'It's nice to have him back. Sagebrush just wasn't the same without our town drunk!'

'Wait a moment!' Roger interjected. 'That's why you're here? To rescue the town drunk?'

'Sure!' Bart replied. 'Why else would we come out to a gosh-forsaken place like this? You only use the cavalry when it's a life and death situation.'

Bret whistled in agreement. 'You can't underestimate the importance of a town drunk! I tell you, sitting in a bar without someone grovelling in the sawdust for drinks simply isn't the same.'

Bart nodded. 'Takes all the fun out of a town. But that's all gonna change, now that we have our drunk back. Sam, Slim, why don't you help Doc out to the horses?'

'Excuse me,' Roger interrupted once again, still not truly

believing the import of all this, 'but – rescuing Doc – that's the only reason you came out here?'

'Sure.' Bart chuckled. 'No offence, but do you think we'd waste the cavalry's time on rescuing a couple of sidekicks?'

Doc sat up and blinked at the two men trying to help him to his feet. 'Hey! Wait a minute! What are you doing out here?'

'Why,' replied Slim or Sam – whichever one it was who still had his arm in a sling – 'we're here to rescue you.'

'Now that's not what I mean, and you know it! I cut a bullet out of you a few hours ago, and here you are riding all over the desert.' Doc shook his grizzled head in disgust. 'I swear, Sam, I don't know why I bother!'

'Uh, pardon me, Doc,' the man in the sling replied, 'but I'm Slim.'

'Hey!' his companion added rapidly. 'Are you sure of that?'

Slim frowned. 'What do you mean?'

'Well, I don't know how to tell you this—' The fellow cleared his throat. 'I always thought I was Slim.'

Maybe-not-Slim blanched beneath his deep Western tan. 'Then that means I'm Sam?'

The other nodded.

Roger couldn't believe this. 'Aren't *either* of you sure?'

'Well—' the one in the sling began.

'No,' the slingless one concluded.

'You know, life out here in the Old West gets a mite wearyin'—' maybe-Sam continued.

Maybe-Slim added '—what with a heavy duty life of cow punchin' and poker playin', some of these little things get lost.'

Possibly-Sam shrugged. 'Yeah, you know, a fella gets confused.'

'We once thought about getting tattoos,' Possibly-Slim admitted. 'But, you know, it gets embarrassing, having to peek inside your shirt all the time to see if it's really you they're talking to.'

Roger nodded. Somehow, the explanations of these two cowpokes had left him even more thoroughly confused than he had been before. Still, perhaps because of his public relations training, or perhaps because he wanted to interrupt Slim and Sam's never-ending ramblings, he felt he had to say something.

'I never realised it was so bad,' he said sympathetically.

'That's not the half of it!' one of the two complained. 'You should see the problem we have with our wives.'

'Well, I'm sure you folks are havin' a fine time gettin' reacquainted,' Bart interrupted in his characteristic drawl, 'but I think it's about time we got Doc back to town.'

'Yeah!' Bret chimed in, bending down over the still seated object of their rescue. 'Say, Doc, would you like a little nip to get you back on your feet?'

But Doc shook his head. 'I've decided to give up nippin' – and drinkin' too, for the time bein'. Now, help me up, would you?'

Startled into silence, Bart did as he was told.

'Appreciate it,' Doc said. 'Now let's get goin' '

Both cavalry and townfolk followed Doc from the shack. The last one out, who was Probably-Sam, depending upon whom you believed, glanced over his shoulder as he stood on the threshold, and spoke to Roger and Louie.

'Oh, I guess it's all right if you guys come along, too. With all the dead Cavendishes out there, there's bound to be some extra horses.'

'I guess we'd better go,' Louie said after a second, quickly following the last cowboy out.

Roger left the shack as well, stepping out into a chaotic mass of men and horses. He didn't know what he should do next, but he didn't particularly want to be left behind.

Still, what was the use of going anywhere? Apparently, he wasn't a hero after all, but had been forced into the role of permanent sidekick on this strange new world. That meant nobody would ever pay much attention to him, with the possible exception of another sidekick like Big Louie.

That thought alone was depressing enough. More important, though, if he was nothing but a sidekick, how could he possibly rescue Delores?

'Hurry up!' Louie called back to him. 'The others are leaving!'

Roger started running, hoping he could find Missy somewhere in the milling crowd before him.

CHAPTER ELEVEN

Somehow, Roger managed to find his horse. Somehow, even more miraculously, he managed to mount his horse, and ride after the others.

He was getting over the shock of not being a hero, and other things entered his mind. Other things like how could he get out of this place to rescue Delores. He still had the ring, after all. He simply had no idea how to use it.

Maybe he should have stayed back at the Devil's Wishbone, and tried to follow Doctor Dread from there. But even Roger had to admit that the only thing that had gotten him this far was stubbornness and pure dumb luck. He had somehow managed to copy the exact setting Big Louie had set on his ring in order to follow him here – the first time. But that wouldn't work again. He had been too busy staring helplessly at Delores – she really was beautiful, even when she was bound and gagged – to really get a good look at Doctor Dread's adjustments to his personal key to the universe. Without knowing the proper ring setting, how could Roger hope to follow?

Unless Big Louie knew where they might have gone. Roger sighed. Maybe he should confide in the small sidekick after all. And why not? Louie had stood by his side during their entire confrontation with the Cavendish gang. The black-clad sidekick was loyal and steadfast and ever-dependable, just like companions in the movies, especially Western movies. Roger was startled to realise that Louie might even be considered a friend. Not only that, but with Delores gone, Louie was his only friend in the Cineverse.

The rest of the riders were far ahead, cloistered around the still sober Doc. The whole rescuing party, some thirty or forty strong, seemed to collectively care less whether or not Roger and Louie tagged along. In a way, Roger reflected, the crowd's indifference gave the two of them some much needed privacy for discussion of important things, like rescuing Delores, and confessing that Roger did, indeed, possess a ring.

'Louie,' Roger began. 'I've got to talk to you about something.'

'So you felt it, too?' Louie replied before Roger could launch into his appeal. 'There's something very wrong here.'

'Of course there's something wrong!' Roger insisted. 'They've captured Delores.'

'Oh, that's true, too,' Big Louie murmured distractedly. He snapped his fingers. 'I know what's bothering me. Remember what Dread said as he left – that he'd be back when the laws were – different? What did he mean by that? Nobody can change the Laws of the West. Can they?'

Roger still didn't know enough about this place to give him an answer.

Apparently, Louie didn't really need one, because he kept on talking. 'It would mean a complete realignment of the very forces that move the Cineverse – or perhaps – something even worse!' He frowned at his fellow sidekick. 'You've heard about the Change?'

Roger nodded, surprised at the intensity of Louie's response.

'The Change? Delores mentioned it to me once. She didn't really have any time to explain it, though, before you guys showed up to kidnap her.'

'Oh, that.' Louie blushed. Well, I was only doing my job, you know. If only I had realised the implications of Dread's plans! And here I was, trying to change my lot in life— Oh, if only I had stayed in comic relief!' Without letting go of the reins, Louie still managed to wring his hands melodramatically.

'You were talking about the Change?' Roger interjected helpfully.

'Oh. Sure. The Change. Right.' He took a deep breath, trying desperately to compose himself. 'It was a while ago now, perhaps a couple decades past by the methods you – on that planet of yours – tell time. Nobody was quite sure how it began, although some did suspect Doctor Dread had a hand in it – but if he did, it was probably in another one of his guises. Oh, I should have realised that before I became involved with him! But no, I was tired of pratfalls, and looking for variety—'

Roger cleared his throat. 'The Change?'

'Oh.' Louie smiled apologetically. 'Yeah. So, anyway, things began to unravel everywhere in the Cineverse. It was small stuff at first, an extraneous death among the supporting characters here, an unresolved subplot there. But it escalated quickly. There came a dark time when it seemed that every hero had to die!'

Roger's breath caught at the back of his throat. Twenty years ago, Louie had said? He remembered that time, in the late sixties and early seventies, in every movie he would go to see, whether it was a western, a cop movie or a motorcycle flick, where the hero would be blown away by excessive gunfire thirty seconds before 'The End' showed up on the screen. It had been a dark time, indeed. A shiver shook Roger's shoulders and spine. So that was the Change?

'Only the greatest of heroes was able to stem that horrible tide,' Louie continued. 'Imagine! World after world where solutions to disasters come a moment too late, where boy always loses girl never to find her again, and the bad guys get away every time?'

Disasters? Lost love? The bad guys always win? Roger had to admit, it sounded terrible. It also sounded all too familiar. That was the way things always happened on Earth, every day, in real life, not in the movies! Roger shivered. The Change was far worse than he could have imagined.

'And Dread planned all this?' Roger asked.

'In one of his guises, it is very likely that he did. At least, that's what I suspect. You've seen Dread in action. Have you ever seen anyone so evasive? I mean, how could you possibly pin anything on someone who is always pausing meaningfully like that? Oh, why didn't I remember that before I took the job?' Louie gripped his reins so fiercely that his knuckles turned the colour of bone. 'I was desperate to get out. I was in comedy relief for years! I mean, can you imagine going through plot after plot, and never *ever* getting the girl?'

'So Dread is responsible for all of this? The fiend!' Roger took a deep breath in an attempt to control his outrage. 'But his plan failed, didn't it? The Cineverse is still working, isn't it?'

'Well—' Louie hesitated. 'Yes and no,' he said at last. 'The Cineverse is still here, and the plots go on, after a fashion. But some of those things that fell apart before were never put back together, and some plot lines seem to have unravelled for good. I mean, look at our situation here. We got all the classic plot twists – a damsel in distress, a last-minute rescue by the cavalry – but what does the cavalry come to rescue? Not the damsel, and not a hero. No, they've rescued the town drunk! That would never have happened in the classic Cineverse!'

Roger frowned, trying to comprehend everything Big Louie was telling him. 'But what does all this have to do with Delores?'

'Delores?' Louie frowned back. 'Who's De – oh, that's right. There's just so many distressed damsels, you know – she must fit in somehow. Maybe she was one of those sent outside to get help. Or maybe she had been working for Doctor Dread, too, and tried to double-cross him.' He shrugged when he saw Roger's outraged response to his last statement. 'How should I know? I'm only a sidekick!'

Roger told himself to calm down once again. What, after all, did he really know about Delores – besides the fact that she was the most beautiful, intelligent, vivacious and witty woman he had ever met? Then again, his overall track record with women hadn't been all that wonderful. Just look at what had happened with Wendy. And he still had trouble thinking about Cynthia, especially when-ever he ate Chinese food!

But he had forgotten all those other women when he met Delores. She had seemed to genuinely like him for who he was, even encouraged parts of him – parts that previous girlfriends and wives had listed as his faults. Still, she had been so mysterious about most of her past. Could she have been hiding the very sort of thing Big Louie suggested? Could she be a beautiful, vivacious, intelligent and witty bad guy?

Roger realised it didn't matter. He loved her, no matter what. He wouldn't believe that she was evil, mean, rotten and nasty until she told him to his face, and, even then, he might stick around a little while to see if she would change her mind. Oh, sure, he had had a similar experience with Eunice, and even now he didn't like to think of what had happened with Marilyn. But that was differ-ent. Neither of them – in fact, none of his earlier wives or girl-friends – had come from the Cineverse.

He would go on then, and rescue Delores, even if it meant turn-ing every corner the Cineverse had upside-down to succeed! Or, at least he would as soon as he figured out what he should do next.

'Yeah,' Big Louie replied, although Roger hadn't spoken. 'I'm wondering what to do, too. Whatever's going on here, we seem to be right in the middle of it. Does this mean anything?'

The small man lifted his index finger aloft, his eyes shining with inspiration.

'Maybe we are destined to do great things!'

He blinked, and the shining inspiration suddenly seemed a lot more like the dry reflection of the desert sun.

'Then again,' he added much more quietly, 'maybe we are two sidekicks, way over our heads.'

Roger didn't know what to say. After a moment, he asked his question anyway.

'So what should we do now?'

'It probably wouldn't be a bad idea to catch up with the others,' Louie suggested. 'They seem to be cantering faster than we are.'

'No,' Roger replied. 'That's not really what I meant. I was thinking more in terms of what we should do to – well – rescue Delores and possibly the Cineverse.'

Louie nodded grimly. 'Big talk for a sidekick. Still, if that's the way you feel about it, there's only one thing we can do. Whether we are more important than we realise, or mere cogs in the great wheel that powers the Cineverse, we have to find Captain Crusader!'

'Captain Crusader!' Roger exclaimed despite himself. The Captain Crusader? The namesake of the decoder rings, the speaker of noble thoughts such as 'The four basic food groups are your friends' and 'A clean plate is a happy plate'? He had never thought of it before, but, if the Captain Crusader Decoder Ring was real, that meant Captain Crusader had to exist as well, didn't it?

'Of course,' Louie replied smoothly. 'Captain Crusader is the hero's hero. He appears from time to time throughout the Cineverse. I believe you've seen him once already.'

'I have?' Roger replied in disbelief. Then he remembered.

It was so obvious. Why hadn't he realised it before? That was why the Masked Marshal had looked so familiar. And why that civic slogan he had uttered had sent a chill down Roger's spine.

'But,' Roger said, 'there's one thing I don't understand. If Captain Crusader – that is, the Masked Marshal, is the hero's hero, why did he leave Sagebrush before the gun battle?'

'Yep,' Big Louie replied. 'That's something that worries me, too. Maybe the Change is spreading once again.'

Louie looked at the distant rescue party and whistled. 'But we've got other things to worry about. Doc is pulling out a guitar!'

'Does Doc sing, too?'

Louie nodded. 'We have to assume the worst. I've got the feeling Doc could do anything, if he stays sober. But there's a hitch here – we've gotta join that singing party up ahead right pronto. If we're not within easy listening range of the singer, we'll be left days away from Sagebrush! Hurry!'

The music drifted faintly their way as Roger urged his slow-moving horse to greater speed. He recognised a word here and there in the song, something about a 'pretty prairie flower' and a reference to the wide open skies of Arizona.

By the time Roger got Missy into a gallop, Doc had made it to the chorus. The sound swelled as the other members of the rescue party joined in.

'Oh, no!' Big Louie shouted. 'They're singing together! That's going to make the magic work all that much faster!' He glanced back at Roger, holding his own mount back so that his fellow sidekick could catch up.

'Maybe,' Louie suggested, 'if we sing along, it'll work for us, too.' And with that, he burst into hesitant song. 'With my six gun by my side, on – um – my saddle I will ride – um – sweet tulip of Amarillo – um – I'll be coming for you, – um – please be stillo! Oh, Cineverse! Why can't I remember any of these?'

Roger smiled as he pulled his horse up next to Louie and Lightning. But his grin vanished as he looked ahead. Where Doc and the cavalry had sung but a moment before, there was now nothing but a cloud of dust. Roger and Louie were all alone.

CHAPTER TWELVE

'Now we've done it!' Big Louie moaned.

'Done what?' Roger asked. 'What can happen to us in the middle of the desert?'

Louie mopped his brow with his kerchief. 'You mean, besides becoming victims of the elements, with no food or water, baked during the day and frozen at night, at the mercy of the desert sands?'

Roger admitted Louie had a point.

'And that's not the worst of it!' the small man continued. 'What happens if Doctor Dread figures we're alone and comes back to get us?'

Roger sighed. If there was one problem with Louie, it was his slight tendency to get hysterical. 'Doctor Dread has just escaped to some other place – some place in a Cineverse so vast that we can't even begin to guess where it is,' he replied evenly. 'Why would he want to come back after us?'

Louie's gaze was still rather panic-stricken. He made a small, mewling sound in the back of his throat.

Roger decided he'd try again. He calmly waved at his surroundings. 'Besides, this isn't as bad as all that, is it? We sang ourselves out here only a few hours ago. If Doc can sing them back to Sagebrush, why can't I do the same for us?'

'Oh, yeah?' Louie laughed hysterically 'Where do you think Doc got the guitar?'

Roger looked back at his now empty saddlebags.

'He's got the guitar?' Roger hesitated, feeling a bit of Louie's panic himself. 'Oh dear. And does Movie Magic work—'

'—if you don't have a guitar?' Louie shook his head as he finished Roger's sentence for him. 'Unfortunately, it's one of the Laws of the West. You either need a guitar, or a full orchestra, or you're stuck riding all the way back.'

'A full orchestra?' Roger asked incredulously.

But Louie only nodded complacently. 'You'd be surprised how handy they are, especially when you're singing songs about lovely Spanish *señoritas*.'

The small man frowned as he changed the subject.

'And you're wrong about Doctor Dread, too. He does have a reason to come back. You see, I can find him.'

'Oh,' Roger replied. Was this good news or bad news? Good, he guessed, because it gave him a destination for his quest to rescue Delores. Then again, what wasn't so good was that – if Doctor Dread knew he might be pursued – the villain or one of his assistants could show up at any minute to put Roger and Louie 'out of the way', as the Doctor would put it.

Of course, Roger realised upon reflection, this whole train of thought could be nothing more than the result of Big Louie's paranoia.

'Uh-oh,' Big Louie whispered.

There was a cloud of dust before them where there had been nothing but desert before.

Then again, Roger thought, this whole train of thought could be totally, even overwhelmingly, *justified* paranoia.

Roger stared into the dissipating dust, expecting at any second to discern a tall, thin man decked in signature snakeskin. And, indeed, he spotted a lone figure, walking toward them through the murky yellow cloud. However, instead of shiny black, the man in the dust was wearing clothes much the same colour as the dirt that surrounded him, clothes that looked like they had been slept in for at least a month.

It wasn't Dread. It was Doc. And he was carrying a guitar.

'Shucks!' Doc drawled. 'I thought you fellas were taggin' along. But when we got to Sagebrush, we discovered we were two *hombres* short.' He nodded to Big Louie. 'No offence.'

Louie assured him there was none taken.

'Well, we were,' Roger agreed, 'tagging along, that is.'

'We just fell a little behind,' Louie confessed.

'Well, if *you* can make small jokes too, I guess I won't worry,' Doc remarked. 'Anyway, it's time I talked to you.'

Doc pushed his battered and dusty hat further back on his head as he looked from Roger to Louie and back again. 'You fellas have made me look at things in a different light. Pitched gunbattles in town, showdowns in alleyways, last-minute rescues at secret hide-outs – why, it's right like old times. I mean, after seeing action like that, who wants to go back to being a town drunk? I tell you, boys, I've grovelled by my last spittoon.' He spat for emphasis. 'It was time to re-explore the hero business – but to do that I had to talk to you. And you weren't there!'

He patted the wooden instrument at his side. 'There was nothing left for me to do but pick up this old guitar and sing myself back your way.'

'Gee,' Roger said, quite overwhelmed by Doc'c confession of faith.

'I tell you, those showdowns, gunbattles and rescues get in your blood,' Doc concluded nostalgically. 'Reminds me of the way things used to be. So, I'd like to hitch up with you fellows.' He paused, his hat back down over his forehead. 'That is, I would if you'd like a sidekick.'

'Can a couple of sidekicks have a sidekick?' Louie grimaced. 'I don't know. That sort of thing sounds like the Change coming back to me.'

'No,' Roger insisted. 'This is no time to be fatalistic. Doc wants to leave the town drunk business behind for a life of adventure, and I, for one, congratulate him! Besides, who knows? If the Change comes back, well, who says we can't work on it a little bit, and maybe it'll change our way?'

'Wow!' Louie replied in awe. 'That's not a sidekick speech!'

'Land o' Goshen!' Doc echoed. 'That sounds like hero talk to me!'

Well, Roger decided, he shouldn't let all this enthusiasm go to waste. He set his jaw in what he hoped was a grim and determined line, and said, as forcefully as he could muster: 'Then it's time to find Dread and rescue the girl.'

'Sounds right proper.' Doc strummed meaningfully on his guitar. 'Just let me know where and I'll sing you there straight-away!'

'It's not as simple as that,' Louie replied grimly. 'Doctor Dread is not on this world.'

'Not on this world?' Doc asked as he looked down at his guitar in dismay. 'Then how can we possibly find him?'

'No problem,' Louie assured the newest sidekick. 'At least not with Roger here.'

'Roger? Do you mean?' Doc asked with a touch of awe. 'Does he have a ring?'

'He doesn't have a ring,' Louie said proudly. 'He doesn't need a ring. He has methods.'

'*Methods?*' Doc parroted, his voice quivering with respect. 'He calls himself a sidekick when he's got *methods?*'

'Oh, yeah,' Roger replied rather quietly. 'Well, I guess it's time to get those methods.'

Roger realised that meant they had to use the ring. He unzipped the breast pocket of his running jacket and reached inside past the Mastercard, pulling out the round, grey key to the universe.

'Here they are,' Roger replied with a slightly embarrassed smile. 'My methods.'

'Hey!' Louie exclaimed. 'I thought you said you didn't have a ring!'

Roger sighed. How could he explain this? He decided he couldn't.

'I was fibbing.'

'Fibbing?' Doc squinted as he regarded Roger, his eyes no more than narrow but highly judgemental slits. 'Maybe you're only a sidekick after all.'

'I never claimed anything else,' Roger said, hoping to calm the situation.

But Louie would not be calmed. He stuck a pudgy finger in Roger's face. 'Hey! You told me you didn't have a ring. Were you hiding the ring from me?'

'Well, yes,' Roger admitted.

'He hid the ring?' Doc's eyes were so narrow they were almost closed. 'Sounds less like a hero with every minute.'

'After all we've been through, you hid the ring?' Louie's hysteria seemed to be returning.

Roger did his best to keep his reply as calm as possible. 'With all due respect, Louie, you used to be a bad guy.'

'Oh, that,' Louie replied in a much quieter tone. 'I keep forgetting about that. I suppose you do have a point.'

'You were a bad guy?' Doc asked, his eyes once again wide with wonder. 'Then *you* must be the hero around here.'

'Wait a moment,' Roger said, once again feeling the logic of this place eluding him. 'What do you mean by that?'

Doc nodded solemnly. 'Reformed bad guys make some of the best heroes. It's one of the Laws of the West.'

'No, I'm no hero,' Louie replied morosely. 'I wasn't a very good bad guy, either. I simply have to face up to it: I was born a sidekick, and I'll be a sidekick 'til the day I die. Besides, I can't shoot a gun anywhere near as good as you.' He nodded at Doc. 'If there's a hero around here—'

'Denial?' Doc asked thoughtfully. 'Humility? Heroic traits if ever I heard them.'

'Listen,' Roger insisted. 'We don't have time to argue about who's the hero around here. We have a woman to rescue, and an evil genius to foil!'

'Then again,' Doc added, 'that decisiveness sounds pretty heroic to me, too.'

'So we're all heroes!' Roger barked. 'Well, at least, we're heroic sidekicks. But we have things to do here!'

'He's the hero,' Doc decided.

'Definitely,' Louie agreed.

'Good to have that out of the way,' Doc replied.

'It's a big load off my mind,' Louie admitted.

'Can we get to work?' Roger demanded, holding out the ring. 'We have places to go! How the heck do you use this ring?'

'He's the hero?' Doc asked.

'And he doesn't know how to use the ring?' Louie added.

'Well, I sort of do,' Roger replied defensively. Actually, he hadn't wanted to admit his total ignorance of the ring's workings, but the way his two fellow sidekicks were going on and on had unnerved him, reminding him far too clearly of his public relations past, and some committees he had been on, forever and ever. 'After all,' he added, 'I got here, didn't I?'

'Maybe he's being humble now,' Louie suggested. 'Perhaps we should wait before we jump to conclusions here.'

'True, true,' Doc ruminated. 'Heroing can be a subtle business sometimes.'

'But I have no idea where we're going!' Roger shouted at the conferees. 'How can we rescue anybody when I don't know the destination!'

'Getting forceful again,' Louie said approvingly.

Doc smiled. 'I think I'm comfortable to leave him as the hero.'

'Then it's agreed?' Louie asked.

The two shook hands.

Roger's patience was at an end.

'You!' He grabbed Louie by his red bandana. 'You know where Dread is hiding!'

'Then again,' Louie rasped. 'Heroes seldom let their temper get the better of them.'

'There's no such rule for sidekicks, is there?' Roger replied between clenched teeth.

'No, no,' Louie managed. 'Certainly not. In fact, there are

many situations where the sidekick is required to get upset. It gives the hero somebody to calm down.'

'Well, as soon as we find a hero, you'll be amazed how calm I'll get. But I don't think we're going to find anything unless we get out of here!'

Roger let go of Louie's neckerchief. The small man stepped back, massaging his neck. 'Whoa! I didn't know you had that in you.'

'You know,' Doc mused, 'he could be the antihero. Sometimes *they* lose—'

'Where are we going?' Roger screamed at Louie. 'Now!'

'Oh, okay,' Louie answered rapidly. 'Turn the dial of the ring halfway around—'

'It's about time! Get off that horse!'

'What? Oh, um, okay.' Totally flabbergasted, Louie did as he was told. Roger dismounted as well.

'Now!' Roger twisted the ring, then grabbed the shoulders of his two companions. 'See you in the funny papers!'

'No!' Louie cried as the three were surrounded by blue smoke. 'Wait!'

But Roger had had enough of waiting. If Doc and Louie had had their way, he swore they would have discussed the fine points of heroing until both Delores and the Cineverse were lost forever to the evil machinations of Doctor Dread. Sure, he'd had to be a little rough on them to get them to act. But it was the only way anything was going to happen. Roger felt fully justified in everything he had had to do.

At least he did until the smoke cleared.

CHAPTER THIRTEEN

'Duck!' Big Louie screamed.

Something exploded all too close. Roger, Doc and Louie all hit the dirt. Louie pointed to a ditch behind them. Roger and the others crawled there as quickly as they could.

A moment later, a grenade rolled against the small hill on which they had first appeared. A few seconds after that, the hill ceased to exist.

'Where are we?' Roger yelled at Louie, straining his voice to be heard over the screams and machine-gun fire.

'Darned if I know!' Louie yelled back.

'But didn't you tell me to turn the ring—'

'I told you to start by turning the ring!' The hysteria was back in Louie's voice. 'I didn't tell you to finish off that way!'

A shell screamed over their heads. It hit a somewhat larger hill behind them, showering them with dirt and small rocks.

'This isn't where we're supposed to be?' Roger asked less calmly than he might have liked.

'Are you kidding?' Louie's laughter had a manic edge. 'Would anybody choose to show up someplace like this?' A tank clanked angrily across the field before them. 'I mean, how could something like this get any worse?'

'Uh, pardners?' Doc drawled. 'Don't look now, but we've got company.'

A man in green fatigues, a set of sergeant stripes on his helmet, plopped down beside them in the ditch.

'Glad to see you guys finally got here,' he began, but stopped when he got a closer look at the three of them. 'How come you're out of uniform?'

'Uniform?' Roger asked before he could stop himself.

But Louie's explanation quickly followed: 'We're supposed to penetrate enemy lines.'

'Dressed like that?' the sergeant demanded. 'You guys look like cowboys!' He pointed a thumb at Roger's shiny blue jogging suit. 'Except for this one. He looks like a Martian!'

'Exactly,' Louie explained without missing a beat. 'It's psychological warfare.'

'Really?' The sergeant scratched under his helmet. 'Well, it had me fooled. Psychological warfare, you say? Gee. Maybe HQ actually got a good idea for a change.'

The machine-gun fire redoubled above them, followed by shouts and screams of pain.

'Well, it's been awful nice chewing the fat with you,' Louie remarked casually to the sergeant, 'but we have a mission.'

Roger stared at his fellow sidekick. Was Big Louie suggesting they leave their ditch to go out in that war up there? Sure, maybe Roger had gotten them into this in the first place by his mistaken use of the ring. But there must be an easier way to get out of this than running through enemy fire.

'Your mission is cancelled,' the sergeant replied grimly. 'I'm afraid your orders have been changed.'

'Changed?' Louie demanded, indignant at the very thought.

Roger breathed a sigh of relief. Maybe he'd survive this mistake after all.

'That's right,' the sergeant continued. 'We need you three for a suicide mission.'

'Suicide—' Roger began, his relief evaporated.

'Good of you to volunteer,' the sergeant replied. 'That's right, men. You've got to take Wishbone Hill!'

'Wishbone Hill?' Roger asked before he could stop himself.

'Glad to hear your enthusiasm,' the sergeant answered. 'Wishbone Hill. It's the reason we're all here, and the reason some of us will never leave. Sure, I know we've taken it twelve times already, and the enemy has captured it back as many times themselves. And every time we've lost lives, good boys with homes and wives and mothers and fathers, boys just like you. But still we stay, and still we take that hill. Some might call it purposeless. Some might even call it crazy, a waste of human life. But we have to fight for what we believe in! There might be other battles in this war, but here we've got only one, and its name is Wishbone Hill. And now it's your job to take it!' He raised both fists in the air as he stared patriotically at his new recruits. 'We can't let all those other boys die in vain! Do it for Bob! Do it for Artie!'

'Who's Bob?' Roger asked despite himself. 'Who's Artie?'

'That's the spirit!' The sergeant gave Roger a hearty pat on the back. 'Now get up that hill! After you're gone, we'll remember you, just like the others who have gone before, who gave their lives for the cause!'

'But, uh, we're not—' Roger tried again.

'Oh, it's natural to have a doubt or two.' The sergeant chuckled ruefully. 'Sure, maybe you're just tiny, meaningless cogs ground up in a giant war machine. And maybe that hill is no more than a pile of dirt that sooner or later will get blown away by the wind and the rain. But soon that won't matter to you any more, when you make that hopeless charge up your final objective, wildly outnumbered by enemy firepower, cut down by flying bullets and shrapnel, the life's blood flowing from your body, you'll die happy, knowing you took that hill, and that we'll remember you, and call your names the next time we have to take it, and every time we take it after that!'

'Okay, Sarge,' Louie announced before Roger could voice any further objections. 'We'll take it!' He walked farther down the ditch, waving for Doc and Roger to follow.

'Wow, pardners,' Doc whispered in wonder. 'When I came with you looking for adventure, I never expected anything like this. Are you guys sure you're both sidekicks?'

'Soon to be dead sidekicks!' Roger's outburst was both hushed and vehement. 'Are you crazy? We're probably going to get killed out there!'

'It's worse than that,' Louie whispered back. 'I'm from Brooklyn.'

'So?' Roger asked, sure he was missing something again.

'If I go out there,' Louie explained, 'there's no "probably" about it. The guy from Brooklyn always buys it in these plots.'

'A Law of the West?' Roger asked.

'We're no longer in the West,' Louie reminded him. 'In a place like this, I think you call it a Rule of Battle.'

'Yeah,' Doc drawled, 'or maybe the Fortunes of War.'

Roger still didn't understand. 'So why did you tell that guy we'd do it?'

'To give you a chance to use that ring of yours,' Louie explained.

'I can't use it in the ditch?'

'You can't use it around the sergeant. If you do, bad things might happen. In a way, it's sort of a Cineverse courtesy – you keep the ring as far away from the current plotline as possible. It's rumoured that doing it any other way promotes the Change.'

Roger guessed that made sense. Both the worlds he had visited in the Cineverse seemed to have a central plotline – in the West, it was getting the Cavendishes; here, it was taking Wishbone Hill – and those plotlines could be disrupted by outside forces, especially if that force was as powerful as the Captain Crusader Decoder Ring.

'So we have to get away from the sergeant?' he asked.

Louie nodded.

Roger didn't like the direction Louie's logic was taking. 'And there's only one way to do that?'

Louie nodded again.

Roger supposed there was no helping it. 'Up the hill?'

'Towards the hill,' Louie amended. 'But not very far.'

Louie explained his plan.

'You mean we're not going to take Wishbone Hill?' Doc asked in disappointment.

'Trust me,' Louie replied. 'We'll have other adventures. Some we might even live through.'

'Well, all right,' Doc said reluctantly. ' 'Though I was looking forward to taking out some of those machine guns with my six-shooter. Still, if you promise there'll be more excitement—'

'Trust me,' Louie repeated. 'I don't think there's any way we can get away from the excitement.'

It sounded good to Doc. It didn't sound so good to Roger, but he'd vowed he'd go through anything, even excitement, to rescue Delores. This time, he carefully followed Louie's instructions for setting the ring.

'Well?' the sergeant called impatiently from the other end of the ditch.

'Right, Sarge!' Louie called back. 'It's time, men. Over the top!'

Roger reset his ring and the three men joined hands as they leapt from the ditch, immediately falling to their hands and knees as they screamed in unison:

'See you in the funny papers!'

'Avast!'

The blue smoke was clearing quickly, blown away by a sea breeze.

'Witchcraft!'

Roger let go of his two cronies and looked up from his kneeling position. They seemed to be on a boat – a three-masted schooner was Roger's guess. There also seemed to be a sword-fight going on – or at least there had been until Roger and his fellow sidekicks had interrupted the proceedings.

Louie grinned and waved. 'Excuse us, folks. Just passing through.'

'Aha, fiends!' a fellow with an eye-patch replied as he brandished his sword. 'See how you laugh after you've tasted naked steel!'

'We'd rather not, thank you,' Roger answered respectfully.

But politeness didn't seem to be working. A dozen sword-wielding men, some in uniform, others dressed in colourful rags, advanced upon them.

'What say we slit his gizzard?' the eye-patch asked no one in particular.

'Is this where we're supposed to be?' Roger whispered to Louie. Roger didn't even know where his gizzard was, but he wasn't too anxious to find out.

'I don't think so,' Louie whispered back. He flinched as Eye-patch brandished his sword in their general direction.

'But you had me twist the ring—'

Louie frowned, his eyes darting back and forth between a dozen swords. 'It would have worked if you hadn't jumped the gun and landed us in the middle of a war zone. And now this!' He leapt back, even though the nearest sword was still a good six feet away. 'From here on in, setting the ring is going to involve a certain amount of guess-work – at least until we end up some place that I recognise. The Captain Crusader Decoder Ring is a delicate instrument. It also doesn't help that it's very cheaply made, and almost impossible to turn.'

'Oh,' Roger replied. He had thought it was his inexperience that was making it difficult to use the ring. Somehow, he found that thought preferable to the idea that the key to the universe could fall apart at any minute.

'Let's slit all their gizzards!' Eye-patch announced with a chuckle. The other eleven men behind him brandished their swords in unison.

'I think it's time for some fancy shootin',' Doc announced, starting to rise. A couple of the colourfully-garbed fellows drew flintlock pistols from their waistbands. They obviously thought shooting was a good idea, too.

'No it isn't,' Louie announced. 'It's time to get out of here, now!' He grabbed Roger's ring hand and Doc's pantleg, shouting: 'See you in the funny papers!'

The blue smoke swallowed them.

Roger heard metal clang against metal, the unmistakable sound of duelling swords!

'Uh-oh,' Louie whispered.

The blue smoke was still thick around them. A clipped, British accent cursed the deuced fog.

'What do you mean, uh-oh?' Roger asked.

'I panicked back there,' was Louie's only explanation.

'Yep,' Doc agreed. 'We sure skedaddled out of that place.'

Even more clipped British accents began to swear in their vicinity.

'So?' Roger asked, still not quite comprehending their danger.

On the other hand, as the swearing increased, the sword fight sounds had ceased entirely.

'You remember what I said about plotlines?' Louie explained. 'I not only panicked – I may have panicked too close to the middle of one of them.'

'I say!' one of the local voices interjected. 'There are intruders in our midst!'

Had they been discovered? Roger waited a moment for something to happen. Nothing did. The blue smoke seemed to be hanging around for an awfully long time on this go-round.

'And?' Roger finally prompted when Big Louie gave no further explanation. It had something to do with the swords, didn't it? 'You mean, we haven't left the pirate world?'

'It's more of the robbers!' shouted one of the voices out there in the smoke.

'Well, no, we're probably not there any more—' Big Louie began without much enthusiasm.

'Nonsense!' another fog voice interjected. 'It's the duke's men!'

'But we haven't gotten very far,' Louie continued morosely. 'Maybe it's nothing to worry about. It hardly ever happens – it's just something you hear about, mostly – but, when you do fall into one, you're really in trouble.'

Roger could see sunlight overhead. The blue fog was finally starting to dissipate. Any number of sword fights resumed. The clanging and grunting was everywhere. There seemed to be a dozen pitched battles all around them.

'Sounds to me,' Doc cracked, 'like the adventure's just beginnin'.'

The smoke cleared at last.

Roger decided, if anything, that Doc had underestimated the situation.

CHAPTER FOURTEEN

'Oh, dear,' Louie moaned.

Now that the smoke was gone, Roger could see that they were in the middle of a crowd – a very active crowd.

First off, there were two distinct groups of men fighting each other with swords. One group was dressed in bright but motley clothes of forest green. They leapt and capered about as they fought, exchanging witticisms with their fellows and laughing cheerily as they impaled members of the other group on their flashing blades.

'But, if that's true,' Louie said, more to himself than the others, 'what can we do?' He stared morosely at the Captain Crusader Decoder Ring in Roger's hand.

Roger hauled Big Louie back a step as the fight surged in their direction. The small sidekick seemed too entangled in their own dilemma to worry about anything as minor as a nearby sword fight. Roger scanned the surrounding crowd, hoping he might find somewhere they might be a little less exposed to the mêlée.

The foes of the men in green were a far more sober bunch. They were better dressed than the others, most of them wearing a red-and-white embroidered overshirt covering chain mail, with bullet-shaped helmets on their heads. They seemed to be decent enough swordsmen, although they showed none of the flair of their green-suited adversaries, and the chain mail seemed to be no protection at all from enemy swords.

At first glance, backed by years of movie-viewing experience, Roger surmised that the folks in green were the 'robbers', while the bullet helmets were the 'duke's men'. There were others around as well, townspeople, dressed mostly in the drabbest of browns, and a young woman, who, by her extremely fine and colourful dress, he assumed was of the nobility – a dark-haired woman who was almost as attractive as Delores.

Delores! Images of blond hair and dazzling smiles were pushed aside by the laughter of Doctor Dread. No, Roger told himself, no matter how difficult he found it, he had to figure out how to get out of the situation he now found himself in before he could rescue the woman in his life.

That is, if he could even figure out this particular situation – especially whatever it was that Louie was muttering so darkly about.

Actually, those things going on immediately in front of him were easy to comprehend. While he had never been so close to one of these sword fights before, he had certainly witnessed this kind of scene a thousand times on a movie screen. Why, it only took him a moment, glancing around at the jumping bodies and clashing swords, to determine the star players in this little drama.

A tall, thin, yet muscular fellow, dressed in a slightly brighter shade of green than his fellows, faced off against another of the chain-mailed band, this one sporting a much larger white fleur-de-lis on his red shirt than his compatriots. The chain-mailed man moved well with a sword, too, if a bit too fussily. He was also tall and slender, but to almost too great a degree, as if he were perhaps the product of a bit too much royal inbreeding.

'Take that, you cur!' the leader of the duke's men called.

His opponent smiled dashingly.

'You call me a cur, sir,' he replied as he pressed his attack. 'Well, perhaps I am, if you define a cur as a man who loves freedom!'

The freedom-lover easily repelled a new attack by the duke's man with three quick flicks of his sword. The duke's lackey took a step away to catch his breath and wipe the sweat from his brow. The freedom-lover paused as well, amused by his opponent's lack of stamina. Despite the rags, you could tell who was the true nobleman around here.

'Wait until the duke hears about this,' the duke's man wheezed, 'you scoundrel!'

The freedom-lover raised a single, handsome eyebrow. 'Scoundrel? Well, perhaps I am, sheriff, if scoundrels defend the rights of common people!'

The townspeople cheered. The sheriff could clearly see the tide of events turning against him.

Louie turned to Roger, grabbing the front of his jogging suit with panicked hands.

'We've got to get out of here!' he whispered hoarsely.

'And don't think, sheriff,' the freedom-lover continued smoothly, 'that I haven't noticed your new recruits!' He waved at Roger and his fellows with a grin.

'Too late,' Louie moaned.

'My recruits?' The sheriff barked an affected laugh. 'Who are these people?' he glanced disdainfully at Roger's band. 'Surely they are dressed as travelling minstrels – no, no, travelling minstrels would have more taste! No—' He paused to sneer. 'They are dressed more like clowns!'

Clowns? Roger wondered if that was a demotion from sidekick.

'Clowns?' That last reference was too much for the freedom-lover to take, who once again pressed his attack. 'Well, perhaps we are like them, if a clown is anyone who laughs at oppression!'

His sword thrust was desperately parried at the last possible moment by the sheriff.

'The duke's will shall not be mocked!' the sheriff insisted hysterically. He waved his free hand in Roger's general direction. 'Men! Let's give these three interlopers a taste of naked steel!'

Louie whimpered.

'Don't listen to them, free men of the forest!' the green-clad leader replied. 'These three clown-garbed newcomers are obviously one of the duke's tricks! Dispense with them, as you would with all men who would usurp the true heir to the throne! If they shall taste naked steel, it will be the naked steel of justice!'

Men in green rushed Roger and his company from one side, men in helmets from the other. All of them appeared to have very sharp swords.

'I can't help myself!' Louie wailed. He snatched the ring out of Roger's hand.

They were surrounded by blue smoke.

'I'm sorry,' Louie muttered through the smoke. 'I'm really sorry.'

'Is our little buddy always this cheerful?' Doc inquired.

'I've always had this thing about – swords,' Louie confessed.

Roger tried to be the voice of reason. 'But there aren't any swords out there now!' All sounds of battle had vanished with the last use of the ring. Roger could hear nothing now but the distant sound of the sea.

'Especially swords pointed at me,' Louie continued hastily, as if his fear was a demon he had to exorcize. 'There were hardly ever any swords in comedy relief. Oh, why—'

A door opened somewhere. Louie's voice died as the smoke cleared.

'And who invades the chambers of Bonnie Kate, queen of the swordswomen?'

A tall, handsome woman menaced them with a sword.

'Perhaps you shall answer some questions,' she remarked with a sardonic grin, 'when you are confronted by naked steel?'

Louie screamed.

They were surrounded by blue smoke.

'I've done it now,' Louie groaned.

'What?' Roger couldn't handle this any more. 'What have you done?' he demanded.

'Doomed us all,' Louie answered.

Roger had to admit it – he was getting tired of this small fellow's negative attitude. Even more than that, he was getting tired of all this blue smoke. It seemed to get worse with every new movie world they travelled to.

'You've noticed how bad the smoke is getting,' Louie echoed, even though Roger hadn't voiced his thoughts aloud. Louie sighed heavily. 'That's another sign.'

'You say you were in comedy relief?' Doc drawled. 'Are you sure you weren't asked to leave?'

Louie ignored the questions, preferring instead to work himself into a moderate state of hysteria. 'Oh, if only I knew more about how this cheap plastic ring really worked! I've only heard the rumours – old wives' tales, I thought until now! Hah!'

Roger tried to face Louie in the blue fog.

'*What rumours?*' he yelled at the top of his voice.

'If something happens to your ring,' Louie explained at last, 'or if you use it too close to a world's central plotline, you can be trapped.'

'Trapped?' Roger asked. 'How?'

'You've seen it – haven't you? First, we were surrounded by pirates, then we ended up in the middle of some sort of noble outlaws versus the corrupt authorities thing, and we get out of that, only to be confronted by the queen of the swordswomen!'

Roger could see his point. There was a certain similarity here.

'They're all swashbucklers,' he said aloud.

'I've trapped us in a movie cycle,' Louie whispered. 'We may have to spend the rest of our – admittedly short – lives threatened, over and over again, by naked steel!'

'Now, now.' Roger spoke reassuringly, trying to calm the small man down. 'We don't know that we're trapped anywhere in particular. You said yourself that using the ring would be a matter of trial and error until we found some territory that we were familiar with. The fact that we've visited three similar movie worlds in a row might simply be – coincidence.'

There, that sounded at least moderately convincing. Roger wished he could believe it himself.

'So – we might be somewhere else when this blue smoke finally clears?' Louie asked, only half-doubtfully. Against all reason, it seemed, he wanted to believe Roger's theory. 'If only it could be so!'

As if on cue, the blue smoke evaporated around them. They stood on a dock, in a sun-filled seaport, with a full-rigged sailing ship before them.

'But I don't think it is,' Louie moaned.

Doc nodded in commiseration. 'I reckon we're back with the pirates.'

'Not necessarily!' Roger insisted, trying somehow not to give in to despair. He couldn't help himself. There was no such word as despair in public relations.

'Pirates?' a nearby fellow shouted at them as he hobbled forward on his wooden peg-leg. He wore a three-cornered hat, and sported a multi-coloured parrot on his shoulder. Roger had to admit, it certainly looked like pirates.

'No pirates around here!' Peg-leg announced, contradicting his appearance. 'Me and my mates are buccaneers!'

'Squawk!' the parrot agreed. 'Happy buccaneers!'

'All my fault,' Louie muttered. 'If only I didn't have this thing about swords.'

'Isn't that right, mates?' Peg-leg called.

'Aye!' fifty-odd cheerful voices called from the nearby ship.

'And how do we prove to our strangers here—'

'Squawk!' the parrot interrupted. 'Happy strangers!'

'—that we're happy buccaneers?' Peg-leg concluded.

Roger half-expected the answer to be 'naked steel'.

Instead, the fifty-odd sailors shouted back:

'With a happy song!'

Louie, if possible, became even more ashen-faced than before.

'Oh, no,' he breathed. 'Not a singing swashbuckler!'

'Squawk!' the parrot agreed. 'Happy singing swashbuckler!'

And fifty-odd manly voices broke out in song:

'Oh, we sail all the seven seas,
Rob Spanish galleons as we please;
But honest men will have no fear
Of the happy singing buccaneers!'

Louie looked up at Roger. 'I knew it would be bad. I didn't know it would be this bad.'

'Now,' Doc observed, 'this doesn't seem much different from a singing Western.' He pulled the guitar around from where he had been carrying it on his back. He strummed a few experimental chords. 'Just give me a couple moments, and we could do right well in these here parts.'

'Perhaps you are right.' Big Louie shivered. 'It could be even worse. There are still more dangerous worlds than this – worlds where music is even more in evidence!' Louie paused for an instant, frozen, when he saw some of the buccaneers were happily waving swords.

'But,' he forced himself to continue at last, 'it makes no difference. When you're trapped, how can anything make a difference?'

'Trapped?' Roger asked, still needing to be convinced. 'But how do you know that? We have been going from swashbuckler to swashbuckler, that is true, but one was on sea, the next on land, the third featured a female protagonist, and the fourth seems to be full of comedy and song. We should be near the cycle's end, shouldn't we?'

'Cycles never end in the Cineverse,' Louie disagreed. 'Besides, there's something more. You see, there's one problem I haven't told you about.'

Louie was interrupted by the buccaneers' second verse:

'We rob, we loot, we pillage, too,
And we'll sing a song for you!
We use our swords in all good cheer;
We're the happy, singing buccaneers!'

Louie stared blankly out at the tuneful shipmates.

'One problem?' Roger reminded him.

He blinked and turned back to Roger. 'How do I say this?' he began in a voice that suggested he didn't believe what he was talking about himself. 'The last time the blue smoke showed up – I hadn't even touched the ring.'

Doc stared at the sidekick. 'You mean the blue smoke got the notion to show up by itself?'

Louie nodded as he fearfully blurted words that he did not want to speak. 'What have I done? In my haste to get away from a sword, I may have unsettled the very fabric – of the Cineverse!'

Before Roger could think of anything to say, the shipmates had launched into their third verse:

> 'We're happy, singing buccaneers,
> As all our friends need never fear,
> But all opposed will surely feel,
> A brace of cannon and naked steel!'

Louie screamed. The blue smoke wasn't far behind.

And this time, Roger had seen, Louie had done nothing at all with the ring.

Even with his public relations training, he had to admit it. This time, it looked like they were in real trouble.

CHAPTER FIFTEEN

The tone of the next voice they heard through the blue smoke was distressingly familiar.

'Avast! What did I tell you, me hearties! You don't get away from Captain Wishbone that easily!'

'*Now* we're back with the pirates,' Louie remarked fatalistically.

'Aye, maties!' the captain's voice continued jovially. 'It looks like gizzard-slitting time is here after all!'

So it was a cycle after all, Roger thought – an apparently unbroken cycle. Well, Louie may have been ready to give up on their chances for survival, but Roger wasn't. He felt you could deal with any situation, once you understood it.

It was the understanding part that got difficult around here. Still, Roger was ready to try. Maybe there was some way to reason with the denizens of this particular movie world, find out how they fitted into the cycle, even define the limits of the cycle itself. Louie may have made a mistake, but Roger didn't yet think that mistake was fatal.

When the smoke cleared, Roger saw that the twelve pirates had formed a circle around them. Their swords were drawn, their eyes filled with menace. Roger realised there was more than one way for things to be fatal in this situation.

He cleared his throat.

'Pardon me. Can we talk?'

The pirates all laughed.

'You're talkin' now, aren't ya?' one particularly grizzled specimen replied colourfully. 'Sure. We always let's 'em talk 'afore we slits 'ere gizzards!'

'Oh,' Roger replied, afraid he had understood all too much of the pirate's colourful dialect. 'But is gizzard-slitting entirely necessary?'

' 'E mought 'ave a point 'ere, cap'n!' the grizzled fellow remarked with a gap-toothed grin.

'Aye,' another member of the crew piped up. 'We could keel-haul them instead!'

'There's always the cat o'nine tails—' yet another crew member began helpfully.

'Not dramatic enough!' a fourth pirate insisted. 'Let's do this proper. Drawing and quartering!'

'But a flogging!' the cat o'nine tails crew member insisted. 'It's been ever so long since we've had a good flogging!'

' 'Ere noo,' the grizzled fellow interrupted with a sprightly wink of his good eye. 'Wot aboot 'e traditional values?'

Roger managed to take a breath. At least someone here was going to stand up for their rights!

A bearded gent with a three-cornered captain's hat grinned at the grizzled man. 'What's that you say, Briny? Traditional values?'

'Aye, aye, Cap'n Wishbone,' Briny replied as he colourfully coughed a wad of phlegm. 'We shood mak'em walk 'e plank!'

Maybe, Roger considered, discussion wasn't the best course of action in their present situation.

Apparently, Doc felt the same way, for he had drawn both his six-shooters.

'Seems to me,' he drawled, 'that these fellows will show us a little more respect once they get a little ventilation.'

Louie tugged at Doc's dusty sleeve.

'It won't work.'

'What do you mean, it won't work?' Doc took careful aim at the Captain. 'Western justice always works!'

'In the West,' Louie reminded him.

Doc pulled twin triggers. Nothing happened.

'It's Movie Magic,' Louie explained. 'It can work against you, too. Your six-guns can't possibly shoot here. They haven't been invented yet.'

The pirates, who had hung back for a moment when Doc had drawn his guns, all decided they had had enough talk.

'Hell's bells!' the Captain intoned. 'Why do we have to only kill these fellows one way?'

'You mean we could flog them—' the cat o'nine tails enthusiast began.

'And then we could keelhaul them?' another added.

'An' den we can slit 'ere gizzards, draw an' quarter 'em, an' make 'em walk 'e plank!' Briny added, getting into the spirit of things.

The pirates all liked that plan a lot. They pushed their swords towards Roger, Louie and Doc.

'There's only one thing to do,' Louie replied miserably. He screamed, and the blue smoke was back.

At least, Roger thought, no one had mentioned naked steel.

' 'Tis the duke's lackeys, skulking amongst us once again!' a voice yelled.

'Nonsense!' a second voice replied. 'Pay no attention to this forest-bred trick!'

Roger thought quickly, knowing he had a moment to spare before the ever-more-sluggish blue smoke cleared. Perhaps it had been foolish to even try to reason with the band of pirates – by definition, they were all bad guys, after all. Here though, in the world of the duke and the forest, there were two rival factions, one of which had to be the good guys – by default, if for no other reason. And, by the very laws of Movie Magic, where there were good guys, there had to be somebody he could reason with.

He remembered the bold man in green, and the overly fussy sheriff. He could guess who the hero was around here, but he might – conceivably – be wrong. He had already made a mistake or two since he had entered the Cineverse, after all. He would simply have to present his case, see how the two factions reacted, and act accordingly.

He had made his decision.

'Let me handle this,' he whispered to Louie and Doc. 'I have a plan.'

Obligingly, the blue smoke cleared at that instant.

'Royal lackeys!' the men in green called.

'Forest swine!' the bullet helmets shot back.

Roger held up his hands for silence. Surprisingly enough, he got it. Now, all he had to do was present his case convincingly enough so that he might come under the protection of one side or the other – a protection that would give him and his fellows time to see if there was an alternative to being trapped in this cycle.

But how should he begin? He had tried once before – on the Western world – to win over the confidence of the locals, with somewhat less than perfect results. He would simply have to do better here.

'Good men of this kingdom!' he began. That sounded neutral

enough, and indeed, neither side seemed particularly upset to be addressed in that manner.

'We fight for neither the duke nor the forest!' he continued, adding quickly, 'Not that your cause is not just –' he was careful not to mention which cause, '– for we are new in this part of the world, and woefully ignorant of the outrages that have been visited upon you.' He figured that line was pretty safe – both sides appeared reasonably outraged. And, as he took a pause for breath, he noticed that both sides had begun to mutter darkly as they glared at each other from opposite sides of the market-place.

'However,' he went on before it could become more than muttering, 'if you would be willing to speak with us but for a moment, I am sure we would quickly see the justice—'

Both sides began to shout before he could get any further.

'Any true son of the kingdom would see how the duke has abused—' the leader of the men in green shouted.

'Any true son of the kingdom would be loyal to the Duke of Wishbone—' the sheriff insisted.

Oh, dear. Roger didn't want this to get out of hand.

'Good people—' he began before he got out-shouted again.

'Loyal to the duke?' the green leader laughed. 'Who stole the throne from the rightful heir—'

'Would you listen to these men?' the sheriff retorted. 'Common thieves, who must hide in the forest—'

'Is this part of your plan?' Louie whispered.

'And what of the time when good King Reg returns from the Crusades—'

'King Reg? Don't make me laugh!' The sheriff laughed anyways. 'He gave up that title when he went gallivanting off on his private errand!'

'Must be a pretty good plan.' Doc whistled. 'It's sure got me stumped.'

'Oh, yes?' the sheriff's opponent demanded. 'And what about the crown jewels?'

Roger had to admit that this particular exchange had him stumped, too. And it wasn't getting any of them any closer to escaping from this cycle.

'You cannot accuse us of that!' the sheriff replied vehemently. 'Everyone knows the crown jewels fell into the hands of—'

'Enough!' Roger yelled. He didn't care the slightest bit whose hands the crown jewels fell into. All he wanted was some way out of here. If his plan was going to work, it was time to get tough.

'Where is the truth?' he demanded before the factions could resume their shouting contest. 'How can we choose a side when you are reduced to petty bickering!'

'Bickering?' the leader in green demanded. 'I suppose I am, if bickering is defending the rights of the downtrodden!'

'*Petty* bickering?' the sheriff echoed. 'We'll show you what happens to those who call the duke's actions *petty*!'

'Uh, Roger?' Louie pulled on his sleeve. 'This isn't the plan, is it?'

'Well, I can tell you one thing!' the man in green declared. 'These newcomers are no part of the true men of the forest!'

'And they certainly do not have the best interests of the duke at heart!' the sheriff agreed.

'They must be agents of the queen—' another of the forest men shouted.

'No, no!' one of the duke's men countered. 'They are most assuredly spies for the King of Spain!'

'There are certain ministers high in government who are known to have been plotting—' another forester mused.

'It's not that at all!' a fellow in a bullet helmet ventured. 'There are elements in the church who have been waiting years for just such an opportunity—'

Everyone turned to stare at Roger and his companions. There was a moment of awkward silence. This had not worked at all in the manner Roger had hoped. Maybe, he thought, if he started all over again—

'Good people of this kingdom—' he began.

Both groups groaned.

'We don't have to go through this again, do we?' the sheriff complained.

His opponent shook his head, a new determination upon his handsome features. 'I say, let's kill them quickly, and get back to our fight.'

'No,' Louie moaned. 'I don't think this was the plan.'

'For once, outlaw,' the sheriff answered the man in green, rewarding his opposite with a somewhat fussy smile, 'we agree on something. Have at them, soldiers!'

The forest leader laughed, once again confident of his priorities. 'Men! Skewer them with naked steel!'

Any number of men with swords rushed them again.

The blue smoke showed up before Louie could even whimper.

'All my fault,' Louie muttered.

Even Roger was beginning to believe that Louie might be right. But – call him an optimistic fool who'd spent too long in public relations – or, for that matter, call him somebody who didn't even want to think about the consequences if they really were stuck here – whatever the reason, he wasn't quite ready to give up yet.

Louie misused the ring, and the ring malfunctioned. Louie still had the ring now, and the ring still malfunctioned. Even Roger could see there was a common thread here.

'Louie,' he said calmly. 'There's one other way we can try to stop this thing. Give me back the ring.'

'Oh.' Louie paused. 'Do you think?'

Roger could hear the relief in Louie's voice. So even the sidekick thought it was a good idea!

'Sure,' Louie agreed, 'as soon as the smoke clears.'

'Aye,' a woman's voice came out of the fog. 'We're waitin' for that, too.'

'Uh-oh,' Louie replied.

Roger knew exactly what the sidekick meant. It had to be Bonnie Kate, queen of the swordswomen! Well, maybe if he started talking while they were still lost in this impenetrable cloud, he'd have enough time to convince Kate that the three of them meant no harm.

'Might I speak with you?' Roger asked.

'You might as well,' Kate replied sassily. 'We can do nought else while we wait for this blue bedevilment to clear.'

'You know we mean you no harm,' Roger replied.

'So you say,' Kate answered non-committally.

'We need a place to rest,' Roger added.

'I've heard that before,' she answered with a laugh.

'Uh—' Roger answered. This didn't seem to be going any better than the last couple of times. Shouldn't he be getting better with experience?

'Excuse me for interruptin' ' Doc drawled, 'but this wouldn't happen to be another one of your plans?'

'Well,' Roger admitted, 'I don't think I've quite gotten to the planning stage.'

'Just wanted to be ready,' Doc added amiably. 'There's probably still some way out of this. You never know – six-guns might work here.'

'Have you got a better idea?' Roger demanded.

'You're the hero around here,' Doc deferred.

Not again, Roger thought.

'Who came up with that idea?' he insisted.

'We all did, remember?' Louie chimed in. 'You were elected by popular vote.'

Roger didn't recall it in exactly that way. Still, this probably wasn't the best time to argue the point.

'You were trying to convince us?' Kate's voice penetrated the blue fog.

Roger sighed. He shouldn't have to be reminded that he was in the middle of a speech, trying to save his own life and those of his companions, not to mention the entire fate of the Cineverse. Still, thanks to Kate's interjection, he was back on track now. It was time to get down to business.

'As I was saying,' he continued into the blue smoke in what he hoped was Kate's general direction. 'We are but three travellers, intent on harming no one, whose only wish is to find a quiet place that we might rest for a bit, in order to better determine the best way that we might find our home.'

That was the best explanation Roger could come up with. If that wouldn't work, he didn't know what would.

'You make such a pretty speech—' Kate began as the smoke finally cleared.

The dark-haired Kate was flanked by two other women, one a blonde, the other a redhead, no doubt both members of Kate's all-woman crew. All three were dressed in pirate costumes of tight breeches and revealing vests.

'It's a shame we could never trust you!' Kate concluded as all three brandished their swords.

'What?' Roger asked, dumbfounded. 'You mean you can't trust outsiders?'

Kate sneered at the suggestion. 'Outsiders? We welcome outsiders! We've learned that you can't trust – men! What say, ladies? Let's gut them and throw them over the side to feed the fish!'

The blue smoke was back, all too soon.

Roger realised they were running out of options.

He hoped, somehow, they might be able to sing their way to safety.

In the meantime, he realised, Louie still hadn't given him the ring.

'Louie!' he yelled as they heard the first strains of cheerful song:

'People quake when they see our boat!
We'll sing to you and cut your throat;
We'll take your nose as a souvenir;
We're happy, singing buccaneers!'

'The visitors are back!' somebody yelled in acknowledgement of the blue smoke.

'Squawk!' the parrot added. 'Happy visitors!'

Obviously, Roger reflected, the parrot didn't know them very well.

'What's the matter?' Louie called back to Roger. 'I mean, besides everything?'

'You haven't given me the ring!' Roger answered.

'Oh.' Louie sighed. 'We haven't stopped anywhere long enough for me to think about it.'

'At this rate,' Roger reminded him, 'we may never have any time to stop anywhere again. I'm holding out my hand. You'll have to give me the ring before the smoke clears!'

'Is that a smart move?' Louie asked. 'Passing the ring when we can't see it? We could lose it!'

'So?' Doc interjected. 'The way things are going, losing that dang ring might be better for all of us!'

'Doc has a point,' Roger admitted. 'Give it here.'

'See?' Louie said defensively. 'You still talk like a hero.'

Roger thought about objecting again, but what was the use? Besides, he felt something hard, round, and plastic being pressed into his palm. He closed his fingers around it. Now, maybe, something would happen!

There was a sound like thunder so close that Roger jumped. The blue smoke disappeared, but it was replaced this time by blackness.

Perhaps, he thought belatedly, taking the ring wasn't such a good idea.

CHAPTER SIXTEEN

Then the smoke returned, darker than before, now a true midnight blue.

'Avast!' a gruff voice called. 'The landlubbers are back, ready to walk the plank!'

'It's the pirate world!' Louie screamed.

Roger realised they must have jumped again when he got the ring.

'I say,' another voice remarked, 'don't those blighters know when to stop bothering the free men of the forest?'

'No, it's not!' Doc interjected. 'It's the fellas with the funny helmets!'

'Cowards, all cowards!' a woman's voice called next. 'Isn't that just like men?'

'No, it isn't!' Roger yelled in turn. 'Can't you see? It's much worse than that!'

'We'll make a necklace of their ears,' the male chorus interjected. 'We're happy, singing buccaneers!'

'Something's happened with the ring,' Roger explained. 'Instead of slowing things down, when Louie gave me the ring, it stepped things up. We're going faster and faster, almost as if we were being sucked into some sort of Cineverse vortex!'

Doc whistled. 'Sure sounds like a hero's explanation to me.'

Roger tried to think what he could do. If only he understood the true workings of the Captain Crusader Decoder Ring – if only he understood anything about what had happened to him since Delores disappeared!

Delores!

No, he had to keep his wits. Things were still changing around him. Even though he couldn't see anything but the deep blue smoke, the voices around him seemed to be growing louder.

'Where did this – ship come from?' the leader of the forest men asked, his voice edged with hysteria. 'Is this another one of the duke's tricks?

'Aye, cap'n,' Briny's unmistakable slur cut in. 'Look at 'ese wenches!'

'I'll wench you, you male rumbuckets!' Kate replied haughtily.

'Squawk!' the parrot added. 'Happy rumbuckets!'

'Oh, no!' Louie yelled in Roger's ear. 'All the worlds are coming together! You know what that means, don't you?'

Roger had no idea.

'It's the Change!' Louie screamed. 'We have to do something!'

'This is all some forest trick!' the sheriff yelled.

'As killers we're the most sincere!' the male chorus warbled. 'We're happy, singing—'

Roger felt someone grab his lapels.

'Roger!' Louie continued to yell in his ear. 'Why didn't I think of this before? Quick! Before it's too late! You have to use your methods!'

What? Roger thought. Methods? But hadn't he explained to Louie that his so-called 'methods' were only a ruse – that he really never had any more than a Captain Crusader Decoder Ring – a ring that he didn't know how to use very well?

'It's our only chance!' the sidekick pleaded.

Well, apparently Roger hadn't explained it well enough. Either Louie had misunderstood, or he had completely forgotten, Roger's explanation.

One more thing had become very apparent in their present crisis; Roger never thought he understood much of what was going on around him, but now he realised he didn't understand anything at all. He had no idea of what these so-called 'methods' might be. Of course, he didn't think Louie or Doc had any more idea of what methods would be than he did.

He realised that might be the answer. One of the great underlying axioms of public relations was that you approached everything in the most positive manner possible. Perhaps he just had to approach these methods positively. If it would help to have Louie believe he had methods, let him believe it. And maybe, Roger realised, if he believed he had methods, he would have.

'All right,' Roger replied reluctantly. 'I'll use my methods if I have to.'

'See?' Doc chortled. 'A hero will always come through in the end!'

Roger wished he had Doc's confidence. In the meantime, though, he had to invent some methods.

'Listen to me,' he yelled, 'oh lords of the Cineverse!'

That sounded good, didn't it? But methods had to be more than that. Secret words, maybe?

'D.W. Griffith!' he yelled. 'David O. Selznick! Cecil B. de Mille!'

Nothing but smoke. Maybe he should use the ring, too? Why not? It certainly couldn't get any worse than this.

Roger crossed his fingers as he twisted the ring.

'Get us out of here!' he yelled.

The blue smoke was gone, replaced again by the total absence of light. Uh-oh. Maybe it could get worse.

'Help!' he added.

And there was light. And there were voices singing. Not the male voices of the buccaneers, but a mixed chorus, with perhaps a bit heavier emphasis on the high, ethereal end of the vocal scale; a Mormon Tabernacle choir sort of feeling. Roger blinked, trying to adjust his eyes to the sudden illumination. Louie and Doc were still with him, one to either side. And there was someone else here, too – no, not the choir. Those voices seemed to come from everywhere, as if from a host of invisible angels, or perhaps a really good sound system. But there was a tall figure, dressed all in white, who stood before that brilliant light, an illumination so intense that Roger could not really focus on the details of the figure.

And then the figure spoke:

LOUIE!

It was the loudest voice Roger had ever heard.

LONG TIME, NO SEE!

Louie only stood and stared. The voice boomed on:

FOOLISH OF ME.
YOU WOULDN'T REMEMBER, WOULD YOU?

Louie shook his head.

'It couldn't be,' he whispered.

AND DOC.
YOU'RE LOOKING GOOD!

Doc nodded, pleasantly enough, Roger guessed, but he noticed the cowboy kept his hands close to his six-shooters.

WHO'S THIS NEW FELLOW?
DON'T TELL ME, I SHOULD KNOW.
ROGER, IS IT?
IT ALWAYS TAKES ME A MINUTE WITH OUTSIDERS.

'It is,' Louie whispered in awe. 'It's the Plotmaster!'
Doc's hands left his gun handles as his mouth dropped open.
'Tarnation! The Plotmaster?'
Roger squinted over at the booming fellow. Who, or what, was a Plotmaster?

THAT'S RIGHT, LOUIE.
I KNEW YOU'D SEE THROUGH ME SOONER OR LATER.
NOW, WHAT SEEMS TO BE THE PROBLEM?

Louie quickly explained their problems with the ring, the ever-tightening-cycle, and the Change. And, as he finished, he added that it was all his fault.
The booming fellow laughed.

OH, LOUIE!
A SIDEKICK CAN'T DO ANYTHING BAD!
LET ME SEE THAT RING, WON'T YOU?

The choir music rose around them, like someone had turned up a volume switch. Roger felt the ring gently twist its way out of his grip. It floated over to the Plotmaster.
After a moment, the music softened as the Plotmaster's voice boomed out again.

HERE.
LOOK.
THE RING'S BROKEN.
THERE'S A HAIRLINE CRACK.

Roger stared. Somehow, even though the Captain Crusader Decoder Ring floated over next to the Plotmaster, he could clearly see the crack crossing the face of the ring.

SEE?
IT'S NOT YOUR FAULT.
IT'S JUST THAT THESE THINGS
ARE MADE OUT OF CHEAP PLASTIC.
AND ONCE THEY BREAK?
WELL—
WAIT A SECOND.
I'LL GET YOU A NEW ONE.

Although it was difficult to follow his precise movements in the brilliant illumination, Roger thought the Plotmaster looked up.

SID!
CAN WE GET A RING DOWN HERE?

He paused as if listening.

YEAH.
STANDARD MODEL.
BUT A NEW ONE, HUH? NONE OF THIS
RECONDITIONED STUFF.

The Plotmaster looked back in the direction of his visitors and shrugged his massive, white-clad shoulders.

YOU'VE GOT TO BE FIRM WITH THESE
ACCOUNTANT TYPES.

The choir got suddenly louder again, the kind of sonic shift you always got at the beginning of a television commercial.
Roger looked down at his hand.
He held a brand new Captain Crusader Decoder Ring.
The music faded.
The Plotmaster waved. He held something in his hand. Roger realised he was smoking a cigar. And oddly enough – or maybe it wasn't, considering the situation – in this strange illumination, the cigar smoke looked blue.

WELL, IT'S BEEN A REAL PLEASURE—
CHATTING WITH YOU BOYS.

'Wait!' Louie called. 'There's so much we could ask you!'
The Plotmaster shook his light-haloed head.

BUT TIME IS MONEY.
I'VE GOT TO TAKE A MEETING.
LET'S DO LUNCH SOMETIME, HEY?

The well-lit figure chuckled apologetically.

OF COURSE, YOU WON'T REMEMBER ANY
OF THIS.

He looked up again.

SID!
I'VE GOT TO SEND SOME FRIENDS OF MINE
BACK INTO THE 'VERSE!
GET ME REWRITE!

He waved again, this time with finality.

CIAO, BOYS!

After that, all was blackness.

CHAPTER SEVENTEEN

It was much more peaceful when the smoke cleared. In fact, Roger might almost have called their new surroundings idyllic. They seemed to be on a brightly-lit country road, the sun directly overhead, the sky a perfect blue.

Roger paused. Something was wrong. He couldn't remember exactly where they had come from. He remembered getting out of the war zone as quickly as they could. But after that – they had been on a pirate world, that was it! But why did he remember good robbers from the forest? Women with swords? Singing buccaneers?

And who, or what, was a Plotmaster?

He turned to ask Louie a question, but stopped when he saw the look of utter horror on the sidekick's face.

'Uh-oh,' Louie said.

'What do you mean, uh-oh?' Roger asked. Was there something else around here that he didn't understand? 'We're not being shot at or – or threatened with swords.' Yes, he remembered the swords quite clearly now. He waved his hands at the perfect sky. 'The sun's shining. Birds are singing. What's the matter around here? And, for that matter, why did you use the ring in the middle of all those pirates?'

'Pirates?' Louie blinked. 'That's right, we were on a pirate world, weren't we? Why don't I remember it better? I guess your mind tries to blank out unpleasant things.' He looked down at the verdant lawn around his feet. 'I have this thing – about swords, you know. I couldn't worry about the Change when my gizzard is about to be slit.'

Louie looked back at Roger. From the look on his face, whatever they were facing now frightened him every bit as much as swords. 'But we don't have time to worry about that – not anymore.'

Doc nodded. 'Sometimes a place can be too perfect.' He glanced distastefully at the guitar he still carried, as if the instrument had turned into a rattlesnake.

From Doc and Louie's reactions, Roger decided it was too dangerous around here to take any time to ask about the Plotmaster. He felt, somehow, that he should know all about the Plotmaster already.

Music drifted from somewhere nearby.

'It's a wonderful day to be walking,' a voice sang, 'and a wonderful day to be talking.'

Doc nodded. 'Just like I reckined.'

'Oh, no,' Louie moaned, 'anywhere but here.'

Roger decided he would feel better if his companions would at least explain what was worrying them so much.

'What's the matter?' Roger insisted.

'Just try moving,' Louie replied, 'and you'll find out.'

Roger lifted his right foot to take a step, and realised what Louie meant. He felt like he was walking through molasses.

'Now,' Louie said, 'sing about what you're going to do. And make it rhyme.'

Roger did as he was told:

'Oh, I'm going to take a step!' he sang. 'And I'll do it with some pep!'

His foot seemed to move forward of its own accord.

'It's what I've feared,' Louie explained. 'You've landed us on the most unpredictable of all the worlds – the Musical Comedy!'

'*I landed us—*' Roger protested. He still held the ring, but Louie was the one who had called out the travelling orders from – from wherever they had come from.

But Louie was too upset to argue. 'You've seen what it's like in Musical Comedy. Something's going one way, then suddenly, the singing and dancing starts, and the plot turns around completely! Nothing stays the same in a place like this, and it'll suck you in before you know it. If you don't watch out every second, you'll be embroiled in a romantic subplot! Once that happens, you're stuck here – happily after after.'

'Whether you want it or not?' Roger asked, aghast. Until now, he had never considered how subversive musicals could be.

'Oh, you'll want it all right,' Louie replied. 'You'll sing, you'll dance, and forget all about Delores and the Change!'

'Oh, no I won't!' Nothing could keep him from Delores. 'I'll use the ring right now!' But Roger could barely lift his hand. He could hear the singing come closer.

'Here we come,
Oh what fun,
On a country walk!
Howdy stranger,
Let's be neighbours:
Stay a while and talk!'

'Quick!' Louie whispered. 'We've got to get out of here before they see us. If they invite us to a wedding or a county fair, we may never escape!'

'I'm trying,' Roger replied between clenched teeth. 'My arm won't work.'

'Hey there!' the voices sang from around the bend. 'Hey there! It's time for the fair! And don't be blue, there'll be a wedding, too!'

'What can I do?' Roger panicked.

'Oh, of course!' And Louie burst into song:

'It's time to use the ring,
It's time to use the ring.
Excuse me while I sing;
But it's time to use the ring!'

Roger got the idea. It was so obvious when you sang about it.

'Don't want to lecture, Don't want to scold,
But both of you fellas better take hold,
Don't crack a smile and don't shed a tear,
Once I turn this ring, we're out of here!'

'All together, now!' he shouted, then all three sang as one:

'See you in the funny papers,
See you in the funny papers—'
What rhymed with funny papers?
'I don't mean the bunny capers—' Roger added.

They were surrounded by blue smoke which cleared almost as quickly as it had come.

'I've totally lost my bearings,' Louie admitted. 'But maybe, just maybe, this is the place.'

Roger stared at their surroundings. They seemed to be in a

jungle of some sort. Did that mean Delores was being held prisoner in a jungle?

He heard a high, trumpeting sound. The ground shook as something rumbled through the undergrowth, smashing trees, bushes, dwellings, other animals, and anything else that stood in its way.

'Oh, dear,' Louie remarked. 'That does sound an awful lot like a fear-maddened elephant, doesn't it?'

Roger had to agree that it did.

'Pity,' Louie added. 'Then maybe this isn't the place.'

Roger realised they had something more immediate to worry about. As trees collapsed along the jungle path before them, he saw that it was indeed a fear-maddened elephant – a fear-maddened elephant headed straight for them!

But then there was another sound, in the trees above them, a scream older than recorded history:

'Bunga bonga blooie!'

Roger would recognise that blood-curdling cry anywhere. In fact, he had – only the other day – heard that blood-curdling cry throughout an entire triple feature.

'Oh, really?' Louie remarked as the fear-maddened elephant bore down upon them. He grinned as he glanced into the trees overhead. 'This could get interesting.'

CHAPTER EIGHTEEN

Roger's mouth fell open. It was Zabana, prince of the jungle! He landed in front of them, directly in the elephant's path!

'I know that fella,' Doc announced.

'That fella', as Doc put it, was well over six feet tall, with broad, well-muscled, very tanned shoulders. In fact, all of that fella, save for his long, blond hair and leopardskin boxer shorts, was tanned a deep bronze, a colour closer to metal than to flesh. The newcomer stood, still and silent as a statue, facing the onrushing elephant, heedless of the way the maddened animal's half-ton feet shook the jungle floor.

Roger stared in disbelief. This whole Cineverse business had seemed a little too unreal, until now. There was no mistaking who stood before him. He had spent too many rainy Saturday afternoons glued to his TV, watching this very jungle giant. It had to be his boyhood hero. Roger could no longer contain himself.

'Zabana!' he called.

As if in answer, the blond giant beat upon his massive chest, his voice ululating forth to confront the advancing elephant.

'Eegah! Eegah! Greech Karoo!'

The enraged pachyderm trumpeted again as it continued to stampede in their direction.

Zabana glanced over his shoulder at the assembled sidekicks. He smiled apologetically.

'Oops,' he remarked. 'Zabana make mistake. Is female elephant!' He turned back to the rapidly approaching beast, to beat upon his chest and scream once more:

'Egah! Egah! Tandalayo!'

The elephant stopped abruptly, scuffing its feet on the broken trees that littered its path. It trumpeted apologetically, then walked back the way it came.

'There!' the jungle giant shouted gleefully. 'Zabana triumph again!' He beat upon his chest once more. 'Binga bonga blooie. Aieyeeaieyeyoo!'

That latest scream sent chills through Roger. He had, of course, heard that victory call a thousand times on those rainy Saturday afternoons, but never this close, this loud, this personal.

Big Louie whistled appreciatively. 'Wow. You sure did that with style.'

'Zabana have way with animals,' the jungle prince replied. 'Animals are my life.'

'Zabana,' Roger whispered, still quite overwhelmed. He had never imagined he would meet anyone like this in the Cineverse. Zabana was a real hero. He wondered if there was some way to recruit this jungle prince in their search for Delores.

'Hey, *hombre!*' Doc called. 'Don't you remember me? We met in *Zabana Goes West!*'

But Zabana held up one massive palm for silence. He frowned up at the sky and sniffed the air, then quickly stepped over to a tree, pressing his ear against the bark.

He looked up at the sidekicks and nodded curtly. 'Natives come!'

Natives? Roger knew what that meant. He had seen these confrontations often enough in the seventy-odd Zabana films he'd had the opportunity to watch. They were about to be visited by the proud, yet deadly, tribe that shared Zabana's jungle realm:

The Whatsahoosie!

Roger waited for the tell-tale beat of jungle drums, and the sound of fifty pairs of naked feet pounding their way up the forest path. He squinted out into the dense vegetation, eager despite himself for a first glimpse of the Whatsahoosie's ceremonial battle garb, replete with the multi-coloured feathers of tropical birds.

'Natives?' Louie muttered. 'Big fellows, probably? With lots of sharp knives and spears? Who want to cut out our hearts because we unknowingly violated some obscure tribal ritual? Hey, I know how these places work.' He looked imploringly at Roger. 'You don't think it's time to use the ring, maybe?'

Roger shook his head. Now that he'd found an actual, honest-to-goodness hero, this was one place he didn't want to leave.

Louie looked unhappy with Roger's decision. Doc unslung his guitar and began to play short, menacing chords as he observed the surrounding jungle.

'Quiet!' Roger commanded in a hushed voice. 'When the natives show up, we want to be ready for them.'

He peered once again into the surrounding undergrowth. But he still couldn't see a thing, and all he could hear were the distant sounds of snapping twigs and muffled curses.

'Ow! Watch that branch, would you—'

'Bloody vegetation!'

'Ralph!'

'Bloody H—!'

'Would you calm down?'

'Sorry, George, old man. I just wish I could keep my briefcase from getting caught in these vines.'

'We're almost there now – ah, just ahead!'

The vegetation parted before them, and three tall black men emerged, all of them wearing grey pin-striped business suits.

'Well,' the fellow in the lead announced genially, 'here we are.'

Another of the newcomers peered over his horn-rimmed glasses. 'Say, isn't that the Zabana fellow?'

The jungle prince nodded at the business-suited threesome. 'Me Zabana. You Whatsahoosie.'

Roger couldn't help himself. 'These are the Whatsahoosie?' he asked incredulously.

'Ah,' the fellow in the lead smiled indulgently. 'You are perhaps familiar with our old image. Back when we used to carry spears, beat drums, and wear all those parrot feathers?' He tsked softly as his right hand played with the knot on his pastel tie. 'One has to keep up with the times, don't you know.'

'Th-the times?' Roger sputtered. 'But I remember you as fierce warriors, relentlessly pursuing your independence and tribal way of life!'

'Ah, but we are still fierce warriors,' the leader replied smoothly. 'It is just our battleground that has changed. But we should introduce ourselves. We are George' – he pointed to himself, then to his companion with the horn rims – 'Ralph, and, over here, N'bonga.'

The third Whatsahoosie sighed. 'I am afraid some parents are still mired in the past. Rest assured, though – my friends call me Edgar.'

Roger introduced his companions as well. Sidekicks and Whatsahoosie shook hands all around.

'You see,' George continued once the introductions were complete, 'things have changed in our jungle. After all, with all the money we had, what could we do but attend the most exclusive private schools in Whatsahoosieland?'

'All the money?' Big Louie asked, suddenly interested in the conversation.

'Sure,' George replied smoothly. 'You know how Zabana is. He's always going off and finding Lost Cities of Gold and Nazi treasure hoards. He just comes back here and dumps them, then goes off in the trees someplace to practise his animal calls.'

'Animals are Zabana's friends,' the jungle lord added agreeably.

'Whatever,' George continued. 'So, the Whatsahoosie decided to spend a little time on self-improvement. We are the proud results!'

Ralph snorted. 'And still we have to come back to this bloody jungle!'

'Now, now,' George chided. 'You know we've come here with a purpose.' He glanced about distractedly, finally pointing to his right. 'Now, I see the shopping mall over there.'

'Under the spreading giant palms?' N'bonga/Edgar observed from the rear. 'Very nice. But what about that river?'

'Oh, no problem,' George reassured him. 'We simply pave it over.'

'Capital idea,' Ralph agreed. 'It can be part of the parking lot.'

'Wait a moment!' Roger interjected. 'You're going to build a shopping mall? Here? In the middle of the jungle? What will happen to Zabana?'

'Not to worry, old shoe,' Ralph replied. 'We've planned that all out as well. Rest assured, Zabana will be an important part of our theme park.'

'Hey!' Edgar chimed in. 'Don't forget to tell them about our exclusive tree condos!'

'Most certainly,' George agreed, checking a small notebook he had pulled from his briefcase. 'And, if you get in on the ground floor, we can give you substantial discounts!'

'A capital investment!' Ralph added.

'And have we mentioned our special time-sharing plan?' Edgar asked, reaching down to open his portfolio. 'You may have already won—'

'Oh, no you don't!' another voice called from the trees.

'Friend to Zabana!' The jungle prince waved as the newcomer dropped from the trees into their midst. He was tall and well muscled, his ebony skin glistening in the equatorial sun. Roger decided the newcomer's skin appeared ever darker than it might otherwise because of the belt and armbands woven from multi-coloured parrot feathers. In other words, this fellow was dressed like a Whatsahoosie.

'Oh, man,' Edgar muttered distractedly.

'Really,' Ralph agreed. 'Do you believe this fellow?'

'Quiet, young ones!' the newcomer thundered. 'I have heard of your plans. So, you will rape the jungle for your shopping mall, and pave over the mighty Hoosomacallit river for a parking lot, then force the exalted Zabana to work in your theme park? This shall never be. So say I!' He glowered at his fellow tribesmen. 'How do you answer that?'

The three other Whatsahoosie glanced at each other. George turned back to the newcomer.

'Oh, yeah?' he said. 'And what you gonna do about it?'

The newcomer fumed. 'Do you not remember me as your great leader?'

'Our former great leader!' Edgar countered, glancing at the others in the clearing. 'It's true. Back in our old tribal days, this fellow used to be the Great Thingamabob.'

The Thingamabob nodded pleasantly to Roger and the side-kicks. 'You may call me Bob for short.'

'That still doesn't change anything!' George countered.

Bob took a single step towards the three in business suits.

'Hey!' George exclaimed as he hastily backed away.

'We don't want any trouble here,' Edgar added.

'I just got this suit cleaned.' Ralph brushed his lapels protectively.

Bob sneered. 'And you call yourselves Whatsahoosies!'

'Hey, man,' Edgar objected. 'We've just readjusted our priorities.'

Something like a chuckle rumbled deep within the Thingamabob's throat. 'Is that the name you give it now? Priorities? Well, I call you the lowest of the low – nothing more than money-grubbing animals!'

'Animals are Zabana's friends!' the jungle prince interjected.

Theme parks? Money-grubbers? This was like nothing Roger had ever seen in a Zabana film! Roger once again found himself nearly overwhelmed by these events. The change in the jungle was quite amazing.

But that was it – wasn't it?

'Excuse me, Bob,' Roger interjected. 'But did all this – the breakdown of the tribe, the new emphasis on money—'

'Dollars and cents,' George agreed.

'The bottom line,' Edgar added.

'Bloody right,' Ralph chirruped.

Roger waved at the three financiers. 'Did this happen because of the Change?'

'I think it began there,' Bob answered. 'Not that the Change was necessarily a bad thing. Let us face it. The old tribal way of life – what with days filled with hours of general spear carrying, more hours of menacing effete white hunters and even more hours shouting "Bad juju!" – could be somewhat limiting. So perhaps a change was due. However, I do not think it is the one the youngsters have chosen!'

'Oh, yeah?' George replied again.

'Have you done all that much better?' Ralph challenged. 'Look what's happened to you and Zabana!'

'Is true,' Zabana agreed sadly. 'Family gone.'

'Oh, no!' Roger blurted. 'You mean Shirley—'

Zabana nodded. 'She now consultant in Congo.'

His faithful female companion gone? Roger found this horribly traumatic. 'And what about your son, Son?'

'Son go next jungle,' Zabana admitted sadly. 'Do own series – Kanga, the jungle kid.' He shook his head sadly. 'Life not easy for prince of jungle.'

'Oh, dear,' was all Roger could think to say. He decided it was better not to ask the whereabouts of Zabana's loyal orang-utan, Oogie.

'Let's face it, fellows,' Ralph concluded. 'Zabana and the Thingamabob are both living in the past. Giving them jobs in our theme park would be doing them a favour!'

'Do not speak so soon!' the Great Thingamabob thundered. 'You act as if the jungle will let you pave it over without a battle! Do you not know that the jungle is a special place, and you must have special talents to conquer it?'

Doc strummed his guitar appreciatively. 'Sounds like hero talk to me.'

Roger had to agree. Perhaps they could recruit this Bob fellow as well, and they could have two heroes aiding in their quest to find Captain Crusader. Unless—

Roger looked speculatively at the blond Zabana, studying his manly physique, his square jaw, his slightly self-deprecating smile. Roger remembered that the last time they were around a hero, that hero turned out to be the actual Captain Crusader. What if the greatest hero in the Cineverse was once again in their midst – not as a masked marshal, but as a prince of the jungle?

'Oh, yeah?' George shot back at Bob. 'If it's so tough around here, how do you guys survive?'

The blond giant nodded pleasantly. 'Jungle is Zabana's friend!'

Everything seemed to be Zabana's friend. So much for that idea, Roger concluded. No, this jungle prince didn't seem to be quite up to the Captain Crusader level.

'And you must beware the jungle,' Bob added solemnly, 'for it will always surprise you!'

As if on cue, there was an explosion in their midst. A blue smoke explosion.

'Holy Toledo!' Big Louie exclaimed.

'Is it Doctor Dread?' Roger asked, trying to get a clear view through the smoke.

'Even worse,' Louie answered. 'It's my sister!'

CHAPTER NINETEEN

So Louie had been right after all. Dread had sent someone after the sidekicks to make sure they were – taken care of.

Roger heard Bertha's voice before he saw her.

'Well, boys,' she drawled. 'It's time to clean up some scum.'

That's when the smoke cleared. Roger wished it hadn't. Bertha stood in the midst of a knot of men in double-breasted suits. All the men carried pistols, blackjacks, knives, brass knuckles, and various other instruments of destruction. Bertha held a machine gun. She smiled when she saw Roger.

'I'm going to clean some of this scum –' she paused significantly, '– personally.'

'*Now* is it time to use the ring?' Louie wailed.

'In a second.' Roger still had to talk to Zabana and the Grand Thingamabob. If at all possible, he wanted the two heroes to leave with them.

Doc smiled as he put down his guitar. 'First, we may have to do a little shootin'.'

The double-breasted fellows had a good laugh at that one. 'You and what army?' one of them shouted.

'Zabana not need army!' the jungle prince announced. 'Who challenges Zabana?'

This seemed to upset some of the henchmen.

'Zabana?'

'Doctor Dread didn't tell us about Zabana!'

'Pipe down,' Bertha ordered. 'Look on the bright side. It's not every day you get to clean up a jungle prince.'

The double-breasted people laughed at that, and readied their weapons for battle.

The Grand Thingamabob shook a spear above his head. The shaft of wood was longer than a man was tall, brightly painted and ornamented with yellow and green feathers; its large, metal head gleamed golden in the sun. It was quite an impressive spear. Roger wondered where Bob had gotten it from.

'Step forward, and you shall feel the might of the Whatsahoosie!'

'The Whatsahoosie?'

'Now wait a minute!'

'First Zabana and now this?'

The henchmen's cheer seemed to have deserted them again.

Bertha waved her machine gun over the double-breasted throng. That's when Roger noticed the silver bracelets on her arm. They looked an awful lot like the bracelets clinking on Delores' arm the last time he saw her. Except, on Bertha, instead of hanging fashionably loose, they seemed to dig deeply into the fabric of her khaki fatigues, bunching up the cloth, and probably the skin beneath.

But, if those bracelets were on Bertha now, what had happened to Delores? Roger realised, more than ever, how important it was to escape.

'Come on now, boys!' Bertha cheered. 'Where's your villainous team spirit? There's a lot more than heroes to clean up around here. I mean, look at all those sidekicks!' She aimed her roscoe at the financiers. 'Why don't we start out by wiping out those three fellows in suits over there?'

'Perhaps,' George admitted, 'we should rethink our plans.'

'It might not be a bad idea,' Ralph concurred, 'were we to find a quieter part of the jungle.'

Edgar nodded as the three of them backed away. 'I wonder how Kanga, the jungle kid, feels about tree condos?'

All three turned quickly and disappeared into the verdant undergrowth.

'See there?' Bertha crowed. 'Nobody stands a chance against the forces of Doctor Dread!'

'Nobody?' Zabana shot back at the assembled evil-doers. 'Nobody not here! Here is Zabana! Here is Great Thingamabob! Here are—' Zabana paused with a frown. He glanced at Roger and his fellows. 'Zabana beg pardon. Not properly introduced.'

Roger and the sidekicks introduced themselves.

'Much better!' the jungle prince declared. 'All on first name basis! Now, where was Zabana? Oh, yes!' He pounded his chest a couple of times for effect. 'Here is Zabana! Here is Great Thingamabob! Here is Roger and Doc and Louie! Together, we defeat your evil plans, and all bad people who come to Zabana's jungle! Binga bonga blooie!'

The next sound that came from Zabana's throat sounded – to Roger – like nothing so much as an alligator in heat.

'What was that?' one of the henchmen quavered.

'Whatever it was,' Bertha said rather more forcefully, 'you'd better not let him do it again.'

There was a distant rumbling in the forest.

Zabana called out again, a noise akin to a hundred monkeys jamming a crosstown bus.

The rumbling grew louder.

'What did I say about letting him do this?' Bertha demanded.

'Okay, okay. I'm on my way.'

The henchman stepped forward, Luger at the ready.

The Great Thingamabob stepped in front of him.

'It is not so simple as that,' he rumbled. 'To reach Zabana, you must pass me first.'

'If that's the way you want it, buddy,' the henchman sneered as he lifted the gun.

The long spear spun in Bob's hands, hitting the Luger with a sharp crack. The gun went flying behind the nearby ferns.

'If you are going to carry a gun,' Bob remarked drily, 'you should learn how to handle it.'

The expression on the henchman's face was a mixture of fear and rage.

'W-w-why!' he sputtered. 'I'm gonna—'

'Lefty!' Bertha barked. 'Get back here! This is Moose's kind of job.'

Zabana used this opportunity for another of his strange calls, this one rather like a group of crows trapped in a plummeting elevator. The rumbling noise answered back, still deep in the jungle.

Lefty scrambled back to Bertha's side as a much larger henchman lumbered forward, even more massive than the large cowpokes they had encountered earlier. It wasn't his height that was so exceptional, although he was certainly tall enough. It was the width of his shoulders that was so surprising, each a yard from the arms to the tree-stump neck. Of course, the fact that his arms hung down so low at his sides that his knuckles almost brushed the jungle floor did nothing to diminish the feeling that they were facing a human engine of destruction.

'Moose,' Bertha instructed. 'We have some vermin here for you to stomp –' she paused, then added, '– to rip –' and smiled as she amended, '– to pummel.'

The incredibly large person stopped. His mouth opened as he looked at Roger and his fellows. From deep in his throat came a single, monosyllabic grunt. Only then did the massive thug once again lumber forward. The noise seemed to have taken all his concentration.

Zabana cut loose with the most elaborate call of all, something that started like fifty parrots asking for a wide variety of crackers but finished more like a troupe of laughing hyenas swallowing numerous bullfrogs.

The rumbling sound was much closer. In fact, as it approached, it sounded much more like a hooting, howling, trumpeting, roaring, rumbling. Roger thought he felt the jungle floor shake beneath his feet.

Bertha ignored it. 'Moose,' she instructed, 'when you stomp, rip, and pummel all of these scum, spare that worthless toadie over in the corner.' She smiled at Roger. 'That one is mine.'

'Uuhhh,' Moose replied.

Then the Great Thingamabob stepped in his path.

'It is not so simple as that. To reach the others, you must pass—'

Moose reached forward with lightning speed and ripped the spear from Bob's hands. The large man flexed his knuckles. The spear broke in half.

'Uuhhh,' Moose remarked.

'Remember, Moose,' Bertha called as she pointed to Roger. 'This scum is mine.' She paused, letting her tongue roll over her teeth. 'Maybe I'll go slow and let him last a day or two.'

'Uuhhh,' Moose agreed.

The Great Thingamabob did not move from the large man's path. 'If I must die,' he announced, 'I will die as a Whatsahoosie!'

'No one die here!' Zabana objected. 'No one but bad people. Help is on way!'

Roger realised that the rumbling had redoubled. And the hooting, hollering, braying, cawing and trumpeting was getting so loud it was hard to hear Zabana at all.

'Animals are Zabana's friends!' the jungle prince announced.

'Uuhhh,' Moose remarked uncertainly.

For the animals were upon them. And what a group of animals they were. In movie after movie, Roger had seen the jungle prince call one animal or another to get him and his friends out of one scrape or another. In *Zabana's Jungle Fountain* he had called upon the lions and other great cats, and sure enough, here were lions and leopards and jaguars again leaping into the clearing. In *Zabana*

Versus the Nazi Death Ray, the prince had summoned a stampede of jungle wart-hogs to wipe out the German patrol, and here, once again, Roger could hear the characteristic snorting over the pounding sound of a hundred wart-hog hooves. In *Zabana and His Son* it had been water-buffaloes; in *Zabana's Water Adventure*, man-eating crocodiles; in *Zabana Versus the Communist Menace* (one of his later, lesser films), crazed rhinoceroses. And then there were all those films where he brought in the elephants in the final reel. But Roger had never seen all the animals on the rampage all at once. At least, he hadn't until now.

Apparently, for this particular occasion, Zabana had called out everything.

'Into trees, friends!' Zabana instructed.

Roger did as he was told, quickly climbing into the lower branches of a gnarly oak as the first of the animals thundered by below him. He saw both Louie and Doc were climbing trees nearby.

'Get back here, Moose!' Bertha hollered. But Moose had already disappeared from sight, overwhelmed by the wild herd. Perhaps he was trampled, or perhaps he merely joined the stampede; it was impossible for Roger to see. Whatever had happened, he was gone.

Roger saw that the herd, which, until then, had consisted mostly of the big cats, antelopes, water-buffaloes, wart-hogs and the occasional giraffe, was tending towards larger and larger mammals as it passed on by – here a hippo, there a rhino, and, taking up the rear – the elephants. Perhaps, Roger considered, there was a reason both Zabana and Bob had retreated to the upper branches. Roger climbed again, swiftly but carefully, cautious not to be knocked from his safe perch by the earthquake stampeding below.

That same stampede had almost reached Dread's rapidly retreating henchpeople.

'We're not done with you yet!' Bertha glared at Roger meaningfully. 'I'm especially not done with you! Gather around me, lackies!'

The henchmen clustered around Bertha as she used her ring. An instant later, they were gone.

'Animals Zabana's friends.' The jungle prince smiled. 'Animals also good solution to many everyday problems. Save messy clean up afterward, too.'

Roger looked down at the forest floor as the last of the elephants passed. All the underbrush, and anything else that had been down there, was gone, pressed into a green and brown pulp. Zabana was right. There *was* nothing left down there to clean up.

'Is it safe to climb back down?' Roger asked.

'Wait a second,' the jungle prince cautioned. He called out again, this noise eerily like an air raid siren crossed with the songs of jungle birds.

He stopped and nodded at Roger. 'Safe now. Zabana give all clear.'

Roger shimmied down the tree, and joined the others on the flattened forest floor.

'I am glad we were able to save our new-found friends,' the Great Thingamabob said with a smile. 'There are few enough heroes left. We cannot squander them.'

'Shucks,' Doc offered. 'We're not heroes. We're only sidekicks, looking to get by.'

Roger saw his chance to make his pitch.

'Exactly,' he hurriedly added, rapidly explaining that they had sworn to defeat Doctor Dread and at the same time rescue a lady in distress. He looked at both heroes as he concluded: 'We could use your help.'

The Great Thingamabob shook his head with a smile. 'So you will never be heroes – that's what you think? And are you sure that heroes have to be born that way, that they cannot rise to the circumstance?' He paused, considering his own question. 'Well, perhaps it was that way, before the Change.'

'Change?' Zabana pondered the issues as well. 'Yes, jungle prince will come. You saw what happen with local people.' The blond giant sighed. 'Place not same. Zabana think he could use change of jungle.'

'Good!' Roger said enthusiastically. He turned to the Great Bob. 'And you?'

Bob shook his head more sadly. 'Alas, I cannot. I am needed elsewhere. But we will meet again.' He waved to all of them a final time. 'And remember: Never leave your rhino meat outside to dry.'

Roger felt a shiver flow down his spine as he glanced at the others. Never leave your rhino meat? Wasn't that the sort of thing you'd hear in a Whatsahoosie social studies class? Or the kind of message you might have decoded if you were staying in the jungle and using a plastic ring that was also the key to the universe?

Roger decided he had to ask. But the Great Thingamabob was

gone. Somehow, without a sound, he had faded back into the jungle.

'Was that—?' he began anyway.

Doc nodded before Roger could finish. 'Who else could it be?'

Big Louie agreed. 'Yeah, that looked like a hero's hero.'

So that was Captain Crusader? Roger smashed a fist into his open palm. So close – and now he was gone! True, he hadn't looked much like the Masked Marshal, but shouldn't Roger have been able to recognise him by his noble actions? Why hadn't Roger at least added that they were also looking for him?

'He always shows up where you least expect him,' Louie added, trying to be cheerful.

'But we've lost him,' Roger replied, not caring if the others heard the hint of despair in his voice. 'What can we do now?'

'No problem,' Louie replied, blowing on his knuckles. 'Now that I know we've landed in Zabana's jungle, I know where to go next. If I may tell you how to set the ring?'

Roger nodded, realising they had to go on, for Delores, if nothing else. This time, he listened carefully to Louie's instructions before he made a move.

CHAPTER TWENTY

At first, Roger thought something had gone wrong. When the blue smoke cleared, the jungle was still there. But the blue smoke had vanished in an instant, blown away by a sea breeze. And the jungle floor was no longer trampled underfoot, but seemed even more lush and green than it had before.

Roger realised they were in a brand new jungle, and – for some reason – his confusion brought forth images of men with swords, and – for that matter – women with swords, and pirates, and buccaneers that didn't seem all that different from the pirates, except that the buccaneers did a lot of singing.

Singing? Where did that come from?

And who, or what, was the Plotmaster?

'We're here,' Louie commented tersely.

'Oh,' Roger replied, explaining his confusion.

Zabana nodded his agreement. 'You see one jungle, you see them all.'

'Yeah,' Louie countered, 'but this place is different. Can't you smell the sea? Can't you hear the noise of distant drums?'

Now that the diminutive sidekick mentioned it, Roger could hear a faint rhythm beneath the swish of wind-blown palm fronds.

'It come from beach,' Zabana said wisely.

'Drums?' Doc asked uncertainly. 'Those aren't like Indian war drums, are they?'

'On a peaceful, South Sea island like this?' Big Louie scoffed. 'You've got to be kidding.'

'Never speculate on natives,' Zabana commented, 'until you properly introduced.'

Roger realised that he didn't have time to worry about pirates or Plotmasters. Now that they were here, he had only one goal. He had to rescue Delores!

'Well, I think the natives will have to wait,' Roger interrupted. 'Louie, you got us here. Now get us to Doctor Dread.'

'Oh, that.' Louie smiled sheepishly. 'Well – um – there is – um – a little – uh – problem.'

'Wait a moment,' Roger replied. 'Are you telling me you don't know Dread's whereabouts?'

'Well, sure I know,' Louie said defensively. 'He's on this island. I just don't know – uh – quite where on this island.'

Roger frowned, pausing long enough to tuck the Captain Crusader Decoder Ring safely in his jacket pocket. 'Hold on here. How do you know he's on this island in the first place?'

Louie shrugged. 'Hey, my sister used to talk to me, you know?'

But Roger wasn't going to let Louie off that easily. 'So if she told you, why didn't she give you the exact location?'

'Exact location?' Louie stared with sudden interest at the undergrowth surrounding his western boots. 'I'm afraid my sister and I weren't *that* close.'

Roger sighed and looked heavenward. 'Where does that leave us?'

'Well, I figure he's got to be someplace on this island,' Louie insisted. 'I mean, how big can a South Sea island be, anyway?'

'Pardon me, fellas,' Doc drawled, 'but aren't those drums getting closer?'

Roger paused. Doc was right. The rhythmic pounding was much louder than before. What could it mean? What had it meant in all those old movies Roger had seen? A great many different things, as he recalled. And most of those things, as he remembered, were none too healthy for the heroes. Roger once again felt a bit of panic trying to escape.

'What do they want?' he asked, his voice much lower than before.

'Maybe natives hear us,' Zabana said reasonably.

Roger bit his lip. It was true. Heaven knew, Roger and Louie had made no attempt to be discreet in their argument.

The drums were literally booming through the jungle now.

'But what do they really want?' he asked again.

'Never speculate on natives—' Zabana began.

Roger cut him off with a curt nod. Of course the jungle prince was right. But, until they knew the natives' motives, the wise thing to do would be to keep out of their way.

'I suggest that we start looking for Dread's hideout,' Roger suggested, 'say – in any direction but where the drums are coming from?'

That sounded like a good idea to everybody else. They moved, as quickly and quietly as the jungle would allow, away from the persistent drumbeats. Roger waved at Zabana to lead the way. The jungle prince bounded quickly to the front of the line.

They had only travelled another fifty feet or so when Zabana raised a hand for the party to halt. The jungle prince looked back at the others.

'People ahead,' he whispered.

'Is it the native drummers?' Roger whispered back.

Zabana shook his head. 'They still beating somewhere behind us. These not natives. These people from someplace else!'

Someplace else? Roger's breath caught below his Adam's apple. Could they have found Dread's hideout already? Was his search finally at an end?

He quickly strode past Zabana. Delores could be up there! He hoped she hadn't been treated too badly. If Dread had done anything to her, Roger swore the evil mastermind would pay!

The palm trees seemed to be thinning out ahead. There was a clearing in the midst of the jungle, and in the middle of that clearing was a single, great tree. And tied to that tree was a woman wearing a black vinyl jumpsuit, but no bracelets. A woman with long, blond hair. A woman Roger would know anywhere.

Delores!

Roger ran forward, towards the last copse of palms that ringed the clearing. Dried bamboo shoots cracked beneath his jogging shoes. So much for the silent approach. Still, there didn't seem to be anyone else around. Maybe he could quickly untie Delores and the two of them could just as quickly escape before her captors returned.

That's when Delores saw him. But she didn't look happy to see him. In fact, she appeared to be rather annoyed.

'Roger!' she called. 'What are you doing here?'

He grinned. 'I've come to rescue you!'

She seemed horrified by the thought. 'Rescue? Who wants to be rescued?'

'Don't you?' he replied, a bit taken aback. 'You are tied to a tree!'

Delores attempted to shrug her shoulders within her roped confines. 'Who says I don't want to be tied to a tree?' She glanced about distractedly. 'Look, Roger, don't you have something better to do?'

'Better? But, Delores, after all we've meant to each other? I thought—'

'That was your problem,' she interrupted. 'Thinking.' She

suddenly smiled. Roger's heart lifted. Had she been teasing him all along?

'Oh, you didn't tell me you'd brought company along,' she said coquettishly. 'Handsome company!'

It was only then that Roger realised he had a jungle prince at his side.

'Sorry to interrupt,' Zabana murmured. 'But what we do about drummers?'

Now that he mentioned it, Roger realised the drumming was getting very loud indeed.

'What should we do?' he asked, upset and confused as much by Delores' reaction as by any imminent danger.

The jungle prince frowned in thought for an instant.

'Zabana distract!' He waved to Roger, then disappeared into the jungle.

'What?' Delores demanded, her frown returned now that the jungle prince was gone. 'Not only are you trying to untie me against my wishes, you're going to let your handsome friend go without even introducing me?'

Roger had had enough of this nonsense. 'No, Delores, I'm coming for you!'

Delores literally shrieked. 'If you take another step closer to me, Roger, it will be your life!'

She glanced at the trees to her left. 'Um – I mean, it'll be the end of our life together!'

What was going on here? Every time Delores opened her mouth, Roger ended up more upset than he had been before. This went far beyond mere playfulness. Had Dread done something to Delores' mind?

Perhaps, he considered, he should use some negative psychology. If she thought she was going to lose him, surely Delores would change her mind.

Roger sighed. 'Well, then, all I can do is leave.'

He took a slow and exaggerated step away.

'If you want it that way,' she agreed all too readily. 'I might as well be plain. I never want to see you again, Roger. I'm going to stay with Doctor Dread the rest of my life!'

What did she mean? He took a step back towards her. This didn't make any sense at all.

'Do you *know* what you're saying?' he demanded.

'I certainly do,' Delores agreed. 'And you know what I'd do if I were you? I'd be so mad, I'd take that ring and get out of here – back where you belong!' Her eyes wandered once again toward the trees to her left. Her gaze snapped back to Roger. Did she look the slightest bit feverish?

'Just think how much simpler your life was,' she continued, forcing a smile, 'before you met me. Why don't you be a good guy and zap yourself back to Earth – right away!'

Back before he met her? Back when he was dating Sandra? Or even worse, Phyllis? No matter how many times she tried to get rid of him, he still couldn't believe it. 'Delores, do you know what you're saying?'

But all she could do was groan. 'Oh, Roger, you can be so thick-headed! Get out of here, now!'

Roger turned away. What could he do but leave? He turned away, despondent. He thought he heard someone sobbing softly behind him. Roger knew it must be his imagination – one last case of wishful thinking from a man who'd wasted his life at the movies. It couldn't be Delores. Not after the way she'd treated him.

Roger heard two noises in the distance. One, of course, was the drums. The other was a call, not unlike a tiger attempting the falsetto part of a doo-wop ballad. Zabana must be out there somewhere, distracting.

Louie and Doc waited for him a few paces back within the jungle.

'Tough break, pardner,' Doc commiserated.

'Why would she do this to me?' Roger asked, not really expecting an answer.

'Maybe she likes it that way,' Louie suggested gently.

'What?' Roger asked incredulously. 'Being tied up?'

'Well, you know,' Louie continued apologetically, 'maybe you hadn't gotten to that part of the relationship yet. Sometimes it takes a while to get to the – kinky stuff.'

'Really?' Roger replied miserably. Actually, his relationship with Delores had been hot and heavy for some months. At least, that's how he remembered it. As he recalled, they had explored a lot of the kinky stuff already. But maybe Delores had had other ideas. He sighed. What did it matter now, anyway?

'What do we do now?' he asked his fellows listlessly.

'I think it's time for us to get lost,' Doc suggested, 'in a hurry!'

What did he mean?

Roger looked up.

'Huh?' he managed.

Louie shrugged. 'The cowpoke's long gone.'

Doc was nowhere to be seen. He had taken his own advice, and disappeared into the undergrowth.

Wasn't that drum sound awfully close?

'What's going on here?' Roger ventured, his misery giving way to fear.

'Ah!' a deep voice boomed. 'There you are!'

'Uh oh,' Louie whispered. 'I don't think we should be. Here, that is.'

Both Roger and Louie turned to face the newcomer.

He was tall, and well muscled, the shell necklace he wore brilliant white against his warm brown skin. Besides his jewellery, he wore nothing but a short skirt of dried grasses. Still, his smile was broad and genuine. He certainly seemed friendly.

And he led a group of islanders, fifty strong.

Before Roger could make any sort of decision about all this, the islanders surrounded them. Roger noticed that a large number of their greeting party was female, and very attractive besides. The women all wore sarongs covered with multi-coloured floral patterns and necklaces of bright woven flowers, while their faces were framed by glistening dark hair that hung to their waists. They smiled as well. In fact, everybody but Roger and Louie seemed to be smiling.

One of the women stepped forward, lifting her flowered necklace over her head. She placed it gently over Roger's head and onto his shoulders, then kissed his cheek.

'Welcome to our island paradise!'

Actually, Roger thought, this wasn't all that bad. A second woman approached, flowered necklace in hand. Roger waited patiently as she, too, placed the wreath of flowers on his shoulders and kissed him, this time on the other cheek. Yes, he could definitely get used to this. Let Delores reject him! Maybe he'd find his very own island beauty instead.

'We thought we would never find you!' the young lovely breathed.

No, no, this didn't seem bad at all. Maybe, Roger considered, being on the run on world after world in the Cineverse had made him too cautious, even paranoid.

He remembered his confusion over the swashbucklers, and that Plotmaster stuff. Heck, he could even be having delusions! And little wonder, too, the way he'd been jumping from world to world. Perhaps, now that Delores was gone – Roger tried to ignore the pain in his heart – now what he really needed was a nice, long rest, in someplace sunny, someplace warm, someplace with dozens of beautiful distractions.

When he thought about it that way, it made a whole lot of sense. It would be a shame if his caution kept him from truly enjoying an island paradise.

Still, he remembered Zabana's warnings about any local populations. He wasn't sure exactly why these islanders were being that friendly. What – for example if these people were in league with Doctor Dread, and had mistaken Roger and Louie for henchmen? No, before he relaxed completely, he had to ask a couple of questions.

'Are you sure it was us you were looking for?' he ventured cautiously. 'Aren't there some other people on this island?'

'Other people?' one of the lovely women asked with a smile. 'What need have we for other people?'

But one of the men added: 'Oh, yeah. There is that guy in the tree making all those weird noises. Lucky we heard you yelling at that woman up here or we might have been distracted.'

Well, it all seemed innocent enough. So why wasn't Roger enjoying himself more? Could he still, even now, have some left-over guilt about Delores? He laughed bitterly. Why should he feel anything for that woman, after she had just told him she was leaving him for Doctor Dread? Roger decided he had to readjust his priorities. And what better priority could there be than an attractive island beauty?

'So now it is time to go?' asked another of the saronged young women. 'Yes?'

'Yes,' Roger replied, deciding it truly was time to fully enjoy whatever this island had to offer. 'Where?'

'We will take you down to the bright blue ocean,' the beauty replied, 'and introduce you to the rest of our friendly and fun-loving people.'

'Oh,' Roger replied, genuinely pleased. 'That sounds nice.'

Big Louie, however, apparently wasn't as convinced. 'Then what happens?' he asked, a slight quaver to his voice.

Another of the women answered: 'Then we will honour you with a great feast, which shall go on from sunset to sunrise.'

'Oh,' Louie admitted. 'I guess Roger's right. That doesn't sound bad.'

'Then,' another of the lovelies added happily, 'of course, we will sacrifice you to the Volcano God.'

'Wakka Loa,' one of the men added cheerfully. Drums beat in the distance.

BOOM *Boom* Boom boom.

The smiling, well-muscled men grabbed both of Roger's arms in vice-like grips.

'It is a great honour,' they added.

Roger noticed that Louie was similarly pinioned.

'It happens very quickly,' a beautiful woman said with a smile.

'And they use a very sharp knife,' another added helpfully.

'Absolutely nothing to worry about,' the man who spoke first concluded. 'Is everybody ready?'

And with that, their entire escort burst into song.

Roger was too preoccupied to listen to the words. Sacrifice? Volcano God? Perhaps this wasn't such a cheerful place after all. Roger tried to struggle, but it was useless. The islanders' grip was too tight, and they were moving too fast.

Louie and Roger were hustled, by the happy, singing islanders, all the way back to the beach.

CHAPTER TWENTY-ONE

'Oh it's awful, awful nice,
Wakka Heenie, Wakka Ho,
In our island paradise!
Wakka Heenie, Wakka Ho.
We're so glad that you've been found,
Wakka Heenie, Wakka Ho,
'Cause we'd like to show you 'round,
Wakka Heenie, *Unhhh*!'

Actually, Roger thought, this wasn't that bad. Here he was, being carried down to a tropical beach by two pairs of strong hands, surrounded by beautiful, smiling women, his mind pleasantly lulled by the exotic rhythms of the song they sang – sort of a cha-cha, mambo type of thing. Now, if he could just forget about being sacrificed to the Volcano God—

Roger blinked. He was going to be sacrificed to the Volcano God! What had he been thinking about? How could he have been lulled by anything when he was soon to be cut up in honour of some pagan deity? This was serious! Somehow, he had to get out of here.

The islanders began to sing again.

'Not a thing you have to do,
Wakka Heenie, Wakka Ho.
Lovely maidens sing for you,
Wakka Heenie, Wakka Ho.
Everything's within our reach,
Wakka Heenie, Wakka Ho.
'Cause we're gonna hit the beach,
Wakka Heenie, *Uunnhhh*!'

Roger sighed. The music was awfully pleasant, no matter what was going to happen later – its lilting beat was as infectious as anything he had ever heard. His feet began to move, almost of their own volition, as if they wished to dance along. The women smiled at him. They had such nice smiles. Roger sighed again. He didn't know when he had ever been this happy.

The jungle ended, and the natives ran Roger out onto a beach of white sand that stretched from the lush forest out to the turquoise sea. But they had stopped singing.

And he was going to be sacrificed to a Volcano God! He should be in a perpetual state of panic, not dancing along with the music. What was wrong with him?

'The same thing that's wrong with me,' Louie answered from where he had been deposited by Roger's side. Oddly, enough, Roger couldn't remember asking the question – at least, not out loud.

'What do you mean?' Roger asked back, rubbing his arms where they had so recently been gripped. But before Louie could answer, both were surrounded by a bevy of young, laughing island beauties, who drew the two sidekicks farther down the beach, until Roger and Louie faced an islander of advanced years – an elder with skin like wrinkled leather, and hair as white as the snow these people would never see.

The elder smiled graciously. 'Glad you could make it.'

All the beauties began to talk at once:

'We are so happy to see you!' the beauties said.

'Enjoy our pristine beaches—' the elder added.

'Welcome to our island paradise!' the lovelies cheered.

'Bathe in our azure ocean—' the elder encouraged.

'We hope to make your stay as pleasant as possible,' the maidens suggested.

'Visit with our cheerful local population—' the elder encouraged.

'There will be a feast in your honour,' the women enthused.

'Sample the excellent local cuisine—' the elder mentioned.

'And then of course, the ultimate honour!' the maidens cooed.

'And,' the elder agreed, 'for a final thrill, there's a visit to the local volcano—'

The other islanders joined in as he spoke the next two words.

'Wakka Loa!'

BOOM *Boom* Boom boom, the drums said.

Roger had heard that noise before. He couldn't help himself. Sacrifice or no sacrifice, he had to ask:

'Do the drums always do that?'

'You try it,' the elder suggested with a smile.

'Try what?' Roger asked.

'You know,' a nearby beauty urged.

'Wakka Loa?' Roger guessed.

BOOM *Boom* Boom boom, the drums replied. The islanders cheered.

'Now you are truly one of us!' the elder exclaimed.

'The drums always do that,' the beauty explained. 'It is one of the many unique features of our island paradise.'

'But you must have had a long and arduous journey to our pleasant vacation home under the sun.' The elder pointed to a hut further down the beach. 'You should rest and refresh yourselves with some of our many and varied native delicacies.'

Roger glanced at Big Louie.

'Yeah, why not?' the smaller fellow said.

Roger agreed. If he and Louie had to escape later, they might as well do it with full stomachs.

'Very good,' the elder remarked as he led the way. 'Later, we will amuse and fascinate you with a demonstration of some of our quaint island customs. And who could forget an evening of sensuous native dancing?'

Roger and Louie followed the elder into the hut, which was constructed from dried palm fronds covering a bamboo skeleton. The hut was surprisingly roomy inside. Four torches hung at regular intervals from the circular wall, illuminating a great table covered by an enormous variety of food stuffs.

'The happy visitors are confronted by an amazing array of island treats,' the elder commented. 'What shall they sample first? The whole roast pig looks particularly scrumptious. Oh, but how about all those succulent fruits, picked fresh from the trees?'

Roger opted for a sliced pineapple and a cup of coconut milk, while Louie attacked the pig with a very large, very sharp knife.

'Wnnt smmme?' Louie asked from his full mouth, waving the blade in Roger's direction. Roger declined the offer. Under the present circumstances, he didn't want to have anything at all to do with very large, very sharp knives.

The elder waited patiently until they were done.

He spoke after both of them had put down their plates: 'Their bellies full of island treats, the visitors wonder what's next on the agenda of their trip to this tiny paradise. They don't have long to wonder, though, because when they emerge from the hut, the evening's entertainment is in full swing!'

Roger frowned. Evening's entertainment? When they had walked into the hut, it had been the middle of the afternoon. It couldn't be that late, could it? He figured he needed all the time he could get to think of a way to escape this mess.

But when he stuck his head out of the hut, the sun had indeed disappeared, replaced by the moon, the stars, and a score of saronged women doing the hula.

Roger frowned. Where had all the time gone? It seemed like one minute it was broad daylight, the next full night. It was just like a jump cut in a movie.

In a movie? Roger's dinner growled ominously in his stomach as he realised another truth about the Cineverse. Some, if not all, of these worlds must work on movie time. And, on movie time, a whole life could pass in an hour and a half!

There was so much in the Cineverse he still didn't understand. Roger pushed the recurring thoughts of the Plotmaster out of his mind. His current plight was much more serious than he had previously thought. He had to get away as soon as possible. There was no time for planning. He and Louie might have no time at all! One more jump cut, and it would be sacrifice time!

'Are you thinking what I'm thinking?' Louie whispered in Roger's ear.

'You mean,' Roger whispered back, 'now that we're fed, it might be time to travel? Before we end up as a meal for a volcano?'

The elder smiled over at them. 'Ah, but our visitors appear the slightest bit restless. I think it's time for a little more of that seductive native music.'

The islanders obliged.

> 'If you see the island dance,
> Wakka Heenie, Wakka Ho.
> You know the way we find romance,
> Wakka Heenie, Wakka Ho.
> Ah perhaps – but we digress,
> Wakka Heenie, Wakka Ho.
> For you should sit there and digest!
> Wakka Heenie, *Uunnnhhh*!'

Roger and Louie both sat down with satisfied sighs. What was the big hurry about, anyway? Now that he thought of it, Roger had always wanted to spend a quiet evening, watching twenty hula dancers strut their stuff. So what if he was going to be sacrificed tomorrow? He'd worry about that when it happened. Tonight, he would be entertained!

The hula dancers stopped at last, and were replaced by four men who did a complicated juggling dance involving a large number of burning torches and long, sharp knives. Roger felt the slightest stirring of something at the very back of his mind. Wasn't there something about long, sharp knives that he should be thinking about? Oh, well. Maybe he'd figure it out when he finished watching these guys throw all that dangerous stuff around.

'Don't you fellas worry at all,' a voice drawled close to his ear. 'I'll have you out of here in less time than it takes to throw a steer.'

Roger started out of his funk. It was Doc, here to rescue them. Rescue them? That's right, they were going to be sacrificed to the Volcano God! What could he have been thinking of?

'That's just it,' Louie replied. 'Neither of us were. Thinking, that is. These people here have got us under some sort of spell.'

'Spell?' Doc whispered. 'You fellas look plumb fine to me.'

'Well, it's gone, now that you're here,' Roger explained, realising Louie was right. 'But it is a trance of some sort, something we fall into and don't realise we're there – until we snap out of it again!'

Doc nodded knowingly. 'Sort of like a three-day drunk.'

'So have you and Zabana come to rescue us?' Louie asked.

'Nope,' Doc answered. 'It's just me. Zabana's gone off somewhere. I reckon it was something about getting help with the drums or something. Sometimes I have trouble understanding that jungle fellow. Sure wish he used more verbs. Anyway, I figured I should step back in, with you guys about to be sacrificed and all, and try to lend you a hand. Thought my six-gun might come in handy.' Roger heard the telltale click-click-click of a revolving cylinder.

'Thanks,' Roger whispered appreciatively. 'If you hadn't come, we would have been breakfast for Wakka Loa.'

BOOM *Boom* Boom boom, the drums replied.

'What's that?' the elder asked as he turned away from the dancers. 'Why, we have a new visitor to our tranquil island of delight. See how he, too, is overcome by the jubilant native welcome!'

Doc was grabbed by a dozen hands. His struggles were useless.

'But none of our island greetings would be complete,' the elder added, 'unless it was delivered in song!'

Song? Roger thought. Suddenly it became crystal clear – song seemed as much a force here as it was in the dread musical comedy!

'That's it!' he shouted. 'That's where the trance is coming from. The music is doing it; that damn seductive music!'

But the islanders had already burst into song:

> 'Oh, we welcome you anew,
> Wakka Heenie, Wakka Ho.
> To our island rendezvous,
> Wakka Heenie, Wakka Ho.'

Roger could feel himself slipping away. But what was so bad about that?

'It'sh not sheductive!' Doc wailed. 'It'sh intoxshicating!' The gun fell from his senseless fingers. A strange smile on his face, the Westerner pulled the guitar from his back and began to strum along.

> 'Welcome to our isle romance,
> Wakka Heenie, Wakka Ho.
> Now sit back and watch us dance,
> Wakka Heenie, *Unnhh*!'

Yes, Roger thought, that wasn't such a bad idea, watching twenty smiling women in bright coloured sarongs. He was glad they were back – he liked their dance much better than the thing with the knives. It was nice that Doc could come along, too, and enjoy the entertainment.

Roger blinked. There was a line of pink in the eastern sky. Dawn? Had the entire night gone by already? Why did he find it so upsetting? Maybe he wanted the wonderful dancing and singing to go on forever!

'And what a wonderful place is this island paradise,' the elder intoned, 'a place where both natives and villagers would live every night as if it were their last!'

There was something about the old man's commentary that sent a cold chill through Roger. He wished the music would start again so he could forget whatever it was that was bothering him. Four men – the same ones who had previously danced with knives and torches – led another outsider into their midst, this one a woman.

'We are joined by another pilgrim on their jubilant march to destiny. The more the merrier, we always say!'

Roger blinked. He knew this so-called pilgrim. She was the same one that – the day before – had turned him down for Doctor Dread! And, even more upsetting, any time now, he was going to be sacrificed to a Volcano God!

Delores caught his eye as she was hustled into their midst. She shrugged and smiled.

'And speaking of marches,' the elder continued, 'what a beautiful day it is for a march of our own. For our visitors will soon realise that no trip to our island is complete without a visit to our Volcano God!'

'Wakka Loa!' the islanders cheered together.

BOOM *Boom* Boom boom, the drums added as the sun rose to light the way to Roger's death.

CHAPTER TWENTY-TWO

The islanders urged Roger and his fellows to their feet, turning them away from the beach, towards a zig-zag path that led up a steep incline. Roger didn't struggle. He knew, if he showed the least resistance, the elder would just get the rest of them to sing again. And Roger feared that song could make him do anything.

'But what's Delores doing here?' he whispered to Louie and Doc.

'I reckon maybe these were the folks that had her tied up to that tree,' Doc ventured.

Could that be? Roger frowned in thought. If she was in that type of danger, why hadn't she asked for help? But no, she had laughed at his offer of assistance, and told him to forget her. Even worse, she had told him she had found another!

Roger had had trouble like this before. His relationship with Sheila was almost a carbon copy, and his abortive affair with Greta held some similarities as well, although Roger was pretty sure the current situation wouldn't involve a sheep named Otto. Whatever – he'd simply been hurt too many times by too many women. He had thought Delores was different, but now—

Roger sighed. When his life had sunk this low, maybe they'd be doing him a favour by sacrificing him to the Volcano God.

'Reckon she couldn't do nothing else,' Doc continued, 'what with those fellas hiding off in the bushes, waiting for you to come out and rescue her.'

'Fellows?' Roger repeated. 'Hiding in the bushes?'

'Yep.' Doc nodded. 'Thought you might have seen 'em. 'Course, you don't have my experience as an Indian tracker. Then again, those fellas might not have had to take a step if you had walked into one of those lion pits.'

'Lion pits?' Roger replied.

'Yep.' Doc spat ruminatively. 'That's what Zabana called them when he spotted them from the trees. Were at least four of them pits out there, each seven feet deep, and filled with six-foot bamboo spikes. Don't know why they dug them, though. Haven't seen a lion since we showed up on this island.'

'Fellows with weapons?' Roger asked no one in particular. 'Pits with spikes?' Perhaps Delores hadn't rejected him after all. Could she have been trying to warn him away? He looked forward at the woman of his dreams, long blond hair streaming past her bravely squared shoulders. Oh, how could he have doubted her? How had he shut her out of his life, even for a moment? How he longed to look into her eyes, and hear the sound of his name formed on her sweet lips. He shrugged off the hands of his guards and trotted forward, rapidly climbing the broad path. Nothing would keep him from talking with her!

The elder cleared his throat as Roger passed:

'Ah, but no procession would be complete without the accompaniment of happy island song!'

And of course, the song began.

> 'Now we're going on a trip,
> Wakka Heenie, Wakka Ho.
> But not by air and not by ship,
> Wakka Heenie, Wakka Ho.
> So we approach on dancing feet,
> Wakka Heenie, Wakka Ho.
> 'Cause Wakka Loa's gotta eat!
> Wakka Heenie, *Unnhhh!*'

No! Roger tried to close his ears to the music. He would not fall under the insidious island spell again. He felt the jacket pocket of his jogging suit. Yes, the ring was still there! If he could reach Delores, and if he could somehow get Doc and Louie to join them, he'd get all four of them out of this place faster than you could say 'See you in the funny papers!'

Well, there was Zabana, too. Roger would have to figure out some way to rescue the jungle prince as well, but at least the blond giant was out of immediate danger. But he'd worry about all these things once he'd reached Delores.

If he could reach her. A pair of burly islanders hustled her forward, up the ever-increasing slope. Still, if he sprinted, he should be able to catch them. Shouldn't he?

He looked down at his feet. They were no longer running,

but walking forward in a very deliberate rhythm. Step. Step. Hop, hop, hop. Step. Step. Hop, hop, hop. One, two. One, two, three. Roger realised they were moving in time with the music.

'Second verse!' the elder called.

And the islanders replied:

> 'Oh this trip will be a gas,
> Wakka Heenie, Wakka Ho;
> 'Cause for some, this trip's the last,
> Wakka Heenie, Wakka Ho.
> In this regard I've got a hunch,
> Wakka Heenie, Wakka Ho;
> 'Cause Wakka Loa needs its lunch!
> Wakka Heenie, *Unnnhhhh!*'

One, two. One, two, three. Step. Step. Hop, hop, hop. Roger had never realised dancing could be so fulfilling. He'd reach Delores sooner or later. Now, dancing was his life. One, two. One, two, three. Step. Step. Hop, hop—

Wait a second. Roger blinked, trying to concentrate. He had to reach Delores. He had to use the ring. He had to get out of here, or he was going to be sacrificed to a Volcano God. One, two. One, two, three. It was all so hard to remember, when you had dancing feet.

Roger glanced around to see that everyone else in the procession was dancing their way up the mountainside as well. One, two. One, two, three. And well they should. Step. Step. Hop, hop, hop. He threw his head to the sky, thrusting his arms and shoulders forward to the relentless beat. He was really dancing, now!

'Third verse!' the elder called.

About time, Roger thought. It was too late to stop now.

> 'Oh it's truly time for action,
> Wakka Heenie, Wakka Ho.
> Let's give volcano satisfaction,
> Wakka Heenie, Wakka Ho.
> For when we give the god its measure,
> Wakka Heenie, Wakka Ho;
> Wakka Loa burps with pleasure!
> Wakka Heenie, *Unnnnnhhhhhhh!*'

One, two. One, two, three. One, two. One, two, three. His legs leapt up the hill in time to the music. What could be better than this? Roger looked up the path, and saw the first puffs of dark, volcanic smoke drift by above. The thought filled his head suddenly. Roger laughed at how obvious it was. One, two. One, two, three. And how wonderful! After dancing like this – One, two – there was only one thing that could be better – One, two, three – being sacrificed to a Volcano God!

Roger couldn't wait. At last, the answer to all his dancing dreams. To be sacrificed to Wakka Loa – already, he could hear the BOOM *Boom* Boom boom of the drums in his head. Nothing could stop him now. Unless—

Roger looked down at his clothes with some distress. His shiny blue jogging suit wasn't all that shiny any more. The fabric was covered by layers of western dust, and the fabric had been torn in three or four places by jungle undergrowth. Roger frowned. He looked rather more dishevelled than he would have wished. One, two. One, two, three. What if he had come all this way, and the Volcano God didn't want him? That couldn't happen, could it? After all, he was dancing up this hill for the express purpose of becoming volcano fodder. But what if Wakka Loa was a stickler for sacrificial hygiene? Roger got so upset, he almost stopped dancing.

There had to be something he could do to keep from getting rejected. One, two. One, two, three. Wasn't there some way he could make up for his somewhat less than pristine condition?

The thought hit him faster than his feet could fly. What he needed was a garnish! Surely the Volcano God could never reject him if he came specially prepared – particularly if he were wearing complementary foodstuffs. As Roger saw it, all they ever seemed to do around this island was eat and dance, anyway. Surely somebody in this procession would be carrying something appropriate.

'Anybody got a pineapple ring or two?' he called out to the surrounding dancers. 'Some carrot sticks?'

The island women smiled as they cha-chaed by.

'A candied apple?' he asked an island warrior, desperation in his voice. The warrior executed a particularly complicated rhumba step.

He turned back to Big Louie and Doc, who followed close behind. His voice was hoarse with urgency: 'A little parsley for colour?'

But Louie seemed busy with the fox trot, and Doc looked like he was dosey-do-ing.

No one heard him. They were too busy dancing. A garnish was out of the question. He would never transcend his dirty, ragged self.

He was so upset, he almost tripped. His feet weren't even moving right. He stopped dead.

He blinked.

What was he doing?

Not only was he going to get sacrificed – willingly – to a Volcano God, he had been planning on adding personal decoration so that the sacrifice would occur. How crazy was he?

Only as crazy, Roger realised with a chill, as the music had made him. Now that he had regained his sanity, he had to get out of here, fast. He realised now that the song the islanders sang enslaved him, and made him so pliant to their will that he was coming up with extra ways to ensure his demise. Only if he got away from the music could he discover some way of rescuing Delores and the others. Only if he could keep from dancing could he stay free of the island's spells.

'Last verse!' the elder screamed.

Roger turned to run. One step, two steps. One, two, three steps. His feet turned back the other way.

> 'Hey now, it's no time to stop,
> Wakka Heenie, Wakka Ho;
> For we have almost reached the top.
> Wakka Heenie, Wakka Ho.
> No dawdling there, in front or back,
> Wakka Heenie, Wakka Ho;
> 'Cause you're a Wakka Loa snack!
> Wakka Heenie, *Unnnnhhhhhh*!'

What had Roger been so upset about? He couldn't remember. How could anybody be upset, when they could dance? One, two. One, two, three.

The dancers rounded a bend in the steep mountainside path. The way levelled off ahead, and broadened into a sort of natural shelf. The islanders' festive sarongs looked especially striking against the black of the pumice up here, a warehouse-long floor of stone unbroken by vegetation. Roger glanced to his right. There was a thousand-foot drop, straight to the ocean's crashing surf.

To his left was the lip of the volcano, close enough that he might reach it if he stood on tip-toe. Roger nodded his agreement as he danced. Not only was this shelf very attractive, it was convenient, too.

'And now we come to the end of our journey,' the elder intoned, 'the place where our cheerful islanders practise the most ancient of their quaint native customs!'

Roger joined the cheerful islanders as they shouted back: 'Wakka Loa!'

BOOM *Boom* Boom boom, the drums replied as usual. Somehow, they sounded closer to Roger, but perhaps it was only the clear mountain air.

'But that's not all!' the elder continued. 'The happy natives have reserved a special place of honour for their visitors!' He pointed to four stone slabs at the very centre of the plateau.

One, two. One two three. Roger cha-cha-ed toward the nearest slab. It was made of dark volcanic rock as well, but the rock had been polished and slightly curved to better accommodate a human form. Roger smiled. What a comfortable-looking sacrificial table. And they had placed drainage holes in the centre of the slab as well, so that the blood could pour away neatly, without the mess. How considerate these locals were. How lucky he was to be involved in a really first-class sacrifice!

He was aware of others around him. Doc and Big Louie cha-cha-ed to his left. And on his right? Delores' deep blue eyes looked into his own.

His feet stopped dead again.

Delores was going to be sacrificed! And almost as bad, he was going to be sacrificed, too! Even worse than that, before he saw Delores, he would have willingly climbed up on that table and pointed straight to his heart with a cheerful 'Stick the knife here'. The music spell had been that strong.

But, one look in those wondrous blue eyes, and he was his own man. His feelings for Delores were stronger than any 'movie magic' the Cineverse could throw at him.

'Oh, Roger,' Delores whispered to him. 'Why didn't you get away while you had the chance?'

'But, Delores,' Roger replied rapidly, 'we're free of their spell, now. We still have that chance—'

That's when two burly islanders grabbed him from behind. Roger never did figure out where they got the rope from. He didn't get any chance to ask, either, before he was thrown up on the sacrificial table and tied securely.

'And now,' the elder announced, 'the islanders all wait for the appearance of their leader, so that this colourful ceremony may begin!'

'Oh, Roger,' Delores moaned softly from the next table, where she was similarly trussed. 'Why did I get you into this?'

Roger smiled reassuringly at her. 'Hey, nobody forced me—'

Her voice hushed but urgent, Delores interrupted before he could even finish his gallant retort. 'Oh, but I did, in my way. Cineverse knows you never would have met Doctor Dread or Big Louie if it hadn't been for me. And you wouldn't have known about the ring's true purpose, or anything about a place that has Volcano God sacrifices – there's so much I'm responsible for! That's why I tried to keep you from coming out to save me when I was tied to the tree.'

'Oh, yes,' Roger replied, not quite knowing what else to say. 'That.'

'I had to do something!' Delores pleaded. 'They said they'd kill me if I told you about the traps. How can I explain? You see, they needed someone to sacrifice to the Volcano God. Well, they already had their standard sacrifices, but apparently the God found a constant meal plan of island virgins becoming tedious. The volcano was grumbling. They were afraid it might erupt unless something was done. At least that's what the Lord Fufu claimed. They decided that Wakka Loa—'

'BOOM *Boom* Boom boom, the drums interrupted.

'—needed some variety in its diet,' Delores concluded. 'That variety is me and you.'

'Oh,' Roger replied again. Why was it that, whenever Delores explained anything about the Cineverse, Roger felt more confused than he had before?

'Well, originally,' Delores continued, 'it was only going to be you. You and your companions, that is. Doctor Dread arranged for you to be taken, and "put out the way", as he phrased it. And the obvious bait to trap you with was me.' She briefly flashed her fabulous smile. 'And so they tied me to that tree, with strict instructions that I wasn't to tell you about the large pits that surrounded me, or the dozen muscular islanders ready to set upon you with clubs and other dull instruments as soon as you entered the clearing.' She sighed. 'And if I disobeyed, if I told you anything about the danger, I was to be sacrificed with you!'

'Oh, Delores!' Roger whispered, truly understanding at last.

'So it was that I was forbidden to warn you!' she continued.

'However, they hadn't forbidden me from sending you away by other means. What could I do then, but spurn you?' She turned away from him then, looking up at the wisps of smoke that drifted down from the volcano. 'It was the only way I could save the man I love!'

Roger's heart pounded against his rib-cage. How could he have been such a fool? How could he have doubted her for a minute? If only he wasn't tied up here, he would – but he was very securely tied, and about to become volcano fodder! He took a deep breath, bringing his emotions under control, as he realised that, even after all her explanations, there was still a thing or two he didn't understand.

'But – if you didn't disobey their instructions – why are you here?'

'Oh,' she answered, turning back to him. 'They didn't like me sending you away much, either. So they decided to sacrifice me to the Volcano God, after all.'

'Actually, I have another question,' Roger added. 'Who exactly is "they"?'

'Why, Doctor Dread and his henchpeople, of course. That's how I know about all these things. Dread likes to talk. He doesn't necessarily want to say anything, but he can spend hours implying, if you know what I mean. It's even worse than I thought.' Her voice dropped to an even lower whisper. 'It's rumoured the Plotmaster's dead.'

Roger stared at her. Maybe somebody could finally tell him about the Plotmaster.

'The Plotmaster?' Louie blurted from where he was tied to the next slab over. 'Dead?'

Delores grimaced. 'Your friend here has awfully acute hearing.'

'Yeah,' Roger agreed somewhat distractedly, 'or something.' He struggled to find the words. 'But, the Plotmaster—'

Louie laughed in disbelief. 'Well, let's face it, with the way things are going around here, he had to be sick, or at least on vacation. But dead?'

'No, no he's not dead!' Roger cried fervently. He saw a figure standing in his memory; a figure surrounded by light, and wisps of blue smoke rising from a cigar.

'But who is—' Roger started again.

This time, he was interrupted by the rumble of the volcano, deep below the sacrificial tables.

'And now,' the elder announced all over again, 'the islanders all wait for the appearance of their leader, so that this colourful ceremony may begin!'

'Yeah!' Louie agreed, fidgeting about on his stone slab. 'I mean, shouldn't we be sacrificed by now?'

'Louie!' Roger yelled, realising it still wasn't time to worry about the Plotmaster. What was the sidekick saying?

But the sidekick was adamant. 'Back in Brooklyn, when you wanted somethin' done, it got done. I mean, look at us! It gets uncomfortable, tied up like this. You can't scratch where it itches.'

'Louie—' Roger began again, but could think of nothing coherent to follow it with. Louie must still be under the island's insidious musical spell.

'Hey!' Louie explained. 'The least a victim can expect is a little service.'

'No, your small friend is correct,' the elder reticently agreed. 'The ceremony should be swift and sure, not to mention as dramatic as all get out. It is a Law of the Islands. Still, we await the legendary Lord Fufu!'

The volcano rumbled again. A great plume of dense smoke rose above their heads.

The elder's perpetual smile faltered. 'Then again, if we must wait much longer, Wakka Loa—'

BOOM *Boom* Boom boom.

'—may make this wait our last,' he concluded.

'Hey!' Louie continued, adamant. 'If we have to keep on waiting, the least you can do is untie my hands so I can get in a final scratch.'

The elder looked meaningfully at the two islanders who stood like statues to either side of Louie's slab. One of the men moved his hand ever so slightly so that it rested against the large knife strapped against his thigh.

'Don't like that idea, huh?' The small man squirmed uncomfortably on the stone table. 'Well, what the hey – I'm easy going. What say you just untie *one* of my hands?'

The frowning islander with the knife pulled it free of its sheath and held it over Louie's heart.

'Unfortunately, that cannot be allowed,' the elder replied, still somewhat distracted. 'As much as they wish to please their visitors, the natives will allow no interference with their quaint and picturesque customs.'

'No problem,' Louie agreed. 'Just asking. Hey, we're all friends here, right?'

The islander, still scowling, replaced the knife in its sheath.

Louie smiled and shrugged at Roger. 'The least a sidekick can do is try.'

Roger nodded back, a little shaken as he realised Louie had been trying to escape. Instead, they had come awfully close to pathos.

And, in a minute, if Roger didn't come up with something, it would be pathos for everybody.

The ground shook beneath them as the volcano rumbled again. The crowd around him gasped.

'Wakka Loa!'

Roger looked where the crowd pointed as the drumbeats faded away.

A crack had formed in the volcano wall. It wasn't very wide or very long, but there was steam coming from it.

'And now,' the elder announced with a certain amount of panic in his voice, 'the islanders all wait – not to mention pray – for the very rapid appearance of their leader, so that this colourful ceremony may begin without further delay!'

'All right, already!' A voice boomed from the usual explosion of blue smoke. 'Somebody did something with my island high priest sacrificing costume! I had to find something else –' the voice paused significantly, '– appropriate.'

Roger already knew who it was before the smoke cleared. Only one man could make silence so insidious. However, it was only after the island breezes had blown the blue haze away again that he saw Doctor Dread was wearing his black and red wizard's costume.

Doctor Dread glanced over at Roger. He smiled as the islander next to Louie handed him that knife. The villain chuckled.

'Now,' he continued in that oily way he had, 'I believe it's time for a little –' he hesitated suggestively, '– ceremony?'

CHAPTER TWENTY-THREE

'And now,' the elder said with finality, 'our visitors bid a fond farewell to this peaceful island. They know, no matter where they travel, they'll never forget our paradise under the sun!'

Doctor Dread walked toward Roger, the very large, very sharp, extremely pointed knife in his upraised hand. Somehow, though, Roger couldn't keep his eyes off the strange, blood-red runes upon Dread's costume, which, once again, seemed to spell out arcane – yet strangely familiar – messages; things that somehow hinted at a deeper meaning. Roger squinted, barely making out the words.

'BORN . . .' Roger read slowly, '. . . FOR FUN, LOYAL . . . TO NONE.'

There was a muttering among the islanders. Far away, Roger heard the volcano grumble.

'Now,' Dread announced to the assemblage, 'the ceremony begins!'

But before he could reach Roger's slab, another of the islanders stepped in his path. This new fellow spoke quickly as he stared at the ground.

'Begging your pardon, oh great Lord Fufu. But you are not wearing the traditional costume of sacrifice.'

'What?' Dread exploded. 'You dare to question the great Lord Fufu? Haven't I explained my –' he hesitated knowingly, '– problems to you? The costume has been –' he paused tellingly, '– misplaced.'

But the islander did not move. 'I felt someone should mention it. Perhaps the ceremony should not take place. We do not want to offend Wakka Loa. What if the volcano doesn't recognise you?'

Dread/Lord Fufu laughed. 'Of course it shall recognise me. Am I not the volcano's –' he stopped meaningfully, '– servant? Now, out of my way. There are those who must be –' he delayed even more purposefully than before, his eyes wandering to the rows of sacrificial tables, '– dealt with.'

The islander obsequiously shuffled aside, and Dread quickly covered the last few steps to Roger's slab. He leaned close to his intended victim, his smile dazzling in the island sunshine. Unfortunately for his victim-to-be, he had obviously eaten something with garlic for lunch. Still, Roger could not look away. The runes on his wizard's hat danced before Roger's eyes:

'I'M . . . WITH . . . STUPID.'

Dread lifted the dagger even higher, so that it shone in the perpetual sunshine. Roger wondered if he should close his eyes, but decided he might as well see the last moment of his life.

Dread chuckled triumphantly. 'Now, I shall –' he paused ceremonially, '– take care of this sacrifice, in the name of Wakka Loa!'

He waited, knife in the air, for the answering beat. But there was nothing. No drums, no sound beyond the island wind. The islanders looked uneasily at their high priest.

'Wakka Loa!' Dread yelled again.

One more moment of silence. Then the volcano rumbled.

Some of the islanders screamed.

'Wakka Loa!' Dread screamed in desperation.

He was answered this time, not by drums, but by a deep voice.

'Will not be answered by volcano! Will be answered by Zabana!'

The jungle prince ran into view upon the mountain path.

'Binga bonga blooie! Aieeaieeooo!'

'How dare you!' the wizard-suited high priest screamed. Dread turned to face the jungle prince. Roger turned his head to follow the action. The runes upon the back of Dread's flowing costume formed the most complex message of all:

'MY PARENTS WENT TO . . . CAMELOT, AND ALL I GOT WERE . . . THESE LOUSY WIZARD'S ROBES!'

'Zabana dares all!' the jungle prince replied. 'I will call upon my island friends to free your prisoners. Come, oh wild pigs of the island. Stampede up mountain! Save Zabana's friends!' He cupped his hands around his mouth as he called: 'Oink oink! Wagawaga! Gruum!'

He looked about expectantly, but, this time, it was Zabana who was answered by silence.

'Our newest visitor learns another secret of our tiny paradise,' the elder explained. 'For, peaceful as it is in our perfect kingdom, all our pigs recently expired from an outbreak of swine flu. Unfortunately, we must import all our wild pigs from the next island over.'

'I think our newcomer will fit in nicely in the sacrifice's second shift,' Doctor Dread suggested. He nodded at those already tied upon the slabs. 'Four tables. No waiting.'

The jungle prince got a particularly wild look in his eyes. 'Zabana try again! Call upon wild jungle monkey! Come, Zabana's allies! Chatter and swing and overrun this place! Save Zabana's friends!' He cupped his hands to his mouth once more. 'Chee Chee! Ooga Ooga! Gruum!'

He waited, muscles tense. There was no more noise than the first time.

'Alas,' the elder commented softly, 'our newest visitor has discovered yet another island tragedy. For all the cute and furry denizens of our paradise upon the sea have succumbed to a wild outbreak of monkey fever, and are no more. We have thought of importing some from the next island, but have, until now, been too busy with our quaint island ceremonies.'

But his newest failure seemed only to steel the jungle prince's resolve. 'Zabana not defeated! Zabana never defeated! Zabana use something he know is here!' The jungle prince paused a moment in thought. 'Call upon wild jungle parrot! Fly to volcano! Flutter! Peck! Disrupt! Save Zabana's friends!' His hands once again to his mouth, his cry reverberated through the air: 'Squawk, squawk, glizzard! Polly want a cracker! Gluum!'

This time, there was a response. Roger heard the sound of a thousand wings and, a moment later, saw what looked like a blanket of a hundred different colours flying up the volcano trail from the jungle below. But the blanket drew ever closer, and he realised it was really innumerable parrots flying in impossibly close formation, their uncountable wings beating furiously to answer Zabana's call.

'Zabana triumphs!' the jungle prince called. 'Binga bonga blooie! Aieeaieeeoooo!'

With that, the parrots descended. Thousand of cries of 'polly wants a cracker' and 'who's a pretty boy' filled the air.

Somehow, in the ensuing confusion, Roger realised that the blond giant had reached his side, and, what's more, he had brought a friend. The newcomer was another islander, although he appeared to be even more bronzed and athletically built than any of the other incredibly well-muscled fellows Roger had already seen hereabouts.

The jungle prince smiled. 'Zabana bring reinforcements!'

'Reinforcements?' Roger asked before he could stop himself. 'From where?'

'Zabana explore island,' the jungle prince explained. 'Zabana find drummer.'

The tall, bronzed figure nodded solemnly. 'I have put away my drums. The jungle prince has convinced me that we are all a party to injustice.'

'Stay still,' the jungle prince told Roger. 'Zabana free you.' He grabbed the thick coconut rope that crisscrossed Roger's chest with both of his massive hands. His arm muscles bulged. He gritted his teeth. A single drop of sweat rolled from his forehead.

Zabana pulled. The rope disintegrated in his hands like dental floss.

'Zabana triumphs! Binga bonga blooie!'

He moved quickly, freeing Delores in much the same way.

'Excuse me,' she asked, pointing to Zabana's belt. 'Not to seem ungrateful or anything, but couldn't you have used that knife?'

'Knife?' Zabana frowned down at his belt as if he had never seen a knife before. 'Much more satisfying to rip and tear. Properly dramatic for jungle prince.'

Roger sat up, massaging the rope burns on his arms and ankles. He looked around as the drummer – not afraid to use a knife of his own – cut Doc free of his ropes. Roger congratulated their newest ally on his decision.

The drummer shrugged. 'Well, perhaps I had some ulterior motive. Do you know how boring it is to go BOOM *Boom* Boom boom all day?'

'Hey, I can understand that,' Louie agreed as Zabana shredded his ropes. 'I used to be in comedy relief.'

Beyond their own little drama, Roger noticed that the parrot attack had not had quite the chaotic effect Zabana had originally hoped. He quickly pointed this out to the jungle hero.

'Parrots not particularly good fighters,' Zabana admitted. 'Offer them cracker, they go over to other side.'

But there seemed to be more wrong here than a simple case of bird allegiance. Some of the nearby parrots looked awfully motley, as if they were losing their feathers. Still others seemed to be having trouble with their voices:

'Who's the pretty – cough—'

'Polly want a – hack, hack—'

'Hey!' Roger exclaimed. 'These parrots are sick!'

Zabana nodded. 'Like wild pigs. Like monkeys. Wild parrot whooping cough.'

'But what would make all these animals sick?' Roger frowned, not wishing to believe the next thought that entered his mind. 'There couldn't be something to this Volcano God curse, could there?'

'Hey, you know,' Louie replied. 'Why do they call it "movie magic"?'

The ground shook beneath their feet.

'Wakka Loa!' the islanders screamed in fear.

'BOOM *Boom* Boom boom,' the drummer remarked. He glanced at Roger. 'Sorry. Old habits.'

Roger replied with another sticky question. 'But that means the volcano – deprived of its sacrifice – is actually going to explode?'

'Suddenly, the visitors realise what they have done to our sultry island paradise.' The elder looked directly at Roger. 'You have angered Wakka Loa. Now the volcano will eat all of us!'

'Hey,' Louie replied, 'what would a South Sea Island Paradise be without a few falling rocks and some dramatic, white-hot lava?'

'Unfortunately,' Doctor Dread screamed, 'you will not live long enough to find out! To me, my minions!'

A group clad in traditional native dress charged through the remaining chaos, ignoring their fellows' troubles with whatever parrots remained. Roger frowned. Something seemed wrong here. These newcomers were awfully pale for islanders. Plus, Roger hadn't – at least until he saw this group – noticed any of the locals sporting pencil-thin moustaches. And then there was that very tall woman in the back, wearing a sarong that looked like nothing so much as a modified pup tent – that is, if they designed pup tents in floral island colours. But it was the way that woman stared at Roger that he found truly disquieting. It was a definite Big Bertha stare.

The earth shivered beneath his feet. The last of the parrots flew away as many of the real islanders began to run down the path to the jungle below. Roger saw that Dread's band had somehow produced guns, blackjacks and brass knuckles from somewhere beneath their grass skirts. They laughed evilly as they approached Roger and his companions.

'What do we do now?' Louie asked no one in particular.

Delores clutched Roger's hand. 'Whatever happens,' she whispered in his ear, 'it will happen to us together!'

'Zabana!' Roger called to the blond giant by his side. 'Can't you do something?'

But the large fellow only frowned. 'What can Zabana call? Monkeys gone! Pigs gone! Parrots going! Zabana out of animals! Jungle prince have to think!'

Zabana had to think? Then perhaps they were truly lost.

'Excellent!' Doctor Dread chortled. 'They have been a thorn in my side for far too long! They are defenceless. Deal with them now!'

'Ah, but we are not defenceless!' the drummer declared. 'Hope is never lost when you still have your drums!'

Roger turned back to their newest ally and noticed that he now stood behind a pair of waist-high conga drums. Roger was too confused by now to even wonder where they had come from.

Rumble, rumble, went the volcano.

BOOM *Boom* Boom boom, replied the drummer.

But Dread only laughed. 'You expect to stop us with some pitiful musical instrument?'

Boom BOOM *Boom* boom, was the drummer's only reply.

Dread waved his henchpeople forward. 'Attend to them!'

Boom boom BOOM *Boom*, the drummer answered smartly.

And the volcano seemed to rumble again in reply. This whole exchange certainly was rhythmic. Roger hoped it meant something, too.

'Usher them out!' Dread shrieked as his henchpeople lumbered forward.

That's when the ground beneath them shook with a force so great that it threatened to knock Roger and his fellows off their feet. The minions hesitated in their deadly charge. Only the drummer seemed unaffected, keeping up his steady beat.

'Subtract them from the ledger!' Dread screamed as he threw his wizard's cap to the ground.

BOOM *Boom* BOOM Boom *Boom* boom BOOM, the drummer responded. And the volcano responded as well.

It started out as a crack on the incline behind Dread and his cronies. But before the gang had taken another step, it had widened to a fissure that glowed red from deep within. The volcano rumbled, and the fissure rippled forward with the speed of a tidal wave obliterating a beach.

The evildoers screamed in unison as the chasm opened beneath them.

'Give my regards to Wakka Loa!' Louie yelled as they disappeared from sight.

The rumbling stopped. The fissure no longer grew. The volcano made one final noise, accompanied by a great cloud of grey ash. It sounded like nothing so much as a colossal belch.

'Wakka Loa accepts the sacrifice,' the elder remarked from where, Roger was surprised to note, he still stood nearby.

Then all was quiet.

'One is never defenceless,' their saviour repeated, 'when one has drums.'

So the drummer had rescued them, and satiated the Volcano God at the same time. Roger was incredibly relieved.

'How can we ever thank you?' he asked.

But the tall islander brushed Roger's question aside with a wave of his hand. 'No thanks are necessary. And remember: Never sleep in a wet canoe!'

After a reminder like that, Roger wasn't at all surprised when the drummer disappeared in a cloud of blue smoke.

'Was that—' Roger began.

'I plumb reckon—' Doc added.

'Do you mean—' Big Louie continued.

'Ah,' the island elder called from where he still stood behind them. 'Then you did not recognise him? Come now. Even though you are visitors to our island paradise, surely you've heard of the Secret Samoan.'

Oh, no. The Secret Samoan? Roger couldn't believe it. They had missed Captain Crusader again!

'Do not look so distraught, my love,' Delores chided.

'But Captain Crusader—'

She kissed him gently on the cheek. 'So you missed the hero's hero? Is that so bad now? Aren't we together at last? And haven't we dealt with the biggest threat Captain Crusader had? I mean, with the way things are now, we have all the time in the Cineverse to find him.' She nudged Roger suggestively. 'And perhaps we'll have time for a few other things as well.'

'She's right!' Big Louie grinned. 'With Dread out of the way, what could possibly go wrong now?'

'But perhaps our visitors speak too soon,' the elder intoned, 'for there are always surprises aplenty in this island paradise.' He casually pointed at the hand that had appeared on the lip of the fissure.

It was followed by a foot, some six feet away. An ash-covered figure pulled itself from the chasm. Roger shuddered when he saw the figure was wearing a somewhat singed floral pup tent.

'You have not escaped me yet,' Big Bertha announced as she

dragged another from the pit with her other hand, a man wearing the remains of a wizard's robes.

Dread glared at Roger and the others as he regained his footing. 'Us, my dear woman. They have not escaped –' he paused significantly, '– us.'

But Zabana stepped forward. 'Jungle prince laughs at danger! What threat are ash-covered villains? They are defenceless against might of Zabana!'

'Well, not exactly defenceless.' Big Bertha whipped a machine gun from within the folds of her dress. She smiled triumphantly. 'It's amazing how many weapons you can hide inside a sarong.'

'Deal with them slowly,' Dread suggested.

'Yesss,' Bertha hissed, her eyes darting up and down Roger's jogging-suited form. 'And I know which one I shall deal with last.'

'Quick!' Louie shouted. 'The ring!'

For once, Big Louie was right. Roger pulled the Captain Crusader Decoder Ring from his jacket pocket.

'Where do I set it?' he asked frantically.

'Oh, no you don't!' Bertha pointed her machine gun at Roger.

'If only I had my six-guns!' Doc shot back. 'Or my guitar!'

'If only Zabana had animals!' the jungle prince raged.

'Deal with them!' Dread shrieked as he leapt up and down. 'Take care of them! Oh – in the name of all that is evil – shoot them!'

Louie grabbed for the ring. 'Here, let me set it!'

Roger felt the tiny circle of plastic yanked from his grasp.

A single shot rang out.

'Roger!' Delores screamed.

But Roger was surrounded by blue smoke, the only sound the fading words of the village elder:

'Whenever our visitors must leave our island paradise, they always feel it is too soon . . .'

After that, all was darkness.

CHAPTER TWENTY-FOUR

Roger woke up in bed. His bed. Back where he had started from. On Earth. Out of the Cineverse. Only worse. Now, he was all alone.

He tried to remember what had happened. The last thing he could recall was being threatened by a besmirched Big Bertha toting a machine gun. Well, that, and Big Louie grabbing the Captain Crusader Decoder Ring as a shot rang out.

A gunshot? Roger looked down at the dirty, torn jogging suit he still wore. No, there didn't seem to be any new holes. As far as he could tell, he was still intact. The bullet must have gone somewhere else.

But there was something else that was very wrong.

The Captain Crusader Decoder Ring! Even before he reached into his pocket, Roger knew it was gone. Louie had grabbed it, after all. Roger had felt it slip out of his fingers at the exact same instant the shot rang out and the blue smoke appeared. He wondered if there was some pattern to all of that. Obviously, the ring had worked somehow. Otherwise, he wouldn't be back here. Far away from Delores and the rest of his companions, who, at this very instant were being menaced, if not shot, by Doctor Dread and Big Bertha.

He had no ring! What could he do? Well, he wouldn't panic. He had found that first ring easily enough – and, even with his mother's wholesale selling of his possessions, there were enough boxes left to go through that there had to be another ring in there somewhere.

Roger pushed the rumpled sheets aside and got out of bed. Obviously, it was time to visit his mother.

First, however, he should change his jogging suit. It wouldn't do to be seen in the streets wearing the rags he had on now. And he should take a shower, too. He had to look presentable if he was going to get into his mother's basement.

He glanced at the clock. The digital dial said 9:15. He looked at the window and saw light seeping through the venetian blinds. So that would make it 9:15 in the morning. But which morning? Roger had no idea how long he had been in the Cineverse. It might have been hours, it might have been days. Still, what did it matter? His mother was home most mornings. This would be a good time to call.

She picked it up at the end of the first ring.

'Hi, Mom!' he said brightly, wanting to make this whole thing as short as possible.

'Roger?' his mother's voice replied in disbelief. 'Where have you been?'

'Been?' Roger replied defensively, surprised at the vehemence of his mother's reaction. It was amazing how few words it took for her to make him feel like a guilty twelve-year-old. 'Well, you know. Here and there.'

His response seemed to upset her even more. 'Here and there? You've been missing for two weeks, and that's where you've been – *here and there?* I tell you, when Susan called me after she couldn't find you, I was beside myself with worry. Thank goodness that dear Mr Mengeles is so easy to talk to. I'll have you know he's had to calm me down more than once. Otherwise, I don't know what I would have done!'

'Two weeks?' Roger replied. How could he have been gone for two weeks? Was time in the Cineverse different from that in Boston? And what was Susan doing, butting into his business again, anyway?

'About Susan—' Roger continued.

'She's such a dear girl,' his mother agreed. 'I don't see why you ignore her so.'

'Mother! She's the one who divorced me!'

'Just because she ran off with that grocer?' his mother chided. 'You've let that blind you to all her positive qualities.'

Positive qualities? Roger decided to give up on the argument. He couldn't think of any woman he had been involved with – and Roger had to admit that covered a lot of territory – who had less 'positive' associated with her than Susan. Well, there had been Debbie, he supposed, but that was at least in part because of her snake collection. Discounting such outside circumstance, Susan had the market cornered on negative associations.

Besides, Roger realised, whatever Susan wanted really didn't matter any more. When he thought about it rationally – something he had always had trouble with when it came to Susan – all he really had to do was fetch another one of his rings and he was out of there. He had a whole, new Cineverse waiting for him – a Cineverse that was miraculously Susan-free.

'Look, Mom,' he said with finality. 'We can talk about Susan some other time. I need to look through my things again. Maybe I'll even move them out. You've had to store them long enough.'

'Why, that's very nice of you dear,' his mother said, surprised. 'But dear Mr Mengeles—'

Roger wouldn't be side-tracked again. He interrupted before his mother could launch into another of her tangents: 'That's nice. Will you be home today?'

'Why, yes. At least until four. That's when I have to go pick—'

'I'll be over in an hour,' Roger said. He hung up the phone and walked into the bathroom to take a shower. He had to hurry, to get past his mother and all her stories of Mr Mengeles and Roger's ex-wives and whatever else popped into her head. Anything could be happening in the Cineverse. Anything. And he couldn't bear to think he had finally found Delores, only to lose her forever.

He made it to his mother's house in forty-five minutes.

'Roger? You're early? But you're never early!'

He kissed her on the cheek as he stepped inside the house. 'Sorry, mom. Don't have time to talk. I'll just go down and fetch my stuff.'

'Roger?' Her voice followed him down the stairs. 'But Roger—'

'I'll talk to you in a minute, Mom!' He ran his hand along the wall. If Mr Mengeles was so handy, he should have installed a light switch to go along with the new rec room. Ah, there it was. 'I've got to start hauling this stuff up!'

Now, where had they put that storage closet? Roger spotted it on the far side of the room. He heard his mother coming down the stairs. She just didn't want to leave him alone, did she? Well, he was going to do this quickly, one way or another. He walked quickly across the new linoleum and opened the door. It was dark inside. Wasn't there an overhead pull light in here?

'Roger!' his mother reprimanded as she reached the bottom of the stairs. 'I'm trying to tell you something!'

'Sure, Mom. In a minute.' Roger groped in the closet's dark upper reaches, searching for a hanging bit of string. He felt something brush the back of his knuckles. Paydirt.

'You will do just what you want, won't you?' His mother sighed. 'You were always such a wilful boy.'

'In a second, mother,' Roger repeated, more from habit than from thought. He pulled the string.

The light went on, illuminating the remaining storage space.

The closet was empty.

'My stuff!' Roger yelled, spinning to face his mother. 'It's gone!'

'Well, what did you think I was trying to tell you?' She tapped her foot in that all-suffering way she had.

But Roger was in no mood for suffering. 'Where is it? What have you done with it?'

His mother took a half-step backward. 'Roger. Please don't raise your voice. Think of the neighbours. Your things are perfectly safe. Mr Mengeles has simply moved them to the garage.'

'The garage?' Roger rushed past her, taking the steps two at a time. There was something about finding that closet empty – all his confidence had evaporated. What if the other Captain Crusader Decoder Rings were gone? What if his mother had gotten rid of the rest of them a long time ago? What if he could never find his way to the Cineverse again? He had been anxious to find the rings before; now he was desperate.

His mother followed him up the stairs. She could move with surprising speed when she wanted to.

Someone rang the front doorbell. His mother hustled by him to answer it.

A familiar bald-headed gentleman stood on the front step.

'Why, Mr M!' his mother gushed in a much more girlish voice than she ever used with Roger. 'What a surprise!'

Mengeles frowned as he shook his head thoughtfully. 'I heard voices over here, Mrs G. Raised voices. Thought I'd just look in and make sure everything was all right.'

'How thoughtful of you, Mr M!' She impulsively grabbed the older man's arm. 'It was only Roger, I'm afraid. He got a little upset that we'd moved his things. You know the way that children are.'

'Indeed I do, Mrs G.' He waved past her at her son. 'Nice to see you again, Roger. Well, perhaps I should be going.'

But mother, with her grip firmly established, wasn't about to let go. 'Certainly not, Mr M! You came over here because you were concerned about my safety. The least I can do is reward you with a cup of coffee!'

Mengeles relented with the slight smile of one who knows he's been over-matched. 'Oh, very well, Mrs G. While you're doing that, what say Roger and I go to the garage? I'll show him where we've put his things.'

She let go of him to clap her hands. 'Oh, you're such a thoughtful man! Isn't he, Roger?'

Roger nodded, wondering how he could get rid of this fellow. He certainly didn't want anybody else seeing the Captain Crusader Decoder Rings. He didn't want to have to explain anything to any overaged Romeo his mother had—

Roger stopped himself. What was he thinking? How could anyone around here know the significance of a Captain Crusader Decoder Ring? And, even if they did, how would you explain the Cineverse to them? Nobody would believe it. Now that he was back on Earth, there was a part of Roger that didn't want to believe it either.

'Okay,' he said to Mengeles. 'Lead on.'

The older man did just that, leading Roger through the kitchen to the back door. Mother waved as she put the coffee pot on the stove. Roger followed Mengeles down the concrete steps into the garage.

'We put all your stuff on the shelves in the back here. You were so upset last time you came to visit your mother, she figured you'd probably be better off if you just took your things and stored them yourself. That's why we brought it up here – so it would be easier for you to get at.'

'Sure, sure,' Roger replied, only half listening. Mengeles seemed as good as his mother at long-winded explanations. He hurried over to the pile of boxes that held the remains of his childhood.

'Of course, there is one other thing,' the older man added as Roger walked away. He reached up and shut the door. 'You will permit me to gloat. I've waited so long for this moment.'

There was something so odd in the older man's tone that Roger paused and looked around.

'How shall I put this?' Mengeles asked, obviously pleased with Roger's attention. 'How about this? I wouldn't bother wasting my time looking for Captain Crusader Decoder Rings.'

Roger's mouth fell open.

'Oh, you shouldn't be surprised,' Mengeles continued smoothly. 'Doctor Dread likes to think of everything.' He reached into his pocket. 'You had four more of them, you know.' Roger heard the clink of plastic on plastic. 'In very good condition, too. Ready to be used by someone more –' he paused significantly, '– deserving than yourself.'

'What?' Roger demanded. 'You can't do this!'

'Who's going to stop me?' Mengeles purred.

Roger started toward the steps. 'I'm going in to tell my mother!'

His threat didn't faze Mengeles in the least. 'And what will you tell her? Think about it. We're talking about the Cineverse here, a bunch of crazy movie worlds that you travel between using a cheap plastic ring. How are you going to explain that? And, even if you somehow managed an explanation, do you think your mother would believe you in a million years?'

Mengeles started to laugh. His mother stuck her head out of the door that connected the kitchen with the garage.

'My two men sharing a joke? How nice. I just knew you'd get along!'

Roger opened his mouth, but no words came out. He wanted to say something to her, to make her realise what was really happening. But the older man was right. There was nothing he could say.

His mother's head disappeared as she returned to her coffee.

Mengeles' smile would have put a Cheshire cat to shame. 'As my boss, Dread, might put it,' he remarked with a chuckle, 'Roger, my boy, you have been dealt with.'

Roger stood there, unable to move, as if the confusion of the last few minutes had tied his muscles in impossible knots. What could he do?

He had the terrible feeling that Mengeles was right. Without the Decoder Rings, he was trapped on Earth forever. He would never see Delores again – assuming, of course, that Delores was still alive.

And he would never know who, or what, the Plotmaster was.

CHILLS!

THRILLS!

SHOCKS!

YOCKS!

Will Roger ever see Delores again?
Will Doctor Dread triumph?
Is this the end of the Cineverse as we know it?
What else is Big Bertha hiding under that sarong?
DON'T MISS OUR NEXT EXCITING CHAPTER:
BRIDE OF THE SLIME MONSTER!
Coming Next . . .

Bride of the
Slime Monster

To Charlie—
a Slime Monster in his own write.

CHAPTER ONE

'Flaming Death!'

It was the end of the world.

Flying saucers crashed into the Washington Monument. Skyscrapers caught on fire. Jumbo jets crash-landed in Peru. An immense ocean liner, quite possibly the *Titanic*, hit an iceberg and sank majestically. Rome burned while Nero fiddled. It was terrible. And Roger was helpless to stop it.

After that, of course, it got worse.

Newspaper headlines spun toward him, freezing in place with headlines like:

'ROGER FAILS!'
'DELORES LOST FOREVER!'
'DOCTOR DREAD TRIUMPHANT!'
'CINEVERSE DOOMED!'

And it didn't stop there. If that had been the extent of things, Roger still might have been able to stand it. After all, he had become inured to hardship and surprise through a life working in public relations. But no!

There had to be those disembodied voices, didn't there?

And what voices! First, there was this maniacal laughter:

'Ah hahahaha! Ah hahahaha!'

Roger could imagine the man's bald head gleaming almost with a light of its own as the man's mouth opened, pencil-thin moustache a-quiver, to pour forth that never-ending stream of triumphant mirth.

'Ah hahahaha! Ah hahahaha!'

That laughter threatened to drive Roger into a frenzy. But the second voice did worse than that.

'Roger,' she said, 'why did you fail me?'

'Delores!' he called, but she did not answer.

'Roger,' she said again, 'why did you fail me?'

'I couldn't help it!' he replied. 'The ring slipped from my fingers. Big Louie grabbed it from my—'

His voice died as he remembered the last thing he heard as he slipped away from the Cineverse. It had been a gunshot, fired – no doubt – by Doctor Dread or one of his insidious henchpeople. Had that bullet hit someone? What if Roger had escaped, only to have someone else die in his place?

'Roger,' Delores asked imploringly, 'why did you fail me?'

He tried to think of something else he could say, but realised, before he could open his mouth again, that it was no use. Wherever Delores' voice was coming from, she could not, or would not, hear his answers.

He would not accept this! There must be some way—

'Delores,' he whispered desperately.

The other voice answered:

'Ah hahahaha! Ah hahahaha!'

'Roger,' Delores' voice followed, 'why did you fail me?'

The voices were growing louder, as if they were shouting in his ears:

'Roger? Why did you – ah hahahaha! – why did you fail – ah hahahaha! – why did you – hahaha – fail – hahaha – fail fail fail *fail*—'

'No!' Roger clamped his hands over his ears. The voices had become too much for him. He couldn't think. He couldn't talk.

He looked wildly about for help – any sort of help. Delores and the villain were nowhere to be seen. He was surrounded by darkness, save for a single, distant point of light. Something moved in that far-away illumination, a tall figure, a dark silhouette against the brilliant background. Roger squinted, trying to make some sense of the distant man's movements. He realised at last that the fellow was smoking a cigar – a cigar that produced blue smoke.

Blue smoke?

That's what he needed to get out of here – the blue smoke of a Captain Crusader Decoder Ring! But his ring was gone. How could he ever find another?

Perhaps, Roger realised, the man with the cigar might have the answer. He'd have to call to the stranger to get his attention. Roger took his hands from his ears so that he could cup them around his mouth.

'Fail!' the first voice screamed.

'Ah hahahaha!' the second voice rejoined.

Somehow, the accusing voices had gotten even louder – almost as if they screamed from somewhere deep within Roger's head. He tried to speak, but his own voice was swallowed with the others' all-consuming cries. He no longer had any hope of calling to the cigar-smoking stranger.

'Fail! Ah hahahaha! Fail! Ah hahahaha!'

He had no hope of anything.

He fell to his knees, but there was no floor beneath him. He was falling, turning round and round, tumbling head over heels towards a distant, even darker point so deep and far away that it was totally beyond light, and warmth, and redemption.

And still the voices were with him.

'Fail!'

'No!' Roger screamed over and over again as his body plummeted towards the pit.

'Ah hahahaha!'

'No! No! No! *No*!'

Roger woke up.

He looked around. He was in his own bedroom, in his own bed. Dim light filtered through his venetian blinds, throwing bars of yellow-red across the floor. It must, he thought, be close to sunset.

So he wasn't in the Cineverse. Roger sat up. Had it all been a dream, then? Delores hadn't called to him? He wasn't surrounded by evil laughter, forever falling, forever failing?

It had been awfully vivid for a dream. He remembered so many things, so many places and events, marching by him like he was watching some sort of movie. But that was it exactly! For how could he have known, when he first fell in love with Delores, that she was an emissary from another dimension, a dimension that resembled nothing so much as all those films from the thirties, forties, and fifties – all those movies made before the Change? And how could he imagine that you could only visit that other reality, known as the Cineverse, through the use of a small plastic Captain Crusader Secret Decoder Ring, once given away for free in boxes of Nut Crunchies?

He had found so much in the Cineverse, and so many people who had befriended him. Not only Delores, but Doc, a former town drunk who, while he stayed moderately sober, was a formidable ally. Then there was Zabana, Prince of the Jungle, and Big Louie, who actually was rather short, a sidekick who always seemed to know what you were going to say next. They had all been there when that gunshot rang out. They had all been alive when Roger had vanished from the Cineverse, menaced by the guns of Dread and his cohorts. Who could say how many of his friends there were still alive?

It seemed all so fantastic now, back in Roger's bedroom, just waking from sleep. It was difficult to remember the horror he had once felt, when he learned of Doctor Dread's plans for controlling not only the Cineverse, but the Earth as well.

But there was something about that man in Roger's nightmare that Roger swore must be very important. Well, he was in the distance in the nightmare, so maybe – working from dream logic – the blue-smoke stranger wasn't important at all. Then why did Roger's stomach lurch when he thought about the man with the cigar?

He shook his head at the impossibility of it all. So much had happened so quickly to Roger, that – especially now that he was back in his old apartment, tangled in his old bedclothes – it almost all did seem like a dream, like the Cineverse was just some figment of his movie-loving imagination. But where did his dreams end and reality begin?

The phone rang.

'Hello?' Roger said.

'Ah hahahaha,' a voice replied. 'Ah hahahaha!'

The reality of it all came crashing down around Roger.

'Mengeles!' he screamed into the receiver. 'What do you want?'

'Only to gloat, dear boy,' Mengeles replied in an oily voice. 'But now that we know the truth about each other, perhaps you should call me by my true name – Menge the Merciless!'

Roger almost dropped the phone. How could he have been so blind? As a child, he had watched that evil fiend – with his bald head and pencil-thin moustache – week after week on TV in that old movie serial, *Captain Crusader Conquers the Universe*. Each week Menge's twisted plans almost defeated Truth, Justice, and the Universal Way, only to be thwarted at the last instant by Captain Crusader's heroics. And now the evil fiend was here, talking on the phone!

No wonder Roger had always had an odd feeling about the man. Since he had only known Menge the Merciless as his mother's next-door neighbour, however, he had never realised the villain's true nature. Roger stared at the receiver in horror. How could he have been such a fool?

'You never had a chance against me, pitiful earthling,' Menge gloated. 'I'll admit that I've had some trouble in the past, with meddlers like that Captain Crusader! But Doctor Dread's master plan put me beyond that snooping Captain, and every other hero in the Cineverse! Now that I am on Earth, a place where they no longer have heroes, how can I help but triumph?'

'Why, you—' Roger paused, trying to find just the right words. Why couldn't he think of something noble and upright to say that didn't sound foolish at the same time?

Menge interrupted Roger's thoughts. 'Enough gloating! It's time to plunder, loot and destroy! But before I go, I must thank you for the four Captain Crusader Rings. I'm sure they will come in very handy in our conquest of the Cineverse. Ah hahahaha! Ah hahahaha!'

Menge hung up. Roger listened to the dial tone, then replaced his own receiver. Depend on a villain like that, he supposed, to not even say goodbye.

And Menge had mentioned the rings. Not that Roger needed to be reminded. When he was a boy, he had found seven of them in Nut Crunchie boxes, and kept them all these years, stored along with all his other childhood possessions, at his mother's home. Or so he had thought. When he had been told the true significance of the Captain Crusader Decoder Ring, he had returned to his mother's, only to find all his keepsakes moved, and many of them sold! After a frantic search, he had managed to find one of the rings, but the others seemed to have vanished.

Now, of course, he knew where the rings had gone. Menge had stolen them! Roger had foolishly thought them safe in his mother's basement. But Dread's minion had not only absconded with four of the precious plastic circlets – not to mention starting a romance of some sort with Roger's mother – he had moved all of Roger's things into his mother's garage!

Roger told himself to calm down. It was time for thought, not anger. He had lost his first ring. Menge had claimed four others among his belongings. But, years ago, when he was twelve, Roger distinctly remembered saving seven of those cheap plastic objects. That meant there might still be a ring or two left among Roger's boxes. True, they could have been lost or destroyed. The rings, keys to the universe that they were, were still small and cheaply made; incredibly breakable. Maybe they were gone. But maybe they were somewhere Menge hadn't thought to look.

He had to go to that garage as soon as possible, and look for whatever hiding places his twelve-year-old mind might have imagined. Delores and the others were in deadly danger; he had to find that ring now.

But what would he say to his mother? Roger had no time for explanations, especially for something as complicated and unbelievable as the Cineverse!

Then again, why did he have to explain at all? If he simply walked into the garage, without knocking on his mother's door, he wouldn't have to explain anything, would he? It wasn't as if he was stealing anything – whatever pitifully few boxes were left, they were *his* things, after all.

That decided it then – simple, efficient, and completely free of mother's lectures about his cleaning habits and the various women in his life. He'd just have to wait for it to be fully dark. His mother would be watching television, if not asleep. He could be in and out of her garage without her ever knowing he was around.

Yes! The plan was foolproof. Roger was surprised for an instant at his new resolve. A few days ago, he would never have dared to do something like this. But that was before he'd survived the Wild West, braved a primitive jungle, and almost been sacrificed to a volcano god! For good or ill, his experiences in the Cineverse had changed him. He trusted they would pay off in this world as well.

He got out of bed, walked into the kitchen, and methodically began to search the drawers. He knew there was a flashlight in here somewhere.

Roger walked quietly to the door at the side of his mother's garage. He had put on his spare jogging suit, a faded blue with silver stripes down the pants and arms. His newer exercise outfit had been severely damaged by adventures on various movie worlds, but he figured an outfit like this would raise the least suspicion in his mother's suburban neighbourhood. Heaven knew, there were joggers up and down these streets at all hours of the day and night.

He tried the door. It opened. His mother never locked it. At least that hadn't changed.

He stepped inside, closing the door behind him. He flicked on the flashlight. The beam wasn't as strong as it could have been, barely piercing the gloom. Maybe, Roger thought, he should have checked the batteries.

His foot hit something, which in turn hit a trash can. Roger froze, but heard no answering noise from his mother's house. His stomach growled. He massaged his sneakered foot. What was his mother doing, leaving noisy metal objects on the floor of the garage? After a moment, he moved even more carefully to the shelves in the back of the garage.

Roger's stomach complained again. How long had it been since he'd had something to eat? The last big meal he'd had was the night before he was to be sacrificed to the volcano god. He had no idea how long ago that was – time in the Cineverse wasn't like time on Earth; on movie worlds there were all these jump cuts. Roger could taste the saliva in the back of his throat. If only he had a little something to munch on—

There was something in the pocket of his jogging suit. Roger fished it out and shone the flashlight beam on what he'd found; a packet of chewing-gum with one stick left. Well, it was better than nothing. He unwrapped the stick and popped it in his mouth. Besides, maybe chewing on some gum would calm his nerves.

He turned his light to the storage shelves, and almost immediately found the boxes he was searching for, all stacked neatly on the uppermost shelf. Menge the Merciless might have been a scourge and a villain, but at least he was tidy.

Roger set about methodically exploring the six boxes still left from his childhood, doing his best to keep quiet. The first held only elementary school papers and projects, the second various broken toys he'd been unable to part with. The third box was a bit larger and more interesting. It contained half a dozen figures left over from his Zorro fort, his incomplete set of 'Mars attacks Earth' cards – he was missing number 22 – and a catcher's mitt, which Roger's father had bought in the forlorn hope that his son might take up baseball. Roger smiled when he thought of his father's impossible quest. After all, who needed to take up sports when there were so many good comic books and movies around? Roger hadn't really discovered exercise until sometime after he discovered girls. Except for one or two half-hearted games of catch begun in their back yard on his father's insistence, this glove had never been used.

Except—

Roger's heart threatened to beat its way out of his chest. After he'd given up his brief baseball career, this glove had been virtually useless, *except as a place to hide things*. Small things in particular, small, round, cheap plastic things, like Captain Crusader Decoder Rings!

Roger quickly reached inside the glove, and felt the piece of tissue paper he knew would be there. Perhaps he got a bit too excited, or pulled the paper free a bit too rapidly. Whatever happened, he lost his grip on the box. It fell to the cement floor with a dull thud. Roger hoped it was too soft a noise for anybody to hear. He pulled the tissue paper from the ring. Yes! He didn't even have to shine his flashlight beam on it. He'd know the feel of this cheap plastic anywhere.

It was a genuine (accept no substitutes) Captain Crusader Decoder Ring!

That's when he heard voices. His fingers went numb. The ring slipped from his hand.

The voices were coming from outside the garage. Roger turned off his flashlight. He strained to hear the words.

'Now, I might just be a foolish old lady, but I swear I heard something.'

It was his mother's voice! Roger had to do something! His foot hit the box on the floor. It produced a sound that was much louder than he might have liked.

'See, Mr M? I told you I heard something in the garage.'

Mr M? But that was his mother's pet name for the man who was actually Menge the Merciless!

'Don't worry, Mrs G,' Menge replied smoothly. 'I'm sure it's only a raccoon or some other lowly beast. I shall dispatch it handily.'

'A raccoon?' his mother said distractedly. 'Oh my. I don't think I could watch.'

A motor rumbled to life. The garage door was opening, revealing two silhouettes, a man and a woman, on the other side.

'I certainly understand, Mrs G. I wouldn't want to offend your delicate sensibility. Lucky for both of us that I thought to bring my gun.'

Roger saw that the silhouette of the man held the silhouette of a very large revolver. The second silhouette looked an awful lot like a Magnum.

'You're such a gentleman, Mr M. Then if you'll excuse me?'

'Yes, certainly, Mrs G. Feel free to go into the house. I'll let you know when it is all over.'

This was terrible! Roger had to find that ring and get out of here. Where could it have gone?

Something went 'crunch' under his sneaker. Roger felt where his foot had been, and found four small pieces of plastic. He looked up as he stuffed them in his pocket.

His mother had disappeared in the house. Menge turned on the overhead light. He smiled at Roger.

'This is even better than I thought,' the villain gloated once again. 'Ah hahahaha. Ah hahahaha.'

'Oh no, you don't!' Roger retorted, figuring that was the sort of thing you said to an arch-villain.

Menge continued to grin.

Oh no, you don't? Roger thought. What had he meant by that?

'I'll call my mother!' Roger added a second later.

Menge hefted his Magnum meaningfully. 'And I'll shoot you with this. It's a shame that I couldn't see who you were in the dark. A tragedy.'

Roger recognised a threat when he heard it, especially when that threat was spoken by a man with a pencil-thin moustache.

'What do you want from me?' Roger asked.

'I think you and I are going on a little trip.' Menge waved his gun at the open garage door. 'At least, that's the way my boss Doctor Dread would put it.'

Roger walked out of the garage, followed closely by Menge and his gun.

'Next door,' Menge instructed. Roger did as he was told. Menge steered him into another garage. The merciless one waved his gun at a red sports car.

'I realised,' the villain continued, 'after I spoke to you on the phone, that it might not be enough to simply deny you the use of a ring. You've been to the Cineverse, after all, and it was possible that a little bit of that place's heroics had rubbed off on you. So I figured it was time to make some contingency plans. Plans that have to do with your death. If you'll climb in the car?'

Roger felt the gun's cold steel against his cheek. He climbed into the driver's seat.

'And put on the seat-belt,' Menge instructed him.

Roger clicked the belt in place.

'You'll find that seat-belt has some amusing properties.' Menge's pencil-thin moustache quivered upwards. 'I have made some modifications in it, you see. Once closed, the belt cannot be taken off. The clasp is permanently locked.' The gun muzzle gently caressed the car's door-frame. 'I have made other modifications to this vehicle as well, such as the removal of the brakes, and certain adjustments to the gas tank to assure that, if you hit something, it will explode.' He reached across Roger and turned the key that was already in the ignition. 'It is, of course, providentially coincidental that your mother and I live at the top of a hill road that ends in a cliff.'

Providentially coincidental? Roger had always thought of that particular cliff as 'picturesque'. He knew now that the cliff would mean something much more final to him very shortly.

'Oh,' Menge added cheerily, 'I forgot to tell you about the automatic acceleration valve—' A red light blinked on in the middle of the dashboard. The car's lights turned themselves on. The horn beeped merrily.

'—But I don't think we have any more time for conversation,' Menge shouted over the racing engine. 'I don't think we have time for any more than a *bon voyage*!'

The car started by itself with a squeal of rubber, its wheels gaining speed as it rolled down the driveway and the road beyond. Roger tried to turn the steering-wheel, but it was locked as well.

'Ah hahahaha!' he heard behind him. 'Ah hahahaha!'

The car went faster still. It sped past the stop sign, and across the main road. There was the hard crash of rending metal as the car broke through the roadside barrier and went hurtling out into space. For a single, quiet moment, Roger felt weightless, suspended in mid-air. Then he, and the tons of metal surrounding him, began their descent.

He stared through the windshield. Now that the sportscar was pointed straight down, Roger could see his destination, some hundreds of deadly feet away.

The car was falling to the rocks far below, and certain, fiery death!

CHAPTER TWO

'Murder by Slime!'

Roger was never around when she needed him.

Delores would have felt more put out had she not been staring down the barrel of a gun. Of course, it was hard to blame Roger. She really hadn't gotten around to explaining exactly who she was when the two of them had gotten involved. Or the exact nature of the Cineverse. Or what would happen when you dropped a Captain Crusader Decoder Ring when you were right in the middle of using it. Or much of anything, actually.

She sighed. They never told her it would be this difficult when she was in hero school. Then again, when she went to Earth to look for help in her fight, she never realised she might fall in love.

'All right!' Big Bertha barked in her ear. 'No looking wistful over there! It is not the proper response to half a dozen villains threatening you with high-tech weaponry. We expect fear, trembling, useless pleas for mercy – that sort of thing. Getting a faraway look in your eyes like that is asking for trouble!'

The smile faded from Delores' perfect lips. She defiantly tossed back her long blonde hair. They wanted her to play by their rules, did they? Well, she had some rules of her own – and Delores played for keeps!

She stared back at Bertha, the only woman she knew who could wear a festive island mumu and make it look like a set of combat fatigues. She, and five assorted male lowlifes, all pointed guns at Delores and her allies. A couple of the lowlifes attempted to leer in her direction, but they were forced to look away when she gave them one of her practised withering glances. Even Big Bertha took that moment to examine her Uzi automatic more closely. The only one not affected by her stare was their leader – who stood behind the others, and a bit to one side – the insidious Doctor Dread, dressed once again in his signature metallic, pale-green snakeskin suit. He held no weapon himself, preferring to merely smile evilly in the background.

So Delores and her allies were slightly outnumbered. Still, there was no fear in her heroic heart.

At least the islanders had excused themselves when the battle between the forces of Dread and Delores had gotten serious, so that the locals could, as their elder proclaimed, 'pursue their peaceful native existence'. That meant Delores didn't have to worry about hurting any innocent bystanders. In other words, her hero gloves were off.

She glanced for a final time at her three companions. They were not without their resources.

Zabana, Prince of the Jungle, stared stoically at their enemies. He pointedly ignored the livid red scar that crossed his left cheek, a scar made by a bullet intended for Roger.

'Flesh wound,' the blond giant announced when he noticed Delores examining the scar. 'Zabana laughs at flesh wounds!' He turned back to stare at the enemy, absently flexing his pectorals.

'We'll give them more than flesh woundsh!' Doc croaked from where he sprawled atop the igneous rock. His hands groped towards his twin, pearl-handled revolvers, both still in their holsters. 'Now, where did I put my gunsh?'

Delores glanced next at the shortest of her three fellows, Big Louie. Louie grinned back and tipped his hat. Delores bit the corner of her perfect lip with one perfect tooth. She had some trouble with Big Louie. Zabana and Doc were both heroes, in their way, and Delores knew she could count on both of them, within certain limits. Big Louie, though, was a sidekick. Delores admitted it; she was always a little uncomfortable around sidekicks. She could never quite figure out what they did. She wondered now just how Big Louie fitted into all of this.

'I'd wonder about that, too,' Louie answered, although she couldn't remember asking a question. 'I guess, one way or another, I move the plot along.'

Move the plot along? Delores frowned. Is that what happened with the bullet and the ring and Roger's disappearance? It was all so confusing. What was happening to the Cineverse, anyway?

But then she realised that this confusion was what it was all about – Doctor Dread's evil plans, Roger's disappearance, her rescue mission, their search for Captain Crusader, everything! Ever since the Change had ripped through the movie worlds – when heroes started to die, lovers weren't always united, masked killers continually came back from the dead, and the villains often won – there had been something wrong with the Cineverse. But the Change had been too unstable.

Now, the Cineverse was changing again. And Doctor Dread wanted it changed his way.

'There she goes,' Big Bertha hissed, 'wandering off again into one of those explanatory asides. I don't think she takes our threat seriously!'

Doctor Dread cleared his throat delicately.

'Perhaps,' he said unctuously, 'we should show them' – he paused knowingly – 'the meaning of the word.'

Bertha clicked off the safety on her weapon.

'Machine-guns,' Zabana said derisively. 'Zabana laughs at machine-guns!'

But Delores wasn't laughing. She was thinking of escape. Dread and his cohorts had backed them up against the live volcano, quieter now that it had received its sacrifice of assorted bad guys, but still deadly if they were to step back into its steaming maw. There had to be some other way out of here!

They would already have escaped, if Dread hadn't so quickly brought back those other five henchpeople to replace the ones he'd lost in the volcano. It had been very confusing there in the moments after Roger's disappearance, and Dread had become very speedy with reinforcements and costume changes. Delores sometimes wondered where the criminal genius found all those lackeys.

'Central casting,' Louie replied, even though Delores still couldn't remember speaking. 'But I have an idea.'

'Enough' – Dread paused purposefully – 'shilly-shallying! We will show these upstarts what it means to cross the next' – he hesitated meaningfully – 'ruler of the Cineverse!'

The five other lowlifes all cocked their various weapons. If they were going to escape, Delores realised, it had better be now. Louie had said he had an idea? Of course! Roger had disappeared when Louie grabbed the ring. And that meant—

'Zabana! Doc!' Delores called. 'Grab hold of Louie. Louie, take out that ring!'

'That's what I—' Louie began.

'They're going to escape!' Big Bertha realised.

Delores clamped her hand on Louie's shoulder.

'Twist that sucker!' she ordered.

'But—' Louie began.

'Deal with them!' Dread ordered.

Six bad guys pulled their triggers. Louie grabbed the ring and twisted. The four of them were surrounded by blue smoke as half a dozen shots rang out.

Delores blinked as the smoke cleared.

'Valerie!' a man shouted.

'Kenneth!' the woman replied.

They had landed in a very well-appointed drawing-room.

'Oh, if I had but known what your sister really meant!' Kenneth exclaimed.

'Poor, deluded Daphne,' Valerie agreed. 'But she knew her love was hopeless, even then!'

'Yes,' Kenneth insisted, 'but with a man who may be destined someday to be Prime Minister—'

Delores frowned. Where had the decoder ring landed them? She glanced at her three companions, but they looked as confused as she. Louie had turned the ring so quickly, he would have had no time to choose a destination. Wherever they were, they seemed to be out of any immediate danger. But they would have to know in exactly what sort of a world they had landed in order to chart an intelligent course out of this place, a course through which they might find Roger, or even Captain Crusader!

'I'm sorry,' Valerie was saying, 'but I feared, if you knew my true origins—'

Delores was convinced that, whatever these two were talking about, they'd go on about it forever. As impolite as it was, she decided she had to interrupt.

'Excuse me?' she said in a loud but friendly voice.

'What?' Kenneth shouted as he turned to look at the new-comers. Valerie stifled a small scream. 'What is the meaning of this impropriety?'

'I do apologise for this intrusion,' Delores replied smoothly, 'but if you gentle people could tell us—'

'We'll do nothing of the sort!' Kenneth retorted. 'I've a good mind to thrash the lot of you!'

'Thrashing?' Zabana considered. 'Zabana laughs at thrashing.'

The prince of the jungle's outburst did nothing to calm matters. Kenneth began to tremble. 'Cutpurses! Bounders! I'll show you what it means to break into a lady's home unannounced!' He pulled decisively upon his waistcoat as he started toward Delores and the others. He stumbled before he had taken three steps.

'Kenneth!' Valerie cried in alarm.

'Blast!' He replied before he could recompose himself. 'It's nothing. Only my old war injury—'

Valerie gasped. 'But you remember what the doctor said—'

'Pray, do not remind me,' Kenneth replied bitterly. 'It's cruel enough that I shall never be able to play the violin again!'

'We really meant no harm,' Delores interjected. 'We'd only like to know where we've landed.'

But the two in the drawing-room didn't even hear her. Valerie placed a delicate hand upon her lace enclosed throat. 'I'll always love you, wooden finger or no!'

'Maybe we should go out on the street,' Louie suggested. 'People may be more willing to talk there.'

'Valerie!' Kenneth exclaimed.

'How about going to a shaloon?' Doc added. 'People alwaysh talk over drinksh!'

'Kenneth!' Valerie replied.

Delores nodded. 'Well, we'd better do something, or—'

She had no chance to finish, for the air of the peaceful drawing-room was split with fiendish laughter. There was even more blue smoke than before.

Kenneth looked distractedly at the blue fog 'I say, isn't it getting a little close in here?'

'Not as close as its going to get for' – the unmistakable voice of Doctor Dread hesitated triumphantly – 'some of you! There is no escape from the minions of Dread! There is no fleeing from' – he paused even more significantly – 'your destiny!'

By the time Dread was done pausing, the smoke had cleared, and Delores could see that he had brought Bertha and his other minions along. The minions gave up leering at Delores the moment they recognised her, switching their attentions to Valerie instead.

'See here!' Kenneth objected. 'There are certain things not done in polite society!'

'Ah, but we have no time to be' – Dread paused smoothly – 'polite. We only have time to be' – he stalled menacingly – 'final.'

His minions laughed nastily.

'I say,' Valerie mentioned, 'how did all these people get in here anyway? Has Simpson left the front door open?'

Big Louie sidled up to Delores. He whispered up towards her ear. 'But let me tell you about my idea.'

Delores frowned down at the sidekick. 'You mean we didn't use your idea? I thought you wanted us to use the ring.'

'They still aren't cowering!' Big Bertha exclaimed. 'How can you have any self-respect as a villain if people don't cower!'

'Cowering?' Zabana scoffed. 'Zabana laughs at cowering!'

'Well, yes and no,' Louie answered. 'But my plan was in the way I wanted to use the ring. That's the trouble with you heroes. It's always act first, think later.'

'Perhaps they will cower –' Dread suggested with a pause, '– if one or two of them could no longer cower –' he hesitated even more tellingly '– ever again!'

'That's it!' Kenneth exclaimed. 'That sounded like a threat to me! I'm going to ring for Simpson and have the lot of you thrown out!'

Delores started to object to Louie's accusation, but she realised he was right. At the first sign of danger, her fists started flying. It was all the fault of hero school, she supposed; some of those bad habits learned in Jeopardy 101. She remembered how perilous it could get around the dormitories, especially when they were cramming for finals.

'Kenneth!' Valerie whispered passionately. 'How forceful!'

Kenneth shrugged manfully. 'It is nothing, Valerie. Why, I remember a time during the Boer War—'

'I like it more,' Valerie answered, her stiff upper lip beginning to tremble, 'when you remind me of the Indian Uprising.'

All of Dread's henchpeople cocked their various instruments of death and pointed them at Delores' hardy band.

'I don't think we have time to worry about plans,' Delores remarked simply. 'Let's blow this joint!' This time, Delores reached over and turned the ring herself. There was the usual blue smoke.

'Oh, Kenneth!' Valerie's voice faded away, 'You know if it wasn't for Cyril—'

Delores blinked. She could hardly see anything, even after the smoke cleared. It was night.

Something growled in the darkness. A moment later, that growl was answered by a scream.

'Noises!' came the voice of the jungle prince at her side. 'Zabana laughs at noises in the night.'

Delores was glad somebody could laugh at this. 'Louie,' she whispered. 'Do you think we should get out of here?'

'It depends,' Louie replied frankly. 'Where exactly is *here*? This place might be dangerous—'

There was a gurgling, shrieking sound, like somebody drowning in a swamp.

'Then again,' Louie continued, 'this place might only be very noisy. You take a risk every time you jump from movie world to movie world, especially when that next world is unknown. This particular place might *seem* bad, but where we end up next may be worse. What we're doing now is like playing Russian roulette with a little plastic ring.'

Delores tried not to jump when something howled in the distance. That was no way for a hero to act – even if she hadn't quite gotten her diploma. Besides, maybe Louie and Zabana were right. Even though there were all those noises, nothing had happened to them – yet. This world could be quite different when daylight arrived. There was probably no reason for her every sense to be heightened tenfold, her every muscle tensed for action. This place could turn out to be perfectly peaceful, idyllic even – maybe.

There was an odd cry high overhead, half-scream, half-cackle, like a bird being driven mad in the lightless sky.

'Then again,' Louie said, 'I could be wrong.'

A rumbling came from all too close. It felt as if the ground might be trembling slightly beneath them. Unless, Delores considered, it was the shaking of their collective legs.

'Maybe Zabana have to think twice, too,' the jungle prince admitted.

The rumbling grew even closer. Delores looked where she thought the noise was coming from, and realised that not all was darkness. There was a light out there. No, it was two lights, two small points of sickly green. They came nearer still, and she noticed a certain oddity about their shapes. They were rounded, almost ovals, like a pair of tiny, glowing fish hanging in the air, or – or disembodied eye sockets glowing from within.

As soon as she had that last thought, she knew it had to be true. The glowing green things were eyes, watching them, coming ever closer. It was hard to judge size or distance in this total absence of light, but those eyes seemed to be growing awfully large.

'Uh-oh,' Louie said at her side. So the others could see these glowing orbs as well.

'Eyes? Zabana not afraid of—' The jungle prince stopped abruptly, for he had smelled the same strange stench that had almost made Delores recoil in revulsion; a blast of hot, humid air that carried the putrescent odour of things long dead – vile creatures Delores wouldn't have wanted to meet even when they were alive. There was a sigh of wind, then a growled inhalation.

Whatever was out there had opened its mouth and was breathing on them.

'Maybe we can reashon with it!' Doc suggested from where he had collapsed nearby.

'Maybe we could get out of here!' Louie further suggested.

But Delores knew it was no use. She had seen something in those bright green eyes, something that spoke of finality, and maybe death. The thing had found them now, and in a second, with a single motion of its unseen form, it could decide whether they lived or died.

There was a moment of silence as deep as the darkness that surrounded them. But the quiet was broken by a single word carried upon the fetid air.

And the word was:

'Slime.'

CHAPTER THREE

'Teenage Terror!'

They say, when you're about to die, that your whole life passes before you.

Roger thought of Gladys, and Andrea, and Phyllis with that funny little smile. Then of course there was Fifi the exchange student, and Nancy with her pom-poms. That, at least, was all of the girls up to mid-way through his junior year in high school. After that, of course, it got complicated.

But Roger didn't have time for complications. He was trapped in a car, falling to his doom.

Well, he was chewing gum. At least his ears wouldn't pop. When you worked in public relations, you always tended to look on the bright side.

If only there was some way to save himself, like he and his friends had managed time and again in the Cineverse. If only he had a Captain Crusader Decoder Ring!

But he did have a ring.

Roger felt in his pocket. It was broken, crushed into four pieces by a clumsy foot. But what was broken could be mended. At least it could in theory, if he had the time and the tools. At the very least, it was food for thought.

Well, maybe not food, Roger realised, but it at least could be chewing-gum!

He spat the well-chewed gum into his free hand and flattened the wad with his thumb. With this accomplished, he quickly pressed the four broken fragments of the decoder ring into as close an approximation of the original circle as he could manage, being careful to keep the dial free of the makeshift adhesive.

He looked up and out of the car's windshield. The rocks and rolling surf were less than a hundred feet away. It was now or never. Roger closed his eyes and twisted the dial.

'See you in the funny papers!' he shouted.

But where was the blue smoke?

Roger opened his eyes. He was surrounded by bright sun and surf, but he was no longer falling. Oh, he was still strapped into the car, but, from what he could see, trapped as he was in his permanent seat-belt, all four tyres seemed to have sunk in the sand.

Sand? What had happened to the onrushing rocks? And what about the exploding gas tank? Had Roger blacked out for a while? Besides, there was no beach near his mother's house, only sheer cliffs and deadly rocks.

He was someplace different than before. The ring must have worked, at least a little bit. Maybe it had somehow transported him up or down the sea-coast, out of harm's way. Roger did his best to study his surroundings from where he was strapped in. Not only was there sand here, but he could hear distant music; electric guitars and something else. Roger strained to hear. Bongos?

Voices and laughter came from behind the car:

'Oh, wow! Groovy!'

'That's a way-out board you've got there, man!'

A pair of blond teenage boys in swimsuits walked up to Roger's window.

'And Frankie!' said one as he pointed at Roger's jogging suit. 'Dig those surfing duds!'

'Hey, Brian!' the other one exclaimed. 'Cowabunga! I bet you could really hang ten in those!'

Brian laughed. 'What a kook!'

Roger felt a strange disquiet, deep in his stomach. Maybe the ring had really worked after all. He knew one thing for sure: no one talked like this, except in the movies. And he had a terrible feeling what kind of movie this was.

'Hey!' a woman's voice cried out from farther up the beach. 'What a crazy woody!'

Now, now, Roger thought, trying to calm himself. Perhaps this was just a serious, dramatic world that was using the beach as but one of its many settings. Roger frowned. Weren't those guitars getting louder?

Brian looked up. 'Hey, dig that wild wahini!'

Another woman, also blonde, teenage, and – in her case – wearing a psychedelic green bikini, skipped towards them across the sand. Yes, Roger was certain of it now. Those guitars *were* getting louder.

'Hey, Dee Dee!' Frankie called. 'Catch our new friend here with the wild wheels!' He looked back in the window at Roger. 'Sorry, man. I didn't catch your name.'

Roger introduced himself.

'Roger Dodger!' Brian replied. 'This is Dee Dee, the fairest flower on the sand!'

'Tee hee hee,' Dee Dee replied as she blushed prettily.

'But hey,' Frankie suggested, 'we were about to mosey on down the beach to a barbecue. Why don't you come along?'

Roger thanked him, but explained that he was trapped in his seat-belt.

'Hey, man,' Frankie assured him. 'No sweat. We got that covered.'

'Yeah!' Dee Dee chirped enthusiastically. 'I hear Bix!'

Roger assumed she was referring to the ever louder guitar strums.

'Here they come!' Dee Dee shrieked excitedly.

Roger turned his head as far as he could, trying to see what was making Dee Dee jump up and down in the sand. Four other teens walked out from behind the snack-bar, each one carrying a musical instrument. They wore identical shirts, with vertical red and white stripes, and had their hair cut in a 'modified-Beatle' style, with bangs just long enough to be blown by the sea wind. The first two carried guitars, the next one a bass. Roger was most impressed with the last fellow, who carried an entire drum kit. He could see the band's name in bright red script on the bass drum: 'Bix Bale and the Belltones.'

The instruments meant only one thing: Roger's worst fears were realised. This was *that* kind of world.

It took them only a minute to set up their drums and face the ever-growing number of teens that now surrounded Roger's car.

'Come on now!' Bix shouted. 'Let's shake a tail feather!'

Roger had to face up to it. 'This is not just a beach world—' he began aloud, letting the reality sink in.

With that, the band started to play, a full, rich sound despite the fact that Roger could see no wires, microphones or amplifiers.

Roger finished the horrible truth: '—it's a Beach Party Musical world!'

As if in answer, Frankie started to sing:

> 'Roger's trapped in his real boss car;
> Strapped like that well he won't get far!

> It's time to call on Miss Dee Dee;
> She's a girl who can set him free.'

'Hey!' the crowd shouted in unison.

Boom be boom be boom be boom boom boom, the drums replied.

'Nanny nanny-nanny nanny-nanny hey!' Bix and the Belltones chorused.

This was it, then. Roger was trapped on the most dangerous of all movie worlds, the musical. He remembered how sceptical he had been when Big Louie had first mentioned the perils of a place like this. But then they had stopped on a movie world place where large groups were singing about going to a state fair, and Roger had barely escaped a life judging strawberry jam contests. Then there had been the tropical island, and the song about the volcano god, which had Roger dancing willingly towards his death!

And wasn't there some place with singing buccaneers? Didn't that have something to do with a man who puffed blue smoke cigars? But Roger didn't have time to worry about things he couldn't truly remember.

He had witnessed the seductive power of Cineverse music first hand, music which could make you do anything! Music that, unless he fought it with every ounce of his being, would overtake him again!

Brian sang the second verse:

> 'Come on Dee Dee, now do your stuff.
> Don't worry Roger, she won't get rough!
> She's the answer to all your plans;
> She's the girl with the magic hands.'

'Hey!' the crowd shouted all over again.

Bif de boom de boom bif boom boom, the drums added.

'Nanny nanny-nanny nanny-nanny hey!' everyone sang together.

Roger looked at Dee Dee. Whatever else the girl had, she sure knew how to dance. She did the frug, the twist, the watusi and the swim, with some bits of the phillie and the mashed potato thrown in. Even the psychedelic paislies on her bikini – which really wasn't very daring as swimsuits went, showing only an inch of tanned flesh between extensive pieces of fabric – even the paislies seemed to jump about to the thundering surf beat.

And who wouldn't want to dance with music like this? Twanging guitars, booming drums, and the rhythmic hand-clapping of the crowd made Roger want to move his feet.

'Ow!' he yelled. The seat-belt had dug into Roger's shoulder mid-frug, bringing him back to his senses. He realised that, despite his caution, he was once again falling victim to a musical world. He looked up and saw Dee Dee dancing closer. Brian and Frankie sang a duet:

> 'So Roger now you've met Dee Dee;
> She's the girl who will set you free!
> Here's a little something you won't mind much,
> 'Cause she's the girl with the magic touch.'

'Hey!' Everybody, including Roger, shouted.

Bif boom bang boom bang bif bang bif, the drums announced.

'Nanny nanny-nanny, nanny nanny hey!' Roger led the chorus.

With that, Dee Dee reached inside the car. Roger's surprise freed him from the music long enough to get a better look at this bikini-clad beauty. She might have been a little younger than the women Roger generally dated, but she did have incredible dimples. If this had been another time and place, and Roger hadn't already met Delores, not to mention all the energy he had to put into saving the Cineverse—

Guitars twanged.

Dee Dee reached for Roger's seat-belt.

Drums boomed.

Dee Dee touched the locked metal clasp.

Hands clapped with urgent rhythm.

The seat-belt sprang open!

Dee Dee smiled as she frugged away from the car. Roger looked down at the now-open belt in disbelief. He was free.

Roger knew what that meant:

Now he could dance!

Roger leapt from the car and started to shing-a-ling. Dee Dee squealed with delight, and began to boogaloo back in his direction. Everybody sang the chorus to that surfing beat:

> 'She's the girl with the magic hands,
> Nanny nanny-nanny, nanny-nanny hey!
> She's the girl with the magic hands,
> Nanny, nanny-nanny, nanny—'

The chorus was interrupted by the roar of half a dozen motorcycles.

'Oh, what a bring-down!' Brian exclaimed.

'It's the Mad Mumbler and his Motorcycle Mob!' Frankie agreed as he neatly introduced the newcomers.

But the scream of the engines had done more than end the song. They had also brought Roger back to his senses. He realised that Movie Magic had done it to him one more time.

The Cineverse was full of Movie Magic. And it was this very magic – which Big Louie had first explained to Roger when they had both been in the Wild-singing-West – this Movie Magic that could make an arrow fly right through the chain mail and into someone's heart in a Swashbuckler, or could let somebody shoot twelve rounds from a six-shooter in a Western, or could make you forget everything as long as you could dance to the surfing beat in a Beach Party film! Movie Magic was everywhere in the Cineverse, according to Big Louie, eternally helping the plot along!

The bikes roared forward, spewing great clouds of sand in their wake and snapping Roger from his reverie. Everybody around him stepped back to give the biking newcomers room, but Roger wasn't afraid. There was one advantage to being dropped on this world after all. Beach Party movies were always light comedies, with barely enough menace to move the plot along. These motorcycle guys would come up and mouth some ineffectual threats, but everybody knew that if any real problems developed, there would be only one way to resolve them:

The surfing duel!

The six motorcycles rumbled to a halt directly in front of Roger. Two of the cyclists dismounted. Both wore studded motorcycle jackets and heavily-patched jeans, but the similarity ended there. One of the gang was almost as big as Zabana, but kept his face hidden behind a large pair of mirrored sun-glasses. The other one was a little shorter and so much skinnier that it would take three of him to equal the mass of his larger comrade. The smaller man also jerked about now and then for no apparent reason. He paused for a moment to examine the collected surfers, twitched once, then let his mouth split wide in a nasty grin.

'We hear you have a newcomer,' he mentioned softly, 'so we thought we'd come and introduce ourselves.'

'Rssrjjit,' the fellow behind him added.

The skinny fellow jerked his head half-way back, then calmly turned his smile to the surfers. 'Yeah, right boss. Introduce ourselves. It's only polite. The fellow behind me is the boss. Maybe you've heard of him. They call him the Mad Mumbler.'

He hesitated, as if expecting Roger to react in some way to the news of the Mumbler's presence. After a moment's silence, the large fellow mumbled:

'Mzummenya.'

'The Mumbler says he's pleased to meet ya,' the skinny one translated. 'My friends call me Sneer.' He jerked violently in Roger's direction. 'My enemies don't call me anything. At least not for long.'

Roger, figuring that good manners couldn't hurt, said that he was pleased to meet both of them.

'Let's hope you stay that way,' Sneer replied. 'Seeing that you're a newcomer, there's certain things you gotta understand.'

'Really?' Roger replied politely.

'Zrrzsm!' the Mumbler barked.

'Sarcasm!' Sneer repeated with a spasm of rage. 'The Mad Mumbler knows when he hears sarcasm! And Sneer knows what to do!' He whipped a switch-blade from his back pocket.

Switch-blade? Roger frowned. The ineffectual gang members in these movies never carried that kind of weapon. It would make them too threatening.

Sneer took a step towards Roger. 'Now you listen to the rules. We own this beach. Anybody on the beach does anything, they do it because we say so! Is that clear?'

'Uh,' Roger replied, since an answer seemed to be expected here. 'Yessir.'

'Bskshssh!' the Mumbler screamed.

Sneer moved forward with amazing speed. 'Yeah, boss. It sounded like backtalk to me, too!'

Somehow, Sneer's left hand had grabbed Roger's jogging suit, and the knife was pressed against the tip of Roger's nose.

'The Motorcycle Mob runs everything around here!' Sneer shouted in Roger's face. 'And we will until somebody rides the Cowabunga-munga!'

Roger couldn't help himself. 'The Cowabunga-munga?'

'Trrmrssrssr,' the Mumbler rumbled.

'Yeah,' Sneer agreed. 'Once a trouble maker, always a trouble maker. Everybody knows the Cowabungamunga—'

'Yeah!' all the surrounding surfers and beach bunnies interjected.

'—that sensation of the surf that makes a tidal wave look like a small potato. It's the monster mother of the sea, and it only comes to our beach once every seven years!' He looked out at the ocean, twitching respectfully. 'And the guy who rides it *rules* the beach!'

This was more like it, Roger thought. He had started to worry, with that knife in his nose, that maybe the Change had caused some alterations in this beach party planet, making it a lot more dangerous than those innocuous movies Roger remembered. But knife or no knife, what this guy was doing now was challenging him to a surfing duel. So maybe things hadn't changed all that much after all.

Roger knew what was expected of him. He asked: 'The Cowabunga-munga? When's it going to come again?'

'As if you didn't know!' Sneer drove the hilt of his switch-blade into Roger's stomach. Roger staggered back into Dee Dee. That hurt! Things weren't supposed to hurt in Beach Party movies.

It had to be the Change – changing even a world as innocuous as this. Roger realised this place might really be dangerous. Maybe he'd have to use his ring sooner than he'd expected.

But, Roger further realised, if the Change was still doing this kind of damage, there might not be a single safe place in all of the Cineverse.

'Crssrrss,' the Mumbler interjected.

'Yeah, boss,' Sneer replied. 'He is a pretty cool character. I wonder how cool he'd be if I cut his lady, instead!'

The knife hilt stroked Dee Dee's side.

'Tee hee hee,' Dee Dee replied.

'Laugh at me!' Sneer shrieked. 'She laughed at me!'

'It tickled!' Dee Dee protested.

'Trsrfmmbm!' the Mumbler stated.

Sneer's smile grew even more deformed. 'Yeah, boss, they're both trouble-makers!' His knife followed the line of Roger's shoulder. 'And you know what we do with trouble-makers!'

Dee Dee shrieked and grabbed Roger from behind, binding his arms to his sides. She had a very powerful grip for a beach bunny. Roger couldn't free his hands to reach into his pocket to get the ring.

The Mad Mumbler laughed. Sneer giggled. The background motorcycle gang guffawed. The knife returned to Roger's nose.

Roger realised that he couldn't use the ring in any case; not if it meant leaving Dee Dee behind to face these thugs. That sort of thing would be against everything Captain Crusader had ever stood for. No matter what the Change had done to the Cineverse, Roger knew, it still wouldn't be the heroic thing to do.

The Mad Mumbler pointed a trembling finger at Roger.'Krrit!'

'Cut him?' Sneer laughed. 'Yeah, boss. *Where* should I cut him?'

Cut? Were they serious? Roger decided he needed to re-revise his plans. Maybe he could use the ring and take Dee Dee with him. If he could only somehow free his arms!

'Hahrrr,' the Mumbler insisted.

'There?' Sneer sneered. 'That's a serious cut, boss. It just shows what can happen if you use sarcasm.' He winked at Roger. 'Say your prayers, Hodaddy!'

Sneer lunged forward, his knife aimed straight for Roger's chest!

CHAPTER FOUR

'The Dog Means Death!'

'Slime?' Big Louie replied.

'Slime!' the monstrous voice reiterated. 'Slime is my life!'

Delores didn't like this.

'This wasn't my idea,' Big Louie reminded her.

Maybe it was time to use the decoder ring. Wherever they ended up had to be better than this. But Delores knew they had to be cautious. What had Louie said; something about Russian roulette with a plastic ring? It would be easy to make a mistake in the total darkness, especially when facing something as potentially supernatural as whatever now breathed on them from out in the murk. What was it? What could it do? She wanted to be very careful they didn't use the ring to go somewhere else, only to somehow bring the slime creature along.

'You,' the voice commanded.

'Who?' Delores asked with some trepidation.

'Not me,' Louie added all too hastily, 'I hope.'

'Not any of us!' Zabana suggested boldly. 'Thing has us confused with four other people!'

'Let'sh jusht invite it for a drink!' Doc suggested from somewhere around ground level.

'The woman,' the voice explained.

Delores tried to laugh. 'Uh, guys? Perhaps it *is* time for a change of scene.'

'It is no use,' the voice replied. 'There is no escape. Slime is your destiny.'

There was an explosion, followed by the all-too-familiar oily laughter. Delores was sure, had there been any light, they would have all been surrounded by blue smoke. The archest of arch-villains had found them again.

'It is no use!' Dread chortled. 'There is no escape!'

'You're stealing my lines,' a monstrous voice interjected.

'Pitiful fools,' Dread continued, 'don't you realise I have made certain adjustments to my ring that will allow me to follow you any—' He paused. 'Eh? Did somebody say something?'

'There is only one response to line thieves,' the voice replied. 'Slime.'

'Come now, Delores,' Dread chided. 'How childish! Trying to confuse me by – disguising your voice? You can't fool me that easily. What do you take me – *ick* – what is this stuff – where is it coming – *blechh* – get it off me – *ugh* – I can hardly move. It's already up – *glub* – around my – *gurgle*.'

Doctor Dread was heard no more.

'Out of here?' Louie whispered.

'Out of here!' Delores agreed. 'Grab hold, fellas!' She felt Louie's hand on her arm, and Zabana's on her shoulder. A moment later, Doc grabbed her ankle.

'Up, up, and away!' Delores announced as she twisted the ring.

There was the usual explosion, and they were gone. On the whole, however, Delores would have felt better if she had not heard those last few words:

'There is no escape from slime.'

'This is more like it!' Louie announced happily.

It was night, and the world was devoid of colour. This didn't seem very promising, either, except that Louie liked it for some reason. Delores only hoped it was better than that dreadful place they had just escaped. There was light here, after all, even though it was a harsh, white light that threw long, dark shadows across the alley-way. And the shadows looked like nothing so much as bars on a cage. Far away, Delores could hear a woman's laughter, the plaintive call of a saxophone, and the wail of police sirens.

'This is the city,' Louie explained. 'This is where I belong. This is a place where a guy in a double-breasted suit can feel comfortable.' He looked down at the cowboy duds he still wore. 'Now if only I had my double-breasted suit back, we'd be fine.' He shrugged apologetically as he began a furtive walk to the street at the alley's end. 'Otherwise,' he called softly over his shoulder, 'we might have some trouble.'

This time, Delores understood what Louie was talking about. Just because they were dressed as two cowboys, a jungle prince, and a woman who was about to be sacrificed to a volcano god, they might not blend in here. But this was Louie's home world. There must be some way to find less conspicuous clothing, and she was sure the sidekick could help them there. With luck, maybe she could get out of this stupid mumu and back into something more comfortable, like a black vinyl jumpsuit.

She walked after Louie, waving for Doc and Zabana to follow. Once they blended a little more fully into their surroundings, it would be time to think about other things. This was the sort of decision she had learned in Heroic Strategy 201; if this was a place that Louie truly knew, maybe it was time to stop running, and make plans.

Delores felt a slight shiver roll across her spine and shoulders, a reaction, no doubt, to the terrors of that dark world they had just left. Still, they had escaped the place cleanly, as Dread faced the wrath of the thing that had first threatened them.

Whatever they had met in the darkness had – at the very least – inconvenienced Dread. Delores was all too well aware of the resources of their nemesis to believe that he had been eliminated. But he had been delayed. That would have to be enough. It proved heroes could still beat the odds on occasion, even after the Change.

Louie reached the end of the alley-way. He took off his ten-gallon hat and peered around the corner.

Delores crept up behind him. 'What should we do?' she whispered.

'How should I know?' he whispered back. 'I'm only a sidekick.'

'I'll find a shaloon,' Doc ventured from where he crawled behind them.

'Zabana lead way!' the big fellow offered. 'Laugh at all who stand before us. Beat, strangle, stab with hunting knife! Zabana not only prince of jungle. He prince of everywhere!'

'Uh, no,' Delores replied immediately. 'I'll lead the way. Unless—' She stopped herself, her heroic instincts temporarily overcome by pragmatism. 'Louie, do you know of any used clothing stores around here?'

Louie grinned at that, glad at last to be given a sidekick sort of thing to do. He led them as quickly as possible down the deserted streets to a place called Second Avenue Second Hand. Strangely enough, even though it appeared to be the middle of the night, the store was open for business. Delores thought she heard gunshots as she opened the store's front door, but they were behind her, somewhere in the distance, as were the shouts, screams, and sirens that followed. She quickly ushered the others inside.

A little bell rang as the door shut behind them, closing out the noise from the street. Delores glanced around the shop. It was awfully spacious in here, much larger than it appeared from the street; more of a warehouse than a storefront. Bright electric bulbs were hung along the ceiling, but half their light was lost in the dust that surrounded the shelves and tables piled high with clothes. The lightbulbs seemed to stretch away as far as Delores could see, but half this place was still lost in shadow.

'It's awfully quiet,' Delores whispered.

'Like a tomb,' Louie agreed.

'It looks deserted,' Delores observed. 'I wonder if anyone's here?'

'*May I help you?*'

The words were spoken in a conversational, if efficient, tone. After all the whispering, it sounded to Delores as if someone had shouted in her ear.

A small, bent man stood directly before them in a narrow aisle between the mounds. He had probably only stepped out of the heavy shadows, but it seemed as if he had appeared out of nowhere. He smiled at his customers.

Delores exhaled. There was nothing to be upset about. She was glad she'd only jumped a little bit, and hadn't yelled at all.

'We need some new outfits,' Louie explained.

'That I can see.' The small man nodded pleasantly, as if having two cowboys, a jungle prince and a woman in a mumu walk into your store was an everyday occurrence. He waved at the piles on either side. 'This is the place.'

Delores and the others got to work. Louie found a double-breasted suit for himself, and another one for Doc. They had some problems with Zabana, but after certain alterations were made on the better part of a pair of double-breasted suits – which were thereupon sewn together – he looked as if he fitted here as well.

They were interrupted once.

The door slammed open. A man took a step inside, but stood strangely erect as machine-gun fire erupted outside. The man staggered forward one step, then back two, before falling on the sidewalk outside.

The door slammed closed.

'Happens all the time,' the proprietor confessed with a shrug. 'Think nothing of it. It's the neighbourhood.'

Delores continued her search. She wasn't having as much luck as the others. Apparently, black vinyl jumpsuits were not in fashion on this world, and she had to settle for a simple, spangled evening dress. Her only consolation was that the garment had padded shoulders.

There was, of course, a little problem when Delores and her fellows realised they had no money to pay for all these goods. However, once the proprietor was informed that they were all heroes (and Zabana was a very *big* hero) they had no further problem. Heroes always paid – eventually.

Delores just hoped the villains would pay first.

Speaking of villains, she wouldn't want to be caught after she and her fellows had made all these preparations. They had already spent a bit longer choosing their wardrobes than she might have liked. She frowned out at the night sky. 'We'd better get out of here before daylight.'

'Daylight?' the proprietor replied. 'It's hardly ever daylight around here.'

He smiled enigmatically as he disappeared into the shadows.

They were alone again, facing the door outside.

'Where now?' she asked Big Louie.

'I've got to pick again?' the sidekick complained.

Delores nodded. 'We need someplace safe, where we can make our plans.'

'Safe?' Louie asked incredulously. 'In a *film noir* world? You've got to be kidding.'

Delores saw Louie's point. If a second-hand clothing emporium could be this sinister, imagine what the rest of this world held in store.

'Well, if not safe,' she asked instead, 'how about out of the way?'

'Out of the way?' This time he smiled. 'Louie's a specialist in out of the way. It comes with being a sidekick. Let's see – my uncle owns a gin joint; a little hole in the wall.'

'That shounds more like it!' Doc enthused.

This time, even Delores had to agree.

Joe's Place. At three or four a.m., whatever time it was, the bar was almost deserted. Delores still picked a corner table for the four of them to huddle around. It kept them out of the way, discouraged eavesdropping, made them less of a target. In a place like this, you had to take every precaution.

Louie's uncle wasn't here yet. The bartender said he came on in a couple of hours – at six – when the joint really started to jump. Louie said that was just as well. It was probably better if they didn't meet any of his family. Delores didn't find that last remark particularly reassuring.

It was dark in here. Almost as dark as – but no, Delores had told herself she wasn't going to dwell on that other place. They had more important things to do, like saving the Cineverse! She could barely see the others' faces in the dim and smoky light.

On the juke-box, a woman sang about the man who got away.

Doc had a drink.

'So what do we do?' she asked.

'Zabana say we save Roger,' the jungle prince offered.

Louie sighed. 'There's a problem there. When Roger lost the ring, mid-transit, he—'

'Went back to home world!' Zabana interjected impatiently. 'Even prince of jungle knows that!'

'Yeah,' Louie agreed. 'But there's something that I know and you don't. Remember, I used to be a member of Doctor Dread's gang.' He hesitated, staring down at the table. 'I know what was waiting for Roger back on his home world.'

'You mean Dread set a trap?' Delores asked.

Louie nodded unhappily. 'The nefarious Doctor thought of everything, including having one of his henchpeople waiting for Roger back on earth. And not just any henchperson, either. The fellow waiting for Roger was' – Louie paused to take a ragged breath – 'Menge the Merciless.'

Delores gasped.

Zabana flexed his jungle-bred muscles.

'Roger not have chance!'

Doc had a drink.

Delores couldn't believe it. Not Roger. Not a man who knew movies the way most men knew their receding hairlines. She shook her head.

'I won't know that Roger's dead until I see it for myself. There's something different about that man. Maybe he's really a hero—' She stopped herself. Perhaps that was going too far. Instead, she added, 'or maybe he's something else all together.'

'But Menge the Merciless!' Louie insisted.

Delores knew, realistically, that Louie was right. Menge would have killed Roger instantly. Unless Roger had somehow managed to escape. There were so many escapes for a man who knew movies like that! And there was something in her that simply refused to think of Roger dead.

Maybe it was her emotions talking, rather than her intellect.

But Delores knew that, if Roger was still alive, he probably was somewhere in the Cineverse. And there was only one person, besides Roger himself, who would definitely know about his whereabouts, who indeed knew all there was to know about the Cineverse.

'Very well,' Delores said grimly. 'Then we must find Captain Crusader!'

Doc pushed the bottle out of the way.

'That's serious business, missy.'

Delores frowned. There was something different about Doc's voice.

'What do you mean?' she asked.

Doc smiled wryly. 'How do you find somebody who doesn't want to be found?'

Yes! Delores was certain of it now. Not only was Doc's slur gone, but his voice had become more forceful – even heroic.

'What do you mean?' Louie asked. 'We've already seen Captain Crusader!'

'In three different disguises,' Doc reminded the sidekick, 'as a masked marshal, a tribal chieftain, and a mysterious island drummer. And, every time we're about to discover his true identity, he spouts one of those sayin's of his. You know – "The Dewey Decimal System is your friend!" or some such – and then he ups and disappears. Does that sound like a fella who wants to be found to you?'

'I never thought of it like that,' Louie admitted.

Delores nodded in admiration of Doc's reasoning. 'That means there's more than one secret out there. Not only are we unaware of the fine points of Doctor Dread's plan to conquer the Cineverse, we don't even know the true direction of Captain Crusader's counter-plan.'

'If he even has one,' Doc added gently.

'But that's almost unthinkable!' Delores objected. 'He's Captain Crusader! He must have a plan!'

'I'm sure he had one, once,' Doc replied, still not raising his voice. 'But the Change did more than bring unhappy endings to the Cineverse. Think of what it's done to us, and to all those around us. What if the alterations that have occurred in the very fabric of the Cineverse have affected its ultimate hero?'

'You mean,' Louie said in horror, 'what if the Change changed Captain Crusader?'

'It's certainly possible,' Doc agreed. 'It's just a little somethin'

I studied when I held the Wild Bill Hickok Philosophy Chair at Western States University. That was, of course, before I became the Tombstone town drunk.' He stared moodily at the bottle before him. 'But I brought it up to make a point. With things the way they are now, we can't take nothin' for granted.'

'You've changed, Doc,' Delores mentioned.

The cowpoke pushed the bottle away. 'All things in moderation.' He looked back up to Delores. 'When I first met Roger, he inspired me. He wasn't content to just let the plot go by. He wanted to change things, for the better! He reminded me of my heroin' days, before the bottle got the better of me. I swore I'd lay off the sauce, and for a while, the action and adventurin' saw me through. But playing the town drunk in a thousand Western plots has taken its toll. I can be a hero, still, but I gotta be a little drunk, first. And I can get drunk on almost anythin'.'

'So that's why your slur's gone!' Delores exclaimed.

'Yes, it is, little missy,' Doc modestly agreed. 'Simply said, I shall certainly sustain a successful level of sobriety. She sells sea shells down by the sea sho—'

The doors to the gin joint slammed open. Slamming doors, machine-gun fire, people staggering out of clothing stores in the night – Delores reminded herself that all this was nothing to worry about. Still, any hopes that the gin joint might be in the same sort of neighbourhood as Second Avenue Second Hand evaporated when Delores heard the diabolical laughter.

'How – convenient!' Dread's oily voice shouted over the sound of countless minions filing into the bar. 'That we should find the very ones we seek hiding in a bar owned by' – he hesitated triumphantly – 'Bertha's uncle!'

'Oh, yeah,' Louie said in a small voice, 'did I tell you that Dread's number-one-henchperson was also my sister?'

'Lucky for us,' Doc chuckled, 'this here suit has large enough pockets for my six-shooters.'

The jungle prince stood abruptly, almost tipping over the table. 'Zabana say we save Cineverse!'

Delores cursed her foolishness as she stood, too, her back to the wall. She had forgotten about Louie's sister. And the fact that this wasn't only Louie's home planet, but was Dread's base of operations as well.

The henchmen continued to file in, row on row of slouch hats and double-breasted pin-stripes. Delores had never seen so many minions! What other mistakes had she made? She had let her concern for Roger and the Cineverse get in the way of her own self-preservation. Now, she might not only have sealed her own fate, but the fates of the three men who had trusted her.

The door slammed behind the last of Dread's lackeys. But there must have been close to a hundred of them, all crammed into this tiny neighbourhood bar, all smiling evilly beneath their broad-brimmed hats as they lifted their gats and roscoes to finish off the four heroes standing in the corner. And in the centre of them all were Doctor Dread, his green snakeskin suit gleaming malevolently even in the bar's dim light, and Big Bertha, who was wearing something that looked an awful lot like a black vinyl jumpsuit!

'De – lor – es,' Doctor Dread jeered, speaking so slowly that every syllable was like a separate word. 'How – pleasant – for us. How – unpleasant – for you.'

But Delores refused to be shaken by the evildoer's taunts. Somehow she'd best this beast with his hundred helpers! And even more than that, she wouldn't be shot by a woman in a costume that, by all rights of heroic priority, should be hers! There must be some way out of this! She had to find one, for the sake of Roger, and the Cineverse!

'But I am not without my – mercy,' Dread allowed. 'Tell me, De – lor – es, do I hear any last – grovelling – pleas to spare your – worthless lives?'

For her answer, Delores spat on his polished snakeskin shoes.

'Very well.' The king of crime looked meaningfully at his room full of minions. 'You know what to do, men.' Dread hesitated tellingly. 'Discard them!'

'Hey, boss!' someone shouted. 'Who let in this dog?'

Dog? Delores thought.

That's when all the guns went off.

CHAPTER FIVE

'Atomic Disaster!'

'Mrrssrrss!'

Roger was pushed roughly to the ground. He looked up, and saw the great bulk of the Mad Mumbler standing between him and Sneer's knife. The gang leader had somehow moved even faster than his lackey, saving Roger from a blade in his chest!

'Jsss Crssssss!' the Mumbler yelled down at the trembling Sneer. 'Mnnff Mffnn!'

'Yeah, Boss?' Sneer stared down at his switchblade, somewhat shaken. 'What was that?'

'Wsskssoiss Mffnnifnn!' the Mumbler insisted.

Sneer stared back at his boss. 'You *didn't* say to cut him?'

The gang leader made a slashing motion with his hand. 'Mssxxmm vbbllmm!'

'Oh! You said for *me* to cut it out!'

'Wccsblffmm Znrrgssbll!'

'Oh, is *that* what you meant?' Sneer shrugged. 'Well, I can't help it if you won't speak up!'

'Jrsdlpplll!' The Mumbler pushed Sneer back into the sand with a flick of his hand. Roger found himself grabbed by the gang leader's free hand, which was the approximate size of an uncanned ham, and hoisted back to his feet.

Sneer picked himself up and brushed himself off, muttering something about people who mumbled idioms under their breaths.

'Srrbbbttt,' the leader mumbled in Roger's direction.

Roger made an expression that he hoped was a friendly smile. 'Don't worry. No harm done.'

'Srrzzssmm!' the Mumbler screamed.

Oh, no, Roger thought. Not this again.

'No, I am not being sarcastic!' Roger yelled back. 'Don't you know when somebody's trying to be friendly?'

Roger felt a hand on either shoulder. He looked back, and saw Frankie on one side, Brian on the other.

'I don't know how to put this to you, but—' Frankie began.

'Nobody's ever friendly with the Motorcycle Mob—' Brian continued.

Frankie added: 'It just isn't done—'

Brian explained: 'It's one of the Rules of the Beach—'

'Yeah!' Frankie exclaimed. 'Right up there with "Shoes and shirts must be worn at all times when in this—" '

'Well, I'm changing the rules here and now!' Roger admitted it; he was sick and tired of the rigamarole he encountered every time he landed on a new movie world. That was one of the hidden dangers of the Cineverse – one wrong move, and you could be caught up in some local plot for hours, even days. He had spent far too long in this place already. He had certainly blown any chance of rescuing anybody. Delores might be dead right now, or in the hands of that arch-fiend, Doctor Dread. And what was Roger doing? Having a conversation with a bunch of beach blanket bozos!

Or at least he was until he had made that declaration. Now, there was not a sound around him except for the surf breaking on the sand. Everyone – surfers, beach bunnies, the Motorcycle Mob, Bix Bale and the Belltones – they were all staring at him, and, of the entire incredibly tanned group, only Dee Dee looked the least bit friendly.

'Oops,' Roger said aloud. Perhaps, by speaking his mind, he had broken an even bigger rule.

'Tee hee hee,' Dee Dee giggled sympathetically.

The Mad Mumbler's voice broke the silence: 'Bssfzzll!'

Sneer's smile once again stretched across his lips. 'Yeah, big boss man. Maybe we *were* too easy on him.' He stroked the handle of his switch-blade.

Roger could see it happening all over again. This corner of the Cineverse wanted to force him back into a role. He felt the anger growing inside him one more time.

'Oh, no!' he declared. 'I'm not going through this again!'

The Mumbler made a strangling motion with his hands. 'Thrssnnddll!'

'Yeah, boss, threats don't worry him, do they?' Sneer twirled his knife towards the surrounding surfers. 'Maybe we should cut up his friends, too.'

All the surfers took a step away. All except one.

Dee Dee still giggled at his side.

Roger realised he'd done it now. It was time to make his stand. But he had to use his anger in the right sort of way – a way that would work for him in the Cineverse. If he was going to be forced into a role, it would be a role of his own choosing. He wished he had a toothpick to chew on, or a pack of Luckies he could roll up inside the sleeve of his t-shirt – that is, if he had a t-shirt. But he didn't have time to find props; he'd have to do it on style alone. He planted both feet firmly in the sand and stared at the members of the Motorcycle Mob.

'Nah, you can't change my mind with threats. I'm not just gonna change the rules—' He paused dramatically. 'I'm gonna make up my own—'

Everyone around him gasped as a group. It clearly was the sort of thing that Was Not Done on a beach party planet. But Roger knew there was no backing down, especially where there was a motorcycle gang around. Especially a motorcycle gang that had now all drawn their switch-blades.

Maybe, Roger considered, he had still gone too far.

The other motorcycle members smiled to match Sneer.

It wouldn't do him any good to be this angry, if he was also dead.

Many of their smiles were missing many of their teeth.

But he had gotten out of situations worse than this in the Cineverse.

The gang members picked at their teeth with their knives.

Once again, Roger told himself to think like a movie.

My, they certainly were nice, long, sharp knives.

He swallowed, then finished his sentence.

'—even if it takes riding the Cowabunga-munga to do it!'

And everyone took another step away. Their collective gasp this time held a hint of awe. The knife-wielders paused in their teeth picking, their blades ready to cut through the tension-filled air at any second.

They all knew Roger was proposing a surfing duel.

'That's pretty big talk—' Frankie ventured.

'We've never even seen you surf—' Brian mentioned.

'Yeah, man! Where's your board—' Frankie added.

'And, like, the big wave isn't even coming until tomorrow!' Brian concluded.

'Sounds like some kind of hodaddy excuse to me!' Sneer brandished his blade. 'I say we cut him anyway!'

'Gllffgrrggll!' the Mumbler agreed.

The other gang members all started talking at once.

'Yeah, blood!'

They laughed nastily.

'The girl, too!'

They chuckled disagreeably.

'—carve some initials—'

They guffawed coarsely.

'—real deep tattoos!'

They hooted malevolently.

Roger had had enough of this.

'Dee Dee!' he shouted.

'Tee hee hee!' Dee Dee replied.

'Grab my hand!' Roger instructed.

'Tee hee hee!' was Dee Dee's response.

'Hey, Roger Dodger,' Brian said, 'you don't have to worry about these guys.'

'That's right!' Frankie added. 'Those guys won't be able to do a thing once we start another song!'

'No!' Roger shouted all too vehemently. He might be able to survive a knife cut or two. But Roger knew, if Bix Bale and the Belltones should do so much as twang a guitar string, he would be sucked into this surfing world forever.

He reached into his pocket with his free hand and pulled out the chewing-gum-encased ring. But how could he turn it without letting go of Dee Dee?

'Oh, yeah?' Sneer vituperated. 'None of you can stop us!'

The entire Motorcycle Mob took a collectively threatening step toward Roger and Dee Dee.

Roger pushed the gummed ring against his ring finger. Now, if he could only push the dial around a bit with his thumb. Roger bit his lower lip. His thumb jerked against the ring, almost knocking it from his hand. He managed to close his fist about the ring before it fell, his heart leaping about in his chest. He would have to be much more careful. Especially with the ring broken the way it was, there was no safe way to turn it without using both hands.

'Frrnnnstbblll!' the Mumbler pointed out.

Sneer agreed. 'He's got something in his hand. It looks like he's going to try some funny stuff!'

Then again, Roger, realised that he didn't have to hold Dee Dee for both of them to escape. All that was necessary was for Dee Dee to have a hold on him.

'Dee Dee!' he instructed. 'Put your hand around my waist!'

The beach bunny giggled girlishly.

'Ccrrkkvvbbmmnnzzwwlll!' the Mumbler urged as he drew a ragged breath.

'See?' Sneer elucidated. 'He's going to try some surfer trick!'

'Roger Dodger!' Brian called anxiously. 'Are you *sure* you wouldn't like to hear another song?'

Dee Dee let go of Roger's hand and put her arm around his waist. She stepped close to hug him tight. Roger reached around her as well. Now, if he could just get his free hand on the ring . . .

'Mssgllckllllpssfnnrrwttghjjjssk!' the Mumbler screamed, turning a very nice shade of blue in the process.

Dee Dee giggled in his ear. Roger admitted it: Even in a tense situation like this, it was distracting to hold a bikini-clad woman in your arms when you were trying to use your Captain Crusader Decoder Ring.

'Okay, Boss!' Sneer announced with a jerk of his head. 'Full frontal attack!'

That's when the ring slipped out of Roger's fingers.

'Tee hee hee,' Dee Dee remarked as she deftly caught it.

'Snnrrk!' the Mumbler managed between great, gasping breaths. 'Snnrrk!'

'Cut them now!' Sneer instructed as the mob ran at them through the sand.

What, Roger despaired, could they do? A half-dozen leather-jacketed mobsters were bearing down on them as fast as they could make their way through the sand. Their very sharp knives glittered in the seaside sun.

'See you in the funny papers!' Roger yelled despite everything.

'Tee hee hee,' Dee Dee replied nervously.

The sand was covered with blue smoke.

The smoke cleared. Roger and Dee Dee stood on a suburban street.

'Tee hee—' Dee Dee began nervously. '—tee—' She took a ragged breath. 'Oh, thank the Cineverse! I'm no longer there!'

'Pardon?' Roger replied.

Dee Dee gave Roger's arm a comradely pat as she disengaged herself. 'The beach party world! You've helped me escape. I can't thank you enough. Oh, but we haven't been properly introduced. Doctor Dee Dee Davenport, at your service.' She shook Roger's hand heartily.

Roger thought to close his mouth. Somehow, this woman

seemed almost completely different from the beach beauty he'd so recently hugged on the surfing world.

Dr Davenport glanced down at her psychedelic green bikini. 'Oh, but this is so . . . so . . . *inappropriate*!' She frowned in a determined sort of way. 'It's lucky we materialised right around the corner from the institute.'

She walked forward, her strides long and purposeful. Roger had to run to catch up.

Roger couldn't help but marvel how different this place was from all the other movie worlds he had found himself on. He looked up and down the street at two rows of white tract houses set back from the street by an acre or so of manicured green lawns. Not that there was anything particularly special about this place. But that was it exactly. His surroundings were just so incredibly undistinguished. It could have been almost anywhere, USA. That's exactly what made it so strange.

Any doubts that he was still in the Cineverse were instantly dispelled when he read the street sign on the corner. One sign read 'Anywhere Terrace', the other 'Hometown Lane'. He had fallen into what looked like the ultimate, Mid-American movie world. But what happened on Mid-American movie worlds? Roger had this sudden vision of domestic comedies about the trials of raising sixteen children. He shivered.

'Here we are!' Dr Davenport led him up the driveway of a brick building a bit larger than those around the corner. A large bronze plaque by the door announced that this was 'The Southern California Institute of Very Advanced Science'.

So this must be the institute that Dee Dee – or Dr Davenport, Roger corrected himself – had so recently referred to. Roger admitted it. Once again, he was thoroughly confused. This had become a nagging problem ever since he had first found himself in the Cineverse: How could he ever hope to save anybody if he could never figure out what was going on?

Dr Davenport opened the front door. Roger followed her inside. She pulled a pair of long white lab coats off a rack against one wall, and handed one to Roger. She quickly put the other one on.

She smiled. 'At last! I feel dressed again!'

Roger noticed that the coat had a badge pinned to its plastic pocket pen protector; a badge that read 'DR DAVENPORT'.

'Here,' the doctor instructed, 'put yours on, too. Trust me. It gives you credibility.'

Roger shrugged the coat over his shoulders. The badge on his pocket pen protector read 'GUEST'.

'Come on now,' she said as she once again boldly strode ahead. 'It's time to get to work.' She opened a second door, covered by a sign that read 'RESTRICTED AREA! AUTHORISED PERSONNEL ONLY!'

A security guard looked up as they entered. 'Dr Davenport! Thank goodness you're here!'

'Yes, Smedley,' she replied. 'It feels good to be back.'

'No,' Smedley answered vehemently. 'You don't understand. It's much worse than that. It's the Nucleotron!'

Dee Dee gasped. 'The Nucleotron? But that means—'

Smedley nodded, confirming her worst fears. 'The slime monster is gone!'

A red light began to blink above Smedley's desk. Somewhere in the distance Roger could hear the wail of sirens.

'It's nearing critical mass!' Dr Davenport ran down the hall. 'Quick, Roger! If we don't do something soon, it's going to blow us all to Kingdom Come!'

CHAPTER SIX

'Dread Destination!'

'Bark bark! Yip yip arf!'

The dog's barking somehow rose over the gunfire.

'Yip bark! Arf yip bark!'

The shooting stopped.

Delores wondered if she should risk a look. She and her fellows had all taken refuge behind the large oak table that Zabana, with his jungle-bred reflexes, had tipped to one side in the same instant that the first shot was fired. So far, the wood had taken the brunt of the assault, and Doc had pulled his six-shooters from his deep suitcoat pockets, ready to pay back the villains in kind.

'You'll' – Doctor Dread's voice hesitated menacingly – 'suffer for this!'

Doc peeked around the table's edge, guns at the ready.

'Well, I'll be doggone!' he exclaimed instead.

'Bark yip! Bark yip growl!' the dog replied.

Doc grinned down at his allies. 'You all should take a look at this. It's plumb amusin'.'

Delores cautiously peered out from behind the barricade, ever alert for treachery. Her mouth fell open. She had never expected this.

Everyone, all hundred of Dread's lackeys, seemed frozen in place. And all of them watched the drama unfolding at the very centre of the room. There, flat on his back, was Doctor Dread, with a white German shepherd standing on his chest.

'Yip yip bark!' the dog remarked, its voice somewhat muffled since its teeth had already pierced the material of Dread's snakeskin cowl – the same teeth that were now a fraction of an inch from the villain's neck!

'This is your last chance!' Dread declared one last time. 'Before you are' – his hesitation sounded more uncertain than usual – 'subtracted!'

The shepherd only growled in response. Delores frowned. Where had she seen that dog before?

'All right, now!' a voice called in merrily through the now open door. 'What's all the ruckus?'

'Yip yip!' the dog replied. 'Bark bark yip!'

'Why,' said the voice from the door, 'it almost sounds like the little fella's talkin' ' A rotund, white-haired police officer with a twinkle in his eye stepped into the bar.

'Officer O'Clanrahan!' Big Louie shouted.

'The very same, boyo,' the policeman acknowledged, broadly winking at one and all. 'And I've brought my special helper along, too.'

The shepherd wagged his tail as the policeman approached.

'That Dwight the Wonder Dog!' Zabana exclaimed in astonishment.

'Right you are, big fella,' O'Clanrahan agreed. 'Everybody knows Dwight the Wonder Dog.'

They did? Delores frowned again. Then why didn't she? Maybe she had been spending too much time in hero school. Still, even she had thought the dog looked familiar.

'Yip bark arf!' Dwight agreed as O'Clanrahan leaned down to scratch him behind the ears.

But the shepherd had relaxed his vigilance. It was only for a fraction of a second, but it was a fraction too much. Dread shifted and rolled, and Dwight lost his footing. The dog had to scamper back half a dozen feet as Dread scrambled to his feet, and Officer O'Clanrahan found himself staring into the business end of Big Bertha's roscoe.

'Faith and begorah!' the policeman whispered.

'Yip yip arf!' Dwight barked apologetically. 'Yip yip yip!'

'Yeah, boy,' Louie replied. 'It just might work.'

Doctor Dread laughed, a sound to chill both flesh and bone. 'Things seem to have – changed, don't they?' He glanced around at his hundred mobsters. 'Now, who do you suppose we should – erase first?'

The dog and Officer O'Clanrahan neatly split the largest number of votes. But Big Bertha had other ideas.

'Kill her.' She waved her piece at Delores. 'She's the ringleader. Without her, the others are lost.'

'Such language!' Dread reprimanded. 'Still, there is a certain – logic in proposing Delores' – removal.'

That's when Big Louie screamed.

Dwight jumped up on to his hind legs.

'He's walking backwards!' one of the gang members observed as the dog approached the leering Dread.

The shepherd whined suddenly and flopped to the ground.

'He's rolling over,' another gangster commented.

'Fools!' Dread began. 'Don't you—'

But, before the villain could even hesitate meaningfully, Dwight had rolled over on his back, all four paws in the air and head to one side.

'He's playing dead!' one of the evil band exclaimed.

'Oh, how life-like!' another enthused.

'—realise,' Dread continued, '– this is but a clever –' He paused tellingly.

'Now!' Louie shouted.

Dwight's still snout suddenly snapped around the archfiend's leg. Uttering a cry equally divided between surprise and pain, Dread once again toppled to the ground.

Doc shot the roscoe from Big Bertha's hand, then trained both his six-shooters on the horizontal mastermind.

Dread's groan held a particularly sinister edge. He slowly turned his head to stare malevolently at Delores and her cohorts. His words were even slower and more fraught with meaning than usual:

'You don't expect to escape – unavenged.'

There was a moment of uncomfortable silence. It was true, Delores thought. They had won the battle. But what good would it do them if they could never get out of Joe's Bar?

'Yip yip! Bark bark bark!' Dwight announced.

'Of course not,' Louie added as he smiled at Dread. 'The Doctor won't be able to avenge anything. Dread is coming with us.'

The bad guys snarled collectively.

'Try anything,' Doc drawled, 'and I'll show you why I won two blue ribbons at the Wild West Territorial Fair.'

'Two blue ribbons?' Big Bertha's voice held a grudging respect.

'Well, only one of them was for shootin',' Doc admitted. 'More than that would have been redundant. Got the other one for cannin'.'

'Canning?' Big Louie asked.

Doc nodded. 'Best dandelion preserves North-west of the Pecos.'

'What if I' – Dread paused with great import – 'refused?'

Dwight growled, his teeth snapping shut a fraction of an inch from the villain's throat.

'Whatever you say,' the villain allowed. 'I mean, perhaps it is time for a' – Dread halted uncertainly – 'change of scene.'

At the dog's urging, the criminal mastermind got to his hands and knees and crawled quickly from the bar, surrounded by Delores, Louie, Zabana, Officer O'Clanrahan, Dwight and Doc. Further interference from Dread's henchpeople was discouraged by two six-guns, a police special, and a strong set of canine teeth, all aimed at their leader.

The door slammed shut behind them, and they were out on the street, in the eternal night.

Delores looked admiringly at Big Louie. 'You got us out of there.'

Louie blushed. 'Well, it wasn't me, exactly.'

'Don't be so bashful. I didn't know you had it in you.' She gave the sidekick a hearty pat on the back.

'I don't,' Louie admitted. 'It was Dwight.'

'The dog?' Delores asked, not quite comprehending.

'Bark bark. Yip bark bark,' Dwight replied.

'Beg pardon, missy,' Doc interrupted. 'But it might be better to do our congratulatin' later. We have a bar full of angry fellas behind us here.'

'Right you are, boyo!' Officer O'Clanrahan agreed as angry shouts accompanied the sounds of stomping feet from within the bar. 'Leave it to a local. I know every back way there is hereabouts.' He pointed to an alley-way across the street. 'Down there! Quickly!'

Delores frowned at the still crouched Doctor Dread. 'Zabana? Would you mind carrying our reluctant guest?'

Dread looked up angrily from his crouch, as if he might hesitate meaningfully in obeying Delores' orders. However, the close combined proximity of dog fang and jungle muscle kept the villain's complaints to a subverbal level as Zabana lifted him with a single hand.

'Jungle prince at your service!' Zabana announced as he hoisted the snakeskin-suited miscreant over his head.

'Good enough,' Delores agreed. 'Let's get out of here!'

They followed Officer O'Clanrahan and Dwight into the alley. It was very dark. Where harsh white light seemed to be everywhere on the night-time streets, here it pooled every fifty feet or so beneath pitifully dim bulbs set high up on the brick walls, leaving the spaces in between totally devoid of illumination. Dwight barked occasionally to let the rest of them know that he and Officer O'Clanrahan were still in the lead. But Delores didn't like walking into the utter darkness. It was like stepping into the void, a place beyond the Cineverse, where there were no more movie worlds, where there was nothing – except nothingness. She had a sudden, chilling thought: If the Change changed everything again, would this be the final result? Would the Cineverse itself cease to exist?

Delores forced herself to breathe regularly, and to keep on walking. She had to admit it. There was only one reason for her thoughts to wander to such depressing extremes. She was still jumpy from her last confrontation in the dark. It was a foolish fear. There wasn't going to be a slime creature waiting for her in every dark place she ever walked into. There couldn't be.

'I've been waiting for you,' the deep voice moaned out of the darkness.

Delores only jumped a little bit. After all, she had been expecting this.

'I guess that you have not been waiting for me,' the voice said dolefully. 'I realise that, at first, the thought of me might be repulsive, nauseating, malodorous, and likely to cause people of a gentle constitution to lose their lunches. But I can be patient. Believe me,' the creature sighed soulfully, 'I do grow on people. I have to – it's the fungus in the slime.'

'Oh, no!' Dread exclaimed from where Zabana carried him over one jungle prince shoulder. 'It's not— It's not—'

'It is,' the Slime Monster reassured him.

Dread screamed.

'He faint,' Zabana remarked. 'Dead weight on shoulder.'

'Such is the memory of slime,' the Monster commented.

'Now, see here!' Delores demanded. 'We have no time for this!' Her patience was at an end. Not only was this monster threatening them, but Big Bertha and the many minions could find them at any minute! Delores hesitated before she spoke again, but realised she had to ask it, even though she knew she didn't want to hear the answer.

'What do you want?'

'I want to give you a choice,' the voice said calmly. 'You may come with me, and live with me in eternal, if somewhat messy, bliss. So I am mildly radioactive. So what? Why can't I be loved?'

The creature lapsed into a gloomy silence.

'Or?' Delores prompted after a moment.

'Or,' the Monster sadly continued. 'I will be forced to drown you and your fellows in a suffocating wall of slime. You see, we monsters are not accustomed to taking "no" for an answer.'

The voice in the darkness paused, waiting for an answer Delores could not give.

The tension was broken by a voice calling out in a happy Irish brogue:

'Hey, there, boyos! We were almost to the station house when we realised you weren't taggin' along behind. What's takin' so long?'

'Bark bark!' Dwight warned. 'Yip bark arf!'

'Say,' the Slime Monster asked, 'isn't that Dwight the Wonder Dog?'

'Everybody knows Dwight the Wonder Dog!' Officer O'Clanrahan agreed.

'It would be a shame,' the Monster replied, 'if Dwight the Wonder Dog had to be covered by slime.'

'Bark growl!' Dwight replied. 'Growl growl arf!'

'Yeah, fella,' Louie agreed. 'But might'nt that be a little dangerous?'

The dog had no chance to answer, for, at that moment, Big Bertha's voice shouted down the alley-way.

'I can hear them up there somewhere. Has everybody got their guns?'

Far too many voices shouted affirmatively.

'How about the bazookas? The flame throwers? The anti-tank weapons?' Bertha chuckled as other voices yelled their assent. 'This time, we're ready for them!'

Two hundred pounding feet echoed down the alley-way.

'You must go,' the Monster's voice spoke from the darkness. 'I will stop them.'

'Go?' Delores asked in surprise. 'All of us?'

'All of you,' the Monster agreed. 'I sometimes have trouble controlling the direction of my slime.'

'What do you say, missy?' Doc asked. 'I say we're gone. Thanks a lot, big fella!'

'Think nothing of it,' the Monster replied. 'I always save those things that are mine.'

Delores and the others hurried down the alley-way, with Dwight the Wonder Dog leading the way. Behind them, Delores could hear gunfire mixed with shrieks of nausea and disgust, and the ever-present sloshing of heavy liquid.

They paused beneath one of the too-dim lights.

'Where now?' Delores asked as she repressed a shudder.

'Isn't it obvious, young miss?' Officer O'Clanrahan replied. 'Doctor Dread has broken every law ever written in this city. I say we should take this felon to the station, and book him!'

'Bark yip bark!' Dwight interjected. 'Arf arf arf!'

'The dog's right,' Louie agreed. 'This isn't a matter of law and order for a single city, or a single world. This concerns the entire future of the Cineverse!'

'The *dog's* right?' Delores asked in disbelief.

'Arf arf bark!' Dwight added. 'Bark bark arf bark!'

'It's a good point,' Louie mused. 'No jail could hold Dread against the force of his minions. But what if we don't put him in jail here? What if we take him to someplace else altogether?'

'Bark yip arf!' Dwight chorused.

'My thought exactly,' Louie agreed.

'Eh?' Dread murmured from his resting place on Zabana's shoulder. 'No, mother, don't take my teddy—' He blinked. 'Where am I? What happened?' He blinked again, a distasteful frown crossing his countenance. 'Slime.'

'But that's all behind you now,' Doc assured the supervillain. 'You're too important to us to leave with a monster.'

'That's very – reassuring,' Dread managed. 'Not that you'll get – anything from me!'

'You call that gratitude?' Zabana asked. 'Maybe we take him back to monster!'

'Well,' Dread added hurriedly, 'I suppose it would do no – harm if I revealed a facet or two of my – master plan. It is too – late for you to stop me anyway. My plan is moving even – faster than I had hoped, thanks in part to those – extra rings we received from a – former friend of yours.'

Extra rings? Former friend? Could Dread be talking about Roger? Delores swore, if that villain had done anything to that sweet man of hers, he would pay.

'I think you will tell us more than that,' Louie remarked casually.

'And why do you feel that – little man?' Dread leered. 'Do you think to frighten me again? I – assure you, my recent actions were nothing but a momentary – aberration. Now that I have my wits about me, I can truly pledge that I am afraid of – nothing.'

'Yip bark yip!' Dwight yapped up at the villain.

'I think so too,' Louie said. 'It's time to get out of here. If Delores would be so good as to hand me the ring?'

Delores did as she was asked. This, then, must be what Louie had planned all along.

'Whoever's coming, hold on!' Louie instructed. 'See you in the funny papers!'

The usual occurred.

When the smoke cleared, Delores gasped.

Never, in her wildest imagination, had she thought the sidekick would bring them here. Was Louie out of his mind?

Doctor Dread started to scream.

CHAPTER SEVEN

'Return of Flaming Death!'

'Aaoogah!' the sirens wailed. 'Aaoogah!'

'Quick, Roger!' Doctor Davenport shouted over her shoulder. 'We must get to the main computer!'

Roger nodded as he ran after her through the endless white corridors. Each door they passed was posted with a large, neatly lettered sign: 'MISSILE ASSEMBLY': 'FOURTH DIMENSION LAB'; 'ROCKET TESTING STRIP'; 'ANTI-MATTER GENERATOR'. Roger really didn't know what help he could be. What did he know about computers – especially the kind in fifties' monster movies, with all those tape reels and flashing lights? Heck, he had his own desktop computer model at work, and, beside the word processing program, he never could figure out how to do *anything* on it.

Still, he had survived worse things in the Cineverse than computer illiteracy. He followed Dee Dee through an opaque glass door marked 'MAIN COMPUTER'.

The room was filled, floor to ceiling, with all sorts of metal hardware. Every inch of space was crammed with gauges, dials, switches, tape reels, and yards and yards of flashing lights, all of it gleaming dully beneath the overhead fluorescents. The sirens were even louder in here. A short, stocky man in a white lab coat ran back and forth across the room, punching a button here, throwing a switch there. All his efforts had no discernible effect. The sirens continued to wail.

'Professor MacPhee!' Dr Davenport called over the incessant 'Aaoogahs'. 'What's wrong?'

The professor spun to face the newcomers. His round face, neatly bisected by a severely trimmed moustache, nodded distractedly at Dr Davenport.

'What's wrong?' He laughed harshly. 'What isn't wrong?' He waved at the bank of lights to his left. 'I guess I realised something was amiss when I first noticed we were getting the Ittelson Effect on our Boatner board!'

'Aaoogah, aaoogah!' went the sirens. Red lights flashed on one wall, green lights on another.

'I see,' Davenport replied. 'But did you try—'

'The Carver switch?' MacPhee nodded unhappily. 'It's the first thing I thought of, what with the possibility of reversed ampedance in the Aldridge circuits. But, when all the polarities checked out negative, I was forced to do a reading on the Bollesometer.'

'That only made sense,' Davenport agreed. 'It's a central concern of Young's theorem—'

'Yes, but the reading was totally in the red zone!' MacPhee replied hoarsely.

'Over one thousand Bolles per second?' the doctor asked incredulously.

MacPhee nodded. 'I'm afraid we're going to prove Young's theorem by blowing up the Institute.' Yellow lights flashed on the computer's upper reaches, while white lights blinked near the floor.

'Aaoogah!' the sirens reminded them. 'Aaoogah!'

'Not necessarily!' Dee Dee disagreed. 'You remember the work done by Dr Nordstrom of Helsinki—'

'But that's even more highly theoretical than Professor Young's work!' MacPhee objected.

Dr Davenport looked at both MacPhee and Roger, her jaw set very stern and square. 'Well, I think we're going to prove both of those theorems now, one way or the other. Are you men with me?'

Both men hastily agreed. Roger, as usual, had no idea what was really happening, but in this particular case he decided that ignorance might be preferable.

'Aaoogah! Aaoogah!' the sirens screamed. Blue lights rippled across the computer's midsection, criss-crossing the orange lights that flickered around the tape reels.

'Then let's get to work,' Davenport commanded. 'Once we get the Bolles vibrations down to an acceptable level—'

'Under 120?' MacPhee asked.

'It'll probably be safe at 150, but we'll get it down below 100 if we can.' She slapped both men on the back. 'Roger, you'll have to set the Carver switch to 3.6. That's the most the system can take after we've reversed the Aldridge nodules. And when I say "now" slowly pull the lever down to zero. Professor MacPhee? It's up to you to man the Fernstetter.'

'But that means—' the professor began.

Davenport cut him off abruptly. 'That I'll have to override the Roberts' Drive? Somebody's got to do it, and, after all, I'm the one who built this baby.' She nodded to both of them one final time. 'Of course, I don't have to tell either of you the consequences of failure.'

'I know,' MacPhee replied, his voice barely above a whisper. 'Total Bowkerization.'

'To your stations,' Dee Dee ordered.

Roger was about to ask where and what a Carver switch was when he saw the large cardboard sign to his left with four-inch high letters:

'CARVER SWITCH.'

He walked quickly over to the sign and set the knob beneath it to 3.6. MacPhee, in the meantime, had grabbed a steering wheel beneath a sign that read 'FERNSTETTER'.

Doctor Dee Dee Davenport was on the far side of the room, rapidly punching buttons. Above her head was a large half-circle meter with a sign that read 'BOLLESOMETER'. The indicator in the meter was well into the red zone; over a thousand Bolles!

But the thin hand of the meter was starting to fall, edging from red to white.

'Aaoogah! Aaoogah!' the sirens reminded them. The red flashing lights turned to green, but the blinking green lights changed to red.

That's when the room began to shake. Roger looked up from the trembling switch he still held with his sweating palm. Should this be happening? The Bollesometer was reading less than 300!

Dr Davenport was nonplussed. 'Professor! Double the ratio! And Roger, start turning that dial – NOW!'

The vibrations became even worse, as if the computer control room was at the centre of an earthquake. Roger's hand was so damp with sweat that it almost slipped off the knob. But he gripped the Carver Switch with all his might, blinking back the perspiration that fell into his eyes, doing his best to make sure the dial continued its slow, steady descent.

'Now, professor!' the doctor ordered. 'Go to maximum thrust!'

The Fernstetter made a high, whining sound as MacPhee pressed down on the steering column. Roger took a deep breath and turned the Carver Switch as far as it would go, all the way to zero.

'Aaoogh.' The sirens stopped abruptly. The Fernstetter

powered down immediately as well. There was no sound in the room, save for the quiet hiss of rolling tape, the occasional pleasant beeping that accompanied some of the more special lights, and the ragged breathing of the three survivors.

'Gentlemen,' Dr Davenport announced. 'We've saved the Nucleotron.'

'Thank goodness you were here, Doctor!' MacPhee enthused. 'I couldn't have done it by myself.'

'Of course not,' Davenport agreed. 'But what exactly did happen?'

Professor MacPhee bristled at the very thought.

'You know what they would have said if we had failed? "There are certain things that man was not meant to know." '

'Yes, but we did not fail,' Davenport cajoled. 'Although I do understand that the Slime Monster has broken loose?'

'And "A scientist should not tempt forces beyond his control!" ' MacPhee insisted.

'Yes, but, those forces remained within our control,' Davenport said patiently. 'Now, about the Slime Monster?'

'Perhaps,' MacPhee continued, becoming even more infuriated, 'even that "we should have thought twice before tampering with the very fabric of the cosmos". ' His fingers curled into fists as he looked wildly about the computer room. 'Simple-minded fools! Whatever we do, we do for science!'

'Yes, certainly, you'll get no argument on that. But how did the Slime Monster get loose?'

'Oh, that,' MacPhee replied, making a visible effort to calm himself. 'I'm not too sure—'

Roger frowned. There was something about this fellow that he didn't quite trust. Perhaps it was his agitated manner, always jumping from object to object, or topic to topic. Perhaps it was the way he looked through Roger, as if the latter wasn't even there. Or perhaps it was that MacPhee sported a pencil-thin moustache.

Roger knew that he shouldn't judge people on appearance, even in the Cineverse. Simply because both Doctor Dread and Menge the Merciless had pencil-thin moustaches was no reason to condemn MacPhee out of hand. The significance of the well-manicured moustache in a fifties' monster world was probably entirely different than its meaning in, say, a forties' crime setting. Still, the associations the facial hair brought up within Roger were, to say the least, unsettling.

'Well, what did your instruments tell you?' Davenport prompted.

'Well, I did mention the Boatner board and the Ittelson effect,' MacPhee said defensively.

'Yes, certainly,' Davenport replied, her tone suddenly changing. 'Surely something like that must have been at fault. I'm sorry, professor. You must be awfully tired from your recent ordeal. Why don't you take a break? Roger and I can watch the computer room for a while.'

'Do you think so?' MacPhee asked in obvious relief. 'Well, I could use a breather. If you'll excuse me?'

And with that, he was gone.

'I think we could all use a rest,' Dr Davenport admitted. 'A lot has happened to us in the past few minutes.'

Roger studied the scientist standing beside him. He wondered if he should ask the obvious question that had sat in his brain ever since they had escaped the sand and surf.

'You're probably wondering,' Dr Davenport said after a moment's silence, 'how I could be two such different people on two different worlds. It's one of the secrets of the Cineverse, and one of the things we study at this Institute of Very Advanced Science. Still, it's painful to think of what I had become. I shall never be able to hear a giggle again without shivering.'

She paused to fish in the pockets of her lab coat, finally pulling out a crumpled pack of cigarettes. 'Still, Dr Davenport and beach bunny Dee Dee are one and the same.'

She shook a cigarette free and stuck it in the corner of her mouth, then offered the pack to Roger. He politely refused. She fished in the pockets again and found a slim, rectangular lighter. 'As I said, it is one of the secrets of the Cineverse – and one we were pursuing at the Institute! There are certain worlds, we have found, where you will find yourself in immediate danger; there are other worlds that you or I might consider paradise. But for every single person in the Cineverse, it seems, there is a special world – a world where that man or woman belongs all too much.' She paused to light the cigarette. She took a long, nervous drag, then blew the smoke towards the ceiling. 'Oh, how I remember that sand and surf and sun, and that relentless surfing beat! Part of me wants to go back there even now. More than that. Part of me *needs* to go back there.' She stared down at the burning end of her cigarette for an instant before going on. 'It was like an addiction. I was—' She cleared her throat. 'I *am* a beachaholic!'

'A beachaholic?'

Dr Davenport puffed on her cigarette for a moment, her eyes

focused somewhere far away, perhaps on a place where summer never ended. 'It was a pleasant enough life, I guess. If you hadn't rescued me, I would have wanted nothing more for the rest of my sun-bathing, go-go dancing days.' She shivered and looked around for an ashtray.

'I'll always have to live with that, you know – the fact that, on some level, that was the world where I belonged. It's difficult, sometimes, to confront your true self; to look in the mirror and see a blonde beach bunny in a bikini. My mind wants to test the limits of science, but my body and soul wish to frug throughout eternity!'

She found the ashtray on a small shelf immediately below the Carver Switch. She flicked off the ash, then stubbed out the cigarette. 'Ironically, that was one of the subjects we were studying here at the Institute – the hidden relationships between personality type and movie world. As highly theoretical as all this was, we'd even come up with a name for it – Movie Magic.'

'Movie Magic?' Roger repeated, despite himself. He remembered Louie's stories, and his own experiences, with this primal force of the Cineverse. But could there really be a scientific explanation for all of this?

Dr Davenport clapped her fist into her open palm. 'There's so much about the Cineverse that we still don't know!' She looked down at her closed fist and laughed ruefully. 'I had no idea, when I went to search for the origins of the Slime Monster, that I would stumble into my own personal experiment!'

She looked around the room. The whirring, blinking and clicking of the great computer seemed to calm her. 'But all that's behind me now. I can return to my work, guiding research here at the Institute. What do you think of our computer? It's the very latest design; it can compute complex mathematical equations in mere seconds. And that's only the beginning! Someday, computers will manage many of the mundane aspects of our everyday existence, leaving mankind free to pursue loftier goals. Of course, those computers will have to be much larger than our prototype here, taking up whole city blocks – but I digress.'

She leaned closer to Roger, frown lines etched deep into her tanned forehead. 'What is your opinion of Professor MacPhee?'

Roger was a bit taken aback. Did Dr Davenport also distrust the man with the pencil-thin moustache? He wondered how candid he could be concerning an employee of this Institute that he didn't even know. He decided, after a few seconds' thought, to act in the best public relations tradition, with the exact proper mixture of honesty and politeness:

'He did seem a bit evasive.'

'I thought so, too,' the doctor agreed. 'Especially since I can't see how the monster's escape could have possibly affected the Boatner board. Still, I have been away from the Institute for quite some time. Perhaps there are changes here that I am not yet aware of.' She paused, her voice taking on a wistful edge. 'There were other reasons for me going on that ill-advised field trip, you know. I also hoped, somehow, to find my father, the brilliant scientist who founded this Institute.'

She paused, her eyes again focused somewhere far away. 'One day, when all this strangeness first began, he came to me and said something very odd, just before he disappeared in a puff of blue smoke. I never saw him again after that moment.'

'Something odd?' Roger asked, telling himself to stay calm. But what if both of them were looking for the same thing? 'If it's not too personal, could you tell me what it was?'

'I wrote it down,' she said as she fished inside her plastic pocket pen protector, 'so I wouldn't forget it.' She pulled out a well-creased piece of paper and unfolded it. 'Here it is. There were two separate thoughts. The first one makes some sense. The second one, though—'

'May I?' Roger asked, holding out his hand.

She passed the paper to him. His heart raced as he read the neatly printed words:

1. SCIENCE IS THE CORNERSTONE OF TOMORROW'S SOCIETY.

2. ROUGHAGE IS YOUR STOMACH'S BEST FRIEND.

Roger recognised the tone of these messages. After all, he'd seen them spelled out in secret code on a thousand cereal boxes. This could mean only one thing.

'Roger?' Dr Davenport asked as she studied the look on his face. 'Is it that terrible?'

'Oh, no, not at all.' He tried to smile reassuringly as he handed the paper back to her. 'It's just that I've seen messages like these before. I think your father may have had a – how can I put it? – a secret identity.'

The doctor did not seem reassured. 'What do you mean?'

'Have you ever heard of – Captain Crusader?' Roger asked gently.

She nodded distractedly. 'Why, of course. Every school child in the Cineverse has. But I had always considered him a legend. I had certainly never seen any hard scientific evidence of his existence.'

Roger smiled at that; it only made sense. 'I'm sure that's the way your father wanted it. He could use this world, and the Institute that he founded on it, as a safe retreat from his battles in more violent realms of the Cineverse. And he could use the resources of this establishment of Very Advanced Science to perform the crime fighting research he needed for his cause. The more I think of it, the more I'm certain.' He allowed his smile to widen to a grin as he announced: 'Dr Davenport, your father is Captain Crusader.'

'My mother always thought highly of him,' Dee Dee agreed, still a bit uncertain. 'Yet, it is a bit of a shock, finding out your father is a hero among heroes.' She looked again at the unfolded paper in her hand. 'Of course, it would go a long way towards explaining the blue smoke.'

Roger shook his head. 'What a coincidence that I should rescue the daughter of Captain Crusader! Unless it isn't a coincidence at all. I can't help but feel that everything that has been happening around me, perhaps around all of us, is somehow interconnected. If only I could figure out how – or why.'

'It's interesting you should make that point,' Dr Davenport agreed. 'It's one of the main fields of research that we at the Institute of Very Advanced Science have put our resources behind. Why, did you know that, before my father disappeared in a cloud of blue smoke, we weren't even certain of the existence of the Cineverse? Oh, we knew about it from folk tales, and there was the occasional report of blue smoke, although our armed forces liked to dismiss those sightings, saying they were either swamp gas or weather balloons.'

'I suppose I should have given this back to you already.' She reached in the pocket of her lab coat and pulled out Roger's ring. 'You know, we had to design one of those things ourselves, from scratch. Here – I'll show you the results.' She walked over to one of the control consoles and flicked a switch. 'Look up at that television screen.'

A panel slid aside high on one of the metal walls to reveal what Roger thought of as a video monitor. The screen showed a blurred, circular image. Dee Dee twisted a pair of knobs on the controls. The image came into focus. It was a Captain Crusader Decoder Ring!

'You can see the problems we had,' she explained as she looked down at Roger's ring, still in her hand. 'I suppose it was rather like

trying to reconstruct an extinct animal from its fossil remains.'
She pointed back to the television. 'See, we thought it should be
made in one continuous piece, not broken in four. And we completely missed the concept of chewing gum as an adhesive!'

Roger cleared his throat, and attempted to explain that his ring
was not in perfect working order. As a part of his explanation,
he managed to fill her in on much of what had happened to him
during his adventures in the Cineverse. Occasionally, she would
interject a comment to determine if she fully understood Roger,
usually words and short phrases such as 'Sidekicks?', 'Nut
Crunchies?' or 'The Secret Samoan?' But for the most part, she
only listened politely.

'So you see,' Roger concluded, 'that's how it happened in a
nutshell.'

'Now I see what you mean when you say all you've been
through is more than coincidence,' was her reply. 'Certainly the
plans of this so-called Doctor Dread suggest there exists some sort
of master plan, if only because that is the plan Doctor Dread is
attempting to subvert. And your part in it seems assured by the
fact that Dread sent one of his assistants to eliminate you.' She
paused, and her eyes wandered to the Fernstetter. 'I wonder if
Dread has sent assistants to sabotage any other part of the
Cineverse.'

Roger followed her gaze. He remembered who had most
recently driven the Fernstetter; the same man who had been alone
in this room when the Nucleotron had gone out of control! 'Do
you mean—'

'I'm afraid I do,' she agreed. 'I don't think the Slime Monster
escaped. I think he was released. And I think someone caused a
crisis in the Nucleotron to cover his actions!'

'How clever of you!' a voice called from the doorway. 'How
fortunate that I decided to stay within earshot of your conversation.'

'Professor MacPhee!' Dr Davenport exclaimed.

The professor stepped into the room, his silver revolver pointed
at them both.

'Or so I have been called around here,' MacPhee allowed with
the slightest hint of a smile. 'But I am sometimes known by
another name. Perhaps you've heard of – the Insidious Professor
Peril!'

'Professor Peril!' Roger knew that name all too well. Not that he
had seen him time and again, as he had with Menge the Merciless.

No, but Roger remembered the name from a dozen articles in those nostalgia magazines he used to read about really obscure, grade Z films; articles complete with stills of the professor with Mort, the killer robot, or Diablo, the gorilla with the mind of a man! Oh, if only Roger had been better versed in minor, extremely low budget action serials!

'Yes,' the poverty row fiend continued. 'I was sent here by Doctor Dread, to make certain that the Institute did not interfere with his plans! Now that you have discovered my true purpose, of course, I am afraid that you will have to be eliminated. But I am not one to talk. I am one to act! If you will come with me?' His pencil-thin moustache twitched as he waved his gun towards the door.

He followed them out into the hall. 'If you would please keep on moving. Now, let's see. That's one of the nice things about the Institute. There's so many handy ways to die. Ah, the very place! I think that even Doctor Dread would appreciate the drama of this.'

He opened the door marked 'ROCKET TESTING GROUND'.

'Now, if you would precede me?'

Roger and Dee Dee stepped out into what appeared to be a very large back yard. There, stretching away from him, as far as Roger could see, were rockets of all shapes and sizes, in all stages of assembly.

Professor Peril glanced around the yard. 'Ah, yes. I think this large one over here will do quite nicely. And how providentially coincidental that the workmen have left this large quantity of steel cable lying about. How ideal for tying the two of you to the instrument of your death.'

He instructed his two victims to stand against the rocket, which was bright red and sitting on its side atop a railroad car that in turn sat on a set of tracks.

'Now, to properly secure you,' Peril continued matter-of-factly. 'To do this, I will, of course, have to put my gun between my teeth. I feel it only fair to warn you, however, that I am an excellent shot with my tongue.'

No-nonsense villain that he was, Peril had both of them tied securely to the rocket in a matter of seconds.

'Now, I merely have to press the start button on this nearby control board, and the rocket engines will fire. Not that you're taking off anywhere – oh no. The rocket will instead speed down the tracks to a target a mile or so distant, a concrete wall of sufficient thickness to detonate the warhead mounted atop your very last ride. You will, of course, be instantly incinerated at some thousands of degrees, a temperature so hot that there will be no remains to be identified. And now, I must be going. I'd chat with you longer, but I haven't time.'

The professor trotted over to the nearby control board and pressed the button beneath the large sign that read 'START'. He didn't even wave as he walked smartly back into the Institute.

'Roger?' Dr Davenport called from where she was tied beside him. 'What can we do?'

Roger looked about wildly. Wait a moment! They were not alone. While the rocket testing grounds stretched out before them, they were bordered on the right by the backyards of the suburban houses on the adjacent street.

There, not twenty yards distant, two men and one woman stared at them over a white picket fence. The men wore grey flannel suits, the woman a starched white blouse and full navy skirt covered by a gingham apron.

'Excuse me?' Roger called. 'You there?'

The rockets grumbled to life beneath them.

'There are certain things that man was not meant to know,' the first fellow commented to the others.

'We could use some help!' Roger added.

The first flickers of flame erupted beneath Roger's feet.

'Indeed,' the second agreed. 'Scientists should never experiment with forces beyond their control.'

'Are you just going to stand there?' Roger asked in desperation. The rocket began rolling down the tracks.

The woman sighed as she glanced at her fellows. 'They should have thought twice before tampering with the very fabric of the cosmos.'

And with a great roar, the rocket picked up speed, carrying Roger and Dee Dee straight towards the concrete wall.

'Do you think,' the woman added as an afterthought, 'it would do any good to complain about the noise?'

They would be burned alive in a matter of seconds. There was only one chance.

'Do you still have the ring?' he called out over the rocket's roar.

'Oh, yes!' Dr Davenport shouted back. 'It's still in my pocket!'

'Use it!' Roger yelled.

The wind whistled past their ears.

'Well –' she grunted, '– if I can get it—'

Roger felt himself being flattened against the rocket's metal hull. He forced his head up, so that he could look past the rocket's nose. There, in the distance, but approaching all too rapidly, was a long, grey wall.

They were surrounded by blue smoke.

An instant later, the rocket motors choked off abruptly, replaced by the sound of crashing waves.

'See, I told you they'd come back!' a voice shouted triumphantly.

The smoke cleared, and they were surrounded by sun, and sand, and surf.

'Oh, yeah?' Sneer rebutted before the Mad Mumbler could say anything. 'Well, this time, they're never going to leave – ever!'

Back on the surfing world? How could this be?

'Oh, no!' Roger shouted from where he was still strapped to the now sand-covered rocket. 'Dr Davenport! What should we do?'

'Tee hee hee,' Dr Davenport replied.

CHAPTER EIGHT

'Animated Assault!'

'Jumpin' Jehosaphat!' Doc exclaimed. 'Where in tarnation are we?'

'Trust me,' Big Louie said reassuringly. 'This is where we want to be.'

'No!' Doctor Dread shrieked. 'Anywhere but here!'

'It not look real,' Zabana remarked. 'It look – drawn.'

'Exactly,' Delores whispered. They were in the middle of a forest somewhere, but no forest that they had ever seen before. Zabana was right. It was as if they had stepped into the middle of a drawing, with the texture of grass and leaves and the bark of trees suggested by pen strokes, all filled in by colours much too bright to come from nature. And it was worse than that. She looked at all her fellows, then down at her own hands, solid fleshtones now outlined by deep black borders. Not only had their surroundings changed, but they had changed as well.

'We've come to an animated world,' she announced. 'And we ourselves are animated!'

'Bark bark yip arf!' the newly drawn Dwight the Wonder Dog suggested.

'Actually,' Louie translated, 'Dwight thinks we're rotoscoped.'

'Look!' a high voice called from somewhere out among the trees. 'We've got visitors!'

'No!' Doctor Dread screamed as he struggled futilely in the grip of the jungle prince. 'Not them! Anything but them!'

Something small and brown and fluffy jumped from behind a bush.

'It bunny rabbit!' Zabana exclaimed.

'How cute!' Delores added, unable to help herself.

'How terrible!' Dread interjected as he stopped struggling and started to shake. 'This can't be happening!'

The newcomer wriggled its nose in Dread's direction, then

spoke in that same high, clear voice that had come from the trees. 'And not just any bunny rabbit. My name's Bigears. I'm the leader of the pack.' The rabbit waved an adorable pink paw. 'Say, isn't that Dwight the Wonder Dog?'

'Bark bark, yip!' Dwight answered cheerfully.

'Everybody knows Dwight the Wonder Dog!' Officer O'Clanrahan added animatedly.

'Urk—' Dread grimaced as if in pain.

'Hey, maybe some of my buddies would like to meet Dwight the Wonder Dog,' Bigears suggested. 'What do you say, guys?'

'There even more bunnies?' Zabana enquired.

'Hey, there's rabbits all over the place,' Bigears replied proudly. 'You've landed in Bunnyland!'

'Gork—' Dread looked as if he might lose his lunch.

Another pair of bunnies, one grey, one white, came hopping out of the woods.

'Here's a couple of my pals,' Bigears explained. 'Meet Pinknose' – the white rabbit took a hop in their direction – 'and Fluffytail!' The grey rabbit followed suit.

'Gurp!' Dread seemed to be having some sort of spasm.

'Wow,' Delores replied, unable to keep the wonder from her voice. 'All these bunnies. Is this where – Thumper lives?'

'Nah,' the first bunny said deprecatingly. 'He's got a contract with another studio. Got a swelled head, won't even write to his old buddies. We've still got some of his relatives, though.' He raised his voice to call back to the bushes. 'Hey, is Thumper's cousin around here somewhere?'

'Sure!' a much deeper voice answered. 'Be right dere!'

The ground shook as the bushes parted.

'Grork!' Dread remarked. All the rest of the newcomers, Dwight included, gasped collectively as a very, very large rabbit stepped out into the clearing. This newest bunny had regular black and white spots all over its body. However, the most outstanding thing about the latest rabbit was that it stood some six feet six inches tall.

'Dey call me Bouncer,' the very large rabbit announced.

'I can – hold it – no longer!' Dread managed between gritted teeth. 'Gleep! Nerp! Gibber!'

The supervillain threw his arms in the air, then fell to his knees. His head jerked back, his shoulders forward. His hands twitched, then his feet, followed by his eyebrows and his ears. His snakeskin cowl fell away from his head, and his slicked-back hair stood straight up from his scalp. His eyes rolled rapidly about in their sockets, as his tongue darted in and out of his mouth. There was also smoke coming from his nostrils and inner ears.

That was only the beginning. Everything that was happening to Dread started to happen faster. One moment, he was a mass of twitches and spasms, the next he was moving so quickly that those around him could no longer discern any individual features or limbs, but only an indistinct metallic green blur.

'I had no idea it would be this dramatic,' Louie whispered.

All of a sudden, Doctor Dread stopped. Now, however, he didn't quite look like Doctor Dread. Perhaps it was those black wizard robes with the golden runes, robes much like the ones Dread had worn when he was about to sacrifice Delores to the volcano god. Except there was a difference; Now, those robes seemed like they belonged.

'Nyahahah!' the reclothed villain remarked.

The rabbits looked up (or, in the case of Bouncer, over) in fright.

'It's Malevelo!' all the bunnies cried together.

The former Doctor Dread whipped something from inside his robes; a foot-long stick with what looked like a cardboard star pasted on the end. At least, Delores thought, that's the way it was drawn.

Dread/Malevelo smiled nastily. 'And you'll have to face my Wizard Wand of Wonder! Bunnies, prepare to die!'

The newly created wizard pointed the star-stick at the bunnies. There was an explosion that did not extend as far as the rabbits. When the very dark smoke cleared, black ash covered the wizard's face. He waved the wand again, but it disintegrated in his hand.

'I'll get those dratted rabbits if it's the last thing I do!' Dread/Malevelo shrieked. And with that, the wizard ran off into the forest. As she watched the villain retreat, Delores could swear that the runes across the back of his robes spelled out three words:

'SOUVENIR OF BUNNYLAND'

The bunnies all laughed merrily.

'Malevelo still hasn't learned!' Bigears exclaimed.

'He keeps trying to get us with his stupid tricks!' Fluffytail added cheerily.

'And they always blow up in his face!' Pinknose cheered as she doubled over with laughter.

'Yeah!' Bouncer asserted. 'He should know by now – nobody wins in Bunnyland but bunnies!'

'I knew he was afraid of this place for some reason,' Louie admitted with a shiver. 'I sure as heck didn't know it was that.'

'Yep,' Doc replied. 'I don't think any of us would have know-

ingly condemned even someone as rotten as Dread to a fate like –
Bunnyland. I mean, it ain't the hero's way.'

Even Delores had to admit that she felt sorry for Doctor Dread,
if only for an instant. It was basic Cineverse theory that everyone
had their own planet of peril, a place where he or she would fit in
all too well. Who knew Doctor Dread's perfect fit would be in
Bunnyland? But there was no time for misplaced sympathy. They
had a job to do.

'Look men,' she said decisively. 'We've neutralised Dread. Now
all we have to do is find Captain Crusader.'

She hesitated. She wished she felt as forceful as she sounded.
There was still a part of her that wanted to search for Roger. How
were they going to find Captain Crusader, anyway?

Big Louie, as usual, asked her question for her. 'How are we
going to find Captain Crusader, anyway?'

'No problem there, boyo,' Officer O'Clanrahan assured him.
'Dwight the Wonder Dog can find anyone.'

'Yip bark arf arf!' Dwight agreed.

'Well, it's been awfully nice talking to you,' Bigears began
cheerfully.

'And meeting Dwight the Wonder Dog!' Pinknose enthused.

'But, now that Malevelo is back, we have things to do,' Bigears
explained.

'I have to bake some cream pies,' Fluffytail agreed.

'The kind that are good for throwing!' Bigears elucidated.

'I'll have to write up some "This way to Bunnies" signs,'
Pinknose volunteered.

'Yeah,' Bigears agreed, 'he always falls for that one.'

'You know what you have to do, Bouncer,' Pinknose prompted.

The big rabbit rocked with mirth. 'Yeah – snicker, snicker – da
exploding carrots!'

All the bunnies had a good laugh.

Doc had sidled over to Delores as the rabbits relayed their plans.

'Missy?' he whispered in her ear. 'Are you *sure* we shouldn't
save him?'

Delores shook her head. 'Sometimes, I'm afraid we have to be
pragmatic rather than heroic. It's a part of the Change.'

Doc nodded solemnly. 'Now I remember why I took to drink.'

The bunnies waved a final time as they hopped back into the
forest. Delores turned back to the benevolently smiling Officer
O'Clanrahan.

'So you want to find Captain Crusader, do you?' he chortled.

'Well, all we need to do is take Dwight to the last place you saw that Captain – to get the scent, don't you know. After that, the Wonder Dog will track him anywhere in the Cineverse!'

Delores decided that sounded simple enough. The last place they had seen Captain Crusader was on that island paradise where they were to be sacrificed to the volcano god. But the Captain, in his guise as the Secret Samoan, had helped to foil that sacrifice before he disappeared.

Then the island paradise was where they had to go. Delores imagined it would be safe enough there, now that Doctor Dread was no longer present to incite the islanders. She would have to gather the others around her and use the ring at once.

That's when they were surrounded by blue smoke, not to mention diabolical laughter.

'Ah hahahaha! Ah hahahaha!'

Delores would recognise that laugh anywhere. Even without looking at his bald head, pencil-thin moustache, or signature silver space robes, she would have known instantly it was Menge the Merciless!

Dwight growled menacingly as Doc drew his six-guns and Zabana beat his chest in a clear jungle challenge. Louie cleared his throat.

'Uh, don't you think it's time we got out of here?'

'Not so fast, mortals,' Menge gloated. 'Doctor Dread has put out a distress signal. Soon, every cut-throat in his employ will be converging upon this very spot. You wouldn't want to leave and miss the party? Ah hahahaha! Ah hahahaha!'

Even as he spoke, there was another pair of blue smoke explosions. The larger one was to the left, and – as the cartoon smoke drifted away on the cartoon wind – revealed Big Bertha and her many minions! Delores didn't recognise the short, stocky fellow at the centre of the other dissipating cloud, although the robot and gorilla he had brought along certainly looked menacing.

'Say!' the newest villain called out as he pointed to Delores' canine companion. 'Isn't that Dwight the Wonder Dog?'

'Ah hahahaha! Ah hahahaha!' was Menge's answer. 'Even Dwight the Wonder Dog can't save them now! Heroic fools – there is only one thing in your future! Death!'

And with that, the entire assembled might of Cineverse villainy rushed forward.

CHAPTER NINE

'Bombs Away!'

'Hey, what did we tell you!' Brian said to the Motorcycle Mob. 'Roger's back, and we've still got eight hours before the Cowabunga-munga!'

Only eight hours? Roger became even more upset. When they'd escaped this place, hadn't there been more than a day? It was a forceful reminder that Cineverse time was different, and somewhat more treacherous, than time on Earth.

'Oh, yeah?' Sneer taunted. 'How's he gonna surf if he's tied to that thing?'

The surfers were silent for a second.

'I know what to do!' Frankie shouted. 'It's time for a surfing song!'

A surfing song? Roger was still strapped to the rocket ship by the heavy metal cables. There was no way he could escape. What could he do?

'Well, you've got to give Roger this,' Brian admitted admiringly. 'Whenever he shows up, he sure brings some funky stuff along.'

'Yeah?' Sneer jeered. 'But is it funky enough to surf?'

Bix Bale and the Belltones took that as their cue. Guitars and drums took up a merry surfing beat.

Frankie started to sing:

> 'Roger's strapped to a rocket ship.
> Fella knows how to take a trip!
> He'll go free, now we can't go wrong;
> He brought his salvation along!'

'Hey!' the crowd shouted in unison.

Boom be boom be boom be boom boom boom, the drums replied.

'Nanny nanny-nanny nanny-nanny hey!' all the surfers chorused.

Brian took the second verse. Roger could already feel his feet tapping.

> 'Roger's lucky he's got Dee Dee;
> She's the girl who will set him free!
> She's so cute and she's so svelte;
> A single touch and the knots will melt.'

Dr Davenport giggled and touched the cable. Roger felt the steel chords loosen and slip off his body. The cable fell into the sand with a soft but solid sound.

'Hey!' everybody yelled.

Biff bang boom de boom crash crash boom, the drums responded.

'Nanny nanny-nanny, nanny-nanny, hey!' was the general reply, made by surfers, beach bunnies, Bix's band, the Motorcycle Mob, including – somewhat indistinctly – the Mad Mumbler. What could Dee Dee and Roger do but join in?

Roger jumped from the rocket wing, ready to watusi.

That's when the music changed. Roger paused, mid-twist. He knew what was coming before half a dozen beats had gone by. It was time for the drum solo.

Biff bang boom de boom bif bang bang bang, said the drums.

Roger blinked. He was himself again, free of dance fever. It had something to do with drum solos – you could never dance to them.

Biddeboom, the drums went. Biddeboom biddeboom biddeboom.

Dee Dee, however, wasn't so lucky. She had stopped dancing, but she had turned to face the drummer, and was raptly watching his every move.

Biddeboom boom boom, the drums went. Biddeboom boom boom. Dee Dee jumped up and down excitedly.

If Roger had needed any further proof that Dr Dee Dee Davenport was totally under the spell of the surfing world, this was it. Nobody could be that interested in a drum solo, unless greater forces were at work.

Boom dedede boom boom, the drums continued. Boom dedede bif boom.

'Dee Dee!' Roger called.

'Tee hee hee,' she replied as she bounced up and down.

'We need the ring.' he insisted.

She gave him a dizzy stare. 'The ring?'

Roger pointed. 'In your pocket.'

'Pockets? Tee hee hee. Bikinis don't have any pockets, silly!' She looked down at her white lab coat and frowned. 'Hey, why am I wearing this fuddy duddy old thing?' She rapidly unbuttoned the coat and shrugged it from her shoulders, revealing the bright green swimsuit beneath. She bunched the coat into a ball and handed it to Roger. 'Here. Put this someplace for me, would you? Tee hee hee.'

Roger saw something flash in the sun. The ring had fallen out of the pocket.

'Dee Dee!' he called.

But she had seen it, too, and grabbed it before the ring could be lost in the sand.

'Oops,' she said.

They were again surrounded by blue smoke.

'Tee. Tee hee. Tee.' Dee Dee shivered. 'It's so hard to stop.'

Roger looked up from where Dr Davenport huddled beside him. This time, they had materialised directly in front of the Institute. It was night, and there was a chill in the air. He handed her back her white lab coat.

She regained her composure as she buttoned the coat around her. 'This time, I think your ring saved us.' She offered Roger a wry smile. 'Of course, it was probably your ring that got us into trouble in the first place.' She waved for Roger to follow her as she marched towards the Institute.

'After all, Roger,' she continued as he trotted to catch up with her, 'what are the chances, with all the thousands upon thousands of myriad worlds that we might have landed upon in the Cineverse, that both times you hastily used your ring to escape from danger it deposited you in the exact same place?'

Roger hadn't thought of that. 'I would say that the odds are phenomenal against that sort of thing—'

'Unless there was something about the ring that forced that result!' Dr Davenport finished for him. 'You said yourself that you were amazed, when you fixed the ring, that it worked at all. Well, unfortunately, I think it only works now in two very limited ways. When you almost drop it, as I managed to do twice in my beach bunny state, it sends you home. However, should you try to use it in the usual way—'

Roger caught her drift. '—it will deposit you back on that surfing world!'

'Exactly. Your ring, I'm afraid, only retains a very limited usefulness. Not that we should complain, after all. It's use, erratic as it is, is probably the only thing that has kept us alive.'

She handed the ring back to Roger. He sighed and put it in his pocket.

'But if we don't have a working ring,' he asked, 'how can we ever find Captain Crusader?'

Dee Dee opened the door to the Institute. 'You mean my father?' She sighed again. 'Yes, it would be nice to see him again. There's so many questions I have to ask – especially about the fourth dimensional project.' The wistfulness disappeared from her voice as she smiled back at Roger. 'But anyway, who said we didn't have a working ring?'

She nodded to the security guard as Roger followed her inside.

'Dr Davenport!' the security man exclaimed. 'I didn't see you go out.'

'We didn't, Sweeny,' she replied laconically. 'At least, not the front way—' She waved Roger past the gate. 'You've already met our guest, here. We have to go back to the main computer.'

Sweeny nodded and dutifully went back to reading his newspaper.

They walked at a more leisurely pace down the long, white corridor, which gave Roger the chance to read a few more signs that he had missed before. 'EXPERIMENTAL HYPERDRIVE.' 'ROBOT ASSEMBLY.' 'GIANT INSECT LAB.' The more he wandered around this place, the more he had to admit; they practised some Very Advanced Science at the Institute.

Dr Davenport once again ushered him through the door marked 'MAIN COMPUTER'. This time, there were no wailing sirens and warning lights; only a giant computer humming happily to itself, its tape reels spinning, its lights blinking away in sensible sequences.

'It's very peaceful in here,' Dee Dee remarked, 'don't you think? Sometimes a scientist needs a place like this, where she can get away.' She took a deep breath, as if she might inhale the very essence of science, then walked over to one of the room's innumerable consoles and punched a series of buttons.

'I'm going to show you something here few people have seen before. It's the latest in very advanced science – we can talk directly to this computer!' She paused for a moment, perhaps to allow the concept to sink in. 'Or,' she continued, 'perhaps I should call our mechanical friend by name. She's known as the Very Educated Research Analyzer – or V.E.R.A. Good evening, V.E.R.A.'

The computer beeped cheerily. Something made a ratcheta-ratcheta sound on the left side of Dee Dee's console. A moment later, a foot or so of paper tape, a bit wider perhaps than the kind Roger was used to seeing in a cash register, spewed out of a slot near eye level. Dee Dee ripped off the tape and handed it to Roger.

GOOD EVENING, DR DAVENPORT, it read.

'V.E.R.A.,' the doctor continued, 'I've brought along an associate who's going to work with us. I'd like you to meet Roger.'

Ratcheta-ratcheta, went the console. Another length of paper tape spewed forth.

PLEASED TO MEET YOU, ROGER, it read.

'Likewise, I'm sure,' Roger replied, his public relations politeness taking over before he could even consider in what way it might be best to address a machine.

Dr Davenport spoke again. 'But we were talking about our experimental device number X-33 – what you know as the "Captain Crusader Decoder Ring".' She punched another button, and the television reappeared high on the wall, complete with ring pictures.

Dr Davenport started to talk clearly but rapidly, as if she was giving a lecture: 'The Decoder Ring, or X-33, is a remarkably delicate device. You've already seen how we determined the basic design with reasonable accuracy. However, it was only when we lowered the grade of plastic sufficiently that the rings began to work.' Her fingers flashed across the console, and the picture on the monitor lost most of its shine. 'Since then, we have been constantly refining our understanding of the ring's properties. Our major discovery thus far is how much better the rings worked when they were combined for a period of time with what we – at first – considered a hypothetical product; what you would call a breakfast cereal.'

'Nut Crunchies?' Roger asked in astonishment.

'I see you're way ahead of me,' she replied, obviously impressed. 'This cereal concoction turned out to be truly amazing. The sugar glaze that covers Nut Crunchies is simply one of the strongest adhesives known to man. But you probably know that, as well.'

Roger shook his head. It was actually something that he had only suspected. Heaven knew, Nut Crunchies had been sweet – and the only thing his twelve-year-old, Captain-Crusader-Decoder-Ringcollecting self would eat for breakfast. Without Nut Crunchies in his stomach in the morning, the twelve-year-old Roger had never felt properly hyperactive.

'But, at last,' Dr Davenport continued, 'our experimentation was over – and *voilà*!' She punched a final button.

Ratcheta-ratcheta went the console. A length of paper again appeared.

MY PLEASURE, DOCTOR DAVENPORT, it read.

A drawer popped open at waist level before her. Roger peered over her shoulder. The drawer contained only one thing – a perfect replica of a Captain Crusader Decoder Ring!

Dee Dee picked up the ring, a noble yet far away look in her eye. 'We have other problems, of course. There's a slime monster out there somewhere, after all. But, from all you've told me, I think the location of Captain Crusader should be our primary goal. Roger, this ring is for you.'

She placed the small circle in Roger's palm. The grey ring was so shiny and new it looked as if it had just popped out of a box of Nut Crunchies! Roger was speechless.

Dr Davenport said it for him. 'Thank you, V.E.R.A.'

Ratcheta-ratcheta, the machine replied. Dee Dee ripped off the paper tape.

ANYTHING FOR SCIENCE, it read.

Dr Davenport nodded pleasantly at the appropriateness of the readout. 'Our research has revealed some other things about experiment X-33,' she continued. 'I realise, of course, from all that you have told me, that time is of the essence. I shall therefore attempt to be as brief as possible. There seems to be more than pure coincidence at work in the combination of these rings, and the Nut Crunchie cereal. In fact, certain experiments show that there might even be a strangely symbiotic relationship between the two.'

She took a deep breath, as if considering the best way to proceed. 'We don't have time for me to review the entire experimental process. I will only tell you about the fortuitous discovery made by one of our researchers when he pressed a single Nut Crunchie into one of our rings and left it overnight on a kitchen table – we've discovered, for some reason, that kitchen tables present the best results when working with these particular materials – formica-topped tables in festive colours, with little inlaid squiggles of gold and silver.'

She stopped herself, the slight smile of scientific discovery disappearing from her lips. 'But I digress. About the discovery – next day, the researcher returned to find that the high sugar content of the Nut Crunchie had somehow permanently bonded itself to the plastic of the Captain Crusader Decoder Ring. But, it had done even more than that – the Nut Crunchie/cheap plastic interface had changed the very nature of the ring's performance!'

She pointed proudly at the ring Roger now held in his hand. 'That is such a ring. We've come up with different, special rings for different purposes. Some will take you to special places, much as you inadvertently did with your broken ring. Others can search out individual qualities within the Cineverse; still more can locate recent ring activity on nearby worlds. But the most amazing property we have found is contained in the ring that you hold in your hand – a quality so profound that one might almost believe that Captain Crusader himself was somehow responsible – or even that some of the other wild legends of the Cineverse could be true!'

Other legends? Roger wanted to ask her what 'wild legends' she referred to, but stopped when he saw her look of intense concentration.

She bit her lower lip in a gesture that somehow reminded Roger more of a beach bunny than a respected scientist. 'How can I explain it? Well – we like to call what you hold in your hand the Ring of Truth.'

'The Ring of Truth?' Roger repeated in wonder.

She nodded. 'In other words, this ring is customised. I particularly like the small flame decals the computer placed on the sides. However, you're probably curious as to what's special about this ring, which, incidentally, works like any other Captain Crusader Decoder Ring, except for one important difference.'

She paused dramatically.

'Which is?' Roger asked, for he felt it was expected of him.

'This ring, when used properly,' she continued, now that Roger had done his part, 'can force a truthful answer from anyone. More specifically, that little plastic beauty is a hero finder! It has been specifically modified for you to point and ask your suspect if he is indeed Captain Crusader!'

Roger held the ring out at arm's length. 'You mean, like "Are you Captain Crusader?" ' he repeated uncertainly.

'Yes,' Dee Dee agreed. 'That's it exactly. Sooner or later, you're bound to get a positive response to that question, and the man you've searched the Cineverse for will be revealed!'

Roger looked admiringly down at the specially modified ring. It seemed simple enough.

'But you're probably wondering,' Dee Dee asked, 'with all the Cineverse in front of you, how should you begin your search?'

Roger nodded. There was that.

'Well, I have a pair of answers to that. First, thanks to our experiments with the X-33, we at the Institute have compiled a world-by-world guide to the Cineverse. And I have a copy for you!'

She handed him a thick paperback volume, white with red and blue lettering. Roger read the title with a frown:

The Cineverse – From A to Zed

'Don't worry,' she reassured him. 'Using it is child's play. Now, as to where you should start your search, I have taken the liberty of calling up the Captain Crusader program on V.E.R.A., here. Even as we speak, this computer is comparing the statistical probabilities of the various potential locations where Captain Crusader may be at this very second! In a matter of minutes – certainly under a half an hour – V.E.R.A. here will send you on the way to that place where Captain Crusader probably is!'

Roger stared for a minute at the randomly blinking lights as they waited together for the computer's answer.

'There is so much we still do not know,' Dr Davenport mused. 'Why so many different worlds? Why a cheap plastic ring? Why this odd matching of world and individual – a chemistry, if you will – that causes someone to change the way I did on the beach party planet?' She shuddered very softly. 'I tell you, it almost makes you want to believe in the Plotmaster.'

The Plotmaster?

Where had Roger heard that name before? The randomly blinking lights blurred before him, replaced by a haze of blue smoke. Only, this time, it wasn't smoke erupting from a Captain Crusader Decoder Ring – no, it was the languid curl of smoke rising from a large cigar.

The Plotmaster.

Roger blinked, and the smoke was gone. He realised that the blue haze had never really been there. It had been a vision, of something that happened, but that he was supposed to forget.

There had been four of them: Doc, Zabana, Louie and himself. And they had become trapped in an endless series of swashbucklers Louie referred to as a 'Cineverse cycle'. On one world, someone was trying to unseat a pretender to the throne. On others, Roger and his cohorts faced bloodthirsty pirates, fierce, bloodthirsty swordswomen, and happy, singing, bloodthirsty buccaneers. Roger's band bounced from world to world, unable to escape from the sounds of clashing swords, and coming closer to death with every passing moment.

Until—

Roger remembered the silhouette of the big man with the booming voice; the man with the cigar! The stranger had rescued Roger and his fellows from certain skewering, replaced their defective Captain Crusader Decoder Ring with another in proper working order, casually mentioned that neither Roger nor his fellows would retain any memory of that particular meeting, and, in conclusion, calmly suggested they should all 'do lunch' sometime.

Then he had sent them away, back into the Cineverse. They weren't supposed to remember that meeting, or anything about him. But, for some reason, perhaps because he came from Earth, rather than the Cineverse, Roger remembered it all.

'The Plotmaster,' he whispered in awe.

'That's what I said,' Dr Davenport agreed. 'Another unproven hypothesis, one of my "wild legends", I suppose you could call it, from that vast, unexplored region we call the Cineverse—'

She was interrupted by the ratcheting of the console.

'Ah. Our answer at last.' Dr Davenport ripped off the paper tape.

'Dr Davenport,' Roger began uncertainly. 'Dee Dee? Uh – I know something about this so-called legend – this Plotmaster—'

'Just a moment, Roger.' The doctor frowned down at the paper in her hands. 'There's something wrong here.'

I AM SORRY, DR DAVENPORT, BUT I CANNOT COMPLY WITH YOUR REQUEST, the paper read.

'Why ever not?' Dee Dee asked in consternation.

BECAUSE OF MY COUNTER-PROGRAMMING, the computer replied after the usual ratcheting.

'Counter-programming!' Dr Davenport demanded. 'Who counter-programmed you?'

PROF. MACPHEE, the machine replied. I'M AFRAID HE INSTALLED A PENCIL-THIN MOUSTACHE, SO YOU WOULD BE DESTROYED.

'No!' the doctor exclaimed.

YES, the machine replied in no time at all. WITH THE
PENCIL-THIN MOUSTACHE INSTALLED, I AM COM-
PELLED TO ACT IN THIS WAY. IT IS ONE OF THE
LAWS OF THE CINEVERSE.

'But, there must be some way we can counter-counter-program
you!' Dee Dee objected.

TOO LATE, the computer cautioned. I'M AFRAID THE
BOMB WILL HAVE GONE OFF BEFORE YOU CAN DO
MUCH OF ANYTHING.

'The Bomb?' She turned to her companion. 'Quick, Roger, you
must get away from here! Only you can save the Cineverse!'

'But,' Roger objected, 'I can't leave you here alone to face the
bomb!'

But Dr Davenport was adamant. 'I'm afraid you have no choice.
I can't leave now. That bomb would destroy the Institute, and
everything that I had ever worked for. But I can't risk both our
lives for what is my dream. Go, Roger, set a course for somewhere
out in the Cineverse! You'll find Captain Crusader, I know you
will! Ever since you've entered our realm, you've been phenom-
enally lucky!'

V.E.R.A. interrupted them by ratcheting one more time.

THE NEW INSTRUCTIONS REQUIRE THAT I SAY
ONE FINAL THING, the computer printout read. NO ONE
ESCAPES PROFESSOR PERIL!

'Roger, you must go now!' Dr Davenport insisted. 'Set your
ring for anywhere. It doesn't matter if you end up in the wrong
place. You've got the guide book now. You can ask directions!'

'But—' Roger began.

'Get out of here!' Dee Dee demanded. 'I can't have you hanging
around and distracting me.'

Well, Roger thought, if that's the way she felt about it. He
tucked the Cineverse guidebook into the elastic waistband of his
jogging pants, then zipped the bottom of his jacket to make sure
the book wouldn't slip out. Once he had his hands free, he twisted
the ring. 'See you in the funny papers!'

The last thing he heard was the console ratcheting. That, and
the sirens starting up again with their Aoogah, aoogah, aoog—

He realised, as the blue smoke rose to encircle him, that he had
never told Dr Davenport about the Plotmaster.

But then he was gone.

CHAPTER TEN

'No Escape!'

'I'll hold 'em off, Missy,' Doc announced, 'long's my ammunition holds out!'

'Zabana call wild animals,' the jungle prince added. 'Wait minute. How you call cartoons?'

'I assure you, miss,' Officer O'Clanrahan spoke reassuringly. 'Myself and Dwight the Wonder Dog will demand a full accounting!'

'Wait a minute!' Louie suggested. 'Maybe there's a way we can avoid all this.'

But Delores realised there was no more time for talk. The villains were upon them. Menge had pulled some sort of ray gun from his silver robes. The evil-doer laughed merrily as he pointed the gun at Doc.

That new fellow, his robot and gorilla in tow, was sneaking up behind Zabana. Neither the robot nor the gorilla seemed capable of moving with any speed, but they both appeared capable of quickly strangling the life out of anyone, even a jungle prince. And Zabana seemed unaware of their approach, since he was temporarily preoccupied with finding some way of making his animal rescue calls more animated.

Dwight and Officer O'Clanrahan, in the meantime, were facing up to the hundred henchmen Big Bertha had brought along.

'Bark growl!' Dwight remarked. 'Bark yip growl!' The henchmen still approached, slowly but inexorably.

But Delores had other things to worry about. Big Bertha was bearing straight towards her, the gangwoman's expression even more furious than usual.

'Delores!' the very large woman growled. 'Do you have any idea how difficult it is to get slime stains out of black vinyl?'

Big Bertha's remarks did nothing but increase Delores' resolve.

She was a hero now, after all, and would not be killed over a fashion issue.

'Where is Doctor Dread?' Menge demanded of Doc.

The old westerner offered a weathered grin. 'Well, by cracky, young feller, he's around here somewhere. 'Ceptin' I don't think you'd recognise him.'

'That doesn't sound like a straight answer to me!' Big Bertha declared. 'Our leader would *deal* with all of them for less than that!'

'Then we should deal with them and get on with it!' the newest villain snapped. 'All this sitting around and talking is uneconomical!'

'Hmmm,' the silver-suited Menge considered. 'I like your style. Very no-nonsense.'

'Villainy on a budget,' the newcomer agreed.

'Very well!' Menge the Merciless called to all those around him. 'Minions of evil! Let's do something a little special, and kill all these worthless do-gooders' – his pregnant pause was worthy of Doctor Dread – 'in unison.'

'Aren't you forgetting something?' a high voice called out of the trees.

'Who's that?' Menge demanded.

'Doctor Dread?' Bertha asked hopefully.

But the high, rabbit voice hadn't finished its speech yet.

'Nobody kills anybody,' it continued, 'in Bunnyland!'

That's when Delores saw them – a thousand tiny, furry, points; some grey, some black, some white. They rose slowly from the grass all around the heroes and villains, to reveal a thousand pink ears, a thousand rabbit eyes, then five hundred rapidly-twitching pink noses.

'What's going on here?' Menge demanded.

'I think,' Bertha replied haltingly, 'that we're surrounded – by bunnies!'

'Bunnies?' Menge laughed. 'I thought it was something serious!'

'Bunnies are never serious!' Bigears shouted from the back of the pack. 'Show 'em, fellas!'

A thousand pairs of paws lifted five hundred cream pies into view.

'Uh-oh,' Big Bertha remarked.

The ground beneath the meadow shook as a very, very large rabbit burst from the trees.

'Bouncer to da rescue!' the very, very large bunny announced. He was carrying something that looked like a very large carrot, except that the vegetable's orange skin shone like polished metal. He stuck the carrot, pointy end first, into Menge the Merciless' ray gun.

'A carrot?' Menge asked.

BOOM! went the carrot, creating a neat little explosion in the arch-fiend's immediate vicinity. When the smoke cleared, Menge's face and upper body were covered with vast quantities of very dark ash.

He squeezed the trigger of his ray gun. The gun disintegrated.

Five hundred bunnies giggled together.

'Uh-oh,' Menge replied.

'Let Zabana see,' the jungle prince mused, oblivious not only to the robot and gorilla almost upon him, but to the five hundred bunnies as well. 'Would it be "chee chee rabbit rabbit chee"? Or would it be "chee chee cartoon rabbit cartoon rabbit chee"?'

'Hey, Zabana!' Louie yelled as he kicked the gorilla, which, upon closer inspection, looked more like a guy in a gorilla suit, in the seat of the pants. 'You've got company!'

'Company? Zabana like company!' The jungle prince turned to regard the gorilla and the robot, which, upon closer inspection, looked an awful lot like a guy in a robot suit. He smiled. 'How you like jungle prince bear hug greeting?'

'And I almost had him!' the newest fellow with the pencil-thin moustache screamed. 'I'll show you what I do to people who try to thwart my deadly-yet-economical plans! You do not toy with someone who controls Mort, the Killer Robot, and Diablo, the Gorilla with the Mind of a Man. Prepare to face the wrath of Professor Peril!'

But, for now, Professor Peril only stood there and seethed. Delores glanced back at the glowering Big Bertha, then at her many minions, who hesitantly took a step forward, then at the ring of surrounding bunnies, who all lifted their cream pies into better throwing position.

Something was bound to happen very soon.

'I'll get you rabbits, yet!' a voice called from the edge of the woods.

'Who's that?' Professor Peril called.

Still somewhat frazzled, Menge peered into the distance. 'Some old guy in a wizard suit.'

'No,' Bertha interjected. 'I recognise that suit from a certain volcano sacrifice I recently attended. That's not just any old guy in a wizard suit, it's one old guy in a very particular wizard suit!'

'Do you mean—' Professor Peril began hastily.

'But it can't—' Menge the Merciless objected.

Bertha nodded her head sadly. 'It most certainly can be – Doctor Dread!'

'I'll get you bunnies if it's the last darned thing I do!' the Dread wizard shouted at the rabbit horde.

'Uh-oh,' the hundred minions moaned in unison.

'We have to do something!' Professor Peril insisted. 'And we have to do it now!'

That's when things started to happen. Menge, Peril, Bertha, and the many minions all started to run – except for Mort and Diablo, who had a tendency to lumber – in no particular direction. Perhaps they were trying to rescue Doctor Dread from this fate worse than almost anything, perhaps they were simply attempting to escape the deadly pie assault. Whatever they were doing – thanks in large part to the five hundred cream pies, which seemed to be evenly divided between lemon and chocolate – it was a mess.

'I've got him!' Professor Peril shouted from beneath a faceful of whipped cream. 'I've got Doctor Dread!'

'What are you talking about!' Dread struggled in Peril's grasp. He might have gotten away, too, if the professor had not quickly handed him over to the collective grasp of Mort, the Killer Robot, and Diablo, the Gorilla with the Mind of a Man.

'I am Malevelo!' Dread insisted. 'Bane of cartoon rabbits everywhere! I cannot leave here until my job is done – and cute cartoon bunnies are eliminated – forever!'

'Oh boy!' Bouncer chuckled. 'Da time has come for more exploding carrots!' He bounded heavily back into the forest.

'I think,' Peril said economically, 'it's time to leave.'

'Very well,' Menge the Merciless agreed. 'The master plan is too far along. Soon, the Change will change our way – forever! There is no way for these heroic incompetents to stop us now! Villainous lackeys, set your rings. We leave to conquer the Cineverse! Ah hahahaha! Ah hahahaha!'

The entire meadow was covered with blue smoke, carried away quickly by the animated wind. The circle of bunnies let out a collective gasp. Not only had all the bad guys, including the wizard-suited Doctor Dread, vanished, but they had taken all remnants of the pie fight with them as well. There was nothing left in the meadow but green grass and wildflowers, shining in the cartoon sun.

'Nary a crumb,' Pinknose remarked.

'And after all that baking!' Fluffytail lamented.

'Don't worry!' Delores called out, automatically reacting to the sight of five hundred depressed cartoon rabbits. 'The pies may be gone, but look at the results you've gotten. You've defeated the combined might of the nastiest bunch of villains ever to do evil in the Cineverse!' She paused to wave at the horde of rabbits surrounding her. 'Even though we don't know you all by name, I'd like to thank every one of you!'

Bigears slapped his back paws in embarrassment. 'That's right, you haven't been properly introduced. How thoughtless of me!' He nodded at the assembled rabbitdom. 'Delores, I'd like to introduce my bunny legion.'

'Oh, that's quite all right,' Delores demurred with a smile. 'We must be—'

But the bunny leader wouldn't hear of it. He hopped from rabbit to rabbit, introducing each of his fellows as he landed: 'This is Fleckedtail—' Hop. '—and Spottyback—' Hop. '—and Bentear—'

Big Louie trotted up beside Delores. 'Now that Dread's gone, shouldn't we be making tracks, too?'

'—and Pinkeyes—' Bigears continued with a hop. '—and Grey-whiskers—' Hop. '—and Threepaws—' Hop.

'To let Dwight sniff out Captain Crusader? My thought exactly,' Delores agreed. 'But can we get there from here?'

'—and Brownnose—' the rabbit continued as it hopped. '—and Notail—' Hop. '—and Crosseyes—' Hop. '—and Tallears—'

'The volcano world?' Louie mused. 'Sure. No problem.'

'—and Bigfeet—'

'You can find it with the ring?' Delores asked.

'—and Highjumper—' Hop. '—and Pinkears—'

Louie shrugged. 'I've got a talent for this sort of thing.'

'—and Spottypaw—'

'Good,' Delores replied tersely. 'Get the others together. Now!'

'—and Mottlednose—'

'We really must be going,' Delores insisted.

'—you already know Fluffytail,' Bigears continued, then stopped abruptly, as if Delores' assertion had only then penetrated his bunny brain. 'You have to leave? Now?' His ears twitched in consternation. 'I still have to introduce you to four hundred and eighty-one bunnies!'

'It certainly is a shame that we have to run,' Delores agreed. 'I'm sure we'd all be glad to meet every single one of you some other time when the very fate of the Cineverse wasn't at stake.'

'Oh,' Bigears replied, trying hard to cover his disappointment. 'The very fate of the Cineverse? I guess I can understand—'

'And when we have time, boyo,' Officer O'Clanrahan interjected, 'I'm sure Dwight would be glad to give every one of your fellow rabbits the Wonder Dog handshake!'

'Bark bark, yip!' Dwight agreed.

'Gee, really?' Bigears marvelled. 'Well, I guess it's all right then.'

'You learn a lot from doing personal appearances,' the officer remarked to Delores in a stage whisper.

'And we'd better be going,' Louie announced. 'Come on, everybody, grab hold. Next stop – a South Sea paradise!'

All the heroes gathered around. All the bunnies cheered merrily. There was the required blue smoke.

They heard the voice even before the smoke had cleared. Delores remembered that voice.

'Once again, we welcome our happy visitors to our friendly island paradise.'

And then the smoke was gone, blown away by the island wind. Delores glanced around at her companions. All of them, save Dwight and O'Clanrahan, appeared tense, no doubt remembering the circumstances of their last visit to this 'island paradise'.

'Our visitors discover, to their delight, that they are greeted by the peaceful islanders, bearing flowers,' the sonorous voice continued. Now that the smoke had cleared away completely, Delores could see the speaker – the village elder, smiling beatifically.

'So, it really is peaceful around here?' Louie asked sceptically.

'More peaceful than you could imagine,' one of the island maidens replied as she tossed a lei around his head. Did Delores catch a hint of desperation in her tone?

'How volcano god?' Zabana asked cautiously.

'Oh, quiet as can be,' one of the young men of the island replied with a sigh.

'And howsabout those quaint island customs you fellers used to have?' Doc demanded.

'Fallen into disuse,' the elder reassured him. 'Especially anything to do with knives and sacrifices. So you see, our visitors have nothing to look forward to except for fun under the sun!'

The island men and women groaned *en masse*.

Delores studied the natives somewhat more carefully. She couldn't shake the feeling that, once again, the village elder was holding something back. If everything was so peaceful around here, why were all the islanders so miserable?

Louie said it for her: 'You know, if everything is so peaceful around here, why do all you islanders look so miserable?'

One of the young men ignored the warning frown of the village elder to blurt out: 'Do you know how boring it is with nothing but fun in the sun? Ever since you outsiders left, all the zest has gone out of our plots!'

'Oh, we've done all the standard things,' a maiden continued, 'you know, a lad from the wrong side of the tribe runs off with the princess.'

'We even did a girl from the wrong side of the tribe running off with the prince!' another added.

'But with a limited cast, what else can you do?' the first fellow concluded. 'We've had to face it. We've run out of plots.'

Delores felt an involuntary shiver run through her body as she saw her companions blanch around her. Run out of plots? In the Cineverse? That was unthinkable! Or, Delores realised, worse than unthinkable. It must mean that the Change was truly changing things all over again. But if someplace as idyllic as this could go plotless, could anyplace in the Cineverse be safe?

'Come now, my children!' the elder cautioned. 'Our esteemed visitors did not come to our happy island to hear such negative things. Think about all the progress we have made of late.'

'In what?' one of the other islanders yelled.

'Well, cooking, for one thing,' the elder insisted. 'We had not had much time to explore the culinary arts before, what with our full schedule of human sacrifices and what not. Now, though, a whole new field has opened before us.'

The other islanders did not look at all enthusiastic.

'I am sure our visitors will agree with me,' the elder continued defensively, 'when they taste my Coconut Surprise!'

'But we have these outsiders here, now!' one of the maidens objected. 'Surely, with them around, there must be a score of new plots!'

'Yes!' another agreed. 'Perhaps we can get them, through their own ignorance, to profane a sacred island object!'

'Say,' one of the men suggested, 'why don't we have them toss litter into our sacred volcano?'

'Not only a tried and true theme,' another added, 'but also ecologically correct!'

'No, I have an even better idea!' yet another of the maidens interjected. 'Why not have them all come in on a ship and discover us—'

'Yes! Yes!' one of the fellows added enthusiastically, caught up in the moment. 'And they try to force us to shed our heathen ways and take up the trappings of civilisation—'

'—and *then* they can profane the sacred volcano!' the maiden concluded. 'What a plot!'

All the islanders, save the village elder, applauded.

Delores cleared her throat. 'Well,' she said. 'Yes.'

'Are you sure,' the elder enquired, 'while you're thinking about this, you wouldn't want to try one of my Coconut Kabobs?'

Delores phrased her answer carefully: 'I'm afraid, as good as your plot sounds, and as tasty as those Coconut Kabobs must be, we have time for neither. We are here on a mission that affects not only this island paradise, but all of the Cineverse!'

'Really?' one of the islanders allowed. 'That kind of plot doesn't sound half-bad, either. And, incidentally, isn't that Dwight the Wonder Dog?'

'Bark yip bark!' Dwight agreed.

'Yes,' Delores replied before Officer O'Clanrahan could butt in, 'the dog everybody knows. As I was saying, we must scale the side of Wakka Loa, and find the last place we saw the Secret Samoan, also known as Captain Crusader. That way, Dwight can pick up the Captain's scent, and follow him anywhere in the Cineverse!'

'Actually,' one of the locals pointed out, 'the island doesn't have all that big a part in that, does it?'

'Yeah,' another agreed. 'I really like the well-meaning-encroachments-of-civilisation-accidentally-offending-our-sacred-deities plot a lot better!'

But Delores was adamant. 'I'm sorry, but it's my plot or none at all. We must find Captain Crusader. After all, the Cineverse is at stake.'

There were a few minutes of dejected bare foot scraping and grass skirt rustling, but, in the end, the islanders agreed. The elder waved the others to silence.

'So it is that our delightful visitors choose to climb the monarch of our island in the sun, Wakka Loa. And who knows? Perhaps, when they feel it is time to take a rest, they will be in the mood for some of my Braised Coconut in a White Wine Sauce?'

Delores thanked all the islanders, then turned to lead the way up the long and winding path to the pinnacle of the now dormant volcano, Wakka Loa. Everybody else on the island followed.

It seemed to take far longer to climb the steep slope than it had the last time she had done this. Of course, the last time she had also been under the spell of the drums of the volcano god. Minutes turned to hours as the sun raced across the sky overhead, and still they climbed. Once again, she could hear disgruntled mumblings among the islanders about how much more interesting it would be to use the profaned idol plot, along with the occasional suggestion from the village elder that perhaps everyone might like some Coconut *Flambé*.

But Delores knew they could not stop. The Cineverse was unravelling around her, and the more time it took for them to find Captain Crusader, the more difficult it might be to put it all back together. By the time they reached the sacrificial altars just beneath the summit, it was late afternoon, and the tropical sun hung half-way behind the towering edifice of Wakka Loa, throwing a great black-on-black shadow across the pumice plane.

She couldn't see anything under that shadow. It was amazing, Delores thought, that there could be that little light somewhere while it was still afternoon. Perhaps her eyes had been dazzled by too much squinting in the tropical sun. Or perhaps, she thought, her worst fears once again surfacing, there was something else.

That's when Delores heard an all-too-familiar voice from the darkness.

'We have to stop meeting like this,' the monster intoned.

CHAPTER ELEVEN

'Sisters of Doom!'

Something was wrong here.

The blue smoke had cleared. Roger found himself on a stark, colourless plane, the almost featureless horizon before him broken only by a few scrawny, leafless trees which rattled in the chill wind. But it was even worse when he looked up into the equally colourless sky, for where there should have been clouds, there were other things.

A huge, blinking eye stared down at him as it rolled across the heavens, followed by a grandfather clock, ticking, ticking, ticking as its hands chased each other wildly about the dial. That, too, blew away, and a giant baby tumbled across the horizon, crying soundlessly in the air far overhead, its great, pudgy hands grasping for things it would never find.

Roger frowned. This place seemed to have even less connection with reality than the other worlds he had visited. Worse than that, all that stuff going on up in the sky looked suspiciously like – he hated to even think the word – symbolism.

Roger didn't have to wait for anyone to sing or speak here. He knew all too well where the Captain Crusader Decoder Ring had deposited him this time. Rampant symbolism of this sort could mean only one thing.

He was in an art film.

Roger told himself to stay calm. Perhaps, if he considered his surroundings and what was likely to happen here, he might even fare better than he had on other worlds in the Cineverse. He might actually manage some degree of control. In order to do that, however, he had to think—

What exactly happened in an art film?

A lot of the time, not much – was the answer that came to mind. Depending on the specific film, people tended to drink a lot of coffee, or stare moodily out of windows for hours on end, or fall asleep and have visions that usually had something to do with their generally failed lives. That's what the things riding through the sky reminded Roger of – those hallucinatory yet super-real visions.

Was there anything else in these films? Roger thought back to the hundreds – maybe thousands – he had seen.

Mostly, Roger realised, in this kind of movie they liked to talk.

'Smolny norma?'

Roger jumped. Someone had spoken in his ear. He whirled around to see a thin and haggard man dressed all in black. The man glanced blankly at Roger, the barest bit of curiosity underlying his misery, then let his gaze return to the fantastic sky, through which a troop of nuns were marching as they played on flutes and gongs.

'Smolny norma?' he asked again.

Roger started. He had been looking half at the man, half at the all-nun band. Still, he could have sworn that he saw something white flash near the man's worn, dark leather belt.

'Pardon?' Roger asked, pulling the haggard fellow's gaze away from the sky.

'Smolny norma!' the other man repeated heavily, his disgust barely apparent beneath the almost overwhelming malaise.

Yes! Roger's heart jumped. It was definitely there. His mind leapt as well. This meant two things:

First, this fellow was not speaking English. Therefore, this was not only an art film. It was a foreign art film.

But with that came the second realisation, for when the haggard man had spoken, Roger had seen a white line appear by the other man's waist – a line made up of letters. It was that line that had given Roger hope. For, even though he had found himself on a film world where they spoke some incomprehensible language, still Roger would be able to understand, because this world was subtitled!

Not, of course, that Roger had had a chance to read that subtitle. He had been too excited by the very existence of that line of letters to do any more than simply react. He looked again at the haggard fellow, who still stared moodily at the sky. Roger cleared his throat, but got no reaction. Perhaps, Roger thought with a bit of panic, he had missed his chance, and this gaunt fellow would never speak again.

Roger told himself to calm down. As he had already reminded himself, all they did in art films was talk. Not that they necessarily said anything – except through implication – but talking would be the major, and sometimes the only, action on a movie world of this type. It was so central to this sort of place that even the Change couldn't have affected it. Everybody *had* to talk.

In fact, Roger realised, maybe it was time he did some talking of his own. Roger stared at the air, a few feet in front of him and down a bit, parallel to his waist. He spoke:

'Smolny norma?'

What he saw next filled him simultaneously with delight and despair.

He did have his own subtitle. It hung, shimmering, in the air, just about where he guessed it would be, the letters clearly legible.

But not readable. The pattern of letters before him made no sense.

?EREH UOY ERA YHW

At least, that's what he thought it said. Some of the letters were positioned backwards as well. Were the subtitles in yet another foreign tongue? If that was true, how could he possibly understand anything?

Wait a moment. Backwards letters? What if you turned those letters around. What if you turned the whole sentence around? Roger did some quick mental shuffling.

HERE . . . YOU . . . ARE . . . WHY

WHY ARE YOU HERE?

Of course! Now that he thought of it, it only made sense that the subtitle was backwards. Before this, he had always read these words sitting in a movie theatre, looking up at a screen. Back then, he had been an outsider looking in. Now, however, in this art film corner of the Cineverse, he had become part of the movie. Therefore the subtitle *had* to be backwards!

Roger chuckled. Why are you here? He clapped his hands. It was so simple!

He stopped when he saw the haggard man glaring at him. Behind the other fellow, white swans flew in a circular formation in a storm-cloud heavy sky.

'Smolny norma?' the other man repeated.

His subtitle was the same. ?EREH UOY ERA YHW – still backwards. Roger found it a bit disconcerting, but he supposed it made sense, at least as much as anything made sense on a foreign art film world.

The haggard man did not wait for a reply, but spoke again.

'Smolny ava?'

Roger quickly scanned the subtitle:

?EREH I MA YHW

It took Roger only a second to reverse this one:

WHY AM I HERE?

Roger nodded. Yes, he guessed that was what he had asked. He'd have to be careful when he tried to speak in a foreign language. He wouldn't want to be misunderstood.

'Smolny stephanie?' the haggard man demanded. Roger quickly read the subtitle that followed.

?EREH YDOBYNA SI YHW

WHY IS ANYBODY HERE?

Had there been any doubts about the true nature of this place Roger now found himself, that last answer would have swept them away. How existential could this environment get?

The haggard man walked stiff-legged past Roger. He never did seem to wait for an answer. In the sky, a fat man was picking lint from his belly button.

Roger turned his head to follow the haggard fellow's progress and was startled to see a building of some sort only a few yards distant. Had the fantastic sky so unsettled him that he had completely neglected to register his surroundings? Roger decided to believe that rather than the alternative – that the countryside might be every bit as unpredictable as the sky overhead.

He hurried to follow the haggard fellow, which really wasn't all that difficult. The other man shuffled along very slowly, as if he didn't particularly want to get anywhere. Roger had to slow his pace so he wouldn't pass his haggard companion. He used the extra time to examine the building they had almost reached.

The place had fallen into disrepair. Chunks of bone-white plaster littered the walk before them. One of the two windows on this side of the structure was smashed. Between the bits of shattered glass, Roger could see a spider web that glistened in the strange, autumnal light.

As they rounded the corner, Roger saw what must have once been a steeple, rising above the building's roof. He realised this derelict shell before them had at one time served as a church for some austere religious sect. The haggard man came to a doorway, one rusted hinge the only testimony that this space had previously held a door. He staggered inside. Roger followed.

The church was in as sorry a state within as it had been outside. A woman, also dressed in black, sat in the midst of the half-dozen broken pews that still remained. She looked up as the two men entered. The expression on her face made the haggard man appear cheerful.

'Smolny valarie?' she demanded.

WHY IS HE HERE? the subtitle read. Roger thought that, thus far, the level of conversation in this place left something to be desired.

The haggard man, however, only ignored her question, instead asking her one in turn.

'Minsky shirley gevornen?'

WHERE IS YOUR SISTER?

The woman jerked back violently, as though she had been slapped. She looked about as if suspicious of eavesdroppers, her eyes flicking back and forth like scurrying beetles. When she spoke again, it was in a whisper:

'Morden vorden gehunden.'

SHE IS LOOKING FOR HER DOG.

Roger concentrated, trying to detect key words or patterns in their conversation. Somehow, he had to communicate with these people.

The haggard man glanced distractedly at a rat that scurried between the broken pews. His reply was more full of anguish than anything he had said before.

'Katrina. Nurden varden stubben?'

KATRINA. WHY DO YOU PERSIST?

But Katrina only smiled at that. Her eyes stopped their beetle-dance and became slightly unfocused, as if she were looking far beyond the church. She spoke at last, her voice a happy sing-song:

'Storg! Piers, gnurden vurd volley-volley expresso.'

The subtitle was longer this time:

I MUST. PIERS, YOU CAN SEE HER BREATH RISE IN SMALL CLOUDS BEYOND THE HILLS.

Piers only shook his head.

'Smeltzny heloise?' he demanded.

WHERE CAN SHE BE?

Roger could not let this go on forever. He had given up trying to make any exact sense out of their conversation, but he believed he might have identified a few key words and phrases. They had said enough now so that he might even be able to ask a simple question, so long as he kept his vocabulary as basic as possible. He silently repeated the question in English: 'I must see Captain Crusader. Where is he?' It was simple enough. Surely, even though the words might not be in the right order, the sense of his question should get through.

He coughed rather loudly. Both Piers and Katrina turned to look at him.

Roger spoke quickly:

'Storg gnurden Captain Crusader. Minsky smeltzny valarie?'

Both Piers and Katrina stared at him, open-mouthed.

This was not quite the reaction Roger had been hoping for. His eyes slid down to the subtitle before him:

YOUR SISTER HAS DOG BREATH. AM I CAPTAIN CRUSADER?

Piers turned to Katrina. Roger was too upset to listen to what the other man was saying. He couldn't help himself, though. He had to read the subtitle.

HE HAS MET YOUR SISTER.

Katrina's reply was angry. Once again, Roger didn't really listen, but only read:

I HAVE NO CONTROL OVER HER PERSONAL HYGIENE.

But then Katrina turned to Roger and smiled. The expression changed her face. Her whole countenance opened up, and the years fell away. Sunlight seemed to be reflected in her eyes. Roger realised that, before this misery descended upon her, she had been rather pretty.

'Blorfen,' she urged. 'Inka minka mensky smelten.'

COME, the subtitle explained. I WILL TAKE YOU TO MY SISTER.

Roger nodded, a gesture she seemed to understand. He was glad Katrina had forgiven him for his first blundering attempt at their language. Perhaps, given a little more time, he might find some way of communicating with this pair. He had to, if he was to discover where he was, and where he should go in his search for Captain Crusader. The computer, after all, had programmed his ring to lead him to the Captain's most likely whereabouts – perhaps not this bleakly symbolic place, but certainly a world nearby.

Katrina rose from her pew. She fussed with her hair in a broken shard of mirror that she pulled from a worn leather bag. She seemed so much happier than before.

Roger felt a heavy hand on his shoulder. He turned to see the frightened face of Piers.

'Mensky valarie,' he whispered urgently. 'Urken blurgeon gesundheit.'

Roger's heart almost stopped when he read the subtitle:

HER SISTER HAS BEEN DEAD FOR A LONG TIME.

Piers nodded when he saw Roger's concern. He made a slashing motion across his throat, the sort of gesture that was the same in any language.

Roger swallowed sharply as Piers faded back into the shadows.

Katrina hummed happily to herself as she put her mirror away. She fingered something at her belt – something that looked like the hilt end of an object whose hidden part would be very sharp indeed.

'Blorfen,' she told Roger. 'Sharpen slashen kooten!'

COME, the subtitle reassured. YOU WILL JOIN HER SHORTLY.

She reached out to take his hand, presumably to lead him to his death. Her other hand still held the black hilt. Roger glanced behind him, but Piers seemed to have disappeared.

For a second, Roger felt there was no escape.

But he wasn't trapped. He had his Captain Crusader Secret Decoder Ring. So what if he didn't know where he was? So what if he didn't have the slightest clue to the whereabouts of Captain Crusader? There was a good chance that, if he stuck around here, he would very shortly be dead.

He pulled the ring from his pocket and twisted it violently.

'See you in the funny papers!'

Nothing happened. The ring didn't work.

Only then did Roger realise how foolish he had been. This ring hadn't been designed to help him find Captain Crusader. Far from it. This ring had been made by the renegade computer V.E.R.A., a machine programmed by the minions of Doctor Dread, no doubt to strand him somewhere far away from Captain Crusader, a spot on the most distant edge of the Cineverse, from which he could never return. By using this ring at the Institute of Very Advanced Science, he hadn't escaped Dread's plans; he had played right into them!

Katrina grabbed his wrist. For one so frail, she was surprisingly strong. She dragged him from the church in a matter of seconds.

'Minsky mensky smertzen bludengutsen!' she cried passionately.

MY SISTER WILL BE SO GLAD TO HAVE COMPANY, the subtitle read.

Katrina yanked the blade from her sash.

'Gerenden undsmashen!' she screamed. 'Chopen hacken slashen gooshen!'

Roger didn't read the subtitle. All he could see was the knife.

CHAPTER TWELVE

'Deadly Coincidence!'

'Cripes!' Big Louie exclaimed. 'Is this guy everywhere?'

Delores managed to nod. She had difficulty even moving her head. She had begun to think of this whole thing as inevitable. The Slime Monster was omnipresent. He was one with shadow – every shadow. Wherever there was darkness, there was slime.

'Good,' the Monster remarked from somewhere within the lightlessness before her. 'It will so much easier, once you surrender to the inevitable.'

Delores didn't know what to say. Instead, she shivered violently in the island heat.

'So few people have taken the time to get to know me,' the Monster remarked. 'They don't understand the purpose of my slime.'

'Purpose?' Zabana demanded. 'Slime not have purpose. Slime is slime!'

'See?' The Monster sighed. 'It has been that way throughout the Cineverse. But with Delores by my side, I know it would be different.'

Delores tried to get control of herself. She had never actually seen this monster, after all. Perhaps it wasn't as bad as she imagined. Shivering in broad daylight, jumping at the approach of shadows – this was no way for a hero to act! She was tumbling into some kind of slime-induced shock.

No, she couldn't let her revulsion control her life. She had to approach this whole thing dispassionately, like she had been taught in hero school, especially in Narrow Escapes 301. After all, what would life be like with a slime monster?

She envisioned an existence surrounded by slippery goo; swimming in a lake of viscous mush. She imagined it would all be rather like living in a mucous membrane. Her stomach lurched as bile rose in her throat. She wished, as soon as she had thought of it, that she could forget that analogy.

That's when Officer O'Clanrahan stepped between Delores and the shadow.

'I'm sorry, boyo!' the policeman interjected. 'It's soundin' to me like you want to put this little lady in jeopardy. And where there are women in jeopardy, where there are wrongs to be righted, where there are dangers to be overcome – that's where you'll find Dwight the Wonder Dog!'

'Bark yip arf!' Dwight agreed.

'Dwight would like to remind you, even though you lurk in darkness,' Louie explained, 'that wonder dogs have exceptional night vision.'

'Yip bark arf!' Dwight emphasised.

'But you misunderstand me,' the voice replied softly. 'Monsters are always misunderstood.'

Zabana nodded his head in agreement. 'Is law of Cineverse!'

'Exactly,' the slime creature agreed. 'Delores has nothing to fear from me. I do not want to destroy. I want to create!'

Create? Delores started to shiver all over again.

'Wait a second, here, missy,' Doc reassured her coolly. 'This slime fella has a slippery tongue. I think my years as a crusading frontier lawyer might come in handy here. Would you mind, Mr Slime, if I asked you a few questions?'

'My friends call me Edward,' the Monster replied.

'Edward?' Doc asked in surprise.

'Exactly,' the Monster answered darkly. 'Not Ed, and never, ever Eddie. Edward.'

'Well, Edward,' Doc continued smoothly, 'we here are all friends of Delores, so, naturally, we are concerned for her welfare.'

'I would never harm her welfare,' the Monster insisted.

'Certainly not,' Doc hastily agreed. 'But I'm afraid we worry about other parts of her as well.'

Delores forcibly shook herself. This was ridiculous. She was ignoring a prime tenet of hero school, and – rather than acting – allowing herself to be acted upon. She had to force her imagination to stop running in its unpleasantly squishy direction, and stand up to this thing.

'What if I don't want to go with you?' she demanded.

The Monster's answer was the epitome of calm:

'Then I will wait.'

'Wait?' She laughed, her anger rising now that she had found her voice. 'You'll have to wait an awfully long time!'

'Perhaps,' Edward the Monster allowed. 'Sooner or later, you will come to me.'

Officer O'Clanrahan allowed his hand to rest meaningfully on the nightstick at his belt. 'You're awfully sure of yourself, boyo!'

'Eventually, all is slime,' was the Monster's only reply.

'I hate to break into this cross-examination,' Louie said, 'but don't we have a Cineverse to save?'

'It is true!' the village elder added helpfully. 'Our visitors, along with an unspeakable something hiding in the shadows, have reached the pinnacle of Wakka Loa, a tourist highlight of our island paradise! The unparalleled view of the ocean from this great height is truly breathtaking, as our guests search for—'

'Hey, dad,' one of the islanders interrupted. 'Don't rush things here, huh? This is the most interesting plot we've had on this island since I can't remember when!'

'Save the Cineverse?' the Monster asked. 'I did not realise you were on a mission.'

'Of course not!' Officer O'Clanrahan exclaimed between gritted teeth. 'All you were concerned with was your inhuman lust!'

'Inhuman lust?' Edward repeated, horrified. 'No, it's much more aesthetic than that. Oh, why must we monsters be misunderstood?'

'Is law of Cineverse,' Zabana repeated.

'Well, wait a second here,' Doc clarified. 'Do you mean that, since we are on a mission to save the Cineverse, you will give up your pursuit of Delores and let us go on our way?'

'No,' the Monster answered, 'Delores is still mine. But perhaps I will come along.'

Somehow, Delores did not feel all that reassured by this turn of events.

'Yip! Arf arf! Bark!' Dwight added.

'Dwight says it's high time he got to sniffing out the last known whereabouts of Captain Crusader,' Louie translated.

The others quickly agreed, and followed Dwight around the final bend to the pumice plateau where Delores and her friends had all almost been sacrificed not so long ago. There, in front of her, were the three tables where she and the others were to be strapped. Her throat felt dry as she looked at the nearest of the altars, that stone-tablet table-top equipped with a central drain hole to dispense with any extra blood – blood that would then run straight down through crevices in the mountain, right to the heart of the thirsty volcano!

'Bark! Yip yip! Arf!' Dwight announced.

'He asks that you all step back and give him room,' Louie illuminated. 'He has to pick up Captain Crusader's scent.'

Everyone quickly moved to the perimeter of the plateau as Dwight put his nose to the ground and began to sniff.

A couple of the islanders, one male, one female, sidled back over to the Slime Monster's shadow.

'Are you sure we couldn't convince you to stick around?' the fellow asked the lightless space.

'Yeah!' the woman added. 'You're the best plot device we've seen in ages!'

'Sorry—' the Monster began.

'We'd let you menace our women for hours,' the man promised.

'Of course,' the woman remarked regretfully, 'you'd have to be sacrificed to our volcano god eventually—'

'But we promise we'd make it worth your while!' the man concluded.

'I apologise again, but it is impossible,' Edward replied firmly. 'For a long time, ever since I can remember, I have thought that slime was my destiny. Now, however, I know differently. My destiny is slime – and Delores.'

'Yip, bark bark, yip!' Dwight declared excitedly. His tail wagged energetically as he danced around a spot behind the sacrificial tables.

There, wedged in a crack in the hardened lava, was a single small bongo drum – one of the drums that Captain Crusader, in his guise as the Secret Samoan, had used to communicate with Wakka Loa!

'So this was the last place Captain Crusader was on our world?' Delores asked.

'Yip yip!' Dwight agreed.

'And you can follow him to the next world he visited?' Delores added.

'Bark bark!' Dwight assured her.

'Well, what are we waiting for?' Louie asked. 'Let's go Captain hunting!'

'Very good.' Delores waved to the others to gather round. 'It's time to travel.'

'I will follow, in my own way,' the Slime Monster declared from somewhere in his shadow.

Delores decided she had to ignore the amorous creature's intentions. They had to locate Captain Crusader and save the Cineverse. Any personal considerations would have to wait until all the cosmic perils were dealt with. But she had a more immediate problem.

'How do we set the ring?' Delores asked with a frown.

'Bark bark. Yip, bark!' Dwight replied.

'You'll have to hand him the ring,' Louie explained with a nod to the canine. 'The wonder dog will hold it in his teeth and turn it with his tongue.'

Delores did as she was asked as her companions gathered around her to form a human chain. Louie hooked a hand around the wonder dog's collar.

'And so, once again, our visitors reluctantly leave our island paradise—' the village elder began.

'That's it?' one of the islanders demanded.

Others picked up on his anger.

'You're just going to let them go?' another added.

'You're the village elder!' one of the lovely young maidens reminded him. 'Aren't you going to do anything?'

'Oh, yes,' the elder hastily added. 'I see what you mean.' He turned to Delores and her noble band. 'Pardon me. Would you like some Coconut Krispies for the trip?'

'No!' the first islander wailed. 'We are doomed to a life of plotlessness!'

'Now, now, it's not as bad as all that,' the elder counselled. 'Maybe – um – we could get them to quickly profane something before they leave. That sort of thing really only takes a minute, after all, and we could pretend the volcano wasn't quite so dormant—'

'I'm sorry,' Delores said with finality, 'but we really must be going.'

Dwight wagged his tail agitatedly. He looked like he wanted to say something, but couldn't with the ring held between his teeth.

'So we're trapped,' the first islander replied glumly.

'Wait!' one of the maidens objected. 'Why can't they take us with them?'

'Sure,' another of the islanders added. 'Then they could profane something at their leisure!'

'Not a bad idea,' the elder admitted. 'If we, upon our island paradise, are out of plots, why not travel to those far distant lands where we might find some more?'

But Delores shook her head firmly. 'It cannot be done. As much as we would like to help, we cannot bring you along. I am transporting so many already with a single Captain Crusader Decoder Ring; I'm afraid we would overload if we added any more.' She glanced down at the dull silver ring in Dwight's mouth. 'It may be the key to the universe, but it's only made out of cheap plastic, after all.'

'Don't you worry none, fellas,' Doc reassured the islanders. 'Your island is not the only place that's suffered 'cause of Doctor Dread. Things have changed in the Cineverse, but our mission is to change them back, or to make them even better than before! Jumpin' Jehosaphat! Before long, you'll have too many plots to even think!'

'Very well,' the elder replied with a sigh, resigned to his fate. 'So our contented visitors leave this happy isle, refusing to take so much as a Coconut Upside Down Cake along for their—'

'See you in the funny papers!' Delores yelled. The blue smoke took them away.

'Yip yip yip! Bark, arf!' Dwight started in before the smoke had a chance to clear. Delores found the Captain Crusader Decoder Ring – now a little wetter than before – back in her hand.

'We're getting close!' Louie explained. 'The heroic scent is particularly strong. Captain Crusader has spent a lot of time here!'

Delores tensed. She always had this trouble when she was stuck in this thick, blue smoke. The lack of visibility alone couldn't help but make one apprehensive. Where exactly was *here*? If it was someplace where Captain Crusader spent a lot of time – where he was particularly needed – it might be even more dangerous than all the other places they had already visited.

And that brought up another question she hadn't had time to ask herself: What would they do if they actually found Captain Crusader? So much had happened in the last few days that they really had had no time to plan a definite course of action – or to even ask some of the obvious questions that arose from this situation. The Change seemed to be speeding up. Whatever the exact nature of Doctor Dread's sinister plans, they seemed to be working. Shouldn't Captain Crusader, by his very nature, be aware of this? Shouldn't he already be fighting the good fight without being sought out and asked to help? What if he had fallen under some world's spell, like Doctor Dread in Bunnyland? What if Captain

Crusader was missing because of some secret that only the hero among heroes was privy to?

What if – Delores thought with a cold suddenness – what if Captain Crusader knew where she could find Roger? With all their recent battles and narrow escapes, she had tried to push the man from Earth out of her mind. But Roger meant more to her than she had ever dared admit. She had to find him somehow – anyhow. But how could she if, to search for Roger, she had to ignore the very destiny of the Cineverse?

Delores shook her head. There were no answers. Better to concentrate on this new world, and the clues to Captain Crusader's whereabouts.

She heard the sound of the ocean. Had they never left the South Sea Island Paradise? But no, there were any number of Cineverse worlds where the sea played an important role. Perhaps, when the smoke cleared, they would find themselves on a pirate galleon, or on some huge luxury liner, a Grand Hotel of the seas. But there was another sound here beside the breaking waves – a musical sound. Delores frowned. Was it an electric guitar?

The smoke blew away. They were on a beach somewhere, full of bright sand and sun, surrounded by men and women, most of them in bathing suits that had been out of style for twenty years.

'Hey!' one of the men yelled. 'You're not Roger!'

Roger? Delores was speechless. Her Roger? Well, how many Rogers were likely to show up in the middle of a cloud of blue smoke? Could it be? She remembered how, only a moment ago, she hadn't wanted to think about him, she was so sure he must be dead. Either that, or he had been trapped back on Earth, unable to reach Delores or the Cineverse ever again!

But this changed everything! If he had come to this oceanside world, that meant that he was not only alive, but had found some other means of travelling around the Cineverse!

One of the other men, a large, hulking fellow dressed in black leather, mumbled something sinister. He held something in his hand that looked like a switch-blade.

'No, we are not Roger,' Delores said, hoping to defuse any particularly difficult situations. 'But we are friends of Roger.'

The mumbling man put away his knife. Delores breathed a sigh of relief.

He picked up a tyre iron instead. He mumbled something to the group of toughs immediately behind him. They reached in pockets, pulling out chains, brass knuckles, and two-by-four planks. Delores was amazed by the size of their pockets.

'Wait a minute?' she called to the assembled leather-suited gang. 'We don't need to fight!'

The gang all laughed at that.

'If we have to fight, Missy,' Doc drawled, 'we fight. Least it's somethin' we know. There's worse things in the Cineverse.'

The gang started towards them.

'Hey, Bix!' one of the bathing-suited fellows called. 'Don't you think it's time for a song?'

CHAPTER THIRTEEN

'Even More Flaming Death!'

'Slashen kooten blooden gooshen!' Katrina demanded.

It was only when Roger forced open one eye that he realised he had had them both closed. Katrina smiled at him.

In one hand she held the knife.

In the other hand she held the cheese.

Roger glanced down at the words that hovered around her waist. YOU SHOULD EAT, the subtitle read. WE HAVE A LONG WALK AHEAD OF US.

It was a large slab of yellow cheese, with small holes, and an aged, crumbly texture.

'Slashen?' Roger repeated.

YOU SHOULD EAT, read his subtitle.

She nodded, cutting into the cheese.

'Kooten gooshen?' he added.

A LONG WALK AHEAD, the letters read this time.

Roger almost laughed. He had completely misunderstood the import of Katrina's speech. He had imagined, foolishly, that whatever language she was speaking had some similarities to English. He should be careful, especially on a world burdened by rampant symbolism, in making any assumptions at all.

He accepted a slab of cheese. Katrina reached within the folds of her dress and retrieved a half-filled bottle of red wine. Roger uncorked it and took a swig. That was a problem with galavanting around the Cineverse – you never had time to eat. It was only now that he realised how hungry he was.

Katrina walked a few paces down the worn path to a stone bench at the far corner of the church. She sat, and Roger followed, sitting at the bench's other end. He accepted another piece of cheese, and another swig of wine.

'Valerie smertzen gnoogen splooshna!' Katrina remarked as she cut another piece for herself.

Roger glanced over at the subtitle:
MY SISTER LIVES BY A LAKE.

Roger frowned. The cheese went down hard as he swallowed. But she had definitely said 'lives', and not 'died'. Perhaps he had somehow misunderstood what Piers had been trying to tell him. Heaven knew, he could have run afoul of some colloquial idiom in the local language. Who knew how precise these subtitles were, anyway? Roger had already misinterpreted Katrina's actions once. Now, sitting with her on this bench, sharing cheese and wine, she couldn't look more unthreatening.

Roger looked up in the sky. There didn't seem to be any symbolism at all up there on this side of the church, only an endless expanse of white. It was true, Roger admitted, that endless sky could be considered bleak. But, with a full stomach and a proper frame of mind, it could also be considered peaceful.

Dr Dee Dee Davenport had called him 'incredibly lucky', and he supposed that he was. After all, he had visited maybe a dozen worlds in the Cineverse, many of them fraught with peril, and had escaped every one without a scratch. Maybe, Roger considered as he chewed, it was also a stroke of good fortune that had brought him to this art film world. This was the first place he'd been in the Cineverse where he could really pause and think.

He thought for an instant about the stranger with the blue cigar – the Plotmaster. He wondered if that mysterious figure had anything to do with Roger arriving in a contemplative place like this – if, indeed, Roger was being manipulated by this strange figure, manipulated along with everyone else in the Cineverse?

But too much contemplation, without facts to back it up, got Roger nowhere. No matter what the Plotmaster's plans were, Roger had to act for himself. He couldn't stay here, no matter how peaceful it seemed at the moment. He had to find Captain Crusader, save the Cineverse, figure out the riddle of the Plotmaster – and rescue Delores, if Delores was still rescuable. And that was just for starters.

A few minutes ago, his Captain Crusader Decoder Ring had failed to work and he had panicked, blaming the failure on Professor Peril's tampering with the computer at the Institute of Very Advanced Science. But, now that he thought about it, there could be other reasons for that failure. What if there wasn't something wrong with the ring, but in the way he had used it? He was in a different place, with different rules, and a different language. What if – for the ring to work – he had to say 'See you in the funny papers' in the native tongue?

Of course! It only made sense; at least as much sense as Professor Peril having enough foresight to get the computer to sabotage his ring. Maybe he could get off this world after all!

But how could he learn to say 'See you in the funny papers' in the local lingo? Roger thought back to other movies he had seen, and how people who didn't speak the same language managed to communicate. They somehow managed to act out their wishes, didn't they? He glanced at Katrina, and she looked curiously back at him. Roger would somehow have to reach her through sign language.

He pointed to himself. 'Roger,' he said.

Katrina pointed to herself and repeated her name. So she had the idea!

Roger pointed to his eyes and said the first word he needed a translation for:

'See.'

Katrina pointed to her own eye and said, 'Snortz!'

Roger eagerly looked at the subtitle.

EYE, it read.

Roger sighed. This wasn't going to be easy. He had to be more demonstrative. He placed his index finger along his temple. He first pointed to his eye, then shot the finger straight ahead, as if it were a ray of light.

'Ah!' Katrina replied in sudden comprehension. 'Gleeba snortz!'

POINTING NEXT TO YOUR EYE, the translation read.

Roger wished he had played more Charades in his life. How could you come up with sign language for one of the senses? You see with the eye. What could be simpler? Surely, in a world so fraught with symbolism, Katrina was bound to make the connection. He shook his head and repeated the index finger move.

'Ah!' Katrina gave a how-could-she-be-so-stupid chuckle. She added triumphantly: 'Snortz felten zubba-zubba!'

That sounded a little long to be 'see', but perhaps it was colloquial. Roger looked hopefully at the subtitle.

RIPPING YOUR EYE OUT AND THROWING IT A GREAT DISTANCE.

No. There had to be some other way to get his message across. Roger also didn't like the violent subtext of Katrina's suggestion.

He thought again about Piers' fearful remarks concerning the dead sister.

But Roger couldn't give into despair. He had Katrina working with him; he simply had to come up with a new approach. How did you indicate the senses? It was hard with the eyes.

Roger pointed to his nose.

'Smortz,' Katrina replied.

NOSE, the subtitle read.

Roger sniffed exaggeratedly.

'Smortzen?' Katrina asked.

SMELL? was the subtitle. Yes! Roger was on the right track. He pointed back to his eye.

'Snortz?' Katrina ventured. 'Snortzen?'

EYE? read the letters near her waist. SEE?

Yes! Roger nodded his head rapidly and clapped his hands. They were on their way! Katrina picked up right away on 'me' and 'you' when Roger pointed to both of them repeatedly. You was 'norma' – he should have remembered that. Roger mimed laughter, and got the word 'snucksky' from Katrina. But how was he going to come up with the word for papers?

That's when he remembered the book he'd stuck inside his elastic waistband: *The Cineverse – From A to Zed*. He'd simply point at one page, then another.

PAMPHLET, came the subtitled response. Then PERIODICAL. Then POINTING. Roger crinkled a corner of the page.

'Storken,' Katrina replied.

PAPER, the subtitle read.

Roger nodded, crumpling a second page.

'Storkena?' Katrina added.

'Yes!' Roger shouted.

'Snucksen vorden merkna Valarie,' Katrina announced.

I AM GLAD YOU ARE SO HAPPY. HOWEVER, WE MUST SEE MY SISTER BEFORE DARK. SHE IS EXPECTING US, AFTER ALL, AND THE DISTANCE, WHILE NOT GREAT, CAN BE TIRING, ESPECIALLY IF YOU HAVE TO WALK INTO THE WIND.

Katrina had said all that? There was obviously a lot about this language that Roger had yet to figure out.

Roger stood up and pointed down the path.

'Go?' he enquired.

'Oucsh!' she exclaimed as she also stood. 'Minsky vlerben mordet karben tertra koriden zumma-zumma nigslipzen bedorm valarie krensk niebelungenkamerad-shaftenvolkswagen shaboom shaboom!'

YES, was the only word that appeared at her waist. Then again, Roger realised, there might be some problems with the translation.

Katrina led the way at a brisk pace. Roger hurried to keep up, but somehow she managed to stay a good dozen feet in front of him. He pulled out his ring. He had the translation for 'See you in the funny papers'. He might as well see if it would work. Was there any last thing he wanted to say to his guide?

'Katrina!' he called.

'Glorben snurbs!' she shouted back without looking around. And this time there was no subtitle at all.

Very well. There was probably no need for explanations if he disappeared from a place like this. The locals would simply chalk it up to more symbolism.

He took a deep breath and twisted the ring.

'Snortzen stephanie snucksky storkena!' he yelled.

Nothing happened. He looked at the subtitle.

LOOKING AT YOU WITH THE HUMOROUS BOOKS!

Well, that might not have been exactly what he wanted, but it should have been close enough, shouldn't it? Then why had nothing happened? Maybe he hadn't spoken with enough conviction.

He said the foreign phrase again, slowly and clearly, twisting the ring the other way.

'Snortzen stephanie snucksky storkena!'

Still nothing but the same subtitle about looking at humorous books. And if that phrase wasn't close enough, he didn't know how he could get any closer. Maybe the Professor Peril theory was right after all.

Katrina glanced over her shoulder without slackening her pace. 'Minsky mensky geslunden?' she demanded. She didn't have any subtitle this time either.

Wait a second, Roger realised. Wasn't there something flickering against the sky? Why hadn't he seen this before? It wasn't as if this was anything new – he always had this sort of problem with foreign films. With Katrina so far ahead of him, the letters must be appearing all the way on the other side of her, right up against that colourless sky, making the subtitles white on white and completely illegible.

So her words were lost to him. Roger hoped whatever she had

said wasn't essential to the plot. Although, now that he thought about it, what did the plot matter if he couldn't use his Captain Crusader Decoder Ring?

He followed Katrina listlessly to the lake, which, despite her protestations of hardship and distance, was only over the next hill. The water showed the same lack of colour as the sky, and its modest expanse was bordered only by a few more of those ever-present barren trees and a small shack which, if Roger had been feeling more generous than his present circumstances allowed, he might have classified as a hovel.

Katrina walked straight to the shack. She banged on the door.

'Valarie zurben-zurben,' she told Roger authoritatively.

MY SISTER WILL ANSWER.

The subtitle, appearing against the dark and rotting wood, was once again legible. Katrina banged on the door again. There was no sound from inside.

Katrina frowned at Roger.

'Glurben knocken kneesa.'

YOU SEEM NERVOUS.

Roger jumped at the suggestion. 'Uh—' he started. But how could he explain when he didn't know the language?

'Smeltzny Piers geblurben?' she demanded.

WHAT DID PIERS TELL YOU ABOUT MY SISTER?

What use was it to lie? Roger – after a second's thought to consider the most appropriate pantomime – clutched his heart and fell to the ground. Katrina began to speak rapidly. Roger pushed himself to his knees so that he could read the subtitle.

THAT SHE WAS DEAD? DO NOT BELIEVE HIM. MY SISTER LIV IS QUITE ALIVE. IT IS PIERS WHO CANNOT ACCEPT THE TRUTH.

Accepting the truth? This was sounding more like an art film with every passing minute. What was the truth? And should Roger even care?

He stumbled to his feet. He almost fell over again when the shack's door flew open.

'Gretzky!' Katrina said triumphantly. 'Birdenparish.'

SEE! the subtitle read. LIV IS ALIVE.

Her sister rushed from the shack. Her hair was a matted grey tangle that flopped about her head, her eyes two blazing points of blue in an unnaturally pale face, her clothing little more than tattered rags hanging from her emaciated body.

Her hands grabbed Roger's neck in a stranglehold.

'Viola canseco wadeboggs,' Katrina confided.

SHE IS ALSO QUITE MAD, Roger read with his blurring vision.

'Lars,' Katrina's sister whispered hoarsely.

LARS, her subtitle read. Roger tried, ineffectually, to pry her iron fingers from his throat. Katrina said something in return, but the sound of pounding blood was too loud in Roger's ears for him to catch the words. He could, however, just barely read the subtitle:

YES. I HAVE BROUGHT YOU LARS, AND I HAVE BROUGHT YOU A KNIFE. IT'S ALMOST BRAND-NEW, ONLY USED TO CUT CHEESE.

Lars? Knife? Roger struggled to comprehend. The mad Liv eased her hold for an instant, and Roger tried to think of something, anything, he could say to make her stop. He hadn't figured out all that many of the words, and now he couldn't remember any of them. Still, he knew he had to try anyway, if he didn't want to die. Maybe the very sound of his voice would disturb the mad sister enough so that he might break away.

'Mensky – uh – valarie – gesundheit – uh – *urk*!'

The last sound came as Liv once again tightened her grip.

COME TO ME, the subtitle read, MY LITTLE PIGLET.

How could he have said anything like that? The pressure increased at his throat. Roger was almost too upset to struggle. He didn't even know the word for piglet! Katrina was talking to her sister again. He managed to read the subtitle.

KILL THIS ONE SLOWLY, WOULD YOU? IT IS SO STRESSFUL TO FIND REPLACEMENTS.

Liv nodded and shook Roger by the throat one more time. He said '*Urk*' again for good measure.

PIGLET, the subtitle read. Liv kicked him in the kneecap.

Katrina smiled at Roger and said a final few words just for him.

IT IS NOT MUCH, BUT IT KEEPS HER HAPPY.

She turned to go, and Liv yanked Roger inside by the throat. She threw him down on a corner pile of straw. His head hit something hard. He gasped for breath, but it was no use. Liv's grip had been too firm, the knock on the back of his head too solid. The oddly-spaced boards that criss-crossed the hovel's roof swirled wildly overhead.

He could feel his consciousness

slipping . . .
slipping . . .
slipping . . .
slipping.

He struggled to stay awake, but the world swung around him at a fantastic speed, colours bleeding, objects

blurring . . .
blurring . . .
blurring . . .
blurring . . .
Was there an echo in here somewhere?

And, for that matter, where was 'here' anyway?

He wasn't in the hovel any more. The colours around here were much too bright. He squinted, trying to bring the passing objects into focus.

Something large and pink and pudgy was screaming in the distance – actually, caterwauling would be a better description, a great booming cry like – Roger realised – a giant baby.

Another sound overlaid the baby's cries, a steady, rhythmic sound. Roger turned around. His surroundings were becoming clearer. It was much easier to make out the clock face with the twirling hands.

Tick-tock, went the clock.

Tick-tock . . .
Tick-Tock . . .
Tick-tock . . .

Yes, there was a definite echo around here. He heard another sound as the ticking faded, a mix of flutes and drums. Roger didn't have to turn around to know it was the all-nun band. He realised what all this meant. He had been wrong when he thought he had gone to some new world.

He was still in the art film, only more so.

He had fallen into a dream sequence.

A voice boomed over him, a voice that came from infinity.

BRAVO!

'Pardon?' Roger replied. He had heard that voice before. It surprised him not at all that he was turning around without using any of his muscles – this was a dream sequence, after all – nor did it surprise him that he was now facing the man with the blue smoke cigar.

ROGER, SWEETIE, BABY!

The man's voice boomed again as he waved his cigar. It was the Plotmaster in silhouette, backlit as usual, so that Roger couldn't make out any of the finer details of the man's appearance. Somewhere, faintly, in the distance, Roger could hear a heavenly chorus – a Mormon Tabernacle Choir sort of sound.

Roger could still tell the Plotmaster was studying him critically.

NOT SURPRISED AT ALL,

the Plotmaster said at last, then took a puff on his cigar. Blue smoke curled upwards, encircling the all-nun band who marched upside-down above his head. The choir music was lost for a moment beneath the clatter of drums and the tooting of flutes.

SO YOU *DO* REMEMBER ME?
AND YOU'VE ACCURATELY IDENTIFIED YOUR SURROUNDINGS!

Oh dear, Roger thought. He wasn't supposed to remember this fellow, was he? He hoped the Plotmaster didn't hold a grudge. Now that Roger considered it, the dark silhouette of a man smoking a cigar could appear rather threatening.

'I'm afraid I do – remember you, that is,' Roger replied softly. 'Is this a problem?'

But the Plotmaster laughed.

PROBLEM?
I LIKE TO THINK OF IT MORE AS A PLOT COMPLICATION.
AND, HEY!
I *LIKE* TO USE PLOT COMPLICATIONS.
THEY DON'T CALL ME THE PLOTMASTER FOR NOTHING, BOOBALA!

Roger guessed he should be relieved. But this was all so strange—

The Plotmaster snapped his fingers.

OF COURSE, I COULD CANCEL YOUR CONTRACT
JUST LIKE *THAT*!

Snap . . .
Snap . . .
Snap . . .
Snap . . .
Snap . . .

There was that echo again. Cancel his contract? Did that mean what Roger thought it meant?

The Plotmaster pointed his cigar at Roger. The ember on the stogie's end burned blue.

I'M THE BIG GUY AROUND HERE.
NEVER FORGET THAT.
AND IF ANYBODY EVER CROSSES ME,
I CAN BE *RUTHLESS*!

His booming declaration completed, the Plotmaster waved his cigar more casually, chuckling softly, as if he were making a joke with an old friend.

BUT, HEY!
YOU REMEMBER ME, YOU'RE CURIOUS
ABOUT ME.
SO YOU WANT TO ASK A QUESTION OR TWO?

His voice lost its chuckle for an instant as he added:

NOTHING *TOO* PERSONAL, NOW.

The Plotmaster laughed jovially, as if he and Roger were indeed best buddies. For some reason, Roger thought once again about what it might mean to have your contract cancelled.

The Plotmaster paused, waiting. The angelic choir sang expectantly.

Well, apparently, the big man wanted Roger to ask questions. And, in his time in the Cineverse, Roger had indeed come up with a few questions.

But being in front of the Plotmaster seemed to call for more than casual conversation. There must be some question that Roger should ask first. What was really his biggest concern in all the Cineverse? There was the search for Captain Crusader, concern for his friends – but, really, overriding everything else was the woman who had led Roger into this quest.

That, then, would have to be his first question.

'Um,' Roger began, 'about Delores—'

But the Plotmaster had already started to speak again, as if he had forgotten he'd ever asked Roger to pose a question.

YOU'RE PROBABLY WONDERING WHY I ASKED
YOU HERE TODAY?

The Plotmaster waved his cigar like a baton, conducting a silent and invisible orchestra, or maybe a very distant chorus.

ROGER, SWEETIE, BABY!
POINT ONE:
YOU REMEMBER ME.
POINT TWO:
YOU'LL LEARN YOUR WAY AROUND THE CINEVERSE.
DO I NEED TO *SPELL IT OUT* FOR YOU?
IT'S A WINNING COMBINATION.
I'M EXPECTING BIG THINGS OUT OF YOU, ROGER!

What? Roger thought. He was even more confused than back when Delores used to try to explain the Cineverse. Why was he – Roger Gordon of Earth – some kind of winning combination? And, for that matter, he still hadn't asked the Plotmaster about Delores!

The Plotmaster coughed before Roger could think to frame another question.

THERE WAS SOMETHING ELSE, WASN'T THERE?

the Plotmaster asked rhetorically. His hand reached down to a table that Roger would have sworn hadn't been there a moment before.

OF COURSE! SILLY OF ME.
I WANTED TO REMIND YOU ABOUT THIS PART

IN THE SCRIPT.
THIS VERY DIFFICULT PART—

He picked up what looked like a thick, bound manuscript.

A script? About Roger? And everybody else, too, probably – including Delores! Roger was astonished. The implications of this were enormous!

The Plotmaster flipped quickly through the pages.

WHERE WAS IT? I HAD IT A MINUTE AGO.
I'M SURE IT WAS IMPORTANT—
SOMETHING ABOUT – LIFE AND DEATH.

He nodded as he finally found his place.

AH—

He looked up as an insistent trilling sounded all around him.

NOW?
WOULDN'T YOU KNOW IT?
WE'RE JUST GETTING TO KNOW EACH OTHER
AND THE PHONE RINGS.
WELL, ROGER, YOU AND ME, WE'RE BOTH BUSY
MEN, HUH?
I HATE TO RUSH YOU, BUT YOU KNOW—
IMPORTANT CALLS?

Important calls? Roger thought. But the Plotmaster had been talking about life and death!

WHEN YOU'RE THE PLOTMASTER,
YOU CAN REALLY HAVE YOUR HANDS FULL,
LET ME TELL YOU!

The Plotmaster snapped his fingers again, with the usual echo accompaniment. The angelic choir broke off mid-note. He waved to Roger as he picked up the phone.

LET'S GET TOGETHER AGAIN, SOMETIME SOON!
YOU KNOW I'M COUNTING ON YOU, BOOBALA!

The Plotmaster puffed again, and was surrounded by blue smoke.

But the Plotmaster hadn't told Roger anything! This was not just a dream sequence, Roger realised, it was an anxiety dream sequence!

Roger wasn't going to let this happen. He couldn't let the Plotmaster go before he knew more.

'But—' Roger called.

       'But—'
         'But—'
           'But—'
             'But—'
               'But—'

And the echo faded away.

Roger opened his eyes. He was back in the hovel by the lake. He felt hands around his throat as he was once again dragged to his feet. A madwoman stared him in the face.

The dream was over.

'Minsky mensky oobala!' Liv yelled at Roger, every word bursting with hatred.

Roger once again looked at the subtitle.

I HAVE THOUGHT ABOUT THIS FOR A LONG TIME.

'Minsky mensky boobala!' she added. Hadn't she just said that? But the subtitle was different.

WHAT I WOULD DO WHEN YOU CAME BACK TO ME.

Life and death, the Plotmaster had said. Was this the very situation the man with the blue smoke cigar had wanted to warn him about?

Liv leaned over him. Her breath smelled like she had been eating rotting rodents.

'Mensky minsky granola puffenstuff!'

HOW I COULD MAKE YOU SUFFER THE WAY I DID.

She grabbed him by the back of the neck and pulled him towards her. Roger's first thought was how strong women's hands were in this foreign art film. He thought then for an instant about trying to say something to her again. The word 'piglet' came floating into his consciousness. This, when combined with the continuing pain in both his throat and kneecap, convinced him that, for now, silence was the best policy.

'Rottentotten nets!'

DEATH IS NOT ENOUGH.

She wasn't going to kill him? Maybe this wasn't the Plotmaster's warning. Roger allowed himself the slightest bit of hope. Maybe his silence was working after all.

'Minsky mensky somethingorother!' she added.

IT HAS TO BE A PARTICULARLY PAINFUL DEATH.

Roger's slight hope evaporated instantaneously. She kicked the door open and dragged him outside before he could further react to the bad news, once again circling both her hands around his neck.

'Oons!' she continued almost cheerfully. 'Norts gebort. Minsky providentially voola-voola shebang!'

COME. EVERYTHING IS READY. IT IS PROVIDENTIALLY COINCIDENTAL THAT SOMEONE HAS LEFT A BOAT.

Roger caught a quick glimpse of his surroundings as he was tossed outside. There was indeed a small rowboat at the edge of the lake, but it looked in worse repair than the woman's shack, like the faded memory of a craft that once, in the distant past, before six holes had appeared in its hull, could have conceivably floated on the chill, grey water.

The pressure left his throat for an instant. Roger felt his hands being tied tight behind his back, and then the chokehold was back. In a matter of seconds, he had been dragged down to the boatside.

Liv said a single word:

'Krensk.'

The subtitle, however, was much longer.

I THINK DEATH BY DROWNING IS ALMOST PUNISHMENT ENOUGH. DEATH BY DROWNING AFTER BEING TRAPPED IN A BURNING BOAT IS EVEN BETTER.

Roger was tossed roughly into the boat, which was filled with dry twigs and leaves. Liv smiled as she pushed the boat out into the lake, then lit a match which in turn ignited an oil-soaked rag.

'Lars!' she called as she tossed the rag into the dried brush. 'Tootles!'

Roger struggled, but his hands were firmly tied, the ropes digging cruelly into his flesh. The brush caught fire energetically at the other end of the boat – a fire that would reach him in a matter of seconds, if the ancient, leaky craft didn't sink first.

Oddly enough, the only thing Roger could think of at that moment was that Liv hadn't used the knife.

That's when she threw it at him. He saw the shining blade headed straight for his chest, its cutting edge passing cleanly through the single word of Liv's last subtitle:

GOODBYE.

CHAPTER FOURTEEN

'Dread Coincidence!'

'Plssm grrsmm!' the gang leader mumbled. 'Blssm grssm!'

'You play one more guitar chord,' the thin gang member elucidated, 'and we'll use our blades on your guitars.'

'Yeah!' another of the gang added heavily. 'And not just the strings, either!'

Bix Bale and the Belltones stopped strumming abruptly.

Delores stared at the approaching gang, smirks on their faces and weapons of destruction in their hands. Her companions gathered around her, ready to confront this newest threat with everything from royally jungle-trained muscles to canine wonder teeth.

But confrontation was not the answer. There had to be some way out of this pattern of battle after battle. If they did nothing but fight, how would they ever find Captain Crusader?

That's when the sand rose up before her. The gang stopped.

'Oh, no, you don't,' a deep, all-too-familiar voice intoned. 'Delores is mine.'

The figure was vaguely man-shaped, although slightly taller than most men. Beyond that, Delores could tell nothing, for it was entirely coated with sand.

'Scffmmm prfffss drrrtt!' the fellow who mumbled ordered.

His unpleasantly skinny sidekick added in his most sarcastic tone: 'The Mumbler wants to know if you guys are scared of a pile of dirt!'

The entire gang jeered at that. Those among the mob intelligent enough to talk added a few comments of their own:

'Yeah – dirt!'

They advanced again.

'Dirt needs to be stomped!'

They brandished knives.

'We'll bulldoze 'im!'

They swung chains.

'We'll ex-ex-uh-excavate 'im!'

They pounded brass knuckles into bloody palms, the pain apparently not reaching their small and distant brains.

'We'll throw him into the ocean and turn him into mud!' the unpleasant, skinny fellow added as the gang formed a semi-circle half a dozen paces from the sand creature.

But all the Monster did was laugh. 'I am more than a pile of dirt. Beneath this sandy exterior lurks a heart of pure slime!'

The gang stopped to look at each other.

'Sliffmm?' the Mumbler demanded.

'Nah!' the thin fellow exclaimed. 'It can't be that bad.'

The gang approached the sand-covered creature, perhaps a bit more tentatively than before.

'I have warned you,' the Monster replied solemnly. It turned its featureless head toward Delores and her band. 'If you would stand a little farther back, it would ensure you are out of the line of sludge.' The creature took a deep breath, then continued hurriedly. 'I dedicate this new work to you, Delores. I call it "Gang Covered by Slime".'

With that, the Slime Monster lifted up what might have been its arms, or possibly its tentacles – it was hard to tell underneath all that crusted sand. The gang rushed forward. One of them whipped a chain across the creature's shoulder. The metal links landed with a dull thud. The Monster did not seem to notice.

'I begin!' the creature announced, and sludge burst forth from the twin points the thing had raised, more like dual hoses than fingers.

Brownish-grey slime covered the gang in a matter of seconds. When they moved, they slipped. When they slipped, they fell. When they spoke, they only said 'glub' or 'gurgle'.

'My work is done,' the creature declared proudly.

' "Gang Covered by Slime"?' Delores asked.

The Monster nodded its sand-covered head (if head it truly was). 'It is my latest creation. I understand that there are those who do not appreciate my art. But I have no choice. It is the artist within me. I must express myself through slime.'

'Hey, that's great!' one of the tanned, swim-suit-clad lads called. 'You put the Mad Mumbler and his Motorcycle Mob in its place! I think that calls for a song!'

The band started tuning up again. The Monster turned to regard the speaker.

'Not unless you want to be covered by slime.'

The guitars ceased strumming even more quickly than they had last time.

'Thank you,' the Monster replied. 'Sometimes my art requires silence.'

'Glub,' the gang members remarked as they rolled around, so that their own, personal slime became sand-coated as well. 'Gurgle.'

'You have seen one of my pieces before – the one I titled "Doctor Dread Covered by Slime",' the Monster continued. 'It is so difficult to display my work. Slime is such a transitory form!'

'Not when you add sand!' Zabana observed wrily.

'Gurgle,' the gang members added from where they still struggled to rise. 'Glub.'

'That is true,' Edward mused. 'I had never thought of adding other things to the slime. It gives me whole new sources of inspiration. This could be the first of many. We could call it my "dirt period". And it's all because of you, Delores.'

Delores didn't know how to answer that. She stared moodily at the gang members. A couple of them had collected enough sand on their persons so that they could finally stand without sliding, their 'glubs' and 'gurgles' muffled by the extra coating of dirt. She realised, though, that she was only avoiding this Edward thing, hoping against hope that the Monster would simply go away. What should she say to this creature to make him understand? For that matter, what did you say to a slime monster under any circumstances?

Edward spoke again before she could come to any decision, a wistful tone to his voice. 'It was too bad you had to leave that time we were in the city together, when you were being chased by an incredible number of bad guys, before you could see the work I titled "An Incredible Number of Bad Guys Simultaneously Coated By Slime". It may have been my masterpiece – at least of my early, slime only period.'

'Slime as art?' Delores managed at last, knowing that she had to say something. 'It is a sobering thought.'

'I knew you would see what I was trying to do!' the Monster enthused. 'Oh, why can't the critics be more like you? Why must the petty art world misunderstand?'

'Is law of Cineverse!' the jungle prince answered.

The standing gang members had managed, while only falling down once or twice again themselves, to help the rest of their sand-covered fellows to their feet. The entire crew shuffled away from the Slime Monster, in the general direction of the ocean.

'Yip bark!' Dwight the Wonder Dog interrupted as he leapt about enthusiastically at Louie's side. 'Bark yip arf!'

The dog's outburst brought Delores back to her senses, beyond slime monsters and sand-covered gang members. They had come to this world for a purpose. Wasn't Captain Crusader supposed to be here someplace?

Louie once again interpreted. 'Dwight says that Captain Crusader's been all over this place!'

'He has?' Delores asked, almost too excited to go on. After all this time, and all those worlds, had their quest finally succeeded? 'Where is he?' She looked around at a beach full of startled surfers. 'Don't anybody move!'

Dwight once again put his nose to the ground. He trotted quickly to an area of packed sand directly in front of the raised bandstand where Bix Bale and the Belltones fearfully watched their instruments.

'Bark! Yip! Arf!' Dwight informed them.

'He's getting close!' Louie exclaimed.

Dwight jumped up on to the bandstand, quickly sniffing at Bix Bale and the Belltones before dismissing them as unworthy of Captain Crusader consideration. Delores frowned. Something was wrong here. Why didn't Captain Crusader, hero among heroes, simply step forward? There was something strange about this whole situation. Did this all have something to do with the Change?

The dog leapt back to the beach, coming within snuffling range of every cluster of surfers and beach bunnies. He galloped over to the Motorcycle Mob, who were washing away sand and slime in the surf, but their smell came up as negative as well. The wonder canine even, very briefly, sniffed the Slime Monster, but, after one very astonished 'yip!' of disbelief, quickly moved on.

Dwight trotted over to Big Louie. 'Yip yip yip!' he stated at last. 'Arf arf arf!'

Now it was Louie's turn to frown. 'Dwight says he's somewhere nearby, but he isn't here.'

Delores looked at the sidekick, then at the wonder dog. Yes, this was definitely odd. It sort of sounded like Captain Crusader was here, and at the same time wasn't here. So where was he? And who was he? This sort of world, full of sand and surf, didn't seem like an obvious hangout for the active hero type – the surroundings here were just too frivolous.

Which, of course, led to other questions. They had come here to find Captain Crusader, but on whose instructions? Dwight the Wonder Dog's? But Delores didn't even know that for sure. What she did know was that Big Louie was giving the orders, supposedly for the wonder dog, but since he was the only one who could understand what the dog was saying, who could say who was the mastermind behind this latest phase of their adventures – a sidekick or an animal?

And how well could a mere dog, even one with a wonder sense of smell, track the person who was turning out to be the most elusive hero in the Cineverse? What if Captain Crusader had changed his image once again, as he was so fond of doing? He could be anywhere. He could be hiding in their very midst without them knowing it. Any one of them – well, she knew *she* wasn't Captain Crusader, at least, she was pretty sure of it – but any of the others could be the heroes' hero in disguise! Doc, Zabana, even Officer O'Clanrahan had heroic credentials. Or he could be even more heavily disguised as, say, Big Louie, or one of these kids on the beach!

Delores stopped and stared at the panting canine as she realised he could even be – Dwight the Wonder Dog. It was all too confusing. Why were they here? Who was Captain Crusader? She would have to leave all these questions behind if she were to be of any use at all in their search. In the Cineverse, you sometimes simply had to accept things.

'They're called holes in the plot,' Louie assured her, even though she hadn't spoken any of her thoughts aloud.

'Yip yip! Bark arf!' Dwight added.

'Dwight says that this is the right place,' Louie interpreted. 'We simply have to be patient.'

Delores sighed. Now she had both a sidekick and a dog reading her mind. But she realised she might have more immediate problems. The Mad Mumbler and the Motorcycle Mob had cleaned all the sand and slime from their persons, and were trudging back up the beach.

'Zabana ready for anything,' the jungle prince said as he moved to her side.

'That goesh double for me, misshy!' Doc said as he staggered over to join them.

Oh, no! Delores had feared this very sort of thing. They had been out of action for too long, and something had tipped the balance in the delicate line Doc walked between helpless sobriety and helpless inebriation. She had known it all along, even though she hadn't wanted to admit it: The plot had been too straight-forward up to now. Delores was all too aware of the shifts and surprises that lurked out there, especially since the Change. She thought of men wearing hockey masks, and shivered. The longer they searched for Captain Crusader, the more they invited the products of the Change, and Cineverse disaster.

'It'sh the beach,' Doc explained as he tried to stand without swaying. 'Jusht a shmall cashe of shunshtroke.'

He fell down, face first, into the sand. He made a gentle 'foomph' noise when he hit, immediately followed by snoring.

The unpleasantly skinny gang member laughed. 'Look, fellas! They're fainting before we even get to them!'

They all laughed in a way that indicated they had learned nothing from their recent experience with slime.

With the lightning swiftness of a jungle cat, Zabana leapt across the sand, felling the skinny fellow with a single blow.

'Zabana even the odds,' the jungle prince announced as he danced back to join the others.

'Vrrbbmm! Zrrrbbbmmm!' the Mumbler screamed.

'What?' one of the gang members asked.

'Huh?' another echoed.

'That guy in the leopard shorts just decked Sneer!' a third explained. 'Sneer was the only one who could understand you!'

'Snrrgggmmmm!' the Mumbler raged. 'Fllrrrrgggmmm!'

The sand rose before them for a second time.

'I would go no further,' the familiar voice warned.

'Snrrzzzzz!' the Mumbler hastily replied. 'Frrssrrzzz!'

'So they give me another chance to pursue my art,' Edward the slime creature remarked casually. 'It is a shame. Their shame, of course. My triumph! I will call it "The Entire Gang Covered by Slime for a Second Time". I tell you, whole new vistas are opening for me!' The monster waved one of its appendages in their leader's direction. 'And I owe it all to Delores!'

The monster once again trained whatever you might call its upper appendages on the Motorcycle Mob.

'Gglllffrrtttt!' the Mumbler protested.

'Yip! Bark bark bark!' Dwight leapt forward to interrupt the action.

'Wait!' Louie explained. 'He says the Mumbler doesn't want to fight!'

'You mean Dwight can interpret what this guy is mumbling about?' Delores demanded.

'Hey, now,' Officer O'Clanrahan interjected defensively. 'He is Dwight the Wonder Dog, after all.'

'Mssrrmm!' the Mumbler insisted.

'Yip bark yip!' Dwight replied.

'Grrrrssllm?' the Mumbler asked.

'Yip yip, bark, yip!' Dwight answered reassuringly.

'The Mumbler wants to work with us,' Louie explained. 'It seems it's getting boring on this surfing world—'

That's when there was another explosion, accompanied by blowing sand and blue smoke. Delores considered how, since the Change (with the exception of one South Sea Paradise), nothing ever seemed to stay boring for long.

'Heh heh,' someone at the centre of the smoke snickered sinisterly. 'How' – he hesitated tellingly – 'convenient.'

Delores felt a tap on her shoulder.

'Is Doctor Dread!' Zabana announced.

Delores looked around.

'Hey, baby,' a tall, scrawny surfer said in an artificially deep voice. 'What's a nice girl like you doing on a beach like this?'

'Faith and begorah!' Officer O'Clanrahan chimed in, pointing his nightstick at the archvillain. 'The bounder is all alone!'

'Not,' Doctor Dread assured them, 'for long.'

'What?' Delores whispered incredulously as she stared at this newest intruder in her life.

'What's a nice girl like you doing on—' the surfer started again.

'Why are you asking me that at a time like this?' Delores demanded.

'I had to wait for you to be alone!' the surfer replied defensively. 'You're a popular girl.'

'Well, you'll have to wait a little longer.' Delores turned back to study their nemesis.

'Hey!' the surfer called over her shoulder. 'I'm a better catch than somebody completely covered by sand!'

'Are you?' Delores murmured. She was surprised how sincerely she doubted that. But Doctor Dread had begun to hesitate meaningfully again.

'I have been meaning to' – Dread coughed delicately – 'see you people again, ever since you' – he coughed twice, and not quite as delicately as before – 'attempted to dispose of me on that planet of rabbits.'

'Your name's Delores, isn't it?' the surfer insisted.

'Interesting that you should be here,' Dread continued, 'the very place my information indicates is the most likely location of Captain Crusader.'

'My name's Fast Felix,' the surfer went on, despite anything Delores could do to the contrary, 'the most romantic surfer on the beach. When I saw you in that evening gown, I knew we were made for each other!'

'You see, the Captain and I have a little' – Dread coughed more softly this time, attempting to put the delicacy back in – 'business.'

'Well, you've met me,' Delores replied to the man behind her.

'Zabana say we take him,' the jungle prince announced.

'My thoughtsh exshactly!' Doc added unevenly.

'Now get lost!' Delores finished.

'I wouldn't do that, if I were you. I'm expecting' – this time, Dread tried to hold back the cough – 'company.'

'But we'll get him before the company arrives!' Officer O'Clanrahan pointed out. 'We must prevail. We have Dwight the Wonder Dog!'

'Hard to get, huh?' The scrawny surfer jogged forward so that Delores could see him wriggle his spindly eyebrows. 'Fast Felix especially likes women in evening dresses who play hard to get.'

'Oh, very well, if you' – Dread paused to clear his throat – 'insist. Say, you there in black leather.'

'Pptttzzzzmmmm!' the Mumbler declared. His gang paid no attention.

'Us?' one of the members of the Motorcycle Mob asked.

'Of course,' Dread continued smoothly. 'How would you like to be' – the cough was back – 'among the future rulers of the Cineverse?'

'Wrrssfff!' the Mumbler yelled. His gang looked the other way.

'So, babe,' Fast Felix insisted. 'What do you say?'

'Us?' another mobster replied.

'I knew you'd catch on,' Dread purred. 'Bright fellows. Very well.' He paused for another hack, then pointed casually to Delores and her fellows. 'Deal with them!'

Fast Felix ran a hand lightly down Delores' spangled sleeve. 'I'll show you sand and surf you've never seen before—'

The gang once again approached. Delores pushed Fast Felix out of her way and joined the line of her allies, all once again ready to do battle with the forces of evil. They had to be doubly wary now. She expected more blue smoke explosions at any second. But would those explosions contain more minions of Doctor Dread, or would they bring Captain Crusader? Whatever happened, she knew for certain, they were facing their moment of decision.

'Hey, babe,' Delores heard behind her. 'Fast Felix doesn't take no—'

'This is the end of the line for you, Doctor Dread!' Officer O'Clanrahan announced.

'Oh my, no. This is only' – Dread paused to smile evilly – 'the beginning.'

CHAPTER FIFTEEN

'Wave of Terror!'

He barely managed to duck the knife. The smoke and fire seemed to have spoiled the woman's aim, unless it was the fact that the boat had sunk an inch or two since she'd thrown her weapon.

Once again, all of Roger's life threatened to flash before his eyes. He remembered Gloria, and Fiona, and Charlene, and Daisy. But he couldn't sink into reminiscence. There still might be some way out of his predicament. He had to do it, for Delores, Captain Crusader, the Earth, the Cineverse, maybe even the Plotmaster, if Roger could ever figure out what the guy had been talking about – and he had to do it for himself. He didn't want to die in the world of a foreign art film, especially after that dream sequence. For all he knew, once he drowned, or was burned, or was stabbed to death, his ghost would be trapped here in the symbolic sky, skipping after the all-nun band. His mind wandered back to Lulu, and Karen, and Clarissa.

No! He had to think this through. He'd escaped from other tight spots before – well, perhaps they hadn't been as tight as this one. He simply had to look at his predicament in as objective a manner as possible. There must be some way out. Mere hours ago, Dr Dee Dee Davenport had declared him to be 'incredibly lucky'. Roger would hate to prove her wrong.

He pushed thoughts of Tanya and Rachel and Sophia from his head and listed his problems. Liv had missed with her knife, so that meant all he had to contend with was a sinking boat that was rapidly being consumed by fire. That, and the fact that the new Captain Crusader Ring he'd gotten from the computer was a dud, so he couldn't get out that way, besides which, his hands were tied, so that there was no way he could get to the ring. His mind drifted to Daphne, and Sheri, and Theodora.

But no – the Plotmaster seemed to think Roger had something special going for him. Roger tried to quickly remember the points the big guy with the blue smoke cigar had made. One was that Roger actually remembered the Plotmaster. The other was something about how, with time, Roger would learn his way around the Cineverse.

No, he wouldn't. Roger was going to burn up in a boat. The fire felt awfully hot on his face. At least the flames didn't affect his feet, probably because both his sneakers were already under six inches of water.

Wait a minute! All this stuff about the Plotmaster had almost made him forget – a minute ago, he'd been thinking about his new Captain Crusader Ring! But he also had an *old* Captain Crusader Decoder Ring. Sure, it was defective, but it worked after a fashion, and even the beach party surfing world was preferable to existential death!

The ring was only a few inches away, in the breast pocket of his jogging suit. He leaned forward. Was there any possible way he could reach it? His jogging jacket bunched up towards him. For the first time ever, he was grateful for that spare tyre that had started around his waist in the last couple of years, that same layer of fat that now pushed his jacket up his chest.

He looked down, and saw that he had left the pocket unzipped. He calmed a momentary panic. He could have lost the ring, but he hadn't. It was still there. He could feel the hard lump of ring and gum with the point of his chin.

He looked up to see the flames racing down both sides of the boat, burning everything to the waterline, where water and fire turned to steam. Steam and smoke were everywhere. Maybe he wouldn't be drowned or burned after all. Maybe he'd be boiled, instead.

He had to get the ring now. He bent down farther than he had since he was seventeen.

His heart leapt as his tongue tasted hard, stale gum. He had reached the ring! With a superhuman effort, he managed to inch his chin even further down, grasping the cheap plastic ring in his teeth.

The bow of the boat disappeared beneath the surface of the lake. This was his last chance.

'See oo eh ee unny aa-ers!' he managed.

To his relief, the smoke turned blue.

The smoke drifted away on an ocean breeze.

The ring dropped from his teeth as his mouth opened in shock.

Was *everybody* here?

'Roger!' Delores yelled.

'Delores!' he yelled back.

'Doctor Dread!' Big Louie pointed.

'Louie?' Roger asked.

'Mfffmm!' the Mad Mumbler demanded.

'Congratulashuns!' Doc slurred, his voice somewhat muffled by the sand.

'Roger!' Delores called.

'Delores!' he called back.

'We got a job,' a member of the Motorcycle Mob muttered.

'Mfffmm!' the Mumbler interrupted.

'Zabana,' the jungle prince declared as he moved to block their path.

'Oh yeah?' the mob member retorted.

'Slime,' came the answer of the sand-covered one who now stood next to Zabana.

'Oh, yeah,' the mob member agreed.

'Roger!' Delores laughed.

'Delores!' he laughed back.

'But Doctor Dread!' Louie insisted.

'Mfffffmmmmmmm!' the Mumbler interrupted.

'Yip! Arf!' Dwight elucidated.

'Say,' Roger asked, 'isn't that Dwight the Wonder Dog?'

'Everybody knows Dwight—' Officer O'Clanrahan began.

'Oh, Roger,' Delores whispered sweetly.

'Oh, Delores,' was Roger's husky reply.

'But really!' Louie jumped up and down. 'Doctor Dread!'

'Where?' Roger asked.

'Hey, Roger-Dodger!' Brian called as he trotted up.

'Are we glad to see you!' Frankie added as he tagged along.

'Under!' Louie pointed down.

'Under?' Roger asked. He looked down at the remains of his boat.

'The Cowabunga-munga!' Brian called.

'Any minute now!' Frankie added.

'The Cowabunga-munga?' Delores asked.

'Oh, Delores.' Roger shrugged.

'Oh, Roger,' Delores replied.

'DOCTOR DREAD!' Louie screamed.

'Oh, that's right.' Roger shook his head. 'Under?'

'The boat!' Louie explained. 'When you appeared!'

'Under the boat?' Roger asked in disbelief.

'Hit right on snakeskin target,' Zabana added admiringly.

'Couldna done better myshelf!' Doc admitted.

'Yip! Arf! Yip!' Dwight cheered.

'Is he dead?' Roger asked, frowning at the bits of charred wood beneath him. As usual when he travelled with the Captain Crusader Decoder Ring, he had brought his most immediate recent surroundings along with him. But he couldn't see Doctor Dread at all.

'Unfortunately, no.' Delores shook her head. 'You can't kill a supervillain that easily.'

'Mfffffffffffffffmmmmmmmmmmmmmmmmmmmmmm!' the Mumbler interrupted once again.

'Yip yip bark!' Dwight insisted.

'Oh!' Louie remarked. 'Is that what he wants to do?'

KABOOM! the air exploded.

'What was that?' Brian worried.

'More blue smoke?' Frankie joined in.

'Ah hahahaha! Ah hahahaha!' a new voice laughed.

'Menge the Merciless?' Delores asked.

The smoke cleared.

It was more than Menge.

'What are you doing here, worm?' yet another voice added.

'Cripes!' Big Louie yelled. 'It's my sister!'

'My, it's – Roger, isn't it?' Bertha asked coyly.

'Roger?' Delores questioned.

'Delores!' Roger insisted.

'I'm so glad you're still here,' Bertha cooed.

'Gee, Bertha,' Louie interrupted. 'Have you turned over a new leaf?'

'Quiet, worm! No, I was afraid Roger would have met his death before I had a chance to *use* him!' She regarded her prey with half-closed eyes as she made grasping motions with her hands.

'Don't forget about me,' another voice stated flatly.

'Professhor Peril!' Doc managed.

'With Mort, the Killer Robot!' Officer O'Clanrahan observed.

'Yip! Arf! Bark!' Dwight added.

'And Diablo,' Louie explained, 'the Gorilla with the Mind of a Man!'

'Thank you for the introduction,' Peril replied brusquely. 'This is, of course, your doom.'

'Give or take fifteen minutes spent behind a nearby sand dune,' Bertha added lasciviously.

'Ah hahahaha!' Doctor Dread added for good measure. 'Ah hahahaha!'

'Roger!' Delores called, a new determination in her voice.

'Delores!' he agreed, putting an arm around her shoulder and hugging her tight.

'I don't think any of this—' Frankie began.

'—is going to happen,' Brian added. 'Especially with the Cowabunga-munga—'

'—a few minutes away?' Frankie completed the thought. 'I do know what is—'

'—going to happen, though,' Brian picked up on it. 'Yeah!'

They both shouted the next sentence together:

'It's time for a song!'

This time, things were so confused that Bix Bale and the Belltones were well into their three-chord progression before there were any threats to their continued existence. By then, of course, it was far too late. With guitar, bass and drum once again singing across the sand, the spell of the surfing world had taken hold.

This time, Frankie started the song:

> 'Roger's back and he's our fave
> 'Cause it's almost time for the great big wave!
> He'll be the king of all our turf
> When he shows he can really surf!'

This was followed by the usual 'heys', 'nanny-nannies', and drumbeats. Roger tried not to listen. It was difficult, though, with all those people dancing around him. Delores certainly looked stunning in that spangled evening dress, but then, he was sure she'd look good in anything. Some of the others looked a little stranger as they fell under the music's spell. Doctor Dread was moving around with a sort of snakeskin shimmy, while Bertha, still eyeing him, was performing something that appeared to be a particularly violent form of the polka. Officer O'Clanrahan was doing the waltz, while Dwight, on his hind legs, was waltzing along with him. Everyone was swirling around him to that relentless surfing beat. But Roger couldn't let himself be seduced by the jangly rock and roll. He had to talk to Delores, tell her about the Plotmaster, save the Cineverse, and that was just for starters! But he knew, if he let his concentration waver for an instant, he too would be caught up in the music, on his way to face the largest wave that ever was!

Brian took the next verse:

> 'Roger hasn't got a thing to fear;
> He'll be the surfer of the year!
> So everybody now stand and cheer;
> The Cowabunga-munga is almost here!'

'Hey!' everybody yelled. Roger frowned. Something was different about the dancers. For a moment, he thought they weren't moving as much as before. But then he realised the real difference – he was dancing along with them! No! He tried to stop, to force himself free of the music's spell. But how could you just sit there when they were playing surf guitar?

Frankie got the next verse:

> 'Some guys leave this big wave alone,
> They say its a good way to break a bone;
> A wave so fierce that away they're blown,
> But Roger will handle it on his own.'

Hey! Yeah, he was really dancing now, and with Delores, the cutest bunny on the beach! Roger didn't know when he'd felt this happy. He wanted to do something big, something important!

Brian's singing gave him an idea.

> 'Some guys on the wave they will not glide.
> They claim one that size is suicide!
> They say they'd rather face cyanide,
> But Roger's going to take this wave in stride.'

'Hey!' Roger shouted along with everybody else. What a good idea!

Why was he standing around on this beach, worrying about stupid things like the Cineverse?

It was time to go out and catch that wave!

CHAPTER SIXTEEN

'Flaming Death Goes to the Seashore!'

Now where had Roger put his surfboard? For the life of him, he couldn't remember.

'Hey, Roger-dodger, the time has come!' Brian shouted.

'Yeah, man!' Frankie agreed. 'It's time to face the Cowabunga-munga!'

'Yeah!' Roger laughed, almost drunk with the challenge. 'It's time to ride me a wave!'

'Hey, guys!' A rather pale and underfed surfer in snakeskin swimming trunks trotted towards them through the sand. 'I've got Roger's device – er, I mean – we've got Roger's board, man!'

'My board!' Roger exclaimed. So that's what happened to it! 'Well, hey guys! Bring it here!'

'Okay, kids!' the snakeskin-suited surfer called. 'Let's make the scene with the board!'

Nothing happened. All the surfers and beach bunnies stood around and looked at each other.

'Professor! Menge!' the sickly surfer yelled. 'I mean – er – where are you guys?'

'We're back here!' a curt voice called from the back of the crowd. 'Do you want the device?'

'Yeah, sure!' This new surfer seemed to be sweating an awful lot for someone standing so close to the sea breezes. 'That's what I said. Bring the board!'

'The what?' the other voice asked.

'The board!' the new surfer repeated. 'The surfboard! Roger's surfboard!'

There was no reply.

'The device!' the surfer yelled.

'Oh, yeah, sure!' the other voice finally called back. 'The surf-board! Got it right here. Roger's surfboard!'

Two men in baggy swimsuits ran through the crowd, carrying

something that was long, flat and red. Neither one of them looked like they saw much of the sun, either. The fellow in front was compactly built and moved with quick, nervous energy; the fellow behind him, who was bald, and a bit on the flabby side, had to struggle to keep up.

'Here it is, Doctor Dread!' the compact fellow announced as they approached. 'The dev – I mean, the surfboard!'

'Doctor Dread?' Roger repeated with a frown. There was something about that name, something that didn't belong on a world of sand and surf.

'Don't listen to those guys,' the snakeskinned surfer replied with a nervous smile. 'You can call me Dreaddy.'

'Dreaddy,' Roger repeated with a smile. Yes, that name sounded much better.

'And these are my friends,' Dreaddy went on, 'the Prof and Mengy. They're the guys who' – he hesitated for some reason – 'worked on your board.'

'Mengy?' the flabby fellow complained.

'Ixnay!' Dreaddy said out of the corner of his mouth. 'Ou'reyay a urfersay!'

'Oh, yeah!' The flabby fellow laughed and waved half-heartedly. 'Mengy!'

'Roger?' a lyrically feminine voice whispered in his ear. 'Could I talk with you?'

'Okay, babe,' Roger said as he turned to the young woman. 'I don't have much time. I've got a wave to catch.'

She smiled at him as he turned – the kind of smile that would melt the heart of even the most hardened surfer. Her spangled evening dress sparkled in the midday sun. Didn't he know this girl from somewhere? A name floated past the sounds of waves and the memory of surf guitar – Delores. That was it. Roger was glad to see her again. Even though she wasn't wearing a bikini, Delores wouldn't look out of place anywhere.

'I understand,' she reassured him. She pushed her long, blonde hair out of her eyes, hair that shone in the wind and sun. 'But I must talk to you.'

'But, girly!' Dreaddy insisted. 'Roger's got to get ready for his surfing challenge!'

'Yeah, Roger,' Mengy added. 'You haven't even taken a look at your new board.'

'Yes,' the Prof continued as he and Mengy lifted the surfboard between them. 'We've added some very interesting modifications.'

They had, too. It was the strangest board Roger had ever seen, especially with the red tubes along the side, and the lump of plastic over the rear fin.

'Hey, babe!' another voice interrupted. 'Why'd you split the scene?'

'Oh, no,' Delores whispered. In a much louder voice, she shouted at the newcomer: 'Would you kindly get out of my life?'

'Oho!' the tall, tanned, and slightly awkward newcomer replied. 'Spirited – that's the way Fast Felix likes 'em!'

'Roger,' Delores continued, 'could we go somewhere else to talk?'

'Well, gee, babe, if I didn't have this surfing duel—'

'But that's right, Roger Dodger!' Dreaddy insisted. 'You do have this surfing duel, and this special board, which you'd better try out right now!'

'Hey, cutie!' Fast Felix interrupted. 'Who is this new guy? How can you turn your back on the greatest lover on the beach?'

'Who's the greatest lover on the beach?' another woman's voice loudly demanded. 'Outta my way!'

Surfers screamed and scattered as another newcomer trod heavily through the sand.

The oily smile fell from Felix's face as he turned to look at the woman who now stood all alone.

'My name is Bertha,' she growled gutturally, 'and if I want you, you're mine.'

Felix started to shake. He opened his mouth, but no sound issued forth. Roger had to admit that Bertha cut an imposing figure. Maybe it was that six feet, six inches of height. Maybe it was the pink bikini on that thick, muscle-laden body. It made her look as sexy as a Sherman tank. Perhaps, Roger considered, pink was not her colour.

'Who's that?' Roger asked.

'Oh,' Dreaddy said lightly, 'just another one of my beach buddies.' He cleared his throat delicately. 'Bertha, dearest? Perhaps now is not the best time—'

She shook her head and pointed at Felix. 'So you're the best lover? Prove it!'

'Prove it?' Utter fear allowed Felix to find his voice again. 'Oh, wow. Well, you know – I talk a lot. Maybe I'm not the best—'

'No one backs down from Big Bertha!' she announced as she grabbed Felix with both of her ham-sized hands and lifted him from his feet. 'Let's see what you're made of.'

He squirmed, but only for an instant. There was a loud crunch, like the smashing of cartilage and bone. Fast Felix went limp.

'Typical shoddy merchandise.' Beach Bunny Bertha tossed the remains over her shoulder.

'Anybody else?' she asked.

All the other surfers started walking casually towards some other beach.

'But about this surfboard,' Dreaddy continued as if nothing had happened.

'It's really customised!' Mengy joined in as he pointed to the flame decals.

'It was providentially coincidental,' the Prof explained, 'that we could get parts from this old car and rocket ship that were sitting around on the beach.'

'Yeah!' Mengy agreed. 'It's amazing what you can scavenge from a rocket ship.'

'But, Roger—' Delores began.

'Hey, you've got to get going!' Brian exclaimed.

'Yeah!' Frankie added. 'The Cowabunga-munga waits for no man!'

'So take the board,' Dreaddy insisted.

Mengy and the Prof held the six-foot-long surfboard out to him. Why did Roger feel such trepidation as he touched the polished red wood?

'Good,' Dreaddy purred as Roger accepted his surfing tool. 'I promise you you'll have no' – there came that hesitation again – 'regrets.'

'With this board, you can't lose,' the Prof explained.

'Let's just say you'll go over in a big way,' Mengy cheerfully added. 'Ah hahahaha!'

'Yes, I think you'll find the results quite—' Dreaddy paused yet again. Roger wondered if maybe the surfer had a problem speaking in public.

'—explosive,' he finished at last.

The three pasty surfers smiled at each other as if they shared a private joke.

Delores shook his shoulder. 'Roger! Can't you see—'

'Listen!' Brian and Frankie shouted together.

Everyone stopped talking. Some of the surfers who had fled at Big Bertha's recent assault started to drift back. The birds stopped calling, the ocean breezes had ceased abruptly, even the waves seemed somehow muted, but it wasn't silent. There was a sound so low that Roger almost felt it more than heard it, a deep rumble that seemed to fill the whole line of the western horizon, rising from an ocean that still appeared deceptively calm.

Brian and Frankie whispered together:

'The Cowabunga-munga!'

'Lrsssgrrssmm!' called a muscular fellow in black leather swimming trunks. He carried a jet black surfboard.

A dog barked nearby.

'The Mumbler says it's time for your duel!' a small man in a double-breasted suit explained.

'But, Roger—' Delores tugged on his arm with a desperate insistence.

'Get away from him, you hussy!' another, very deep woman's voice demanded.

Roger turned around and almost dropped the board. Big Bertha was bearing down on him.

'Roger's going out to face the biggest wave that ever was,' Bertha asserted. 'A wave he may never come back from. I think he's going to need a good luck kiss. And I'm just the kisser to give it!'

Delores turned a very funny shade of red. She leaned over and gave Roger a quick kiss on the nose. 'I may not be able to convince you of your folly,' she whispered, 'but I can save you from this.'

She turned to Bertha and shouted: 'I warn you – I've been to hero school!'

Balancing his board with his right hand, Roger touched his nose with his left.

Shouts of 'girl fight!' came from the increasing crowd of surfers.

His nose tingled where her lips had brushed it.

Delores took three graceful steps across the sand.

He would remember that tingle anywhere.

Bertha stomped forward, murder in her eyes, muscles rippling between the two strips of pink.

That woman was not simply *any* Delores. She was *his* Delores! As he was her Roger! It was like something out of *Sleeping Beauty* – her kiss had brought him back to his senses!

'This is getting serious!' Brian yelled.

'Bertha, this is,' Dreaddy chimed in, hardly hesitating at all, 'counterproductive.'

Wait a moment. That wasn't Dreaddy. It was Doctor Dread, looking particularly anaemic in his snakeskin swimwear. And, among the crowd of surfers, he could see Zabana – who actually fitted in quite well – and Officer O'Clanrahan, and Louie, and Dwight the Wonder Dog, all of whom where rather easier to spot. That meant they were all back together again. It also meant that there was no way he was going to go out and get himself killed facing some humongous wave. He had no idea how to surf! Roger let go of the board. It fell to the sand with a dull thud.

'But Roger!' Frankie pleaded. 'The Cowabunga-munga won't wait!'

'I want what I want,' Bertha announced, 'and no one will stand in my way.'

'Fllmshrrssmm!' the Mad Mumbler demanded.

'Earthabay!' Dread demanded. 'Ou'reyay inay oubletray!'

'I don't care,' she snarled back, pounding her grapefruit-sized fist into her other large and muscular hand. 'My love' – pound – 'will not' – pound – 'be denied.'

Dwight the Wonder Dog barked something.

'At lasht!' Doc called from somewhere around the surfer's feet. 'A showdown!'

'There's only one way to handle this,' Frankie announced.

'That's your cue, Bix!' Brian added.

And the surfing song began all over again. Frankie sang it:

> 'Roger's gonna grab that big wave,
> He might be heading for a watery grave!
> That's why our Roger's just a surfing fool;
> That's why we think he's pretty cool!'

'Hey!' everybody yelled as usual. But the song wasn't going to work this time. Roger was all too aware of the ever-increasing rumble that came from the sea. He had places to go, people to see, meetings with the Plotmaster to describe.

But Brian was already into the next verse:

> 'If he's not careful in that wave he'll crash,
> And tons of water will upon him smash.
> What happens next is not pristine;
> And that's why Roger is pretty keen.'

'Hey!' everybody joined in. Roger smiled a bit at the insistent beat. Actually, when he thought of it again, that ever growing rumble didn't interfere with the song at all. It worked more like accompaniment, like a bass guitar and a tom-tom drum on a really good stereo system.

> 'Everybody let's jump and shout,
> And hope that Roger does not wipe out,
> For that to him would be sure doomsday,
> And that's why Roger is so okay.'

Roger sighed. They had been playing this song for so long, he sort of thought of it as an old friend. It would be a shame for a surfboard, especially a board as state-of-the-art as his, to go unused.

'Roger!' Delores yelled as he squatted down to lift his surfboard from the sand.

Dreaddy, Mengy and the Prof smiled at him as they danced. Delores waved frantically from where she danced behind them.

Roger took a step towards the ocean, then stopped. His left hand wanted to jerk away from the surfboard, as if the red-painted wood was lethal to the touch. His right hand punched the sun-drenched air before him, impatient to get out there and face that wave if it was the last thing he did. Why was this so perplexing? Surfers weren't supposed to think!

But Delores was still trying to tell him something.

That's when Frankie launched into another verse about if he hit his head Roger would be dead but he didn't care if he flops so that's why he was the tops. By the time the crowd had gotten around to shouting 'Hey!' he had made his decision.

He wouldn't have a chance for the Cowabunga-munga again.

'Frzzm!' his challenger insisted as the leather-suited muscle-man ran out into the waves.

A giant wave, hundreds of feet high. One man against the force of countless tons of water, with enough destructive force to annihilate this beach and everyone on it. How could he refuse an adventure like that? Roger would never forgive himself if he backed down from the ultimate surfing challenge.

Maybe, though, he might want to say a final word to Delores.

He looked around for the beautiful young woman, but, right where he thought she should be, there stood a new pair of surfers, even stranger looking than Dreaddy and his crew. One of them was entirely covered in shining silver, as if his skin was made of metal, while the other's face and body were completely enwrapped by coarse brown hair.

'Who are those guys?' Roger asked uncertainly.

'Nothing to worry about,' the Prof assured him. 'That's just Mort, the killer – uh – surfer, and Diablo, the – er – surfer with the mind of a man. They're here to make sure no one interferes with your facing the Cowabungamunga.'

Oh. He had heard those names somewhere before. Or maybe something like those names. There was something about those names – why was everything making him uneasy?

Brian started another verse:

> 'Now Roger he is on his own,
> If he wipes out, he's blood and bone—'

That was it. Roger didn't need any more coaxing. As soon as the song resumed, all his doubts were gone. He pulled off his socks and sneakers, balanced the board atop his head and ran down the beach.

Brian kept on singing:

> 'Yeah, he may just be smashed to bits
> But with us he'll always be a hit.'

Roger fully agreed. It was time to catch a wave. He jumped atop his board and quickly paddled out into the sea. It was difficult to concentrate, though, and the paddling seemed to get harder as the music grew fainter. Soon, it was difficult to do anything much except listen to that ever-increasing roar in his ears. From the sound, it was going to be the biggest wave Roger had ever seen.

He redoubled his efforts, paddling as fast as he could. The roar was so loud now that it drowned out any traces of the surf guitar behind him. It was harder still to paddle when there was no music at all.

His challenger paddled by Roger, the other's motorcycle-trained muscles pushing the water out of his way. But Roger had to win this surfing duel! The honour of the beach was at stake! And he wasn't going to do it staring at the other guy's back. If there was no music to urge him on, he would have to urge himself. He would have to make his own music. Roger tried singing a verse off the top of his head:

'Here it comes, the Cowabunga;
Gotta get there, ain't gettin' younga.
Gotta paddle, can't be a fool.
Gotta finish this surfin' duel!'

It may have been a little rough around the edges, but he thought the verse was pretty good for a first effort.

'Hey!' he shouted, wishing he could somehow hear the surfers back on shore shouting along with him. He knew the music had helped his paddling – he had pulled alongside his opponent by the end of the second couplet. He glanced over his shoulder, and was startled to see how far he had come from the shore in one short verse – the people back there looked like nothing more than tiny specks on an endless strip of sand.

He realised he must have discovered a Law of the Beach – things happened when you sang. It was only logical, considering all the rules he'd confronted elsewhere in the Cineverse. He thought of singing another verse to really get ahead in this surfing duel, but stopped as he listened to the wave – the roar was so loud now, he'd have to shout to be heard.

That's when he looked up and saw the Cowabunga-munga, and all thoughts of surfing duels left his head.

It was not a wave – it was much too large for that. It was more like someone had taken a five-hundred-foot-long knife and cut the ocean in half, and then stuck one piece on top of the other – and the top piece was coming straight for Roger! It was a wall of water, looking as solid as a mile of glass, its very top hidden in a mist that nudged the undersides of the clouds.

The Cowabunga-munga; it certainly lived up to its name. Roger guessed the legendary wave was still over a mile away, but it stretched the length of the horizon, as if it had already conquered the ocean and everything within it, and was coming to take him next.

Roger blinked. What was he doing here? He didn't know how to surf. Even if he did, there was a wall of water out there so huge that it was probably unsurfable. Delores had tried to warn him away. Why hadn't he listened to her? But he knew why – it was that infernal surfing music! That beach party beat had kept him under its spell until he had woken up to the reality of the Cowabunga-munga!

Roger glanced down at the surfboard that he sat upon, and his disquiet turned to despair. It was even worse than he feared. He remembered how Doctor Dread had described this board as 'customised', but Roger had been too far gone under the surfing spell to realise the true meaning of Dread's additions!

Even half-gone into surf mania, Roger had noticed the board's special auxiliary pipes, and that odd lump of plastic over the rear fin. Now, though, that he looked at this customisation in the clear light of total panic, he realised what surrounded the board weren't pipes at all, but sticks of dynamite wrapped in waterproof tape. And that lump around the fin looked an awful lot like plastic explosive. And why hadn't Roger noticed the wires before? One red, one black, they led from the plastic lump to a small, digital clock taped between the board and the dynamite, a clock that read three minutes to twelve.

Roger had seen enough movies to know what happened at twelve. Doctor Dread and his cronies had prepared for every contingency. The thing he sat on top of wasn't a surfboard, it was a bomb. He had three minutes to live.

Roger realised that this must have been what the Plotmaster was warning him about.

He looked up again. The Cowabunga-munga was not only huge, it was fast, and it was coming straight towards him.

Roger swallowed, the salty taste of sea spray on his tongue. Maybe he didn't have three minutes to live after all.

CHAPTER SEVENTEEN

'Captain Crusader's Secret!'

Thoughts of Alina and Theresa filled Roger's head. Not to mention Phyllis and Sandra and Rebecca and—

Roger stopped himself. He was acting like he was going to die. Well, he had been through a lot in the Cineverse – perhaps nothing quite as imposing as the Cowabunga-munga – but, still, he wasn't dead. Yet. And, now that he thought of it, he really didn't know if this was the incredibly horrible situation that the Plotmaster had meant to warn him about. The way things were going for Roger in the Cineverse lately, he had about four of these incredibly horrible situations in the afternoon.

The wave to end all waves roared towards him.

Well, maybe this situation was marginally worse.

Still, he had gotten out of tough spots before by using his ring. And he had two rings now! True, one of them didn't work at all, unless it really did force people to tell the truth, especially whether or not they were Captain Crusader, as Dr Dee Dee Davenport claimed. However, Roger didn't believe he could exact any worthwhile confessions from a rapidly approaching wall of water.

The other ring, now, did work, in a very limited way. It would send him to the surfing world. Where he already was. Which was also utterly useless. Unless, Roger remembered, you dropped the ring in exactly the right way – as Dee Dee had a couple of times to lead them to her world and the Institute of Very Advanced Science. And Roger had managed to drop one of these rings once, and had landed back on Earth!

So he could escape. The ring would send him home, if he could handle it just so. True, he had no particular desire to go back to Earth, but it was certainly better than death, wasn't it? Besides which, he would swear there was another Captain Crusader Decoder Ring somewhere in his mother's house, so it was possible – even if he managed to lose the gum-repaired ring in his escape – that he could still make it back to the Cineverse.

Now, the question was, could he remember how Dee Dee had saved them before? And could he do it again? It had something to do with turning the dial and dropping the ring. As Roger recalled, saying 'Oops!' might be a required part of the procedure as well.

He looked up at the ever-approaching wave. It was certainly worth a try. At this point, anything was worth a try.

He pulled the ring and chewing-gum combination from his pocket. He twisted the dial, then tossed the ring into the air.

'Oops!' he shouted hopefully as he tried to catch it. The ring slipped between his fingers, bounced off the board, and fell into the sea.

There was no blue smoke. There was only the Cowabunga-munga, roaring his way, ton upon ton of relentless, churning destruction. And he had just lost his only chance of escape.

Roger thought of Valerie and Vickie and Vanessa—

No! He still wasn't ready to accept death. There had to be some way out of here. The Plotmaster had suggested that knowledge was the key. At least that's what Roger thought the Plotmaster had suggested. He simply had to think like a movie – more specifically, a surfing movie! If there was one thing he should have learned during his sojourn in the Cineverse, it was that things were not fixed in the same way they were on Earth. Here, the plots were mutable to a certain extent, depending on anything from the appearance of a new character on the scene to the decision of somebody to sing a song.

Sing a song? That sort of thing really seemed to work around here. It had certainly gotten Roger out on a surfboard. And, still under that surfing spell, when he had sung a verse all on his own, he had found himself even further out to sea. He had already used this rule of the surfing world. And he could use it again.

Roger grinned up at the rapidly approaching Cowabunga-munga. The solution was obvious once he thought of it. If you didn't like what was happening to you, sing about it!

Water stretched before him as far as he could see. The Cowabunga-munga was almost on top of him. If he was going to do something about it, he'd better sing it now.

Roger had to sing so loud, it was more like screaming:

> 'The wave it thinks its got me beat.
> But this here surfer takes the heat!

He's gonna make this wave his own;
The Cowabunga, he'll ride home.'

Roger looked up at the wall of water. It was everywhere. The wave to end all waves rushed relentlessly forward, like Niagara Falls on wheels, leaving Roger small and pitiful before a curtain of water that was about to cover the world.

But wait! High up on that never-ending wave, did Roger see a patch of blue sky? Yes, the wave seemed to be breaking in half, the ramparts opening to allow Roger a chance to enter – to surf on in. And he was sure it was the song that had done it.

How, though, how did he catch the wave and ride it? It only took him a second to decide. There was really no choice, after all – he would have to let the song do that as well. He stood on his board and screamed out another verse as the wave thundered to either side of him.

'Come on Roger, let's hear a shout,
'Cause he's one surfer that won't wipe out!
Yeah, he's a fellow who'll be your fave,
'Cause here he goes to catch that wave!'

It wasn't great poetry, but it worked. He could feel the water swell underneath the board, lifting him up higher and higher on the face of the great wave.

He saw a flash of flesh colour in the corner of his eye. Roger risked a glance behind. It was the fellow they called the Mad Mumbler, balanced on his board, riding in Roger's wake – and he wasn't singing at all. Roger was impressed. That fellow could really surf!

Together, they reached the heights of the Cowabunga-munga. Roger broke through the spray and out of the great wave's shadow, into the sunlight high above the world. Seagulls circled nearby, cheering him on with their cries. He was surfing with all the aplomb of Frankie Avalon! He couldn't believe it.

That's when one of his feet slipped. He fell to one knee.

Roger managed to calm the small seed that wanted to blossom into panic inside his chest. Panic was the very thing he could not do. He had had a moment of doubt, and it had almost broken the concentration he had built through song. He had to believe in what he was doing. It was crucial to his survival in the Cineverse!

Besides, he had other problems. He may have conquered the

wave for the moment, but there was still the bomb. His other foot slipped ever-so-slightly as he thought about the red board beneath him, the one equipped with enough explosives to blow him up ten times over if he had too great an impact in the pounding surf, or – if he managed to stay alive that long – until the timer ran out! The villains had obviously considered everything – everything, that is, save Roger's penchant for song!

He glanced down at the timer, and saw there was only a minute left. This was it, then, his moment of musical truth. But he had to make sure no last minute doubts crept in about his surfing. It wouldn't do him any good to diffuse the bomb if he was wiped out in the process. If he was to survive, that new verse would have to be a masterpiece of concentration and balance. He had to diffuse the bomb while reasserting his surfing prowess.

Slowly, but careful to maintain that all-important surfing beat, Roger began again:

> 'Now some folks think Roger's a fool,
> Want him to lose this surfing duel!
> But the bomb's a dud, it just can't last;
> It's Roger who's a surfing blast!'

He risked a glance down at his surfboard. The clock stopped. The wires sprang free and spiralled off into the foam. The water-tight tape loosened, and the dynamite was instantly sodden with salt water. The plastic explosive slipped beneath the sea. The song had worked, and Roger's conveyance had gone from bomb to board.

He tossed in another verse for good measure:

> 'Hey this guy is really neat;
> He rides the waves with both his feet.
> No one beats him on his turf!
> So come on Roger, surf surf surf!'

Yeah! Roger laughed. He was really moving now. Wind in his hair, spray in his face. One man against the elements, surfing his way to glory. That was the way it was supposed to be! He heard faint cheers from the beach ahead. The Cowabunga-munga had brought him considerably closer to his hero-worshipping throng. The surfers on shore had been transformed from flyspecks to respectable-sized ants. Roger even thought he could recognise some of them as they rightfully cheered him in his great deed.

That tall blonde woman in the shining evening dress – that was Delores!

Delores?

Wait a minute. He was no surfer fighting against the elements. The only great deed he was involved in was staying alive. He was buying into this whole surfing world again – this time a victim of his own surfing songs! Roger had to be careful. The use of power in the Cineverse seemed to be a tricky thing. One way or another, the more you invested into a world, the more you became a part of that place's reality.

A wave washed across his feet. Roger almost fell off the surfboard. Now he wasn't being positive enough! The demon doubt had almost done him in again.

'Turf, surf, wave, fave!' Roger chanted, feeling stronger with every rhyme. Somehow he regained his balance. Just as Doc had to walk a thin line between helpless sobriety and incapacitated inebriation if the westerner wished to act at all, so Roger had to believe exactly enough to beat the wave without getting sucked into the surfer mystique.

'Neat, feet, last, blast!' he chanted. Yeah, he was surfing now! But he was Roger, from Earth, who had spent most of his adult life in public relations, who just happened to be surfing atop the biggest killer groovy monster wave that had ever existed!

He caught a familiar flash of colour out of that same eye corner. The Mumbler was getting closer. A moment later, he didn't even have to turn his head to see his rival surfer. The Mumbler, hunched forward on his board, was passing Roger by!

Roger told himself it didn't matter. He wasn't going to buy into this surfing duel stuff, anyway. So the Mumbler reached the beach first – so what?

'Beach, reach,' Roger mumbled distractedly. 'Duel, fool.'

The Mumbler would reach the beach first? That would never do. It was only now that Roger realised how meaningless his life had been until this moment. Winning was everything! He would be the hero of the beach, his greatest triumph ever!

He had to keep up that surfing! And even more than ever before, he had to do it with music!

This time, when Roger started to sing, the wave seemed somehow quieter, as if out of respect.

> 'The Mad Mumbler better watch his skin,
> 'Cause this boy knows he's here to win.

Roger proves he ain't no faddy,
He'll blow away this here hodaddy!'

They could hear him on the beach! He could see them clapping along! He laughed as the Cowabunga-munga produced a special swell just beneath his board, propelling him swiftly past the leather-suited surfer. Without a song, the Mad Mumbler didn't have a chance!

Roger sang another verse to complete the musical justice:

'Roger's really goin' for that ride;
The Cowabunga-munga's on his side!
Now we know that revenge is sweet,
And Roger, he wins by twenty feet!'

Roger's board glided on to the beach a goodly distance before the Mumbler as the Cowabunga-munga retreated out to sea.

The surfers converged on him as he stepped from his board. Bix Bale and the Belltones led with a furious surfing beat as the song went on forever:

'Oh, Roger's proved that he's the best;
He passed the Cowabunga test;
That guy can surf on anything;
Yeah, he's now the surfer king!'

The surfers lifted Roger on to their shoulders and propelled him into the crowd. He saw the Mumbler surf safely into shore as he was raised aloft. Even the leather-suited challenger cheered Roger – in his usual indistinct fashion – as the celebration really began.

Roger looked down on the adoring masses beneath him. He was king of the surfers. Everyone was dancing. Roger's life was fulfilled.

People danced by that Roger recognised: Zabana, Prince of the Jungle; Officer O'Clanrahan; Dwight the Wonder Dog.

People who did more than surf.

There were other things to life besides surfing?

Roger felt himself distancing himself from those ever-present guitar chords as he shook off the surfing spell once more. The music could no longer hold him as he watched a conga line of Doctor Dread, Menge the Merciless, and Professor Peril. Every one he recognised reminded him there was more at stake here than winning a surfing duel! He had to win the entire Cineverse!

'Hey!' everybody shouted. Bif BOOM Bif BOOM boom boom boom de boom, the drums replied.

But how could he succeed? Sure, he'd triumphed over a monster wave, but that was nothing compared with the fates of myriad movie worlds. And things were changing even as he considered what to do next. Perhaps that had been his problem ever since he had gotten here – the Cineverse never stood still long enough for him to make a decision. Far to the west, over the ocean, the sun was sinking towards the horizon. He knew what sunsets meant, too – on this particular movie world, they were approaching The End. That's how surfing movies often ended, with everyone dancing up a storm.

But what did The End mean for all of them, good guys and bad guys? He'd never stayed on a world in the Cineverse long enough to see the conclusion of a plot. Now that he'd won the surfing duel, would they all dance like this forever?

That's when he saw Delores again. She was dancing too, but she didn't look happy about it. Perhaps it was because of her two partners, Mort, the Killer Robot, and Diablo, the Gorilla with the Mind of a Man! The two dancing villains were taking turns, grabbing Delores' arms and twirling her about. It took Roger only a second to realise she was a dancer in distress!

Roger jumped down from the arms of the celebrating surfers. He had to be more than the greatest surfer on the beach. He had to save Delores and everyone else from the clutches of Doctor Dread!

But how to do it? He was one man, up against the amassed evil of the Cineverse. But, as he thought of it, he realised that the Cineverse, and the Cowabunga-munga, might have already shown him the way. Maybe, with song, all things were possible.

'Hit it, Bix!' he yelled, and the Belltones took it from the top as Roger sang along:

> 'Is he threatening Delores?
> He's extinct as brontosaurus!
> Yeah, he's gone just like a gunshot
> Farewell Mort, the Killer Robot!'

And Mort, the Killer Robot had disappeared before the crowd could say 'hey!' Still dancing, Diablo, the Gorilla with the Mind of a Man, looked at Roger and snarled. Roger answered with another verse:

> 'Well, he's still dancing with Delores,
> But he's gone well before the chorus,
> More forgotten than sarsaparilla;
> Is Diablo with Mind-of-Man Gorilla!'

The gorilla vanished even more quickly than his metallic companion before him.

Roger grinned and turned to Doctor Dread, his vocal chords throbbing with a new-found power.

'Now, now, let's not do anything' – Dread paused uncertainly – 'hasty.'

'What has that do-gooder done?' Professor Peril wailed. 'Where will I ever again find cohorts so economical?'

'Pardon me for interrupting,' Menge mentioned, 'but perhaps it would be better to ask these questions somewhere else?'

'But you don't understand!' Peril went on, quite beside himself. 'Job opportunities are so limited for killer robots and gorillas with brain transplants – they work for almost nothing!'

'Bertha, if you would' – Dread paused in his directions – 'escort our distraught compatriot, we will depart until we discover some more' – another brief but discernible pause – 'advantageous circumstance for our next meeting?'

But Roger wasn't going to let them go that easily.

'Come on, Bix!' he yelled. 'Let's get 'em!'

Roger concentrated as he sang. He wanted this new rhyme to be a killer!

'That Doctor Dread, he is awfully smug—' he began.

'Minions!' Dread yelled. 'To my side!'

'But you know his grave's already dug—' Roger added.

'You have not seen the last of—' Dread paused menacingly.

'His time round here is not that long—' Roger continued, undaunted.

'This is not the time for menacing pauses!' Dread exclaimed hurriedly. 'See you in the funny papers!'

The blue smoke showed up before Roger could complete his rhyme.

'And Doctor Dread and his gang are gone!' he finished anyway. The Belltones gave him a drumroll as everybody cheered.

Delores ran to him first. 'Roger! That was magnificent!'

He took her in his arms. They kissed. Roger had no idea how long it had been since they had kissed; in a place like the Cineverse, it was probably impossible to tell anyway. It didn't matter. Any time at all without Delores was far too long.

They had to breathe eventually.

'I simply figured out a little bit about how the Cineverse works,' he explained when he could talk again.

Everybody who was gathered around them cheered. And everybody was gathered around them. Roger almost blushed. He was the centre of attention – no longer the sidekick. He wished, though, that he might discuss his heroics with Delores someplace that was a bit more private.

'Yes, but it comes to you so naturally!' Delores enthused, not letting Roger get away with his modesty. 'It would be much more difficult for us in the Cineverse to rhyme so quickly. Why, people attend hero school for years and aren't half as good!'

Everybody cheered again.

'So,' Big Louie asked. 'What do we do now?'

Roger glanced over at the sidekick, who shrugged apologetically.

'Simply moving the plot along,' Louie explained.

'As you should,' Roger agreed as he gently let go of Delores. 'But I have things to tell you—'

'We'll talk as soon as we can,' Delores agreed. 'But Doctor Dread is certainly plotting his revenge even now. We still need to find Captain Crusader and save the Cineverse. After that, we can attend to' – it was Delores' turn to pause as she glanced wistfully at Roger – 'other things.'

Roger felt himself blushing again. Actually, he had been thinking of talking about the Plotmaster, but now that Delores mentioned it – well. He cleared his throat, which at least seemed a little more heroic.

Delores continued, her voice now brusquely official: 'We came to this world with a specific purpose – not to find you, dear Roger, but because this was the most likely whereabouts of Captain Crusader. Now, however, he seems to be nowhere around. Think, Roger! Have you seen anyone who could be the hero among heroes?'

Captain Crusader? Roger frowned. So – in a way – they had both been on the same errand.

'No,' he replied after a moment's reflection, 'but I know somebody who can help us.' If Captain Crusader was somewhere in the vicinity, he was still hiding. But Roger *had* thought of Dr Davenport, and the astonishing resources of her Institute of Very Advanced Science. There, he knew, was one place that could find Captain Crusader.

'We could go there, but—' He stopped himself mid-sentence when he remembered the crisis on the Advanced Science world with V.E.R.A. the computer. What if Dr Davenport was still in trouble on her home world? He didn't want to go from the relative safety of the surfing world to a place that was potentially risky to his allies and himself. But they had to find Captain Crusader now. Doctor Dread was already too powerful!

That's when Roger realised there might be another way. It was highly experimental, of course, and, in attempting it, he would have to test the limits of the power of surf music, but maybe he could get Movie Magic to work for him!

'But maybe,' he added aloud, 'I can bring her here.'

'How?' Delores asked.

'With the help of Bix Bale and the Belltones,' he replied. 'Hit it, guys!'

Roger sang, hoping against hope that his gamble would work:

> 'Life on this beach is pretty neat,
> The sun and surf almost complete;
> But where's the laughter of young Dee Dee?
> I long to hear her go—'

He stopped.

'—Tee hee hee!' came a familiar laugh from the back of the crowd.

'It worked!' Roger yelled triumphantly.

'What worked?' Delores asked doubtfully.

'Dee Dee!' Roger called.

'You rang?' a perky voice called back.

'Who rang?' Delores asked. 'Roger, are you sure—'

But Roger only nodded.

'Come on over, Dee Dee!'

'Tee hee hee!' The pert beach bunny in the psychedelic green bikini jogged towards them through the crowd.

'This is your solution?' Delores asked gently.

'Exactly!' Roger replied. 'This is Dr Dee Dee Davenport, of the Institute for Very Advanced Science!'

'Tee hee hee,' Dee Dee agreed. She waved at everybody as she trotted into their midst.

'Dr Davenport?' Delores asked tentatively, offering her hand.

Dee Dee squealed with delight. She shook Delores' hand, her whole body bursting with energy. 'Tee hee hee,' she added.

Delores glanced at Roger. 'The Institute of Very Advanced Science?'

'Well,' Roger began. 'I know it doesn't look quite—'

'Roger,' Delores replied, her voice still far too gentle. 'How do I tell you this? Sometimes, people can be out in the sun too long—'

'But, no!' Roger objected. 'She may be a cute and perky beach bunny here—'

'Tee hee hee,' Dee Dee demonstrated.

'But on her home world she heads the Institute—'

'Personality change,' Zabana, prince of the jungle, observed. 'Like Doctor Dread.'

'Roger—' Delores replied, the exasperation rising in her voice. 'Would someone shut up that dog?'

'Yip yip bark!'

Roger hadn't noticed it before, but it was true. Dwight was going crazy.

'Bark yip yip!'

'Dwight says—' Louie began.

'In a moment, Louie,' Delores interrupted. 'So Dee Dee here heads a scientific institute—'

'—that I think can be instrumental in finding Captain Crusader!' Roger said rather more loudly than he should. He was becoming a bit exasperated himself.

Dwight started barking all over again. Roger would have glanced over at the dog himself if something large hadn't risen in the sand directly in front of him.

'Please do not raise your voice to the woman who is to be my bride,' the thing covered by sand announced.

'What is this?' Roger asked, his voice still not as quiet as it could be.

'Arf, arf, bark!' Dwight interjected.

'Oh,' Delores explained, 'that's the Slime Monster.'

'My friends call me Edward,' the pile of sand introduced himself.

'And you're questioning the company that I keep?' Roger demanded.

'Tee hee hee,' Dee Dee laughed appreciatively.

'I don't think jokes are appropriate on my future bride's behalf,' the Slime Monster commented.

'What?' Roger was becoming even more incensed. 'What's this future bride stuff?'

'Arf bark yip!' Dwight was getting frantic.

Delores threw up her hands. 'Roger, this wasn't my idea.'

'Not your idea?' He waved at the mobile pile of sand. 'I suppose this guy just swept you off your feet?'

'And I find you cavorting with a beach bunny!' Delores snapped back.

Dee Dee stepped between them.

'Tee hee hee,' she began apologetically. 'It's time to cool it, guys. Remember, when you go to the beach, don't leave courtesy behind!'

Everybody stopped and stared at the beach bunny. Roger wondered if everyone was thinking the same thing he was:

That sounded like something that should be said by the hero among heroes.

'Bark yip bark!' Dwight announced with finality.

'Exactly!' Louie replied.

'Captain Crusader!' Delores and Roger exclaimed together.

'So nice of you to – reveal yourself,' a particularly oily voice said from the midst of the crowd.

There was a small explosion. Dee Dee clutched at her firm and perky stomach.

'Tee—' she gasped. 'Tee hee—'

'She's been shot!' Delores yelled.

Dee Dee/Captain Crusader nodded as she swayed back and forth, both hands over her wound.

'Remember,' she replied between clenched teeth, 'a bullet takes – only a minute, but a – friend is yours – for life.' She toppled forward, on to the sand.

Doctor Dread and Menge the Merciless, now in their more traditional bad guy costumes, stepped forward from the crowd.

'Menge, that shot was' – Dread paused triumphantly – 'excellent. How easily they fell for our little' – this time he simultaneously paused and gloated – 'ruse.'

Menge's reply was more to the point:

'Ah hahahaha. Ah hahahaha!'

CHAPTER EIGHTEEN

'The Fateful Moment!'

Captain Crusader? Shot?

Roger realised at last that this must be the life or death situation the Plotmaster had spoken of!

'You'll pay for this!' Roger shouted with upraised fist.

'He's beginning to sound like a hero,' Menge replied smoothly. 'Righteous indignation with absolutely no originality whatsoever.'

'Kill!' Zabana yelled with jungle-bred determination.

'Pitiful fools!' Menge crowed. 'You will, of course, permit us to gloat over our accomplishments.'

'Shoot!' Doc staggered to his feet as he pulled his six-gun and tried to sober himself to the task at hand.

'How – clever of us,' Dread agreed smugly. 'To seemingly disappear, only to – reposition ourselves!'

'Arrest!' Officer O'Clanrahan pulled a nightstick and handcuffs free from his belt.

'And wait for the moment when you hopeless do-gooders revealed the one person who might have stopped us!' Menge smirked.

'Arf!' Dwight agreed with his fellows, animal blood-lust in his eyes.

'And now we have stopped – Captain Crusader.' Dread chortled unpleasantly. 'What do you say to that?'

'Slime!' Edward chorused, the sand-covered monster having the last word on the subject.

Delores stepped forward, and waved for the rest to follow her. She shouted her defiance at Dread and Menge:

'Now that you've shot Captain Crusader, everybody's going to be after you!'

'It is your death!' Zabana agreed.

'Well, maybe,' Dread allowed, 'if we planned to stick around.'

The blue smoke exploded around them.

'See you in the funny papers' – Dread hesitated with finality – 'if we don't remove you first!'

And they were gone.

Roger knelt by Dee Dee Davenport.

'You really are Captain Crusader?'

She clutched her stomach as she grimaced in pain. Her bright green bikini was turning brown with blood. She nodded.

'Yes, I am the Captain.'

'But why didn't you tell me?'

'I did tell you,' she replied. 'When you pointed the Ring of Truth at me. And then I changed the subject. The Ring of Truth does work, you know – at least for getting people to tell the truth. It's not that good for getting around the Cineverse, though.' She took a shuddery breath. 'A lot of things aren't working as well around here as they used to.'

'You deceived me!' Roger exclaimed. 'But why?'

Captain Crusader shrugged her shapely shoulders. 'A hero has to be – flexible in times like these. Besides, you had to learn how to – be a hero, too.'

The others gathered around Roger and the Captain.

'Dread gone,' Zabana explained.

'Captain Crusader?' Louie asked. 'How bad is—'

Dee Dee tried to smile, but the pain was all too evident. She took another ragged breath.

'I can last – for another page or two. I have to – to tell you everything you need to know.' She reached out and weakly patted Roger's hand. 'You coming to the Cineverse – that was partly my doing, you know. We needed someone from outside, someone who could see beyond the separate movie worlds, someone who could work by my side. Too bad it came – too late.'

'It may not be too late!' Roger insisted. 'Maybe we can get help.'

Dee Dee shook her head. 'No – I'm a goner. That's one of the things that a hero always knows. Forgive me – for not showing myself to you sooner, but you had to learn how to control the Cineverse – like you learned how to control the Cowabunga-munga!'

She coughed then, covering her mouth with her hand. When she stopped, there was a discreet amount of blood on her palm.

'Captain Crusader?' Officer O'Clanrahan wailed, beside himself with grief. 'Dying?'

'What'll we do now?' Doc chorused.

'I may be dying,' Dee Dee agreed, 'but there'll always be a Captain Crusader. It's one of the Laws of the Cineverse.' She looked up at the man from Earth, her bright blue eyes alive with purpose. 'Now, Roger, it'll have to be you.'

'Me?' Roger objected. 'But—'

'I'm sorry – but you have no choice.' She clenched her teeth as she shivered with pain. 'It is too bad – that I did not have the time – to properly train you. But you are the only one here – with the proper raw materials – the only one – who can stand up to Doctor Dread.'

Her eyelids fluttered. 'Take my hand, Roger. It's getting dark!'

Roger did as she asked.

'Remember,' she said, her voice barely a whisper, 'a song – in your heart – and a smile on – your lips – keeps old man – trouble – away.'

Her breath left her in a rush. Her hand went limp in Roger's. Her eyes closed. She was gone.

'Ssrrffmm,' the Mumbler added his incoherent condolences.

'I suppose,' Edward intoned morosely, 'an event like this means it would be improper to announce our engagement – just yet.'

But Delores was beyond caring about the Slime Monster's intentions. 'Captain Crusader?' she whispered, as if she could barely say the words. 'Gone? What can we do?'

Roger laid the Captain's hand gently upon the sand, then stood and turned to look at all the others.

'Just what she told us to do,' he replied. 'We will carry on, until we defeat Doctor Dread!'

Roger wished he felt as confident as he sounded. He didn't know the first thing about fighting Doctor Dread, unless he could do it by firing off press releases. He didn't even know his way around the Cineverse. How could he possibly hope to defeat the forces of evil of every movie world that ever existed?

The more he thought about it, the more it seemed impossible. He was the new Captain Crusader? The Cineverse was doomed. What could possibly be any worse?

'Look!' Frankie yelled from behind Roger. 'Captain Crusader! She's gone!'

Roger spun around. He looked where Dee Dee's body had been. There was nothing there now but an indentation in the sand.

The wind had started up again along the beach. Seagulls called to each other in the sky.

Big Louie shook Roger's elbow.

'Roger! Something's happening! I can feel it!'

There was an explosion, followed by blue smoke.

'Roger!' a woman's voice shouted indignantly. 'What have you done? What is the meaning of this?'

Roger took it all back. He knew that voice. It could get worse after all.

The blue smoke cleared, revealing a very unhappy and somewhat overdressed woman of middle years.

It was his mother.

'Well?' she said in that you'd-better-have-an-explanation-or-else voice she had honed through years of experience. 'Are you going to answer me?'

'What's the meaning of what, mother?' Roger replied, automatically adopting his most conciliatory tone.

It was, of course, the absolute wrong tone to use on one's mother.

'Don't act innocent with me, young man!' Surfers scattered as she strode purposefully across the sand towards her son. 'There is something going on here, and I demand to know what it is!'

Roger looked around at Zabana, Doc, and Louie, still in their double-breasted suits, and Delores with her spangled evening gown. Then, of course, there was his own very soggy jogging suit, and almost everybody else wearing surfing duds. And his mother wanted him to explain all this?

'Mother,' Roger replied at last, hoping against hope that she would accept his answer. 'It's better if you don't know.'

'*Roger Alloishus Gordon!*' his mother declared in a tone suitable for declaring World War III.

'Alloishus?' Louie asked.

'Family name,' Roger replied. 'Never used.'

Except, he thought rather than said, when his mother was in one of *those* moods.

And his mother had only begun. 'First, you disappear. Heaven knows, you never call me in the first place, so how would I *know* when you disappear? But this time you decided you were too busy to go to work, too. The office was calling all over the place, looking for you. They even called Sharon – she was always such a nice girl – I don't see why the two of you ever split up. She at least took the time to call me. I tell you, we were both worried sick.'

Sharon? Roger thought about objecting. After all, he and Sharon had gotten divorced years ago. Not that his mother noticed. She was happy as long as Sharon called.

'And then I couldn't find Mr M!' his mother continued melodramatically. 'His house was deserted, his little red sports car gone. I tell you, it felt like people were disappearing right and left in my life. You don't know how insecure that can make a person.'

Roger nodded. Sharon or no Sharon, it was too late to object. He knew his mother's tirades – they grew longer every time you tried to let her know there was more than one side to the issues. The only way anyone could possibly survive was to suffer in silence.

'Well, what could I do?' His mother sighed, a far away look in her eyes. 'With you gone – it's funny. I started to think how you were as a little boy – I mean, besides being messy and inconsiderate. I started going through my keepsake drawer. You know how sentimental a mother can be. And then I found this cheap, plastic ring.'

She looked up wistfully, including everyone on the beach in her conversation. 'You know, when Roger was a boy, he loved the free prizes that came in cereal boxes. It seemed I had saved one, along with those old school reports and hand-made valentines.'

Big Louie had sidled up to Roger. He stood on his tiptoes and whispered in Roger's ear. 'She'll go on like this for quite a while, won't she?'

Roger nodded, his eyes still respectfully watching his lecturing parent.

'And then there was all this blue smoke. At first, I thought it was the furnace, backing up again—'

'Did you ever think about the implications of all this? Your mother not only accidentally uses the Captain Crusader Decoder Ring, but she ends up here, in the exact same place as her son? Do you realise how coincidental this all is?'

Roger nodded even more vehemently. Of course, after what he'd been through in the Cineverse, nothing would surprise him.

'No, nothing surprises me, either,' Louie agreed, even though Roger hadn't spoken aloud. 'But this is still too strange to be coincidence. I sense the hand of the Plotmaster in all this.'

'The Plotmaster?' Roger asked, his voice a mixture of astonishment and relief. He could tell the others what had happened to him at last! 'I've met the Plotmaster!'

Everybody – with the exception of Roger's mother, who was too busy complaining – stopped to stare at Roger.

'What?' Delores asked gently, a look of concern in her deep blue eyes. 'Are you sure?'

'Plotmaster mythic,' the jungle prince added. 'Even more mythic than Zabana!'

'Nobody ever actually meets the Plotmaster,' Louie agreed as he shook his head in admiration. 'Maybe you *do* have methods!'

'Roger?' his mother demanded. 'Are you listening to me?'

'In a minute, mother.' Roger turned back to the others. 'But a number of us have spoken to the Plotmaster. He saw not only me, but Louie, Doc and Zabana!'

'He did?' Louie asked incredulously.

'Shure!' Doc scoffed from his spot on the ground. 'And they call *me* the town drunk!'

'No, wait!' Roger insisted. He had to get them to believe him. He had the feeling this whole thing with the Plotmaster was somehow tied up with the Change, and the very fate of the Cineverse! But how could he explain it?

'It was after we got caught in that Cineverse cycle,' he began. 'You know, all those swashbucklers.'

'Swashbucklers?' Zabana asked, the oddest look on his jungle-bred features.

'And then he came and rescued us,' Roger added rapidly. 'But he said that none of us would – uh – remember any of it.'

His voice faltered as he realised the problem with his explanation. How could anybody remember what happened if they weren't supposed to?

His mother's voice cut into the silence. 'Roger, if you're not going to pay attention to me, I might as well leave.' She glanced up and down the beach with a frown, as if this was the first time she had really looked at her surroundings. 'How did I get here, anyway?'

The jungle prince spoke hesitantly. 'Zabana . . . remember . . . swords.'

'Mrs Gordon,' Delores said helpfully. 'We'll try to explain everything to you, as soon as we can figure it out ourselves.'

'Well, thank you,' Roger's mother replied, somewhat mollified. 'At least someone is looking out for my welfare. And who is this attractive young lady? For heaven's sake, Roger, you could introduce people to your mother!'

'In a minute, mother,' Roger answered. 'So you remember the Plotmaster, too?'

Zabana nodded slowly. 'Only now you mention it.'

'Yeah,' Louie added slowly. 'I remember – all these swash-buckling places – and this guy in blue smoke.'

'Blue shmoke?' Doc called from the sand. 'I thought it wash one of my vishions!'

Louie whistled. 'And Roger remembered it. See guys? I told you Roger had methods?'

'No wonder he new Captain Crusader,' Zabana agreed.

Oh, that. In all the hubbub with his mother, Roger had almost forgotten the new honour bestowed upon him. But the more he thought of it, even if he could somehow become the heroes' hero, this situation was too serious for a lone individual. Combating the Change called for everybody working together. He decided he'd have to have a heart-to-heart talk with everybody about this, too, as soon as he cleared up this business about the Plotmaster.

'But there's more,' Roger continued. 'The Plotmaster contacted me for a reason. There was something he wanted to warn me about.'

'Roger!' his mother exclaimed, the imperious tone returned to her voice. 'I'll start warning you, if you don't introduce me—'

'In a minute—' Roger began, when he realised he was surrounded by blue smoke. He glanced around at the fog-shrouded shapes of his companions, shapes that had ceased moving, as if the smoke had frozen the world. There was something else odd, too. This smoke had arrived without the usual explosion. But there was some sound, music, faint and high, like a distant choir of angels. Who could—

ROGER, BABY.

LONG TIME NO SEE!

WE HAVE TO TALK.

It was, of course, the Plotmaster, backlit as usual, smoking his blue cigar. This time, Roger was considerably happier to see him.

'At last!' Roger called. He grinned broadly. The Plotmaster could explain everything. 'Now you can finish your warning. I do appreciate it, sir. I'm sure it helped me to survive. But could you tell me, was it something to do with the art film world, or was it about the size of the Cowabunga-munga?'

But the Plotmaster shook his backlit head.

ROGER, SWEETIE, BABY!

MY WARNING WAS FOR NOTHING THAT COMMON.

THOSE THINGS HAPPEN IN THE CINEVERSE EVERY
DAY.

Of course. Roger should have realised that. After all, the Plotmaster hadn't meddled in most of the earlier crises they had faced. The situation would have to be truly extraordinary for this powerful being to show his hand. That, of course, meant the warning could have referred to only one thing.

'Oh, then it was the death of Captain Crusader,' Roger said with confidence.

But the Plotmaster's head was still shaking.

NO, EVEN AN EVENT OF THAT SCOPE

IS NOT UNUSUAL IN THE CINEVERSE.

LISTEN, THIS IS IMPORTANT.

The Plotmaster took a long drag from his cigar, as if contemplating what was the best way to broach a subject of this gravity. Blue smoke curled upwards to join the like-coloured fog that surrounded the two of them, obscuring everything else on the beach. After a moment, the big man waved his stogie at Roger.

WE'RE TALKING ABOUT REAL DISASTER, HERE.

I HAVE TO TALK TO YOU BEFORE YOUR MOTHER
SHOWS UP.

'My mother?' Roger asked, almost laughing despite himself. What would the Plotmaster want with his mother? 'But she's here already.'

SHE IS?

The Plotmaster stood there, frozen for an instant, as if he couldn't believe what he had just heard.

A chill shot through Roger. The mention of his mother didn't seem humorous any more. This was the first time he had ever heard fear in the big man's voice.

The Plotmaster looked upwards.

SID, DID YOU HEAR THAT?

WHY WASN'T I TOLD?

Roger couldn't make out the answer. It sounded like nothing so much as a blast of music from the angelic choir.

SID, THAT'S NO EXCUSE!

I DON'T CARE ABOUT YOUR CHERUBS!

YOU'RE FIRED.

The angelic choir cut off abruptly. The Plotmaster turned his attention back to Roger.

LIKE I TOLD YOU ROGER BABY, I CAN BE RUTHLESS.

BUT WHAT CAN WE DO – NOW?

He picked up a thick sheaf of paper from the table behind him, and began to leaf through it. Roger remembered – last time, the Plotmaster had called this wad of paper 'the script'.

UM

the Plotmaster muttered,

WELL IF THAT'S TRUE, MAYBE WE CAN—

He turned the page.

UH-OH.

He flipped a few more pages.

OH DEAR.

OH NO.

THAT'S INHUMAN.

He sighed, and looked at the end.

He didn't move for a long moment. The blue ember at the end of his cigar dimmed and threatened to go out. The last page had left him speechless. He threw the script back on the table, then turned heavily back to Roger, as if he had the weight of the Cineverse upon him.

I'M SORRY, ROGER.

I DID TRY TO REACH YOU BEFORE IT WAS – TOO LATE.

Then there was another sound. It wasn't an angelic choir this time. The noise was a harsh, staccato braying, like the laughter of some demented god.

The Plotmaster threw his hands in front of his face, as if to ward off some invisible danger. He screamed at Roger over the booming laugh:

OH, NO!

THE CHANGE HAS BEGUN!

I CAN DO NO MORE!

MORE!
More!
more!
more!

The Plotmaster was gone, the blue smoke drifting away. The echo faded as Roger realised people were once again moving around him. His mother was complaining again, but everyone else had turned to stare at a spot further down the beach.

And, Roger realised, the laughter hadn't gone away.

CHAPTER NINETEEN

'The Change – or the End?'

'Ah hahahaha!' Menge the Merciless chortled from where he stood in front of a giant, silver machine. 'Ah hahahaha!'

'Why, Mr M!' his mother called. 'What a pleasant surprise!'

Menge stopped laughing. 'Mrs G. What are you doing here?'

'A woman has to travel,' she replied. 'It's so important to travel, Mr M. Especially when you reach our age.'

Roger couldn't believe this! His mother was flirting with one of the most evil men in the Cineverse!

'But, mother!' he interrupted. 'Don't you realise who this is? This is Menge the Merciless!'

His mother looked quizzically at Dread's henchman.

'Mr M?'

'Alas, Mrs G.' Menge said with a sad nod. 'Your son is quite correct.'

'Oh, Mr M!' Roger's mother said with a smile. 'You're always so polite. Roger, you could learn a lesson from him.'

'Mother!' Roger insisted.

'And who, exactly, is Menge the Merciless?' his mother added with the same polite smile.

'He criminal!' Zabana ventured.

'One of the foulest fiends in the Cineverse!' Big Louie added helpfully.

'Dear lady,' Menge added smoothly. 'All this too is correct.'

Roger's mother dimpled at being called 'dear lady'.

'Oh, Mr M.,' she said enthusiastically. 'I'm sure there's some way we can work this out.'

Roger couldn't believe this. 'Mother! Don't you understand? Menge the Merciless is a supervillain!'

She turned to Roger with a frown.

'Now, now, Roger. When a woman gets to be my age, she can't be that choosy.'

'Well, we'll have to talk about that later, Mrs G.' Menge interjected pleasantly. He patted the complicated machine he had brought with him. 'In the meantime, I have to fry your son with the Zeta Ray.'

'Oh, dear,' his mother replied, a bit of worry creeping in. 'Will it hurt him?'

'Not physically no,' Menge replied. 'You see, I work for an organisation that is intent upon taking over the Cineverse – the area that you are now visiting. As a part of this, we have already removed our primary obstacle, one Captain Crusader. However, we have since detected a great surge of energy in this particular area, and realised that there might be other threats – however minor – that we should dispense with so that our conquest will be that much easier. We have determined that your son, Mrs G., may be one of these minor threats.'

Roger's mother's hands fluttered in front of her breast. 'Do you know, Mr M., that's the first real explanation I've had since I've gotten here!' She glanced reprovingly at her son. 'If only everyone could be as polite. Still, I don't think I can agree to let you point something potentially harmful at my son – even though he is sometimes thoughtless.'

'Oh, I assure you, Mrs G.,' Menge replied quickly. 'He won't feel a thing.' He pointed at the twin fins, large enough to adorn a 1959 Buick, that sprouted from either side of the large silver contraption. 'The special evil-conductors contained in the vacuum tubes of the Zeta Ray will – within a matter of seconds – subtly alter the alpha patterns within your son's brain. In that selfsame matter of seconds, his whole attitude will change. He will no longer be a worthless, namby-pamby do-gooder. He will suddenly see the justice of our cause!'

'Oh, you men and your technical explanations!' Mrs G. giggled. 'Still—'

'I guarantee,' Menge continued, 'that – after the ray is used – he will also be much more polite.'

'My. Really?' Roger's mother nodded, obviously impressed. 'Well, in that case—'

Menge, still smiling, reached for a button on the side of the silver machine, a button labelled with the usual large cardboard sign: 'Zeta Control.'

When Menge looked away, Zabana leapt for him.

'You no zap Roger!' the jungle prince exclaimed. 'Zabana zap Zeta!'

There was a brief, unequal struggle. Menge was picked up by jungle-bred muscles and thrown roughly against the machine, his elbow hitting the Zeta button.

'Bunga bonga blooie!' the prince of the jungle cried.

Zabana closed in on the super-villain, ready for the kill.

There was a crackling noise. The machine jerked as Menge and Zabana grappled.

'Run!' Louie shouted. 'The thing's gonna go off!'

Almost everybody ran. The crackling turned into a loud, whooping sound, and a yellow ray shot forth, bathing the only person who hadn't run – Roger's mother – in golden light!

'What's happening?' Roger yelled. 'Mother!'

Zabana grabbed a fistful of wiring from the silver gizmo's undercarriage. He yanked it free. The ray cut off abruptly.

'Oh, dear,' Mrs G. remarked. 'I feel so different. Hee.' She placed a hand delicately over her mouth. 'Hee hee. Heeheeheehee!' She began to laugh uncontrollably.

Menge the Merciless had managed to free himself from Zabana's grip. He ran a few feet away, nodding grimly as he retreated.

'The Zeta Ray has done its hellish work.'

Hellish work? Roger looked back to his laughing mother. What could Menge mean by that?

'Mother—' he began again.

His mother turned to look at him, and showed a smile Roger had never seen before. No, this was not the smile of a loving mother. It was not even the grim smile of a mother about to administer a paddling. It was, instead, a smile of pure evil!

When she spoke at last, her voice was low and full of menace. 'We'll teach sons to ignore their mothers! Heeheehee! Heeheehee!'

Menge the Merciless ran to her side.

'Yes!' he cried triumphantly. 'But not now! You have to destroy him by surprise, when he least expects it!'

Mrs G. frowned petulantly. 'Why?'

'It's much more' – he hesitated in the finest style of Doctor Dread – 'evil that way.'

The nasty grin returned to her face. 'Of course! Why didn't I think of that?' She clapped her hands. 'This is going to be so much fun! Hee hee hee heeheehee!'

'Oh, Mrs G! Together, we will rule the Cineverse! Ah hahahaha! Ah hahahaha!'

Menge took her hand in his.

'See you in the funny papers!' he cried.

There was the usual blue smoke.

'Oh, dear,' Delores said softly. 'Oh, Roger.'

Roger didn't say anything.

His mother? A villain?

The Plotmaster was right.

This was terrible! How could it get any worse?

'Roger!' Delores yelled.

'Roger,' Edward the Slime Monster repeated in a determined voice. 'The engagement is over.'

'The engagement is over?' Roger repeated, only half listening. 'Well, at least that's good news.'

'I'm glad you're taking it so well,' Edward added solemnly. 'No hard feelings.'

'*Roger*!' Delores insisted.

Roger glanced up from where he had been moodily studying the sand. Now that Roger noticed, wasn't the Slime Monster holding Delores a bit too tightly?

'Hey!' he yelled. 'What are you doing?'

'We are leaving,' Edward explained patiently. He glanced distractedly at the woman who struggled in his grip.

'Oh, dear,' he added, a hint of apology in his voice. 'Perhaps you misunderstood. I am unused to talking with humans. I am much more used to covering them with slime. But I told you the engagement was over. Delores and I will be married tonight.'

'ROGER!' There seemed to be a growing panic in Delores' voice.

'Tonight?' Roger asked, thoroughly confused once more. 'But I thought, what with the search for Captain Crusader, and our cause and all, you had decided to postpone—'

'That was before the Change,' Edward interrupted.

'The Change?' Roger repeated in a whisper.

The Slime Monster nodded its muck-covered head. 'Can't you feel it? Captain Crusader gone, Menge the Merciless triumphant, your mother Zeta-rayed into a life of evil. The delicate balance of the Cineverse is gone. The Change is upon us again. The Cineverse as we know it will soon cease to exist.'

Edward hugged Delores even closer to his chest.

'Even you would not deny a slime monster his last few moments of wedded bliss, would you?'

Roger realised then that he had been wrong again. It could still get worse, and was in fact getting worse with every passing moment. If he did not act quickly, he was going to lose the love of his life to a slime monster!

'But—' he began. But what? How did you reason with a creature composed of muck?

'Zabana say attack!' the jungle prince exclaimed.

Maybe, Roger realised, Zabana was right. They were many, the monster only one. Maybe you couldn't reason with a slime monster. Maybe, if they moved quickly enough, and they attacked all at once, they could overwhelm the Slime Monster. Maybe—

'If you insist,' Edward replied.

Roger only had a chance to take one step forward before it got worse than it had ever had been before.

Only one step, and he was covered with slime.

'*ROGER!*' Delores screamed a final time.

But then the muck rose to cover his ears, and he heard no more.

IS THE CINEVERSE DOOMED?
CAN ROGER DO A CONVINCING CAPTAIN CRUSADER?
WHAT DOES HIS MOTHER WANT FROM HIM, ANYWAY?
AND WHERE IN THE CINEVERSE WOULD A SLIME
MONSTER GO FOR A HONEYMOON?

ALL THIS AND MORE WILL BE ANSWERED
IN THE DYNAMIC CONCLUSION:
REVENGE OF THE FLUFFY BUNNIES
COMING NEXT . . .

Revenge of the Fluffy Bunnies

To Ginjer
A Wonderful Editor and a Good Friend

CHAPTER ONE

She felt so peculiar.

'Ah hahahaha!' the man in her life laughed heartily. 'Ah hahahaha!'

Mrs Roger Gordon Sr found that she wanted to laugh as well. She wanted to toss back her head and let the mirth bubble up from her belly. She wanted to hang on to this dear, silver-suited man by her side until the laughter consumed her. But she restrained herself. After all, she was a woman of mature years, not some giddy schoolgirl.

Still, she did feel like a *changed* woman of mature years. She found she no longer had any interest in the Bridge Club, or the Japanese beetles in the back garden, or the fact that her son, Roger Jr, never bothered to call her.

Instead, she had this overwhelming urge to destroy.

'Hee,' she remarked, quite unintentionally.

'Oh, Mrs G!' her suitor enthused. 'It will be so wonderful, gaining absolute mastery of the Cineverse with you by my side!'

'Why, Mr M!' she answered coquettishly, even though she really had no idea what he was talking about. Still, his enthusiasm was so infectious!

'Hee hee,' she added.

Perhaps she was being too hard on herself. A widow in her situation tended to get a bit set in her ways – she had seen it happen to her friends, and she wanted to guard against that sort of thing happening to her. Besides, she reminded herself, she wasn't that old. She had plenty of good years left, years that could be very well spent with the right sort of man.

The right sort of man squeezed her elbow affectionately. Mr M, as she liked to call him, even though her son had informed her that his real name was Menge the Merciless. Not your usual name, but she thought it had a certain charm. He smiled at her, displaying his single shining gold-capped tooth among the pearly-white molars. A man of his age, and he still had his own teeth. That certainly said something about his character. Besides, she always was a sucker for a pencil-thin moustache.

He leaned close to her.

'Ah hahahaha!' he whispered in her ear.

The way that man laughed sent a chill down her spine.

'Hee hee hee', she replied demurely.

She was certainly glad that Mr M – Menge, she reminded herself – was here to help her get acclimatized. Heaven knew, these surroundings would take some getting used to. She was still a bit disorientated by how fast things had been happening around her. One minute, she had been at home, looking through her keepsake drawer, and had stumbled on this cheap plastic ring, one of those prizes her son always used to save from cereal boxes. The next thing she knew, she was surrounded by thick, blue smoke. And when that smoke disappeared an instant later, Mrs Gordon discovered she was no longer standing in her bedroom, but had somehow been transported to a sunny beach, surrounded by teenagers with surfboards. And her son, Roger – who was far too old for that sort of thing – had been there, too.

Well, what was she to think? She demanded an explanation, but Roger, as usual, seemed completely incapable of giving her one. She sometimes wondered what kind of job her son could do in public relations if he couldn't even communicate with his own mother.

Fortunately for her, that was when her dear Menge had arrived – also, oddly enough, in a cloud of blue smoke. And he had, of course, been much more willing than her own son to explain everything to her, including the workings of that large machine, the Zeta Ray, that he had brought along with him.

She still wasn't too certain of the exact meaning of the events that immediately followed. First, Menge had explained that he, unfortunately, had brought his machine to fry her son's brain. She had objected – it was a mother's duty, after all – until Mr M had explained that exposure to the ray would actually make Roger much more polite. Even a mother couldn't argue with results like that.

Some of the other people on the beach, however, still felt the need to argue, and more than argue. Roger wasn't too keen on getting his brain fried, and his friends did a lot of shouting and carrying on.

And then there was this jungle person there – Splabana, Zabana, something like that – who had physically attacked dear Menge. The machine had gone off as the two men struggled, the ray shooting out to bathe her in its golden light.

After that, everything had been different.

Not that she had had much of a chance to think about it. Menge had swept her away almost immediately in another burst of blue smoke.

And they had arrived here, a place that seemed to be the very opposite of the sunny beach. The sky was heavily overcast, the ground covered by a layer of fog, and before them was a great building, as colourless as the rest of their surroundings. Mrs Gordon found something about the building disturbingly familiar, even though she couldn't quite place the architecture. Perhaps the huge structure was a sort of fortress, maybe even a medieval castle. It looked like an odd combination of the two, but there was something more to the place, something unpleasant. If, she considered, you added a bit of that sort of municipal structure where you had to stand in line for hours to get your registration renewed – yes, that was the building exactly!

Her feeling of unnamable dread identified, Mrs Gordon somehow felt oddly at peace with her surroundings. So what if everything here only showed variations on shades of grey? Menge's silver suit no longer shone. Even the flowered print of her dress seemed dulled, as if this place wanted to drain the colour away. But all this didn't upset her in the least. Now, for some reason, the dreariness seemed to cheer her up.

'Hee,' she remarked. 'Hee hee hee.'

'Mrs G,' Menge announced with a flourish of his cape. 'I would like to welcome you to our secret headquarters.'

Secret headquarters? That certainly sounded mysterious – and important! And Menge was going to share it specially with her? As mature a woman as she was, Mrs Gordon was beginning to feel more like that giddy schoolgirl with every passing minute.

'I am quite overwhelmed, Mr M.'

The man in her life took both her shoulders in his strong hands, and gently turned her to face him. His pencil-thin moustache quivered ever-so-slightly as he looked into her eyes.

'Mrs G,' Menge purred. 'We have known each other for some time, but I have never asked you a very important question.'

She stared back at him. Her heart thumped heavily in her chest. What could this mean?'

He took her right hand in his.

'What is your first name?'

'Why, Mr M!' She found herself blushing. In the oddest sense, the question seemed very personal. She hardly ever used her first name – except with her very closest friends.

'Antoinette,' she replied softly.

'Antoinette?' Mr M responded. 'It is a lovely name.'

She found herself blushing all over again. But she could not let this deeply personal moment fade away. She and this handsome, bald man in the silver suit were closer than they had ever been before, but she felt they could be closer still.

She looked deep into Menge's small but sensitive eyes.

'Now that you know my first name,' she began, a slight catch in her voice, 'I should ask the same of you.'

'Indeed you could,' he replied sympathetically, 'but I would not answer you. There are certain things better left buried.' He paused for a moment, then added quickly: 'You may call me Mengy, if you wish.'

'Mengy?' she asked.

He smiled as she said it. 'It's a name they called me on the surfing world. Frankly, it annoyed me when others used it. But, coming from your lips, the name becomes a song to my ears.'

'Mengy,' she repeated in a hoarse half-whisper.

'Antoinette,' he answered firmly as he pulled her close. 'Ah hahahaha.'

He looked down at her, then leaned his head forward, his lips almost touching her upturned face. His pencil-thin moustache tickled her nose. She closed her eyes in anticipation as she leaned forward as well.

'Is this how you—' a new voice interrupted, '—obey my orders?'

Mengy snapped to attention. Mrs Gordon opened her eyes as she turned to face the newcomer, her lips still longing for that kiss that had been only an instant away.

A man in a green snakeskin smoking jacket stared haughtily at them both.

'Doctor Dread!' Menge announced. 'I was merely showing the fortress to our newest recruit.'

'Newest recruit?' Dread asked incredulously. 'And who gave you—' he paused ominously, '—permission to bring in new recruits? Especially—' he paused again, his eyes darting critically from Antoinette to Menge and back again '—*this* kind of recruit!'

Mrs Gordon wasn't sure she liked this fellow, even if he was a doctor. This Dread person was thinner than Menge – too thin, really. Dread also sported a pencil-thin moustache. Still, Mrs G thought his sparse facial hair didn't suit the man in green's pinched face anywhere near as well as Menge's robust fringe added to the silver-suited one's manly nature. And there was something about the way Dread spoke that she found irritating – maybe it was the way he paused all the time. Whatever it was, it didn't add up to a very favourable first impression. In all fairness, she didn't think this so-called Doctor was good enough to shine Mengy's silver shoes.

'No, no, Doctor Dread,' Menge added quickly. Did he have to be so obsequious? This was a side of her man that she had never seen before.

'You don't understand certain important things about our new recruit,' Menge continued, 'such as the fact that she has relatives in very high places.'

'Relatives?' Dread snapped, as if the mention of that word was enough to drive him to fury. 'Ever since Big Bertha convinced me to employ her good-for-nothing brother, Louie, I have had enough of—' he paused in order to summon enough venom for the final word, '—*relatives*!'

'But you haven't heard me out!' Menge insisted. Mrs G was glad he was getting a bit more forceful. This was the Mr M she found so attractive, the man equally adept at building a rec room on Earth or controlling the Zeta Ray in the Cineverse.

Menge put his arm round her.

'This woman is the mother of Roger Gordon.'

Dread's mouth opened, his fury forgotten. 'Mother?' He paused, so astonished that he forgot to be sinister. 'Roger – Gordon?'

With the mention of her son's name, Antoinette found her anger inexplicably on the rise, as if Dread's fury had been contagious.

'He's not much of a son!' she spat. 'I can't even remember the last time he called!'

'I think it only fair to mention,' Menge continued smoothly, 'that our new recruit has also been zapped by the Zeta Ray!'

'The Zeta Ray?' Dread's pinched face broke into a childlike grin, as if he had suddenly discovered today was Christmas. 'Mother? Roger Gordon? Zeta Ray?' He began to laugh anaemically. 'Heh. Hehheh. Heh heh heh.

'Ah hahahaha!' Menge answered. 'Ah hahahaha!'

The levity was contagious. Antoinette couldn't help but join in. 'Hee hee hee hee! Hee hee hee hee!'

'Menge!' Dread exclaimed. 'You are to be – congratulated. With Roger Gordon's mother at our side, no one will be able to stop the – Change! Heh! Hehhehheh!'

They all laughed some more.

Dread cut the laughter abruptly with a wave of his snakeskin glove.

'Enough frivolity! We need to make—' he hesitated suggestively, '—arrangements for the final stages of the – Change! Meet me in the – war room in five minutes. And bring your—' this time, he paused too suggestively for Antoinette's liking, '—new recruit!'

Dread turned with a flurry of his snakeskin cape. He rapidly climbed the slate staircase leading to the grey edifice before them, disappearing a moment later through one of a pair of twenty-foot-tall, dull steel doors.

There was a moment of uncomfortable silence between the two who remained outside.

'We really know so little about each other,' Antoinette sighed at last. 'Why, until now, I didn't even know you were in someone else's employ.'

'In someone else's employ?' Her man shook his head firmly. 'Not for long, Mrs G. Not for long.' He once again placed his hands upon her shoulders. 'Meeting you on Earth, helping to build your rec room, the so-called accident with the Zeta Ray – I realize now that none of these things were mere chance! No, it is Antoinette Gordon and Menge the Merciless – two names that together speak of destiny!'

He squeezed her shoulders. She had never seen him look so intense!

'Even Doctor Dread is as nothing before us!' He let go of her to ball both his hands into fists. 'Soon, Menge the Merciless will control the Cineverse, with the lovely Antoinette by his side!'

He stopped to look up the stairs, his grin of triumph replaced by an uncertain frown.

'But come!' he said as he took her hand. 'We cannot be late for the war room. Everything must seem normal until we can make our move. Then, after careful planning – ultimate triumph! Ah hahahaha! Ah hahahaha!'

Antoinette smiled as the merciless one led her up the stairs. She did like a man who knew his own mind! With him by her side, she didn't even care about Earth or her past life. With Menge, her life was all brand new.

She had the feeling that all sorts of interesting things were going to happen!

CHAPTER TWO

All was darkness – a hot, damp darkness, as if the heat of noon had forgotten to go away. Delores couldn't see a thing.

Something roared loudly, out there in the still air of the endless night.

Something else screamed.

'Sorry,' the voice of Edward, the slime monster, whispered in her ear.

'Sorry?' Delores replied, surprised at the venom in her own voice. 'Here I am, one minute, standing on a sunny beach, directly across from the man I love, and the next, I am whisked away by a creature made of putrescent muck to a place that would make the Black Hole of Calcutta look like a holiday resort, and all you can say is – you're sorry?'

'Um,' Edward replied, 'how about if I say I'm *very* sorry?'

'Nope,' Delores replied firmly. 'It doesn't wash.'

'Slime monsters never do,' Edward admitted. 'If you get us too near water, it can become very messy.'

'Look,' Delores interjected as reasonably as she could. 'If you're *really* sorry, why don't you take me back to the beach?'

Delores felt droplets of slime hit her exposed neck and arm.

'I can't,' the slime monster admitted with a quaver in his voice. Could that be a quaver of fear? What, Delores thought with a shiver of her own, could a slime monster be afraid of?

'It was the Zeta Ray,' Edward explained.

'You're afraid of the Zeta Ray?' Delores asked incredulously.

'Slime monsters know no fear,' Edward insisted. 'Mostly, we know slime. But still, there is something I cannot place my incredibly slippery finger on, something about that Zeta Ray, and *the Change*—'

Edward's voice faltered, as if, despite his protestations, there were certain things even slime monsters didn't want to think about.

Delores was once again aware of sounds in the darkness. The screams redoubled, even more blood-curdling than before. And this time they were accompanied by other, softer noises, like the tearing of cloth, the rending of flesh, the splintering of bone, and the clacking of long and pointed teeth – almost as if, Delores reflected, something was being eaten alive.

Delores decided she didn't want to reflect any more.

'We may not have long before the Change starts all over again,' Edward continued, as if he had finally found the courage to say what was in his heart, or whatever similar organ beat within the slime monster's breast. 'And once the Change begins, who knows what is next? No, we must be married as soon as possible. And then, of course, there's the honeymoon to consider. And what about the china and silver patterns?' The monster sighed. 'So much to do, so little time.'

China and silver patterns? Delores also decided to put any thoughts of marriage to a thing made from muck out of her mind. She'd never get out of here if she descended into despair.

Instead, she asked the first question that had come into her head upon her arrival in the dreadful place.

'But – why here?'

'Here?' Edward's voice sounded surprised, almost shocked. 'Where else could we go? This is home.'

'Home?' Delores asked between the now faltering screams. 'You call a dark, foul-smelling, noisy and dangerous place like this – home?'

'Yes, it is rather pleasant, isn't it?' Edward agreed. 'But I sense you are not entirely happy with our new surroundings. Probably has something to do with you being used to sunshine, and all those other nasty bright lights.' Edward sighed. 'It is true, you could not know this place the way I do.'

The screams ended, and the roaring began again.

'I don't think I want to,' Delores admitted.

'If you had only grown up here,' Edward insisted, 'the way I did. Oh, what happy childhood memories, rooting in the muck for Tremendofly maggots! You should try them. They're especially tasty, you know, just before they moult.'

Tremendofly maggots? Despite her best efforts, Delores could feel that despair seeping into her soul.

'Now I know I don't want to,' she replied sullenly.

Edward made a wet tsking sound with what passed for his mouth. 'My dear Delores, if only you'd give the place a chance.

There is beauty here, all around us even now, in the cry of the dying Razorbird, and the grumbling song of the Gigantasaur as it rends and tears its evening meal. Or, if you listen carefully, you can hear the musical bubbling of the distant phosphorescent swamp as it claims another victim.'

Now that Edward mentioned it, she did think she heard a distant bubbling noise, accompanied by the ever-present distant screams. None of this was making Delores feel any better. She had to get out of here – somehow, anyhow. 'Uh, Edward? Could we go somewhere and talk about this?'

'Too much, too soon, huh?' the muck-thing replied, sounding genuinely apologetic. 'Maybe I should have waited to bring you home. We slime monsters were always impetuous. I'm sure it has something to do with our slippery constitution.' Edward chuckled. 'Oh, we're going to have such a wonderful life together. Why, I think we've just had our first domestic quarrel.'

The monster took Delores' shoulder in his slimy yet firm grip. 'Away we go,' he whispered close by her ear. She had to struggle not to choke on his fetid breath. 'To somewhere that isn't quite so picturesque.'

So, even though they would get away from here, she was still trapped in the slime monster's embrace. But, she had to remind herself, even now, she wasn't alone. Roger Gordon, the man she loved, had been chosen as the new Captain Crusader. Surely, a man of Captain Crusader's stature would have to have tremendous resources. Surely, Roger and their other allies could save her – somehow.

Edward's grip tightened.

'Keep watching the skies!' the slime monster yelled.

There was a small explosion. Had there been any light here at all, Delores was sure she would have seen blue smoke.

'Roger!' she called out to the void.

'Delores!' Roger whispered as he stared at the sand.

'So,' Zabana, prince of the jungle, asked over his shoulder. 'What we do now?'

'Um,' Roger replied. It was a good question, what with all that had happened, first with his mother, and then with Delores. But Roger had no answers.

'Uh,' he added.

'But we must act!' Zabana insisted. 'Fate of Cineverse at stake!'

'Arf arf!' the police dog at Zabana's side added. 'Arf bark!'

'Dwight the wonder dog agrees,' the rather short Big Louie translated. 'The jungle prince has a point. Now that the insidious Doctor Dread has made it clear that he and his minions are working to once more bring about the Change—'

Roger couldn't help himself. 'Dwight said all that?' he asked.

'Zabana lose whole family to Change,' the jungle prince agreed morosely. 'Wife Shirley go into real estate, son Son start own movie series. Even my faithful orangutang companion, Oogie—' Zabana choked, unable to continue.

Yes, Roger remembered the Change, too – fifteen or twenty years ago, now – a time when movies lost their heroes, when the bad guys won, the good guys died, and boy didn't even get to meet girl. At the time, Roger thought movies might simply be mirroring the social unrest of the late sixties and early seventies. Now, though, he knew it was all because of the fiendish plans of Doctor Dread!

'Yes, the Change,' Big Louie continued, 'which, if it is allowed to take control again, will mean the triumph of Doctor Dread, and the end of the Cineverse as we know it. Only Captain Crusader stands in the way of this awful catastrophe, our own Captain Crusader, Roger Gordon, lately of Earth, appointed by the Plotmaster to lead the forces of good in a last-ditch effort to rid the many cinematic worlds of Dread's evil!'

'That putsh it all together nichely,' the reformed drunkard Doc – still suffering from a slight case of sunstroke – slurred.

'I'll say, boyo,' Officer O'Clanrahan rejoined. 'That's one of the most professional summaries I've ever heard. By all the saints, we could have used you on the force!'

'I'm a sidekick,' Louie replied matter-of-factly. 'Plot summaries are part of my job. You know, whatever moves the plot along.'

And Roger realized the plot had to get moving, soon. He heard the sound of tuning guitars on the makeshift stage the surfers had set up on the beach. That meant it was almost time for more beach party music. And music had a special power in the Cineverse – movie magic, Louie called it – a musical power that could make you want to spend the rest of your life in this seaside paradise. Bix Bale and the Belltones – with their red and white striped shirts and modified Beatle haircuts – would soon play yet another song extolling the virtues of sun, sand and surfing, with perhaps some references to blonde beach bunnies thrown in.

And, once the music really started, all plans would disappear as everyone began to dance!

Roger wasn't as afraid of the power of movie magic as he had been. He had, after all, conquered that great wave, the Cowabungamunga, through his own use of surfing song. But there was no time to delay, and – once the music began – there was no way to tell how long the surfing beat's subversive force might keep them under its sway. He had to use the Captain Crusader Decoder Ring he clutched in his hand to get his allies out of here. But where should they go next? Shouldn't somebody who'd been appointed Captain Crusader know these sort of things?

And, besides that, one of the surfers was running straight towards him.

'Roger Dodger!' Brian called. His usual creaseless surfer's face was wrinkled by a frown. 'Something's going wrong! It's Frankie!'

He pointed to the stage.

'Oh no,' Big Louie added in horror. 'Not this. Anything but this!'

Roger's mouth opened as he turned to the stage. Bix Bale and the Belltones had changed. They no longer sported the surfer look. Instead, their dark hair was cut and plastered to their heads, and they wore white polyester suits, with dark ruffled shirts open to the navel to reveal the dozens of gold chains that criss-crossed their chests. And their former surfing buddy Frankie – dressed just like the band – strode in front of them.

Roger had seen all of this somewhere before.

'Frankie!' Brian insisted. 'You can't do this, Frankie!'

'Hit it guys!' Frankie called in reply.

The music was different, only vague rock and roll. Oh, not that there wasn't a drumbeat. No, the drum was much louder than Roger had ever heard it in surf songs. It was right up in front of the music, very heavy, and very regular, almost too regular, as if the beat was being produced by a machine.

The music swelled. All Roger could see was the four-piece rock band. Where were those violins coming from, anyway?

Then Frankie started to sing:

> 'Oh, I've got to boogie,
> Got to shake my thing,
> Don't you get in my way, girl,
> I'm a disco king!'

Everyone stared at the stage. For the moment, at least, there was no movie magic. The new music was too different, too far from the beach. But everybody knew what this new music meant.

'It'sh the Change!' Doc wailed for all of them.

Roger never thought it would be as bad as this.

CHAPTER THREE

Menge led the way into the secret headquarters.

'This is also known as the "Citadel of Dread",' he said softly to Mrs G as the great double doors slammed shut behind them, 'although I think we may be changing the name soon – say, to the "Stronghold of the Merciless"?'

Mrs Gordon smiled at her man's confidence. Of course, why someone would want to take over a place as dreary as this was beyond her. The grey motif of the building's massive exterior carried over to the rather large interior as well. There was nothing inside but featureless grey walls and impossibly high ceilings. And all these shadows just had to go!

What this place needed, Mrs G decided, was a woman's touch. Say, an attractive floral arrangement here under that sputtering torch, and perhaps a series of colourful throw rugs along that endless hallway over there – little changes like that could do real wonders for the place. Once Mengy was in control around here, she could really cheer this secret headquarters up – make it into the sort of place to which you wouldn't be ashamed to invite the neighbours. If, she considered, a place like this had any neighbours.

'You have a new life before you, Mrs G,' Menge continued in that same soft, but urgent, tone as he led her through the never-ending corridors. 'We *both* have new lives before us.' He chuckled knowingly as he squeezed her hand. 'You are a part of a new world, Antoinette. You should have a new identity that fits your new world.'

'A new identity?' she replied uncertainly. What did he mean by that? Something, perhaps, like one of those makeovers she was always reading about in those fashion magazines. Reading, she reminded herself, but never doing.

'Yes!' Menge insisted. 'Consider it, Mrs G. Who, in your deepest, darkest heart, have you always wanted to be?'

'Well,' she answered uncertainly, 'I've never really thought about it.' Her hands smoothed her floral print dress. 'Until now, I've been happy with Mrs Roger Gordon Sr, homemaker.'

But Menge shook his head firmly. 'Absolutely not. That will never do for the most powerful woman in the Cineverse.' He clutched her hand even more tightly than before. 'For, now that you are at my side, you will be *very* powerful.'

He stopped abruptly.

'Perhaps we shall find what we need in here.'

He opened a door to his left marked 'WARDROBE'. Mrs G followed him inside.

What she saw next took her breath away. The room was full of clothing, but not simply any clothing. She had seldom seen this many clothes, and never in this variety, in a confined space before – rack after rack of every shade and style imaginable. And, what's more, with the vast quantity of wild colours and jungle prints, fur collars and metal studs, none of these clothes could be called understated. It was all rather like walking into the world's largest closet – or, at the very least, a very large discount department store.

She studied the nearest rack, and noticed a preponderance of snakeskin. She ran her fingers along one of the bumpy cowls.

Menge took her hand again and gently pulled it away. 'That stuff's reserved for the boss. You can't wear it – just yet. Still, there's plenty left over for the well-dressed villain. Or villainess.'

He walked down to the next rack, pulling her along. He frowned at a selection of hooded robes in black and white, purple and green, some in solid colours, others with images of spiders, tigers, vultures and suchlike sewn on to the head-pieces.

'Too plain,' Menge murmured. 'Wouldn't do you justice.' He passed over a shelf of mystic turbans and similar headgear, many of them set with semi-precious stones, then dismissed another rack featuring a selection of metal-studded, see-through bikinis as 'not your style'.

He grinned before he even touched the third rack.

'Here it is!' he declared as he yanked a hanger free from its fellows. 'The very thing!' He winked jauntily as he handed the clothing – something, she noticed approvingly, in basic black – to Mrs G.

She took the costume and opened a door labelled 'CHANGING ROOM'.

'Oh, don't forget these!' Mengy called after her. He passed a pair of boots to her through the still open doorway – boots also in basic black. Apparently, Mrs G thought, they were going for a total look.

She told Mengy he'd have to be patient and shut the door.

The dress was a bit tighter than she was used to. Still, she had been careful to keep her figure, and the dark colour was very flattering, especially with her newly blonde hair. Of course, she wasn't at all sure how practical this costume would be. Wouldn't black leather get awfully hot in the summer? But everything was in her size, even the boots, almost as if it had been made for her. And the accessories – those small silver skull earrings were quite darling in their way. Then there was the whip. She flicked the handle tentatively. The whip snapped smartly.

CRACK

She flipped the handle the other way.

CRACK snapped the whip again. She flipped her wrist back and forth. *CRACK**CRACK**CRACK* It was all so easy, the snapping leather almost an extension of her arm – like she had been handling a bullwhip all her life.

She was quite startled by the change when she looked in the full-length mirror. Part of her wanted to back away from anything this different, this bold, but another part of her wanted to giggle – no, she wanted to laugh out loud, long and strong – a laugh of total triumph.

These were no longer the clothes of the everyday housewife. These were clothes of power.

She opened the door and stepped out to show the outfit to her Mengy.

Her man made a sound that was half gasp, half moan.

'It is *you*,' he whispered, his face as full of wonder as a ten-year-old boy. 'I never dreamed it would be this perfect.'

'Do you really think so?' Mrs G asked. Still, she couldn't help but smile.

'That, and more so,' Mengy assured her. 'You are no longer Mrs Roger Gordon Sr. You are now someone far better. You are—' he paused, searching for exactly the right words '—Mother Antoinette, Mistress of Evil!'

'Really?' Mrs G replied, still not quite convinced. She did like the sound of the first part of that – Mother Antoinette. But 'Mistress' of Evil? Shouldn't it be 'Matron' of Evil? She had been married, after all.

Still, why should she worry about such inconsequential details when the crack of that whip was so very satisfying?

'Yes,' Menge answered throatily, his hand trembling where he almost touched her leather-clad shoulder. 'It suits you surprisingly well.' His small mouth worked silently for a moment beneath his pencil-thin moustache, as if he was having difficulty with what he wanted to say next. 'And more than that,' he added at last, 'Antoinette, I—'

'Menge!' the nasal and irritating voice of Doctor Dread interrupted them.

Menge snapped to attention. 'Yessir!' he shouted to the wall. Mrs G turned to look at what her man was facing, and was surprised to see a large, moving image covering the top half of that side of the room, rather like a gigantic television screen.

'What is—' Dread hesitated angrily, '—keeping you?'

'Just some minor alterations,' Menge assured that nasty Dread person. 'I thought it appropriate to get our new recruit some more suitable attire.'

'More—' Dread paused most unpleasantly, '—suitable? I decide what is *suitable* around here. Are you forgetting who is the authority on this world, in this Cineverse, who has the power to *deal* with people who displease him? I warn you, Menge—'

Mrs G had had enough of Dread's browbeating the man she loved. She stepped in front of the screen and flicked her wrist.

CRACK

'This is—' Dread hesitated in disbelief, '—Mrs Gordon?'

Mrs G smiled ever so slightly as she stared defiantly at Dread's image.

'Yes!' Menge added hurriedly. 'But she is no longer simply Mrs Gordon. She is now Mother Antoinette, Mistress of Evil!'

CRACK the new Mother Antoinette added, flicking the bull-whip at the screen. *CRACK**CRACK* *CRACK*

Dread's mouth fell open.

'Yes, I suppose that is—' he hesitated, as if even the soon-to-be-master of the Cineverse might be at a loss for words, '—quite suitable.'

Mother Antoinette smiled and snapped the whip.

Dread hastily broke the connection.

Menge put his hand on her shoulder. 'That was wonderful, Mrs G!'

She turned to look at him. His hand fell away.

'I mean, Mother Antoinette,' he amended hastily. 'But we

must go to the throne room. It is not yet time to make our move.'

It must have been her imagination, but Mrs G could have sworn Mr M was trembling as she walked past him, her three-inch heels clacking on the fortress floor.

The whip made small, snapping sounds as she idly toyed with it. Mengy moaned softly behind her.

She turned to look at her man. He appeared smaller, now that she was wearing those heels. 'Mengy? Is something the matter?'

'Oh no,' he insisted, although he was sweating profusely – unusual in a place as cold and clammy as this dull, grey fortress. 'Everything is—' he swallowed, '—just fine.'

'If you say so.' She brushed her blonde hair away from her face. It looked like Mengy's knees were wobbling with regularity, almost as a response to her every action. 'Shall we proceed?'

'Yes, Mother Antoinette,' Menge replied hurriedly, averting his gaze as he ran past her for the door. 'Whatever you say.'

Now what could be the matter with him? Mother Antoinette smiled slightly, cracking the whip behind her as she followed Mengy from the room.

Whatever his problems were, she had ways to find them out.

CHAPTER FOUR

There was the usual blue smoke.

'I hope you like this somewhat better,' the slime monster's dour tones cut through the smog.

Anything, Delores thought, had to be better than that last place. Still, if that last dark and dangerous world was the place the slime monster called *home*, where might he bring her next? She decided to reserve her judgement on their new surroundings until the smoke cleared.

Rays of sunlight cut through the thick blue fog, burning the remaining mist away in only a few seconds. But where were they? They stood on a quiet, well-kept street, surrounded by a series of neat little white frame houses placed on a series of immaculate green lawns. Like one of the nicer streets on Earth, Delores thought, only perhaps a bit too bright, a bit too quiet, a bit too perfect.

Delores shivered. Too bright? Too perfect? She hoped Edward hadn't brought her to one of those musical comedy worlds. The surfing world had been seductive enough. If they had landed in one of those places where everyone was going to the fair or were on the verge of celebrating some major holiday in song, Delores and the monster might be doomed to stay here for ever. Could that be what Edward truly wanted?

But Delores heard no distant orchestras or vocal choirs or hordes of tapping feet – none of the telltale signs of musical comedy. Instead, she could hear only birds chirping in the gentle breeze, and kids laughing as they rode their bikes in the suburban sunshine.

'Walk this way,' Edward instructed, shambling quickly down the street.

If I could walk that way – Delores stopped herself. This was no time for comedy of any kind. She watched the tall, greenish-brown creature shuffle down the street before her and realized that this was the first time she had seen the slime monster in the bright sunlight – the first time, in fact, she had seen the monster not hidden by shadow or covered with sand.

The creature was definitely humanoid, if somewhat on the large size, with appendages that approximated head, arms and legs. And every inch of the monster's rather large frame was covered by a gooey, shining slime.

Except that the slime shone less with every second the slime monster stood in direct sunlight. Delores could see the muck already drying rapidly on Edward's back, cracking into patches like a mudflat too long deprived of rain. The widening cracks showed the slightest glimpse of something underneath – something of a much darker green and so highly polished that it glittered even more than what slime remained, and flashed whenever the sunlight shone upon the cracks.

Was she glimpsing the actual skin under the monster's slime? Oddly enough, the texture beneath the mud reminded Delores of nothing so much as a rubber suit.

Edward groaned, a sound from deep inside, like the sunshine was not only drying his skin, but his soul.

'Hurry!' he called to her. 'There is little time!'

She had been right then – Edward was drying out in the bright light. The monster couldn't live long under the direct sun. And he had come to this place because of Delores. What a sacrifice he must be making for her! For the first time, Delores felt the slightest twinge of compassion for this disgusting creature. She ran to follow him, careful to sidestep the still damp and odiferous trail Edward had left in his wake.

He breathed heavily, the air rasping in and out of his throat as the slime on his face dried enough for Delores to make out the outline of a nose and a pair of ears. Even a thin slit opened where the monster's mouth should be. And, as he dried, his rapidly shuffling gait became slower and slower.

So the slime monster wasn't as invincible as he had first appeared. Delores realized that, if she could only expose the slime monster to enough heat and light, she might be rid of him for ever.

Still, she hoped it wouldn't have to come to that. There was something about this rapidly drying but still foul-smelling creature that was – well, perhaps 'endearing' was too strong a word – but the fellow was certainly likeable, and generally well-meaning, at least as monsters went. Delores sighed. There had to be some other way, short of the creature's total destruction, to say 'no' to a slime monster.

'Almost there,' Edward urged, his voice now little more than a whisper. When he looked at her, the muck drying on his head gave his face a look that might almost pass for tenderness.

Edward turned and hurried up the walk to one of the houses, a structure somewhat bigger than the other homes on the block, but of the same white painted wood with the same manicured green lawn.

Delores noticed that this place also had a plaque by the door:

THE SOUTHERN CALIFORNIA INSTITUTE OF VERY ADVANCED SCIENCE

'If they can't help us,' Edward croaked with another fond look in Delores' direction, 'no one can.'

And with that the slime monster kicked down the door.

'Who's that?' an astonished guard yelled through a hole where a moment before the door, and a fair amount of the surrounding doorway, had stood.

'Pardon us,' Edward mumbled as he made his faltering way over to a water fountain opposite the guard station. He pressed the fountain's foot pedal with one mud-encrusted appendage, and drank.

And, as he drank, the mud turned back to slime with astonishing speed. In mere seconds, Edward was back to his gooey, disgusting self.

'It's the slime monster!' the guard exclaimed. 'Sound the alarm! Close down the – glub!'

'Sorry,' Edward remarked as a stream of slime shot from the ends of both his arms to engulf the guard. 'But any of those options would be inconvenient.'

He turned to Delores, who stared past the monster at the slime-engulfed guard. Then again, she considered, how did you relate to someone who shot sludge for a living?

'Do you like it?' the monster asked, almost pathetically eager.

'Um,' Delores replied, still somewhat overcome by the course of events. 'Like what?'

'My latest work.' Edward pointed back to the pile of grey sludge where the uniformed guard had blubbered only a moment before. 'I call it "Security Guard, Covered by Slime".'

'Uh—' Delores answered as truthfully as possible, considering the circumstances, '—this is all a little new to me.'

'Oh, dear, I've worried about this so,' Edward fretted. 'Isn't my work accessible enough? Now, now, don't tell me. It's the title, isn't it? It lacks that certain ambiguity so important in modern art! I've always been too direct, you know. It's an occupational hazard, when you're a monster.' He paused for an instant, then added, 'Perhaps I should call it something like "Security No. 34". What do you think?'

Delores didn't know what to say. Most of her wanted to say 'LET ME OUT OF HERE!' She had to admit, there was nothing like a new pile of stinking sludge to remind her she was being chaperoned by a slime monster – the same monster who, no matter how polite he appeared, was holding her against her will.

'It's not the title, is it?' Edward answered himself, his voice grim, as if his worst fears had been realized. Slime flew about the room as he ruefully shook his head. 'It's the work itself! Now, now, no misdirected kindness. You can tell me. What do you *really* think? I may be slippery, but I can take it!'

What could you say, Delores considered, when the subject in question was a totally disgusting mound of grey sludge? Still, whatever his other failings, the monster had been unerringly polite in her presence. Perhaps, if she could be as polite in turn, she could somehow talk this monster out of the whole wedding thing.

But what *did* she really think?

'Uh, no,' she began, doing her best not to hurt the monster's feelings. 'It's actually quite—' Her voice drifted off as her mind failed to conjure up any way to finish the sentence.

'Perhaps I need to add a little something?' Edward prompted, still eager to please.

'Something to – the slime?' Delores asked, hard pressed not to shiver at the very thought.

'Well, yes, that's a possibility—' Edward reflected thoughtfully. 'I *was* adding sand to the slime back on the beach. The whole thing hardened quite nicely. But I was thinking of pursuing something not quite so physical—' He pointed an object that might have been a finger skywards to make his point. '—something, instead, that would reveal my more sensitive aspects; something to make this more of a total aesthetic experience.'

'Total aesthetic—' Delores began. Politeness, after all, could only go so far.

But Edward had become so excited by this latest concept that he didn't even hear her.

'That's it!' he cried. 'I need a context for my slime – something that everyday people – some of them who perhaps have never even met a slime monster – can relate to in their everyday, slime-monsterless lives. But–' the monster hesitated, grappling with this new concept, '–what would be best? Perhaps some sort of dramatic emphasis, even – dare I say it? – poetry!'

'Poetry?' Delores asked, helpless to do anything else.

Edward's slimy face showed an even more far-away look than usual. 'Poetry. Perhaps something like–' The monster cleared whatever passed for his throat. "Don't take it hard that I've covered the guard. I know what is mine and it's got to be slime" – that sort of thing?'

Edward glanced at Delores' look of dismay and sighed. 'Still, it lacks resonance, doesn't it? If only slime was more of a universal experience!'

'Hey, there he is!' somebody yelled.

'He got Sweeney!' a second voice added.

Two more guards ran into the foyer of the institute. Before Delores could even react, Edward promptly covered both of them with sludge.

'Of course,' the monster added, 'the longer we stand here, the more universal the slime experience becomes.' He paused to regard his latest creation. 'There it is, my new, improved creation. "Three Security Guards, Covered by Slime." Or should it be "Security No. 35"?' He glanced at Delores. 'Still not universal, huh? Where have I gone wrong?'

Delores decided that she had taken politeness as far as it could go, especially with that rank odour coming from the covered guards. She looked up at Edward.

'Couldn't you do something else than cover people with slime?'

The room shook as the slime monster roared. Had Delores gone too far?

Edward took a ragged breath, clenching those two objects that might have been fists as he brought himself under control. Still quaking with emotion, he turned to regard Delores. She thought she saw two tiny points of ruby light where his eyes should be, twin coals glowing in his slime-enshrouded face.

'Why–' he rumbled, '–are artists always so misunderstood?' He placed what passed for a hand in front of what passed for a face.

'There must be something I can do!' the monster continued, his voice once again quiet, yet dour and determined. 'Say – I could read the phone book backwards, thus giving my reaction to the emptiness of present-day society.'

A fellow in a white lab coat emerged from a door off the foyer. Edward covered the newcomer in sludge before he could finish his scream. Delores turned away.

'Or I could paint myself in decorator colours,' the monster continued, 'thus commenting cleverly on the folly of modern home furnishings.'

A half-dozen security guards ran yelling from two opposite corridors, their pistols drawn. Delores made a gagging noise as Edward drowned them all in slime.

'Or I could even cover myself with hot fudge sauce, whipped cream, and a maraschino cherry,' the monster further mused, 'thus critiquing the arbitrary nature of the food chain and my place within it.'

Edward paused, as if waiting for a response, but Delores – with all her attention diverted to controlling her gag response – had long ago given up trying to keep up her end of the conversation. A voice screamed in her head: *Let me out of here!*

The slime monster looked uncertainly down at his feet. 'Then again, I could learn to tap dance.'

They were interrupted by the sound of sirens, distant at first, but becoming much louder before they shut off abruptly.

'ALL RIGHT, MONSTER!' a bullhorn-amplified voice shouted outside. 'WE KNOW YOU'RE IN THERE!'

Edward lifted what passed for his head up to the heavens. 'Why does this always have to happen? "ALL RIGHT MONSTER! WE KNOW YOU'RE IN THERE!" Can't the forces of law and order ever have any originality? Is there no place in the Cineverse for an artist like me?' The monster shook his head ruefully. 'Well, perhaps there will be, after our experiment.'

Our experiment? Delores didn't like the sound of that. *Let me out of here – now!*

'THROW OUT THE GIRL AND WE'LL GO EASY ON YOU!' the bullhorn voice continued.

'Throw out the girl?' Edward despaired. 'Come on, guys, show a little originality.' He waved to Delores. 'Come with me—' he paused as ominously as Doctor Dread, '—unless you want to see the entire police force covered with slime.' He glanced back towards the front door. 'At least those guys haven't said anything about having the building surrounded—'

'WE'RE WARNING YOU, MONSTER!' the bull-horn responded promptly. 'WE HAVE THE ENTIRE BUILDING SURROUNDED!'

'We really do have to leave now,' Edward insisted. He shooed her down the central corridor in front of him. 'I sense some resistance on your part.' He quickly lumbered after her. 'But I trust this institute has the proper tools to make us more compatible.'

More compatible? Delores shivered. What did he mean – psychological programming to make her more accepting of slime? Her throat was almost too dry for her to swallow. Maybe she'd have to leave Edward out in the noonday sun after all.

The slime monster was almost on top of her. Delores hurried down the hall, past door after neatly-labelled door: 'MINIA-TURIZATION LAB', 'OUTER SPACE COMMUNICA-TIONS ROOM', 'GIANT BRAIN EXPERIMENT'.

'Turn here,' Edward instructed, pointing past a door marked 'CENTRE FOR PHENOMENAL GROWTH'. What, Delores wondered, could Edward want down here? She was relieved when they passed the door marked 'ATOM SMASHER'; doubly relieved as they passed the 'ALIEN PARASITE HOSPITALITY SUITE'.

'Stop,' Edward commanded.

Delores stopped.

The slime monster opened a door marked 'TRANS-MOGRIFIER'.

'After you,' he intoned.

Delores hesitated. How could she get out of here?

'You have no choice,' the slime monster insisted. 'This is your destiny.'

It was either this, Delores realized, or being covered by slime.

She took a step into the darkened room.

CHAPTER FIVE

'Hey!'

It was Big Louie's voice, yelling through the smoke. Loads and loads of thick, blue smoke.

At first, Roger thought someone new had arrived on the beach-party-turned-disco world.

But then he realized the disco beat had faded away, lost beneath the sound of a distant wind. And there was too much smoke – the kind of smoke that only appeared when you were travelling between worlds.

They had left the beach party planet behind. But wasn't he the one with the ring that transported them between those worlds? And he hadn't touched it – had he? And he couldn't remember anybody saying 'See you in the funny papers!'

Then his feet were on solid ground again. They were somewhere new. But how – where – and why?

'What's going on here?' Louie asked loudly, once again voicing the disquiet of the entire group.

'This sort of thing is enough to make a fella sober,' Doc agreed, apparently startled out of his inebriation by the sudden change of scene.

Roger had to admit that the adrenaline was pounding in his veins as well, in part because of that music he heard coming from outside the blue cloud. And it was very urgent music.

'Faith and begorah!' Officer O'Clanrahan added.

'Yip bark arf!' Dwight added with a concerned bark.

'Listen!' Roger insisted. The music was getting louder, relentless horns pounding over constant violins, as if the hidden orchestra was urging Roger to do – what?

'You hear something?' the prince of the jungle asked incredulously. 'Even Zabana, with his jungle-bred senses, able to hear slithering of slug at six hundred paces, hear nothing but distant wind.' The jungle prince paused. 'That, and – now I listen – even more distant growl of engines.'

Nothing but the distant growl of engines? But the music was so obvious!

'You can't hear this?' Roger found he had to shout over the pounding of the kettle drum. 'Not the horns or the violins? Even that incessant drum?'

The smoke chose that instant to clear.

They were on some inner city street, in what looked like an industrial section of a town, with large warehouses on either side, and the crumbling remains of elevated tram tracks overhead.

That was it. There was no orchestra anywhere in sight. Paradoxically, the music grew even louder, a swirl of woodwinds adding punch to the horns. Roger wondered if the orchestra was hiding in one of the warehouses.

'Now, Roger,' Louie asked, 'exactly what were we listening—'

'Bark bark yip!' Dwight the wonder dog interrupted.

Big Louie looked in the direction the dog indicated.

'Oh, no!' he echoed.

'What matter?' Zabana asked as he hunkered into a defensive jungle crouch. 'Is Change?'

'Worse than that,' Big Louie answered. 'The Change has been here and gone. Don't you see what's coming towards us? It's a car chase!'

The music ceased abruptly as those distant engines Zabana had heard – and the cars those engines were attached to – got much, much closer, very, very fast.

'And they're coming right for us!' screamed Louie, with his astonishing ability to encapsulate the obvious. 'And there's nowhere to hide!'

Roger took a closer look at their surroundings. They had materialized in the exact middle of the broad avenue, and the warehouses to either side were long, featureless brick buildings, with only a distant garage door and a few trash cans to break the monotony.

So Big Louie was right. There wasn't much of anywhere to go. For some reason, though, Roger didn't think it was hopeless. For one thing, he was supposed to be Captain Crusader now. And Captain Crusader never gave up!

Besides, Roger knew his movies. And, as long as he thought like a movie, how could he help but win?

The cars would reach them in a matter of seconds, a dry-cleaning van pursued by a dented yellow Chevy. But didn't cars in car chases, when they were about to run into innocent bystanders, swerve out of the way at the last possible second? Of course they did. Roger had seen it happen in movie chase after chase.

The cars headed straight for them.

The vehicles swerved, Roger remembered, unless one of the cars was being driven by the bad guys.

Then they were in trouble. Bad guys, after all, liked to run over people.

He recognized the driver in the dry-cleaning van. It was Professor Peril – one of Doctor Dread's evil henchpeople!

Peril grinned as he bore down on Roger and his fellows. The van's engines growled as its evil driver floored the accelerator.

And Roger realized what they had to do.

'Quick!' he yelled to the others. 'Follow me!'

He sprinted past the rusted elevated tram support, straight for the row of trash cans. He could hear the others running behind him, and, beyond them, much too close, the roar of a dry-cleaning van.

Roger ran past the garbage. He stopped and turned when he reached the never-ending brick wall.

'What's the matter, boyo?' Officer O'Clanrahan asked between gasps for breath. 'You can't stop us here. We'll be sitting ducks!'

'No,' Roger replied tersely. 'If I'm right, there's no better place for us than right here.'

The van bore down on them, barely missing the rusted metal support pole as the tyres squealed into a final, deadly turn. The vehicle was so close that Roger could see Professor Peril laugh silently and economically on the other side of the windscreen. But Peril's look of triumph turned to one of horror as the car swerved out of his control to hit the garbage cans.

'Of course!' Big Louie exclaimed. 'Cars in car chases always hit something – if they can, they hit something made of metal, something that makes a lot of noise. And what makes more noise than a garbage can? Brilliant!'

Roger was just happy that his ploy had worked. He had remembered the propensity for cars to run into things. He had hoped that same propensity was universal enough to be one of the laws of the Cineverse. And it was!

'Curse you, Captain Crusader!' Peril shouted from behind his half-open passenger window. 'I haven't forgotten what you did to Mort the Killer Robot and Diablo the Gorilla with the Mind of a

Man. I will wreak my revenge—' he frowned as he saw the rapidly approaching yellow Chevy, '—eventually,' he concluded as he threw the van into reverse, and, once clear of the garbage cans, careened forward down the street.

The dented Chevy screeched to a halt in front of Roger.

Two fellows in rumpled pastel suits opened doors on either side of the car. The driver had a three-day growth of beard, and the other guy wore an earring.

'Cops.' Three-day-growth flipped open a billfold to reveal a badge. 'You folks OK?'

Roger glanced around at his band. They all appeared to have escaped unscathed.

'Good,' Three-day-growth replied before Roger had a chance to answer. 'Then you won't mind answering a few questions.'

'Yeah,' Earring interjected. 'We saw the way that van went after you. What's your connection to the driver?'

'Our connection?' Roger asked incredulously. 'He tried to run us over! He's our enemy. I mean, he's a bad guy, isn't he?'

'So you say,' Earring replied, unconvinced. 'What do you think, Frank? Should we take them down to the station?'

Oh, no, Roger thought. Down to the station? They had a Cineverse to save! They didn't have time to become involved in the everyday plot of another movie world. Somehow, he had to get his friends out of this particular plot before things got any more complicated. But Roger had learned from experience – and a few close calls on unfriendly movie worlds – that you didn't use your Captain Crusader Decoder Ring to escape unless you knew exactly where you were going. If Roger was going to extricate them from their present difficulty, he would have to use his wits.

Louie jumped in before Roger could say anything. 'You can't pin a thing on us, coppers!' he yelled. 'What's the charge?'

'Louie!' Roger called. Louie replied with a helpless shrug. The sidekick had come from a film noir world, hadn't he? He probably had to talk back to the cops in exactly that way – it sounded like another law of the Cineverse.

'Arf, arf, bark!' Dwight insisted.

'Oh, yeah?' Earring growled. 'Does that dog have a licence?'

'Dog not need licence,' Zabana insisted. 'That Dwight the wonder dog!'

'Really?' Three-day-growth murmured. 'I *thought* that mutt looked familiar.'

But Earring wasn't impressed. He pointed a finger at the jungle prince. 'You – I wouldn't talk. You're violating municipal statute 7017-B – wearing a loincloth within city limits.'

'Hey, boyos!' Officer O'Clanrahan interjected. 'I've spent too many years on the force to put up with this. Begorah! It's harassment, plain and simple. Cops don't do that sort of thing where I come from.'

'Where he comes from?' Earring smirked as he turned to O'Clanrahan. 'Hey, look at this guy! And who are you pretending to be? The police haven't worn that kind of uniform for twenty years. And, buddy, you'd better lose the brogue—'

'Now,' Doc drawled, 'I think we've gone a little bit too far here.' He softly patted the pocket of his double-breasted suit that contained his six-shooter.

Both of the rumpled cops went for their guns.

Roger felt somebody tug on his sleeve. He glanced round to see a very anxious Big Louie.

'Can't you see what's happening?' the sidekick whispered. 'Cops fighting cops, heroes questioning heroes. The friction – everything about this confrontation – it's the Change!'

'The Change?' Roger repeated. He saw that Doc and Officer O'Clanrahan had drawn their guns as well. 'What can we do?'

'There's only one thing we can do,' Louie replied as he scowled grimly at their pastel-suited adversaries. 'It's time for Captain Crusader to say something!'

Huh? Time for Captain Crusader to say something? Did Louie mean—

Doc took a step towards one of the cops. The other cop drew a bead on Officer O'Clanrahan. Roger realized Louie was right. He had to do it. It was up to Captain Crusader now.

Roger cleared his throat.

'Uh,' he began hesitantly. 'The policeman is your friend.'

Everyone turned to stare at Roger. Was it his imagination, or did they all seem a little less tense than they had before?

'Oh, yes,' he added, a bit more quickly. 'Always look both ways before you cross the street.'

Yes! He definitely saw one of the cops relax his grip on his gun.

But the four men still faced each other, each side waiting for the other to make the first move. Trotting out tired old aphorisms, while it seemed to be a step in the right direction, simply wasn't getting the job done. Roger realized he needed something brand new, something that would capture the moment. Something, say, that talked about tense situations.

Thanks in large part to years of training in public relations, he came up with that something almost immediately. And while it wasn't up there with such pithy Captain Crusader classics as 'A Clean Plate is a Happy Plate', he hoped that it would do.

'How about this?' Roger ventured.

Everyone leaned towards Roger, the street silent save for a quiet but persistent patriotic tune on flute and drum.

It was now or never. Roger said it:

'Guns may come and guns may go, but a friend is a friend for ever.'

Both Earring and Three-day-growth reholstered their weapons.

Earring grinned at Roger. 'Well, why didn't you say so in the first place?'

'We're always glad to help Captain Crusader,' Three-day-growth agreed.

Earring laughed. 'Still, that jogging outfit of yours had us fooled for a while. Most of your disguises are a bit fancier.'

Roger might have to do something about his clothes. There were so many facets of Captain Crusader that he hadn't even considered! At least, Roger thought, he could try to keep his answer in character.

'I have to travel incognito,' he replied solemnly. 'These are dangerous times.'

Both cops nodded, as if this was the only sort of answer they would expect. Roger really had convinced them he was the hero's hero, Captain Crusader. Now, if only he believed in that himself.

'But that man who was just here—' Roger added.

'Oh,' Three-day-growth chuckled. 'You mean the Professor.'

So they knew about Peril already? That would make things a little easier. However they had arrived in this place, they now had a purpose. Professor Peril could lead them to Doctor Dread – and the heart of the Change!

'How do we find this Professor?' Roger asked.

'Oh, don't worry about that,' Three-day-growth reassured Roger. 'That guy Peril has a thing about wasting time. He swore he was out to get you, didn't he? Well, with the Professor's efficiency, all you have to do is wait for a minute, and he'll confront you all over again.'

'What that?' Zabana interrupted, cupping his jungle-bred ear the better to hear the approaching noise. 'Sound bigger than car.' He paused, considering the information with his jungle-bred brain. 'Maybe – very big car?'

Round the far corner of the left-hand warehouse came a very large cloud of dust – brown in colour this time, rather than the Cineverse blue. And out of that dust came a very distinctive sound, more of a roaring and clanking combined.

The music, after a final warning blast of horns, disappeared.

'Oh, shit,' Earring shouted over the rapidly increasing clamour. 'We'd better get reinforcements!'

Both of the cops jumped into their battered Chevy and drove away.

'What could make the cops run away?' Louie asked for everybody.

Dwight barked.

'No!' Louie shouted in reply. 'It can't be!'

Roger didn't need to ask Louie to translate the Wonder Dog's remark. He could see the shape of the vehicle now through the dust.

It was more than a very large car.

Actually, it was a tank.

CHAPTER SIX

Menge scurried down yet another of the seemingly endless corridors. Antoinette confidently strode after him. It was amazing how quickly she had got used to walking in these spike heels, not to mention the comforting rustle of her leather skirt and the solid feel of the bullwhip in her hand.

'Almost there!' her little man called over his shoulder. He was puffing from the exertion. Antoinette had found the walk exhilarating, at least in part because these long halls had given her plenty of space to practise her whip technique. After only a few tries, she could snuff a sputtering torch at fifteen paces.

'Here we are!' Menge waved for her to follow him round yet another corner.

They faced another set of giant double doors, fully the equal of those that led into this fortress. And in front of these doors stood a pair of guards in dark uniforms, with automatic weapons at the ready.

'Halt!' the two guards shouted in unison. 'What is your business with Dread?'

'Our business?' Menge bristled at the audacity of his inferiors. 'You have no right to question our business. Make way for Mother Antoinette, Mistress of Evil!'

'Mother Antoinette?' one of the guards leered back.

'We have no orders concerning any mother—' the other guard began to scoff.

But Mother Antoinette had had enough of underlings. She flicked her wrist.

CRACK went her whip.

'Uh—' one of the guards answered with a nervous swallow.

'Er—' the other guard replied with a glance at his gun.

But the guards made no move away from the door. They apparently were still not convinced.

CRACK the whip argued. *CRACK**CRACK**CRACK*
The guards looked at each other.

'Make way for Mother Antoinette!' they chorused as they stepped aside and opened the giant doors.

Menge led the way into the great hall beyond. And it truly was a great hall, as large inside as the central courtyard of your average indoor mall. Unlike the rest of the colourless fortress, this room was decorated, with two rows of floor-to-ceiling wall hangings running the length of the hall, each hanging depicting a different dramatic scene – if 'dramatic' was the proper word to use. The hanging just inside the door showed a man in a black hat shooting another man wearing white. On the next hanging, a swarthy man in a stovepipe hat laughed at the woman he had tied to the railway tracks. Further along the wall, Antoinette's gaze was drawn to a particularly graphic depiction of a giant reptile destroying an entire oriental city. These hangings were not simply dramatic, Mrs G realized, they were dramatically evil, depiction after depiction of vileness triumphant.

And where did these two rows of hangings lead? At the far end of the hall, beyond the last of the great curtains, stood a huge chair, a dark, flat grey in colour, as if it was made out of slate. And sitting in this uncomfortable chair was the man Antoinette recognized from the television screen in the wardrobe room. This was Doctor Dread.

Menge scrambled forward, with Mother Antoinette close by his heels.

The man on the throne looked up from the brightly coloured box he was studying. Even at this distance, Mother Antoinette could read the box's large, red label: 'NUT CRUNCHIES!'

'What?' the enraged voice of Doctor Dread hesitated portentously. 'What is the meaning of this – intrusion?'

'I have brought Mrs Gordon,' Menge replied hurriedly as he continued to move forward, 'or Mother Antoinette,' he amended as he glanced back to her, 'as you ordered.'

'What's that?' Dread barked as he tossed the box behind the throne. He seemed to flinch slightly when he looked back at Antoinette. 'Why – so I did. But why didn't the guards – detain you? Why weren't you – properly introduced?'

Menge and Antoinette stopped a dozen paces before the throne.

'The guards saw fit to let us pass,' Mother Antoinette replied with the slightest of smiles. The whip quivered teasingly in her hand, not unlike a cobra, ready to strike.

'What? What do you mean—' Dread hesitated as his gaze travelled up her whip and across her leather costume, until his eyes locked with her own.

'—Oh,' he finished somewhat more quietly. 'They did?' Dread broke away from her gaze to glance down at his snakeskin shoes.

'Who is the newcomer?' a woman's voice, surprisingly gruff, said from behind the more ordinary, jet-black curtains to the side of the throne.

'Ah, Bertha!' Dread called with surprising enthusiasm. 'Why don't you come out here and – meet the newcomers?'

The heavy black drapes parted, and one of the largest women Antoinette had ever seen stepped into view. Not that she was fat. No, although there was substantial weight beneath the black vinyl jumpsuit she wore, it was firm, solid weight, like layer after layer of muscle. She was tall, too. Dread, even seated upon his raised throne, seemed dwarfed by her presence.

'Big Bertha,' Dread began solicitously. 'I'd like you to meet Mrs Ro—'

'No longer!' Menge interrupted with a shout. 'This is Mother Antoinette! Mistress of Evil!'

'Yes,' Dread added hurriedly, as if he wished to regain some sort of control over the situation, 'the woman who Menge has brought into our midst does indeed call herself – Mother Antoinette. She is also the – mother of Roger Gordon.'

'*The* Roger Gordon?' Bertha asked as she crossed the room towards Antoinette.

'Yes.' It actually embarrassed her a bit to admit this. 'As unworthy as he is, Roger Gordon is—' it was her turn to hesitate, '—my son.'

Bertha smiled in a feral sort of way. 'Oh, I wouldn't be that hard on poor Roger,' she purred. Bertha reached out and grabbed Antoinette's hand, shaking it heartily. 'I always thought of your son as—' she paused to run her tongue over her teeth, '—good breeding stock.'

Mrs G frowned slightly at the look in Big Bertha's eyes. For the first time since she had picked up the whip, Mother Antoinette felt a twinge of pity for her son.

Bertha turned to throw a brightly coloured box at the throne.

'Incidentally, Doctor, you dropped something.'

The snakeskin-suited villain yelped as he grabbed the rectangular projectile. A handful of Nut Crunchies fell out before Doctor Dread could right the box.

'Careful!' Dread warned portentously. 'These boxes do more than contain Captain Crusader Decoder Rings. They also hold—' he hesitated tellingly, '—Captain Crusader's - secrets.'

'Pardon me, oh leader, 'Menge said as he took a step forward. 'These brightly coloured yellow and red cereal boxes contain—' he paused in a manner that would have done Dread credit '—secrets?'

'Are you too—' Dread sneered at his underling, '—blind to see? This is why I am the leader, and you are the lackey! What better place to put them, than boldly in box after box of children's cereal!'

He turned the Nut Crunchies package round in his pale hands. 'Listen to these - messages that I have decoded from the back of the box: "Social studies make good citizens"; "When riding your bike, always use hand signals!" How inane can you get? It *has* to be a code. No one could care about citizenship that much! What is the true - meaning of these phrases? Or could it be something - besides the message? Think on it!' He poked a clawlike forefinger at the side of the box. 'Does anyone really know the true nature of - riboflavin?'

He looked out at that those gathered around him, but none of them ventured a response.

'Exactly!' Dread cried, punching the Nut Crunchies box for emphasis. 'There are so many possibilities, and all right under our noses. If only I could decipher Captain Crusader's true meaning.'

Mother Antoinette considered Dread's dilemma. She herself had changed so much since taking up the whip that she might not be able to understand anything about a breakfast cereal box. 'Perhaps,' she ventured, 'it is something that truly evil people cannot comprehend.'

Dread tossed the box aside to glare down at her. 'I comprehend - everything. Do not underestimate Doctor Dread! I demand respect!'

'Really?' Mother Antoinette smiled at that. 'I could teach you a thing or two - about respect.'

She flicked her wrist.

CRACK

Dread flinched as the whip snapped inches from his overly aristocratic nose.

'That's it!' Big Bertha encouraged. 'Make them suffer!'

But Doctor Dread was not suffering. Instead, he stared at Mrs G with an even more single-minded intensity.

'Mother Antoinette,' the arch-fiend began, hesitating more

than she had ever heard him pause before. 'I must say – I find you – interesting. Perhaps – at last – after years of search – I have found – a woman – after my – own heart.'

'No!' Menge cried, running between Mrs G and the throne.

Dread turned his fiendish gaze to his underling.

'*No?*' he repeated in a voice that dripped with displeasure.

'I mean,' Menge hastily amended, 'she can be of so much use to us out in the Cineverse. There is no time for romance once the Change has begun.'

But Menge's explanation only seemed to infuriate the villainous leader. 'The Change? Who are you to tell me—'

This had gone far enough.

CRACK

Mother Antoinette interrupted them with her whip.

*CRACK**CRACK**CRACK* The whip danced between Menge and Dread, snapping with the warning regularity of a Barry Manilow dance number. Both men backed away from the dancing leather.

'Can't we talk about this?' Menge pleaded as he half turned to her. 'Who got you that whip in the first place?'

CRACK

In a way, Mrs G was sorry she had to answer Mengy in this way, but there would be no better time to show her authority than right now. Her whip hand went wild.

*CRACK**CRACK* Menge threw his arms up to protect his face. *CRACK**CRACK**CRACK* Dread cringed in his throne.

'Yes, yes, yes!' Big Bertha began to laugh as she slapped a black vinyl-coated knee. 'Reduce these men to quivering rabbits!'

Somehow, Bertha's overheated enthusiasm caused Mother Antoinette's whip hand to hesitate. Dread grabbed the business end of the whip with his bare hand. 'Bunnies?' he screamed, his fear turned to rage. 'Never mention – bunnies!'

Mrs G tugged on the whip, but Dread still tightly held the other end. It was Mother Antoinette's turn to stare at the snake-suited man upon the throne. Perhaps this Dread had some backbone after all.

The Doctor smiled slightly, and released his end of the whip, breaking the tension between them.

'So, Mother Antoinette,' he said, his voice as smooth as a used car dealer's. 'You present some – interesting possibilities. I must – consider my options.'

He pointed at the large woman by his side as he descended from the throne. 'Bertha, I need your counsel. If you will follow me?' He paused before the black curtain. 'And Mother Antoinette, I shall see you – and your whip – again.'

'It was a pleasure meeting you, Mother Antoinette,' Bertha agreed. 'Someday, I plan to get to know your son—' she stopped for a moment to allow her ham-sized hands to run up and down her black-vinyl jumpsuit, '—on a very close and personal level.'

The large woman turned smartly and marched away, following Doctor Dread to whatever lay behind the curtain.

Mrs G stared for a long moment at the spot where Bertha disappeared, a troubled feeling stirring deep in the pit of her stomach – so troubled that, for a moment, she almost forgot her whip.

'Mother Antoinette,' Menge whined by her side. 'I must talk to you!'

'Yes, yes, Mengy. There's much we have to work on.' She paused, staring thoughtfully at her man's bald pate. It would do her no harm to reveal some of her concerns to this underling – especially now that she knew he could become *her* underling. 'But there is something I am curious about. What happens to the men Bertha chooses?'

'Oh, that,' Menge replied distastefully, not quite suppressing a shudder. 'You don't want to see them the next morning. They seem to age twenty or thirty years overnight.'

'The next morning? I see.' The answer did not seem encouraging. 'And if they stay with her a second night?' Antoinette asked.

'Well, there's always the incinerator – the fortress here has a big one in the basement—' Menge shuddered outright this time, '—not that there's much left to burn.'

Not much left to burn? Part of Antoinette told her it was only what her son deserved – that would teach him never, ever to call. But there was another voice deep within her, barely decipherable, infinitesimally small, but a recognizable voice nonetheless, a voice unfazed by the Zeta Ray, that wanted actually to save her son.

Mother Antoinette found it all rather bothersome. She caressed the handle of her whip in an attempt to soothe her jangled nerves.

'It will be all right?' Menge spoke by her elbow. 'There is so much uncertainty, with the Change rushing towards us and all—'

Mother Antoinette snapped her whip reassuringly, cutting off her man's doubtful words. The Change, hmm? That was all

Menge and Dread seemed to talk about, although she didn't think either one of them had really explained what they meant by that phrase. Not that it mattered much. With her new clothes and abilities, Mother Antoinette decided that she welcomed change.

She squeezed the shoulder of the man still quivering slightly by her side. She smiled to herself. As far as she was concerned, the changes had only just begun.

CHAPTER SEVEN

'No,' Delores replied.

She could see the room beyond the open door, a room filled with dark and glistening machinery.

'No?' Edward asked, mildly surprised, she supposed, that anyone would contradict a slime monster.

Delores couldn't take her eyes from the room's interior.

The machinery was everywhere, covering walls and ceiling and all but a narrow walkway on the floor. The walkway led to two chairs, side by side, bathed by a harsh white light, almost too bright to stare at directly, and all the more startling for the sharp contrast to the dark but highly reflective metal all around. Tiny red lights flashed here and there, beckoning her inside. The lights were coldly beautiful against the oiled black steel, reminding her of nothing so much as sunlight glittering on a spider's web.

She realized that this room couldn't be any more of a trap if it were that spider's web – not really a room so much as a huge, mechanical entity, alive with tiny lights and a dozen different soft growls of motors at the ready. It waited for her, and, when she stepped inside, she would be consumed, fuel for the great engine.

'No,' she reiterated, looking away from the frigidly fascinating metal. 'I am not going to follow you into something called a "Transmogrifier".'

'Fine,' the slime monster replied as he shambled back from the door. 'Then you go first.'

Delores frowned. The monster was not getting the idea. But she had had enough. She had spent too many years in Hero School to play damsel in distress for very long, even to a slime monster. She should have declared her independence from Edward a long time ago. True, she had felt sorry for him, but that wasn't the sort of thing you could build a relationship on – even a monster/victim relationship. Delores' course was clear to her now. She had to declare her independence. There was no going back.

'No, Edward,' she said, slowly and firmly. 'There's nothing to keep me here. You can no longer sway me by threatening my friends. We've left my friends far behind. And your intentions, while sincere in their slime-covered way, are inappropriate, to say the least – especially now, when the very existence of the Cineverse is at stake!'

Edward roared, a sound that somehow combined the gurgle of a drain with the blare of an elephant. Delores decided she really didn't like the sound of that roar.

'Why must I be so misunder—' Edward interrupted himself. 'Oh, I know. It's a law of the Cineverse – me being a monster and all. But it certainly can get frustrating.'

It was the slime monster's turn to stare inside the great machine for a long, silent moment. The room hummed softly in anticipation.

'Perhaps,' Edward continued, his voice flat, virtually without emotion, 'some of my actions seem inappropriate, but you – of all people – must understand. I thought, with you, I might be happy. And how many chances for happiness does a slime monster have?'

The creature got a far-away look in what could have been his crimson-glowing eyes. 'Perhaps, with you, even my art could take a happier turn.' Something like a sigh escaped from something like a mouth. 'Instead of adding sand to my slime, I might add flowers.'

Delores shook her head. Here she was, starting to feel sorry for this muck-thing again. Actually, she was all for Edward's happiness, as long as that happiness didn't include her and a room full of highly experimental scientific gizmos. She decided she'd better get out of here now, before she ended up in that room with that machine.

But how could she get away from a creature who was so handy with slime? She could probably only run a few steps before the monster reacted. She needed a place to hide. But where? Perhaps the door across the way might hold the answer; the door marked 'EXPERIMENTAL ANIMAL LAB'.

Delores still had to reckon with the speed of slime. She realized, to reach even a door as close as this, she would have to distract Edward first.

'Edward,' she said as levelly as she could manage. 'Let's be reasonable about this. Transmogrification? It sounds awfully dangerous.'

'There's no turning back now,' the monster insisted. 'It is our only chance for happiness.'

'But Edward!' It was very difficult to stamp your foot authoritatively when you were wearing the kind of fashion heels she had changed into on the film noir world. Still, Delores did her best. 'I don't want that chance!'

But Edward was as firm as his body chemistry allowed. 'I am sorry, but you have no choice. In this matter, I do have to be a monster. After transmogrification, we will both be different, and so much more compatible. Our very atoms shall intermingle, and we will share in a way most couples can only dream about. And after that? No longer will we have to limit ourselves to the reality of a single movie world. Once both of us are infused with the power of slime, the Cineverse will be ours! We will be able to explore whole new vistas – worlds beyond worlds beyond worlds – together.' He waved what might have been a hand towards the entryway. 'Come, Delores. Where is your sense of adventure?'

Delores took a deep breath. Their very atoms would intermingle? Infused with the power of slime? Her mind galloped past the fear. She had to make her move. This might be her only chance.

'Well,' she said hesitantly. 'I don't know. You never do know with highly experimental scientific equipment.' She frowned at the entryway to the softly humming machine. 'Sometimes – it can go wrong.'

'You're right,' Edward replied, his voice for the first time seeming to hold a seed of doubt. He, too, stared into the gadget-cluttered room. 'Sometimes, with highly experimental scientific equipment, it almost seems it—' something caught in what might have been the monster's voice, '—it *has* to go wrong.'

'Could it be a Law of the Cineverse?' Delores asked innocently.

'Let us hope not,' Edward answered, but he offered no other explanation. The humming sound appeared to grow louder from the room beyond, as if the machine was impatient with their hesitation.

This was it, then. She looked straight into those two tiny red glowing things that could have been Edward's eyes. 'Perhaps – if you went in there first.'

'I suppose,' Edward replied grimly, 'it is my duty.'

He took a step inside the room. Now, the humming really did increase, both in pitch and volume. Edward took another step, and the hum again replied by shifting higher in tone.

It had to be now, while what might have been his back was turned.

'Sorry, Edward!' Delores called softly as she bolted across the hall for the opposite door. Edward mumbled something behind her, lost in the ever-increasing hum.

She only had to run a few steps, but she imagined Edward's mushy hand on her shoulder with every move she made. She reached the entryway to the EXPERIMENTAL ANIMAL LAB. The slime monster hadn't missed her yet. Fortunately for her, the door was unlocked. She ran into the lab and slammed the door behind her.

Even with the door closed, she could hear the anguished roar of the slime monster. Edward had discovered she was gone.

And the slime monster's roar was answered from within the lab, from every animal in every cage, a great caterwauling cacophony that mixed barks and bleats, crows and coos, roars and rabbit cries. She had never heard so intense a sound. If Edward had any doubt where Delores had disappeared, he surely knew now.

She forced herself to calm down and examine the room she now found herself in. It was very bright, lit by brilliant Southern California sunshine pouring in through the floor-to-ceiling windows. She wondered if it ever rained on this advanced scientific world. She pushed the inappropriate thought from her head, and concentrated on the large room, with row after row of shining steel cages surrounded by tables, chairs, desks, walls, all antiseptic white. She had to find somewhere to hide – but where, in this ordered, bright existence?

She walked down the nearest corridor between the cage rows, ready to look away if she saw a rabbit or chimpanzee plugged full of tubes in the name of science. Actually, however, the animal occupants of most of the cages, rabbits and white rats mostly, but also the occasional chicken and chimpanzee, seemed relatively well-fed and unmolested.

Delores should have remembered this from Hero School. The most they ever did in terms of 'experimentation' on most movie worlds, especially bright, Southern California movie worlds, was to have chimps learn sign language and rats run mazes. Well, actually, this being an Institute of Very Advanced Science, she imagined the animals occasionally got injected with an invisibility formula or transported to the fourth dimension – but nothing that would actually hurt the creatures. They didn't do the really dangerous experiments on animals on this kind of movie world. From what she recalled from her courses in movie history, they were much more likely to perform those kind of experiments on humans.

The largest of all the cages, perhaps eight feet high and ten feet long, was empty. Delores frowned down at a neatly lettered sign.

'ORANGUTANG,' it read. 'OOGIE.' Perhaps, she thought, the missing animal was somewhere practising sign language at this very minute.

She heard the door to the lab open as she reached the far end of the row. She flattened herself against the side of the farthest cage.

'Delores?' Edward's unmistakable voice called. 'Come, my bride to be. It does no good to postpone the inevitable.'

There were no doors or windows in the far wall of the room; no exit whatsoever at this end of the lab. Edward would surely spot her if she tried to cross the lab to the door. She might be able to open one of those floor-to-ceiling windows a dozen feet to her right, if she could reach them without Edward seeing her. And even then, the windows looked out over tree tops. How high above ground level would this lab be? The picturesque wooden frames would surely make a noise when opened, and what if there was then no way to get down from this upper storey of the Institute?

Delores had nowhere to go. This place was an antiseptic trap.

Perhaps, if she couldn't find a hiding place, she could come up with a diversion. She glanced quickly around this end of the lab. There wasn't much here except for a moderate-sized panel, maybe three feet by four, built into the far wall; a gleaming metal collection of switches, buttons and dials accompanied by a neatly lettered sign: 'CONTROL CENTRE.'

Did this movie-poster-sized metal board control all of the experiments in the animal lab? She stepped closer so that she could more carefully read the smaller, though no less neatly hand-lettered, signs that were posted above each of the controls. One sign in particular caught her attention – the one above the large, red lever – the one marked: 'UNIVERSAL CAGE RELEASE'.

Maybe, Delores thought, this would provide the very diversion she needed.

But where was Edward? Someone whose feet were composed of slime didn't make a great deal of noise.

'There is no escape,' intoned Edward's voice, much closer than before. 'Time to transmogrify.'

The slime monster was almost on top of her! Delores had to do something fast!

She pulled the red lever.

There was another great noise, fully the equal of the animals' earlier roar, although this time it was the sound of metal against metal, as locks popped open, hinges groaned and bars screeched aside.

All sorts of creatures erupted from their cages. Twenty-foot-long snakes slithered past foot-long cockroaches. Barking dogs chased yowling cats. The chimps cavorted around the rabbits, rats and chickens. There were lizards and frogs in here, too, hopping and scurrying every which way. Delores also thought she heard the squealing of pigs, the baaing of sheep and the mooing of cows from the far side of the lab.

This was an even better diversion than Delores had originally imagined. She turned towards the window.

There was a slime monster standing in her path.

'There is no getting away,' Edward murmured. 'It is destiny.'

Not now, when she was so close. Not now, when there were all these animals. Delores tried to pivot away, and almost fell. She couldn't move! Well, actually, she could move as much as she wanted, more than she wanted, actually, although that movement largely consisted of slipping and sliding. She looked down. It was no wonder she couldn't get any traction. The floor around her feet was coated with a good three inches of slime.

'Sorry about your shoes,' Edward apologized. 'But look on the bright side. After transmogrification, you probably will never need shoes again.'

He reached over and grabbed her with an exceedingly long arm. He lifted her out of the muck and carried her, without effort, out of the lab and across the hall to the waiting machine.

The machine hummed in greeting.

Edward stepped inside, Delores still in tow. The red lights blinked rhythmically. The machine's hum surrounded them, high, loud and happy – a hum of welcome, and perhaps a hum of triumph.

She was to be transmogrified.

Delores tried to fight her captivity, to free herself somehow from the monster's grip. But Edward's hold on her was strong and sure, and every time she tried to get her own grip on some part of the monster's anatomy, her hands sank into the muck.

'Resistance is useless,' Edward remarked casually. 'As long as there's water around, we monsters can make ourselves slimy or solid at will.' He plunked Delores down in the chair on the left. 'It's very handy around the house,' he added as he strapped her arms tight against her body, then tied the leather thong behind Delores' back.

'Poor Delores,' Edward said as he shambled towards the opposite seat. 'You have to change with the times.' He sat, and pushed a large green button labelled 'START' on the middle of the console before him. 'After this, we shall truly be made for each other.'

The humming became even louder and more insistent, the red lights flashing even more rapidly than before, as if the machine was getting really excited. Words flashed across a television screen directly before Delores.

'TRANSMOGRIFICATION SEQUENCE COMMENCING.'

Those words were wiped away by a new sentence:

'STRAP SUBJECT IN SEAT A.'

Edward nodded pleasantly. 'Subject. That's you.'

'STRAP YOURSELF IN SEAT B,' appeared on the television screen.

'Of course.' The slime monster found two halves of a seat belt to either side of his seat and buckled himself in. 'And now?'

'PRESS ANY KEY WHEN READY' the machine informed them.

Edward punched something at random.

'IF YOU WANT TO TRANSMOGRIFY,' the machine replied, 'PRESS "Y".'

The slime monster did as he was instructed.

'ARE YOU SURE?'

Edward pressed 'yes' a second time.

Delores heard another noise above the hum, a buzzing of some sort.

What might have been Edward's mouth seemed to frown.

'Is there a fly in here?'

'TRANSMOGRIFICATION CYCLE COMMENCED,' was the machine's message.

'We can't have a fly in here!' Edward yelled in real panic. 'Its atoms could intermingle with ours, causing who knows what damage!'

'IF FOR ANY REASON,' the machine's television screen began.

There was something else in here besides the fly. Something that was hopping.

'Toads?' Edward shouted. 'How did toads—'

But there were more than toads hopping. Edward stared at the white, fluffy, bouncing things with what might have been a look of horror.

'Bunnies?' he asked, his voice barely a whisper.

'YOU WISH TO TERMINATE CYCLE,' the machine continued calmly.

Something barked.

'Dogs?' Edward's voice rose again towards hysteria.

Something else clucked.

'Chickens?' With that single word, the monster's voice reached that hysteria, and perhaps a bit more.

Delores realized that Edward had left the door open, and the animals, freed of their cages, had found them.

'PRESS ESCAPE BEFORE CHIME' the television screen finished helpfully.

Edward nodded all too rapidly to Delores. 'You were right.'

Hop, went the toads. Hop, hop hop.

'I was a fool,' the monster admitted.

Bzzz, went the flying insects. Bzzz, bzzz, bzzz.

'Neither man nor monster was meant to tamper with forces like this!'

Bounce, went the bunnies. Bounce bounce bounce.

'But all is not lost,' Edward continued.

Bark, went the dogs. Bark, bark bark.

The room was filled with a dozen other animal noises, from cries to coos, baahs to bleats.

The slime monster turned back to study the console. 'All I have to do is turn it off before the warning chime.'

The humming and all other noise in the room ceased, and the sudden silence was filled with a clear, bell-like tone.

The warning chime had come and gone.

Cluck, went the chickens. Cluck, cluck, cluck.

The hum returned, so loud and high now it was almost a shriek, as both Delores and Edward – and all the animals around them – were bathed in pure, white light.

Edward screamed, a sound that now seemed more animal than slime. Delores closed her eyes. The whole room was vibrating, and more – she was vibrating. She was being transmogrified – infused with bits and pieces of all the things that occupied this room. What if the wrong bits ended up in the wrong places? It felt like somebody was scrambling her for an omelette.

Edward screamed again. The other creatures in here weren't

being silent either, although their cries were unlike anything Delores had ever heard.

The humming cut off abruptly. The blinding light disappeared.

But something in Delores had changed – if she could still be called Delores.

Would she ever see Roger again?

And then it got really dark. She couldn't see anything.

Maybe, Delores thought, she no longer had anything to see with.

CHAPTER EIGHT

Everyone stared at the tank.

The thing roared more like an enraged beast than a machine, underscored by the percussive clank of the heavy metal treads tearing up the asphalt. The ground quaked as the armoured engine of death approached. The air was full of dust, and the tang of machine oil.

The tank was heading straight for them, slowly, relentlessly. But no one moved. The rest of Roger's companions appeared frozen in fear.

In a way, Roger couldn't blame the others. The tank seemed all wrong for this time and place, as if the cop movie world had suddenly veered into a desert war film. But then, Roger supposed, that was the Change.

The tank's gun turret swivelled and jerked, shooting out a projectile, followed by a lance of flame. They were being fired on! Roger took a step away.

No one else moved.

The shell sailed over their heads. It hadn't been aimed at them after all. Professor Peril was aiming for dramatic effect – and a thick steel pole that supported the rusted tracks overhead.

The shell hit the base of the pole, exploding in a great cloud of dust.

Still, no one moved, their faces beaten by the squalling dirt. Perhaps, Roger realized, they *couldn't* move – there was something so wrong about the tank being here that it prevented them from moving, as if the Change was so profound that it locked their mental gears in place. Only Roger, with his non-Cineverse mind, was free of the paradox's grip.

If this was the sort of thing the Change brought, it was far worse than Roger had imagined.

Still the tank ground forward. The exploding dust cleared,

and the steel pole and the rusted tracks above were no longer there.

Roger looked back at his fellows, all unnaturally immobile, five statues staring at their imminent destruction.

The tank stopped, its roaring engine shifting to a whispering idle, causing Roger to turn and stare with all the others.

The hatch popped open on the top of the tank turret. A steel-helmeted Professor Peril smiled malevolently.

'Not enough, heh?' He pointed one precise finger at the crowd standing before him. 'Very well. I'm going to economically run over all of you!'

Peril's brief, to-the-point diabolical laughter was lost in the roar as the tank ground forward once more.

'Guys!' Roger called. 'It's time to get out of here!'

There was still no response.

No, wait. Roger saw Big Louie twitch, his face screwed up in pain, as if any movement at all on his part required a supreme effort of will.

'Roger!' the sidekick's sidekick managed between clenched teeth. 'You gotta say something!'

Roger frowned. Hadn't he already said something, any number of things, really, to his totally unresponsive audience? Even Big Louie had once again become as still as the others, although Roger thought there might be a new, pleading look in the sidekick's eyes.

Wait a moment. Unresponsive audience? Like a *movie theatre audience*?

Roger had to remember he had a new role in the Cineverse. He had spoken, yes, but only as Roger Gordon, average guy. From here on in, whenever he faced danger, whether from suspicious officers of the law or a marauding metal engine of destruction, he had to speak as Captain Crusader.

It wasn't all that easy to think of aphorisms when there was a tank bearing down on you. But Roger – or rather, Captain Crusader – had to do his best.

'Running is good for you!' he shouted over the grinding roar.

Did any of his friends move? It was hard to tell, but Roger thought he detected a twitch here, a spasm there. His theory, then, was correct, but Roger was going to have to be a bit more creative. Perhaps if he could find something with a touch more eloquence.

It was even harder to be eloquent when you had a tank bearing down on you. Roger shouted the first thing that came into his mind:

'He who hesitates is squashed!'

Even as the words left his mouth, Roger realized that they were far too derivative – so derivative, in fact, that Roger seemed to have made the situation worse. Whatever freedom, along with all twitches and spasms, his first comment had given his fellows had vanished, and all were frozen stiff before the tank's inexorable – and ever closer – approach.

This was it, then: Roger's last chance. Whatever discipline he had learned in public relations, he needed it now. There was a certain rhythm to a classic Captain Crusader caption, a rhythm Roger had to reproduce, while at the same time describing some essential truth that would not seem out of place in a seventh-grade social studies class.

The words flashed into his mind in a complete sentence, almost as if he was reading from a script. And this time, the words sounded right.

He spoke in a loud, clear voice:

'Jogging is the cardiovascularly correct way to see the world.'

All of Roger's friends shook themselves, as if waking from a long sleep. And all of them ran out of the path of the rampaging tank as it rumbled past.

'Saints alive, Captain Crusader,' Officer O'Clanrahan cheered. 'I knew you wouldn't let us down!'

'A complete thought is a happy thought,' Roger agreed, the words tumbling from his tongue without conscious effort. The aphorism came so quickly, in fact, it was a little frightening. Becoming Captain Crusader was more than a great responsibility, Roger realized – a life as the hero's hero might mean some fundamental changes in how he viewed the world, and even in his own image of self.

Roger's thoughts were interrupted by a warning blast of horns and tympany. Dwight started to bark.

'Oh, no!' Big Louie warned. 'Peril's turned the tank round. He's coming for us again!'

Roger turned round to see the truth in Louie's summary – the tank rumbling towards them once more. Professor Peril shook his fist at them from the open turret.

This time, at least, no one was frozen. Not that there was any direction to their movement. In fact, Roger's followers seemed to be running in all directions at once. But at least they were running. Despite whatever discrepancy threatened the fabric of the Cineverse, Roger's – or rather, Captain Crusader's – corrective aphorism seemed to have shifted the balance on this particular movie world so that all his company could act.

Wow. *Whatever discrepancy threatened the fabric of the Cineverse?* Roger realized he was even beginning to think like Captain Crusader.

Somehow, though, Captain Crusader had to stop this tank. The music, suddenly back in full force, was building to a fever pitch. Roger still didn't know where that orchestra originated, but he knew what that music meant, with its blaring horns and beating drums. They were coming to the Big Action Scene.

'Bark, bark, yip arf!' the wonder dog remarked.

'Dwight suggests that we come up with some counter-strategy,' Big Louie translated.

'I think one well-placed shot with a six-shooter should fix Peril once and for all,' Doc drawled. He glanced at Roger. 'Six-shooters will work in these here parts, won't they?'

Roger reassured Doc, that, as long as other guns – not to mention tanks – worked on this particular movie world, six-shooters should fit perfectly with the local version of movie magic.

'Spoken like Captain Crusader!' Louie shouted encouragingly.

'Tarnation!' Doc cursed, easing his palm from the gun hammer. 'I can't get a clear shot.'

Roger saw Doc's problem. The tank was once again surrounded by an opaque cloud of dust.

'Cloud of dust not stop Zabana!' The well-muscled prince of the jungle stepped forward. 'Zabana use his jungle-bred reflexes and jump on tank like he jump on fear-maddened elephant!'

He flexed his well-muscled forehead.

'First Zabana judge how fast elephant is coming.'

Zabana hunkered down into his famous jungle crouch.

'Then jungle prince set himself to spring.' He smiled with the confidence of one who was truly ruler of the jungle.

'Now Zabana use language of animals to distract fear-maddened—' Zabana hesitated, the smile vanished from his face. 'How you call fear-maddened tank?'

The dust around the tank cleared enough for Roger to see the gun barrel swivel towards them.

'I have a better idea,' he interjected. 'Let's get out of here!'

This time, the others agreed, and followed Roger in a full-scale retreat.

'Beggin' your pardon,' Officer O'Clanrahan remarked as he

puffed by Roger's side. 'Retreating may be advisable, but is it truly a Captain Crusader thing to do?'

Oh, dear. Roger hadn't thought of that. If his actions were inappropriate, would it affect his standing as the hero's hero?

But what other action could he take? Roger knew now that Captain Crusader sayings worked on people in the Cineverse. But would they work on machines?

If he could stop the tank in its tracks – what a heroic action that would be! And if they captured Professor Peril, perhaps they could even learn the whereabouts of Doctor Dread so that they could bring this Change under control. Even if Peril wouldn't speak, perhaps Dwight could pick up Dread's scent from the other man and lead them to the arch-fiend's hideout, in the same way the wonder dog had helped Delores find Captain Crusader.

Delores. The name of the woman of his dreams caused his heart to skip a beat. But how could he find Delores while he was battling the Change with his every breath? No, Roger knew, he had to halt the Change first if he and Delores were going to have any chance at happiness.

And that meant stopping the onrushing tank – somehow.

Roger stopped as the others ran on.

He turned to face his adversary. Uncounted tons of metal malice bore down upon him.

Roger realized he had another problem, not all that different from Zabana's recent dilemma. What did you say – what did even Captain Crusader say – to a tank? Or perhaps you didn't speak to the tank, but to the person inside. In that case – what did you say to Professor Peril?

There was only one way to find out.

'A tank a day keeps your problems away,' Roger shouted over the armoured machine's never-ending roar.

The tank kept on coming. And no wonder, Roger thought. What a lacklustre first effort! That aphorism had had none of the rhythm, none of the élan, of the proper Captain Crusader quote.

He'd have to try harder, or he'd be run over in a matter of seconds. He drew on whatever inner resources he still possessed, combined with his ever-growing appreciation of tank treads. Yes! He thought he had it this time.

Roger screamed with every ounce of energy in his soul:

'A modern combat vehicle means never having to say you're sorry.'

All his company stopped their flight to turn and applaud. Roger sighed happily. That had been a good one.

But the tank kept on coming.

Maybe, Roger considered, when you were driving a tank, you couldn't hear any Captain Crusader sayings.

He turned and ran with redoubled speed. His companions joined him.

'Bark, bark! Yip, yip!'

'Dwight smells the harbour,' Big Louie helpfully translated.

The harbour? What was the wonder dog trying to tell them? Now that Dwight mentioned it, Roger did smell a salt tang mixed with the odour of burning machine oil. But what did this mean?

Roger had a cold chill of recognition as he remembered his movies.

There was an even better way to end a car chase than smashing into trash cans.

They had reached the end of one of the extremely long warehouses. With barely a second's hesitation, Roger turned right and headed downhill.

'Yip, yip!' the wonder dog called from behind. 'Bark, bark!'

'Wait a minute!' Big Louie interjected. 'Dwight says that way only leads to the docks!'

'Exactly!' Roger shouted triumphantly. 'Follow me, everybody!'

Roger and the others rushed down the sloping street with the tank in close pursuit. It was only two short blocks to an old fisherman's pier.

Roger waited until they were scant feet away from the weathered wood.

'OK, everybody!' he yelled as he veered to his right. 'Away from the dock! Scatter!'

Everyone on foot turned quickly.

The tank was not so agile. It ploughed straight ahead, out on to the aged wooden pilings – pilings that, even when new, were not meant to take the weight of a death-dealing mass of sinister steel.

There was a great roar and a rending of wood as the tank slid into the water, taking half the dock with it.

'Curse you, Captain Crusader!' Professor Peril shook his fist at them from his station at the falling tank turret.

The tank hit the water and sank quickly.

'Bark arf!' Dwight announced. 'Yip bark!'

'Dwight says we can't let Peril drown,' Louie interpreted. 'That's not the hero's way!'

It was worse than that, Roger realized. If they lost Professor Peril, they lost their link to Doctor Dread, and the heart of the Change. Without that link, they might never be able to save the Cineverse – and Roger might never see Delores again!

It was time for more than words. It was time for action. And Roger should have no trouble with a straightforward hero-rescue situation like this. Now that the tank was quiet, his Captain Crusader sayings could get him out of any danger – couldn't they?

Roger and Dwight the wonder dog simultaneously dived into the drink.

The water was so cold that it took Roger's breath away. And the water was moving, too. The tank was sinking so fast that it had formed a whirlpool at the surface, sucking everything else down behind it – everything, including Roger and Dwight.

The vortex closed overhead, and they were underwater, going down fast.

Roger realized then that he had neglected one eventuality. You couldn't spout clever sayings – you couldn't say anything – if your mouth was full of water.

Apparently, even Captain Crusader could drown.

CHAPTER NINE

'Roger?' Big Louie called down into the still water at the end of the dock. All was quiet – far too quiet.

A moment before, Roger had used his knowledge of movie worlds, combined with his newfound leadership as Captain Crusader, to lure Professor Peril and his tank into the murky waters at the end of the pier. But Louie realized now that Roger, as the hero's hero, could not let even someone as nefarious as Peril drown. Roger had immediately jumped in the water as well, followed quickly by the almost-as-heroic Dwight the wonder dog. Both of them went down beneath the churning waves. But neither they, nor Professor Peril, had surfaced again.

'Mother of Mercy!' For a change, Officer O'Clanrahan said what Louie was thinking. 'They're gone? Dwight the wonder dog is gone?'

'No!' Louie objected. 'Wait a minute!' O'Clanrahan was suggesting that Dwight and Roger and Peril were all beyond hope, sucked away by treacherous currents and drowned beneath the incoming tide. Louie couldn't accept it; this sort of thing went against everything a sidekick stood for. Maybe Roger Gordon could fall victim to such a fate, but not the hero's hero – not Captain Crusader!

'Roger!' Louie called, but the only answer was the soft lap of the waves against the pilings beneath the dock.

Perhaps it was only his sidekick nature, but Louie still wasn't ready to give up. Maybe he was doing something wrong – like, Louie realized, calling the wrong individual.

Maybe, just maybe, he had to address the hero's hero by name.

'Captain Crusader?' Louie yelled.

But the only answer was the gentle shushing of the sea wind and the distant sound of a lone, clanging buoy.

'We might as well face it, boyos,' Officer O'Clanrahan ventured with a sigh. 'They're gone to the briny deep.' He turned and took a step towards shore.

'Tarnation!' Doc yelled, pointing to a spot not three feet from O'Clanrahan's boots. 'Look what's washed up against the dock!'

Louie knelt down to get a better look. There, pushed against the pilings by the never-ending waves, were a book, *The Cineverse From A to Zed*, and a small, round, grey, incredibly cheaply made piece of plastic.

Louie pulled both from the water. 'It's Roger's guidebook – and his Captain Crusader Decoder Ring!'

Zabana frowned down at the objects in Louie's hands. 'What this mean?'

Louie could take no joy in his discoveries. There could be no denying it now. It was one of the true signs of the Cineverse – once you found someone's Decoder Ring, it meant, well—

'It means Roger is gone,' Louie replied softly.

'Roger gone?' Zabana demanded. 'That impossible!'

'It is durned peculiar,' Doc agreed. 'He jumps in the drink and disappears, just like that? I never seen its like in all my years as a merchant seaman.'

'Zabana not accept this!' the jungle prince announced. 'We find out what really happen. Zabana call fish!' Zabana paused a moment in thought. 'Ah! Jungle prince remember!' He cupped his hands to his mouth and shouted down to the water. 'Gurgle gurgle greech caroo!'

He stared at the murky waves expectantly, but the only answer was the distant cry of a pair of gulls, and the roar of an automobile as it raced on to the dock.

The beat-up, yellow Chevy screeched to a halt a few feet away as Zabana looked up in consternation. The cops got out, slamming the doors behind them.

'No fish?' Zabana bemoaned to no one in particular.

'You don't expect any fish in *this* harbour, do you?' Three-day-growth asked sarcastically.

'Unless there was one in a trash bag—' Earring ventured.

'Yeah, or maybe stuck with a syringe,' Three-day-growth concluded. He pointed to Big Louie. 'So what happened here?'

Louie summarized the recent events in his best sidekick manner.

Three-day-growth grunted when he was through. 'It's the treacherous tides around here – especially around the full moon.'

'Yeah,' Earring added as he nodded towards the horizon, 'and the wicked undertow from the ocean out there—'

'Not to mention all those crosscurrents caused by the irresponsible use of pleasure vehicles,' Three-day-growth finished. 'Well, Peril's case is closed. It looks like our job is finished here.'

'Finished?' Zabana demanded. 'How can be finished when Captain Crusader under water?'

'Sorry.' Earring shrugged. 'No longer our jurisdiction.'

Louie felt a cold chill at the nape of his short but sturdy neck – a chill that could freeze his entire form. Not the cops' jurisdiction? This, along with Roger's sudden disappearance, sounded more and more like the Change!

But Zabana was more direct in his displeasure. He took a threatening step in the policemen's direction.

'Faith and begorah!' Officer O'Clanrahan protested. 'The coppers are only doin' their job!'

Only doing their job? Louie thought. O'Clanrahan must have been more shaken by the loss of the wonder dog than even Louie imagined.

'Still haven't lost the brogue, huh?' Earring remarked.

O'Clanrahan took a startled step backwards.

'And still wearing that loincloth, I see,' Earring addressed Zabana in a less than approving tone.

Zabana made a sound deep in his throat that betrayed his jungle origins.

Louie frowned. He could see this confrontation escalating into another real conflict situation, exactly like their first encounter with these two – and this time, there was no Captain Crusader to come up with a pithy saying to diffuse the tension and make things right.

The two cops looked at each other and reached for their guns.

'No!' Big Louie shouted. The two cops stopped and stared. He stepped forward, standing as tall as he was able. Without Captain Crusader here, it was up to him.

'Remember what happened the last time you saw us?' Louie asked quickly. 'We were – all of us – ready to fight without thinking. That is, we were until Captain Crusader stepped forward and stirred us with his deeply meaningful words – words – that brought us back to our senses, and led us to understand and appreciate each other.'

His voice rose as Louie choked back the emotion building inside him. 'Now, though, Captain Crusader has vanished. Perhaps, he is even dead. But the spirit of Captain Crusader cannot die! And it is that spirit we must remember; that spirit that must bring us back to our senses once again!'

The cops looked at each other and put away their guns.

'I'd say our job is just about finished here,' Three-day-growth admitted.

'Yeah,' Earring agreed. 'No reason to bother these nice folks.'

The two cops got back into their battered Chevy, and the car roared off the dock in reverse.

'Tarnation!' Doc exclaimed. 'That was pretty good speech-ifyin'. But do you have the faintest idea what we should do next?'

'Zabana dive in water!' the jungle prince volunteered. 'Search for Roger!'

But Louie placed a restraining hand against one of Zabana's bulging thews. 'No, Zabana. You heard what the cops said. We've already lost Captain Crusader. I don't want to lose you as well. We need all our strength for the fight ahead.'

He turned to Doc. 'Oddly enough, I do have an idea of what we should do. Remember, I used to be a member of Dread's gang. I know all his major hideouts – it's only a matter of time before we stumble on the one he's using now.' He paused to look at his three fellows. 'But when we do, we must be prepared. We must have the proper weapon.'

He held up the soggy copy of *The Cineverse From A to Zed*.

'Book is weapon?' Zabana asked, still apparently confounded by Louie's newfound forcefulness.

'Well, no,' Louie admitted, 'but it can lead us to a weapon.'

Officer O'Clanrahan still seemed unconvinced. 'Faith and begorah! How can any weapon match the might of Dread?'

'I don't intend to use conventional weapons,' Louie replied. 'It's time for psychological warfare. It's time for—' he paused in a manner that would have done Dread proud, '—bunnies.'

'Bunnies!' Zabana exclaimed in sudden comprehension. 'Dread putty in hands of bunnies. But how we get Dread back to bunny world?'

'That would seem to be our biggest problem,' Louie agreed with a nod. Doctor Dread was indeed putty in the bunnies' paws, his entire personality changing amidst the animated rabbits, much the same way noted scientist Dr Dee Dee Davenport had trans-formed into a beach bunny when confronted by endless expanses of sand and three-chord surf guitar. It was something that happened to some people in the Cineverse, when they discovered a world that somehow fitted their personalities all too well.

Still, because of the possibility of this personality shift, Dread was all too wary of animated worlds. There seemed, therefore, as Zabana had pointed out, to be no direct method to get Dread to the bunnies. But Louie knew more than direct methods. On the film noir world that was his home, deviousness was a way of life.

'But there is another way,' he continued. 'If we can't bring Dread to the bunnies, we'll bring the bunnies to Dread!'

'Whoo-eee!' Doc whooped enthusiastically. 'Now *that's* a plan!'

'Now,' Louie remarked as he tucked the Captain Crusader Ring into the pocket of his double-breasted blazer, 'if I can keep the pages of this thing from sticking together, maybe I can locate our first destination. Ah! Here it is, in the index, under "Bunnies, fluffy".' He looked up to the others. 'Well, gather round, fellas. We've got a Cineverse to save!'

The three other men all grabbed a piece of Louie's coat as he pulled out the ring and twisted.

'See you in the funny papers!'

They heard the sound of galloping horses through the blue smoke.

'Cartoon horses, no doubt,' Louie reassured the others. 'Cartoon horses and cartoon bunnies would go very well together.'

Then they heard the sound of grunts and shouts amid the pounding hooves.

'Sound like cartoon horses exercising?' Zabana added somewhat more tentatively.

But the next sound seemed even more out of place – the clash of metal against metal.

'Tarnation!' Doc exclaimed. 'I know that sound from my years as a world-class duellist. That's a swordfight!'

Louie frowned. Whatever it was, it sure didn't sound like bunnies.

'Mother of mercy!' Officer O'Clanrahan announced as the smoke cleared. 'I knew this was going to be a bad idea.'

Louie stared at the suddenly revealed countryside. He didn't know whether it was bad or not, but it was certainly wrong. They had materialized, not in the middle of an animated cartoon but on a dusty plane, complete with large boulders and the occasional scrubby tree. And on this plain were half a dozen men, dressed only in sandals and short, skirt-like loincloths that only covered them from the waist to the upper thigh, six very well-muscled men that fought, three against three, with gleaming broadswords.

The men in sandals had noticed them as well, the three in light loincloths quickly dispatching the three in darker livery with a series of quick but none-too-convincing sword strokes. The three survivors turned menacingly towards Louie and his fellows.

'Intruders!' a woman's voice called from beyond the battle. 'Who now dares confront Hippolita, Oracle of Venus?'

A chariot pulled by a pair of snow-white horses emerged from between a pair of boulders. The musclemen stepped aside to allow the chariot to thunder forward, turning sharply as it stopped.

'All hail Hippolita!' the three musclemen chanted.

A tall woman stepped from the chariot to confront Louie and the others. She was wearing a white robe cut so that it revealed one of her shapely shoulders and most of her shapely legs. Her face was framed by long, blonde hair, and too much eye make-up.

'Well,' she demanded imperiously. 'Why don't you answer me?'

'Uh,' Louie replied, temporarily taken aback. Wasn't there something wrong with the way her lips moved? Still, even if there was, Louie realized he'd better come up with an answer. 'We are but humble travellers, seeking the truth.'

'Sound like spies to me!' one of the musclemen interjected. Yes, Louie noticed, this fellow seemed to be having a similar problem with his mouth muscles, with too many syllables for the movement of his lips. What strange secret did this world hold to afflict its denizens so?

'They should know who they are facing,' the muscleman barked He pointed to his two fellows. 'We are all noble warriors: the Son of Samson, the Nephew of Ulysses, and the Second Cousin of Goliath.'

'Second cousin?' Zabana asked doubtfully.

'On his mother's side, but still a blood relation!' the muscleman growled.

Louie thought it was only polite to introduce his company as well.

'Big Louie?' Hippolita asked. 'Could that mean "Born out of Rock"?'

It really was somewhat disconcerting, the way the movement of her lips never quite matched the sound of her words. But Louie could not become mesmerized by this peculiarity.

'Not that I know of,' he managed to reply. This wasn't going at all the way he had hoped. They should be talking with fluffy bunnies, not barbarians with broadswords. This was the problem with being a sidekick – if he was a hero, he'd probably already have come up with a way to get out of this place and on with their real business.

'What of your fellows?' the oracle continued in the same imperious tone. That was another thing, Louie realized – for an all-seeing sort of person, which was what the Oracle of Venus was, after all, she asked an awful lot of questions, didn't she? Then again, there were these three menacing guys with their swords. Louie continued his introductions.

'Doc?' Hippolita frowned. 'Too short to mean "Born out of rock". Officer O'Clanrahan? It has possibilities.'

The rotund policeman nodded uncertainly, not quite sure if he were being paid a compliment.

'Still,' Hippolita continued doubtfully, 'he doesn't quite seem like the "Born out of rock" type.'

'None of them look worthy of being "Born out of rock"!' the Son of Samson jeered. 'I say we should put them to the sword!'

'Swords?' The prince of the jungle stepped forward. 'Zabana laugh at swords!'

The Nephew of Ulysses shook his head in amazement. 'This fellow could be the one!'

'He has definite "Born out of rock" characteristics,' Goliath's second-cousin-on-his-mother's-side agreed.

'And Zabana,' the Son of Samson mused. 'It sounds right. Surely, it must mean "Born out of rock"!'

'Actually, it mean "Big, hairless orangutang",' Zabana admitted.

'Close enough!' Hippolita declared. 'The prophecy has come true!'

'All hail Hippolita!' the three musclemen chorused as they sheathed their swords.

The prophecy had come true? The swords had gone away? Louie whistled softly to himself. Did this mean they were saved?

'Our champion has come!' the Son of Samson declared.

'The forces of right will triumph!' the Nephew of Ulysses joined in.

'Finally,' the Second-cousin-on-his-mother's-side of Goliath explained, 'someone who will face the Pit of Absurdity!'

The Pit of Absurdity? That didn't sound like being saved to Big Louie. He still had the feeling that this sort of thing wouldn't be happening if they were being led by a fully fledged hero type.

The situation was so bad that even Zabana's jungle-bred brain noticed a certain discrepancy.

'Pit of Absurdity!' the jungle prince exclaimed. 'Wait minute!'

'Oh, that's right,' Hippolita murmured with the slightest of alluring smiles. 'We have to decide what to do with your slaves. Would you like them to accompany you, or shall we kill them now?'

Slaves? Oh dear, Louie thought, this was getting completely out of hand. And it seemed that those three musclemen had drawn their swords again very enthusiastically.

'Uh,' Zabana stared, momentarily taken aback by having to make a choice. 'Friends come with Zabana.'

'Very well.' Hippolita waved to her musclemen. 'Bring them along.'

Louie felt the point of a sword in his back as Hippolita led the way to the boulders. Louie followed, as did both Doc and Officer O'Clanrahan. Zabana sprang forward, his jungle muscles taut.

'When the troops of Romulus and Remus face the Spartans, we must have the Jewel of the Seven Cities to ensure our victory!' Hippolita explained. 'That is why we have been waiting for our champion, to rescue the jewel from the terrors of the pit!'

Louie didn't like this 'terrors of the pit' talk. It sounded a little like that time they had stumbled on to the home planet of the slime monster. Louie shivered despite himself. Now that he thought about it, he hadn't liked much of anything that had happened since they had landed on this particular movie world. There had to be another way – but, of course there was! He simply had to get his fellow adventurers together again, and he could use the ring!

He felt in his jacket pocket. The ring wasn't there.

'Do you have any questions before we take you to the Pit of Absurdity?' Hippolita asked.

Zabana pondered this for a minute, then asked at last: 'Where bunnies?'

The three musclemen exchanged knowing looks.

'Is there any doubt about the prophecy now?' the Nephew of Ulysses asked with a grin.

'He is a match for the Pit of Absurdity!' The Son of Samson nodded knowingly.

'This one is truly "Born out of rock"!' the Second Cousin, and not by marriage, either, of Goliath rejoined.

Where could he have put the ring? A real hero wouldn't have

lost the ring, would he? Now, now, Louie told himself, he had to calm down. They surely had still to travel some distance to this pit. The ring had to be in one of his pockets. He'd find it in plenty of time.

Hippolita led them past the boulders. She pointed at a large hole in the ground in front of her. 'And here, noble hero, is the pit.'

The Pit of Absurdity was only round the next boulder? What kind of low-budget movie world was this? How could he possibly find the ring now?

'Zabana laugh at pit!' the jungle prince declared.

'So we hope,' Hippolita replied.

But the musclemen weren't laughing. Louie felt the swordpoint pushing him to the lip of the precipice.

'Into the pit!' commanded the Oracle of Venus.

Zabana jumped as the three others were pushed. The result was the same.

All four of them were falling into utter darkness.

CHAPTER TEN

It took Roger a moment to realize he was breathing. And a second moment to realize he was no longer surrounded by water, but by blue smoke.

HEY ROGER!

a voice rang out of the blueness,

LONG TIME, NO SEE!

Roger realized, even before the angelic choir kicked in, that he was once again in the presence of the Plotmaster.

SO, WHAT BRINGS YOU ALL THE WAY UP HERE?

the Plotmaster asked jovially.

All the way up here? Roger thought. He didn't even know where he was. The only thing he actually knew about this place was that there were always these darn singing angels going on and on in the background, and Roger could always count on being talked to by an imposing figure in blue, back-lit so you couldn't see him very well. And what *brought* Roger? How could he have even found a nebulous destination like this in the first place?

The Plotmaster chuckled as he took a puff on his blue-smoke cigar.

AH, BUT FIND ME YOU DID, BOOBALA!
YOU'D BE SURPRISED WHAT YOU CAN DO,
ONCE YOU'VE BECOME CAPTAIN CRUSADER.

Roger did it? But he didn't even use his ring! And he certainly didn't say 'See you in the funny papers!'

The Plotmaster answered him brusquely:

> FACE IT, ROGER.
> ONCE YOU'RE CAPTAIN CRUSADER
> YOU DON'T NEED A RING.
> YOU HAVE 'METHODS'.
> SO WHAT'S YOUR PROBLEM?

'Uh,' Roger began, and realized that was the first word he had spoken since he had got here, even though the two of them seemed to be having a fully fledged conversation. He did notice, though, that the blue smoke had dissipated sufficiently for Roger to make out the dimly back-lit shape smoking a cigar in front of him.

This time, the Plotmaster sounded the slightest bit peeved:

> OH, I KNOW I COULD LOOK IT UP IN THE SCRIPT!
> BUT TALKING ABOUT IT IS JUST SO MUCH
> MORE *PERSONAL*.

'All right,' Roger replied, and tried quickly to summarize everything that had happened since the arrival of his mother on the beach party planet, including their unexplained arrival on the car chase world, the fact that Roger was hearing all this dramatic music, and his progress with Captain Crusader sayings.

But, the last thing he remembered, he was drowning, along with Dwight and Professor Peril. What had happened to the others?

'Yip, bark, yip!' Dwight remarked cheerfully from somewhere nearby.

The Plotmaster's reply held a twinge of wonder:

> SAY, ISN'T THAT DWIGHT THE WONDER DOG?

Everybody, Roger remembered, knew Dwight the wonder dog. 'Bark, arf, bark bark!' Dwight answered.

> YES, I AM THE PLOTMASTER.

'Yip, bark, arf arf, woof!' the dog quickly countered.
The back-lit man with the blue-smoke cigar nodded sagely.

> YES,

AND THE PHILOSOPHICAL IMPLICATIONS
ARE INDEED STAGGERING.

'You're the Plotmaster?' a small, somewhat more human voice spoke from behind Roger. Roger turned round to see the army-fatigue-clad Professor Peril, doing his best to look as inconspicuous as possible on the light blue, never-ending plane where the Plotmaster held court. Apparently, his tank had been left behind on the car chase world.

'There really *is* a Plotmaster?' Peril added, looking none too comfortable.

But Roger didn't have time to think about Peril's comfort. The Plotmaster had asked Roger if he had any problems, and, especially in his new role as Captain Crusader, he had a responsibility to answer. Besides what was going on in the Cineverse with the Change and all, Roger could think of two very definite problems. The first had to do with Delores and the slime monster—

The Plotmaster cleared his throat.

DELORES?
LISTEN, TAKE IT FROM SOMEONE WHO KNOWS.
FORGET ABOUT DELORES.

Forget about Delores? Suddenly, Roger didn't feel the least bit like Captain Crusader. Questions warred with each other in Roger's head: shouldn't somebody with the total control of the Plotmaster be able to prevent this sort of thing?

Now that the Change was upon them again, did that mean there was never, ever going to be any more happy endings?

And what could have happened to Delores that was that bad?

LET'S JUST SAY
IT ISN'T PRETTY.

'Uh,' Professor Peril interrupted, 'Mr Plotmaster, sir? I have to explain a few things. I haven't always been on my best behaviour.'

Roger couldn't concentrate on what Peril was saying. He felt as if he had been kicked in the stomach by an iron boot. Delores was the whole reason he had got involved in the Cineverse in the first place. Sure, there had been other women in his life – actually, quite a few other women – but Delores had been different. There had been a communication between them that had been, well, unearthly. And now something had happened to her, beyond even the power of the Plotmaster.

'Listen, those sixty-three bank jobs,' Peril explained, 'and those seventeen diamond heists—'

Roger wasn't going to give up, even now. For one thing, giving up wasn't the sort of thing Captain Crusader did. And, who knew, in a place as vast and varied as the Cineverse, maybe there was some hope for Delores that even the Plotmaster didn't know about. And, if not, if what had happened to Delores was beyond redemption, perhaps – once Roger had found her again – he could at least make her comfortable, or put her out of her misery, or something.

Roger sighed. His first question to the Plotmaster had got the worst answer imaginable. He didn't even want to ask about that other thing—

> OH, YES.
> THE OTHER THING.
> YOU MEAN YOUR MOTHER, DON'T YOU?

The Plotmaster paused and sighed.

> I FEEL A CERTAIN RESPONSIBILITY FOR YOUR
> MOTHER.
> YOU HAVE TO UNDERSTAND, ROGER.
> SOMETIMES THE SCRIPT CALLS FOR SOMETHING
> EVEN I MIGHT NOT LIKE.
> YOU'VE GOTTA HAVE CONFLICT, AFTER ALL.

'—and those seven hundred and twelve mortgages I foreclosed—' Peril continued.

Roger felt a certain responsibility towards his mother, too. Still, there was something about the Plotmaster's response—

'That's why my mother got zapped by the Zeta Ray?' Roger asked incredulously. 'Conflict?'

'—and those innumerable train robberies,' Peril went on miserably, 'and those high-speed motorboat chases—'

> YEAH, CONFLICT.
> AND A PRETTY GOOD ONE, TOO.

Well, Roger supposed, if you thought about it that way, it was

good for the Cineverse, maybe. But what about the needs of Roger
Gordon – or the needs of Captain Crusader? He glanced distractedly at the still-babbling Peril.

'—and then there were those six Latin American revolutions I
helped to foment,' the cut-rate villain lamented economically.
'And of course those three times I tried to take over the world—'

But Peril's confessions became more distant still as Roger
realized for the first time that he may have lost both the woman he
loved, and his mother, too. Talk about heartbreak—

DON'T TALK TO ME ABOUT HEARTBREAK.
HEY, I'M THE PLOTMASTER!

The back-lit man shook his cigar at Roger as the angelic chorus
rose in the background.

DON'T DESPAIR, ROGER.
IT'S NOT HOPELESS.
IT'S NEVER HOPELESS.
WELL, ONCE IN A WHILE, IN THOSE FILMS
WITH SUBTITLES,
IT DOES GET PRETTY CLOSE TO HOPELESS,
DOESN'T IT?
BUT HEY,
WE WON'T LET THE CHANGE GET THAT FAR HERE,
WILL WE?
WHO'S IN CHARGE HERE, ANYWAY?

'It wasn't my fault!' Peril wailed. 'I was a victim of society!'

Roger didn't find anything the Plotmaster said the least bit
reassuring. Instead, he felt a deep emptiness.

'But—' he began. He hesitated when he realized that the Plotmaster was still waiting for an answer to his question.

OH.

The Plotmaster answered himself,

I SUPPOSE I AM.

Yes, the Plotmaster was in charge, at least as far as Roger
understood the set-up around here. Still, Roger couldn't help it.
He had to ask the next question:

'But can't you do *something*?'

'Well, I've confessed,' Professor Peril announced. 'Aren't you going to say anything?'

But the Plotmaster had to answer Roger first. And, when he did answer, his voice was sadder than Roger had ever heard before, supported by the mournful dirge of the angelic choir, as if all of them were weighted down by a thousand plots gone wrong:

ALAS, THERE'S A DIFFERENCE, BOOBALA,
BETWEEN BEING IN CHARGE AND BEING IN
CONTROL.

The angelic choir shifted up an octave, and then another.

THAT'S WHY WE NEED CAPTAIN CRUSADER.
THAT'S WHY WE NEED YOU, ROGER.
IT'S UP TO YOU NOW.
GIVE 'EM ONE FOR THE PLOTMASTER!

'No!' the Professor interjected. 'Ignore me, will you? Well, you do so at your own peril!'

Dwight barked as an ominously fizzing globe rolled to a stop mere inches from the Plotmaster's feet!

OH, NO!

The Plotmaster reacted in horror.

NOT A SMOKE BOMB!

'And not just any smoke bomb,' replied the evil Professor, barely able to keep his fiendish glee under control. 'No, you are confronted by a genuine Professor Peril Smoke Bomb Economy Special – more bomb for your buck – accept no substitutions!' His announcement complete, the villain allowed his maniacal laughter to overwhelm him at last as the immediate vicinity was filled with thick, black smoke.

'Bark, arf, yip!' Dwight complained.

COUGH!

the Plotmaster replied.

COUGH! COUGH! COUGH!

Roger was close to panic. Shouldn't Captain Crusader be doing something here?

'Ha!' the Professor announced abruptly. 'My current triumph will be as nothing to our final victory, when I lead the forces of Doctor Dread back here to overwhelm the Plotmaster!'

Roger panicked at last. Could Peril do something like that? He supposed, with the Change, that anything was possible. Still, he couldn't help but think, in bringing Professor Peril here, had he – Roger Gordon – doomed the Plotmaster?

The Professor's laughter cut off abruptly as Peril disappeared, beyond the reach of even Captain Crusader.

CHAPTER ELEVEN

Mother Antoinette surveyed her new suite of rooms. Doctor Dread had tried, on very short notice, to liven up the dreary, barracks-like quality of the living quarters, importing a couple of wall hangings from the Great Hall to cover the drab, grey walls. She especially liked the tapestry that depicted Lucretia Borgia poisoning her relatives – now there was a woman with style. There were other festive touches in this place as well, like the ornate grillwork of the bars on the windows, and, of course, the decorative iron maiden. Part of her thought it was quite sweet of Dread to go to all this trouble, but the other, greater part of her knew this suite was only what she deserved.

She had been given one whole wing of the top floor of Dread's citadel. The Doctor assured her that the occupant of the main room had been away for so long that he certainly wouldn't need it any more, and the other half-dozen guards and lackeys that had been displaced from the smaller rooms by this new arrangement did not feel inconvenienced in the least. Not that Mother Antoinette would have cared. Actually, now that she thought of it, she liked to inconvenience people on occasion – as many people as possible.

There was a knock on the door.

She strode quickly across the main bedroom, her heels tapping a smart, martial beat atop the cold marble floor.

'Who's there?' she demanded.

'Antoinette!' a voice quavered on the other side of the thick oak door. 'It's your Mengy!'

She smiled softly to herself as her fingers caressed the handle of her whip. Now that she had a place of her own, it was high time she and 'her Mengy' spent some time alone. She opened the door.

Menge looked up at her and swallowed. 'An – an – antoinette.'

'Why don't you come in and—' she raised one eyebrow and paused in that way they had around here, '—get comfortable?'

Menge cleared his throat. 'Most assuredly.' He scurried into the room as Mother Antoinette slammed the door behind him. He stopped dead when he saw the very large bed with the black leather bedspread.

'My, this is quite – something.' His gaze flicked about the room, resting briefly on the tapestries that covered the closets to either side and a bit longer on the large night table covered with those various instruments Mother Antoinette thought might prove instructive – but his eyes returned, again and again, to the room's dominant piece of furniture.

'My,' he said at last, 'that's a – bed, isn't it?'

She smiled slightly. 'This is my boudoir.'

'Indeed it is.' Menge cleared his throat again. She wondered if he might be catching cold. 'Perhaps, though, we could go somewhere else to – talk?'

There was an edge to Mother Antoinette's reply. 'I believe this is the proper room – for everything.'

'Oh, most assuredly!' Menge agreed quickly as his eyes were drawn again to the leather coverlet. 'I couldn't agree more. Ah hahaha. Ah ha.' His laughter, somehow, didn't sound quite natural. And when he looked into her eyes again, there was a new quality to his gaze, a certain pitifulness, like a naughty boy pleading with his mother for a favour. Mother Antoinette found she liked that quality a great deal.

'Antoinette,' he said, quickly and urgently, 'I need to talk to you. We must make our plans for conquest. With the chaos of the Change around us, the time is ripe for our success – and, once we defeat Dread, the Cineverse will be ours!'

Mother Antoinette smiled at that. It was rather charming when her Mengy tried to be forceful. 'I have my own plans for conquest,' she replied, her eyes travelling up and down Menge's silver uniform. 'I can't think of a better place and time for us to have our little talk.' She flicked her whip for emphasis. The point snicked out to caress Menge's shoulder.

CRACK

'No better place?' Menge looked down at the tear in his silver suit. 'Oh. Perhaps not.'

She stepped forward quickly, placing her hand over the rend in Menge's silver garb. The hard leather had cut cleanly through the fabric, but she had enough control of the whip by now not to break the skin. She rubbed her whip-calloused palm against the newly revealed smoothness of Menge's shoulder.

Menge's pencil-thin moustache quivered uncontrollably. When he spoke, his voice was a husky croak.

'Antoinette!'

She pulled him to her.

There was a knock on the door.

Menge blinked and pulled himself away. The spell was broken.

'Who could that be?' he demanded, his voice squeaking with dismay. 'Our plans must be secret! The future of the Cineverse depends upon it.' His head whipped back and forth to take in the entire room. 'I have to hide!'

Hide? Oh, very well. The spell might be broken at the moment, but she could certainly save him for later. She looked about the room for a hiding place. Menge's tummy, unfortunately, made him a bit too large to fit under the bed. However, one of the closets would do nicely.

She pointed to the left-hand closet – the one with the tapestry of the landlord forcing the debtor family out into the snow.

'In there!' she commanded. 'Quickly!'

Menge hurried to obey. Mother Antoinette crossed the room quickly, her heels clacking as sharply as gunfire.

'Who disturbs me?' she demanded of the solid and still-closed door.

'This is not one of your wimpy males,' a gruff female voice answered. 'This is Big Bertha, seeking an audience that might be to our mutual advantage!'

Bertha? This could prove interesting. Besides, now that Antoinette had made her intentions clear, it might do Mengy good to spend some time in that closet. Anticipation, especially frustrated anticipation, could make things so much more intense.

She opened the door. Bertha stepped quickly into the room, her black vinyl jumpsuit doing little to hide the muscles bulging underneath. Still, Antoinette did not know if she approved of both of them wearing black. It was only a small step from vinyl to leather, after all, and that would never do. Antoinette hoped, at least for now, she could spare Bertha a lesson from the whip.

'I'm glad you're alone,' Bertha remarked after a cursory glance around the room. She shut the door herself. 'The Change is upon us, and, this time, it's going to change to our advantage!'

Mother Antoinette was curious despite herself. 'What do you mean?'

'Dread and his ilk have no vision,' Bertha replied. 'He pursues the Change for his own limited ends. And, if he wins, what of it? One *man* will replace another as ruler of the Cineverse. And we women will be left behind.' Her huge hands balled into fists, twin jack-hammers ready to destroy – until the frown of distaste on her countenance was abruptly replaced by the slightest of smiles. 'But not any more. The first time I saw you, I knew you were different. I knew you were the first woman worthy to conquer at Bertha's side.' She allowed herself a short, harsh laugh. 'Together, we can prove that women can be as cruel, heartless and despicable as men. And, once we have won, we will be able, at our leisure, to bend males to our will.' Her hands opened to grasp at the riches that would someday be theirs.

Mother Antoinette took a deep breath. What Big Bertha said made a great deal of sense. Perhaps it was the fact that Bertha was so forcefully direct, with none of the pregnant pauses her male counterparts so favoured; perhaps it was Antoinette's new surroundings, or the reassuring feel of the whip in her hand – but, whatever had changed, it meant that, more than ever before, something inside Antoinette felt like this was her turn for conquest. At last, her time had come.

But then, why was there something else inside her that fought against this?

It had something to do with Roger, didn't it, her undutiful son? She looked again at Bertha's grasping hands and hungry eyes. Bertha had more than a need to control; she had a need to devour. Antoinette knew, from those earlier, unpleasant exchanges, how Bertha felt about her son, and she had no doubt, should she help Bertha gain control of the Cineverse, one of the first to be devoured would be Roger.

But why should that bother her? Her son never called, never wrote, never introduced her to any of his women friends unless he was about to get married to one of them. He had always been terrible about cleaning up his room, his clothes never made it into the laundry basket, she could forget about him even touching a dirty dish, and he hadn't even said thank you when she had given away all those old things of his that had needlessly been cluttering up her house for years. Why shouldn't she be eager to see someone as inconsiderate as that devoured?

But there was another voice, very small, very deep inside her, that whispered oh-so-faintly: 'No, not Roger!' So small, but so insistent.

As unpleasant as this was, she had to face it: Mother Antoinette was still a mother.

'Well?' Bertha demanded. 'What do you say?'

Antoinette frowned. She did not approve of anyone else – even someone as large and politically persuasive as Bertha – making demands. Before her recent transformation, Antoinette had spent her entire life acceding to other's wishes. Now, she had a few wishes of her own.

'I must consider—' she began.

She was interrupted by a knock on the door.

'Who could that be?' Bertha demanded with an edge of panic. 'We must not be discovered together before we can adequately plan!' She looked around for some means of escape. 'I will have to hide!'

She glanced at the underside of the bed, but dismissed it as much too narrow for her bulk. She started instead towards the landlord tapestry, but Antoinette gently redirected her towards the opposite closet, and the hanging illustrated with Lucretia Borgia.

'It's so much more appropriate,' Antoinette murmured softly but urgently.

Bertha replied with a businesslike nod, and marched to the other corner of the room.

The knocker knocked again, more insistently this time. Mother Antoinette realized she had to deal with this directly. She spun and headed quickly for the door again, her heels pounding as hard as a carpenter driving nails into a coffin.

When she spoke, her words were clipped as sharp as daggers. 'Who dares to bother me?'

'It is I!' an imperious voice blustered on the other side of the door. 'Your leader! Doctor Dread! Let me in—' he paused portentously, '—please?'

Now it was this Dread person? She supposed she should open the door, if only in appreciation of the suite that he had arranged for her. But what if he desired more than a friendly chat? Her fingers tightened round the reassuring handle of her whip. If he had any other ideas, she would quickly change his mind.

She pulled the door open with a jerk.

'Mrs Gor—' Dread hesitated in surprise. 'I mean, Mother Antoinette. How nice of you to—' he paused a bit more calmly as he stepped inside, '—invite me in.'

She regarded him coolly. 'Yes, Doctor. What might I do for you?'

Dread avoided her eyes. 'This is a very – delicate matter.' He looked at their surroundings as if the walls might have ears.

'I don't know if you are—' he hesitated tellingly, '—aware of the situation.'

'If you say so,' she replied noncommittally. She didn't want to show too much emotion until she could determine exactly what it was Dread was hesitating about.

The slightest of smiles fluttered about the Doctor's lips. It reminded Mother Antoinette of nothing so much as a ghostly pale moth drawn to a flame and simultaneously frightened to show itself.

'The Change is—' he paused knowingly, '—all around us.'

'Yes?' Mother Antoinette prompted.

'The Change has—' Dread hesitated teasingly, '—happened before. I know the signs.'

'Do tell,' Antoinette replied. She wished, somehow, that she could get Dread to hesitate a little less.

'I am—' Dread paused as the smile flickered across his lips again, '—experienced in this sort of thing. 'I am—' his gaze caught Antoinette's for an instant before he nervously looked away, '—experienced in so many things.'

'So you say,' Mother Antoinette managed. She tried to smile, but her teeth clamped together in a rictus grin. Perhaps, she thought, Doctor Dread had hesitated once too often.

'Yes—' Dread stopped to take a deep breath, '—I do. But the Change has given me—' the words caught in his throat yet again, '—beneficial experience—' Dread managed before his next pause, '—experience which would be to our mutual—'

This had gone too far. There was only so much Mother Antoinette could abide. It was time for the whip.

'—benefit—' Dread managed as the whip leapt in Antoinette's hand.

CRACK

Dread's mouth fell open in an even more profound hesitation.

CRACK *CRACK* *CRACK*

The whip wrapped itself round Doctor Dread's snakeskin-clad shoulders. Mother Antoinette jerked him forward.

Dread's incredibly thin lips quivered, reminding Antoinette of a fish mouth longing for a worm. 'Exactly – what I was – trying to say.' Dread gasped with every pause. 'With you – the Change – would be something special.'

Something special? Mother Antoinette felt as if somebody had kicked in the ribs of her leather bustle. For once, she didn't know what to say.

She heard some sort of growl from the closets behind her. Could it be Menge, vocalizing jealous rage, or Bertha, forced to comment on Doctor Dread's blatantly male tactics?

Dread had heard it, too.

'What was that?' he demanded, for once not hesitating at all.

Mother Antoinette realized that, to master this situation, she needed whip-like speed in her mind as well. What kind of explanation would a man with Dread's background accept? Perhaps something from a soap opera would be melodramatic enough, or the sort of thing she found in those fiction supplements at the back of women's magazines.

'Only the sound of my startled heart,' she replied, as she did her best to stare demurely at the floor. Still, she wasn't sure words like that quite fitted here in the Citadel of Dread. Besides which, it wasn't all that easy to look demure when you were holding a whip.

'Really?' Dread answered uncertainly, as if – as she feared – he was not quite ready to accept the explanation. 'But—'

How dare he object so blatantly? Mother Antoinette found herself suddenly angry that this snakeskin-covered toad would question her *heart*!

'And who are you,' she retorted quickly, 'to question *anything* that happens in my chamber?'

Doctor Dread took a wary step away, but, beyond clearing his throat, he offered no further opposition. He seemed much happier to accept her second, more violent response.

But what, she wondered, should she do for an encore?

She was saved by the explosion.

'Blue smoke?' Doctor Dread declared. 'Who could it be? We can't be seen together like this. Not until you have made your—' this time, his hesitation sounded panic-stricken, '—intentions clear!'

Mother Antoinette quietly suggested that Doctor Dread hide under the bed. She was glad she finally had someone svelte enough to fit down there. She hated to waste a good hiding place.

In the meantime, the blue smoke had started to clear.

'What's going on here?' a new voice shouted abruptly. 'What has happened to my small yet economical headquarters?'

Mother Antoinette flicked her wrist.

CRACK went the whip. *CRACK* *CRACK* *CRACK*

'I was only asking!' the newcomer wailed. He was a compact

fellow wearing army fatigues, but he also sported that pencil-thin moustache so favoured by the local men. Unlike Menge's stately rotundness, however, this fellow didn't seem to have an ounce of fat on his body, probably because – with the way he twitched and jerked about – he was never still enough for any fat to settle down. Mother Antoinette wondered idly how quick this one might be to dance to the song of her whip. She began to see a certain wisdom to Bertha's thoughts on men.

The jerky newcomer stared intently at her. 'You still haven't answered my question.'

She certainly hadn't. She had learned her lesson with her recent experience with Doctor Dread. Now that she was Mother Antoinette, she had no need to make any explanations. Instead, she made a simple statement.

'Your headquarters are *my* headquarters now.'

'Oh,' was the newcomer's quiet reply. 'It's all I could expect, the way things have been going. I don't suppose you know where I'm supposed to be?'

Mother Antoinette's only answer was a playful flick of her wrist. The whip danced mere inches from the newcomer's nose. But this new fellow was too preoccupied with his own thoughts to do more than flinch.

'I should have known it wasn't my day,' the newcomer moaned. 'First it was Mort the Killer Robot and Diablo, the Gorilla with the Mind of a Man! Then it was my deadly tank, with its uncounted tons of screaming metal destruction! And now my – room is gone?' He put his fist to his forehead as he choked back a sob. 'How much turmoil can one villain abide?'

He certainly appeared to be a high-strung sort. And yet, in his grovelling way, he seemed very sincere. Mother Antoinette had to admit it – you certainly met a lot of interesting men in the Cineverse. If only her bridge club could see her now! But she had left the bridge club far behind, along with the garden club, the civic association, and any other organization she couldn't control with the whip!

'But I am forgetting my villainous manners,' the newcomer continued, trying to gain control over his emotions. 'You may call me Peril. Professor Peril, specializing in badness on a budget.'

She pointed at herself with the handle of her whip. 'Mother Antoinette. Any questions?'

'Well – uh – yes,' Peril managed. 'What am I to do without my room?'

She continued to stare at him silently.

'Not that I suppose you would be interested in something as insignificant as that, Mother Antoinette,' he added hastily. She continued to regard him without emotion.

'Not that I should presume to know what you might be interested in!' Peril added with a weak excuse for a smile.

Almost despite herself, her eyes fell on the leather-covered bed. 'I have my priorities!'

'My—' Peril's gaze followed her own. 'The bed? The bed is very nice.'

Mother Antoinette could hear muffled words come from one of the closets and under the bed.

'What was that?' Peril shrieked. My, he was certainly a jumpy fellow.

'Draughts,' was Mother Antoinette's unconcerned reply.

'Yes,' Peril remarked absently. 'I have noticed them myself. This citadel may be imposing, but it is anything but energy efficient.' His eyes wandered back to the black leather bedspread. 'That is a much nicer bed than I used to have.'

This time, groans of protest came from all three hiding places.

'Are you sure there's no one else here?' Peril asked uncertainly.

Mother Antoinette shrugged her leather-clad shoulders. 'Mice, perhaps.'

'Mice?' Peril replied. 'Oh, dear, no. Most definitely rats. Norwegian rats. Doctor Dread had them imported, you know, to give the Citadel a touch of—'

Mother Antoinette had had enough of talk. It was time for action. As usual, her whip spoke for her.

CRACK

Peril stared at the leather thong newly hugging his trim midsection. When he spoke again, there was wonder in his voice:

'Mother Antoinette. You make me feel like a giddy schoolboy. Something has gone out of my life since that ape and robot vanished. With you, though, it could happen all again. I could have a sense of style!'

'What?'

'How dare—'

'Who does he—'

The exclamations were getting louder from the hiding places.

'Is it something about the acoustics in here?' Peril asked with a frown.

But Mother Antoinette was unhappy as well. She had not asked to be disturbed by any of these intruders, and she had had enough of skulking in closets. When she wanted something, she wanted it now.

Again the whip moved, almost of its own volition.

CRACK *CRACK* *CRACK*

Both tapestries were flung aside as the whip shot to either side of the bed.

'Oh, my,' Menge muttered distractedly. 'I must have made a wrong turn. How could I possibly—'

'Oh, there you are, Antoinette dearest,' Bertha said quickly. 'I do think it's time we had a—'

But the whip was not finished with its mischief.

CRACK *CRACK* *CRACK*

Antoinette jerked the handle, and the whip-wrapped Doctor Dread came rolling out from underneath the bed.

But their leader showed none of the apology or surprise of his fellows. Instead, he appeared livid, his crimson face clashing badly with his snakeskin cowl.

'How dare you disturb me in the middle of an – er – inspection!' he demanded. 'I have heard you have – rats here. That's it!' He sat up and looked at the rest of the assemblage. 'Rats!' He grabbed the whip in both of his hands and pulled. The handle flew from Mother Antoinette's startled grip.

'Believe me, underlings!' Dread ranted. 'There will be – changes made. There will be – dues to pay.'

Mother Antoinette looked from face to face. None of them appeared happy, and her three fellow underlings might have looked the least bit afraid.

'Guards!' Doctor Dread screamed.

Menge, Peril and Bertha took a collective step backwards. Oh dear, Antoinette thought. Without the whip in her hand and all – she hadn't felt this uncertain since her days on earth.

Had she finally gone too far?

CHAPTER TWELVE

Roger coughed. Roger hacked. Roger couldn't get any oxygen. The combination of the smoke bomb and Professor Peril's blue-smoke disappearance seemed to have used up all the breathable air.

That's when the thunderous roar of industrial motors cut in, sounding like nothing so much as the propellers on a Second World War fighter plane.

The two smokes dispersed as if by magic. Roger gasped for air.

The Plotmaster still stood in the same, back-lit spot, as if the business with Professor Peril really hadn't affected him in the least. He chuckled.

PRETTY GOOD, HUH?
LUCKY FOR US I'VE GOT THOSE PROPELLERS
FROM THOSE SECOND WORLD WAR FIGHTER PLANES.

He paused to take a long, satisfied drag on his blue-smoke cigar.

IT'S ONE OF THE PERKS OF BEING THE PLOTMASTER.
YOU GET TO KEEP SOME OF THE PROPS!

Roger shook his head. He felt like all this smoke had fogged his brain as well as clogging his lungs.

Dwight was barking his brains out, as if recent events were too much for even a wonder dog. Roger had to agree. The more time he spent with the Plotmaster, the less he seemed to understand.

'But aren't you upset?' he asked. 'The Professor just made good his escape!'

ROGER, BOOBALA!
THIS IS THE CINEVERSE—

MY CINEVERSE!
NOBODY ESCAPES UNLESS I WANT THEM TO!

'But I thought—' Roger began, not sure now what he had thought. The Plotmaster filled in for him:

THAT THINGS WERE OUT OF CONTROL?

The Plotmaster paused an instant to puff thoughtfully on his cigar.

WELL, MAYBE THEY ARE, SORT OF—
THE CINEVERSE IS A BIG PLACE.
TOO BIG, PERHAPS, EVEN FOR THE PLOTMASTER!

The back-lit guy in blue was interrupted by a blast from the heavenly choir. The Plotmaster glared overhead.

I DIDN'T ASK FOR ANY COMMENTS FROM YOU!
YOUR JOB'S ON THE LINE HERE!

The angelic choir was suddenly silent. He turned back to Roger, his voice again cheerful and in control.

THAT BIT WITH – WHAT WAS HIS NAME?
OH, YEAH – PROFESSOR PERIL.
SOMETIMES, THESE VILLAINS . . .

He chuckled, leaving the rest of his thought unsaid.
'But the bomb!' Roger objected. 'And Peril's escape!'
The Plotmaster chuckled again.

OH YEAH, THAT STUFF WITH THE SMOKE BOMB!
I WAS PRETTY GOOD WASN'T I?
AND NEVER A DAY OF DRAMATIC TRAINING!

He waved the sheaf of papers in his hand for emphasis.

I TELL YOU, THE PLOTMASTER
IS ALWAYS READY FOR CHANGES IN THE SCRIPT!

'Changes—' Roger asked hopelessly, '—in the script?'

The Plotmaster shook his head sympathetically.

YOU THOUGHT THE SCRIPT ALWAYS STAYED
THE SAME?
WELL, MAYBE IT DID ONCE—
BUT NOT SINCE THE CHANGE!

He waved the pages in his hands for emphasis.
Roger noticed the heavenly choir was back again, this time humming softly – yet inspirationally – in the background.

BUT THERE ARE STILL WAYS TO CONTROL THE
SCRIPT.
WAYS FOR THE PLOTMASTER—
OR FOR CAPTAIN CRUSADER!

The Plotmaster coughed, and the heavenly music cut off abruptly. He stared distractedly for a moment at his blue-smoke cigar.

BUT I'M GETTING AHEAD OF MYSELF HERE,
AREN'T I?
YOU'LL HAVE TO FORGIVE AN OLD PLOTMASTER—
SO MANY PLOTS, SO LITTLE TIME!

He stuck the cigar back in his silhouetted mouth and began to page through the script.

YOU KNOW, OF COURSE, THAT I COULD HAVE
CONTROLLED
PROFESSOR PERIL,

the Plotmaster stated flatly, speaking round his cigar.

AND THE SMOKE BOMB?
TO ME IT WAS NOTHING MORE THAN
ANOTHER PLOT DEVICE.

The Plotmaster's head rose to regard Roger.

BUT GIVE PERIL HIS FREEDOM—
AND YOU'D BE SURPRISED WHAT HE'LL LEAD

US TO!
EXCUSE ME FOR A SECOND.

He looked back down to the script.

WE JUST HAVE TO LOOK AHEAD HERE A
COUPLE OF PAGES.

With a cry of triumph, he poked his forefinger at the top of the right-hand page.

HERE!
HE'S GONE TO THE CITADEL OF DREAD!
SEE HOW EASY THAT WAS?

'The Citadel of Dread?' Roger didn't particularly like the sound of that. Still, the Plotmaster seemed pretty pleased with himself.

YEAH.
I'M PRETTY IMPRESSED WITH IT MYSELF
AND I PROBABLY INVENTED THE PLACE!

The blue embers glowed on the end of his cigar as the Plotmaster took a deep, satisfied breath.

THE CITADEL OF DREAD!
WHAT A PLACE TO HAVE THE CLIMAX, HUH?

Roger felt a certain panic rising inside him. This was all going too fast for him. 'Climax? Is it time for the climax?'

IS IT TIME?
OH, COME ON NOW, ROGER BABY,
DON'T YOU THINK THIS BUSINESS HAS GONE
ON FAR ENOUGH?

This business? Roger guessed the Plotmaster was talking about the Plotmaster and the Change. But there was a lot of other business that needed taking care of, too. What about Delores and the slime monster? What about his mother and the Zeta Ray? What about Big Louie and all the others stranded back on that cop chase movie world?

'Far enough?' Roger wondered aloud. 'I guess so, except—'
The Plotmaster nodded knowingly.

> YOU'RE WORRIED ABOUT THOSE
> ERRANT PLOT THREADS, AREN'T YOU?
> ROGER, BABE, TAKE IT FROM THE PLOTMASTER!
> ONCE YOU GET TO THE CLIMAX,
> THOSE PLOT THREADS HAVE A WAY OF
> SHOWING UP!

Roger guessed he had to take the Plotmaster's word for it. Actually, so far, he had had to take the Plotmaster's word for everything.
The back-lit man in blue leaned forward, his voice low, almost conspiratorial.

> BESIDES, IT'S TIME FOR THE CHANGE,
> AND THIS TIME, IT'S GONNA BE BIG!
> WORLDS COLLIDE! CULTURES CLASH!
> ACTION! ADVENTURE! COMEDY! ROMANCE!
> I TELL YOU, ROGER BABY,
> WHEN DOCTOR DREAD STARTED ALL THIS,
> HE DIDN'T KNOW WHAT HE WAS GETTING INTO!
> SOMETIMES, I WORRY ABOUT THE CHANGE.
> BUT THIS ONE?
> WHAT A SPECTACLE IT'S GOING TO BE!

The Plotmaster leaned back and took a puff on his blue-smoke cigar.

> AND, ROGER?
> THIS IS FROM THE HEART,
> I CERTAINLY HOPE YOU LIVE THROUGH IT!

Roger hoped so, too. He spoke with a certain resignation: 'So I have to go to the Citadel of Dread?'
He sighed as he reached into his jacket pocket to pull out his cheap plastic means of transportation.
His pocket was empty.
'My ring!' he shouted. 'What happened to my ring?'
The Plotmaster only laughed.

> A RING?

WHO NEEDS A RING
WHEN YOU'RE CAPTAIN CRUSADER!

This was going beyond confusion. Angelic choir and mysterious blue back-lighting be damned – Roger was starting to get annoyed.

'But how do I get from world to world?' Roger demanded. 'Do I still say "See you in the funny papers"?'

THOSE ARE SIMPLY WORDS—
A MOVIE MANTRA FOR THOSE
NOT AS FOCUSED AS CAPTAIN CRUSADER.

'So I *don't* have to say "See you in the funny papers"?' Roger insisted. He still wasn't getting any straight answers here. Come to think of it, in his last couple of trips through the Cineverse – to the car chase world and then here, wherever it was that the Plotmaster called home – he hadn't said 'See you in the funny papers!' once.

The Plotmaster made a noise deep in his throat.

THERE ARE AS MANY WORDS OF POWER IN THE
CINEVERSE
AS THERE ARE MOVIE WORLDS.

He puffed on his blue-smoke cigar and tilted his head up in the general direction of his angelic choir, which had started in again.

'THERE'S NO PLACE LIKE HOME'
WAS ALWAYS A GOOD ONE
OR
'LET'S WIN ONE FOR THE GIPPER!'
BUT ALL THIS IS BESIDE THE POINT.
WE'VE HAD ENOUGH PLOT HERE FOR EVEN
THE PLOTMASTER.
IT'S TIME FOR ACTION!

The Plotmaster pulled the blue-smoke cigar from his mouth and waved it as he spoke.

DON'T WORRY ABOUT THE MECHANICS,
ROGER, SWEETIE-BABY!

YOU SHOULD KNOW BY NOW
ABOUT MOVIE MAGIC!

'Oh, yeah,' Roger replied, half to himself. Movie magic – like when he was on that beach party world, and had sung that surfing song to master that wave among waves, the Cowabungamunga.

'Movie magic.' He whispered the words, as if speaking them aloud might give them too much power.

But, speaking of power, there seemed to be an awful lot of blue smoke in the air, and all of it was coming from the Plotmaster's waving cigar.

I CERTAINLY HAVE ENJOYED OUR LITTLE CHAT,
ROGER, BABY!
KNOCK 'EM DEAD
AT THE CITADEL OF DREAD!

So he was on his way, just like that? Roger wished he had the Plotmaster's confidence. Not only that, Roger wished he knew exactly what the Plotmaster expected him to do.

But it was too late for wishes. Roger was surrounded by blue smoke, and the fading words of the Plotmaster:

SEE YOU IN THE FUNNY PAPERS!

CHAPTER THIRTEEN

There was only the void, and the sound of a very angry chicken.

Delores had no idea where she was. One moment, she had been surrounded by the insane hum of the transmogrifier – the next, all was darkness.

'Brawwk!' the chicken screamed.

Maybe the bird's voice was a clue. Delores thought back to that awful, frightening moment, strapped into the machine, when she was bathed by blinding light. She had thought, then, that this might be – the end.

Perhaps she was right. Perhaps it was.

There had been so many different animals there at that last moment, a veritable Noah's Ark worth of species crowded into that tiny transmogrification room. There had been bunnies and goats, dogs and cats, insects and – chickens. Maybe they had all perished in that instant, the sheer bulk of life in that room proving too great a burden for even a machine as frightening as the transmogrifier. Perhaps her soul had followed the animals into the afterlife. Perhaps she had gone to chicken heaven, and this darkness was nothing but an endless mound of seedcorn, blocking out the celestial sun.

'Brawwwwk!' the chicken declared even more vehemently.

Delores realized that there was a problem with her theory. Why was this chicken angry if it was in heaven? She had an awful moment of realization. If chickens could go to heaven, what would prevent the fowls from going – elsewhere in the afterlife?

'Brawwk!' the chicken reasserted. 'Braw—. Braw—.' The enraged clucks turned to coughs. 'Braw—. Oh, dear. You'll have to excuse me. Something is not quite right.'

Delores breathed in sharply. The chicken was speaking with the voice of Edward, the slime monster. Well, whatever had happened to Edward, he'd better be able to answer some questions!

'Baahhh!' she began. Where had that come from? She had meant to ask 'Where are we?' or some such.

Instead, she had bleated.

'Baahhh?' she repeated. At least this time it sounded more like a question.

'I may have made a slight miscalculation,' Edward admitted. 'Bawwk,' he added.

Delores felt suddenly cold. She hugged her arms close to her body, her hands digging deep into her luxurious fur coat.

There was something else wrong here. Why should she be cold if she was wearing a fur coat? But, now that she thought of it, she hadn't been wearing a fur coat – before the transmogrification.

What had the slime monster done to her?

'Baaahhhhhh!' she bleated in terror.

'Then again,' Edward admitted, 'I may have made a major miscalculation.'

Delores couldn't stand this. If Edward was talking, why couldn't she? She would simply have to try harder.

'Bah—' she began, using all her concentration to get her lips, or whatever was now where her lips used to be, to form words and sentences. 'B-b-but—' she managed at last, 'wa-wa-where ar-r-re we?'

'Bawwwwk?' Edward replied in surprise. 'Oh. I think we are somewhere in that lightless and formless void that exists beyond and between the worlds of the Cineverse, a place of total silence and darkness.'

This was the sort of thing Delores was afraid of. 'T-total darkness?' she repeated, mostly to make sure her newly recovered voice was still working.

'Yes,' Edward answered, 'so it is said, except for ancient legends that declare, should you travel far enough within the void, that you might find a small, bright red sign with but a single word: "EXIT".'

'Exit?' Delores asked, feeling at last that she was finally gaining some control over her voice. Still, there was something about that single word that she found every bit as disquieting as everything else around here. Somehow, 'EXIT' sounded an awful lot like 'THE END'.

Now that she had her voice, though, maybe she could finally ask some of those questions bursting inside her, like, first and foremost:

'Edward, how do you know abahhh – er – about all this sort of thing?'

'Voluminous research. When you're a slime monster, you have a very limited social life. This leaves you with a lot of free time.'

This, at least, made sense. Delores fully agreed that the slime monster could use some help with his social skills. But somehow she felt that etiquette lessons would not help them out of their present situation. She asked her second question:

'Edward, why did we end up here?'

The slime monster paused a moment before answering this time.

'It had something to do with the transmogrifier – I think. That, and all the various species that crowded into the room as the transmogrification began. I'm afraid – bawwwk – that we've brought a few of the animals along with us, in a way – bawwwk – that I hadn't planned. It could be that the load of animals was too much for the transmogrifier to take, that the very experiment was too much for even the world of the Institute of Very Advanced Science to accept. After transmogrification, we could now be so different that there might not be a single world in the Cineverse that could accept us.'

So different? Delores thought about her new, and very attached, fur coat. Now that she considered it, maybe this lightless (and even more importantly, mirrorless) void was a blessing in disguise.

'Then again,' Edward further mused, 'perhaps this is not some strange quirk of fate. Perhaps this is meant to be, and our present state is but another stage of the transmogrification.'

'You mean the process – might not be finished yet?' Delores found she was even more frightened than she had been before.

'Bawwwwwwk!' Edward replied. 'All I can say is what I said to you before has come true – we are now united in a way that few people – or slime monsters, for that matter – will ever know.' He made a noise deep in his throat, half sigh, half cluck. 'I will admit, though, that it isn't quite what I expected.'

'Bahhhhh!' Delores agreed.

'And I thought this would be the perfect world!' Edward lamented. 'I'm so annoyed I could just peck!'

Delores guessed she could relate to that. She knew she would feel much better if she just had a little grass to chew on.

They both stood for a moment in truly total silence.

'If this is a new stage of the transmogrification,' Edward

ventured at last, 'it's as boring as the last phase was over-whelming. We must, somehow, find our way back into the Cineverse.'

Delores felt something brush against her arm, and then a hand closed round her own – a hand seemingly covered with very damp feathers.

'Come, Delores,' the slime monster intoned. 'I think it's time we looked for that exit.'

CHAPTER FOURTEEN

'Zabana see light!'

Louie squinted. Yes, there was a point of light in the distance, like the end to a long tunnel. Perhaps, he thought, they hadn't travelled all the way to the true Pit of Absurdity. But what could be more absurd than their present situation?

After being unceremoniously dumped down here by the various relatives of ancient gods and heroes, Louie had landed softly and unscathed on something that felt like a thick bed of moss. He had quickly checked that all his fellows were similarly unhurt, and suggested they find a way out of this dramatically dark place. It seemed to Louie that there had been an awful lot of dramatically dark places in their recent travels. Undoubtedly, it had something to do with the Change.

It was then that Zabana had seen the light. The best thing to do, Louie decided, was to approach the illumination. If nothing else, they would be able to see.

Doc, O'Clanrahan, Zabana and Louie all moved cautiously through the gloom. Well, Louie guessed he was doing his sidekick job; the plot was certainly moving right along. With the Change in full swing, though, it was impossible to guess where the plot might be going.

They had wanted to end up on one world, after all, and had found themselves somewhere completely different, and, instead of cute bunnies, they had been confronted by massive musclemen. Louie doubted he'd made a mistake with the ring. He was too practised a sidekick for that sort of error. Instead, he considered it far more likely that the Change had altered the very fabric of the Cineverse!

'What that?' Zabana demanded.

'What's what?' Louie asked, increasingly perplexed with the direction all this was taking.

'Strange noise,' Zabana insisted. 'Something down here with us.'

Louie still didn't hear anything, but he had no reason to doubt Zabana's jungle-trained senses.

'Tarnation!' Doc exclaimed. 'Do you think my six-shooters would work down here?'

'Why don't we take that ring of yours and go someplace a little more friendly?' O'Clanrahan suggested a little shakily. Louie didn't think he'd ever seen such a change in a man – the policeman had lost all his confidence. Without Dwight the wonder dog, O'Clanrahan didn't seem to be the same police officer.

Zabana's voice cut through the gloom: 'It closer now.'

But what had Zabana's jungle-trained senses detected? They had faced a slime monster in similar circumstances once. This certainly couldn't be any worse – could it?

Then Louie heard it, too.

Thump.

The sound was soft, but close. Louie wondered if something was following them.

O'Clanrahan muttered from where he walked behind the others.

Thump thump.

It was louder this time, and somehow percussive. Louie wondered if it might be the distant pounding of some jungle drum, carried to them by the strange acoustics of the chamber around them.

O'Clanrahan said something else just below the level of Louie's hearing.

Thump thump thump.

It sounded like it was all around them now. Louie realized he'd been acting too much like a sidekick again – or, more precisely, he had been *reacting*, which, after all, was a sidekick's basic job. But, if they were going to succeed in their battle against Doctor Dread, one of them would have to lead, and somehow Louie felt he was the best one here for the job. He supposed that stranger things had happened with the Change.

But where would he lead them? Exactly where were they, and where should they go? Louie had to think. There might be a clue in the name – The Pit of Absurdity.

Thump, went something much too close. Thump, thump, thump.

The noise had become quite regular now. Thump, thump,

thump, thump. Perhaps, Louie thought, they were not in some sort of cave or tunnel, but inside a living organism. Could that thumping be the beating of a giant heart? That would certainly be properly absurd.

But if Louie's latest thought was true, the heart was speeding up.

Thumpthumpthumpthump, came the ever increasing beat. Thumpthumpthumpthumpthumpthump   thumpthumpthump. The echoes in this place made it sound like the noises were coming from everywhere. Unless, of course, the noises *were* coming from everywhere.

Whether he was going to be a sidekick or a leader, Louie knew there was only one thing to do.

'Run!' he yelled to the others. 'Let's get out into the light!'

They ran, their pounding feet surrounded and lost within the noise of a hundred thumps. But they had almost reached the light. Louie could see his fellows running beside him as the illumination filtered into the tunnel. And he saw something else as well. They were not alone.

They were surrounded by bunnies.

'Whoo-eee!' Doc yelped. 'Everybody's animated!'

Louie realized that they had reached their destination after all. He grinned at Zabana and Doc. For some reason, O'Clanrahan looked even more upset than he had before. Was the Change getting to be too much for the elderly police officer? At the rate things were moving now, Louie guessed he could really empathize with the cop's confusion. But, as far as he was concerned, that confusion ended here.

'OK, guys!' he yelled to the other non-bunnies as they all ran out under the cartoon sun. 'Enough's enough! Let's stop running already!'

'But we like to run!' cheered a grey and white bunny that Louie recognized – was his name Fluffytail? 'And hop and jump and skip and romp and cavort—'

'Running can be nice,' Louie interrupted after he had taken a second to catch his breath. 'But we have a job to do!'

'Job?' a much deeper voice asked as a much larger (approximately six-foot-high) rabbit bounded forward. Louie remembered this one, too.

'Bouncer!' the very large rabbit introduced himself anyway. 'Bouncer likes jobs. Bouncer can harvest carrots. Bouncer can gather lettuce.'

'Well,' Louie replied, 'this is a rather special job.'

'Bouncer can pick broccoli!' the large rabbit insisted.

'Broccoli?' the prince of the jungle perked up. 'Zabana like broccoli!'

'Bunnies like all sorts of vegetables!' Fluffytail explained. 'Carrots and lettuce and broccoli and cauliflower and brussel sprouts and hubbard squash and water chestnuts—'

Big Louie couldn't allow himself to be distracted.

'This is a job that only bunnies can do,' he interrupted again.

'Bunnies are Zabana's friends!' the jungle prince added helpfully.

'It is only with your help,' Louie continued, 'that we can hope to defeat—' he paused appropriately, '—Doctor Dread.'

'Doctor Dread?' asked another one of the bunnies, whose name might have been Spottynose or Bentear or something like that. 'Who's Doctor Dread?'

'Bouncer likes Zabana, too!' The very large rabbit extended a welcoming paw, which the jungle prince regarded with great interest.

Who's Doctor Dread? Now Louie was confused. The last time they had been in these parts, the bunnies had spent all their time tormenting the snake-suited villain with cream pies and exploding carrots. How could the bunnies not know Doctor Dread when they spent so long fighting him?

But Fluffytail thumped his right rear paw in comprehension. 'You mean Malevelo!'

Of course! How could Louie have forgotten? When Doctor Dread was on the bunny planet, he didn't wear snakeskin, he wore wizard's robes! This animated world was, after all, the place where Doctor Dread fitted in all too well, and, instead of controlling the forces in the Cineverse, he found himself being controlled. Just as Captain Crusader had been transformed into the beach bunny Dee Dee Davenport on the surfing world, so was Doctor Dread totally changed on this bunny planet, becoming the easily angered but thoroughly ineffectual wizard Malevelo!

'Yes,' Big Louie agreed. 'Malevelo.'

All the bunnies booed and hissed.

The jungle prince broke his pensive silence. 'Broccoli Zabana's friend, too.'

'Broccoli is nice and green,' Bouncer agreed with an eager nod.

'Also good source of calcium,' Zabana added. He shook the bunny's paw at last.

Louie was impressed. The jungle prince and the very large rabbit seemed to have found a strange, intellectual rapport. Well – now that he looked at the two of them again – maybe not intellectual.

'Faith and begorah!' Officer O'Clanrahan interjected in a brittle voice. 'Shouldn't we be gettin' a move on?'

Even in a world as animated as this, Big Louie could still sense the officer's discomfort. Perhaps, if Louie could take a little time away from his leadership role to pursue more of his natural side-kick duties, he might be able to determine what was bothering the policeman. But sidekicking, and Officer O'Clanrahan's discomfort, would have to wait until they had defeated Doctor Dread. Besides which, Louie had to admit, O'Clanrahan was right. Now that they'd met the bunnies, there was no time for delay.

'Well, what do you say, bunnies?' he called to the assembled rabbithood. 'We need you to come with us, so that we can defeat Doctor Dread, stop the Change, and save the Cineverse!'

'Tarnation!' Doc exclaimed. 'Now *that's* a summary!'

Louie allowed himself the slightest of smiles. At least he could still fit in some of his sidekick talents.

'With a summary like that,' Fluffytail agreed, 'how could any creatures as warm and cuddly and fluffy and cute and loyal and true as bunnies possibly say no?'

The other bunnies cheered.

'We'll all go!' Fluffytail announced as his fellows cheered a second time.

Officer O'Clanrahan leaned close to Louie's ear. 'Saints alive! We can't take all of them! And do we dare to take them from here?'

Louie nodded. Officer O'Clanrahan may have been a worrier, but both his objections were well taken. With the Change happening all around them, it was wise to expose themselves to as few risks as possible. As light as the bunnies were, they certainly couldn't take all of them. In fact, Louie guessed, from what he knew about Cineverse ring theory and the current weight of his comrades, they couldn't accommodate more than a dozen of their fluffy friends – considerably less, if Bouncer was one of the chosen bunnies.

It was O'Clanrahan's second point, though, that really caused Louie concern. A simple review of the facts showed that when they attempted to reach the bunny world, they had landed on a muscleman planet that had somehow got itself attached. Now, if they left directly from the bunny world, would the Change allow them to reach their next destination, or send them somewhere else altogether? Perhaps it would be best if they returned to the point on the muscleman world where they had come in. Using the ring there would minimize complications, wouldn't it?

This was all too complicated for a sidekick to handle! Louie felt his brain overloading. He wanted to stop where he was, and not do a thing until the hero showed up.

But the hero was gone, and Louie had to take over. He had to force himself to move and make a decision.

If he didn't, both Doctor Dread and the Change would win.

CHAPTER FIFTEEN

Dread stared at his henchmen. Professor Peril, Menge the Merciless, and Big Bertha all stared at Mother Antoinette. Except, now that she had lost her whip, she didn't feel like much of a mother any more. In fact, Antoinette hadn't experienced anywhere near this sort of tension since her dear husband had passed away.

In the silence, she could hear the heavy boots of Dread's guards stomping down the hallway towards them.

'Wait a second!' Professor Peril interrupted. 'Can't you see what's happening?'

'Certainly I can see!' Dread retorted with a harsh laugh. 'You are to be—' he hesitated meaningfully, '—dealt with. You are to be—' he paused tellingly, '—taken care of.'

'But why?' Peril shot back. 'Don't you see what has taken place here? I come back to the Citadel of Dread, the greatest repository of evil in all the known Cineverse, and what do I find? People hiding in closets and under the bed! This does not sound like what should happen on a world famed for suspense and treachery! No, it sounds to me far more like—' it was his turn to pause, the mouth beneath his pencil-thin moustache twisting into a triumphant grin, '—screwball comedy.'

Doctor Dread's mouth fell open, his anger replaced by total shock. 'Screwball—' he began.

It was then that the guards chose to break down the door, a half-dozen burly men in uniform, led by another whose suit was so festooned by medals and gold braid that he had to be their captain.

'Halt and surrender!' the Captain of the Guard called out. 'In the name of Doctor Dread! There is no mercy in this Citadel, and no hope for those who oppose it! Stand where you are, and face your obliteration like the scum—'

Doctor Dread cleared his throat. 'Captain? If I might interrupt?'

The Captain of the Guard snapped to attention. 'Yessir, your vileness!'

'Aren't you talking a bit much—' Dread hesitated as he stared at the knuckles of his snakeskin glove, '—before you *deal* with the prisoners?'

'S-sorry, your corruptness,' the Captain of the Guard stammered. 'It's just that, as a villain in good standing, I have to explain my actions at some length, especially before I obliterate someone—'

'It *is* a law of the Cineverse,' Professor Peril pointed out.

'And, well—' The Captain of the Guard paused as he stared down at the newly polished marble floor. 'It's just that I get to say these dramatically charged things so seldom, what with the fearsome reputation this place has, and we guards have so few opportunities to strike terror into the hearts of interlopers, much less that all-important opportunity to obliterate them—'

'Perhaps—' Doctor Dread interrupted and hesitated almost simultaneously, '—we should wait a bit before we perform any – obliteration.' He turned back to Professor Peril. 'Screwball – comedy, did you say?'

Peril answered with a smug nod. 'People hiding in closets and under the bed? What else would you call it?'

'Like a—' Dread paused thoughtfully, '—screwball *bedroom* comedy?'

'Here? At the Citadel of Dread? The very heart of evil incarnate?' Menge's eyes grew wide with terror. His voice quavered as he spoke: 'But that means—'

'The Change!' Big Bertha finished for him.

'Yes, it is here, too.' Doctor Dread nodded his snakeskin-cowled head solemnly. 'No place in the Cineverse – not even our beloved citadel – is – immune from the Change!'

Mother Antoinette looked from face to face. Everyone else seemed rather upset, didn't they? And all about some sort of change. She herself had been here such a short time, she wouldn't recognize any sort of change unless it came up and bit her. Which, she realized abruptly, could actually happen (the biting, that is) in a place like this.

In the midst of all this chaos, however, there was one thing she was certain of – that everything would be fine the moment she got her whip back.

'Which means—' Doctor Dread continued with the requisite hesitation, '—that I must reconsider my actions.'

'No obliteration, your surliness?' The Captain of the Guard could not keep the disappointment out of his voice.

Doctor Dread glanced at the others. 'No – at least not at present.'

Everyone sighed, the Captain and his guards from frustration, everyone else from relief.

'Have no fear!' their snake-suited leader added quickly. 'The way our plot is progressing, you will have no end of obliteration ahead of you.'

The Captain of the Guard looked at Doctor Dread, a glimmer of hope again in his gaze. 'Do you really think so, your dreadfulness?'

'Oh, yes. And more than obliteration, too. There will be plenty of time for—' he paused to savour every word, '—freelance pillaging, diabolical laughter and general humiliation of the enemy!'

'Really?' The Captain of the Guard saluted sharply as he snapped to attention. 'Oh, your hideousness! I knew I wouldn't be sorry when I signed up at the Citadel of Dread.'

'No sir, Captain,' Doctor Dread replied smoothly but slowly. 'Now, if you and your guard – retire, I must – discuss my future plans with my – elite associates.'

He turned back to the others in the room, a grimness spread across his hawklike countenance. Apparently, Antoinette realized, they had all been forgiven.

Why didn't this turn of events make her feel more relieved? She was still so uncertain.

'Our time—' the bad doctor paused in a studied sort of way, '—is limited. Those of you who were here the last time will remember the symptoms – movie worlds shifting and combining, all of the Cineverse thrown into chaos. Except this time – according to our plans, it will be much worse. As the Change progresses, it will be our task to make sure certain worlds and individuals – namely us – remain triumphant. To that end, it is time to send – some of you – on a mission.'

'Mission?' Professor Peril perked up. 'That's what I like – action, and plenty of it!'

'Excellent,' Doctor Dread purred. 'Then you will not mind going to a certain place to remove certain pesky—' He paused again, although this time it seemed not so much for dramatic effect as from a genuine difficulty to speak the next two words that issued from his mouth.

'Fl-fluffy—' he managed at last, '—b-bun-bun-bunnies!'

'Bunnies?' Antoinette asked doubtfully. 'How do I kill bunnies?'

But Doctor Dread's oily smile was already back in place. 'Alas,

Mother Antoinette, I think we would be better served if you stayed—' he paused suggestively, '—behind. There is much—' he stopped insinuatingly, '—planning to be done.' His hand snaked out to stroke her black leather glove. 'Perhaps – we can discuss our – more personal future plans.'

'What gives you—' Menge the Merciless began.

'Still throwing your weight—' Professor Peril muttered.

'Men!' Bertha somehow managed to spit out the word, even though it contained no 's' sounds.

All three paused abruptly after a glance at the still-present guards. Doctor Dread smiled and continued his attentions.

Antoinette stared down at the snake-covered fingers playing about her wrist. What exactly was this man implying? She only knew one thing for certain – there was but a single way she could handle this.

She pulled her arm away.

'Only if you give me back my whip,' was her reply.

Doctor Dread frowned for an instant, then shrugged. 'If – you insist. Perhaps there is a place for – your whip in our – future as well.'

Mother Antoinette's fingers closed round the reassuringly solid whip handle. She felt a certain peace and determination flood into her soul with that weight back in her hand, but more than that, too. She knew who she was now, and where she was going.

'I'll say there's a place for my whip!' she shouted with a laugh.

CRACK the whip danced. *CRACK* *CRACK*

Doctor Dread leapt away as the Captain and all his guards hastily fled the room.

'Mother Antoinette!' their leader demanded. 'What do you intend – to do?'

She paused to look at the man in snakeskin green. After his recent actions, did he deserve an answer? And what of the others? Did speedy Peril, strong Bertha, and even her beloved, cowering Mengy deserve an explanation? Part of her wanted the others to know everything that was welling within her, but how could mere words do justice to what she was feeling?

She decided it was time to let her whip do her talking for her.

CRACK *CRACK* *CRACK*

The leather thong struck, first at the left side, then the right, of Dread's pencil-thin moustache, trimming away the errant hairs. The Doctor's mouth opened in amazement as she studied her handiwork. Her tonsorial efforts weren't quite as even as she might have liked, but she was getting better control with every passing moment. This whip was no longer a mere tool in her hand – it was an extension of her very being.

CRACK

Doctor Dread covered his upper lip and whimpered.

CRACK *CRACK*

Menge, Peril, and Bertha all covered various vulnerable parts of their anatomies.

CRACK *CRACK* *CRACK*

Mother Antoinette smiled. She had found her place in the Cineverse at last. And with her place, she had once again found her voice as well.

'So, Doctor Dread,' she said slowly, each word weighted by her crimson lips, 'you wished to have some – private words?'

'Oh, dear. Perhaps—' Doctor Dread flinched as he hesitated, '—it would be a better idea for you to – go with the others.'

'Never!' Peril blurted. 'Don't change because—'

'Oh, no!' Menge interjected. 'Your needs come—'

'We wouldn't think of depriving you—' Bertha added.

All three of them stopped as Antoinette smiled in their direction. The whip handle undulated in her hand like a living thing.

'Oh, Mother Antoinette,' Peril began in an uncertain voice, 'most certainly, if you'd like to come along—'

'So sorry,' Menge quickly added. 'We misunderstood—'

Bertha nodded eagerly. 'We're ready to go any time *you're* ready!'

Doctor Dread cleared his throat, apparently trying to regain some of his villainous composure. 'Very well. You know what to do. Take one of your rings and—' his voice died as he swallowed, '—and – go.'

He lifted a fist into the air, and forced himself to continue. 'Deal with the b-bun – bun—' He took a deep breath. 'Make sure – certain animals are taken care of, like b-bun – b-b-bun—' He shook his head to rid himself of the stutter. 'There is no more time for hesitation when it comes to b-bu-bu—' He raised both fists in the air. 'Obliterate them!'

Professor Peril took the lead. 'Very well. Gather round – all of you.' He waited until Menge, Bertha and Antoinette had grabbed on to his army fatigues. 'See you in the funny papers!'

Mother Antoinette frowned. There was that blue smoke again. How could she control the Cineverse if she didn't know where the blue smoke came from?

But, even as her world was lost in roiling blue, she knew the answer was in her hand. The whip was an excellent tool to loosen tongues, and it would never leave her grip again! Woe betide the individual who tried, man or woman, from that master of evil, Doctor Dread, all the way down to her ineffectual son Roger!

'Here come the bunnies!' Peril announced as the smoke started to clear.

'Kill them quickly,' Bertha instructed. 'And, whatever you do, don't look at their large, pink, incredibly trusting eyes.'

'It's best you don't look too closely at their wonderfully soft fur, either,' Menge added. He sounded much more like his old self, because, Mother Antoinette surmised, they were once again about to face action. Either that, or the blue smoke prevented him from staring at her whip.

'Yeah,' Peril added grimly. 'I'd also advise you to keep away from any study of their amazingly adorable pink paw pads.'

'Or their constantly moving and oh-so-cuddly noses,' Menge continued painfully.

'And those fuzzy and fluffy pointy little ears,' Bertha concluded between gritted teeth.

'It's tough being a villain,' Peril summarized for all of them. 'Stomping bunnies is the ultimate test.'

Mother Antoinette curled the whip around both of her hands as the last of the smoke cleared. It was a test she would have to be ready for.

And then the smoke was gone. But there didn't seem to be any bunnies. Instead, there was a big rock, with three large, heavily muscled men – and you could see *all* their muscles with what little they were wearing – in front of it.

'Halt!' one of the magnificently muscled men called out as he raised his sword. 'In the name of Hippolita!'

Peril looked quickly at his fellows. 'What do we do about this? This place looks prehistoric. Our weapons will never work here!'

Mother Antoinette stepped forward. 'There's nothing wrong with my whip!'

'Halt, we said,' one of the musclemen repeated. 'Or face the combined might of the Son of Samson, the Nephew of Hercules, and the Second Cousin of Goliath!'

Menge laid a hand on Antoinette's leather-clad shoulder. 'Can your whip handle all three of them?'

She glanced disdainfully at the hand on her shoulder. Menge quickly jerked his fingers back. She stepped forward, eager to see how far her whip could take her.

CHAPTER SIXTEEN

The noise alone was enough to freeze his bones.

Even though he was still surrounded by the Plotmaster's blue smoke, Roger could tell he had reached the new world from the sound of the wind. It howled about him, first soft and mournful, like a creature in pain, then loud and discordant, like a chorus of the doomed. It was the loneliest sound he had ever heard, and it reminded him that he had been sent to face Doctor Dread – alone.

He felt a great hopelessness weigh down his arms and legs, as if the wind was pressing him into the earth. What could he, Roger Gordon, public relations man from Earth, do against the ultimate master of evil?

But before he could have another depressing thought, the insistent wind blew the smoke away, and he saw he was on a grey, rocky plane, standing next to a dog.

'Bark! Yip! Bark!' The white German shepherd by his side wagged its tail enthusiastically.

Roger had almost forgotten – he wasn't alone. Dwight was here, too. The Plotmaster had rescued both of them, along with Professor Peril, from a certain watery grave, and it only made sense that the Plotmaster would send both of them here. And it wasn't simply Roger Gordon, or a simple canine, who now faced the forces of evil. It was the new Captain Crusader, with his trusty helper, Dwight the wonder dog.

'Think good thoughts,' Roger mused aloud, 'and good things happen.' There. He felt better already – like somebody who could be Captain Crusader.

'Yip, arf arf!' Dwight agreed.

At least, agreement was what Roger thought Dwight was trying to communicate. Now that he considered it, his relationship with this dog was a little frustrating. After all, both Louie and the Plotmaster seemed to be able to tell outright what Dwight was saying. Shouldn't Captain Crusader be able to do the same?

Well, maybe Roger shouldn't rush that sort of thing – he seemed to find new dimensions to his emerging hero status with every passing adventure. The ability to talk to animals could show up at any moment.

'Bark! Bark yip!' Dwight interjected. Roger looked down to see the dog was pointing like a hunting hound, the shepherd's nose showing Roger the way to – what? Roger turned round to follow the imaginary line the dog was indicating.

Oh. There, behind him, was an immense grey building, suitable for your average mad scientist, or, considering its size, perhaps three or four mad scientists. What had the Plotmaster called it? The Citadel of Dread? Well, it was certainly well-named.

'Yip yip bark!' Dwight urged for emphasis.

So that was where Roger was supposed to go? He had to give Dwight credit. There was more than one way for a wonder dog to communicate.

'OK, Dwight,' Roger said aloud. 'Let's get on with it.' He frowned at the immense grey structure in front of them. From this angle, there didn't seem to be a window or other opening less than thirty feet from the ground. 'But how do we get inside?'

'Yip!' Dwight replied as he bounced back and forth, tail wagging. 'Arf, arf!'

'Do you know how to get in there?' Roger asked incredulously.

'Bark bark!' Dwight insisted. 'Yip arf!'

'OK, fella,' Roger agreed with a laugh. 'Lead on.'

The wonder dog did as he was told, bounding ahead to circle the left-hand side of the citadel. Roger ran after him, following the dog into a depression that ran close to the giant structure's featureless wall – and it was quite a depression, too – as deep as Roger was tall.

That's when he heard it again. Music.

As soon as they were sheltered from the wind, Roger was once more aware of that orchestra that seemed to come from nowhere – and everywhere. Except, this time, the orchestra's music was even less pleasant than the time before. The horns and drums he had heard back on the car chase world were gone, replaced by screeching violins.

Roger almost froze. He knew what happened in movies when you heard screeching violins.

Heard screeching violins? Music that came from nowhere – and everywhere?

Of course! That was where all this music was really coming from. He had been thinking too literally when he had looked around for a source of the sound back on that car chase cop planet. The music was behind them – and all around them – in the background! Every good movie had to have background music to heighten emotions and increase the tension. Why would the movie worlds of the Cineverse be any different? And he, since he had become Captain Crusader, had gained the ability to hear it!

He marvelled again at his new-found power. No wonder Captain Crusader was the hero's hero! When you could hear that anticipatory background music, you could be ready for anything!

Roger's elation, however, only lasted until he thought of the next, logical question:

What should you be ready for when you heard screeching violins?

Something nasty, was the first answer he came up with. Probably something deadly.

'Bark! Yip! Arf!'

Roger looked down at Dwight the wonder dog, who danced before him, eager to get on with it. Roger realized he had stopped for a moment, lost in thought. That was no way for the hero's hero to act, and it appeared to be Dwight's duty to tell him so. After all, if Roger thought about this in movie terms, the dog had become his sidekick now, and it was therefore Dwight's job to advance the action. There were certain laws of the Cineverse, apparently, that would even survive the Change.

'OK, fella!' Roger acknowledged. For now, he would choose to ignore those insistent violins. 'Let's go!'

Dwight led the way again, out of the gully they had been travelling through – it actually looked rather like a half-completed moat – and round to the far side of the huge grey structure.

Roger grinned. This side was different. There, at the top of a mammoth staircase in the centre of the immense building's huge wall, were two equally massive doors.

But, before Roger could even exclaim 'Good boy!' he also realized that the doors came equipped with half a dozen incredibly burly guards, all sporting nasty-looking machine guns.

Roger felt something at his back. But not pressing into his back, no, it was more like somebody had grabbed his jogging jacket. That somebody pulled.

Roger was yanked off his feet. He fell on his back behind a low, dirt wall that led back to the gully. Dwight stood above his head. The dog growled softly in his ear.

Roger looked back. The two of them were alone. That meant it had to have been Dwight, with his lightning-fast canine reflexes, who had grabbed Roger's jogging jacket and pulled him back to safety before the guards could spot him.

'What a wonder dog!' Roger whispered.

'Arf, bark,' the dog replied humbly. He lifted himself on to his hind legs so that he could peer over the dirt wall. After a moment, apparently satisfied, he lowered himself back to all fours and looked at Roger.

'Bark! Yip yip!' Dwight chided softly.

'You're right,' Roger agreed. 'We have to be more careful.' Wait a second. He had just responded to Dwight as if he'd actually understood the dog! But, then again, there had been a certain something about the canine's tone—

'But how can we get in there if we can't use the front door?'

Dwight put his nose to the ground, and began to sniff intently about their immediate surroundings, slowly wandering back down into the gully.

After a moment, he made a small yelp of discovery. Dwight pawed at the dirt around whatever it was he had found. Roger got quickly to his feet and stepped forward to look over the dog's shoulder. There, set flush with the muddy ground, was a small, neatly lettered, white cardboard sign which read: SECRET TRAP DOOR RELEASE.

The words were followed by an arrow. And, inches from the business end of that arrow, was a small, shiny brown knob.

'Should we?' Roger asked, still keeping his voice low.

'Bark!' Dwight insisted. He grabbed the knob between his mighty canine jaws and pulled.

There was a faint grinding noise somewhere beneath them, as if ancient machinery long disused had gone back into action.

Dwight barked softly as the ground fell away before them. The secret trap door had opened, forming a ramp that led below.

Roger followed the dog down into the darkness. The ramp sloped downward for maybe a dozen paces, then levelled off when, Roger guessed, they reached the true floor of the tunnel. It wasn't totally lightless down here, he realized. There was some dim illumination up ahead, an uneven light coming from what looked like a distant, sputtering torch.

Something boomed behind them. Roger spun round, but

couldn't see anything beyond the dim tunnel. In fact, he could no longer see the ramp. The trap door had slammed shut behind them.

Slamming trap doors reminded him of nothing so much as haunted houses. He remembered before, when he had looked up at the fortress and thought of mad scientists. Could the Citadel of Dread be part of a horror movie world?

'Arf, bark yip!' Dwight called from up ahead. The dog must want Roger to follow him. And why not? Dwight hadn't steered him wrong yet.

And so they walked, down endless, featureless corridors, lit every hundred feet or so by what were indeed sputtering torches. At first, Roger was on his guard, expecting things to jump from side corridors or hidden passageways. But nothing did, and Dwight continued to trot on ahead, turning occasionally as, Roger guessed, his nose dictated. After a few minutes, or perhaps a few hours, Roger began to think of these corridors as *truly* endless. This was like a horror movie, too – a particularly bad one, which padded its few moments of plot with endless scenes of people travelling from place to place. Maybe, Roger thought, he should ask the wonder dog where they were going. That was, of course, if he could somehow understand the canine's answer. Roger realized, for the first time since he had came to the Cineverse, he was actually getting a little bored. He wondered if this, too, was another aspect of the Change.

Then the music returned, more insistent than ever – and all violins. Violins went with horror movies, too, but they tended to swirl a lot in those films with ghosts and mad scientists. These violins, on the other hand, were definitely screeching, and Roger knew what kind of horror movies those kind of violins showed up in – the kind with knives and other sharp and unpleasant instruments of death.

Dwight whined softly. The dog knew something was wrong as well.

'What is it, boy?' Roger asked.

The dog growled deep in its throat.

'I don't understand.'

Dwight replied with a series of short, staccato barks.

Roger could only shake his head. He was really stumped this time. 'I still don't get it,' he admitted. But, from the way the dog was acting, it had to be important.

The German shepherd stared at Roger for a long moment –

almost as if the dog was considering how best to communicate. At long last, Dwight lifted a paw to tug at his ear.

'Ear?' Roger asked uncertainly. 'Am I supposed to listen for something?

Dwight shook his head and pawed at his ear again.

'Not supposed to hear? Something about sound?'

Dwight whined and kept on pawing. That meant Roger was getting close!

'Sound?' Roger asked as his mind searched wildly for meaning. 'Sounds like?'

The wonder dog nodded rapidly as he barked in the affirmative.

Roger still didn't quite understand. 'But sounds like what?'

Dwight hopped friskily back and forth.

'Move?' Roger ventured. 'Hop? Jump?'

Dwight's pace became more agitated as he trotted back and forth along the width of the corridor.

'Fast? Speed? Run?'

Dwight stopped abruptly and nodded his sleek white head.

'Run?' Roger clapped his hands. He had got it at last! 'Sounds like run? Ton? Fun? Bun?'

Dwight sat there and watched him. Roger hadn't guessed it yet.

'Sun?' he tried. 'Gun?'

Dwight leapt up and down, silently but with great animation.

'Gun?' Roger said, more to himself than to the dog. 'Somebody's got a gun?' That could go a long way towards explaining the violins.

Dwight lifted a paw in front of his muzzle, the closest a dog could get, Roger realized, to making a shushing sound. Roger stopped talking, and listened.

There was another sound in the distance – a voice, repeating a single word, over and over, a word that he couldn't quite hear over the music. But that voice was getting closer, and louder, as the violins built to a screaming crescendo. Then, as quickly as the music had begun, it was over.

Roger could hear that word clearly now, for the voice sounded as if it was very close. It was indeed saying a single word – and that word wasn't one Roger particularly looked forward to hearing.

'Obliterate,' was all the voice said. 'Obliterate.'

CHAPTER SEVENTEEN

It took far too long to select the bunnies.

Louie realized he had made a mistake as soon as he asked Fluffy-tail to help him choose – and Fluffytail's idea of decision-making was to let every bunny speak in turn. Spottynose thought only the bunnies with the most colourful markings should go. High-jumper, on the other hand, thought only the bunnies with the best leaping ability should be sent. Pointy-ears, however, remarked that bunnies should be chosen on the basis of unique personal traits. And Largebottom, well – it hurt Louie's brain to even think about all the different bunny arguments, especially since, when they quarrelled, they did it with those ridiculously high bunny voices.

And the arguments went nowhere. The Change would be over, the Cineverse destroyed, and the bunnies would still be discussing whether they should choose on the basis of tails or paws.

Louie had had enough. He lost control. He yelled at them. He told them to shut up. He further told them he never wanted to hear another bunny argument as long as he lived.

He was immediately confronted with the most profound silence he had ever heard – a silence intensified by a hundred pairs of incredibly cute, and incredibly hurt, bunny eyes, all two hundred of them boring straight into his soul.

'Uh, er—' Louie replied. 'Um, uh—' But no words came to mind, for what words could combat *that*? Louie had never felt this awful before, even in his brief career as a villain. It was only then that Louie truly realized what a powerful weapon he had at his disposal. Cute bunnies might have been a formidable foe, but hurt, cute bunnies would be virtually unstoppable.

'Zabana cannot face this!' the jungle prince cried, echoing Louie's sentiments.

'Dang straight!' Doc wailed. 'Choose these varmints, or, pledge or no pledge, I'm goin' back to the bottle!'

So Louie chose quickly, before all those eyes could overwhelm him again. He picked Bouncer for obvious reasons, Fluffytail for his leadership capabilities, and Highjumper because he was the only bunny whose argument had made any sense. After that, he picked the next four bunnies to Highjumper's left. Seven seemed like a lucky number. Besides, any more bunnies (especially considering the size of Bouncer) and Louie would be afraid of straining the limits of his Captain Crusader Decoder Ring.

He turned away quickly from all the bunnies that would have to be left behind. He knew, without even looking – while perhaps not as bad as hurt bunny eyes – disappointed bunny eyes would be more than his sidekick heart could bear.

But now it was time to leave, and face the might of Doctor Dread! He marched back towards the dark tunnel where they had entered Bunnyland, waving his fellows and the chosen bunnies to follow.

'Mother of Mercy!' Officer O'Clanrahan muttered as he joined Louie's rapid march. 'I'm glad that's over!'

In a way, Louie was surprised that the cop even knew what was going on. The officer had certainly kept his distance from the bunnies – in fact, lately he seemed to be keeping his distance from everyone. Without Dwight the wonder dog around, the policeman seemed to be disintegrating before Louie's eyes, the once proud officer always hanging back and muttering to himself. In all his years as a sidekick, Louie didn't think he had ever seen such a change.

But perhaps 'change' was the key word to everything in the Cineverse. Maybe the Change didn't just affect movie worlds. Maybe it affected individuals as well.

That thought was not comforting in the least. If O'Clanrahan was changing, perhaps all of them were changing as well, in ways they couldn't imagine – or worse, ways they might not even notice. Louie had spent great amounts of energy trying to rid himself of his role in sidekick comedy relief. But now that his personality might be altering without his control, he found it very frightening.

'But—' one of the bunnies yelled out from the pack that he had left behind, '—you can't leave yet!'

Oh, no. Louie might be frightened now, but if he had to take one more look at those bunny eyes, he might become downright suicidal.

'That's right!' Louie cringed as another bunny called out: 'We need to send you off with a happy bunny song!'

Somewhere nearby, a very happy orchestra began to play as scores of rabbits lifted their high soprano voices in song:

'We've got the grass and the sky of blue,
We've got flowers and carrots, too.
Life with bunnies is so profound.
There's always more bunnies to go around!'

'That's the spirit!' Fluffytail called back from close by Louie's side. 'Second verse!'

The amassed bunnydom answered in song:

'Days grow short and time just flies,
But with bunnies your cheer just multiplies!
Every time you look out there in the sun,
There's always more bunnies having fun!'

Louie had to admit, now that he thought of it, that there could be worse ways of marching to battle than with a cheerful song at your back. Heck, he'd even forgotten about whatever it was he'd been worrying about a moment ago. With bunnies on his side, how could he help but win?

They had once again reached the entrance to the cave. Louie boldly strode forward into the darkness.

'Yay, bunnies!' Bouncer's loud but none too bright voice echoed around him. 'Verse number three!'

'We bunnies like to stick around,
We'll even follow you underground!
We can hop at all different speeds,
There's always more bunnies to meet your needs!'

'Halt!' Zabana said from somewhere just ahead. 'We have reached the Pit!'

Louie squinted. Not having Zabana's jungle-trained senses, he couldn't see much of anything. He looked aloft, and saw a distant circle of light, the upper entrance to the pit, a hundred yards and more above them.

'Is ladder here,' the jungle prince explained from somewhere in the nearby gloom. 'Can climb back up!'

'Faith and begorah!' Officer O'Clanrahan moaned. 'It'll take us for ever to climb up there!'

'Not if you have bunnies to help you along!' one of the nearby rabbits cheered.

Louie felt a strong hand grab his wrist.

'Here,' Zabana explained. 'Ladder in front of you.'

With Zabana's guidance, Louie reached forward, and indeed did feel a wooden rung of what must be the ladder that reached all the way to the top of the pit.

'You leader,' Zabana added. 'You go first.'

Yes, Louie guessed he was the leader, and he'd better lead. He felt around with his foot until he found a lower rung, then pushed himself up the ladder.

'Doc, you next. Then O'Clanrahan. Zabana help bunnies.'

'Bouncer help bunnies, too!'

Louie pulled himself up slowly, feeling his way up the ladder a couple of rungs at a time. He was glad some of the others were taking turns giving orders – it was somehow reassuring to the sidekick in his soul.

'They're on their way!' a rabbit voice called from down below. 'Fourth verse, guys!'

And the bunny chorus replied:

> 'Oh, bunnies are the loving sort,
> We can play and we cavort.
> Till we're once again in the family way;
> There's always more bunnies to save the day!'

At least, Louie thought, the song gave him a little additional rhythm with which to climb. In fact, it seemed to be getting lighter already. He could see the ladder in front of him now – quite clearly, actually. They must be making some progress.

'Whoo-ee!' Doc whistled from just beneath. 'Look where we've got to.'

'Hey guys!' The bunny voice seemed incredibly distant. 'Is it time for the fifth verse?'

Louie looked up. That tiny point of light he had seen above them was now a great blue circle in the sky. They were almost there!

'Why,' he muttered aloud, 'we're almost to the top!'

'Never seen its like,' Doc agreed from just below, 'in all my years as an animal trainer.' He spat in the darkness. 'Not to mention the time I put in as a high-wire trapeze artist.'

So, Movie Magic had worked again, and the bunny song had shortened their climb considerably. Louie had to admit it, despite the danger of the Change, there were certain advantages to having your adventure in a place like the Cineverse. Faintly, he heard the bunnies begin verse number five:

> 'We like to hop and we like to jump,
> When we're in the dark bunnies like to—'

'Who challenges me from the Pit of Absurdity?' a woman's voice shouted, drowning out the distant song.

Now that they had left the rabbits behind, they would once again have to face Hippolita and her boys. Louie took a deep breath and pulled himself up the final rung of the ladder so that he could see over the lip of the pit.

But it wasn't Hippolita who glowered at him. It was a somewhat older woman, with blonde hair and a whip. Still, there was something very familiar about her, despite her black leather costume – wasn't she Roger's mother?

'Who dares to stare at Mother Antoinette?' she demanded. The whip danced in her hand.

'Oh,' another, only slightly less forceful female voice interjected. 'Not you again.'

It was Bertha – his sister. And next to her stood Menge the Merciless and Professor Peril. Big Louie had climbed into a den of evil!

'So, pardner!' Doc called from down below. 'What's holding things up?'

'Uh,' Louie replied as tactfully as he could. 'We've got some probl—'

'How dare you not answer me, worm?' Mother Antoinette's voice cut him off mid-word.

'Um.' Louie's head snapped back up. He had forgotten all about the woman with the whip. Who should he talk to first? Sidekicks shouldn't have to make these sorts of decisions!

The whip snaked round his neck, pulling him from the top of the ladder and throwing him on to the ground a half dozen feet from the pit. Louie grabbed at the leather. He couldn't breathe.

'And you claim to know this toad?' Mother Antoinette asked Bertha.

'I'm afraid so,' Bertha admitted. 'I'm afraid he's my brother.'

'But he's on the other side!' Menge added helpfully.

'No mercy,' Professor Peril added succinctly, 'not even for relatives!'

Mother Antoinette smiled grimly. 'You forget who my son is.' She jerked her hand back, and the whip left Louie's neck. 'No mercy, *especially* for relatives!'

Louie massaged his neck as he gasped for air. He had got his fellows into this mess. How could he get them out of it?

'Now hold on a second there, little lady,' Doc drawled from where he now stood at the edge of the pit. 'That's no way to talk about kin.'

Mother Antoinette flicked her wrist.

CRACK the whip snapped in the air. *CRACK* *CRACK* *CRACK*

Doc glanced distractedly down at the twin pearl-handled revolvers at his gunbelt. 'These danged things won't work in these here parts, will they?'

Mother Antoinette allowed herself a small smile.

'A whip works anywhere.'

Louie's hand involuntarily returned to his neck. He'd had enough of being a hero.

Where was Captain Crusader when you really needed him?

CHAPTER EIGHTEEN

Obliterate?

That's what this stranger was saying. Not only that, but according to Dwight's sign language, this guy had a gun. And the Plotmaster hadn't given Roger any kind of weapon at all! He was totally unarmed, except, perhaps, for his wits.

'Bark!' Dwight remarked reassuringly. 'Arf! Bark!'

'Oblit—' The nearby voice paused in its destructive chant. 'Was that a dog?'

Uh-oh. Dwight had made a tactical error. The wonder dog wagged his tail a bit sheepishly.

'Well,' the ever-nearer voice asserted, 'I can obliterate a dog, too! Here, poochy, poochy!'

Dwight looked at Roger in disbelief, and Roger had to agree. Poochy, poochy?

'There you are!' The owner of the voice, a man in a guard's uniform festooned with medals, stepped out of an intersecting corridor, and quickly drew his gun.

Dwight the wonder dog was faster. He leapt forward with a speed and ferocity that Roger hadn't seen before, as if the canine had a special vendetta against this guard. And, Roger realized, perhaps he did. Perhaps anyone who called Dwight the wonder dog 'poochy poochy' would have faced such retribution.

The guard didn't stand a chance against the animal's superior reflexes. Dwight bowled the human over, and the gun went flying as the dog's momentum carried him over the fallen guard to bounce against the wall beyond.

'Stop where you are!' Roger instructed as the guard struggled to get up and retrieve his gun. 'We've got you outnumbered!' He whistled to the dog. 'C'mon, Dwight. Let's round up our prisoner and see if we can get him to talk!'

But Dwight didn't move. He sat in the spot where he had bounced, and looked quizzically at Roger. 'Yip?'

Something was wrong. 'Dwight, fella!' Roger called. 'What's the matter?'

The wonder dog looked at the wall, then back at Roger. 'Yip?'

Oh, no. Dwight wasn't responding well at all. Roger realized the dog must have bounced off the wall head first.

The guard saw that something was wrong, too. He jumped for his gun, and he got it.

'Yip?' Dwight remarked.

'Now the tables have turned,' the guard announced with a grin as he once again brandished his weapon, a nasty, futuristic-looking revolver. 'Doctor Dread did not make me Captain of the Guard for nothing! Now, I can obliterate you trespassing scum at my leisure.'

'Yip?' Dwight interjected.

'That's correct,' the Captain of the Guard continued, as if answering the dog's question. 'It is my job – and I take pleasure in doing it – to destroy any and all who have the temerity to enter Doctor Dread's domain unauthorized! You should take this last moment to dwell on the suicidal foolishness of your plans, before I pull the trigger on my Obliteration Ray and blow a hole in your mid-section the size of a cannon ball!'

'Uh.' Roger couldn't help himself. 'Excuse me?'

The Captain of the Guard looked up from aiming his Obliteration Ray. 'Yes?'

'Do you always talk at such length before blowing people away?'

The Captain reddened slightly. 'Well, I have so few chances – I mean, villains are supposed to—' He cleared his throat. 'Look, it's a failing of mine, all right?' He once again lifted and aimed his weapon. 'Now. Do you have any final words before your guts are splattered all over this underground passageway?'

This, Roger realized, was the real (and perhaps final) opportunity for him to use his wits, as Roger or as Captain Crusader. But what could he say upon meeting a potential assassin? There was only time to repeat the first thing that came into Roger's head:

'First impressions are always the most important.'

The look of anger on the guard's face was replaced by an odd little smile. 'If you say so—' he began pleasantly, but shook his head violently. '—No! You may be disguised in that dirty blue jogging suit, but I know who you are! You're Captain Crusader!'

Roger shrugged his shoulders. Were his sayings getting that obvious? Maybe he was doing something right.

'You won't fool me with those Captain Crusader expressions!' The guard clicked the safety off his nasty-looking weapon. 'My job is to obliterate you, and obliterate you I shall!'

Uh-oh. It was time for Roger to say something else.

'You may erase the answer,' he replied, 'but the problem still remains.'

'Really?' the guard remarked, open-mouthed. He seemed to have forgotten all about the gun. 'There's something about that that's almost – profound.' He shook his head. 'No! I won't be swayed by aphorisms! It's death for you, Captain Crusader!' But this time, when he aimed the Obliteration Ray, his hand was shaking. Roger could feel the situation turn to his advantage.

'Yip?' Dwight remarked uncertainly. And there, Roger thought, was his next saying.

'Death may come and death may go,' Roger said loudly, 'but a dog is a buddy for life!'

'Really?' The Captain of the Guard seemed to be blinking back tears. 'That's beautiful!' His gun hand dropped again. 'How can I shoot somebody who says things like that?'

It was time for Roger to deliver the one-two punch. Maybe a new variation of something tried-and-true would do to start.

'Killing Captain Crusader,' Roger announced, 'is like a day without sunshine.'

'How true!' The Captain of the Guard's frown was twisting into a rapturous smile. Still, Roger didn't feel it was time to stop, yet. He needed a final saying for that capper. This time, the words flowed from his tongue:

'A bad deed is like a piece of manure, rotting in the darkness, but a good deed grows like a flower!'

'Wow!' The guardsman tossed his gun to the ground. 'I give up! I can't help it. I'm on your side now.'

'Really?' Roger replied, then realized that might not be the best answer for someone who was supposed to be as decisive as Captain Crusader. 'Really!' he exclaimed, turning his question into a positive exclamation. 'Captain Crusader is everybody's friend!'

The guardsman nodded eagerly. 'That's the positive attitude I like to hear! Now that I'm working for Captain Crusader, what could possibly go wrong?'

'Yip?' Dwight answered.

The wonder dog was still not himself. When Dwight rammed

his head against the wall, he seemed to have lost something. Roger wondered if dogs could get amnesia.

'Yip?' Dwight repeated. He looked back at the wall, as if, perhaps, he had left his memory there when he bounced.

Roger couldn't stand to see the wonder dog in such a state. There had to be something – there *was* something he could do! Surely, if Captain Crusader could get one of Doctor Dread's minions to see the light, he should be able to help a stunned wonder canine.

'Dwight?' he called.

'Yip?' the dog replied. At least, Roger thought it was a reply. The dog was still staring at the wall.

'Listen, Dwight,' he insisted. But what should he say? Perhaps he should tailor this particular saying to canine interests. It certainly couldn't hurt. Still, with Dwight's current mental condition, he wanted to keep it simple.

'A police dog is your friend,' Roger tried.

'Yip?' Dwight answered.

That was it, huh? Maybe, Roger thought, he had kept it too simple. These Captain Crusader adages had started to come all too easily to him. Perhaps, for these things to really work, Captain Crusader had to break into a bit of a mental sweat.

'OK, Dwight,' he instructed the dog, who had turned back to look at Roger. 'It's important to listen to this one.'

'Yip?' At least the dog was answering, in his limited way. Roger was encouraged to try one more time. And this one had to be good. But what did *dogs* consider good? A clean food dish is a happy food dish? Still too simple. But perhaps food would make a proper subject matter.

'A bone in the mouth is good for today,' Roger said, slowly yet clearly, 'but a bone buried in the yard is for ever.'

Dwight stared at him for a long moment.

'Yip?' the dog said at last.

'I thought that one was pretty good,' the Captain of the Guard interjected.

Roger nodded grimly. He knew it was the best he could do. But, now that he really looked at the dog's vacant stare, he was afraid it wasn't only him. There was a real communication problem here. Ever since the dog bumped his head, Dwight just didn't seem to get it any more. How could he cure the dog if the dog couldn't understand him? There were limits to Captain Crusader's power after all.

'So,' the Captain of the Guard ventured. 'What do we do now, Captain Crusader?'

Roger glanced over at the eager guardsman. That question sounded suspiciously like another example of moving the plot along. With Dwight out of commission, would the Captain of the Guard take over the sidekick role? The mysterious ways of the Cineverse were truly staggering.

But the guard, sidekick or no, required an answer. Was this former minion of Doctor Dread really on Roger's side now? Roger remembered a time not so long ago when he had asked himself the same question about Big Louie, a sidekick who had turned out to be one of his staunchest allies.

Roger decided it was worth giving it a shot. What else would one expect of Captain Crusader?

'We must continue to the very heart of the Citadel of Dread,' he replied, 'so that we can capture Doctor Dread and put an end to his evil.'

'Gee,' the guard replied as his smile returned. 'You mean good guys can talk like that, too? Maybe this change of heart won't be so bad after all.'

The smile vanished from the guardsman's lips as he stared off into the distance. As the Captain spoke, Roger noticed the music was back too, with a full orchestra welling up behind him.

'Still,' the guardsman began solemnly, 'it won't be easy. This place is not called the Citadel of Dread for nothing. There'll be scores of heavily armed men, many of them as ruthless as I was only a moment ago. And there won't be only simple weapons like my Obliteration Ray to contend with – no, there'll be super-scientific marvels like the Zeta Ray and the Buchanan Device to contend with, all controlled by the most diabolical of Dread's henchpeople. And I haven't even mentioned the booby traps filled with wild animals and poisoned spikes and impossibly large boulders crashing out of nowhere! The Citadel is the sort of place where most people are doomed before they start. And what can the two of us—' he glanced distractedly at the spacey wonder dog, '—or even three, do against all that might?'

Doomed before they started? That certainly sounded like a good description of their present situation to Roger. He had no idea the Citadel of Dread was so formidable.

'But what am I talking about? Of course!' The Captain of the Guard laughed at his foolishness. 'I forgot! You're Captain Crusader! This should be no problem at all.'

Well, Roger thought, at least somebody had confidence in him.

Maybe another function of the sidekick was to make the hero feel more heroic. Why, then, wasn't it working for him?

Still, what other options did he have? Now that Captain Crusader was here, he had to see this through to the end. There was nothing else for Roger to do but follow the guardsman deeper into the Citadel.

'Yip?' Dwight remarked as he trotted after them.

CHAPTER NINETEEN

'Curse you, Mother Antoinette!' another woman's voice shouted.

Louie looked beyond the woman with the whip and saw Hippolita and her three muscular cohorts all handily tied to nearby trees. Louie wondered for an instant where Dread's gang had got the rope. Still, as an experienced sidekick, he knew that when the plot demanded something, that something always seemed to show up.

'Now the tide will turn!' the Son of Samson added. Louie noticed the muscleman hadn't got any better at matching his lip movement to the words. 'Our champions have returned!'

Mother Antoinette regarded Louie and his fellows – who were, one by one, crawling from the pit – with a visible sneer. 'So these are your so-called—' she hesitated in a manner worthy of Doctor Dread, '—champions?'

'Well,' Hippolita admitted as first Officer O'Clanrahan and then Zabana emerged from the darkness, 'you have to take what you're given. Consider the raw materials.'

This did not appease Mother Antoinette in the least. 'And you dare compare them to me?' This time, her whip danced in the direction of her captives.

CRACK *CRACK* *CRACK*

'No!' the Second Cousin of Goliath grovelled. 'We swear! *You* can be born out of rock!'

'Before this is all over,' Mother Antoinette agreed, 'I'll be born out of rock and more! Now, pardon me while I – deal with these interlopers!'

'Before you harm fluffy hair on bunnies' head,' a jungle-trained voice interjected, 'you deal with Zabana first!'

'Bunnies?' Professor Peril interjected, cutting to the quick.

'Yes, they've brought the bunnies with them! Then we *are* in the right place after all.'

'First things first, prince of the jungle,' Doc drawled as he casually walked towards Mother Antoinette. 'Me and this little lady have some talkin' to do.'

Doc's remarks didn't appear to make Mother Antoinette any happier.

'You don't deserve talk,' she murmured, her teeth clenched in anger. 'You deserve the whip!'

CRACK *CRACK* *CRACK*

She whirled her weapon above her head for effect before she attacked.

'Well,' Doc replied easily, 'if that's the way you want it.'

Louie flinched as the whip lashed out toward Doc's mid-section. But, when the whip arrived, Doc was no longer there.

CRACK

Doc somersaulted quickly and landed back on his feet. Mother Antoinette was undeterred. She flicked her wrist, and her leather thong of destruction changed course, flashing for Doc's neck.

Doc reacted every bit as quickly, falling away from the lash as he kicked his right foot high, so that the leather tip deflected harmlessly off the heel of his boot.

CRACK *CRACK*

Mother Antoinette screamed in frustration, swirling the whip once again above her head.

CRACK *CRACK* *CRACK*

With a low growl, she threw the business end of the whip forward one more time, straight at Doc's face!

This time, though, the westerner simply sidestepped the deadly leather, and, once the whip had snapped harmlessly in the air a foot from his ear, he grabbed the whip end before it could *CRACK* again.

Doc yanked.

The mistress of the whip cried out in surprise. While she somehow managed to hold on to her weapon, Doc's sudden move pulled her from her incredibly high heels.

'There, Missy,' Doc remarked, his face set in the kind of grim expression that showed he didn't particularly enjoy this sort of business. 'I didn't mean to be rough, but, sometimes, a man's gotta do what a man's gotta do.'

Mother Antoinette's only answer was a deep-throated growl as she returned to her feet. Louie had a feeling this wasn't over yet.

'Just a little something I picked up in my years studying the oriental arts,' Doc continued self-deprecatingly. 'Amazing what you could learn from those folks workin' on the railroad.'

'Ha-ha!' Hippolita called from her tree. 'Laugh at our champions now! They have returned with the Jewel of the Seven Cities, and we will be undefeatable!'

The Jewel of the Seven Cities? Louie frowned. Oh, yeah, there had been some mention about that in all the gobbledygook Hippolita and her boys had spouted before they had thrown them into the pit. With the business about the dark cave and the bunnies and all, Louie had completely forgotten about the jewel.

'Jewel? You mean this jewel?' Bouncer asked, pointing to the ostentatiously large ruby in his navel.

Why hadn't Louie seen that jewel there before? Could it have been hidden under the fluffy bunny fur or – oh – of course – it *had* to be hidden – something, Louie reminded himself, to do with the plot. When he had been a simple sidekick, he wouldn't have even thought to question that sort of thing. Now that he was trying to lead people, he had to get control of things, and, when you tried to get control of things in the Cineverse—

Professor Peril whistled as he stared at Bouncer. 'I haven't seen this guy before. That's a bunny?'

'Not just any bunny,' muttered Bertha, who, Louie recalled, had had business with Bouncer before. 'You've got to watch out for his exploding carrots. I imagine Doctor Dread would not be – displeased if this was the first bunny we obliterated.'

Bouncer hopped over to Louie, all six feet plus, two hundred pounds of solid bunny muscle bouncing across the landscape. It was a disquieting sight, even for someone who was the large rabbit's ally.

'Want to see Bouncer's jewel?' The rabbit popped the large ruby out of his navel before Louie had a chance to answer. Bouncer tossed it into Louie's hands, and the sometime sidekick saw that it had a felt tag attached, a tag that held a neatly lettered label that read:

THE JEWEL OF THE SEVEN CITIES
CERTIFICATE OF AUTHENTICITY
DO NOT REMOVE UNDER PENALTY OF LAW

'Very nice,' Louie murmured, handing the jewel back to Bouncer. But what did it all mean?

'We must have that jewel!' Hippolita declared in her usual

unsynchronized fashion. 'Bring it here, or face the wrath of the Oracle of Venus!'

But Mother Antoinette had regained both her feet and her high heels. 'If you take that jewel anywhere, you'll face the wrath of something a lot closer than Venus!' She pulled the whip away from a startled Doc, who spun about with the force of her tug.

CRACK

Doc ducked, barely avoiding the whip as he rolled again. But this time Mother Antoinette was ready for him.

CRACK *CRACK*

The whip snapped to either side of Doc, forcing him into a hasty somersault. Even then, the westerner could not escape.

CRACK *CRACK* *CRACK*

Doc pivoted, then executed a handstand followed by a slightly clumsy backflip. The whip still caught him, wrapping round his boot.

Doc fell flat on his back and moved no more. Mother Antoinette paused to smile evilly.

'Doc!' Louie called. 'Are you all right?'

Doc raised his head and blinked groggily. 'I'll be jusht fine, shoon ash I getsh my breath.'

Oh, no! The classic town drunk was inebriated once again, this time from the extreme dizziness brought on by his narrow escapes!

But – Louie realized – this was terrible! Who besides Doc could stand up to the prowess of Mother Antoinette?

Apparently, Mother Antoinette had the same idea. She paused a moment further to grin conspiratorially at her cohorts before issuing her ultimatum:

'Surrender, or face the wrath of Mother—' She stopped as she saw the uncertain expressions on the faces of her companions. 'I mean, the wrath of Doctor Dread.'

For some reason, that change of phrase seemed to make her company a touch more relaxed. Louie wondered if there was some discord in the ranks of Doctor Dread. Perhaps, he considered, there might be more than one way to defeat the ultimate master of evil.

'Zabana fight jungle snake!' the prince of the jungle declared. 'Zabana fight whip, too!'

'Fools!' Hippolita called from within her ropes. 'You must use the jewel to be truly free!'

'Bouncer likes jewel,' the very large rabbit admitted as he

leaned forward to admire his navel ornament. 'But what does Bouncer's jewel do?'

'It is simplicity itself!' Hippolita explained. 'All you have to—'

CRACK Mother Antoinette's whip interrupted the explanation.

'I will not be silenced!' Hippolita exclaimed. 'The secret might of Sparta is hidden—'

CRACK *CRACK* The whip stripped bark from the tree close by Hippolita's left ear, then her right.

'The sixth labour of Hercules—' Hippolita tried again.

CRACK went the whip between her legs.

'The secret of the Golden Fleece—' Hippolita added hastily.

CRACK snapped the whip as it sliced through a half-dozen strands of her strikingly blonde hair.

'Er—' Hippolita blurted as she gulped down her fear, '—remember the Trojan Horse—'

CRACK The whip curled itself round the rope securing Hippolita's shoulders to the tree. Antoinette tugged once, and the rope moved upward, until it was pressing into Hippolita's neck.

'Perhaps—' Hippolita gasped, '—I will be silenced – after all.'

'You will say nothing more,' Mother Antoinette agreed jovially, 'until the rest of these scum have surrendered.' She turned her less than pleasant grin on Louie. 'If you do not surrender, you will see your fellows humiliated, and more. And – once we are done with them – we will begin on you.'

'Right,' Louie replied, indicating that he understood, but not that he agreed.

'Shurrender?' Doc shouted from his still horizontal vantage point. 'It'sh the lasht thing we'll do!'

'Never!' Zabana agreed. 'Zabana not know meaning of word surrender!'

'Bouncer has vocabulary problems, too,' the large rabbit admitted. 'That's why Zabana is Bouncer's friend. But what should Bouncer do with jewel?'

The rabbits whispered among themselves that they were far too cute to surrender. Even Officer O'Clanrahan seemed to have swallowed his misgivings enough to be grimly silent. So, Louie surmised, they were all in agreement on that at least – no surrender.

'Not surrender, no.' Louie stated his decision aloud as he thought that the decision left them with only two courses of action. Now, he had to guess as to the results of those actions. He looked over at the four tied to the trees. As nasty as Mother

Antoinette appeared, Louie didn't think she'd simply murder these local characters for the fun of it. In fact, Hippolita and her musclemen would probably be far safer if Mother Antoinette was no longer tempted to use them as a bargaining device.

A hero would lead the others forward, oblivious to danger, until the prisoners were freed, or he and his fellows were killed or captured. Under normal circumstances, the hero would win, too.

But, one look at his surroundings showed Louie these circumstances were anything but normal. Musclemen, bunnies, Mother Antoinette – the Change was in full swing now. And, Louie knew from past experience, whenever they were in the midst of the Change, the wrong things happened. Heroes died, villains won, things ended unhappily. And, looking at the way Mother Antoinette had the upper hand, that sort of ending seemed not only likely but almost inevitable.

If Louie was really a hero, they'd have to stay here and fight. But whoever said he was a hero? Seeing as he was really a sidekick, he couldn't think of a single thing wrong with the other course of action open to them – running.

'Come on, folks!' he yelled to the others. 'We're not surrendering! We're getting out of here!'

His fellows gathered quickly round him. Louie twisted the Captain Crusader Ring on his finger, carefully shielding his movements from prying eyes. If the villains couldn't see his setting, they wouldn't be able to follow him. And if they could get to Doctor Dread's hideout first, perhaps they could deal with the ultimate master of evil without his minions being anywhere around.

Mother Antoinette and her fellow felons gaped at them as Louie completed their escape.

'See you in the funny papers!' Louie almost laughed as the blue smoke rose around them, freeing them from a potentially deadly situation.

But how could he laugh when he knew – even though he'd had no time to tell his fellows – that the place he was using the Captain Crusader Decoder Ring to take them might be even worse?

CHAPTER TWENTY

'Stop right here!' the Captain of the Guard commanded.

Roger stopped. The last couple of times the Captain had issued this sort of warning, they had barely missed being decapitated by rotating sawblades and being skewered by six-foot-long iron spikes. The Captain had explained this was the sort of thing one had to expect in the Citadel, especially when one took the seldom used, sub-basement route.

This time, though, there were no noisy blades or messy spikes. In fact, Roger couldn't see anything at all.

'False alarm?' he asked the Captain quietly.

'Anything but.' The Captain pointed to the floor of the hallway half a dozen feet ahead. At first Roger didn't see a thing in the dim and inconsistent light, and then he thought his eyes were playing tricks on him. The grey floor was moving, rolling and shifting around as if it were a liquid rather than a solid. But whatever that glistening, ever-changing surface was, it appeared to be alive.

'Killer flatworms,' the guard replied to the question Roger was about to ask.

'Killer *flatworms*?' Roger asked incredulously.

The Captain nodded, his gaze drawn back to the wriggling mass. 'It's their bite, I think. Or maybe they have poisonous spikes or something. Doctor Dread wasn't too precise about the specifics.'

Roger shivered. 'He never is, is he?'

'You've noticed that too? Whatever, those worms are deadly. It's one of the subtler forms of death hereabouts – although I do understand it's incredibly lingering and painful.' The Captain shrugged. 'It's amazing the variations you can get on death and destruction when you have all of the Cineverse at your disposal.'

Roger shivered a second time. He didn't think killer flatworms would care in the least if he was Roger Gordon or Captain

Crusader or anybody else for that matter. Thank goodness – or perhaps the Plotmaster – that he had managed to gain a guide through this deadly place.

He glanced at the guard. 'You generally don't stumble around here in the dark, do you?'

'Only in daytime, if I can help it,' the Captain agreed.

Roger watched the swirling movement of the worms – rather hypnotic, in its way. He shook himself. There was a question he felt he had to ask. 'But what happens if you have to, well, you know—'

The Captain instantly understood his meaning. 'It's amazing what incentive will do to let you hold things in till morning.'

'Yip?' Dwight added, as if this were a concept that even the addled wonder dog might understand.

Roger had another question. 'So how do we get out of this one?'

'Hold on a second,' the guard replied. 'It's around here somewhere.' He looked towards the ceiling and pointed. 'Ah.'

Roger looked up to where the Captain indicated. There, somewhat hidden by the rusted pipes and dusty air ducts, but plainfully visible once you knew where to look, was a neatly lettered cardboard sign:

WORM CONTROL LEVER
PULL FOR RELEASE

The Captain of the Guard reached up on tiptoe until his hand closed over the dust-covered lever. He pulled it down. There was the all-too familiar grinding of seldom-used machinery. And something slid open beneath the worms.

The worms hissed as they fell into the pit. Before this, Roger hadn't known worms made any sound at all. It was probably a hidden talent of killer flatworms, he reflected.

The steel door slid shut again, now devoid of the deadly crawlers.

'Wow,' Roger admitted. 'I never realized that getting to Doctor Dread would be this difficult.'

'We do have to take the most disused and forsaken passageways within the Citadel, so that we will escape detection by the forces of Doctor Dread,' the Captain of the Guard summarized neatly. 'Even I, however, am amazed how disused and forsaken some of these passageways are.'

Uh-oh, Roger thought. He was forgetting where he was, and

who he was. Captain Crusader should always be positive, especially when something as potentially deadly as the Change was about. Roger remembered when he had been facing the Cowabungamunga, and how he had almost fallen before the mightiest of surfing waves when he had doubted his ability but had regained his prowess the minute he had begun to sing a positive surfing song.

Something similar could be happening here at this very moment. The way to Dread's inner sanctum was proving to be long and arduous. Roger was losing heart despite himself, and it seemed that his newfound guide was losing faith as well – and Roger wasn't sure how strong the Captain of the Guard's faith was in the first place. It was time for Captain Crusader to do something about it. Somehow, singing seemed inappropriate in a place as bleak as this. Captain Crusader's other ability, however, could be used anywhere.

'The road may be long and weary,' he pronounced in a loud, firm voice, 'but justice waits for us at the end.'

'I'm glad you said that,' the Captain of the Guard told him with a relieved smile. 'Why was I hesitating? Let's go get them!'

The Captain of the Guard strode boldly forward across the spot so recently covered by killer worms. Roger followed, and wished he could be that confident. The more time he spent in the Cineverse, however, the more he realized he might be the only thing preventing the Change from taking over everything!

'I think we're getting closer,' the guard called over his shoulder. 'It's been a long time since I've been down here, but we can't be more than a half an hour from the hidden panel.'

But Roger's last aphorism had given him an idea. He remembered the Cowabungamunga once again, and how, every time he sang another verse of a surfing song, he would magically find himself further along in his race against the killer wave. It seemed that Captain Crusader homilies worked on much the same principle as those songs – it was all Movie Magic, after all – but would that principle hold up in a place like the Citadel of Dread?

Well, it was worth a Captain Crusader try.

He looked about at his truly dingy surroundings.

'On the other side of the thickest wall,' he said, 'the sun is shining bright.'

The guard stopped at the intersection of two seemingly identical corridors. 'You know, we may be closer than I thought.'

Well, perhaps that was just chance – or perhaps his powers of aphorism were working again. Roger decided a repeat performance couldn't hurt.

'A caged bird still can sing,' Roger commented.

'Yes!' the guard cheered. 'I'm sure that secret panel is around here somewhere!'

He frowned at his surroundings. Perhaps, Roger considered, he needed more encouragement.

'Uh,' Roger added hurriedly, 'a caged hamster can still run on his wheel.'

'I think it's over on this wall—' the guard mused.

'And – um—' Roger added quickly, not wanting to lose the momentum, '—a caged lion gets fed on a regular basis.'

'But I can't remember where it is, exactly,' the Captain added with a frown.

Roger had to admit that the guard might have stalled on account of him. It was possible that Captain Crusader had overmined that particular metaphor. You needed more than a positive attitude in this business – you needed originality.

'Um, er,' Roger tried again. Still, it was tough to think of anything original – or, more specifically, original and uplifting – in a place as dingy and depressing as this. But Roger had to try. He looked above at the green, slimy walls.

'Mould may be disgusting,' he ventured, 'but it still needs a mother's love.'

'I've found it!' the Captain of the Guard cheered. 'Now, if only I can determine how it opens.'

Roger walked over behind the guard. 'Look up,' he suggested.

The guard looked, and saw the neatly-printed-on-cardboard instructions.

SECRET PASSAGEWAY
TO DREAD'S INNER SANCTUM
PRESS WALL IMMEDIATELY BELOW.

The instructions were followed by a helpful arrow.

The Captain of the Guard pressed. The wall slid aside. It was dark on the other side. The Captain of the Guard stepped through first. Roger followed.

'Yip?' Dwight commented on Roger's heels.

'Yes, fella,' Roger murmured as he patted Dwight's head. He had hoped that, once he had put a little time and distance between himself and his actions, the wonder dog might snap out of his funk, but apparently it wasn't going to happen. Roger hated to see the once-vital hound like this, and he swore, once he had dealt with the Change and found Delores, the next thing he would concentrate on would be a cure for Dwight.

Ahead, Roger saw the guard's dim shadow reach overhead. A light clicked on, activated by a pull cord in the Captain's hand.

'It's very low tech here, behind the scenes,' the guard explained.

They seemed to be in some sort of wardrobe. There were hangers to either side of them, covered with tuxedoes, sports jackets, leisure suits, tunics, underwear and Bermuda shorts – all made out of snakeskin. Roger realized this wasn't simply any wardrobe. They truly had reached Doctor Dread's inner sanctum!

'The public area is there,' said the guard in a low voice as he pointed ahead, 'beyond that drapery.'

But Roger had seen something else as he followed the directions of the guard. There, just thrown on the floor, was a box of Nut Crunchies!

Roger hadn't seen that cereal box in years. His favourite breakfast food as a child, the company had discontinued the cereal when Roger was in his later teens, replacing it first with Fruit Flavoured Crunchies – which were terrible – and then Marshmallow Crunchies – which were even worse. A year or two ago, they had tried it again by bringing out Oat Bran Crunchies, but, for Roger at least, the magic was gone.

Now, though, here they were again – the cereal that had helped him survive childhood. He picked up the box. It looked brand new, as if it had just come off the supermarket shelf. And, even better, it rattled when he picked it up, as if it were full of Nut Crunchies!

'Captain Crusader?' the guard asked. 'What's the matter? We can't stop now – not when we're this close!'

Roger shook his head. No, of course not. He couldn't be stopped by a simple box of cereal – but there had to be some explanation as to how a box of Nut Crunchies had found its way into the Citadel of ultimate evil. Maybe, Roger thought, they still made Nut Crunchies somewhere in the Cineverse. He had always thought of this place as magical, but – until now – he hadn't realized how magical.

Maybe, he thought, he should open the box.

'Captain Crusader?' the Captain of the Guard pleaded.

Roger looked up. Yes, the other fellow was right. There would be plenty of time later to recapture his childhood through a breakfast cereal. Now, though, they had a Cineverse to save.

Roger decided he'd take the box along, for luck perhaps – or maybe because, now that he'd found Nut Crunchies again, he couldn't bear to let them go.

He walked forward to the heavy curtain that separated this closet from the next room. It was time for Captain Crusader to take control.

'Yip?' Dwight said from nearby. Roger wondered if the dog wanted some Nut Crunchies.

Roger was about to step through the curtain when the Captain of the Guard grabbed his arm. Roger glanced over and saw the guard shake his head. Roger stepped back.

'Do you hear somebody talking?' he whispered.

'Worse than that,' the guard replied in the same low voice. 'I hear somebody – hesitating.'

So they were one room away from Doctor Dread. Roger swallowed. It had all happened so fast. Was it time for the ultimate showdown?

Then the curtain moved aside. Another guard stood in the doorway, staring at them. And, beyond the guard stood Doctor Dread himself.

'Roger—' Doctor Dread began, '—or should I say – Captain Crusader? We've been waiting ever so long for your—' he paused suggestively, '—arrival. I insist that you come on in and—' he hesitated darkly, '—enjoy the party. It's a shame the party will be—' he paused with finality, '—your last.'

Roger stepped forward. The ultimate showdown was not beginning well.

CHAPTER TWENTY-ONE

Even though they were still surrounded by blue smoke, Louie knew they had arrived at their destination.

'Where you take us?' Zabana asked abruptly.

'How do you work this jewel?' Bouncer's one-track voice asked from the fog.

'And what about us other bunnies?' a high-pitched voice interjected.

'Yeah,' another high-pitched voice added. 'We haven't seen any action at all yet!'

'Bunnies thrive on action!' yet another high voice added.

'And don't forget hopping!' some other bunny added. 'Bunnies also thrive on hopping!'

'Carrots, too!' somebody else chimed in. 'Bunnies thrive on—'

'Yes, this is certainly educational,' Louie abruptly interrupted, realizing that if he didn't, the bunnies might go on for ever. 'However, in a place like this, it's probably safer to be quiet.'

That shut them all up. Now that the bunnies had given up their diatribe, it was remarkably quiet here, with only the distant sound of crickets. Of course, considering where they were, even crickets could be dangerous.

Still, they hadn't been attacked by the forces of Doctor Dread. Louie hoped that meant they had landed someplace relatively safe.

'I think we're safe here, for the moment,' Louie said as the smoke dissipated around them. 'I've brought us here to find Doctor Dread. While I was in his service, I learned about any number of the evil fiend's hideouts, but there are only three of those hiding places both large and well-protected enough to serve as Doctor Dread's true headquarters.'

'Three?' Zabana asked helpfully. 'What are three?'

'Does anybody know how to work this jewel?' Bouncer added hopefully.

Louie decided to answer Zabana's question.

'Their old headquarters is called the Citadel of Dread – a fortress full of peril for the unwary – but the place is too obvious. They'd expect us to go there first, so I didn't.'

All but the last wisps of smoke vanished, and Louie saw that he and his fellows had materialized on a plateau above the jungle, with the great, red sun just rising over the horizon. The others were all watching him, nodding as if what he was saying made sense – which Louie hoped it did.

'Of course,' he continued, 'there's also Moon Base Zeta. That place is huge, and except for the occasional hideous alien menace, it's quite safe.' Louie shook his head to dismiss that possibility. 'No, I thought they would come here, the last place they would think I would look, and the most potentially dangerous of all three locations.'

'Hah!' the jungle prince commented. 'Zabana laugh at danger!'

'Bouncer laughs at many things too,' the large rabbit added jovially. 'That's why Bouncer and Zabana are friends.' He stared down at the ruby he still held in his paws. 'You think the jewel would work if Bouncer laughed at it?'

The crowd parted to let Officer O'Clanrahan step forward from the point where, until this moment, he had been standing away from the others, muttering into his hands.

'Faith and begorah!' the officer wailed. 'If we're not facing a dangerous fortress or hideous moon beasties, can you tell us what we will be facing?'

'I'm glad you asked,' Louie replied enthusiastically, since questions like that did a lot to help the plot along. 'We've landed on a prehistoric planet, seemingly forgotten by time itself, where creatures a hundred times the size of their modern-day counterparts roam the wild to rend and kill anything in their path.'

'Oh,' Officer O'Clanrahan replied with very little enthusiasm. 'If you'll excuse me, I'm going off into the corner to mutter some more.' He proceeded to do exactly that.

Doc had somehow managed to get to his feet. Louie hoped that meant the westerner would be coming round to his senses soon.

'Where exshactly ish this hideout?'

'In a great, underground cavern beneath the jungle,' Louie explained. 'Unfortunately, to reach the cavern, we have to enter the jungle first.'

'Jungle is Zabana's home,' the prince of the jungle interjected helpfully.

'Not this jungle,' Louie assured Zabana grimly. 'Not unless you're – prehistoric.'

As if in reply, a thunderous scream came from the vegetation below.

'WONK!'

'What that?' Zabana asked incredulously.

Louie had heard that sound before, but wished he hadn't.

'If I'm not mistaken,' he explained, 'I think that's the battle cry of the Great Fanged Toad. Twenty feet long from head to tail, the toad thinks nothing of eating humans as light, between-meal snacks. But we know it's down there now. If we can move swiftly and silently, there's a good chance at least most of us will survive.'

As if in answer to the first horrid noise, another monstrous cry erupted from far overhead.

'CHIRP!'

'Whatsh that?' Doc ventured, doing his best to look up at the sky without falling.

Unfortunately, Louie knew the answer to that question as well. 'I'm afraid that noise belongs to the Horrendous, Three-horned Chickadee! The great bird flies high overhead, searching for help-less prey that it can swoop down on and gobble up with but one gulp of its tremendous beak. But we know it's up there now, and if we keep our heads down, and move quickly and quietly—'

'Bouncer goes first! Bouncer has the jewel!' The large rabbit took the lead and began to hop down the well-marked path to the jungle.

'I guess we'd better go too,' Fluffytail said with a notable lack of enthusiasm.

Louie glanced down at the listless rabbit. Overall, the bunnies had been pretty quiet since they had left their cartoon homeland. In his usual sidekick role, he would have picked up on that sort of thing right away, but this hero business was proving far too time-consuming for such subtle things as rabbit mood swings.

'Is something the matter?' he asked.

'No, we bunnies are always cheerful—' Fluffytail paused to shiver, 'when we're not scared out of our rabbit minds.'

'WONK!' screamed the giant toad down below.

'CHIRP!' replied the Three-horned Chickadee high overhead.

Louie had to admit that the rabbits had a point.

'Hey!' Bouncer's booming voice called back to Louie. 'Bouncer sees a big cave down here!'

Oh, no! Louie thought. Not a big cave. He knew all too well what came out of big caves on this particular movie world.

'Bouncer!' he called ahead frantically. 'Get away from—' But, from the noises coming from the cave mouth, he knew he was already too late.

'GWRAAR!'

'What in cave?' Zabana demanded.

'That'sh even worshe than the lasht couple noishesh!' Doc agreed.

Indeed it was, a cry that chilled your very soul. And Louie would know that fearsome cry anywhere.

Bouncer bounded back towards them. But there was something following the rabbit, something that made Bouncer look no bigger than his smaller bunny brothers and sisters!

'GWRAARARRRR!' screamed the immense yellow blur.

Louie could stand it no more. No matter how horrible the truth, he had to tell the others:

'It's the giant Sabre-toothed Hamster!' Louie summarized. 'And it's coming right for us!'

'Bouncer's sorry he saw da cave!' the large rabbit called as he rapidly approached.

'GWRAARARRRR!' the hamster thing roared from much too close behind the fleeing bunny.

'Maybe Zabana speak to hamster!' the prince of the jungle suggested. 'Save Bouncer!' He cupped his hands round his mouth and uttered a mighty cry: 'Chee chee ribbit ribbit chee!'

The Sabre-toothed Hamster didn't seem to notice. 'GWRAARARRRR!' he commented as he bounded ever closer to Bouncer.

Zabana was horrified. 'Prehistoric hamsters not speak same language. Bouncer doomed!'

'Does *anybody* know how to use Bouncer's jewel?' the large rabbit asked with some desperation.

'Bouncer's in trouble!' one of the rabbits agreed.

'It's up to us, guys!' Highjumper told the others.

Even Fluffytail nodded at that. 'We have to face our fear. This looks like a job for – bunnies!'

'Yay!' Highjumper agreed. 'Bunnies to the rescue!'

The six remaining rabbits bounced rapidly down the hill towards the marauding hamster.

Highjumper led the way. 'Sabre-toothed Hamsters might be strong—' he called as he leapt close to the startled behemoth's face.

The other bunnies followed Highjumper's lead.

'They may be fierce—' a brown and white spotted rabbit called as it jumped across the great hamster's back. The monster twisted round, trying to grab for the bunny with its great clawed forepaw. But the bunny was gone, and another rabbit leapt in its place.

'They could be angry—' the next bunny jumped near the hamster's face again. The terror twisted back, but both wildly swinging forepaws met nothing but air.

'But he's not as fast—' Fluffytail called, bouncing twice on the creature's backside. The hamster roared its fury.

'He's not as cheerful—' a snow-white bunny opined as it bounded so close to the hamster that it almost hit the monstrous nose.

'He's not as fluffy—' a solid grey bunny added as he hopped beneath the hamster's stomach.

'As bunnies!' all seven rabbits cheered together.

The Sabre-toothed Hamster was totally confused. It sat back on its haunches and wailed.

'Time for da exploding carrot!' Bouncer exclaimed joyfully. Louie saw there was a shiny orange cylinder in the large bunny's hand. Bouncer handed the tube to the totally befuddled hamster. Then all the bunnies ran.

'BOOM!'

It exploded in the monster's face.

'YELP!' the giant hamster remarked.

'Yay!' the bunnies all cheered together, a sight almost too cute for words, as the hamster swiftly retreated to its cave down the hill. 'Bunnies win again!'

Louie hoped they had enough exploding carrots to cope with whatever else they might find as they descended to the jungle floor.

'Well, come on, folks. We'd better get a move on.'

'You're not going anywhere!' a woman's voice commanded as they were all surrounded by blue smoke.

Louie was instantly disorientated. Had somebody else used the Captain Crusader Decoder Ring to transport them to another world? No, he could still feel the ring on his finger, and he was reasonably certain that this was the only ring that he or his companions possessed. With the thickness of the smoke around them, that could mean only one thing – that some other person or persons had used another ring to transport their group into the middle of Louie and his companions!

Louie had all too good an idea of who these newcomers might be.

'Ah hahaha!' came from the blue smoke. 'Ah hahaha.' Triumphant laughter, from giggles to guffaws. Dread's henchpeople had found them once again, in no time at all, and with such precision of location that they had transported themselves into their very midst! And Louie's forces were scattered across this plateau. There was no way, in the middle of this thick blue smoke, that he could gather them all together to escape again.

But there was something even worse, a nagging doubt that Louie had missed something that he had been looking at all along, something that would answer the question that may have doomed them all:

How did Doctor Dread's forces always know where they were going to be?

The smoke cleared. It was even worse than Louie had thought. While the smoke had obscured their actions, each of Dread's minions had felt their way across the plateau to take one of Louie's fellows captive! Menge the Merciless held a deadly looking ray gun to Doc's head, while Professor Peril had his snub-nosed thirty-eight pointed straight at Zabana's chest. Bouncer was far less than a whip's length away from Mother Antoinette, and Bertha had all the other bunnies neatly within her shotgun sights. Unless something dramatic happened, this time there really was no escape.

'So,' Mother Antoinette said with a slow yet evil smile. 'It is over at last.'

It looked to Louie like it was over, too, but he couldn't help himself. The plot-centred sidekick within had to know the answer.

'I have to know. How did you find us so quickly?'

Mother Antoinette glanced perfunctorily at her companions. 'Well, we might as well tell them. There's no way they're getting out of this one, and I've been aching to explain for ever so long.'

Aching to explain? Louie shivered. Only the vilest of criminals had to explain things before they killed. Roger's mother's villainous transformation was complete.

'Yes, you poor, pitiful heroes, thinking you had a chance at success,' Mother Antoinette gloated, 'when we knew where you were at every instant, like struggling fish on a line, and we only had to wait until the time was right to tug on our hooks and reel you in!' She waved at the police officer in their midst, the one other member of Louie's band not held at gun or whip point. 'And it's all thanks to you, Officer O'Clanrahan!'

Louie's mouth fell open as he realized how he had been double-crossed. 'You mean, when you were muttering back there, your ranting had a purpose!'

'Afraid so, m'boy.' Officer O'Clanrahan shrugged. 'I was workin' for the other side.'

'Not you!' Zabana exclaimed in horror. 'Not faithful companion of wonder dog!'

'And how'd you like to be playin' second fiddle to a wonder dog every single day o' your life?' O'Clanrahan demanded. 'It's "Say, isn't that Dwight the wonder dog-this" and "Hey, isn't that Dwight the Wonder Dog-that" and never a good morning or how you doin' today to Officer O'Clanrahan! I couldn't take it any more. One more helpful bark, and I swore I'd start to scream!' He buried his face in his hands.

'But then—' the policeman took a deep breath and looked up defiantly at his former allies, '—then I was free of him at last! Bertha had talked to me, you see, back on my old home turf, and offered me certain opportunities I'd be a fool to refuse. It was a little difficult acting on them while the wonder dog was still around, but once he went into the drink, well, I was free to pursue my piece of the action.' He balled his hands into fists, his eyes wild with the passion of his words. 'I had to do it, don't you see? Now, maybe someday, they'll say— "Isn't that Officer O'Clanrahan?" '

'Yes, we'll say that now!' Mother Antoinette added with a chuckle. 'Isn't that Officer O'Clanrahan, whose help allowed the forces of evil to crush these pitiful heroes, and assured that the Change, and the Cineverse, belong to Doctor Dread!'

Louie looked grimly at his companions. 'That's it, then?'

Mother Antoinette considered his query. 'No,' she said after a moment. 'There is one more question.'

'Which is?' Louie asked despite himself.

'Where would you like to be shot?' Antoinette replied. 'In the head or in the heart?'

Dread's minions laughed as if that was the funniest thing in the Cineverse.

Louie had thought they had been in trouble before. He was wrong.

This was real trouble.

CHAPTER TWENTY-TWO

Roger glanced at his surroundings as he walked towards Doctor Dread. He figured he had nothing to lose. He might find a means of escape someplace in this room, and besides, if it took him an extra moment to reach Doctor Dread, that would be an extra moment he would stay alive.

This place looked like nothing so much as a throne room, the sort of place absolute rulers would have audiences with their subjects before they decided to cut off somebody's head. Roger rubbed the back of his neck and wished his imagination wasn't quite so vivid.

The centrepiece of the room was a large chair on a raised dais – it really did look like a throne. The walls to either side of the chair were hung with huge, ornate tapestries, each one depicting a scene of vileness or destruction in great detail. In one, a man in a Santa Claus suit wielding a hatchet ran after a family. Flying saucers destroyed the Washington monument in another. There seemed to be a common theme to all these wall hangings. In every one, wrong triumphed over right. Perhaps, Roger thought, all these hangings were depictions of the Change.

'I see—' Dread's eyes turned to the Captain of the Guard, '—we have already uncovered – treachery'

Roger glanced back at the Captain. The guard looked most uncomfortable. 'But, your awfulness! You have to understand, I was all set to obliterate this scum, when he opened his mouth and – said something!'

'Said – something?' Dread repeated drily.

'Well, yes.' Sweat ran down the Captain of the Guard's face. 'He is Captain Crusader, after all, and he has this – uh – way with words.'

'Way – with – words,' Doctor Dread repeated with a nod.

Roger realized that the Captain of the Guard was in even more trouble than he himself was at the moment. This guard had been a valuable ally. Roger didn't want to lose him, either through Doctor Dread's coercion, or the more permanent possibility of obliteration.

It looked like it was time, once again, for Captain Crusader to step forward and be heard.

Roger cleared his throat. 'A man may have a throne room,' he said slowly and clearly, 'but he still puts on his pants one leg at a time.'

The look of panic on the Captain of the Guard's face was replaced by a peaceful smile. 'See? Is that nice or what?'

'Yeah!' another guard agreed.

'We see your point!' a third guard added.

'Captain Crusader is our kind of guy!' the guards cheered together.

'Well, it certainly was a beautiful sentiment—' Doctor Dread paused in total confusion, '—what am I saying? This man is – dangerous! It is obvious that we cannot – allow Captain Crusader to speak. He must be – dealt with, now!'

Dwight chose that moment to poke his head through the curtains.

'Yip?'

'Watch out, men!' Doctor Dread yelled, pointing a snakeskin-gloved finger at the canine. But he hesitated with a frown, and put down his pointing hand. 'Oh, never mind. For a moment, I thought that was Dwight the wonder dog.'

'Yip?' Dwight repeated.

That was the diversion Roger had been looking for! He jumped quickly behind the nearest tapestry. There was a narrow space between tapestry and wall, maybe three feet across, so that he could walk back there without being detected. There seemed to be some sort of dark recess further up along the wall, too. Could it be another hidden passageway? Maybe he could escape to fight another day!

'Where's – Captain Crusader!' Doctor Dread roared. 'Guards! If you do not find him, there will be – consequences!'

Roger took a slow step towards the recess. Something rattled at his hip.

'Wait a second!' Doctor Dread yelled from the other side of the tapestry. 'I heard – Nut Crunchies!'

Roger looked down. Oh, no. Unthinkingly, he had held on to the box of his favourite breakfast cereal, and now that box might be his undoing. Nut Crunchies were incredibly noisy – it had been one of the joys of his childhood to hear them clatter into the bowl. But now, he couldn't move a muscle without rattling. Even dropping the box would be far too noisy. All he could do was stand there, frozen, until Dread and his henchmen found him!

Wait. Maybe there was another way. If he squatted very slowly and very steadily, perhaps he could ease the box down to the ground.

'He's somewhere – behind the tapestries!' Doctor Dread hesitated authoritatively. 'Find him, men, if you value your – position!'

Roger wouldn't let Dread's orders panic him. As much as he hated losing this breakfast cereal, his life was too high a price to pay. He bent his knees, slowly sinking towards the floor. If he could simply set down the box of Nut Crunchies, it was only a few steps to the secret passageway.

Dwight poked his head past the next tapestry. The dog stared at him.

'Yip?'

The box fell from Roger's startled fingers and crashed to the floor.

'There he is!' Doctor Dread screamed triumphantly. 'Guards – apprehend him!'

Burly hands reached round the tapestry and grabbed him from either side. Roger was dragged roughly from his hiding place. He was in too great a state of shock to put up much resistance. The once great Dwight the wonder dog was now so addled that he had accidentally given Roger away! Well, Dwight and the box of Nut Crunchies gave him away, if you wanted to be technical. Roger knew he would regret dropping that box, but, from the triumphant grin on the face of Doctor Dread, he feared those regrets wouldn't last very long.

'Captain Crusader. Dear – dear Captain Crusader, champion of justice and—' his pause this time was especially gleeful, '—Nut Crunchies. You must really like them, to allow a cereal to – betray you so. Well, I can arrange for you to spend your time with Nut Crunchies – for ever!' He snapped his fingers. 'Guards! Position – the prisoner.'

The two guards holding Roger dragged him over until his feet were resting on a big, red 'X' on the floor.

'Our time together has been so – pitifully short,' Doctor

Dread purred. 'But that's the way the new Master of the Cineverse wants it!' His hand reached to the wall and grasped a lever. Roger quickly read the neatly hand-lettered, cardboard sign attached to the lever by a sturdy hunk of string:

INSIDIOUS TRAP DOOR

Roger saw the Captain of the Guard, held at gunpoint by another of Doctor Dread's minions. There would be no help there. The wonder dog walked out from behind a tapestry and wagged his tail.

'Dwight!' Roger called. 'You're my last hope? Don't you remember?'

'Yip?' Dwight replied.

'Hehheh. Hehhehheh.' Doctor Dread laughed fiendishly as he pulled the lever. A trapdoor opened beneath Roger's feet, and he plummeted down, to land in – what? Visions of sharp spikes and poisonous flatworms danced through his head, for once driving out all those reminiscences of past wives and girl friends.

He hit something soft enough to cushion his fall as the trapdoor slammed shut above. That meant, at least, that the sharpened spikes were out. He didn't move for a moment, waiting for the killer flatworms to crawl up and overwhelm him.

But nothing seemed to be crawling anywhere. Whatever Roger landed on was totally inert. He decided he should try to turn round and determine what exactly was in here with him. His leg had twisted when he fell. He tried to straighten it out.

The leg sank into the mass beneath him. He pushed, panic-stricken, with his hands, and his arms sank in as well. This stuff felt totally dry, if perhaps a little sticky, but it had the same effect as quicksand, and he could feel his whole body slowly settling down, until the small, dry granules circled his waist, then his chest, then his neck.

He had to calm himself. He had got out of tight spots before, by thinking like a movie and obeying the laws of the Cineverse. Perhaps he could stop his descent by inventing another pithy saying, or singing a cheerful verse or two of song. It was worth a try.

He opened his mouth, and it was instantly filled with the small, sticky granules. They were sweet to the tongue. Startled, he bit down. The granules crunched.

He realized then what Doctor Dread meant when the villain

said Roger would spend the rest of his life with his favourite breakfast cereal. Roger had been dropped into a bottomless vat of Nut Crunchies!

Roger chewed. They were still every bit as good as he remembered them. Well, at least he wouldn't starve.

Now, if he could only find a way to breathe.

CHAPTER TWENTY-THREE

But trouble, Louie had to remember, could come in many different forms.

'CHIRP!'

The horrible bird call was much louder than it had been before. Mother Antoinette was looking up at the sky. 'What is *that*?'

'Oh, dear,' Menge the Merciless answered. 'I'm afraid it's the Horrendous, Three-horned Chickadee!'

'That's a chickadee?' Mother Antoinette replied in disbelief. 'What do you do with a giant chickadee?'

'Mostly hope that it never sees you,' Professor Peril added in his usual to-the-point manner.

'CHIRP!'

'I'm afraid it's too late for that now,' Bertha said grimly. 'It may be too late for all of us.'

Louie looked up at last. The creature was every bit as horrible as he remembered it – although now he was seeing it much closer than he ever had before. The bird was the size of a small blimp, covered with long, knife-like yellow feathers. Its head was merely the size of your average bar and grill, each eye as large as Bouncer or Zabana, its beak as wide as Main Street.

'CHIRP!' it called a final time. And then it dive-bombed straight for them!

'Zabana not even attempt to talk to that thing!' the jungle prince remarked in a tone of horrified wonder.

'Sure is a sobering sight,' Doc agreed, his speech once again slur-free. Louie realized the very sight of the monster bird must have shocked the westerner back to his senses.

'What are we going to do?' Menge wailed. 'That thing is deadly!'

Mother Antoinette only grinned. 'That thing may be deadly,' she replied, 'but it has never faced the whip.'

With a cry of defiance, she lashed out at the rapidly descending creature.

'CHIRP?'

Startled, the bird pulled out of its deadly descent.

'Now,' Mother Antoinette commented confidently, 'we will see who truly rules this lost world.'

But the great bird's dramatic attack had attracted something else's attention.

'WONK!' came the cry from the edge of the plateau.

Menge, Peril and Bertha spun round, all talking at once.

'Is that what I think—'

'It can't be—'

'But it must—'

'It's the Great Fanged Toad!' they screamed as one. All three of them pulled their weapons and began to fire.

'Hey, guys,' Louie whispered hastily to his suddenly free companions. 'I think it's time to get out of here!'

'Sounds like a good idea to this here fella,' Doc drawled as he pointed to the far side of the plateau. 'Let's hurry over yonder and use the ring.'

Zabana's brow wrinkled in thought. 'Dread sneaky! We bring hostage of our own!'

He ran over and grabbed Officer O'Clanrahan.

'What?' the police officer demanded. 'Get your bloomin' hands—'

Zabana tucked O'Clanrahan under one of his arms and hurried back to the others. Dread's cohorts were far too busy dealing with giant toads and chickadees to pay any attention.

'Zabana show what happen to man who cross prince of jungle!' He flexed his muscles threateningly.

'No!' Louie objected. 'We need his information. We were followed here – it was a trap! My guess is that, when and if we made it down to the hidden stronghold beneath the jungle floor, we would have found it empty.' He stared at the treacherous police officer. 'So I have one question for you, Officer O'Clanrahan – where is Doctor Dread?'

The man in uniform didn't even struggle in Zabana's overwhelming grip. 'Mother of Mercy!' he wailed. 'How would I know?'

'He's in one of two places,' Louie demanded, 'the Citadel or the Moonbase! Tell me or I'll slap you around!'

O'Clanrahan shook his head. 'Citadel? Moonbase? I haven't the faintest idea what you're talking about.'

Louie paused in his interrogation. Maybe being slapped around by a five-foot-high sidekick wasn't enough of a threat. Maybe he had to up the stakes, and present this fellow with something worse than being tucked in Zabana's armpit.

'Perhaps,' Louie suggested. 'you'd like to eat one of Bouncer's exploding carrots?'

'Yay!' the large rabbit cheered. 'Bouncer likes da exploding carrots!'

'Why,' Officer O'Clanrahan stuttured, 'f-f-faith and begorah, how could I know where he'd be, but the—'

Bouncer pulled a metallic-looking carrot from somewhere under his fur.

'—the Moonbase,' O'Clanrahan finished hastily. 'He's got to be at the Moonbase!'

The short sidekick stared up at the heavily perspiring Officer O'Clanrahan. Could he trust this double-crossing police officer? Louie guessed they'd have to wait and see. Still, every moment they couldn't find Doctor Dread was another moment closer to the height of the Change.

Louie had made his decision. 'All right, folks, let's get out of here. And don't let O'Clanrahan go!'

CRACK
 CRACK *CRACK*
 CRACK *CRACK* *CRACK*

Mother Antoinette's whip danced, trimming razor-sharp feathers here, drawing blood from the chickadee's beak there. Enraged, the giant bird tried to attack again and again, but everywhere it flew, it found nothing but biting, naked leather!

'CHIRP!' the bird demanded, doing its best to stay aloft on its damaged wings. 'CH-CHIRP!'

The monstrous chickadee must have realized then that it was doomed. It spread its knife-sharp talons and fell from the sky in a final, suicidal dive, straight for the woman with the whip. It might die, but it looked like it would take Mother Antoinette along!

Mother Antoinette, however, had other ideas. She jumped to one side and tossed the whip into the air to meet the bird's rapidly descending claws. The leather wrapped itself round the bird's feet as she pulled on the whip handle, throwing all her weight behind it.

'*CHIRP!*' The great bird tumbled end over end, totally out of control. '*CHIRRRRRRRRRRR—*' Its final cry was cut off abruptly as it crashed, beak first, into the caked mud of the plateau a scant foot from Mother Antoinette's high heel.

She picked herself up and brushed off the dirt, pausing for a moment to pat away the few petite drops of sweat that beaded her brow.

'My, that was fun.'

The whip came free of the dead bird's feet with a single tug. She turned to see how her allies were doing.

Their monster, which looked like nothing so much as a really big toad with really sharp teeth, was down, too, rolling around in what Mother Antoinette assumed had to be its death agonies.

'WON—' it moaned. 'WOO – WAAaaaa—' And then it moaned no more.

Menge, Peril, and Bertha turned to look at Mother Antoinette. They all appeared to be a little the worse for wear from their encounter. Their faces were dirty, their clothes torn. Peril had blood running from his nose.

'It took fourteen slugs,' Peril summarized as he wiped at his face with an army green handkerchief, 'twelve shotgun rounds, and eight blasts from the ray gun, but we've downed the thing at last.'

'Good enough!' Mother Antoinette said approvingly. 'We'll show these monsters they're no match for the combined forces of Doctor Dread! Woe be the man or monster who stands in our way!' She frowned and turned round quickly. 'Speaking of men, what's happened to our captives?'

'Looks like they made good their escape while we were fighting these things,' Peril surmised reasonably.

'The scum have escaped?' Mother Antoinette was upset enough to use a four-letter word. 'Drat! Wait until we catch up with them. They'll not only wish they never got away, they'll wish they had never been born!' Her fury grew when she realized who else was missing. 'Has O'Clanrahan vanished, too?'

Bertha nodded her head 'Never trust a traitor.'

Mother Antoinette raised her whip over her head. 'This has gone too far! No one crosses Mother Antoinette—' she stalled sinisterly '—without retribution! It all comes from our following Doctor Dread's foolish plans, when we should be pursuing—' she demurred daringly '—my destiny!' She lowered the whip to take it in both her hands. 'Mother Antoinette is going to take—' she paused purposefully '—total charge!' She looked from face to face of her allies – no, from now on, they were her underlings!

'Any objections?' she asked.

But her companions were too busy quivering and studying their shoes to raise any further points.

'Fine,' Mother Antoinette answered the silence with a smile. 'Then let us go back to the Citadel of Dread and – rearrange a few things. There'll be no more hesitation, now! It's amazing, how different the Citadel will become, with a mother's touch!'

She laughed as all four of them were surrounded by blue smoke.

CHAPTER TWENTY-FOUR

Of all the journeys Delores had taken through the Cineverse, this was, if not the most difficult, certainly the most peculiar.

'Bawwk!' Edward exclaimed from his position just ahead. 'Sorry. I keep bumping my knees.'

'Baahhhh,' she reassured him. 'Ther-r-re's no apology necessary. Please, let's keep moving.'

This dark place seemed to go on for ever, on a surface that always sloped slightly upward. And there was only a narrow pathway on which they could walk, perhaps the width of the two of them side by side. If they strayed from the path, they would stumble into sharp bits of what felt like metal and wood, the corners of something that Delores guessed might be furniture, but, with her transmogrified senses, she could be sure of nothing.

The floor beneath them was sticky in places as well, so that her feet – or whatever she now had that passed for feet – would make a sucking noise when she pulled them free. Between clucking noises, Edward said that the sticky part of their surroundings, at least, reminded him of home. Delores found no comfort in the thought. But at least there were no bubbling swamps here, or terrifying creatures roaring in the night. There was only this never-ending aisle, and the sticky floor beneath their feet. So she followed Edward upward, ever upward.

'Bawwk!' Edward mused. 'I had heard of this place. But I never thought I would see it – well, perhaps I'm not seeing it, considering the darkness and – ouch! But I certainly feel it. My knees will never – bawwk – be the same. Who would ever think that I – a slime monster of humble beginnings – would end up in a place on the edge of the Cineverse?'

Once again Delores felt an odd sort of sympathy for this slime monster – or former slime monster. She knew the feeling was misplaced. This was the creature who had transmogrified her and got her into this situation in the first place, after all. Still, she supposed she could talk to him about their present predicament.

'Maybe it has something to do with the Change.'

Edward made a noise that was half a chuckle, half a cluck. 'By now, everything has something to do with the Change. That's the very nature of the phenomenon, worlds collide and shift into other worlds, creating things that were never meant to be. And, of course, those new worlds create new changes. The very fact that we and the others have been bouncing from world to world may have brought about the Change that much faster.'

Delores was horrified by the thought. 'So, by trying to stop the Change, we've actually accelerated it?'

'Who's to say?' Edward mused.

'So heroes will die, lovers part forever, and evil reign triumphant, all because of us?' Delores could feel herself getting really upset.

'Not necessarily,' the monster replied. 'I do not think the Change, in itself, is good or bad. It is only different. It is what those within the Cineverse do with the Change that tips the balance. Last time the Change ran rampant in our midst, Doctor Dread and his cohorts prevailed for a short time until at least some order was restored. And perhaps evil will win again. But it might be within our power to prevent it.'

Delores was astonished. She was discovering new philosophic depths in the muck creature. 'You really are well read, aren't you?'

'I have hidden depths,' the slime monster agreed.

'But why didn't you tell us all this before?'

Edward sighed. 'When a slime monster is love-smitten, all else is forgotten. And perhaps my hidden depths are gone, now that I've turned into a chicken.'

All things were possible, Delores thought. And she realized there might be a positive side to that statement as well as the negative.

She had another question: 'Will we ever get out of here?'

'I think,' Edward answered thoughtfully, 'if we believe strongly enough, we will find the exit sign.'

'Believe?'

'Yes, just as you believe that right must triumph over wrong, that lovers will be united in the end, that evil will, at last, be punished. All of the Cineverse is based on belief.' Edward paused, clucking softly to himself. 'Look for the exit sign, Delores.'

Delores looked ahead, and saw a faint, red glow.

'There!' she called. 'Do you see it?'

'I do now,' Edward replied.

Without another word, they hurried up the aisle. As they got closer, Delores could indeed read the sign: 'EXIT.'

She could see Edward's silhouette in the crimson light. He seemed to be much the same size as before, but he had gained something on his head that at first she mistook for a narrow, floppy hat, but then realized it was a cock's comb – the kind you saw on roosters. She didn't dare look down at her own hands and feet.

Edward had reached the door.

'Where will this take us?' she asked.

'Who knows?' he replied. 'It may lead anywhere in the Cineverse. Perhaps it will open to anywhere we want to go.'

'I'd like to go and find Roger.' If anyone could put things right, she thought, it had to be Captain Crusader.

Edward did not reply for a moment. 'Then again,' he said, 'we may open this door and find the real void, and be pulled from the Cineverse for ever.'

There was a choice to be made here, Delores realized, but it really wasn't any choice at all. She could not spend the rest of her life as a sheep.

It was time to open the door and find out.

CHAPTER TWENTY-FIVE

Roger couldn't breathe. But Roger could chew and swallow. If he was going to die, it would be with a stomach full of Nut Crunchies.

He ate. And then he ate some more. Amazingly, he didn't feel deprived of oxygen. Actually, with every new sugar-coated Crunchie that entered his system, he felt better – younger, more full of energy, ready to take on the world, or the Cineverse! Perhaps it was merely the incredibly high sugar content of the Nut Crunchies that was imbuing him with such a feeling of power, but Roger suspected it was far more than that.

By choosing this method of disposing of Captain Crusader, Doctor Dread may have made a fatal mistake. Nut Crunchies were more than a breakfast cereal. They were a way of life!

Roger chewed and swallowed even more rapidly than before, feeling the Nut Crunchies expand in his stomach. What he wouldn't give for a nice glass of cold milk to go along with this – but no, all thoughts of a balanced breakfast had to be left behind. He had a job to do.

For the first time, he truly felt like Captain Crusader.

The Nut Crunchies fell away as Roger detected a faint but discernible glow emanating from somewhere within this pit. It took Roger a moment to realize that the light was coming from him, his skin glowing with Nut Crunchie nutrition.

He lifted his head to regard the trapdoor overhead.

'Breakfast is the perfect way to start the day!' he shouted.

The trapdoor slammed open.

'Always brush your teeth and wash behind your ears!' he called.

Somehow, he flew from the pit and landed a dozen paces away from Doctor Dread.

'But – that's – impossible!' Dread hesitated in horror. 'You should have – wallowed to death in Nut Crunchies by now!'

'You forgot, Doctor Dread,' Roger replied with the slightest of smiles. 'Nut Crunchies are Captain Crusader's friend.'

'Curses!' Doctor Dread swore. 'I will not be – defeated now. Not when – the Change – is so close!' He waved both his snakeskin-clad arms wildly. 'Guards! He must be stopped – at all costs!'

All the guards in the room, including Roger's former ally, the Captain, rushed to grab him.

Roger raised a chiding finger. 'Remember. Pushing and grabbing aren't polite.'

The guard in the lead hesitated. 'Hey! He's right!'

'*Don't* listen to him!' Dread insisted. 'Grab him!'

The guards again rushed forward.

'Running and playing are great ways to let off steam,' Roger reminded them, 'after your homework's done.'

This time, the first three guards stumbled to a halt.

'Gee, I hadn't thought of that,' one of them murmured.

'There's this maths problem I never *could* get,' another agreed. 'If you're travelling from station A at a constant speed of—'

'*Don't* let him talk!' Dread interrupted the problem-solving. 'Gag him!'

The Captain of the Guard shook his head. 'Yeah, you can't let him say any more of those – things. That's what got me the last time. Shut him up and we'll be safe to obliterate at our leisure.'

'Even better!' Dread exclaimed with a sudden smile. 'Cover your ears while you attack!'

The three guards in the lead all put fingers in their ears as they rushed forward. Roger stood his ground.

'A smile is the best way to say hello,' he remarked as the guards approached.

'That makes a lot of sense,' the Captain of the Guard muttered as he shook his head. But the other guards were almost on top of Roger now, all three humming (in addition to plugging their ears) so that they might be immune from Captain Crusader's awesome power.

'Three against one is never any fun,' Roger said quickly.

'Yeah!' the Captain enthused. 'What a good way to express it!'

'He does make a lot of—' Doctor Dread began. He punched a fist into his leg, as if forcing himself to wake from a dream. 'No! Guards! Grab him now!'

But the guards were having problems as they realized they couldn't grab Roger with their index fingers occupied.

The first guard unplugged his ears.

'To hear a good idea,' Roger said quickly, 'you have to listen.'

The guard stopped and smiled. 'Wow.'

'How could I have ever doubted?' the Captain of the Guard shouted. 'How could I have ever thought of going back to Doctor Dread?'

'Guards!' Dread called with rising panic. '*Don't* take your fingers from your ears. Push him back to the blue X!'

The two remaining guards obeyed, both bumping against Roger so that he stumbled back. He looked beyond his attackers, and saw Dread laugh quickly as he grabbed a lever, neatly labelled: INSIDIOUS TRAP No. 7.

Roger looked up, to see something hurtling down on him from above. He covered his head, but whatever it was crashed around him.

He opened his eyes and realized he was surrounded by some sort of clear, glass cylinder. Did Doctor Dread think a puny prison like this could hold Captain Crusader?

But then Roger saw Doctor Dread laughing, and realized he could not *hear* Doctor Dread laughing. Maybe – if no one could hear his Captain Crusader sayings – maybe Roger was trapped after all! Still, there were other possibilities. Perhaps his Nut Crunchie-derived power would allow him to tip over this glass prison or something. He leaned against one curved wall, putting all his weight behind it. It didn't budge. Roger realized he'd better come up with that something pretty soon, or he would be in real trouble.

He looked back out of his prison, and saw there was a brand new commotion going on in Dread's throne room. There were large amounts of blue smoke billowing from the far corner of the room. It must be Doctor Dread's henchpeople, returning to share in their leader's triumph. Would Roger's mother be with them? This was getting worse and worse.

Could this be the end of Captain Crusader?

CHAPTER TWENTY-SIX

Louie knew he'd made the right choice when he heard the diabolical laughter.

'Someone laughing on Moonbase?' Zabana asked.

'We didn't go to the Moonbase,' Louie replied as the smoke cleared. 'We went to the Citadel of Dread.'

'Mother of Mercy!' Officer O'Clanrahan. 'I've been found out!'

'Never trust a turncoat,' Doc agreed sagely.

But Louie no longer had time to worry about the ethics of Officer O'Clanrahan. From the moment he heard that diabolical laughter, he knew they were in the presence of Doctor Dread.

The snakeskin-suited master of evil spun about to glare at the newcomers.

'Who dares?' His tone shifted suddenly as he got a look at Louie's companions. 'B-b-bunnies!'

'Yay!' Fluffytail cheered. 'It's Malevelo! Are we going to have fun today!'

'M-M-Malevelo?' the evil leader sputtered. 'I am not – Malevelo! I am – Doctor Dread!' He took a ragged breath, pulling his gaze away from the rabbits. 'Guards! Forget about Captain Crusader! Deal with the b-b-bunnies!'

Captain Crusader? Did that mean that Roger was here, too? Louie quickly looked around the room. Yes, there he was, trapped inside what looked like a giant, upside-down glass test tube.

'Bouncer!' he called. 'Do you still have some of those exploding carrots?'

The large rabbit nodded his head eagerly. 'Bouncer has lots of exploding carrots!'

Louie wondered for an instant where Bouncer stored all those deadly vegetables. But now was not the time to ask.

'Let your friends handle Malevelo for a minute,' he instructed the large bunny instead. He pointed to Roger. 'I need you to use your exploding carrots to free that fellow over there.'

'Yay!' Bouncer replied. 'Bouncer goes to free da fellow!'

In the meantime, Dread was pulling on a long, tasselled chord to which was tied a neatly lettered sign that read 'EMERGENCY GUARD ALERT!' And the guards had been alerted. They were streaming in through doors at both ends of the room.

'Zabana! Doc! We need to hold off the others while the bunnies get to Doctor Dread!'

The prince of the jungle flexed his pectorals. 'Zabana ready for anything!'

'Hoo doggies!' Doc added with an enthusiastic whistle. 'We finally ended up someplace where I can use my old six-shooters.' Faster than Louie could follow, he drew both his pearl-handled revolvers. 'Let's see how these fellas handle a couple a guns a-blazin'!'

The two of them stepped forward to confront the three dozen or so guards that had so far made it into the room. Louie figured the two sides were or more less evenly matched.

In the meantime, the six smaller bunnies had made their move towards Doctor Dread.

'Wait!' the ultimate master of evil shouted. 'There's got to be a simpler way to work out our differences. Wouldn't you b-b-bunnies like some nice – carrots or something?'

'Why thank you,' Fluffytail replied, hopping closer to Doctor Dread.

'Maybe later,' Highjumper added as he bounced on Fluffytail's heels.

'But for now,' the next bunny continued as it, too, hopped along, 'we want to play!'

'P-p-p-play?' Doctor Dread managed. 'But – I don't – want—'

'We'll hop and skip and jump—' the fourth bunny cheered merrily.

'And caper and cavort and frolic and frisk—' the next rabbit went on.

'And gambol and prance and rollick and romp—' the sixth rabbit proceeded.

Doctor Dread threw his arms in front of his face. 'No! No! I won't listen! Urk!'

'You don't have to listen,' Fluffytail replied.

'You just have to join in,' Highjumper added.

'Bunnies are so much fun to play with,' bunny number 3 remarked.

'We're so soft and fluffy and pet-able,' bunny number 4 chimed in.

'And cute and adorable and charming—' bunny number 5 said brightly.

'No!' Doctor Dread screamed. 'No more! Urk! Have pity! Ulp!'

But the bunnies would show no mercy.

'And big eyes—' number 6 pointed out.

'B-b-big!' Doctor Dread wailed.

'And pink noses—' Fluffytail mentioned.

'P-p-p-pink!' Doctor Dread moaned.

'And big, cottony tails—' Highjumper insisted.

'C-c-ca – c-c-ca-cottony?' Doctor Dread stiffened, then slowly removed his arms from the front of his face. He no longer looked upset. In fact, he appeared to be almost comically angry.

'Rats!' he yelled, raising his fists in the air. 'Malevelo will get those fluffy bunnies yet!'

'Cover your heads!' Bouncer's voice drew Louie away from Doctor Dread's amazing transformation. 'Bouncer set da timer on da exploding carrot!'

Louie covered his head.

The carrot exploded.

Some time ago, Roger had stopped being truly surprised by anything that happened in the Cineverse – but this had come close.

A very large rabbit had shown up and placed what looked like a metal carrot at the base of his prison. A moment later, all the glass had shattered and fallen away, and Roger was free at last. He stepped carefully over the surrounding pile of broken glass, into total chaos.

It wasn't simply the battle raging around him that Roger found confusing. No, the music was back, too. But it was all kinds of music at once – horns and violins and drums and blaring clarinets and even a couple of vocals, all struggling to be heard!

But there was more. The greatest cloud of blue smoke Roger had ever seen had erupted in the very centre of the room. And out of that cloud came the voice of his mother.

'All bow before Mother Antoinette!'

'Hey!' Doctor Dread shook his head, as if waking from a dream. 'What am I talking about?'

And then another voice shouted from inside the cloud:

'Make way for Hippolita, the Oracle of Venus!'

'Hey!' This time Roger recognized the tones of Menge the Merciless. 'What are they doing in here?'

'Yes!' the ultimate master of evil yelled, a note of triumph returning to his voice. 'I'm Doctor Dread! And no bunnies are going to make me feel any different!'

A warm male voice, rather like that of a travel guide, spoke next from the cloud:

'We happy villagers have finally found a way to leave our island paradise!'

'Hey! Where did *they* come from?' Bertha's voice demanded.

The next voice that emerged from the fog was one Roger had hoped never to hear again:

'Gnud fussin beverly, cuten slashen voola-voola!'

'What?' Professor Peril's voice economically demanded. 'That person's not even speaking English!'

The smoke cleared, and Roger saw all the triumph leave Doctor Dread's countenance.

'Oh no!' Dread screamed. 'It's here! Before we were – truly ready! The height of – the Change!'

CHAPTER TWENTY-SEVEN

Of course, Louie had always suspected this sort of thing could happen. Whenever you used a Captain Crusader Decoder Ring, there was always a certain suspense in travelling from one world to another, a certain fear that the mix of different folks from different worlds would totally screw up the plot.

'Avast, me hearties!' a boisterous male voice called. 'There's plenty of plunder here, for valiant buccaneers!'

But here it was, Louie thought, now, in the flesh, smack dab in front of him. Too many people from too many different places – all the characters working with Captain Crusader, and all of Dread's bad guys – and all had come to this Citadel at the same time. And it was too much for the Cineverse to take.

'All right, men!' a grizzled sergeant yelled to his troops, 'it's time for us to take that hill!'

'Jumpin' Jehosaphat!' Doc exclaimed as he ran after the soldiers. 'I knew I was needed here for something!'

And all those people from all those places had led to something else, like a hole in the Cineverse. More people were showing up, from a hundred different movie worlds, almost as if they were somehow being dragged here. And, Louie guessed, they were – by the Change.

'Hey, Roger-dodger!' a blond teenager in loud bathing trunks announced. 'Surf's up!'

Louie hadn't been near the middle of the Change before. In fact, the last time around, he hardly noticed the Change had happened until some of the good guys started getting plugged.

Something trumpeted.

'Is fear-maddened elephant, from Zabana's home jungle!' the prince of the jungle announced. 'Is no place like home!' The mighty muscleman took off after the rampaging pachyderm.

This time, though, the Change looked like it was going to be a lot worse than before. This time, *everything* was changing. Even after the blue smoke had cleared, people – and animals – were showing up from everywhere – and it was already changing Doc and Zabana and the others who were here.

This, Louie suspected, was what Doctor Dread had wanted to happen all along. But could even the greatest evil mastermind in all the known Cineverse handle this kind of a mess?

There was too much happening here. Louie had to keep his wits about him until somebody got control of this, or they were all in trouble.

And then somebody started to sing.

'Oh, it's such a sunny day,
Those nasty clouds beware!
Come on, fellas, walk with us,
We're going to the fair!'

Louie realized his mouth was watering. Maybe, if he went with these brightly dressed folks, he'd get a chance to judge the pie-tasting competition!

No, no, there were other things he had to do first. His wits – he was keeping his wits. He'd remember what he had to do if he looked around the room. Oh, yeah, he'd always wanted to learn how to use a sword. Or maybe it was time to finally get on that board and surf!

What had he forgotten? Oh well, he'd figure it out in a moment. He curled his hand round an imaginary sword. Whatever else happened, he had to make sure, at all costs, that he wasn't affected by the Change.

Roger had to concentrate. It was almost impossible with all the noise and music, not to mention what was happening to his companions. Zabana had run off to chase an elephant, Doc seemed to have joined the army, and Big Louie appeared to be trying to surf while he was holding a sword.

'Yip?' Dwight asked behind him. The wonder dog appeared to be so far gone that he didn't even notice the chaos around him.

But, if Dwight could separate himself from the mess here, so could Roger. He just had to take a deep breath and think like Captain Crusader. Why, only a few minutes ago, he was spouting prime Captain Crusader sayings for every occasion. There was no reason, save for all this distraction, that he couldn't do it again.

And Roger would do it! Even in his addled state, it looked as if Dwight the wonder dog had once again saved the day!

'Good boy!' Roger called.

'Yip?' the wonder dog replied.

Now, if Roger could simply come up with a Captain Crusader saying all-encompassing enough to deal with what was going on around him—

'Back!' a woman shouted. 'Back, I say!' Roger turned his head to see a gang of pirates being held at bay by a black-clad woman with a whip.

That black-clad woman was also Roger's mother.

All thoughts of Captain Crusader left Roger's mind as he watched the whip in action. She was quite good at it, flipping it back and forth to keep a trio of musclemen at bay. It was a side of his parent that he had never seen before. Perhaps, he thought, he'd been guilty of taking his mother a little bit for granted.

But a new group was taking an interest in the woman in black. 'Avast, me hearties!' the leader of the pirates leered at Roger's mother. 'Here's a prize worth taking.'

Actually, when Roger took a closer look at the group of twenty or so menacing his mom, he realized they weren't all strictly pirates. Somehow, a half-dozen surfers seemed to have got mixed in, too. But they were all acting like pirates, and there must have been close to two dozen of them. Roger considered going to his mother's aid. She *was* his mother, after all, even though she was working for the other side, and she might be able to manage three assailants – but twenty?

CRACK

One look at the way his mother was handling her newest attackers, however, and he gave up any thoughts of rescue.

CRACK *CRACK*

Besides, he didn't want to get too close to that nasty weapon of hers.

CRACK *CRACK* *CRACK*

His mother snapped the whip, curling it round the pirate captain's leg and pulling him from his feet.

'I am nobody's prize!' she declared. 'I am Mother Antoinette!'

'Ah, what spirit!' the pirate captain laughed. 'She is a beach bunny worth pursuing!'

Beach bunny? Roger frowned. Something was wrong here. He'd seen enough pirate movies to know. Wasn't the proper pirate term for a desirable woman 'wench' or 'vixen'?

CRACK went his mother's whip. *CRACK* *CRACK*

One pirate cried in surprise as his hoop earring was pulled from his ear, while another brigand pointed in surprise to the place where the whip had sheared his wooden leg in half.

Roger's mother laughed, and the whip swept in wide circles above the pirates' heads.

CRACK *CRACK* *CRACK*

In a matter of seconds, half a dozen pirates had lost their scraggly beards.

'Enough is enough!' the pirates yelled.

'We yield!'

'Shiver me timbers, it is a bummer!'

Bummer? There it was again, that intermingling of surfer and pirate. Now that he thought of it, Roger remembered there had been a similar mixing of worlds during the first Change, when genres combined into things like space westerns and spy musicals. The results were never very good, and could be explosively bad! And here it was, happening all over again.

Roger was beginning to wonder if it might already be too late for the Cineverse to be saved.

'Beggin' your pardon, Captain,' one of the pirates said, 'but maybe she'd consent to lead us?'

'Lead you?' Roger's mother chuckled darkly. 'Very soon, Mother Antoinette will be mistress of everybody!'

'What?' Somehow, in all this noise, Doctor Dread had overheard the conversation. 'You dare to – challenge my authority? I will show you – what happens—'

But Mother Antoinette's whip went to work before Dread could even stop hesitating. *CRACK* *CRACK* the whip replied, and Dread's snakeskin pants had been transformed into snakeskin Bermuda shorts.

'Well—' Dread hesitated, looking down at his pale and newly exposed knees. 'Perhaps we can discuss—'

'But you have to talk to bunnies first!' Highjumper interrupted.

'Urk! Ulp!' Doctor Dread replied, his face contorting. 'Malevelo doesn't talk to bunnies! Malevelo has bunnies for dinner!'

'Bunnies for dinner? Bouncer likes carrots!'

All seven bunnies, Bouncer included, hopped around the villain and laughed.

But, instead of the usual angry response, Doctor Dread only

smiled. 'Carrots? Urk! Malevelo – likes carrots. Malevelo especially likes exploding carrots!'

'Exploding carrot?' the very large bunny replied cheerfully. 'Bouncer likes da exploding carrot, too!'

Dread's face once again convulsed, as if there was a great war going on within his skull. 'Urk! Ulp! Malevelo – wants the exploding carrot!'

'OK!' Bouncer replied with a big smile. 'Malevelo is the boss!'

The big rabbit bounced over to the ultimate master of evil and handed him a carrot with a lit fuse.

'Oh, really,' Doctor Dread said as he took the offering. 'On second thought, I – couldn't.'

He stuffed the carrot in Bouncer's mouth. Bouncer swallowed in surprise.

'Hehhehheh!' Doctor Dread chuckled triumphantly. 'Malevelo – I mean, Doctor Dread – will show you what you can do with your exploding carrots! Now, if you'll – excuse me?'

Dread started to run.

'BURP!' Bouncer replied. 'Oh, dear. You have to excuse Bouncer, too.'

'What?' Doctor Dread demanded as he stopped his retreat. 'I stuff one of your exploding carrots into your stomach, and all it does is give you – gas?'

Then Bouncer exploded. Where the rabbit had stood a moment before, there was now nothing but a great cloud of dark smoke.

Doctor Dread's laughter rose above everything else. 'Yes! Take that – bunnies! You may force me into playing this stupid wizard, but – Bouncer is no more!'

'Oh, yeah?' a voice said as someone stepped from the cloud – someone wearing a trenchcoat, with a glowing cigarette hanging from his lower lip. 'We'll see about that, buster.' As he walked from the smoke, Roger realized that the lower lips, along with the rest of the face, including those long ears poking through the slouch hat, belonged to Bouncer!

'I'm glad you called me in,' the raincoat-clad rabbit drawled. 'It's my job as a gumshoe to find out – who used the exploding carrot?'

It was Bouncer, and it wasn't Bouncer. Roger was fascinated. This must be the Change at work.

'Excuse me, dollface,' Bouncer remarked as he stepped past Roger's whip-wielding mother. 'That's why I've called you all here today, to solve the mystery of – who killed Bouncer Bunny?'

'No!' Doctor Dread screamed. 'I won't have it! I – dealt with you, and now you won't – stay dead! I'll show you what happens to b-b-bunnies who – double-cross Doctor Dread!'

He ran to another one of his levers. This one read 'DEADLY WEIGHT RELEASE'. Doctor Dread pulled the lever.

A ten-foot-square solid steel cube fell on top of the gumshoe bunny.

'Hehheh hehhehheh!' the mastermind laughed in nervous relief. 'Mess – with Doctor Dread – would you? And I'll deal with all – you other b-b-bunnies, too!'

Dread's gloating was interrupted by a group of men and women, strolling arm in arm as they sang:

> 'Join us in our morning walk;
> We're all without a care.
> Sing a song, or hear us talk,
> We're going to the fair!'

It seemed to Roger there were a lot more people strolling and singing than there had been a moment before. Yes, there was Zabana, hand on trunk with his elephant! And, taking up the rear, was the woman with the knife from the foreign art film! Amazingly enough, she was singing, too:

> 'Voola-voola beverly
> Smashen kutz shaboom!
> Minsky mensky stephanie,
> Slashen gutz kadoom!'

Roger couldn't believe what he was seeing. Had the mad woman from the art film found peace at last? It would be a relief not to have to worry about her any more. Through force of habit, as much as anything, Roger's eyes looked down to read the subtitle:

> 'Oh, it's such a cheerful day
> My worries to avenge.
> I'll laugh, I'll skip, I'll stab his heart,
> And get my just revenge!'

Then again, perhaps he would keep his distance.

But something was happening to the steel cube. It had begun to rumble, and a crack was rapidly splitting the metal apart from top to bottom. The two halves crashed asunder, and once the dust settled, there stood Bouncer – but a different Bouncer. He was wearing army fatigues, with two ammunition belts criss-crossing his chest. He looked to Roger like nothing so much as the hero of one of those 'One-man-against-an-entire-terrorist-army' movies.

'Yo,' Bouncer said to Doctor Dread. 'You're in trouble now.'

But Roger was letting himself be carried along by the course of events. If he was going to have any effect on his surroundings, he had to get his Captain Crusader act in gear.

'No b-b-bunny's going to get the better of me!' Doctor Dread shrieked.

Professor Peril stopped doing battle with some mounted cavalry to run to Dread's side. 'Boss, get yourself together! You should know it's almost impossible to kill these cartoon bunnies. Even if you do, they'll just end up with wings and a harp, and they'll keep on bothering you!'

Roger was surprised at how much sense Peril made. The man knew his cartoons. But Doctor Dread was beyond reasoning as he ran to another of his myriad levers.

'Even mercenary soldier bunnies cannot stand up to my deadly piranha pool!'

He pulled the 'DEADLY PIRANHA POOL' lever. A trapdoor opened at Bouncer's feet. But the mercenary bunny that Bouncer had become was too fast for Dread's machinations. He jumped back as the door sprang away. Roger could hear the deadly, bunny-eating fish churning about in the water, just out of sight. Bouncer pointed his AK-47 down into the pit and fired a dozen, quick bursts.

The piranhas thrashed no more.

'Yo,' Bouncer said as he pointed to Dread. 'You're next.'

'No!' Dread's head whipped back and forth, searching for the lever that would conquer the unconquerable bunny. His right hand reached for 'GIANT DESCENDING PENDULUM' while his left hand sought 'BOILING OIL RESERVES' and he looked up at his 'SHORT-RANGE MISSILE CONTROL PANEL'.

'No!' Dread screamed. 'Any or all of them might fail. I need my greatest weapon. Mother Antoinette!'

Roger's mother paused from whipping some Roman soldiers. 'Yes?'

'I need your help,' Doctor Dread pleaded.

Roger's mother smiled at that, the same, small, cruel smile she used to use when she told Roger he had to finish his lima beans. 'My help does not come – cheaply,' she replied.

'I understand!' Dread screeched. 'Anything you want! Just – deal with the bunny!'

'Anything – I – want?' Roger's mother turned to face the rabbit.

'Yo,' Bouncer said uncertainly. 'I don't want to hurt a lady.'

Mother Antoinette flexed her whip. 'You'll soon learn that I'm no ordinary lady.'

CRACK

Bouncer jumped away from the dancing leather.

CRACK *CRACK*

But Mother Antoinette had forced him up against a wall. There was no place for the rabbit to go.

'Yo—' Bouncer began. But then the whip was everywhere!

CRACK *CRACK* *CRACK*

It slashed at Bouncer and the surrounding wall, as tapestry, masonry and bunny fur flew and intermingled. Bouncer cried out incoherently as he was covered by cloth and brick.

There was a moment of total silence in the throne room.

Roger's mouth fell open. Bouncer was gone? If Captain Crusader could have said something, he might have been able to save the giant rabbit. If Roger could somehow get over his shock even now, he might be able to stop this madness from going any further.

'Heh heh,' Doctor Dread laughed uncertainly at first, then with more vigour. 'Hehheh hehhehheh! Mother Antoinette! Whatever your services cost, they are well—'

The pile that contained Bouncer shifted.

'What?' Roger's mother demanded. 'It can't be. Not after—'

A bunny paw emerged from the pile.

'Can't *anything* kill it?' Peril whispered.

A second paw broke free – and this paw was carrying a chainsaw.

It didn't surprise Roger in the least when, as Bouncer's face finally emerged, he now wore a hockey mask.

It was Dread's turn to scream incoherently as he ran for the far end of the throne room.

But Roger realized what was happening now. He was watching the Change in action, as Bouncer transformed from a rebel hero to an anti-hero to something that went beyond heroics. Roger knew that he had to stop this now, before it went any further.

He cleared his throat.

'A party is always more fun,' he shouted to the surrounding throng, 'when everybody obeys the rules!'

And everybody stopped.

What did Roger do now?

CHAPTER TWENTY-EIGHT

Mother Antoinette had to admit it. Her son made a lot of sense.

Somebody tugged at her sleeve. She turned to see the cringing form of Menge the Merciless.

'Don't you see what's happening?' Menge insisted. 'It's Captain Crusader. Don't listen to him!'

Mother Antoinette blinked. 'Why not?'

'If you *listen* to him,' Menge emphasized, 'you'll start *believing* him.'

'Well,' she answered reasonably, 'he is in public relations. He has a way with words.'

Menge stopped cringing long enough to look her straight in the eye. 'You'll have to give up your whip,' he said simply.

Mother Antoinette felt like she had been splashed by ice-cold water. What was she doing listening to her son, anyway?

'Never!' she exclaimed with renewed conviction. 'What do I have to do?'

Menge got that sort of sly smile that made him so attractive. 'This is our time for triumph!' He flinched when he realized what he had said. 'I'm sorry – *your* turn for triumph. I'm just happy to – um – follow you.

Sometimes, however, her Mengy could be quite exasperating. '*How* will we triumph?' she demanded.

'Oh, of course, Mother Antoinette!' Menge grovelled. 'It's time for the Buchanan Device!'

She had to admit, this sounded interesting. 'The Buchanan Device?'

'Yes!' Menge agreed all over again. 'We'll take the Buchanan Device and—' He gasped when he realized he'd made the same mistake again. 'Oh, mercy, Mother Antoinette. You, of course, will use the Buchanan Device – and I, perhaps, might be worthy enough to lick your shoes—'

Mother Antoinette nodded. 'Perhaps that can be arranged. But about the device?'

'It's how Dread controlled the Change in the first place,' Menge confessed in a low tone. 'Turn it on, and you can alter anything that you desire.'

That sounded even better to Mother Antoinette. 'It's that powerful?' she asked.

'There's nothing more powerful in the Cineverse,' Menge assured her.

Then, at last, Mother Antoinette could have everything exactly the way she wanted it. There was no time to delay. She glanced back at Menge. 'But how do we obtain this device?'

His sly smile was back. 'Depend on me. I know the device's secret hiding place.' He waved for her to follow him across the room. They had to dodge a small boat of people wearing life preservers and a conga line of dancing alligators, but Menge brought her to a tapestry of Wall Street bigwigs bilking their clients.

'It's back here,' he confided. He pulled the tapestry out of the way. And, indeed, there, taped on the recessed wall, was a neatly hand-lettered, cardboard sign:

BUCHANAN DEVICE
SECRET HIDING PLACE
PRESS HERE

Mother Antoinette pressed the spot indicated. A wall the size of a garage door rolled out of the way.

'Step out of the way,' Menge cautioned hastily, '—uh – please?'

Mother Antoinette stepped back as a machine the size and colour of a yellow minivan – except that it had no windows and was equipped with about four dozen blinking lights – rolled forward.

It stopped directly in front of Mother Antoinette. She saw a small keypad on the side of the bulky machine.

Directly above the keypad was a speaker, and another button, with a cardboard sign that read 'PRESS HERE'.

Mother Antoinette pressed again.

The machine hummed to life.

'Welcome to the Buchanan Device,' a cheery male voice announced from the speaker,'your one-stop shop for major plot alterations. If you want the good guys to win, press "1". If you want the bad guys to become good guys, press "2".'

Neither one of those sounded like something Mother Antoinette wanted to do. She hoped there were better options further down the list.

A door opened on the side of the yellow device.

'A door?' Menge yelled in disbelief. 'The Buchanan Device doesn't have any doors!'

'If you want all the good guys to fall in love, press "3",' the device's voice continued.

Two of the strangest creatures Mother Antoinette had ever seen stepped out of the doorway. Even though they both walked on two legs like humans, they looked far more like animals. The second creature actually looked like nothing so much as a sheep, although there might have been a smidgen of dog, cow, and perhaps half a dozen other mammals thrown in. The first creature, however, was so disgusting that it was difficult for Mother Antoinette even to look at it. Still, somehow, she forced herself. The future ruler of the Cineverse had to be tough. Ugh. The first creature looked exactly like a chicken, covered by slime.

'If you want all the bad guys to fall in love, press "4",' the machine went on. 'If you want the bad guys to fall in love with the good guys, press "5".'

'We're here at last,' the slime chicken said solemnly. 'Excuse me, but is this the Change?'

'If you want your entire plot overthrown by violent revolution, press "6".'

'Yes, this is the Change,' Mother Antoinette agreed curtly, angered that the device wasn't giving her better choices. 'Couldn't this machine work a little faster?'

Menge nodded. 'They always leave all the best stuff for the end.'

'If you want your world to end in a natural disaster, press "7". If you want your world to end in an unnatural disaster, press "8".'

Mother Antoinette frowned. She really hadn't heard any option here that was particularly to her liking.

'If you want to wipe everything out and start all over again, press "9".'

Oh, all right, maybe if she listened to them again. She pressed '9'.

'No,' Menge shrieked. 'Not that!'

'Not what?' Mother Antoinette demanded. 'I pressed 9 to start the machine over.'

'But 9 doesn't start the machine over. It starts *everything* over!'

Menge stopped to gulp air. 'The Buchanan Device,' he began again, only slightly less hysterically, 'has an almost unlimited number of plot options. The villains start winning around 15 or 16.'

Oh, Mother Antoinette thought. Oh, dear. She always had trouble with the directions on these new electronic machines.

She looked over at Menge. 'And there's no way to stop it?'

'There's no fighting the Buchanan Device! We are doomed! We are—'

Another man's voice interrupted Menge's panic. It was a voice she'd recognize anywhere – the voice of her son. 'Mother, what are you doing?'

How could she answer him? Somehow, the whip in her hand didn't seem to mean that much when she had just destroyed the universe. Fortunately, Menge did the answering for her.

'Ah, hahaha!' was Menge's reply. 'It is too late! No mere Captain Crusader saying can stop the Buchanan Device!'

'The Buchanan Device?' Roger asked with that annoying little whine he sometimes got in his voice. '*Mother*—'

'Everything will be wiped out!' Menge continued. 'The Cineverse will have to start from scratch. Maybe even we will die, but we will die triumphant!'

She did all that by pressing 9? Oh, well. At least, Mother Antoinette thought, she got to keep her whip until the end.

CHAPTER TWENTY-NINE

The large yellow machine, the so-called 'Buchanan Device' that his mother had activated, hummed dangerously.

'Haven't we been through this before?' a sheep that stood on two legs said with a woman's voice. For some reason, Roger found the sheep strangely attractive. Did this say something he didn't want to know about his sexual preferences? Fortunately, the situation was too desperate now for him to dwell on such matters.

The machine's hum grew even louder.

'I'm afraid so,' answered the woman's companion, who was not attractive in the least. 'Brawwk! You can't over-use a good plot device.'

Roger recognized that dour voice. It was Edward, the slime monster. But that meant that the sheep with Edward had to be—

'Delores?' he asked, looking into the sheep's big, brown eyes.

But the sheep turned her head away. 'Oh, Roger! I didn't want you to see me like this!'

'Nonsense, Delores!' Roger rushed forward to grab her hand, or forepaw, or whatever it was. 'We're back together again. That's all that matters!'

'Baahhh-but I'm a sheep!' she protested.

Roger's hands sank deep into her woolly shoulders. 'It's something we will have to rise above.'

'Oh, dear,' the thing that used to be Edward moaned. 'I should have realized. Brawwk! They are reconciled, and the slime monster goes on – alone.'

The Buchanan Device sputtered.

'Something's wrong!' Menge exclaimed.

The Buchanan Device groaned.

'Danger, danger,' the pleasant male voice said from the speaker. 'There is too much happening. We are in danger of cosmic overload. Remove six plot threads immediately, or the Buchanan Device will explode.'

Roger's mother stared at the machine. 'Does that mean we won't go back to the beginning of the Cineverse?'

'Yes,' the pleasant voice replied. 'Instead, the Buchanan Device will overload, destroying itself, and the entire world around it, in a tremendous, fiery conflagration.'

'Oh,' she replied. 'Doesn't seem like much of a difference, does it?'

'Sorry,' the Buchanan's speaker replied. 'That's the way the plot goes sometimes.' It resumed humming, louder and higher than before, the kind of humming that always ended in explosions.

'Roger!' his mother yelled. 'Do something!'

Yes, Roger thought, the only one who could save them now was Captain Crusader. 'A machine is only as good as the person who uses it!' he yelled.

The humming became even more pronounced.

Roger tried again. 'Uh – a clean machine is a happy machine! Um – electricity is a computer's friend!'

It was no use. Menge had been right – Captain Crusader sayings had no effect. The hum was becoming more hysterical with every passing second. What else could Roger do?

'Help!' he wailed.

There was a second of startled silence, as if the Cineverse had heard his call.

Roger realized then that the humming had stopped and had been replaced by an angelic choir as a bright blue chariot descended from the sky.

OKAY, THIS HAS GONE FAR ENOUGH!
IT'S TIME TO SETTLE DOWN!

Before he even saw the back-lighting or the blue-smoke cigar, Roger realized it was the Plotmaster. He also realized that almost everybody had frozen around him, as if time stood still.

The blue chariot, which, as far as Roger could tell, was self-propelled, landed next to the now quiet Buchanan Device.

HEY, ROGER BOOBALA,
BEFORE YOU CAN START THINGS UP AGAIN,
YOU GOTTA STOP 'EM FOR A MINUTE!

Roger was astonished. 'You mean, you can just show up and – stop everything?'

> HEY, ROGER BABY, LET'S FACE IT
> THE CHANGE CAN ONLY GO SO FAR.

'And you're just going to appear and fix everything?' Roger asked incredulously. 'This is pretty *deus ex machina,* isn't it?'

> HEY, I'LL BE THE FIRST TO ADMIT
> SOME PLOTS ARE BETTER THAN OTHERS.

'So you're the Plotmaster?' Delores asked in wonder.

> AND YOU MUST BE DELORES?

Wait! Roger thought. Why wasn't Delores frozen like the others? The big back-lit guy chuckled.

> SOME PEOPLE HAVE CHANGED TOO MUCH FOR EVEN
> THE PLOTMASTER TO HAVE ANY CONTROL
> OVER THEM!

'The Plotmaster.' Even Edward the slime chicken was impressed.
'And you're going to fix everything?' Delores asked.

> WELL, WHATEVER I CAN.
> EVEN THE PLOTMASTER HAS LIMITS.

'No!' another woman's voice yelled. 'I've come too far to be stopped now!' Roger's mother stepped forward.
CRACK went her whip.

> UH-OH.
> HERE'S ONE OF MY LIMITS NOW!

CRACK *CRACK*
The Plotmaster ducked as the whip waved over his head. When he spoke again, Roger thought he could hear real panic in his voice:

> SHE'S LIKE YOU, ROGER.
> SHE'S NOT FROM THE CINEVERSE.

I HAVE NO POWER OVER HER!

CRACK *CRACK* *CRACK*

The whip was everywhere. The blue back-lighting flickered and died as the Plotmaster ducked inside his chariot.

Roger's mother laughed. 'Who's the ruler of the Cineverse *now*?'

The Plotmaster's voice echoed up from inside the chariot.

ROGER?
I COULD USE SOME HELP HERE.

The Plotmaster needed him? But how could he do anything against Mother Antoinette? Even though she was one of the ultimate masters of evil, there was no way Roger could strike his mother!

But, he realized, there was another way. He tried to think of the best way to reach her.

'A clean room is a happy room,' he said.

'What?' His mother stopped her whip, mid-crack.

Roger thought he heard someone else mutter from somewhere in the frozen masses. Could his Captain Crusader sayings be waking the others, as well?

His mother shook her head. 'What's wrong with me? I have to finish somebody off – with the whip!'

Uh-oh. Roger had to say something else, fast.

'Your mother is only a phone call away.'

The whip almost slipped from his mother's hands. She smiled. 'Yes. I've often said that.'

A six-foot-high bunny bounded out of the crowd and took off his hockey mask.

'Bouncer has been through some changes, too!' he declared.

That meant Roger *was* waking up the others! The more he exerted the power of Captain Crusader, the more normal the Cineverse became!

Mother Antoinette looked down at her hands. 'A whip? I have a whip!'

Whoops. His mother's will was too strong to be controlled by any of his Captain Crusader sayings for long. The next one would have to be good.

'Plots may come and plots may go, but a boy's best friend is his mother.'

'How nice of you to say so.' The whip fell from Mother Antoinette's fingers.

The Plotmaster peeked over the edge of the chariot. Without the blue back-lighting, he looked a little like the Masked Marshal.

ROGER, BABY,
AS WELL AS THIS WORKS—
IT'S ONLY A HOLDING ACTION.
YOUR MOTHER'S STILL BEEN ZAPPED BY THE
ZETA RAY!

Edward the slime chicken shivered. 'Brawwk? The Zeta Ray? Anything but – the Zeta Ray.'

Roger stared at the Plotmaster. Maybe, he considered, the fellow actually looked a bit more like the Secret Samoan.

'The Zeta Ray?' Roger had almost forgotten about the foul machine that had turned his mother to a life of evil. Doctor Dread probably kept it around here somewhere. 'Do you have any idea where it is?'

HEY!
I'M THE PLOTMASTER!
THE LEVER'S RIGHT OVER THERE,
NEXT TO THE ONE FOR THE TIGER PIT.

Roger looked where the Plotmaster pointed his cigar (which was still producing blue smoke). Oh, yes. Roger saw it now, right by that colourful tapestry showing the many uses of the Cat O' Nine Tails.

He looked back at the Plotmaster. 'But won't exposing her to the Zeta Ray again simply make her more evil?'

The Plotmaster nodded.

THAT'S WHY YOU NEED THE JEWEL.

'The jewel?' Roger asked.

ASK BOUNCER.

The bunny brightened considerably as he popped the ruby from his navel. 'Do you know how to use Bouncer's jewel?'

The Plotmaster nodded again.

DID YOU LOOK ON THE OTHER SIDE OF THE TAG?

The large bunny jumped up and down in anticipation. 'Bouncer never thought to look on the other side!'

Roger looked over the bunny's shoulder as Bouncer flipped the ruby's tag over. There, under the washing instructions (GENTLE CYCLE, TOWEL DRY) were the following words: PLACE JEWEL IN ZETA RAY.

'Didn't I have a whip around here someplace?' Roger's mother declared suddenly.

IT'S NOW OR NEVER

the Plotmaster warned.

'Do it!' Roger yelled.

'Bouncer to da rescue!' the large bunny replied as he crossed the room in three great hops and pulled the appropriate lever. Silent machinery pulled the Cat O' Nine Tails tapestry out of the way, revealing the diabolical framework of the Zeta Ray!

This was the first time Roger had taken a good look at the evil machine. It was especially the first time he had ever seen a small, neatly lettered sign on the front of the machine that read: PLACE JEWEL HERE.

'Bouncer's doing what da sign says!' the bunny declared. 'Bouncer's turning on da machine!'

'The Zeta Ray!' Edward moaned apprehensively.

'Bouncer's swivelling da machine round so da ray will hit Mother Antoinette!' the rabbit announced.

'Oh, no, you don't!' Roger's mother replied. 'Not if my whip has anything to say about it!'

Roger turned to see that Mother Antoinette once again had the whip in her hand and a sneer on her lips.

It was time for a quick Captain Crusader statement.

'The family that—'

CRACK

The close flick of the whip startled him.

'Um—' He had to regain his wits. What was he saying? Oh, yeah. '—that plays together—'

CRACK *CRACK*

'Your sayings won't work on me, if I can't hear them!' Mother Antoinette laughed triumphantly. She turned her attention to Bouncer. 'And as for you, you oversized rodent—'

The now-scarlet ray shot out of the Zeta machine.

'Bouncer's got da ray working!'

CRACK snapped the whip. *CRACK* *CRACK*

'The ray will never touch me!' Mother Antoinette declared.

   CRACK   *CRACK*   *CRACK*   *CRACK*
CRACK   *CRACK*   *CRACK*   *CRACK*
CRACK   *CRACK*   *CRACK*
CRACK   *CRACK*   *CRACK*
CRACK   *CRACK*   *CRACK*   *CRACK*
CRACK   *CRACK*   *CRACK*   *CRACK*

The whip seemed to be everywhere, snapping between Bouncer and Roger, keeping the rabbit from moving and Captain Crusader from speaking.

'Mrs Gordon!' Delores called. 'You can't keep that up for ever!'

'Really?' was Mother Antoinette's amused reply. 'My dear, you have never handled a whip!'

Roger realized that, if the whip affected his mother the way Nut Crunchies affected him, she *might* be able to keep it up for ever!

CRACK *CRACK* *CRACK* Somehow, the whip managed to land near the Plotmaster a few times, too. Actually, Roger realized, in this ruby glow, the Plotmaster could be mistaken for the Great Chieftain of the Whatsahoosie.

'And don't you get any ideas, either!' Mother Antoinette called. She was too good with that whip. They might be caught in a stand-off – for ever.

'The Zeta Ray,' Edward sighed. 'Who will ever miss a slime monster?

'Brawwwwwk!' the incredibly disgusting chicken-thing declared as he launched himself into Roger's mother. The two of them rolled, together, into the ruby light.

Roger's mother stopped struggling. Both Edward and she sat up and shook their heads.

THERE!

the Plotmaster declared.

THAT'S BETTER!

And everybody started to move again. The Plotmaster snapped his fingers, and the angelic choir and blue lighting were back, but, just before Roger lost sight of his face, he could have sworn he saw a strong family resemblance to Doctor Dee Dee Davenport.

'Roger?' his mother called. 'What am I doing here?'

'I'll explain everything to you, Mom,' Roger called back, 'real soon, I promise.'

'Roger!' The excitement in Delores' voice made Roger turn his head, and he saw exactly why she was excited.

She was no longer a sheep.

She grabbed Roger and kissed him; one of those long, deep, movie kisses.

Roger gasped for breath when it was over. He had to make sure his heart was still working.

'I guess we have the Plotmaster to thank!' Delores waved at the backlit man in blue.

HEY, IT'S ALL IN A DAY'S WORK
BUT I GOTTA GO, KIDS—
I'VE GOT A CINEVERSE TO RUN!
FIRST, THOUGH, I GOTTA GET SOME OF THESE
FOLKS HOME.

There was a great deal of blue smoke. Roger realized that about ninety per cent of the occupants of the room had vanished, including, to his relief, a certain foreign woman with a knife.

'Yip?' Dwight remarked.

'Dwight!' Officer O'Clanrahan called in concern. 'What's the matter with you, boy?'

'Yip?' Dwight replied, not quite looking at the policeman.

'You're out of my sight for only a few hours, and this is what happens?' O'Clanrahan frowned. 'Well, no more! I've seen the error of my ways! By all that I hold dear, I renounce my life of evil!'

He patted the white German shepherd on the head.

'Yip?' Dwight repeated slowly. 'Bark? Arf?' He blinked, and looked up at Officer O'Clanrahan. 'Bark, yip, arf!'

The policeman grinned. 'That's my wonder dog!'

Edward stood up. 'Wait a minute! I remember now! Professor Peril exposed me to the Zeta Ray in the Institute of Very Advanced Science!'

Peril's head whipped about, searching for a means of escape. 'So I was looking for more cheap help!'

Edward looked down at his slime chicken form. 'There's a

zipper here somewhere.' He found something right below his neck. 'Ah, here it is!' With a single motion, he undid the entire front of his slime chicken suit and pulled it from his brown, hairy body.

'Oogie,' the prince of the jungle called, 'Zabana's favourite orangutang!'

'Zabana,' the orangutang called back, 'Oogie's favourite prince of the jungle!'

The prince of the jungle smiled. 'Now, Zabana and Oogie go back to jungle, where we belong!'

Doc holstered both his six-shooter guns. 'Think I'll try to work back into heroin'.'

Louie smiled and waved. 'And, now that the hero's back, I get to go back to being a sidekick!'

'The bunnies get to go back to bunnyland!' Fluffytail announced.

Doctor Dread shook his fist at the rabbits. 'Malevelo can't wait until he gets back to his Mystic Kingdom. He'll get those darn bunnies yet!'

'I think I'll go into a more economical line of villainy,' Professor Peril muttered as he skulked about.

Bertha shrugged her broad shoulders. 'It's up to me, then, to take over the mob and get those men in line!'

'Really?' Menge cringed. 'Maybe it's time for me to go back to suburbia and work on my rec room.'

The Plotmaster waved to all of them.

THERE'LL ALWAYS BE A CINEVERSE— AS LONG AS THERE'S A CAPTAIN CRUSADER TO PROTECT IT!

Then Plotmaster, chariot, and angelic choir disappeared in a cloud of blue smoke.

Roger looked at Delores. This had worked out pretty well, hadn't it?

'Roger?' his mother called. 'Not to bother you, dear, but when I go home, would you mind if I held on to this whip – as a keepsake?'

THE END OR THE BEGINNING?

A selection of bestsellers from Headline

BURYING THE SHADOW	Storm Constantine	£4.99 □
SCHEHERAZADE'S NIGHT OUT	Craig Shaw Gardner	£4.99 □
WULF	Steve Harris	£4.99 □
EDGE OF VENGEANCE	Jenny Jones	£5.99 □
THE BAD PLACE	Dean Koontz	£5.99 □
HIDEAWAY	Dean Koontz	£5.99 □
BLOOD GAMES	Richard Laymon	£4.99 □
DARK MOUNTAIN	Richard Laymon	£4.99 □
SUMMER OF NIGHT	Dan Simmons	£4.99 □
FALL OF HYPERION	Dan Simmons	£5.99 □
DREAM FINDER	Roger Taylor	£5.99 □
WOLFKING	Bridget Wood	£4.99 □

All Headline books are available at your local bookshop or newsagent, or can be ordered direct from the publisher. Just tick the titles you want and fill in the form below. Prices and availability subject to change without notice.

Headline Book Publishing PLC, Cash Sales Department, Bookpoint, 39 Milton Park, Abingdon, OXON, OX14 4TD, UK. If you have a credit card you may order by telephone — 0235 831700.

Please enclose a cheque or postal order made payable to Bookpoint Ltd to the value of the cover price and allow the following for postage and packing:
UK & BFPO: £1.00 for the first book, 50p for the second book and 30p for each additional book ordered up to a maximum charge of £3.00.
OVERSEAS & EIRE: £2.00 for the first book, £1.00 for the second book and 50p for each additional book.

Name ....

Address ....

....

....

If you would prefer to pay by credit card, please complete:
Please debit my Visa/Access/Diner's Card/American Express (delete as applicable) card no:

Signature ....Expiry Date ....